*Breath of Scanda...*

"We're breaking all the rules, you know." Eden rested her head in the hollow of Neil's shoulder. She felt, rather than heard, his low laugh.

*Sigh of Surrender*

She swallowed hard as Neil's hand stroked the back of her neck, sending an involuntary shiver down her spine. "I think you're trying to seduce me," she whispered.

*Ecstasy of First Love*

Neil raised his head, viewing the woman in his arms through eyes of molten gold. He hadn't meant to take them this far this soon, but now ... he wrapped Eden in his arms and, over her fearful protests, sank with her to the floor. "Gently, love." Neil's voice roared in her ear. "You're ready, more than ready ..."

# Promise Me Love

## Lynn M. Bartlett

**AVON**
PUBLISHERS OF BARD, CAMELOT, DISCUS AND FLARE BOOKS

PROMISE ME LOVE is an original publication of Avon Books. This work has never before appeared in book form.

AVON BOOKS
A division of
The Hearst Corporation
959 Eighth Avenue
New York, New York 10019

First Avon Printing, October, 1982

For my mother, Verna,
for her endless support and
For my Father, Roy,
for all those stories about the "olden times"

And for Derek,
who taught me that life and love go on

# Contents

# BOOK I
## 1873–1877

They know not I knew thee,
  Who knew thee too well:—
Long, long shall I rue thee,
  Too deeply to tell.

—BYRON

# *Chapter 1*

A soft spring rain fell gently from overcast skies, bending the leaves of the massive maple tree that partially concealed the bedroom window and landing against the glass panes with a soft, fat plop . . . plop . . . plop. The street was quiet, with only an occasional passing carriage sending up sprays of water from the rapidly forming puddles. Few of the gentlemen living in the mansions that lined this street had ventured out to test their vigor against the inclement weather and—heaven forbid—a lady of means would not so much as set foot beyond her salon on a day such as this. The lower floor of the house was silent, and in the second-floor front bedroom the flurry of activity—which had kept several maids, one seamstress and an anxious mother dashing from bureau to jewelry box to wardrobe and back to the two girls standing stiffly in the middle of the room—had at last abated and the various participants had retired, leaving the girls to sip their hot chocolate in peace.

"How can you be so perfectly calm? I declare, I'm so excited I don't know how I can bear it until the ball. Ouch! Drat those horrid little pins—I do hope these awful scratches disappear before then." Margaret Lawson—Meg to her friends—carefully probed the broken skin beneath the cloth of her sleeve, gave a tiny wince of pain and asked, a trifle peevishly, "How do you manage to stand so long without moving? Every time I have a fitting my nose itches or a strand of hair drops into my eye. Eden . . . oh, Eden Thackery, you're not even listening to me!"

The tall, slender figure at the window turned slowly, an indulgent smile lifting the corners of a perfectly shaped mouth. As usual, Meg thought resentfully, Eden was unshakable, despite the madness of the afternoon. Only the dressing gown tied at Eden's tiny waist, and the fact that Eden's golden hair had escaped the confines of its chignon to fall in a glorious cascade to her hips, betrayed the fact that Eden had taken part in the organized chaos.

"Ah, but I am, dear Meg," came the soft reply. "You were wondering if the grievous damage done by madame's pins is

permanent." Gray eyes that moments before had been wistfully
watching the rain's descent now turned their misty depths upon
the seated girl. "You are too impatient, Meg; that is the problem. Patience and practice."

Meg wrinkled her upturned nose. "You sound like Mama.
She has been lecturing me on that same subject since we returned two weeks ago."

"You are lucky to have her," Eden admonished softly, and
Meg flushed guiltily for having forgotten her friend's orphaned
state.

Eden's own mother had died six years earlier, leaving a
painfully shy ten-year-old Eden in the care of an uncaring
father. Now, watching Eden glide to the fire, Meg could vividly
recall their first meeting. After his wife's death, Locke Thackery had had no time to waste on so unprofitable a project as
raising a daughter—especially a daughter who scarcely spoke
more than two words to him whenever they dined—and had
promptly shipped Eden off to Miss Rosehart's Christian Seminary for Young Women.

Meg already had been at Miss Rosehart's for a year, as had
Jane Gregory, Hope Chandler, Kate Marlin and others from
New York, when Eden had arrived, and their unquestioned
authority had already been firmly entrenched. It was to Jane
that Meg's thoughts now turned—beautiful, spiteful Jane with
her honey hair and melted-chocolate eyes, who had instantly
recognized a rival in Eden.

"Jane will be at the ball," Meg said almost idly, but her
green, gold-flecked eyes were alight with an unspoken question.

For a long moment the only sound in the room was the
ticking of the clock on the bedside table and Meg wondered
if Eden had even heard the comment; but when Meg caught
the sudden hardness in the gray eyes and the almost imper-
ceptible tenseness of the finely molded features, she shuddered
inwardly. Oh, yes, Eden had heard.

"I know," Eden's normally gentle voice replied coolly.

So Eden, too, was recalling the past. Had it really happened
only two years ago? Meg thought, striving to remember how
they had looked at fourteen. To Eden's credit, she had endured
Jane's snide comments with more good grace than Meg herself
ever could have. For nearly five years Eden had never retaliated
with a scathing retort, only with a slight lifting of her head.

The circle in which the girls traveled always had held Jane in awesome regard; the others had, in truth, been more than a little afraid that Jane would turn on them if they tried to defend the stoically silent Eden.

Who would have guessed what was being planned beneath that calm exterior? How could anyone have known that Eden had inherited the cold-blooded vengefulness which so many had feared in her father while he lived? Locke Thackery had been a man to reckon with, and it was Jane's misfortune that she mistook Eden's reticence for weakness.

"Jane deserved it," Eden said sharply, her thoughts exactly matching Meg's own. "You know she did, Meg."

Meg nodded in silent agreement, her dark curls bouncing around her face. They all should have guessed, on that early spring day, that Eden's patience had reached its end. Eden had said little, as was her nature, but there had been an aura of expectancy surrounding her when the girls had retired to the garden to work on their embroidery. Even now, Meg could see the five girls as they arranged themselves in the chairs around the table. For a time they had stitched in silence, occasionally exchanging random small talk and thoroughly enjoying the warmer weather—until Jane had wearied of the peaceful companionship.

"I understand your father sold the last of his slave ships before he died, Eden." Jane's eyes had glittered in the sunlight.

Eden had slowly looked up from her stitchery, her gray eyes expressionless. What should have warned Jane was the hint of a smile that flickered briefly over Eden's lips.

"I suppose that makes you feel you are our equal now," Jane had continued, carelessly brushing a strand of thread from her skirt.

"On the contrary." Eden had carefully laid aside her material and fixed her gaze upon Jane. "I have *always* considered myself *your* equal."

Needles had stopped, poised in midair; nervous glances were exchanged; even Jane was momentarily disconcerted by the unfamiliar note in Eden's voice. Then Jane laughed. So it had finally happened. After four long years timid little Eden had decided to make a stand. The other three girls had settled back, like Romans of ancient times, to watch the spectacle unfolding before them. Meg's heart had leaped painfully against her ribs—do be careful, Eden, she had wanted to warn her friend.

Only Meg knew how deeply Jane's comments had wounded Eden; only Meg, in the room she shared with Eden, had heard her muffled sobs late at night.

But the first attack had been launched; the two gladiators had squared off. The others were already sure of the outcome—Jane had a history of victories in the arena, and her path was littered with the crushed egos and bruised pride of other, less experienced opponents.

"My equal," Jane had laughed, incredulous; then her voice had turned harsh. "Your father bought his way into polite society with money earned by the transporting of blacks from Africa. And your own mother's father was a slaveowner—perhaps your mother even owned a slave or two before she left Louisiana."

"Perhaps," Eden had agreed quietly. "She lived in a time and place where owning a person of color was acceptable. But I don't wish to discuss my parents with you, Jane, so kindly refrain from mentioning them."

This second, quiet warning was also totally lost on Jane, who had plunged ahead. "Do not presume to tell me what I may or may not discuss," she had said haughtily. "I do as I please!"

"You will regret it." It was Eden's third and last, warning. "Mine isn't the only family with skeletons in the closet. Do you still wish to discuss buying a place in society?"

The insinuation had been too much for Jane to bear in front of her followers, and she had sprung to her feet, a bright spot of red coloring each cheek. "Your father was a dirty flesh-seller," she had spat out, "and your mother was a southern strumpet!"

The others had gasped at Jane's insults and, as one, had turned in horror to watch Eden's reaction. Of them all, Eden was the only one who had appeared calm and unmoved. How can she do it? Meg had wondered, with a mixture of admiration and pity—but her pity had rapidly evaporated when she noticed the strange, vengeful gleam in the depths of Eden's suddenly hard eyes. Something cold had then touched Meg's spine.

"The more common name for your father's profession," Eden had continued ruthlessly, "was pimp—procurer, if you will; that's the polite name for it. But that was only after he stopped supplying guns and alcohol to the Indians in the West. Oh, he's very proper and respectable now—his fortune is clean, as are his hands, and he married into one of the oldest families in New York." The even, relentless voice had paused briefly, and Eden had given a mirthless smile. "Would you like me to continue, Jane. I find your family tree particularly fascinating."

All the color had drained from Jane's face and she gave a short, jerky shake of her head. Eden rose and calmly collected her sewing.

"You don't frighten me, Jane," Eden had said at last. "You never have. Your jokes, made at my expense, I have tolerated. The snide remarks, the snickers—none of that mattered. But you made a mistake when you thought I would stand by and let you slander my family. Unless you want your family's dark secrets revealed, I suggest you refrain from amusing yourself at my family's expense." Her face grim, Eden had fixed each girl in turn with a cold stare. "I'm sure our friends have already forgotten our little conversation here today, but I want you to remember it, Jane. Because if you don't"— Eden had leaned forward so that Jane could not possibly mistake the warning flash in the mist-gray eyes—"believe me, I have only scratched the surface of your background."

From then on, Eden had been the unacknowledged leader of their small band. Oh, Jane had retained the semblance of command, but it was Eden to whom the girls would turn for approval when Jane made a suggestion. And that, Meg reflected as she watched Eden pour another cup of chocolate, was what still rankled Jane. And Eden? Eden had never referred to the incident; had never again argued with Jane—or with anyone else, for that matter. In the six years of their friendship, Meg had seen Eden's cold, unforgiving anger only that once, and that had been quite enough, thank you. You could never tell what Eden was thinking; she was too self-contained, too much in control of herself.

Meg shrugged off the memories and brought her attention back to the present. "Is Hugh coming for you?"

Hugh Colter, her guardian for the past three years, had deposited Eden at the Lawsons' front door that morning.

"No." Eden moved back to the window and began to trace the path of a fat raindrop on the pane. "He arranged with your father for me to use one of your carriages."

"Why don't you spend the night?" Meg offered. "You can send a note to Hugh and not have to brave that awful rain."

"That's kind of you, Meg, but no. I have things to do at home, and I promised Hugh I'd have dinner with him."

"You're so horribly obedient it's frightening," Meg laughed, dispelling the last shadows hovering in the room. "Don't you ever wish to escape? Don't you long for an adventure—just one—before you marry some promising young banker or broker or—"

"—or candlestick maker?" Eden finished with one of her rare, genuine smiles. "Meg, you dream too much, a direct result of those novels you smuggle past your mother." Having neatly evaded the question, Eden set her cup down with a sharp clink. "Now help me find my cloak, Meg; I think it's buried under this pile of petticoats."

The rain had turned into a light drizzle by the time Eden was handed into the Lawson carriage, and she gave a small sigh of relief as the carriage lurched forward. Her finely arched brows drew together; her fingers toyed with a wisp of her glossy hair as she considered Meg's question. An adventure? She, Eden Thackery, throw caution to the wind and follow one of the daring impulses that occasionally seized her mind? In the shadowy interior of the carriage, away from prying eyes, Eden smiled ruefully. To be free, she thought sadly. To be unrestricted by conventions, by society; to do whatever I please; to be what I want to be, rather than what others desire. Her frown returned as she glanced out the carriage window. A few more blocks and she would be home. Hugh would be waiting for her in the study—his refuge, as he was fond of calling it—but he wasn't expecting her for another hour or so....

Eden rapped loudly against the ceiling, and almost immediately the carriage halted. The driver was new, Eden remembered, so it was unlikely he would argue with her order, unless Mr. Lawson...

The driver scrambled down and opened the door. "Yes, miss?" The sound of his voice, so loud in the small coach, startled Eden, but she controlled the erratic jumping of her nerves and arranged her demeanor into the unmistakable manner of authority.

"I . . . I've changed my mind." If the driver noticed her hesitation he gave no sign, and Eden gathered the courage to give him a different destination. "Do you know the place?"

"Yes, miss, the old Thackery mansion—but that's in the opposite direction from—"

"I'm aware of that," Eden interrupted icily. "Take me there and then deliver my packages to Mr. Colter's home, if you please."

The driver hesitated briefly, then nodded, closed the carriage door and sprang back up to the driver's seat. Women, he complained silently as he turned the team and whipped them into a trot. Not a one of them what had a grain of sense. He thought longingly of the warm fire he had left and the pint of rum sitting beside his chair, and as his passenger swept through the front door of the Thackery mansion he wondered bitterly why he had sold his cab.

In the dark entrance hall, Eden paused to give her eyes time to adjust and to steel herself against the flood of bitterness this home unleashed.

"Miss Eden!" A woman of immense proportions lumbered into the hall, a black wool dress stretched to its limit over her curves. "Lord, child, what are you doing here? Is Mr. Colter with you?"

"No, Katrin, I came alone," Eden replied with a tiny smile. Katrin, the housekeeper, had been responsible for the few happy memories she had of this house—Katrin's freshly baked bread smothered with jam for an afternoon treat, Katrin's cool hand placed upon a child's feverish brow in the middle of the night. Eden longed to embrace the smiling, familiar figure, but the years of training and restraint had done their work too well; instead she extended a slender hand to the older woman. "How are you, Katrin?"

"I'm just fine, Miss Eden, and you're prettier than ever."

"Thank you." Eden drifted through the hallway, the heels of her shoes tapping loudly in the deserted mansion. "I'd like to be by myself, Katrin."

The housekeeper nodded in understanding. "When you're ready, miss, there's tea in the kitchen," Katrin called, and with a shake of her head waddled back to the pantry.

Eden walked down the hallway leading to the back of the house; no need to open the doors of the rooms, to reveal that which had carefully been hidden from the eyes of strangers. On the right, her father's library, his office, and finally a gaming room; to Eden's left, the ballroom and music room, divided by a folding panel. She could still recall the exhausting hours spent in that vast, empty room under the vigilant eyes of her piano instructor and dance master, excelling in both disciplines, not because she wanted to, but because it was expected of her.

How often had she stood at the double doors of the ballroom watching her mother twirling around the floor in the arms of her guests while Locke Thackery conducted business on the sidelines, never glancing in his wife's direction? How often had her father caught Eden watching the gaiety and brusquely sent her back to her room with an imperious wave of his hand?

With a sudden, violent motion Eden threw open the massive doors, wincing inwardly as the crash reverberated through the house. The grand piano still stood in front of the row of French doors, its shape a ghostly outline beneath the white dust cover. This time no dance master waited impatiently, no piano teacher toyed with his metronome, nor was her father sitting rigidly upright on the satin-covered sofa, waiting for her to begin the torturous weekly recital, ready to pounce at her smallest mistake. Eden turned abruptly on her heel and let herself out through the rear door leading to the garden.

The garden had been her mother's pride and joy while she had lived. All the love and care for which the child residing in the third-floor nursery had yearned had instead been lavished upon rows of flowers. But now the flower beds contained little more than the withered skeletons of the past, and the once carefully tended paths were yielding to the weeds which grew between the paving stones. Past the flower beds, around the gazebo to the pair of willow trees planted so long ago when Adria Jessup Thackery had come to New York as a bride. Beneath the trees two marble stones, separated by some unknown artist's conception of the angel Gabriel, bore simple, untruthful inscriptions:

|  |  |
|---|---|
| ADRIA THACKERY | LOCKE THACKERY |
| BELOVED WIFE AND | BELOVED HUSBAND |
| MOTHER | AND FATHER |
| 1835–1867 | 1827–1870 |

A vase of fresh flowers standing beside Adria's headstone brought a wry smile to Eden's lips. The unknown admirer, faithful to the end. Since the day of Adria's death a vase of flowers, without a card, was delivered every morning, in all kinds of weather, seven days a week. While Locke was alive he had tried in vain to discover who sent the bright flowers, and upon his death his inability to solve the mystery was probably the one thing he regretted, the only failure of his life.

Eden plucked a solitary bud from the vase. "I should think he would have stopped sending them after all this time," she remarked softly to a squirrel who was studying her with great interest. "After six years, his florist bill must be enormous. I wonder if she knew?"

Eden left the garden, retracing her steps across the sodden lawn. She ignored the tempting warmth of the kitchen, as well as the fondly remembered parlor on the second floor, and instead found herself standing just inside her mother's bedroom. In this room, too, the furniture had been draped with white dust covers. Eden had been born in this room, yet how seldom she had visited it—three times in all, counting the night her mother had died. Lovely, fragile Adria, whose patrician features and blond hair Eden had inherited, was little more than a vague memory to her daughter.

Eden flicked aside the cloth on one of the chairs and sank gracefully onto the cushion. Hers had not been a happy family. Eden could not think of it without a sharp stab of pain. Father's first love had been money . . . lots and lots of money. Eden could vividly recall the morning on which the outbreak of the war had been trumpeted in the newspapers.

"Hah!" Locke had exclaimed, banging the palm of his hand on the breakfast table. "I knew those damned Southerners would do it!"

"Locke, please," Adria had objected softly, "not in front of Eden."

"Why not?" Locke had demanded. "The child will hear the words eventually. But never mind. Do you realize what this war means, Adria? The army will need guns, bullets, cannon, material for uniforms, medical supplies—the possibilities are endless!"

"And young men will kill and be killed, thousands will be horribly mutilated, homes will be destroyed, the land will be left scarred and barren. Oh, yes, Locke, I know what it means," Adria had answered, but her sarcasm had been wasted. When Locke left the table he was whistling.

Four-year-old Eden had timidly ventured, "Daddy happy."

"Why shouldn't he be?" Adria had sighed. "He'll find a way to turn misery into profit."

Adria had paid dearly for any spark of defiance she had dared display, and gradually the strain between her and Locke began to tell. Little by little her health failed and she kept to her rooms so much that a place was no longer set for her at meals. Soon Adria left her sanctuary only when her presence was required at one of Locke's dinner parties. The final blow was the Union victory over the South. When the majority of Adria's letters to childhood friends at home were returned marked "deceased" or "whereabouts unknown" she knew that there was no reason to accept Locke's offer of a visit to her beloved South. There remained one final duty for her to discharge, and Adria Jessup Thackery clung tenaciously to life for the two years it took her to fulfill that obligation. Adria managed, with amazing subtlety, to secure in Locke's mind a prominent position for Hugh Colter. And, in turn, Hugh's protection for Eden. That accomplished, Adria died as unobtrusively as she had lived.

Unheard by Eden, a second visitor arrived at the mansion. His silver hair sparkling with raindrops, Hugh Colter stood at the doorstep and cursed silently at having forgotten his hat.

"Well, Katrin," Hugh growled when the housekeeper let him in, "where is she?"

"Somewhere in the house, sir, but I don't know where," Katrin answered frankly. "I tried to keep track of her, but she seemed, well, rather odd, sir."

Hugh glared. "Odd? How?"

"Well," Katrin hesitated, "rather like her mother before the end came. Just walking through the house—you know, sir."

Hugh's lips thinned angrily at the reference to Adria. Common gossip had labeled Adria as mad, but she hadn't been. At least not to Hugh, just returned to New York after four long, bloody years of war. Irish by birth, American through immigration, Hugh had spent the past fifteen years as a soldier. Before that he had tried the life of a farmer out West for a year, and before that, two years as a longshoreman on the docks of New York. Not exactly the proper training for a man in his early thirties who suddenly found himself with more money than he had ever dreamed of possessing.

It had been at Locke's insistence, Hugh recalled as he searched the rooms on the first floor, that Hugh had agreed to remain in New York, and it had been through the wizardry of Locke's careful investments that Hugh's fortune had grown.

The idea had been immensely attractive for the formerly impoverished Irishman—Hugh had had his fill of smelling like a horse and finding entertainment in dance halls. Hugh's hands had been far from clean when he had met Adria—his money had been won at the card tables of saloons in the West and from the bounty that was paid for Indian scalps—but she had understood that the circumstances made the man, not the other way around. So the fragile, transplanted southern belle had taken the rough Irishman under her wing—had smoothed his jagged edges, taught him how to read, how to dress, which fork to use, how to speak without letting his Irish brogue steal into his voice. And, in the final two years of her life, Adria had entrusted the daughter for whom she dared not display affection—out of fear that Locke would separate them—into Hugh's care. Less than a month after Adria's death, Locke had legally named Hugh as Eden's guardian.

Hugh slowly climbed the staircase to the second floor, the freshly oiled banister slippery to his touch. Though the continued growth of Hugh's wealth was due now to his own hard work at his shipping company plus a few shrewd investments in real estate, he was also the trustee of Eden's inheritance—which included the firm of Thackery Ltd. When Locke had succumbed to a heart attack three years ago, Hugh had wasted no time removing Eden to his own home; he wanted to be close at hand when the composed girl gave vent to her grief. The well-meaning precaution had been unnecessary; to Hugh's knowledge Eden had never wept for her parents. Adria's words had come back to him then: Make her happy, teach her to laugh. But dear Adria had underestimated the strength of the shell Eden had been forced to raise around herself for protection. Gradually, carefully, over three long years, Eden had learned that Hugh demanded nothing from her, that she was surprisingly free to enjoy whatever she desired. And Hugh's tender care had had its rewards as Eden—slowly at first, and then with increasing frequency—had allowed the shell to fall away when Hugh was present.

At first it had been a simple matter for Hugh to include Eden in his household. At thirteen, despite her wariness, she had been starved for the attention and affection Hugh found so easy to give her. But this last year had been a kind of torture for the burly Irishman. When Eden had returned from school during the Christmas holidays, Hugh had been severely jolted by the realization that she was no longer a child—Eden had somehow, by some miraculous transformation, blossomed into a willowy beauty, slightly taller than the average woman, with an alabaster complexion that seemed to cry out for a man's touch. Hugh's chest constricted. It was like a sordid joke; the older guardian in love with his youthful ward and unable—because he knew such a union stood little chance for happiness or success—to declare himself. So Hugh concealed his love for the enchanting creature under his protection and forced himself to smile benevolently at the young, ardent suitors who beat a path to his door. Not one of them was good enough for his Eden; not one.

Hugh stopped just short of the bedroom doorway. There she was, sitting motionless in the murky twilight filtering into the room. Softly, so as not to frighten her, Hugh murmured, "Eden."

Mist-gray eyes swiftly focused on Hugh's powerful form. Eden's expression relaxed ever so slightly when she recognized the intruder. "What on earth are you doing here, Hugh?"

"I might ask you the same thing," Hugh answered as he crossed the room. "Whatever prompted you to come here?"

Eden shrugged. "I really don't know. I was on my way home when suddenly I had this . . . this urge to see the house." She gave Hugh a small smile. "Odd, isn't it? Somehow I expected it would look different after all these years, but it hasn't changed at all. Here it stands; my father's monument to the world."

Hugh raised an eyebrow at the bitter comment. "It's a beautiful house; tastefully decorated—"

"Oh, yes," Eden cut in, "we Thackerys are noted for our taste in furnishings. We do everything properly—we go to the right schools, patronize the arts. My mother was an absolute genius at giving parties so that Father would get whatever he wanted from the men she so charmingly dazzled."

"Eden," Hugh eyed her sadly. "It's over, dear heart; they're dead and buried."

"I know," she said in a shaky voice, the defensive shell disappearing for the present. "I never mourned for them, Hugh! I never shed one tear when they died—and I still haven't. Why? Why can't I mourn? Why can't I cry? They were my parents, Hugh, I should feel—*something*, some emotion besides this . . . this bitterness, this hatred!"

Hugh firmly quelled the desire to pull Eden into his arms, and instead lowered himself onto the bed. "Would it help to know your mother loved you very much? And . . . and your father, too, in his own way." The lie stuck in Hugh's throat, but he could do nothing less for his sweet Eden.

"In a pig's eye," Eden retorted in a steely voice. "My father was a cold-blooded reptile and you know it."

"Such language, Eden," Hugh groaned and ran a huge hand through his damp, silver mane, a hint of Ireland touching his voice. "Maybe it was a mistake, my being appointed your guardian. You need a woman around, not an old bachelor who's too set in his ways to teach you what you should know. I understand that you're hurting, dear heart, and I just don't know what to do to help you."

"Oh, Hugh!" The guilt in his voice brought Eden out of her own bitter reverie. "Hugh, that simply isn't true—I don't think there is anyone else in the world who could have done for me what you have." Eden leaned forward and brushed her fingertips over Hugh's clenched hands, giving a small, uncertain laugh. "Do you remember how you used to tell me those awful jokes when you came to visit? And the stories you'd tell about Ireland? When I knew you were coming I'd watch for you from my window. And when I saw you turn in the drive, I'd fly down the stairs and wait for you in the library. I still have the carved horse you gave me for my eleventh birthday." Unexpected tears welled in the gray eyes and clung to the thick, dark lashes. "I've never told you before how much I enjoy your company, and I should have. I'm very lucky to have you, Hugh."

Hugh fumbled inside his jacket for a handkerchief and handed it to Eden, feeling his heart expand and contract painfully while he watched her dab at her eyes. She did care for him, but as a child would care for a father; that knowledge plus the tears coursing down Eden's cheeks defeated Hugh's resolve and he pulled Eden's head against his chest. Damn! Hugh lamented angrily. I want her love, not her gratitude.

At length Hugh pushed Eden away but retained a firm grip on her shoulders, his blue eyes strangely bright as he studied her. "Dear heart, that's the kindest thing you've ever said to me."

Eden returned Hugh's smile, then suddenly jumped to her feet, dismay written on her face. "Hugh, look, it's nearly dark!

Your friends will be arriving at the house soon—we'd better hurry."

When Katrin shut the door behind them, she was surprised to hear Hugh's rumbling laughter floating back to her on the wet air.

# Chapter 2

The week that followed was pure hell for Hugh. Eden, having admitted Hugh into her most private thoughts, seemed to drop all the walls between them and made an effort to show her appreciation of his guardianship. Her well-meaning attention strained Hugh's willpower to its limits, as it only served to remind him that Eden was more and more a woman and less and less a child. Watching Eden drift through his home or greet his rough—and often bawdy—friends from his impoverished days with the same unwavering smile with which she met her own acquaintances, Hugh found that he dreaded knowing there would come a time when this graceful creature would marry, leaving him alone in a house far too large for his own needs. There was a simple answer to that problem, of course. At forty Hugh Colter was still young enough to be considered an excellent catch. His body was lean; the powerful muscles developed through the years of hard physical labor still were firm. The only evidence of the encroaching years was the stunningly silver hair, although that, too, could be an advantage, since it contrasted strongly with Hugh's suntanned face and his piercing blue eyes, with the fine lines radiating from their corners. Even the deep grooves on either side of his mouth did not detract from the strong line of his jaw. All told, Hugh felt certain that if his physical appearance didn't attract one of New York's well-endowed younger widows, the size of his bank account would.

So it was with a certain amount of determination that Hugh set forth with Eden to still another debut at the St. Nicholas Hotel. What might otherwise have been a trying evening—it set Hugh's teeth on edge to watch Eden being fawned over by a pack of stripling youths—could, with a little effort, very well turn out to be enjoyable.

"You look awfully pleased with yourself," Eden remarked at Hugh's sudden smile as he settled more comfortably against the leather cushions of the carriage. "I should think that with the depression you'd be dour as a Scotsman."

"Since when do young ladies bother their heads with busi-

ness?" a surprised Hugh asked. "You're supposed to worry
about dresses and such—speaking of which, dear heart: Have
you decided on a gown for your debut?"

"Hugh, I'm serious." Eden leaned forward, her eyes round
with concern. "I know you feel it's your duty to protect me,
but it's impossible for me to ignore closed businesses and
notices posted about receivership. Some stores and wholesalers
are offering their entire inventories at reduced prices just to get
ready cash. I may be young, Hugh, but I'm neither blind nor
stupid. Tell me honestly: Are you in trouble financially?"

"What would you do if I were?" Hugh countered with a
grin.

"Well," Eden said thoughtfully, "I...I could sell my
father's house—it should bring quite a bit, even in today's
market. Or I could find a job, or..."

"Wait, wait," Hugh said, laughing at the eager proposals.
"Your concern is most touching but totally unnecessary, I assure you. If there's one institution I basically distrust it's a
bank. I don't believe in putting all my eggs in one basket, or
all my cash in one bank. Investments are the key—as your
father so often pointed out to me. Good, solid investments such
as land, factories and mines all give a good return on money
invested—you can buy cheap, then sell at a good profit. But
never give up a sizable cushion of cash to fall back on in case
one of your ventures goes sour—remember that, Eden. And
now, dear heart, what about your coming-out ball?"

Eden shrugged and smoothed her skirt. "Must I have one?
Oh, all right, I know I must, and I know the date has already
been set, but I resent being put on display like a side of beef
in a butcher's window. I keep waiting for someone to ask how
much I run per pound. It's humiliating!"

"But necessary." The carriage had stopped and Hugh
jumped out, then reached up to assist Eden. "It's one of the
social evils you must live with. But aside from that, among
the men who attend these affairs is your future husband. I do
promise, however, not to arrange a match unless the man meets
with your approval."

"If you're not careful, you'll find yourself with a spinster
on your hands—and a spoiled one into the bargain!" warned
Eden as she handed her cloak to Hugh, but inwardly she was
thankful. She refused to think what a loveless marriage would

mean—the memory of her parents' attempt at matrimony still was too fresh to allow Eden to contemplate her own marriage.

The grand ballroom was already filled with the best of New York's society when they entered, and as they made their way through the press of people Eden nodded politely to several acquaintances. The relaxation she had felt in the privacy of the carriage was gradually disappearing, and Eden felt herself slipping into the polite, detached woman everyone knew.

"You look far too serious, dear heart." Hugh's quiet voice drew Eden's attention and she smiled faintly as Hugh presented her with a glass of champagne. "Not too much, and drink it slowly, Eden. Margaret Lawson has been waving frantically ever since we came in. Didn't you see her?"

"I saw her; she's with Kevin Davis—he's home from Harvard for vacation—and Tim and Jane Gregory, and another man I don't recognize."

"Don't you want to join them?"

"Not particularly." Eden wrinkled her nose in distaste. "Jane and I aren't exactly the best of friends—even if Tim does have the misguided notion that he's in love with me. Can you picture me as Jane's sister-in-law?"

Hugh laughed softly. "I have a feeling you'd come out on top. Better brace yourself, Eden. Tim's coming this way and from the look on his face I'd say he intends to carry you back to that happy little group. Enjoy yourself, dear heart."

Eden shot him a disgusted look but Hugh simply grinned and disappeared into the crowd.

"Good evening, Eden." Tim Gregory stood beside her, the smile on his face oddly shy despite the fact that he was six years older than she. Tim's features and coloring matched his sister's, but his gentle brown eyes lacked the malice that was so much a part of Jane's personality.

"Hello, Tim," Eden said quietly, resting her hand on his proffered arm. "You look very handsome tonight."

"Why . . . thank you, Eden." Tim looked extraordinarily pleased with her compliment and flushed slightly, causing Eden to think how truly fond she was of this uncertain young man. "You look beautiful—Jane will be green when she sees your gown. Mother made her wear white again, with only ribbons for color."

Eden glanced down at the organdy-swathed neckline of her gown. The low, curved neckline—made in the latest fashion—

lay off her shoulders, baring a goodly expanse of creamy flesh in both front and back. Of blue-shot silk, the long, tight-fitting basque bodice accented Eden's small waist, while the peplum fell in graceful folds over her narrow hips. An elaborately draped overskirt of the same material was drawn back just below the hips to cascade over the bustle and fall downward, ending in a yard-long train, but the silver tinsel underskirt was, to Eden, the most striking feature of her gown. The tinsel shimmered when she moved, reflecting the colors of everything she passed and lending a perfect counterpoint to the blue silk. The gown was a small act of rebellion on Eden's part—she was heartily disenchanted with the custom of wearing white until one's debut.

"Jane's found a new prey that's keeping her busy," Tim said ruefully, mistaking Eden's silence. "She's going to land in a lot of trouble if she keeps flitting around like a drunken moth—especially if Dan finds out about it."

"Isn't he here tonight?" Eden asked in surprise.

"He had a business meeting with some out-of-town clients," Tim replied with a shrug. "You know Dan Miller's philosophy: business before pleasure. Did I tell you Dan asked Father for Jane's hand? She's been lording it over Meg all evening and I think Kevin is hoping the earth will open up and swallow him."

"I don't understand," Eden said, puzzled. "If Jane is practically engaged, then why is she making such a fuss over . . . what did you say his name is?"

"Banning, Neil Banning. And you'll see soon enough what all the fuss is about. Only promise me that you, too, won't fall at his feet!"

"I'm hardly the falling type," Eden retorted drily; then fixed her lips into a polite smile as they joined the quartet. Eden already knew the others, and Tim introduced her to Neil Banning.

"Charmed, Miss Thackery." The rich, precise voice surprised Eden, and she looked up into a pair of brilliant, golden eyes that reminded her of twin candle flames. The hand holding hers was sun-browned and lean, with long, tapering fingers that exerted a firm but gentle pressure. "I understand now why Tim was so reluctant to rejoin us."

To her chagrin, Eden felt her cheeks warming beneath Neil Banning's gaze, and as gracefully as possible she quickly removed her hand from his grasp. "You're too kind, Mr. Banning." Turning slightly, she smiled affectionately at Meg and Kevin. "Hello, Meg. Kevin, welcome home."

"Eden, you're late," Jane purred as she reclaimed Neil's arm. "How unforgivable of you."

Kevin and Meg took advantage of Jane's diverted attention to slip away from the group, and Eden fixed Jane with a frosty stare.

"Had I known you were waiting for me," she said smoothly, "I would have arrived earlier. I do hope you weren't inconvenienced, Jane."

Jane started to make a biting comment, but thought better of it and instead said sweetly, "Neil is from Mexico, Eden. Isn't that exciting?"

Eden glanced at Neil Banning, wary of anything and anyone who fascinated her adversary. "You're a long way from home, Mr. Banning. Have you come to make a profit from our economic depression or is your visit purely for enjoyment?"

Intrigued by Jane's reaction to this newest arrival, Neil Banning stared down into cool, gray eyes for a moment before answering. "A little of both, Miss Thackery. I assume you aren't against private enterprise?"

The conceited note in Neil's voice unaccountably rankled Eden. "Not at all—and *I* assume you have enough cash reserve to see you through should any of your investments fail?"

"Very good," Neil smiled appreciatively. "Since you seem well versed in economics, why don't we take this dance and you can tell me what might give me the best return on my investment."

Before she had a chance to reply, Neil swept Eden into the crush of dancers, pointedly ignoring the outraged looks both Jane and Tim sent his way. But Neil could not ignore the reproof he saw in the gray eyes that were so calmly regarding him.

"If looks could kill, Miss Thackery," Neil said lightly, "I think I'd be dead by now. Did I insult you so badly?"

"Perhaps in Mexico one does not have to ask a woman's permission for a dance," Eden replied tartly, "but here it's considered in bad taste simply to do as one pleases. I, for one, prefer to be asked."

Neil had the audacity to grin at her and he tightened the arm he held around Eden's waist. "It's bad form in Mexico, too, but you must admit we could hardly strike up an acquaintance with Jane and Tim hanging on our every word."

"You presume a great deal, Mr. Banning," Eden said in a tight voice. From the corner of her eye Eden had caught sight of one of the worst gossips in New York directing pointed looks at herself and Neil, and she groaned inwardly. "I would appreciate it, Mr. Banning, if you would return me to Tim."

"Call me Neil; the way you say 'Mr. Banning' makes me feel as if I were a doddering old man of eighty." God, but she is lovely, Neil thought. With her flaxen hair and flawless, milky skin Eden was a decided contrast to the fiancée waiting for him back home. As a rule Neil had little use for these cold, haughty *norteamericano* types, but he was a thousand miles from Mexico and this one—ah, this one was different.

"Mr. Banning, you are holding me far too closely. Kindly keep to a respectable distance," Eden demanded, desperate now to be free of this annoying man who seemed oblivious to the conventions of polite society.

"Better and better," murmured Neil, drawing her still nearer so that her breasts brushed against his chest. "I was wondering if you were as tepid as your friend Margaret."

"You're not that lucky," Eden responded in a sugary tone just as she drove the sharp heel of her shoe into the arch of his foot. Neil gave a low grunt of pain and Eden found herself, thankfully, free of his embrace. To quell the curiosity exhibited by a few of the other dancers Eden said loudly, "Forgive me, Mr. Banning; I do apologize for my clumsiness." Her eyes held no trace of apology, however, as she looked up at Neil Banning and allowed him to see the indignation flashing there. "Now, Mr. Banning, if you will excuse me?"

It took every ounce of willpower Eden possessed to walk sedately from the dance floor. Indignation rapidly gave way to anger as she weaved a path through the crowd toward the doors opening onto the terrace. The night air was cool, a welcome relief from the warmth of the ballroom and its nearly overpowering odor of women's perfume and men's cologne, and Eden allowed the faint breeze to drive the heat from her cheeks. The man hasn't a shred of common sense, Eden thought furiously as she began to pace the terrace. Is Mexico so lacking in polite society that a woman's reputation means nothing?

"Call me Neil," she mimicked acidly to the night. "Hah! I hope I broke every bone in his foot."

"You very nearly did." Neil's clipped voice came softly from the shadows behind her, and Eden whirled about with a small gasp of alarm. "You surprise me, Eden. I had no idea young ladies of good breeding knew such tricks. You really should be ashamed of yourself."

Eden controlled her rising temper with an effort. The arrogance of the man! "Had you done as I requested, that trick, as you call it, would not have been necessary. I don't enjoy being the subject of gossip, Mr. Banning, but since you ignored my protests you left me no other recourse. And now you have compounded the problem by following me here."

Eden made the mistake of trying to brush by Neil and immediately her arm was caught in an iron grip that made her wince inwardly. For a long moment Eden struggled wordlessly to free her arm while Neil drew her inexorably closer to him, a mocking smile curving his lips. A flicker of pain crossed Eden's face and abruptly Neil relaxed his grip.

"You don't give an inch, do you, Eden Thackery," Neil remarked, more as a statement than an inquiry. She is a challenge, he admitted to himself as he watched Eden regain her composure. He had not failed to notice the rare smile that had broken the reserved expression of Eden's finely boned, oval face when she had greeted her friends, yet since that moment Eden's mien had revealed no true emotion. The other women Neil knew would fall at his feet when he flashed his particularly winning smile, but Eden seemed totally immune. Maybe he had been too secluded on the hacienda these past two years; with only the eager serving girls on whom to exercise his charms it was possible, just possible, that he had lost his touch.

"Are you quite finished with me, Mr. Banning?" Eden's tone was glacial, but inwardly her heart was pounding like a sledgehammer.

"Afraid, Eden?" Laughter danced in the depths of Neil's golden eyes as he sensed her reaction to his closeness. "Afraid because I treated you like a woman of flesh and blood instead of like some damn virgin goddess?"

"I don't know what you mean," Eden told him stiffly, shocked by his language as well as by his choice of topics.

"You will," Neil assured her, the knuckles of his right hand lightly brushing the ivory skin of her cheek. "And God help us when you do."

Unwillingly Eden felt her defenses giving way to the mag-

netic attraction that arced between them like a living thing.
Neil was tall and lean, but his broad shoulders—emphasized
by the elegant cut of his swallowtail coat—hinted at the
strength concealed by the material. He was a man to be reck-
oned with, perhaps even feared, and as Eden studied his aristocratic features she had the uneasy feeling that he could read
the thoughts whirling through her mind. He was so handsome,
so totally different from the young men who came to court her.
Eden found herself toying with the idea of letting him kiss her.
Would she like to be kissed by Neil Banning? Would it be
enjoyable? Would she like to be enfolded by those strong arms,
to feel herself pressed tightly against that taut, masculine body?

Neil asked softly, "Have you ever been kissed by a man,
Eden?"

"Of course," she answered sharply, annoyed by the question
and by her own reactions.

"No, sweetheart, I don't think you have. Oh, Tim has probably kissed you, and maybe one or two others like him have
tried, but they weren't much, were they? A quick, rather sloppy
kiss stolen when no one could see you; probably a bit off the
mark, too, so that your teeth cut into your lip and you had to
use a cold compress to reduce the swelling?"

The question dropped into a silence which Eden stubbornly
maintained, adamantly refusing to give Neil the satisfaction of
knowing how close he was to the truth. Her eyes slid down
from Neil's and she stared sullenly at the pleated white front
of his shirt. Neil watched the expressionless mask settle over
Eden's face and after a long moment he chuckled and cupped
her chin in one hand, forcing the cool, gray eyes to meet his
own golden gaze.

Eden found herself helplessly trapped by his gaze, and even
as she fought against the attraction she felt for him, she knew
it was useless. Was it the cobra that hypnotized its prey before
it struck? Eden wondered irrelevantly as Neil's face lowered
toward hers.

"Here you two are. Whatever happened, Neil? You've been
gone for ages!"

At the sound of Jane's voice Eden recoiled from Neil's
touch only to find his hands on her arms, controlling her instinctive reaction. Neil gave Eden a warning look before turning
to speak over his shoulder to Jane.

"Miss Thackery felt a bit faint," Neil answered smoothly. "She thought some fresh air would do her good."

Neil had circled to Eden's side and now Tim hurried forward, his expression mirroring his concern.

"Eden, are you all right?" Tim asked as he chafed her hands between his own. "The way you ran out . . ."

"Yes, of course," Eden replied quickly. "As Mr. Banning explained, I suddenly felt faint and he was kind enough to make certain I had recovered. We were just about to return—"

"I should hope so," Jane cut in imperiously, then turned to Neil with a pout. "You've already missed two of the dances you promised me, and I shan't allow you to neglect me further."

With a brilliant smile Neil offered Jane his arm. "Dear lady, I beg your forgiveness, and since Miss Thackery feels so much better . . ."

The rest of Neil's words were swallowed up by the orchestra as he and Jane returned to the ballroom. Eden shook her head to clear the cobwebs that still seemed to paralyze her even though Neil had disappeared from sight.

"Would you like to go back inside now?" Tim gently touched her arm. "We can stay out here if you prefer—it's a nice night."

Eden drew a deep, steadying breath. "No, thank you, Tim. I'd like to go back," she replied, refusing to acknowledge her own chaotic emotions. "We haven't danced tonight either."

Tim was graceful and considerate as they waltzed around the ballroom, but Eden was acutely aware of Neil Banning as he drifted almost constantly into her line of vision. Whether he did this intentionally or not, Eden couldn't be sure, but the mocking smile Neil bestowed upon her whenever their eyes clashed sent the blood rushing to Eden's cheeks.

"Are you certain you feel all right?" Tim asked as he led her from the floor. "You're as pale as a ghost one minute and bright red the next. Would you like me to call Hugh?"

"Oh, Tim! Let it be, can't you?" Eden blurted out, annoyed to no end by his attitude. "I'm fine, fine, fine!"

Tim looked at her in disbelief. "What's gotten into you tonight, Eden? Did Banning try something? By God, if he did . . ."

"No, no," Eden hurriedly interrupted. "I'm sorry, Tim, I didn't mean to snap at you; but I have to stop depending upon Hugh for everything, don't you see?" She rushed on, desperate to placate Tim and to change the subject. "Three years ago I was dumped into Hugh's lap—a ready-made family he hadn't expected—and I upset his entire life. It's time he was able to live the way he wants to without having to worry about me. I'm sixteen now and I'm perfectly capable of handling my own life—of making my own decisions."

A hopeful gleam came into Tim's eyes, all thoughts of Neil Banning vanishing as rapidly as they had appeared, and he grasped eagerly at Eden's hand. "There *is* a way you can give Hugh back his freedom. You know how I feel, Eden, I've made no secret of it. I swear you'll never regret making this decision—Eden, marry me."

Taken aback by his proposal, Eden could only stare wordlessly at Tim, her throat constricting in panic at the thought of marriage. Images of her mother flashed through Eden's mind, bringing with them a terror so great that she barely heard Tim's words.

"I'll make you happy, Eden, I promise. I'll be a good husband to you—you'll never want for anything. There's some land for sale near my parents' house; we could build our home on it. Would you like that? You could decorate it exactly as you please..." Tim's words trailed off as he waited for some indication that Eden accepted his offer, but she merely watched him, her expression frozen.

Eden's thoughts were in such turmoil that she failed to see Tim's expectant look. Oddly enough, for all of her terror of marriage, Eden Thackery was a romantic. She firmly believed in her heart of hearts that one day she would meet a man and they would fall passionately in love. Her imaginary lover would be easily recognized, for he would send Eden's heart beating wildly, and his very presence would make her feel warm and secure. To this one man Eden would be able to open herself completely; she would be able to cast off the restraints it had been necessary for her to adopt in order to survive. In marriage Eden would find freedom—but not in marriage to Tim; that would be a dreadful mistake for them both.

"Oh, Tim," Eden said softly. "I'm flattered, truly I am. You're very sweet and I'm terribly fond of you. I value your friendship and you are dear to me, please believe that."

The flame went out of Tim's eyes, to be replaced by a look of pain. "But your answer is no, isn't it?"

Tim's pain hurt Eden deeply, and she shaded the truth to

spare him. "For the present, Tim, it's the only answer I can give you. Let me have time to discover the world now that I'm out of school. In a year, say, if your feelings are the same, ask me again—maybe my answer will be different then."

For a moment Tim looked undecided, then finally he gave a quick nod of his head. "A year, then, but I shall make a down payment on the land anyway, just in case."

Eden was about to dissuade Tim from the investment when Jane, Neil at her side, descended upon them.

"Tim, dear," Jane purred, "you look positively grim. Eden, what have you done to my poor brother?"

"Not a thing," Tim snapped at his sister.

"My, my, aren't we in a black humor," Jane commented caustically with a look at Eden. "I was going to invite you both to come with Neil and me, but . . ." She left the sentence unfinished and raised her shoulders in an eloquent shrug.

With a nervous glance at Neil, Tim objected quietly, "You can't leave and you know it. What will Dan say?"

"Who cares?" Jane answered pettishly. "It will teach him a lesson. Dan's already two hours late, and if he thinks I'll stand around and wait for him, he's wrong!"

"Well said," Neil applauded in mocking, precise tones. "We had planned a midnight carriage ride through Central Park; Jane tells me it's quite enjoyable this time of night. You're welcome to join us if you like."

Tim turned to Eden and she saw the indecision in his eyes. He didn't approve of Jane's suggestion, but neither could he allow her to leave the ball with a stranger. Looking up, Eden caught the challenge gleaming brightly in Neil's eyes, and for an instant she was tempted to take up the gauntlet Neil so obviously had thrown at her feet. Common sense prevailed, however, and at last Eden calmly shook her head at such foolishness.

"I think not," Eden said evenly, her eyes locked with Neil's. In a tone which sounded much like an indulgent mother allowing her children to run outside and play, she continued, "But you three go ahead. I'm sure Mr. Banning will find the Bethesda Fountain by moonlight positively spellbinding."

"Do you find it so, Miss Thackery?" Neil questioned lightly, but his look carried an unspoken message. *If you do, then why are you refusing?* One dark eyebrow arched baitingly. *Because you are afraid . . . of me?*

"It's a magnificent sight, Mr. Banning, but I've seen it before." And in far more pleasant company, she added silently. Neil Banning bowed mockingly and, with Jane on his arm, went to collect their wraps and hail a carriage.

Above the high, starched collar of his shirt Tim's face turned an unbecoming shade of red as he wrenched his gaze away from his sister and back to Eden. "Eden, I'm sorry but—"

"But you simply must run after Jane and save her from herself," Eden finished impatiently.

"I'd do the same for you," Tim protested.

Eden favored Tim with her most glacial look. "I should hope I have more sense than to place myself in such an untenable situation."

"You're not being fair," Tim said stiffly. "Jane doesn't mean any harm—she's just upset because Dan allowed a business meeting to spoil her plans."

"I understand exactly how she feels," Eden replied sarcastically.

Tim sighed and glanced anxiously at the door through which Jane and her escort had disappeared. "Eden, I know I'm leaving you stranded here, but you know as well as I do what will happen to Jane's reputation if I allow her to leave alone with that Banning character."

"She'll be ruined." Eden's tone held no pity, although she shuddered inwardly. In New York, a harmless ballroom flirtation was enough to shred a woman's reputation, and every eligible young woman—including Eden—lived in mortal fear of crossing the fine line between being charming and amusing and being labeled scandalous. No matter how much she disliked Jane, being "cut" by society was a fate which Eden would literally not wish upon her worst enemy. "You'd better hurry, Tim, before she gives the dragons their evening feast."

"Eden, you're wonderful." Tim smiled gratefully, but he was already edging away from her. "I'll make this up to you."

Tim was out of sight before Eden had a chance to reply. With a resigned shrug, she pasted a smile back onto her face and made her way across the ballroom to join the small cluster of debutantes who were sitting out this waltz. This latest incident had crystallized Eden's determination not to marry Tim and she wondered, as the remainder of the evening whirled past in a rapid succession of dancing partners, exactly how to phrase her decision when the time came to tell him once and for all.

Distracted as she was, Eden found her thoughts straying back to Neil Banning and their moments together on the terrace. None of the other men she knew produced that wild jarring within her—that feeling of being so . . . so alive! A ridiculous thought, Eden promptly chided herself. His arrogance threw me off balance, that's all. Women find Neil Banning extremely attractive and he knows it, and he made that clumsy advance because I didn't fall at his feet like Jane. It's a relief to be free of Neil Banning and his odious presence.

Yet, as Hugh's handsomely appointed berlin rolled through the gaslit streets long after midnight—with a complacent Hugh dozing in the corner—Eden found herself wondering if Jane still were enjoying Neil Banning's company. And then Eden wondered why she should care.

# Chapter 3

It was early morning when Eden descended from her rooms for breakfast. This was the one routine that had taken her by surprise when she had first entered the household—Hugh had never lost the habit of rising with the sun, and Eden had soon learned that if she wanted a warm morning meal it would be waiting for her in the family dining room. Breakfast in bed was reserved for when she was sick, not for when she overslept.

"Good morning, Hugh." Eden's voice was husky, betraying the yawn she tried to stifle.

"Top o' the morning, Eden," Hugh replied with an exaggerated brogue, his blue eyes dancing as he caught Eden hiding another yawn as she helped herself to the food on the sideboard. "Sleep well?"

Eden shrugged as she slipped into her chair. "Not very—Tim and I had words last night . . . and then, spending time with Jane always puts me out of sorts."

"Well, that's not surprising. You two never have gotten along, expecially after you dragged up her father's past."

Eden nearly dropped her fork. "How did you find out about that?"

Hugh puffed his pipe and smiled at her through the smoke. "It seems Jane cried on Daddy's shoulder and he in turn decided to take it out on me. Best laugh I'd had in years, especially since he couldn't deny a thing. But how did you find out about him?"

With a great show of concentration Eden poured a cup of coffee and carefully added a measure of cream before answering. "My dear departed father had a habit of keeping files on his business associates—"

"I destroyed those," Hugh broke in. "When your father died I found the files and burned them."

"I know." Eden smiled a bitter smile. "If you were hoping to spare me the knowledge of how my father did business, you were too late. But, to return to my answer, that's where I found out about the honorable Mr. Gregory. Believe me, Hugh, I never would have brought up his sordid past if Jane

31

hadn't . . . well, she said some things about Mother that I didn't particularly care for."

"I see." Hugh knocked the ash from his pipe. "Tell me, dear heart: In your curiosity, did you happen to read any of the other reports?"

"If you mean yours," Eden said frankly, "yes, I did. Like my father, I find it helpful to know about the people who surround me."

Her voice was so cold, so completely devoid of any emotion that for a moment Hugh had the uneasy feeling that Locke Thackery had found a way to return from the dead. But the impression rapidly faded, and Hugh smiled at the delicate beauty gracing his table.

"Did it shock you?" Hugh rose and led the way to his study, where he settled himself at his desk and began sorting through the sheaf of papers awaiting his attention.

Eden wandered aimlessly about the room, her fingers trailing over the curved backs of the French Renaissance armchairs before she perched on the seat in front of the bay window.

"Your past?" Eden halted, searching for the right words. "You've had a very . . . checkered life. Dock worker, farmer, soldier—no one can say you were born with a silver spoon. No, Hugh, I wasn't shocked. Surprised, perhaps, but then I think I always sensed that you've had to fight for whatever you wanted. Maybe that's why I've always admired you. You knew what you wanted from life and you got it. I wish I could do that."

"You can." Hugh leaned back in his armchair, blue eyes sparkling in appreciation as he watched the sunlight create a burnished halo around Eden's face. She hadn't bothered to pin up her hair at this early hour and the long, flaxen curls tumbled gloriously about her face down to her waist. With an effort Hugh dragged his thoughts back to the conversation. "I know that at sixteen it seems like the whole world is against you, but it won't always be this way. What you don't realize yet is that with your not inconsiderable inheritance you have more freedom than most people. Even when you marry you won't have to be dependent upon your husband. At least that's one thing you can thank your father for—although I admit I somehow doubt he ever planned for you to be financially independent."

Eden nodded but said nothing; instead she turned and gazed out the window. Receiving no response, Hugh resumed working, the scratching of his pen filling the otherwise silent room. As a diversion, Hugh had started an import business that dealt exclusively with goods from the Orient. Statues, carpets, folding screens, furniture, paintings—all found their way to the New York wharves and from there to Hugh's warehouse. It was more a hobby than a business interest, but as he totaled the ledgers Hugh discovered that most of the goods had been sold to retail houses at a good profit and the firm was solidly in the black.

Which reminded him: "End of the month in a week, Eden. I'll want to go over your accounts then. Are your books in order?"

Even while he asked, Hugh knew the question was rhetorical. The household accounts, as well as Eden's personal account were always up to date, and in three years Hugh had learned that Eden was no spendthrift. In fact, Eden's personal account showed a reserve that would make a bank president smile. Usually Eden would respond to Hugh's question with a laughing comment, but today she simply nodded and continued looking out the window. Hugh shrugged and returned to his paperwork—Eden could be moody at times and it would do no good to press her.

"Hugh?"

"Umm?" Hugh's pen tracked its way across the paper.

Eden's voice was soft when she spoke, but every word exploded like a bomb in Hugh's brain.

"Hugh, Tim asked me to marry him."

The pen gouged into the paper before Hugh could bring his hand under control and he stared dumbly as the ink sank into the blotter.

"Hugh? Did you hear what I said?"

She was crossing the room now and Hugh frantically collected his fragmented thoughts. It wouldn't do for Eden to see he was upset.

"Yes, Eden . . . I heard you." Eden stood in front of his desk, her hands clasped demurely in front of her as she waited for his next words. "What did you tell him?" Hugh managed to croak. A hundred good reasons for delaying the marriage sprang to mind and Hugh had to force himself to remain silent.

"I said no—but Tim looked so very hurt that I asked for some time." Eden looked at her guardian helplessly. "What else could I have done? He asked me last night at the ball and I couldn't very well cause a scene there."

"How long before you have to give Tim your final answer?"

"A year. Hugh, what am I going to do? Tim thinks I'll change my mind, but I won't. Can you believe that he's putting money down on some land near his parents' home? My God, the man won't even give me room to breathe, and all because I went and told him that I felt it was time I started making my own decisions—that I felt responsible, even a little guilty, for being such a burden on you these past years. Admit it, Hugh, it was terribly unfair of my father to name you as my guardian when you were just starting to enjoy your wealth. Precisely what you needed to make your life complete—one daughter, courtesy of Locke and Adria Thackery!"

"I never thought of it that way," Hugh said sharply. "And neither Locke nor Adria could have convinced me to take you into my home if I hadn't wanted you! So don't get the idea that you're some kind of cross I have to bear; and don't think that I'm sitting on pins and needles waiting for you to get married because . . ." this was coming too close to his feelings and Hugh finished lamely, "because I'm not. Don't worry about Tim; if in a year you still feel the same way, we'll find a way to deal with him."

Eden visibly relaxed. "Thank you, Hugh. You have no idea—I spent most of last night wondering how I would handle Tim when my year was up. Oh, Hugh, I had such a miserable evening."

Hugh reached out to pat her hand. "Now that you know, you can stop fretting. Dear heart, you're sixteen; you should be enjoying yourself. There will be plenty of time for you to plan and worry when you're older. What I'm trying to say, Eden, is that there comes a time when you've got to stop hiding behind that wall you've put between yourself and the rest of the world. You have to learn to trust people, my sweet."

"But I do!" Eden protested. "I trust you and Meg."

"How about Tim?"

Eden hesitated, then shook her head.

"The girls you went to school with—aside from Meg?"

Again Eden shook her head.

"Any of my friends?" Hugh continued relentlessly.

"No. Well, perhaps Ian." Eden toyed with the humidor on the desk. "I don't make friends easily . . . acquaintances, yes, that's simple, all I have to do is be polite and laugh at the proper time. But . . . I suppose it's just not in me to trust others as easily as you do."

"All it takes is practice." Hugh sighed and firmly returned the humidor to its place. "Whoever said that youth is wasted on the young was right. Lecture's over for today. Now why don't you spend the rest of the day indulging yourself—God knows you have enough money in your account. Buy a new dress or whatever it is young girls like these days."

"How about one of those beautiful silk caftans that your ship brought in this week?" Eden asked with a mischievous smile. "I hear they are deliciously wicked."

"Absolutely not," Hugh thundered in mock rage. "They're not . . . appropriate for someone your age."

Eden affected a pout, then went to Hugh's side and brushed a kiss on his cheek. "I'm off then. I'll take your advice and spoil myself outrageously." At the door Eden turned and teased, "What would you do if you were fifteen years younger, Hugh?"

Before he could stop the words, Hugh heard himself replying, "I'd marry you, Eden."

For a moment Eden looked shocked and then, sure that Hugh was teasing her in turn, she gave a light laugh and disappeared.

Massive Trinity Church, its tall steeple rising far above the plebeian affairs being conducted in its presence, tolled the hour of ten, the mellifluous sound reminding the throng on the sidewalks below that fortunes were waiting to be made . . . and lost. Here stood the financial institutions of the country; it was behind the windows of these brick and stone buildings that bankers and stockbrokers kept their fingers on the pulse of the nation's economy. It was here in the not-so-distant past that some of those men, upon learning about the collapse of Jay Cooke & Company, found that their empires were crumbling as well. A few—such as Hugh Colter—who had been wise enough not to invest too heavily or trust too completely in the policy of overexpansion that had prevailed nationwide accepted their losses philosophically and set about the process of rebuilding. Others who were less shrewd and less fortunate watched their resources dwindle with growing desperation and chose another route—they died, either quietly, in the privacy of their homes by putting bullets in their brains, or spectacularly, by taking a final, fatal step out of the window of their offices. To them, death was infinitely preferable to the public humiliation of bankruptcy and poverty.

Despite the depression—and in some cases, because of it— well-dressed men still frequented the establishments lining Wall Street. Here Neil Banning alighted from a hansome cab and, after first consulting the brass nameplate on the building which read Thackery Ltd., Financial Consultants, paid off the driver.

The outer office was empty save for a young man seated at a massive, oiled-walnut desk, and Neil waited impatiently for the secretary to acknowledge his presence.

"Yes, sir, may I help you?" Weak blue eyes challenged Neil's right to invade the quiet sanctuary.

Neil returned the stare arrogantly, the short fuse on his temper igniting. In a soft, inflexible voice Neil replied, "My name is Neil Banning. I have an appointment with Mr. Kelly. Announce me."

The secretary hesitated for perhaps half a minute longer while he referred to his calendar; then, obviously impressed with the notation beside Neil's name, he left his desk and disappeared through a door in the back of the office. He returned almost immediately, followed by a balding, middle-aged man.

"Mr. Banning? Matthew Kelly—a pleasure to meet you." Kelly extended his hand and ushered Neil into his office.

Neil settled comfortably into a leather armchair and smiled slightly, declining to open the conversation. Instead he focused his attention on the oil portrait of Locke Thackery which hung on the wall behind the manager's desk.

Matthew Kelly looked uncertainly at the dark, silent man, inwardly cursing his secretary's abrasive nature and hoping this Neil Banning had not been so insulted that he would refuse to do business with the firm.

"Now then, Mr. Banning," Kelly assumed a professional air, "how can we of Thackery Ltd. be of service to you?"

Neil considered toying with Kelly—nothing upset a broker more than knowing a potential client had been affronted and might take his capital elsewhere—but eventually Neil rejected the idea. He was sick to death of New York and wanted only to complete his business and return to Mexico.

"Your firm was most highly recommended to me," Neil began, pausing to light a cigar. "I recently came into a considerable amount of money for which, shall we say, I have no immediate need. I am prepared to invest the entire sum based upon your advice—provided you can assure me a handsome return."

"I see." Kelly steepled his fingers thoughtfully. "You are not a gambler, then, Mr. Banning?"

Neil shrugged. "I indulge occasionally, but I prefer to have the odds in my favor. Don't mistake my intentions, Mr. Kelly; I can well afford to lose the money, but I would rather not. Do I make myself clear?"

"Very," Kelly answered drily. "But I am sure you understand that in this business there are no guarantees. Within the limitations you have set, I can recommend two courses. One, you can invest in an established business. This is the safer of your choices; you are practically assured of a profit, though not a very large one, I'm afraid. The business in which you would invest would be conservative, with a small but consistent growth rate. Your other choice is precisely the reverse. You can back a new, struggling firm—I won't lie, Mr. Banning, it's a risky proposition, but after the initial growing pains have subsided, your return would be a great deal larger than it would be on your first alternative. Of course, you realize you also run the risk of losing your entire investment should either business fail. The choice is yours, Mr. Banning."

"And if I choose to buy out a firm that will shortly be filing for bankruptcy?"

Matthew Kelly expelled his breath slowly. "That is an alternative—but I would advise against it unless you plan to remain in New York and personally supervise the reorganization. Are you willing to do that?"

Neil shrugged. "If all goes well, I won't have to." From his jacket Neil pulled a sheet of paper and handed it to Kelly, who studied it intently. After a moment Neil asked, "Are you familiar with the firm, Mr. Kelly?"

Kelly nodded and said quietly, "I had no idea. This firm has always appeared so stable. How did you come by this information? Are you quite certain it is reliable?"

"Absolutely. I attended college in England with the owner's son—hence my information." Neil relaxed in his chair and fixed Kelly with his golden stare. "I am more than willing to pay the asking price and the son has already agreed to take over the leadership. The only change I intend to make in the company's policy regards cargo. During the war, and for some time thereafter, this shipping line turned a sizable profit. The reason? They carried primarily munitions, supplies, and, in some cases, troops. They relied too heavily on government contracts. When the government sailed into rough seas, so did the line. Under my ownership, government contracts would be limited to less than 1 percent of the business. I intend to continue using the old ships strictly as cargo vessels; in addition, I would like to add several passenger ships. For years, the well-to-do have extolled the virtues of world travel, but I plan to make it possible for members of the middle class to return to the homeland of their fathers, or the land they left years ago and long to see once more before they die. There's a whole new untapped reservoir of potential buyers out there, and I intend to take advantage of the situation."

Matthew Kelly was understandably shocked by Neil's recital and he cleared his throat nervously. "You have obviously thought this through, Mr. Banning, so may I ask why you came to us?"

Neil grinned. "I needed a sounding board—a professional who would tell me whether or not my thinking was basically sound. Your firm has quite a fine reputation, Mr. Kelly." It was obvious that flattery would not mollify Kelly, who saw his commission disappearing right before his eyes. Greed was a vice with which Neil was accustomed to dealing, and he added in a faintly disgusted voice, "For drawing up the necessary papers and attending to a few other minor details—such as seeing to it that my share of the profits is deposited quarterly in a bank in Mexico City—I will pay you an initial fee of ten thousand dollars plus a percentage of the first year's profit, and in addition an annual fee for as long as you continue to represent me. Is that agreeable?"

Matthew Kelly didn't have to be asked twice—he rang for his secretary and had the papers drawn up immediately.

It was known as "Ladies' Mile"; it ran along West Twenty-third Street from Fifth Avenue to Eighth Avenue and it contained every type of shop imaginable. It was possible to walk the length of the street and buy a dress, hat, gloves, shoes, jewelry and books, all from different shops. The mere mention of the "Mile" was known to cause husbands to groan and frantically try to persuade their wives and daughters to spend the day at home.

Hugh had never faced such a problem with his ward. Eden rarely spent a day pleasure-shopping; extensive though her wardrobe was, she was surprisingly frugal, buying new dresses only for special occasions or when she felt an old dress was hopelessly out of style. Eden was not impulsive, but today—her spirits buoyed by the fact that she could depend upon Hugh to stand by her in her refusal to marry Tim—Eden found herself gaily purchasing four new gowns with matching shoes for which she had absolutely no need.

Her protesting stomach reminded Eden that it was nearly lunchtime, but after a longing glance through a restaurant window she crossed the street to the jeweler she frequently patronized. A tiny silver bell over the door announced her arrival, and as Eden stood in the doorway allowing her eyes to adjust from the sunlight, the jeweler stepped from behind one of the counters to greet her.

"Welcome, Miss Thackery." He grasped Eden's hands in both of his affectionately. "Since you were last here I have added a great many pieces you might be interested in—a ring, perhaps, or a necklace, or a pair of earrings?"

Eden laughed softly, fully aware of her weakness for the delicate, sparkling beauty created in this shop. "You are terrible, Marcel; if I purchase one more thing from you I shall have to buy another jewelry box. Now tell me: Is it ready?"

Marcel nodded. "I finished the case yesterday and it is a work of art, if I do say so myself." He led Eden to a counter running the length of the shop. "Browse through this display; I won't be long."

The jeweler disappeared behind the curtained rear doorway and Eden turned her attention to the dazzling array beneath the glass. Had she less willpower, Eden would have purchased every piece of jewelry that caught her eye. The value of the gems was meaningless to Eden; rather she enjoyed the way diamonds trapped and reflected the light in an endless show of colors, and the way a ruby glowed blood-red when she looked at it long enough. These precious stones and more Marcel had set in intricate works of silver and gold that winked invitingly at her. So engrossed was Eden that she didn't bother to look up when the bell above the door signaled another customer—but the rich, mocking voice caused her to turn.

"I thought I recognized you through the window. May I say you look positively ravishing this morning?" Neil Banning's eyes raked her from from head to toe.

"It's afternoon, Mr. Banning," Eden informed him coolly, her high spirits vanishing.

Neil shrugged and laughed. "Morning, afternoon, evening, it makes no difference. You still are the most beautiful woman I've met in New York. Don't blush so, Eden, or these good people will think I've said something indecent to you."

Eden regained her composure with some difficulty. "In which case, Mr. Banning, I thank you for the compliment."

"Lovely, aren't they?" Neil indicated the display.

Unnerved by his presence, it took Eden a moment to decide whether to be civil or cut him dead. Remembering the night before, Eden had just decided to shun him completely when she heard herself say, "Yes, they are. Marcel is very talented—his designs are very popular."

Neil smiled slightly, as if sensing Eden's confusion, and pointed to a pair of silver earrings which were a bit too gaudy for Eden's taste. "Do you like these?"

Eden looked at him ruefully. "Not particularly."

"A bit ostentatious, aren't they?" Neil agreed, an odd note creeping into his voice. "But I promised my . . . my sister a present from New York, and unfortunately she doesn't have the most discriminating taste. The showier the better."

Eden was saved from responding by Marcel returning from the workroom. He placed a square, velvet-covered box in front of Eden, eyeing Neil curiously as he did so. Eden glanced at Neil's brooding expression and smiled reassuringly at Marcel.

"Marcel, this is Mr. Neil Banning. He would like to see those, ah, interesting silver hoops with the large drops of diamonds and turquoise."

Eden drummed her fingertips on the counter as Marcel placed the earrings on the glass. She studied the jewelry with undisguised curiosity. The pieces lacked Marcell's distinctive touch, of that Eden was certain, and she glanced questioningly at Marcel.

Marcel nodded. "One of my apprentices; he has a flair for working in silver but he knows nothing at all about using gems. He's young; he'll learn soon enough. If I might make a suggestion, Mr. Banning . . ." Marcel deftly steered Neil along the case.

Shaking her head, Eden slowly opened the box in front of her. Hugh's birthday was two weeks away and this was to be Eden's special gift to him. The lid snapped back to reveal a large pocket watch, its gold case artfully filigreed and scrolled. The face of the watch was decorated with Roman numerals, each accented by a small emerald. The back of the watch opened as well, and inside the back lid was an ink miniature of Eden along with a slender lock of hair she had carefully braided. Facing the portrait were engraved the words:

AS EVER,
EDEN
1873

Eden smiled at her reflection in the highly polished gold as she returned the watch to its box. Dear Hugh. Would he understand that this was her way of thanking him for the guidance and affection he had given her over the past years? It hadn't been easy for Hugh; Eden knew she had often been moody and withdrawn, yet Hugh seldom lost his patience or temper. Somehow Hugh had found his way through Eden's protective barriers and had shown her the affection she had never received from her own parents. She owed Hugh a great deal, and she would be eternally grateful to him. Perhaps Hugh was right, she thought irrelevantly, maybe she should be more trusting of others.

"Is it satisfactory, Miss Thackery?"

Eden shook off her thoughts and smiled at Marcel, genuinely pleased. "More than satisfactory, Marcel, it's truly a work of art. Thank you so much—I know I didn't allow you much time."

Marcel shrugged. "For you, Miss Thackery, it was no trouble at all. Did you find anything for yourself?"

"Marcel, you're a greedy devil," Eden chuckled, then sighed. "There are several pieces I like . . . but I'm afraid I shall have to pass this time. I'm trying to curb my impulses and, believe me, it isn't easy. And, Marcel, please be sure you address this bill to me."

The jeweler nodded and moved on to another customer as Neil approached.

"You look pleased," Eden commented, noting the packages Neil held in one hand. "Did you get the earrings?"

"I am and I did. I closed a profitable business venture this morning and I plan to celebrate. Why don't you have lunch with me, Eden?"

"That's very kind of you, Mr. Banning, but..."

"Have you already eaten?"

"No, but..."

"Then you must allow me to buy you lunch."

Neil's smile was so engaging that Eden's heart stopped a beat. "I'm sorry, but no. I have plans for this afternoon."

"But not for lunch," Neil persisted. He propelled her to the door and out onto the street, where he regarded her with amusement. "You're worried about your reputation, is that it? Then explain how our having lunch in a public place could possibly damage you. I can hardly rape you in a restaurant."

Eden sighed heavily. "You really are impossible, Mr. Banning."

"The name is Neil and I wouldn't say impossible—more like persistent." Neil watched Eden patiently, waiting for her answer. Eden did look lovely. The sunlight burnished her hair into a pale, flaxen flame and in the slight breeze the dove-gray dress with long, full sleeves molded provocatively to the curves of her body.

This Neil Banning, even with his outrageous sense of humor, was far more to Eden's liking than the arrogant man she had met last night. At least this time he was waiting for an answer instead of simply whisking her off. Regretfully, for she found this sudden change intriguing, Eden shook her head but allowed herself to smile. "I am sorry, but I can't."

"Not even if I apologize for my behavior last night?" Neil's eyes bored into Eden's and his voice deepened. "I do apologize, Eden. My only excuse is that I want to get to know you, and my time in New York is limited. Am I forgiven?"

Neil took her hand and once again Eden felt that unique jarring sensation pass through her at the contact. "My behavior was deplorable as well," Eden said softly. "Gossip is rife in New York, Mr. Banning, and exceedingly cheap. To hold a lady as closely"—she colored delicately—"as closely as you held me can do irreparable damage. Nonetheless, I did over-react."

"So we're even." Unconsciously Neil stroked Eden's hand with his thumb. "Shall we start again, Eden?"

It was tempting—oh, *so* tempting—to forsake the guests Hugh had invited for tonight in favor of this tall, handsome man, who for some unknown reason made Eden feel as if they were the only people on this crowded street. A simple lunch, Eden thought, weakening. What harm could be done? The housekeeper and butler had the preparations for the party well in hand—Eden's presence wasn't necessary. But she veiled her eyes with her lashes as a far more decorous thought crossed her mind. A well-bred lady did not accept a gentleman's first invitation, no matter how attractive she found him. One simply could not risk appearing too eager. Accordingly, Eden withdrew her hand and moved away from Neil, compelling him to follow.

"I thank you for your invitation, Mr. Banning," Eden said graciously, a charming, practiced note of hesitancy coloring her speech. "But today, unfortunately, my time is not my own." They had, without Neil realizing it, reached Eden's panel-boot victoria and as the coachman sprang down to assist her into the vehicle Eden turned and smiled sweetly at her companion. "I hope the duration of your visit is not so brief that we shall not meet again. Good day . . . Neil."

She was driving away, with only the top of her head visible above the collapsible leather hood of the victoria, before it struck Neil how perfectly he had been maneuvered by a mere slip of a girl. Left standing on a street corner, he should have been annoyed, but instead he found the situation amusing. Chuckling, Neil touched the brim of his hat in a mocking salute to the departing carriage, but his golden eyes gleamed wickedly. "Next time, Eden Thackery, you won't escape so easily."

The Eden who critically oversaw the preparations within the Colter mansion was far different from the girl who had flirted so demurely with Neil Banning. Although technically the housekeeper was responsible for the management of Hugh's home, in reality Eden had run the house since her graduation from the seminary. Few if any decisions were made without Eden's approval, and the staff had learned early that their employer's ward ruled with a velvet-covered iron hand.

Upon returning from the "Mile" Eden had gone first to the

kitchen and then to the game room, to insure that the vigorous cleaning which was being done met her standards. Eden was well satisfied during her inspection, but her expression was cool as she examined the game room and its furnishings. The blue brocatelle draperies with their accompanying lace sheers had been taken down, cleaned and replaced, and the gilt cornices had been polished, but Eden confirmed the butler's story by giving the fabric a vigorous shake. With a slight nod of approval Eden moved on to the white Carrara marble mantel and matching marble-topped petticoat tables, all of which met Eden's white-glove test. The Aubusson carpet had been aired and beaten and now occupied a large portion of the freshly waxed mahogany floor. Rosewood Belter armchairs, intricately carved with scrolls and flowers, matched the draperies and stood at intervals around the room. A rosewood game table, surrounded by four side chairs, was placed squarely in the center of the carpet, the table's polished surface glowing in the afternoon sunlight. Wordlessly Eden walked to the walnut double doors and surveyed the room as if she had never seen it before.

"Very well, Simmons," Eden said at last to the hovering butler. "Everything seems to be in order. You've done an excellent job."

"Thank you, Miss Thackery." Simmons, too, surveyed the room, wincing inwardly at the thought of what would soon take place in such elegant surroundings. "Will there be anything else, miss?"

Eden looked at him sharply, well aware of the English butler's thoughts. Well, Hugh was Hugh, and Eden wouldn't change him for the world. In a tone guaranteed to freeze his blood, Eden added, "Make certain you have enough Bourbon brought up, Simmons. You will recall that last time you ran short and the gentlemen were forced to wait until you returned from the wine cellar. It must not happen again."

Simmons meekly inclined his head. "Yes, Miss Thackery."

"I'll do the flower arrangements myself, later this afternoon. Please see to it that everything I need is in the game room by five o'clock."

Satisfied that the butler would keep his distaste for the events of the evening to himself, Eden retreated to her bedroom to attend to her own preparations. When Eden entered her sitting room the young woman who was industriously straightening the books on top of the sofa table looked up and smiled warmly.

"Good afternoon, Miss Eden."

"Hello, Millicent." A genuine smile curved Eden's lips as she removed her hat and handed it to her personal maid. A quick glance around the well-ordered room drew a chuckle from Eden, and when Millicent returned, Eden teased, "You've been doing the housemaid's work again, Millicent. The sitting room was a mess when I left it this morning. Thank you."

"Not at all, miss," Millicent beamed, her brown eyes sparkling. "It's a pleasure for me and I know you like your things tidy. Besides, there were only a few books and magazines to be picked up."

"Nevertheless, it was thoughtful of you." Eden sighed and allowed the peace of the room to surround her. Unlike the rest of the house, which was done in various shades of blue and green, Eden's sitting room and bedroom were decorated in rich damask rose accented only in a blue so pale it appeared gray. Eden smiled—the colors were an odd mixture of lush and austere but she preferred these neat surroundings to the current jumble and clutter of her contemporaries. She was, as Meg often pointed out, woefully out of step with the times.

Eden shrugged, turning her thoughts to the coming evening. "I'm going to rest now, Millicent. Please wake me at three and have my bath ready."

"Yes, miss. Which gown will you be wearing tonight?"

Eden paused in the doorway to her bedroom, a slight frown creasing her brow. "The new teal-green silk, I think. Yes, that will do nicely. See that it's pressed. Oh, and, Millicent," she added with a groan as the maid started past her, "I'll have to corset tonight so you'd best check the laces on that hideous contraption."

While her mistress rested, Millicent moved silently about the bedroom. She placed the gown in the sitting room, to be pressed later, after she completed her other duties. The much-maligned corset was unearthed, and Millicent chuckled to herself. Eden, flouting all dictates, refused to be trapped inside this punishing undergarment except when absolutely necessary. Not that she needed the whalebone restrictions, Millicent thought admiringly. Eden's natural form was so slender, her waist so tiny that few if any could tell whether she laced or not.

Millicent tiptoed from the room and softly closed the door. Unlike the other servants, who knew Eden Thackery only as their employer's prudish ward, Millicent was fiercely devoted to her mistress for she knew what the others did not—that for all Miss Eden's icy politeness and cool speech she had a soft heart. Who would know better than Millicent herself? The two were nearly the same age and because Millicent's mother worked for Hugh in the kitchen, Millicent had been hired as a companion for Eden when she had joined the Colter household. Over the years a friendship had developed between the girls, in spite of the differences in their stations. The new gowns which filled her wardrobe were the result of the bolts of material Miss Eden had given her on her birthday. Every year at Christmas Millicent received a cash bonus from Mr. Colter—which went to help support her family, as did her monthly salary—but from Miss Eden she received a very personal gift. Whatever the gift—a book, perfume, a scarf—it was always beautifully wrapped and seldom was shared with the members of Millicent's family.

As she labored over the ironing board Millicent wondered again, fleetingly, if she would still be in Miss Eden's employ within the next year. She desperately hoped that when Miss Eden married Tim Gregory—as she undoubtedly would—that Miss Eden would include her in the new household.

Promptly at five-thirty Hugh Colter arrived home and immediately availed himself of his private bathroom. Eden had her own bath as well, but the luxury of indoor plumbing was not the object of childlike glee for her that it was for Hugh. But then, why should it be? Hugh thought as he spun the faucets and watched the water spill into the enamel tub. Eden had never been burdened with the chore of carrying bucket after bucket of water from stove to bathtub. Hugh smiled wryly as he settled into the tub. Eden took this sort of thing for granted—another example to add to his mental list of the differences between himself and his love. He was keeping a tally with almost grim determination, though its effect on his heart was by no means certain.

Half an hour later Hugh stood in the doorway of the game room, the gaze from his blue eyes warmly caressing the slender figure who was putting the final touches on a floral arrangement at one of the petticoat tables at the opposite wall. Eden took a step backward, her head tilted to one side, and viewed her handiwork. Apparently satisfied, she placed the scissors and discarded greenery on a tray, and Hugh realized it was time to make his presence known.

"You have a flair for that, dear heart." Hugh strode across the room and, unable to resist the temptation, lightly kissed Eden's cheek. "Not that Ian or the others will notice, but still, fresh flowers add a nice touch to a room." He paused, noticing the faraway look in her eyes, then added teasingly, "And what young man are you daydreaming about?"

To their mutual horror Eden blushed. Hugh's laughter froze in his throat and Eden, turning quickly away to regain her composure, failed to see the pain that spasmed across Hugh's face. She had, indeed, been indulging in fanciful thoughts about Neil Banning, but she could hardly admit such a thing to Hugh! How could she possibly explain that she was unaccountably attracted to an arrogant man she had met only the night before?

"I . . . I wasn't thinking about a specific young man," Eden managed finally. "I was just comparing the various attributes of the men at the debut last night." It was at least partially true—Eden had found herself comparing Neil Banning to Tim all afternoon, and so far Tim was suffering by the comparison.

"I see." Hugh studied Eden's profile and fought to control his jealousy as her coloring returned to normal. He knew Eden well enough to know when she was being evasive. He had, unintentionally, struck a nerve, but Eden would tell him nothing if he pried further. Still, knowing that another man occupied her thoughts soured Hugh's mood. With an effort, he changed the subject. "Is everything ready for tonight?"

"Yes." Relieved, Eden looked at Hugh and smiled. "I've instructed Simmons to set up the buffet fifteen minutes after Ian and the others arrive. Do you approve?"

Hugh nodded brusquely. "Fine." His tone was shorter than he had intended and Eden looked at him curiously. Hugh cursed silently. If he didn't control himself *she'd* soon be asking *him* what was on his mind! "I could use a drink," he announced, turning away.

A trace of Ireland colored his speech, alerting Eden to the fact that Hugh was troubled. The remaining wisps of her wool-gathering vanished and Eden watched, concerned, as Hugh tossed down a glass of Bourbon and poured himself another.

When Hugh seated himself at the game table, Eden followed and took the chair to his right. "What is it, Hugh?"

"Nothing that a night of cards and pleasant conversation won't set right," Hugh growled.

"I don't believe you," Eden said quietly, without heat. "This morning you were your usual cheery self and now..." She purposely left the sentence unfinished, which forced Hugh to meet her gaze.

Hugh sighed, torn between cherishing and hating the tenderness in her voice. "I've a ship due from Hong Kong that's two weeks late. It's just business, dear heart; nothing to lose any sleep over."

Eden believed the lie itself, but not the part about there being no reason for concern. Hugh's import business, though financially solvent, was still in its infancy, and the loss of a shipment could be a fatal blow. But, Eden decided, since Hugh appeared determined not to discuss the matter any further, she would simply have to trust his judgment. Hopefully, Ian and the other guests would lift Hugh's spirits. All Eden had to offer until they arrived was a recounting of her day at the "Mile"— with Neil Banning's presence carefully edited out.

Hugh's guests arrived promptly at seven, their hearty laughter announcing their presence and causing the properly dignified Simmons to show his distaste when he showed them into the game room. Hugh immensely enjoyed these monthly affairs, but his staff rolled their eyes in horror and wondered aloud why such ruffians were even allowed in the house.

"Thank you, James." The largest of the four men clapped the butler on the shoulder with an audible smack. "I'm sure we could never have found Hugh without your help. Needn't hang about looking down your nose at us, James. If we need you, we'll yell."

The door closed discreetly after the butler, and the red-haired giant laughed and shook his head. "I've often wondered where you found that one, Hugh. He has all the humor of a corpse."

"He might be friendlier if you called him by his correct name. It's Simmons, not James. I don't know why you can't remember that, Ian."

Ian Garrison lifted his massive shoulders in a shrug. "James, Simmons, it makes no difference. He's English and I've no love for any Englishman, even if he does work for someone from home." The frown quickly left his face and he grinned widely at Eden. "There's my girl! Sure and you're the prettiest thing on this side of the Atlantic, Eden. Come here and let me have a look at you. Aye, lovely as ever and getting ready to break all the men's hearts, I'll wager. You'll have your hands full with this lassie, Hugh."

Eden smiled ruefully at the big man's teasing. "You've been kissing the Blarney stone again, Ian. Or else your eyesight is failing." But she chuckled when Ian pulled her into a bone-crushing hug. "What's the matter with the rest of your rogues' gallery, Ian?"

Ian turned to the three men still standing by the door. "Davey, Liam, Brian! What ails you? You've met Eden before and she's not so fearsome that she'll take your heads off."

The men greeted Eden rather sheepishly, but despite the distance between them she caught the unmistakable fumes of whiskey. It didn't make any difference to her, Eden thought, because this night would end like the other monthly get-togethers, with Hugh's friends stumbling blindly home in the wee hours of the morning after a night of food, poker and drink. Hugh wouldn't be in much better shape, Eden knew from firsthand experience. Tomorrow morning his eyes would be red-rimmed and his sense of hearing so acute that Eden would speak mostly in whispers.

When the buffet was in place, the men piled their plates high with food and ranged themselves around the game table while Eden looked on fondly. Coats and ties were slung over the backs of chairs, carelessly discarded in favor of shirt sleeves and comfort while the men applied themselves with great relish to the meal. Eden only nibbled at the food on her own plate, seeing to it that the supply on the buffet did not diminish and that the decanters of Bourbon were constantly replenished by an aggrieved Simmons. Conversation ebbed and flowed, covering a wide range of topics but centering mostly on Hugh's import company—where the four men were employed—and the possible effects the depression could have on it.

"Not that it bothers me, mind," Ian said blandly as he washed down a quantity of roast beef with a tumbler of whiskey. He jerked his thumb toward the others. "But Davey here, and Liam and Brian, they've families to think about. Hell, I could always go back to scouting for the army, but these three can't uproot kith and kin like that."

"It won't be necessary," Hugh stated firmly, and Eden gave a sigh of relief that something had at last brought her guardian out of his dark introspection. "I'll pay their salaries out of my own pocket if I have to, but I'll not fire a single man. This depression can't last forever, and the company is well into the black. We'll weather this without too much trouble."

"I hope so," Brian added sourly. "Most of my neighbors have gotten the boot already and what jobs there are aren't open to Irish. Times like these make me wish I'd never left home."

Hugh nodded gravely. "We've all of us felt that way at some time. When I came over at the ripe old age of fourteen I thought that the streets of America would be paved with gold and that I would no longer have to break my back working a barren plot of land. Instead I worked fourteen hours a day on the docks, loading and unloading ships for a pittance that barely kept body and soul together. The signs were up then, too—No Irish Need Apply—so we took whatever we could and were thankful for it. Any heavy labor or dirty job that no one else would touch—why, there was always one of us cold enough and hungry enough to be happy for the work."

"But things were no better at home," Ian broke in. "And we knew it; that's why we came to America and that's why we've stayed. Look to yourself, Hugh. When I first met you, you were flat broke; you'd lost everything trying to make a go of farming out West. A more miserable sight I've never seen than when you walked into the fort to sign on as a scout." Ian's laughter rattled the china, and Hugh reddened. "Scout my bleeding arse! The closest he'd ever been to an Indian was the wooden one in front of a cigar store. Eden, lass, did Hugh ever tell you how we met?"

Eden refilled Ian's glass and smiled mischievously. "Hugh has never told me much of anything about his life in the army— except for a few stories that I suspect he made up strictly for my benefit."

"I'm sure Eden isn't interested in my ancient history," Hugh said gruffly, painfully aware that one of Ian's yarns would only highlight the chasm which put Eden beyond his grasp. "All that happened twenty years ago—it doesn't even make a good story."

"It makes a splendid story," Ian protested. "You should have seen him then, Eden; nineteen years old and skinny as a fence post with a line of blarney as long as your arm. Oh, he was a charmer in those days, our Hugh—"

"That's enough!" Hugh slammed his glass on the table. Ian opened his mouth to object, but after one glance at the expression on Hugh's face he thought better of the idea and closed it with a snap.

"Hugh," Eden cajoled, "let Ian finish. I'd enjoy hearing—"

"Well, I wouldn't. I was there, remember, and I don't want to hear about it all over again. Now, shall we drop the subject? If you're finished with your meal let's play some cards."

"But, Hugh . . ." Eden was bewildered by his attitude.

"The matter is closed, Eden," Hugh repeated harshly. "Have the plates cleared away and then you may leave us."

Eden's knuckles whitened around the neck of the crystal decanter, and she lowered her head to conceal the pain and confusion in her eyes. "As you wish, Hugh. Gentlemen, enjoy your game."

Eden retreated to the safety of her room and stood for a moment in the doorway. From below came the sound of the men's conversation and laughter, with Hugh's voice loudest of all when he called for another round of drinks.

When at last—with Millicent's help—Eden was freed from the biting corset stays and propped up in bed with a book, she puzzled over Hugh's behavior. It wasn't like Hugh to lose his temper like that, especially in front of others. Eden reviewed her conduct of the evening but could think of nothing she had said that might have angered him. There was nothing in Hugh's past to be ashamed of, Eden was certain of that, and Ian was one of his oldest friends.

"Whatever could be wrong?" Eden demanded of the room. It hurt her to think Hugh was angry with her. He was one of the few people she genuinely cared for, and his feelings mattered greatly to her. Frowning, she gave up all pretense of reading and blew out the lamplight beside her bed. "He'll tell me tomorrow if I've done something wrong," she mumbled into the pillow. "Maybe he was just in one of those black Irish moods I keep hearing about."

By two in the morning Davey, Brian and Liam, their eyes red from cigar smoke and Bourbon, had bid their host a slurred good-bye, and Hugh and Ian had settled down to polish off the final decanter. Hugh sat slumped in his chair staring wordlessly into space as he downed glass after glass of liquor as if it were water.

"You're in a rare mood tonight," Ian said at last. "I didn't know you made a practice of terrifying children."

"I'm entitled," Hugh snapped. "And Eden's no child. It's high time she learned to fend for herself."

"Oh, aye, she must be all of sixteen. Why not throw her out and let her make her own way in the world?"

"Go to hell, Ian. It's none of your damn business anyway." With a convulsive movement, Hugh hurled his glass into the empty fireplace. "God *damn* it!"

Ian moved the remainder of the Bourbon and his own glass out of harm's way. "Ease up, Hugh. Something's been eating at you all night. Are you going to spit it out now, or do you want to finish off your whiskey supply first?"

Hugh shook his head wearily, running his fingers absently through his hair. "I've got a bad temper, Ian, you know that."

"But not with the lass. I've never heard you speak that way to her before."

"I never have, before tonight." Hugh laughed grimly. Then abruptly, he confessed, "I caught her daydreaming today, Ian, about a man, I've no doubt. I've always known that Eden was only mine for a little while, but I never thought it would be so hard to let her go."

It took a while before the full impact of Hugh's words hit Ian, but when it did he sat bolt upright in his chair. "Good God! You can't mean that you're in love with her? Hugh, that's mad; she's your ward!"

"Don't you think I know that? Don't you think I've been over it and over it in my mind? I know what you're thinking, what everyone would think if they knew—that I'm a disgusting old lecher drooling after the innocent child left in my care. But it's not like that, Ian; I love Eden, I want to marry her." Hugh raised a hand to silence the outburst he knew would be forthcoming. "I'm well aware of all the reasons why such a marriage wouldn't work—the age difference, for one thing. I don't think either of us could ignore a gap of twenty-four years, and even if we could, I doubt our so-called friends would allow us to forget it. And then there's the difference in our backgrounds; Eden has been raised to take this kind of life for granted, to accept butlers, maids, cooks and thirty-room mansions, while I find it hard to believe I'll never have to worry about where my next meal is coming from. But she's been happy here with me, and she runs the house as efficiently as Adria ever did."

"Now, there's the heart of the matter," Ian reflected. "You fell in love with Adria and she with you, but neither of you did anything about it. Now the mother is dead and suddenly the daughter's a young woman, beautiful, eligible, and she even resembles her mother to a certain extent, although there are times when I swear she's Locke all over again. What I'm asking, Hugh, is this: Are you settling for Eden because you couldn't have Adria? If you are, it would be a terrible thing, not only for you but for the lass as well."

Hugh sighed and pushed himself out of the chair. He walked over to open the windows and stared up at the heavens for a long time before answering. "I've thought about that too. Maybe at first Adria's memory had something to do with my feelings for Eden, but that doesn't mean my love for Eden isn't real. I'm trapped, Ian; I can't declare myself to Eden because she'd be horrified, yet it's getting harder and harder to pretend that I don't mind all those young bucks sniffing around." Hugh bit a knuckle as he contemplated the night. "She's so damn vulnerable, Ian," he said quietly. "She doesn't show it very often, but she is, and I don't want to see her hurt."

"A noble sentiment to be sure, but hardly practical. You can't hide the lass away from the world, much as you may want to. Let her go, Hugh, before you lose control and hurt the both of you."

Hugh smiled thinly. "I really don't have any other choice, do I, Ian?"

# Chapter 4

Eden woke shortly after the sun's first tendrils of light found their way into her bedroom, rolled to her back, stretched catlike until every muscle felt smooth and supple and then slowly opened her eyes. Muted sounds came from below—the servants were probably already at work restoring order to the game room. Hugh's parties never failed to leave a pall of smoke in the room, which meant that summer or winter the windows had to be thrown open to allow the room to air, and on occasion a broken glass or two could be found on the carpet.

Hugh. Eden's forehead wrinkled. What kind of mood would he be in this morning? If past hangovers and last night's rage were any indication, the answer was simple: He would be in a foul mood. Eden was sorely tempted to pull the sheet over her head and go back to sleep rather than face Hugh before his brain had cleared. They rarely fought, but when they did Eden felt as if Hugh somehow had betrayed the trust she placed in him. Well, she wasn't about to lie in bed waiting for the ax to fall. This Friday morning she had too much to do. Determinedly she threw off the covers and reached for her wrapper.

Somewhere in the distance silverware clattered rudely onto china, the sound magnified by some mysterious means, sending wave after wave of pain crashing and reverberating through Hugh's eggshell-tender skull. He groaned and gingerly lifted his head from the protective shield of his hands. The silver coffeepot reflected a ray of sunlight, sending sharp, hot daggers deep into his eyes. Carefully Hugh shifted his gaze to his cup. Empty. He considered the options: ringing for a maid, or trying to reach the coffeepot under his own steam. If he used the bell resting close by his left hand the noise would surely blow off the top of his head, but the coffeepot was too damn far away. The thought of moving made Hugh's stomach churn and he returned his head to his hands.

"Try this."

Hugh pried open an eye and regarded the glass held between two slender hands. "What is it?" he croaked.

"The usual—hair of the dog that bit you." Eden's voice

was soft, her smile gentle as she coaxed, "Do try it, Hugh, you'll feel ever so much better. Then I'll get you some toast and more coffee."

Hugh gave in, draining the glass in four generous swallows. A shudder ran dangerously through his frame before his stomach gave a final lurch and settled back into place. Now if his head would only return to its normal size.

"Here." Eden set a plate containing two pieces of toast in front of Hugh and refilled his cup. "Eat slowly. You know the routine."

"Thank you." Hugh caught her hand as Eden turned, carrying it first to his lips, then to his cheek. "That feels good; my head feels like it's ready to explode."

Eden placed her free hand on Hugh's forehead. "You're a bit warm. You're not coming down with something, are you?"

"No, no." Hugh leaned back in his chair and closed his eyes, enjoying the coolness of Eden's hands. "Never underestimate the force of the bottle."

Eden massaged Hugh's temples. "Simmons is wearing his properly horrified expression this morning."

The corners of Hugh's mouth twitched. "He'll survive. The question is: Will I?"

"You always have," Eden replied indulgently. "Come on now, try to eat something."

"Eden." Hugh trapped both her hands in one of his and smiled weakly. "About last night, dear heart, I do apologize. I had no reason to talk to you the way I did."

Relief flooded Eden and she squeezed Hugh's hand lightly. "It's my fault, too. I shouldn't have pressed the matter. I'm sorry."

"No need to be. You were curious. It's an affliction shared by people all over the world. But be aware, Eden, everyone is entitled to their privacy, their own secrets that they wish to keep from the rest of the world."

"Even you?"

"Everyone," Hugh repeated, looking away from the calm eyes and wondering how long he could keep his own secret.

With the aid of breakfast and a headache powder, Hugh was well enough restored to announce that he would spend the morning at his company, completing the inventory of the warehouse he had been working on for the better part of the week.

Eden saw him off with a smile and a gentle reminder that they were expected at a garden party in the afternoon. Next Eden conferred with the housekeeper regarding the weekend menus and Hugh's rather limited entertainment calendar.

At nine o'clock Eden left orders for the carriage, retired to her bedroom, bathed and sat impatiently while Millicent swept her waist-length tresses into a perfect chignon with a few curls at the back to soften the severity of the style. Once again Millicent laced Eden securely into a corset over her chemise, held the petticoat while Eden stepped into it and tied the padded bustle in place at Eden's waist. A bright yellow underskirt was buttoned next, followed by a one-piece bodice and overskirt of diagonally striped navy blue and yellow. The long sleeves of the bodice ended in frothy lace cuffs, matching the lace jabot which tumbled from Eden's throat to a point just above her waist. Eden's lisle-stockinged feet slid easily into her pointed-toed boots, whose cloth tops matched her overdress, and while Millicent diligently plied a button hook, Eden perched a blue-trimmed yellow hat over the front of her hair and secured it with two wickedly long hatpins. After checking her appearance in the mirror, Eden looped the strings of her reticule around her wrist, picked up the matching striped parasol and left the bedroom.

The panel-boot victoria and its driver were waiting at the front door, and when Eden was comfortably settled on the leather seat she gave the driver the first address on her list. As the carriage rolled along the streets Eden found herself reflecting—most unkindly—on the demanding obligation known as "calling." In her reticule were cards upon which only her name appeared, engraved in a black, Gothic script. At each of her destinations she would descend from the vehicle—slowly and gracefully, for it never would do to appear hurried—knock on the door, nod to the butler and solemnly place one of her cards in his hand. Then she would return to her carriage, dash to the next address and repeat the entire scene. At least today she would be spared the usual fifteen-minute visit at each home—the Chandlers' garden party thankfully precluded that social necessity—but next week she would be forced to endure the short conversations which were all but mandatory to "calling."

Eden's list of addresses was lengthy, and in spite of her driver's expert handling of the team of matched bays, two hours passed before Eden alighted in front of Delmonico's. The doors to this public but frighteningly exclusive restaurant opened just as she reached them, and Eden nodded her thanks to the door-man as she glided past. As arranged, the manager, Mr. Fletcher, came forward to greet Eden and whisk her away to his office—though not before some of the gentlemen seated in the private rooms bestowed appreciative looks in her direction.

While she disliked the business of "calling," Eden found this task even less to her liking. She was here today to make the final arrangements for her debut, a ritual she could not escape no matter how much she privately despised it. By New York's standards her ball was an intimate affair—only six hundred fourteen people would be invited. The average number was one thousand or more. As she reviewed the guest list, the seating arrangements, the menu, the orchestral selections and the floral decorations, Eden longed for the courage to add Ian Garrison to the guest list. She had developed a genuine affection for Hugh's old friend and it pained her—as Eden knew it did Hugh—to restrict Ian's presence to private evenings in Hugh's home.

"Caroline Astor and her blue bloods tolerate me because your family and fortune were here long before the Civil War," Hugh had told Eden on one occasion. "Because of you, neither she nor those so-called Patriarchs dare cut me; but on the other hand, I don't dare alienate them because of my position as your guardian. I've explained all this to Ian, dear heart, and he understands. When you're properly married I can go out and do as I please, but in the meantime neither Ian nor myself have any complaints."

Eden set aside the final page of the checklist with a word of approval to Mr. Fletcher. Thus was Ian Garrison consigned to his rented room on the night of her ball, while Mrs. Astor and the twenty-five gentlemen she had labeled "Patriarchs" would be in attendance.

The manager rose and escorted Eden from his office to the door of the establishment. There was a small delay while they awaited Eden's carriage, and he took advantage of the moment. "I must ask one more thing of you, Miss Thackery."

Eden felt like groaning, but she merely nodded and began pulling on her gloves. "I wasn't aware we had overlooked anything, Mr. Fletcher."

"This does not pertain to your debut." Mr. Fletcher's voice

dropped to a confidential note. "In the future, Miss Thackery, it would be far more appropriate if you would allow your guardian to attend to these matters. I am certain you understand."

Except for the sudden flintiness of Eden's eyes, her appearance was unchanged when she replied, "I'm afraid I don't. Please explain yourself, Mr. Fletcher."

"Miss Thackery, I am certainly in no position to address myself to the subject of a young lady's deportment. However—" Fletcher threatened to continue a lecture which Eden had no intention of hearing.

"You are so correct, Mr. Fletcher. Your position scarcely allows you the familiarity of a tutor." Eden's tone was icy, and the manager paled visibly. She smoothed the gloves over her fingers, her eyes never leaving his while she continued, "Delmonico's was Mr. Colter's choice, not mine. If you have any objection to dealing directly with me, you should have voiced your opinion at our first meeting. Since this is, after all, *my* debut, I intend to arrange it to my satisfaction. If you find working with me so offensive, I will be happy to withdraw my reservation."

Fletcher gulped. "I have no objection to working with you, Miss Thackery," he protested hastily. "But you must understand my position. The young ladies with whom I confer also have their mothers present."

"How convenient. But I, as you know, have been without a maternal cushion for several years." Eden knew what Fletcher was driving at—a man and woman alone together behind closed doors? Scandal! She *should* meekly accept the chastisement and leave—but under Hugh's guardianship she had grown far too independent for that. Hugh had no time for vacillation, from either men or women, and he considered chaperones unwelcome encumbrances to be placed upon only those young ladies who seriously lacked common sense. Thus Eden, with Hugh's encouragement and approval, had far more freedom than other girls her age.

Fletcher anxiously cleared his throat. "I only meant, Miss Thackery, that perhaps next time you would kindly..." The cool gray gaze disconcerted him so that he finished weakly, "kindly bring along a companion?"

A mischievous smile tugged at the corners of Eden's mouth.

Leaning toward the manager she softly inquired, "Why, Mr. Fletcher, are you planning to do me harm?"

Fletcher paled, then turned red as a beet at such audacity. That was how Eden left him: speechless, staring, frustrated and unable to say a word about the exchange to anyone because he had, indeed, overstepped his limits to an extent that could cost him his job. Fletcher squared his shoulders with an effort and returned to his office.

In one of the private dining rooms, Eden's departure had not gone unnoticed. And the interest she had aroused in Matthew Kelly's luncheon companion had been quickly observed by the older man. "That is Miss Eden Thackery," he informed his client. "Sole heir to Thackery Ltd. My employer, if you will."

"Really," came the murmured reply. Remembering the oil portrait which dominated the reception room of the firm, the client added thoughtfully, "She bears little resemblance to her illustrious forebear."

"No, she looks more like her mother, thank God. Except for the eyes." Matthew Kelly shivered involuntarily, a reaction not missed by his companion.

Neil Banning's attention—half a world away during the meal—abruptly concentrated on Kelly. "Locke Thackery was, I take it, a difficult man?"

"Ruthless. The place has been somewhat less frantic since his demise." Elated by the interest which had replaced Banning's previous indifference, Kelly hurried on. "Thackery Ltd. is in trust right now, under the administration of Miss Thackery's guardian. A nice enough fellow, I suppose, but hardly—"

"Guardian?" Neil's mind caught and hung on the word. "The young lady is an orphan?"

Matthew Kelly nodded. "First her mother died, then her father. She'll be coming out soon, I believe, but it's simply a matter of going through the motions. I expect her engagement to Tim Gregory will be announced at the close of the season."

Neil had gleaned as much from Tim himself during that endless ride through Central Park. What a waste of a lovely woman, Neil thought—to be shackled to Tim and his petulant sister for life.

"Would you like to meet her?"

Neil jerked his thoughts back to Matthew Kelly, aware that

the man had been talking away yet he hadn't heard a word that he'd said.

Neil's scowl only reinforced Matthew Kelly's determination. Perhaps if the new client met, and liked, Eden Thackery, his opinion of Thackery Ltd. would raise substantially. The meeting could prove most profitable for Matthew Kelly and Thackery Ltd. "Miss Thackery," Matthew resumed when Neil did not answer, "is a most personable young lady. If you are free this afternoon I would be happy to arrange an introduction."

The scowl vanished and a speculative gleam—misunderstood by Kelly—entered the golden eyes. Neil sipped his brandy and then smiled. "It just so happens, Mr. Kelly, that I haven't any plans for this afternoon."

The Chandlers' garden party was an unqualified success— at least to its hostess, Harriet Chandler. The lush back lawn unfolded majestically before her gaze, but the real triumph was the hedge maze, which contained at its center a newly constructed wrought-iron gazebo. A smile of satisfaction appeared on Harriet's face as she watched the younger guests wind their way over the paths between the hedges. Hope's friends were undoubtedly enjoying the game, and while the maze allowed the strolling couples a modicum of privacy, they were still exposed to full view from the terrace. All the proprieties had been strictly observed. Still smiling, Harriet turned to greet another guest.

For Eden, wandering aimlessly over the paved paths, the affair was anything but pleasant. She had spent the past hour ducking Tim and his profuse, heartfelt apologies for deserting her the night of the ball, and now she was totally lost in the Chandlers' maze. Her sense of direction had failed her long ago and now, when she reached yet another dead end, Eden gave an exasperated sigh and simply dropped onto the wrought-iron settee at the end of the path. Tim might trap her here, of course, and short of climbing over the hedge she would be unable to escape him, but at the moment she honestly didn't care. She was impatient with Tim and with herself, but most of all she was impatient with their inane game of half truths and false assurances. Why couldn't she simply come right out and tell Tim that she was done playing second violin to Jane? If Tim wanted to play watchdog to his sister, that was fine, but Eden had no intention of waiting around until he happened to find a spare moment for the woman he supposedly loved.

Eden smoothed the bright green poplin skirt of her garden dress, recalling her earlier conversation with Tim. She had accepted Tim's apology in a less than gracious manner and Tim, sensing that he was not wholly forgiven, had taken it upon himself to tell Eden what had happened during the midnight carriage ride.

"Honestly, Eden, I've never met such a rude fellow as Banning. He barely answered Jane's questions—in fact, in more than one instance he refused to answer altogether. All we learned about him was that he was born in Mexico but was educated in England. Oxford, I think he said. At any rate, he's on his way home to Mexico—from England—now, and I find that rather odd, don't you? I mean, 'Banning' is hardly a Mexican name, is it?"

Tim hadn't given Eden a chance to answer; instead, he had charged right into another apology. It was when Tim had gone to get her a cup of tea that Eden had ducked into the maze and that, in retrospect, had been a mistake. Apologies notwithstanding, she might have been able to find out more about Neil Banning; but instead, here she sat, tired, thirsty and wishing this day were over.

"Well, well, what have we here? A tree nymph?"

Eden gasped and looked up to find Neil Banning standing at the intersection of the paths. He strolled toward her, an engaging smile on his lips, and Eden was forced to notice all over again how attractive he was. Above the gray cutaway coat his face was tanned and angular, handsomely accented by the waves of thick, dark hair, and the thin, high-bridged nose and firm mouth lent more than a trace of arrogance to his features. But it was the eyes that fascinated Eden—golden eyes beneath dark swooping brows. They commanded attention and when, as now, they were fixed on a certain object, their effect was devastating.

"My mistake. The tree nymph has disappeared and left in her place the lovely Eden Thackery." Neil's smile widened into a grin and he gestured toward the settee. "May I?"

"By all means." Eden slid graciously to one corner of the seat and collapsed her lace parasol, her actions concealing her surprise at Neil's unexpected appearance. "I'm sorry about your wood sprite."

"Don't be—I happen to prefer mortal women." Neil settled

into the opposite corner. "So does Tim Gregory, it seems. He's tearing up the grounds looking for you."

Eden started. "Is he in the maze?"

"Not yet; but it's only a matter of time before he employs the same method I did in order to locate you." Neil turned and gazed at Eden. "Why do I get the impression that you're hiding from Tim?"

"I'm not hiding...exactly," Eden replied, her color rising at the mocking gleam in Neil's eyes.

"From what I heard, Tim left you for a moment while he went for refreshments and when he returned you were gone." Neil raised an inquiring eyebrow. "That sounds suspiciously evasive to me."

"Nonsense. I simply decided to investigate the labyrinth." *Why* couldn't she stop blushing?

To Eden's chagrin, Neil laughed aloud. "You really must practice the gentle art of subterfuge, Eden; you eyes and your coloring give you away."

"Unlike Jane?" It was a waspish thing to say but Eden, feeling childishly defensive, couldn't stop herself. "She's here, you know, and I'm certain she'd be overjoyed to see you again."

The laughter had disappeared from Neil's face and he regarded her seriously. "You're jumping to the conclusion that the feeling is mutual." He leaned a little closer to Eden and, with a wry smile, added, "It isn't."

"Oh." Eden swallowed and looked away.

"Now I've embarrassed you, and I didn't mean to," Neil said earnestly. He took one of her hands from the parasol handle and held it in his own. "I've made no secret of the fact that I find you attractive, that I would like to know you. Jane Gregory has nothing to do with the way I feel." The delicate hand he held relaxed slightly and Neil pressed his advantage. He rose, forcing Eden to do likewise. "Come with me."

"Where?"

"Out of this maze." Neil drew her arm through his as they began walking. "You realize, of course, that the terrace offers a perfect view of the maze." Neil grinned as Eden glanced anxiously over her shoulder to confirm what he'd said. "I was right. You *are* hiding from Tim."

Eden sighed. Neil had already guessed the truth, so there was little point in being evasive. "I'm not avoiding Tim as much as I'm avoiding his apologies. He's determined to make amends for deserting me in order to chaperone you and Jane."

"I take it you haven't forgiven him."

"But I have," Eden protested in exasperation. "It's just that Tim—oh, never mind; it isn't worth discussing."

"I think I understand. You and Jane don't get along and Tim is caught in the middle." Neil ignored her startled look. "There's a simple solution, Eden. Slip away with me now and Tim will have no idea where you've gone."

"And neither will my guardian." Now it was Eden's turn to laugh. "You think of some very impertinent ideas, Neil."

"But I've made you laugh, which I've noticed is something you do quite rarely." The offer had been teasingly made but Neil still felt a twinge of disappointment at her refusal.

He was tall, Eden thought irrationally, much taller than she remembered. Her head just reached Neil's shoulder, and using her own height as a gauge Eden guessed Neil stood at least three inches over six feet. He moved with catlike ease, so self-assured, so controlled . . . Eden was so wrapped up in her own thoughts that she failed to see the loose paving stone in the path. One minute she was walking gracefully at Neil's side and the next her right ankle had twisted painfully beneath her. She was pitching forward, the Chandlers' well-manicured lawn rushing up to meet her, when Neil's hand seized her upper arm at the same time he curled a steadying arm around her waist. With negligent ease Neil lifted Eden out of the fall, spun her about so that she faced him, then firmly planted her back on her own two feet.

"Thank you." Eden's voice was breathless, an effect she hoped Neil would attribute to the accident. It was, in fact, caused by the fact that he was still holding her, and Eden found his touch most unsettling.

"My pleasure." Neil stared down at Eden, the laughing comment he had been about to make dying as he lost himself in twin pools of fathomless gray. Something hammered at his chest and it took several moments before Neil realized the sharp thudding was his own heartbeat. "Are you all right?"

"Yes." The spell was broken and Eden began to breathe again. "You may let go of me now."

"More's the pity," Neil murmured, drawing his hands away. At Eden's bewildered look he smiled gently and bent to retrieve her parasol from the ground. Straightening, he saw Eden wince in pain as she tried to take a step, and he quickly placed a hand beneath her elbow. "What's wrong?"

"I'm afraid I've twisted my ankle." Eden sighed. "A perfect end to a perfect day."

"The gazebo's not far. You can rest there." Neil grinned. "I can carry you if you like."

"My ankle is twisted, not broken," Eden replied with a smile. "You needn't take such drastic measures."

"Drastic for you; enjoyable for me." Neil shifted his grip to a more secure position. "Here, use me as a crutch." He shortened the length of his steps, pacing himself against Eden's hesitant gait.

Awkward as the arrangement was, it worked, and they reached the gazebo without further mishap. Neil helped Eden up the half-dozen steps and deposited her on one of the wrought-iron chairs, taking the chair next to her when she was comfortably settled.

"Better?" Neil asked.

"Yes, thank you." Eden eyed him curiously. "Are you a doctor, Neil?"

"What makes you think that—because I know how to help someone with a sprained ankle?" Neil shook his head and laughed. "I have done it before, on battlefields. I do, however, have a brother who is a doctor."

Eden considered the information as well as the man beside her. "At the risk of prying, which battlefields? You're not old enough to have been involved in the Civil War."

"Is that a roundabout way of asking my age?"

"No! Not at all, I only—" Eden stopped, seeing the teasing glint in Neil's eyes.

Neil leaned forward and toyed with one of the pale curls at Eden's temple. "I'm twenty-eight, and if we were in Mexico your guardian would see to it that you weren't left alone with me for a minute."

Eden shot him a wicked look. "Should I be frightened, or are you simply comparing countries?"

"Just comparing," Neil admitted, smiling. "I saw you in Delmonico's today. You were lovely, aloof—in Mexico your behavior would never have been tolerated. Nor in England." At Eden's openly inquisitive look Neil explained, "I was educated in England. I'm told it's evident in my British inflection."

"Then you certainly have heard of the suffragette movement," Eden replied spiritedly.

An expression of mocking amusement spread across Neil's face. "Radicals—they represent a vocal but extremely small group of women. Spinsters, to be exact; women who carry a grudge because no one ever placed a ring on their finger."

"How wrong you are!" Eden exclaimed. "Their grudges are more than justified. For centuries women have been treated as second-class citizens; we have been told we are capable of running a household and raising children but not of entering the professional or academic worlds."

"And in return you are given free rein within the home and in the shops so dear to your feminine hearts." Neil settled back in his chair, enjoying this heated but obviously foolish confrontation. So Eden was a suffragette, enamored of the rabble's politics. He had expected more of a woman of such breeding—but then, this was not Mexico. Eden was not a *criollo* whose bloodlines could be traced back through the generations to the Spanish Empire. Blood will tell.

"Home and shops?" Eden shook her head in disbelief. "Contrary to popular masculine opinion, women's thoughts are not limited to Paris fashions! And why should we stand meekly by until men decide to *give* us certain rights, such as the right to vote, which should be ours at birth?"

"Because that's the way the world is." Neil laughed at the outrage his words produced in Eden. "And please don't bring up the worn-out examples of Queen Elizabeth and Queen Victoria. If you notice, all their advisers were, and continue to be, men."

"Oh, you're impossible, just like every other man I know. Except, perhaps, my guardian," Eden added thoughtfully. "He at least understands the double standard and tries to avoid it."

"In which case you're both terribly naïve. Admittedly a double standard exists, but it's for your own protection. Women are beautiful creatures, but you are also"— Neil paused, searching for the right word–"emotional, mercurial. You are given to excesses, fits of pique; you need the stabilizing influence of men."

Eden looked exasperated. "Ivan the Terrible and Napoleon were men. I'd hardly call either one of them stable," she countered.

"They are exceptions and you are being unreasonable."

Eden sniffed. "Being unreasonable is a purely masculine trait, one I wouldn't care to assume. But the attribute I dislike most about your gender is that you kill with such impunity. For example, take the custom of dueling. Why two supposedly mature people would stand still and shoot at each other is beyond comprehension. I don't think that is the act of a *reasonable* person."

"Honor and pride demand a great deal of a man," Neil stated quietly, intently. "And more often than not the cause of a duel is a woman."

"I wonder how often the woman is asked if she feels honored by being the object of a duel?" Eden turned and stared at Neil. "'To the victor go the spoils,' isn't that the phrase? Would you like to be regarded as a trophy? To have your own life arranged to someone else's satisfaction?"

A chill passed through Neil. *Put yourself in her place.* She couldn't know—did not know!—his background, the demons which hounded him. So how was it possible for Eden to touch upon the wound which tormented his soul? "You know everything . . . and nothing," Neil said at last. "The idealism of youth fades with each passing year until, eventually, you weary of the struggle and become what others have always known you to be. Then you become a cynic."

The bitterness in his voice caused Eden to hesitate. "I'm not certain I understand what you mean," she said slowly.

"I hope you never learn," Neil replied, his eyes hooded. "You're far too gentle to suffer such macabre disillusionment." The gray eyes that locked with his probed, questioned, sought responses he was not prepared to give. "Don't ask—not now, not yet."

"You open subjects only to close them before anything can be revealed; that's very frustrating and unfair." Eden tilted her head to one side, considering, and then added in a lighter tone, "But for now I'll let it go without comment—except to say that I don't believe you're the cynic you claim to be."

Neil's smile was noncommittal. "If you're up to it, we should rejoin the party." Eden's ankle was much recovered, but she did not refuse Neil's assistance. They walked in silence, arms linked, until they came within view of the main body of the guests. Reluctantly, Neil released Eden's arm and gazed down at her. "I'd like to see you again. May I?"

"You *are* given to abrupt departures," Eden responded.

"Just as you are prone, it seems, to looking beneath surface appearances." His parry was satisfactory, but Neil felt compelled to add, "Tim has spotted us. It's only a matter of time before he arrives, followed closely by his sister. Frankly, I would prefer not to meet either of them again. But may I see *you* again?"

"Yes," Eden replied promptly, acknowledging both to herself and Neil that the time for coyness had long passed. "Every Sunday at one o'clock I go to the Mall in Central Park to hear the afternoon concert. If you like, we could meet there."

Neil was disappointed. "Not tomorrow?"

"I'm sorry. My guardian and I have plans for Saturday."

"You're very devoted." Neil winced inwardly the moment the sarcastic words were spoken.

To Neil's surprise his words were met not with anger but with a smile. "My guardian is very deserving of devotion and somehow I feel that you, of all people, understand prior commitments."

"I do." *Tell her now,* an inner voice prompted Neil. Tell her of Constanza, of the wedding that is just two months away, before she begins thinking the impossible. Neil could not. "Sunday at one. Until then, Eden."

He bowed over her hand—an Old World gesture so completely at odds with the man Eden thought she knew—and quickly melted into the rest of the guests. Eden smiled gently, already anticipating their next meeting.

"Eden, your behavior is unforgivable!" Tim's voice was strident as he and Jane bore down upon Eden. Tim grasped her upper arm. "To leave me standing on the terrace looking for you is one thing, but to desert me in favor of a rendezvous with that Mexican fellow is beneath contempt. If you don't care about your own reputation, you should at least care for mine."

"Since you did not come charging after me to save me from myself," Eden countered icily, "I gather my transgression pales in comparison to causing a furor at a debut." Tim reddened and Eden took advantage of his discomfort. "Let go of me, Tim."

Tim complied but Jane was not so easily sidetracked. "At least I had the decency to be accompanied by a chaperone. And I was *invited* to share a gentleman's company! I did not throw myself at him. Honestly, Eden, you must be more circumspect."

Eden smiled coldly at Jane. "I don't need to defend my actions . . . particularly not to you." She glanced at Tim. "Nor, in light of your wild accusations, do I feel you deserve any type of explanation."

"Since you are Tim's fiancée, I think at the very *least* you should explain why you and Neil spent so much time in the gazebo," Jane smirked.

Eden stiffened, then leveled her gaze on Tim. "You push too hard, Tim," came the soft, inflexible reprimand.

"I told you about my plans in confidence, Jane. In confidence!" Tim glowered at his sister. "You swore you wouldn't say a word to anyone."

"To anyone outside the family," Jane amended with a catty smile. "Besides, you can hardly accuse me of betraying your secret marriage proposal when Eden herself is the blushing bride-to-be." Despite her bravado, Tim's ominous frown warned Jane against pursuing the subject further. A strategic retreat was called for, Jane decided; she had set these two at odds and that in itself was enormously satisfying. "You will excuse me, won't you? Katie Marlin just returned from Boston and I promised to tell her all the latest gossip."

Eden stared at Tim, barely aware of Jane's departure. She could feel the anger surging through her veins, turning blood and flesh alternately hot and cold as she carefully chose her words. "Tim, I gave you an answer which you refused to accept. Then, because I didn't want to hurt you, you will recall that I asked for more time. You agreed."

They argued—or rather Tim argued, pleading his case before a remote Eden. He hadn't meant to tell Jane about his proposal; the words had simply slipped out before he realized it. He shouldn't have caused a scene in front of Jane, but didn't Eden understand how upset he was when she slipped away and then reappeared with Neil Banning? Half of New York expected their engagement announcement at the end of the season, and for heaven's sake, didn't she care about *appearances?* Eden listened silently, withdrawing further with each word, remembering another man who had delighted in cataloguing her sins and transgressions. Once again she was an ornament, an asset to be listed beside stock purchases and company mergers. Flawed ornaments were unacceptable; unreliable assets were quickly unloaded. Eden had *had* to accept her father, but she had no intention of letting another man place her in the same box her father had. Eden stared at Tim, seeing him clearly for the first time. Despite his protestations of love, Tim would eventually want only the ornament, not the woman.

Eden snapped her parasol open. "I've had a tiring day and your lecture has given me a splitting headache. Quite frankly, I don't care a fig about your opinions of my behavior. Good day."

Eden turned on her heel and walked away, leaving Tim stunned in her wake. She went directly to Hugh and circulated at his side for the remainder of the party. Hugh was curious but unquestioning, accepting her presence with a smile and a light squeeze of her hand. Her actions were cowardly, Eden silently admitted, but when the inevitable confrontation between herself and Tim came, it would happen in private. Besides, the conversation swirling around her required only mechanical answers and vague smiles—otherwise she was wonderfully free to daydream. Neil's touch had been gentle, yet it had set her heart pounding. Eden wondered, with a mixture of hope and fear, if Neil would attempt to kiss her the next time they met. It was a pleasant, thoroughly scandalous speculation.

Neil Banning poured himself a second cup of coffee and touched a match to the end of his cigar, his golden eyes half closing as he contemplated the events of the day ahead. The thought of having Eden Thackery all to himself for an entire afternoon brought a smile to his lips. She was an amusing diversion, with her serious expression and contained manner; quite different from Constanza. Neil's smile faded rapidly; the idea of spending the rest of his life tied to Constanza and her pack of greedy, grasping relatives was as welcome as the prospect of facing a firing squad.

Unfortunately, Neil had little choice in the matter. He had a responsibility to fulfill—that of producing a son to carry on the family name. Constanza came from a family whose bloodlines were impeccable, albeit impoverished. Each of them, Neil thought bitterly, was well aware of what the other stood to gain from the marriage. And as soon as he'd taken care of the matter of insuring the continuation of his name, Neil would find himself a beautiful, volatile woman and install her as his mistress.

It wouldn't be hard; any woman with half a mind would leap at the chance. An intriguing thought occurred to Neil. Would it be possible to persuade Eden Thackery that she would enjoy such a life? Not on a permanent basis, of course; but perhaps for a year or so, until Neil tired of her and, after settling a considerable amount of money on her, sent her packing. What a sensation an American mistress would cause among his friends!

Neil sighed regretfully. Enticing as the fantasy was, it was also impossible. Eden Thackery might lack his own aristocratic bloodlines, but she was not without standing in New York. Tampering with this debutante could only lead to problems.

A soft tapping on his door broke his concentration and Neil was still scowling irritably when he opened the door. "Yes, what is it?"

A woman, heavily veiled and dressed completely in black, stood before him. "I must speak with you, Mr. Banning." Her voice was low, as if she feared someone might hear, and she took advantage of Neil's surprise to brush past him into the room. "Be so kind as to close the door."

"Like hell I will!" Neil swore angrily. "What do you want?"

The veil lifted to reveal Jane Gregory's smiling face. "Good morning, Neil."

"Oh, Christ," exclaimed Neil, hurriedly closing the door.

Jane cast an appraising eye at his dressing gown as she stripped off her gloves. "If I'd known you were such a late riser I wouldn't have come so early. Umm, coffee. May I?"

Neil gestured impatiently. "Help yourself. I repeat, Jane: What do you want?"

Jane sipped at her coffee and returned the cup to the table with a rude exclamation. "Terrible, absolutely terrible. How on earth can you drink this swill?"

"I've tasted worse. Come on, Jane, out with it. What brings you here all decked out for Halloween?"

Jane flushed angrily and hurled herself into a chair, but when she spoke her tone was civil. "I came to offer you a . . . a wager of sorts. You are a betting man, are you not?"

"At times," Neil acknowledged, still standing. "But I don't see how that affects you."

A small, pink tongue darted out as Jane nervously wet her lips. "I saw you Friday afternoon in the maze with Eden Thackery. You seemed quite taken with each other." She looked expectantly at Neil, waiting for a comment. Neil eyed her coldly, refusing to satisfy her curiosity. Jane shrugged carelessly. "I don't blame you, of course; Eden is . . . fairly attractive, in her own way. But I do hope you realize how such an innocent scene could easily be misconstrued by some people. And gossip is the main source of entertainment in New York; it would be most unfortunate if Eden's name were bandied about with yours."

Something flickered in the depths of Neil's eyes. "I'm sure no one would take such talk seriously. Miss Thackery's behavior is beyond reproach."

Jane giggled. "But who knows that besides you and Eden? We're a very closed society here, Neil. Surely you can understand that, being from an aristocratic family yourself." She smiled engagingly.

A muscle worked in Neil's cheek. "Come to the point, Jane. You're leading up to something that smells to me like blackmail. Why don't you tell me straight out how much you want."

"Blackmail!" Jane's eyes widened in affected shock. "Good heavens, I never . . ."

"Save it," Neil snapped. "Say what you have to say and then leave."

"How direct," Jane murmured, a malicious glint coming into her eyes. "Let me start by giving you a brief history I think you'll find interesting. Little Eden Thackery has been a thorn in my side for years, a thorn that is threatening to imbed itself even deeper. For God knows what reason, my brother has taken it into his head to fall in love with her and he's decided to marry her." Jane's features arranged themselves into lines of distaste. "I'm sure you can see why I'll never allow such nonsense to take place."

"Why not?" Neil relit his cigar and sat down, relaxing as he sensed a personal vendetta in Jane's visit. "Eden Thackery seems to be a perfectly suitable candidate for a bridal gown."

"Maybe so, but not with my brother," Jane returned scathingly. "I have no intention of going through life with an iceberg for a sister-in-law."

Neil's eyebrows shot up. "Indeed," he commented with interest. "Forgive me, but I fail to see what I have to do with your private feud."

"I simply want to discredit Eden in front of Tim—but I can't do it alone. Aside from Tim you're the only man for whom Eden Thackery has shown more than a passing interest. I'd like you to reciprocate that interest, intrigue Eden still further. It shouldn't be that difficult, not for a man of your obvious . . . assets."

Neil chuckled mirthlessly. "What do you plan to do? Hide Tim and yourself under the bed so you don't miss anything?"

"Nothing so crude," Jane sniffed. "Tim flew into a rage when he merely saw you and Eden together in the maze. I think that if he sees you two together again—in a meeting that was obviously prearranged—Tim will quickly sour on Eden Thackery. We can arrange it so simply, Neil. Name a time and place and I'll see to it Tim and I are there."

Neil didn't believe Jane's explanation, not for a minute. Cynic that he was, Neil sensed Jane's ruthlessness. Not only would Tim abandon any plans of marrying Eden, but Neil was certain Jane would twist the story of the innocent meeting until Eden's reputation would be soiled beyond repair. Neil could be ruthless, too, when he so desired, but he had no intention of participating in Jane's sordid play.

"No thanks." Neil rose and tossed Jane's gloves into her lap. "I'm not fond of melodrama."

Jane stamped to the door, her face set angrily, where she paused briefly. "You had better reconsider, Neil; if I choose to, I can make your stay here very miserable."

"Sorry, Jane," Neil grinned, "but I wouldn't waste my time if I were you. I'll be leaving New York in a couple of days— besides, as you say, gossip is cheap here, so I doubt anyone would take your remarks seriously. Go home, little girl, you're out of your depth here." Neil was still laughing as Jane slammed the door closed behind her.

Millicent pinned the final curl in place and stepped back to survey her creation, her eyes meeting Eden's in the mirror. "There now, Miss Eden, you look lovely. Your young man will fall at your feet when he sees you."

The idea of Neil rolling over like a pet dog brought a chuckle from Eden and she corrected lightly, "He's not *my* young man, Millicent, he's just a friend."

"It takes more than a friend to make your eyes sparkle like that," Millicent said knowingly. "You never fuss this way for Mr. Gregory."

"Mr. Gregory wouldn't notice if I wore sackcloth and

ashes." Eden rested her chin in her hands and studied her reflection. "You don't think it's too much, Millicent? It's not too fussy, too overdone?"

"Certainly not," Millicent's lips pursed disapprovingly at the question. "You're a young lady now; it won't do for you to go running about with your hair hanging down your back. In fact, miss, you shouldn't be going out with this young man at all until Mr. Colter meets him."

Eden sniffed. "Mr. Colter allows me to choose my own *beaux*, Millicent. Besides, you're accompanying me to the park, so everything will be nice and proper."

Millicent was not mollified. "Accompanying you, yes; but you said we're to separate in the park and then meet at the carriage at five o'clock. I ought to remain with you—at a discreet distance, of course—all afternoon."

"Absolutely not! I won't have my friend thinking I need a wet nurse. What kind of an impression would that make?"

"A very good one. He'd know you aren't one to be dallied with. That you're a lady of some consequence. If you ask me—"

"But I didn't," Eden snapped, suddenly impatient, "and if I ever do require your advice, I shall ask for it. Until that time, kindly remember your place."

Millicent's head bowed. "Yes, Miss Eden," she said in a crushed voice.

"Oh, Millicent, I didn't mean it." Eden extended her hand. "I'm just nervous, I guess—today is so important to me and I want everything to be just right. Please, Millicent, try to understand."

"I do, Miss Eden; I know how you feel," Millicent replied earnestly. "I have a young man myself. It's different where I come from; girls learn early to fend for themselves. But you, you've been sheltered and protected all your life. If you don't mind my saying it, Miss Eden, what will you do if he makes improper advances?"

Eden's eyes widened in amusement. "Improper advances? I'm shocked that you'd even think such a thing, Millicent."

"If it's a man you're going out with, you'd best think of these things yourself. It's you I'm thinking of, miss. I don't want to see you hurt."

The laughter vanished from her eyes and Eden said softly,

"I appreciate your concern, Millicent, but please don't worry. I can take care of myself."

Any further protests Millicent might have made were silenced by the expression on Eden's face. Eden would tolerate only so much interference, and Millicent had reached her limit. Millicent might be resigned to silence, but that didn't mean she had to allow Miss Eden to place her reputation in jeopardy. Her mind was made up. Whether Miss Eden knew it or not, she would have a chaperone today.

Eden and Millicent arrived at Central Park fifteen minutes before one o'clock. Eden waited until Millicent disappeared into the crowds on the carriage concourse before she turned in the opposite direction and walked to the ornate pagoda which served as the music pavilion. The New Yorkers were starting to gather for the concert, and Eden eagerly scanned the faces of those she passed. Neil was not among the bystanders, nor did she see him in the distance. Eden gnawed at her bottom lip. The esplanade ran a quarter of a mile in length, and her directions to Neil had been less than precise. It was entirely possible that he was waiting at the opposite end of the Mall, in which case they would miss each other entirely. He would think she had deliberately stood him up and she would, in all probability, never see Neil Banning again.

"Hello there." Eden gasped, whirled, and found herself gazing into Neil's golden eyes. He was hatless today, as he had been at the garden party, and the sunlight danced through the loose, natural waves of his dark hair. Neil grinned, amused by her direct appraisal. "You're prompt. I like that."

Eden laughed softly, her heart soaring at the vague compliment, for she had the feeling Neil gave them rarely. "One of the lessons taught by my guardian: There is no such thing as being fashionably late."

"I agree," Neil said, recalling that Constanza always kept him waiting, sometimes for an hour or more. He pushed the thought aside, studying the young woman in front of him. Eden had dressed simply for their meeting. The pale blue poplin gown abandoned the formal over- and underskirts in favor of the less elaborate, one-piece skirt which fell over a diminished bustle. The neck of the gown was high, the sleeves wide and full-length, and both were edged with lace. The color, Neil decided, lent a startling clarity to Eden's already crystalline eyes. The sight of Eden took Neil's breath away, though he hated to admit it to himself. "You're lovely, Eden." Unable to resist the impulse, Neil reached out and touched her cheek with his fingertips.

Eden's smile was genuine. "Thank you." Neil's hand lingered, his thumb caressing her jawline, as an odd tension filled the air between them. They were surrounded by people, yet strangely enough, Neil's touch seemed to isolate them from the crowd. His actions were improper, totally unacceptable to Victorian society—but Eden felt no sense of outrage. Instead, she was sorely disappointed when Neil's hand fell away.

Neil took Eden's arm and by tacit mutual consent they walked away from the pavilion, away from the crowds.

As they strolled along the paths, thoroughly enjoying the late spring air and sunshine, Eden felt the reserve between them ebb away. They said very little, commenting infrequently on some object that drew their attention, and for once the silence wasn't oppressive but rather companionable in its nature. The day was warm, and Eden watched enviously when Neil pulled off his jacket and swung it carelessly over one shoulder. Her own fingers toyed with the ribbons of her bonnet. She would feel so much more comfortable if she could bare her head to the light breeze.

"Why don't you take the damn thing off?" Neil had caught her gesture and now flashed Eden a brilliant smile. "You're missing the best part of nature being all bundled up like that."

As he spoke, a gust of wind tossed Neil's hair into unruly curls and Eden could do nothing but return his smile.

"No well-bred lady would be caught dead without her bonnet." Eden struck an affected pose. "Don't you like it?"

Neil eyed the confection of ribbons, bows and lace with obvious distaste. "Somebody ought to give it a decent burial. Here." With a quick flick of his fingers the bow was undone and the bonnet discarded. "Now if you would only take the pins out of your hair and let it blow free, I could almost imagine we're on some isolated hillside instead of in the middle of the city."

Eden looked surprised. "A romantic streak, Neil? I never guessed that about you."

"My bad English blood coming out." Neil's face hardened into an expression so bitter it struck at Eden's heart. Though she longed to ask what he meant by the remark, Eden prudently held her tongue. She would not press.

As they walked on, it seemed natural to gravitate toward the lake, one of Central Park's main attractions. A variety of craft—from rowboats to guide-pedaled swan boats to large omnibus launches—could be seen traversing the shimmering water, and when they reached the boat rental and Neil raised a questioning eyebrow, Eden quickly nodded.

The man renting the boats wore a pink and white striped apron, and with his full white beard and merry eyes he looked like a displaced Santa Claus. Neil folded his jacket and placed it on the seat in the rowboat as a cushion for Eden, and as he helped Eden into the boat she caught the knowing wink Santa exchanged with Neil.

Eden leaned back in the bow, her eyes half closed against the glare from the water, watching admiringly the play of the muscles across Neil's chest and arms as he drove the oars into the water. Neil was a magnificently attractive man, Eden found herself thinking with a newly discovered sensuality. He had the natural grace of an athlete—that was obvious from the easy way he carried himself—and it was clear from his tanned face that Neil spent a great deal of time out of doors.

"Like what you see?"

Neil's laughter jolted Eden from her musing and she reddened.

"I was wondering about your English blood," Eden told him truthfully.

"Why?" Neil's voice was harsh and he applied himself angrily to the oars.

"Because you claim Mexico as your home, yet you speak more of England, and you don't bother to explain how the two come together. And, female that I am, you make me curious." Eden paused. "Is that part of your fatal charm, or is it deliberate on your part?"

Neil rested his arms on the oars. His gaze was intense, as if he found the question a personal assault. Eden held her breath, afraid of the violence she sensed in Neil, releasing it only when he spoke. "You are nothing if not direct, Eden, which is rare in a woman. Most women deceive themselves and those around them, and a lot of people get hurt in the process—a lot of innocent people." Neil's tone was so bitter that Eden was vaguely relieved when he took up the oars again and had something to occupy his hands. "You enjoy romance?

Sure you do; all women dream about it. Well, let me spin you a tale guaranteed to bring a tear to your eye.

"Some thirty years ago the oldest son of a very old, very respected British family became bored by life on the country estate and the gaming houses in London and decided he needed a change of scenery, a bit of excitement in his life. He'd already had a walking tour of Europe, so the Continent held no attraction for him, nor did America. But there was one place that struck his fancy, fired his imagination. Mexico. Land of the *conquistadores*. A country that had been torn by revolutions for years and was at best highly volatile. So he packed his bags and headed for Mexico, half a world removed from England.

"Whatever he expected to find, he was sadly disappointed. The golden Mexico of the legends didn't exist; Indians weren't dressed in colorful, feathered costumes but instead wore rags. The children were dirty and starving; sickness and disease were everywhere. The sun was so hot during the day that it took him nearly two weeks to adjust to it; and when the sun finally did set, bands of thieves roamed the streets, attacking anyone foolish enough to be abroad without protection. He soon discovered there was very little about Mexico he liked—the climate was hot, the women were cold, the men were arrogant, the food was inedible. There was one bright spot, however; *criollo* society—that's people of pure European blood who are born in Mexico—greeted him with open arms. Rank and wealth do have their advantages. Have I bored you yet?"

Neil's mocking tone stung Eden deeply. Sensing that the recitation was painful for Neil, no matter how he made light of it, Eden gave a quick shake of her head and Neil smiled grimly.

"That's unfortunate . . . I suppose you want to hear the rest." Neil shipped the oars, his golden eyes growing cold and flat, and allowed the small craft to drift aimlessly.

"Among the *criollos* he met a young Mexican woman, the fiancée of one of his new friends. She was, to say the least, beautiful, the most beautiful woman he had ever met and she in turn found him equally fascinating. I'm sure you can guess what happened. Supposedly it was love at first sight, if such a thing exists. They were very noble about it, of course never seeing each other alone, meeting only at parties or public functions and pining away for each other the rest of the time. Eventually the strain became too much, the sacrifice too great, and, convinced that no one could fault them for their . . . love, they bravely declared themselves to her father.

"They had guessed wrong. The old man flew into a towering rage; he raved and ranted for an hour, reminding his daughter of her race and heritage, the pride of the family name she was attempting to disgrace. He had every right to be angry; he was an honorable man who was horrified that his daughter would even think of betraying the family honor by loving an outsider, a foreigner—and an Englishman in the bargain. So he did the only thing he could: He locked his daughter in her room and ordered her lover never to see her again, making it quite clear that if he did so the old man would kill him."

"How awful," Eden murmured involuntarily. "To be so cruel to your own child. How could he do such a thing?"

"Because he knew what was best for his daughter! He knew that such a misalliance could bring only misery, shame, dishonor . . ." Neil was practically shouting, and he brought himself under control by a supreme effort of will. "But his reasons aren't important, are they? And the best part of the story is yet to come—after all, what romance is complete without a tragedy?

"A week after the confrontation the young woman managed to escape with the aid of her lover. They fled north, toward Texas, stopping long enough in some isolated village to be married by some priest. The old man sent men after them, and so did the abandoned bridegroom, but the lovers managed to cross the Rio Grande just a few steps ahead of their pursuers. They were free—for a time.

"The young man wrote to his father, asking for money so he could bring his wife and himself back to England. He did not know that his father-in-law had also written a letter to England, and his father had finally run out of patience. The father offered his son not ship fare but an ultimatum: Annul the marriage and come home, or stay in Texas and be damned. The son and his bride chose to stay in Texas. They purchased a bit of land with what money they had and tried to make a go of it.

"The Mexican *patrón* didn't give up as easily as the English lord. It took over a year and God knows how much in bribes but he finally obtained an official annulment of the marriage. In the meantime, the jilted bridegroom had located his runaway fiancée and he shared the information with the *patrón*. They gathered a few handpicked men and rode into Texas. They had to wait for a week, but eventually the Englishman left his wife alone in the house.

"She fought them, of course, biting and scratching, screaming at them to leave her alone, to let her live out her life with the man she loved. The ex-fiancé put a quick end to her protests by knocking her senseless and throwing her over his saddle. They left two men behind to give the Englishman a lesson in manners when he returned, along with a note saying if he ever tried to see his wife again he would be killed.

"He went back to England—a little older, a little sadder— and after a time he married again, properly this time, to a woman chosen for him. When his father died he took his place in the House of Lords. He's content now, I suppose—lands and a title do bring a certain amount of comfort and compensation."

A muscle worked violently in Neil's cheek as he stared intently at Eden. Damn! Why had he felt compelled to tell her this story? It wasn't any of her business—she couldn't possibly care about this bit of ancient history, even if it did gnaw at his guts like a malignant, living thing. Neil fought back the surge of anger and hatred that always waited near the surface, ready to break through the barriers of indifference he had learned to construct long ago. It wasn't easy; Neil possessed a flaming temper and it took very little to set it off—as evidenced by the number of duels, fistfights and even gunfights in which he'd been involved.

"Neil?" Eden was frightened by the rigid set of Neil's jaw but her curiosity outweighed her fear. "Neil, what happened to the woman?"

"She returned to Mexico," Neil said in a tight voice. "She married the man she should have married in the first place, gave him a son and lived the retiring life of a dutiful, quiet country matron until her death a few months ago." Neil's smile was twisted and it hurt Eden to see it. "Ah, I see you're still confused, Eden, still curious. Allow me to clarify the story.

"You see, the annulment—though valid—arrived too late to prevent certain . . . consequences, the most notable of which was my birth, exactly one month before. My stepfather was very reasonable about my existence: Although he didn't adopt me I was raised in his household alongside his son, my half brother, as a true *criollo* of Mexico. But despite his generosity, all of my stepfather's friends were well aware of the circumstances of my birth. Thanks to my mother's impetuosity I have the dubious honor of being the first legitimate bastard in history."

Eden waited until Neil had taken up the oars again before she asked, "Don't you think you're being just the tiniest bit unfair, Neil? Your mother must have loved your father very much to risk all that she did for him. Few women would take such a chance."

"Love!" Neil snorted. "My dear Eden, 'love' is a word people use because it's more genteel and refined than admitting a sexual attraction. 'Lust' is by far a more honest word than 'love.' And as far as finding either love or lust in marriage, I am convinced that particular combination does not exist. When I marry, the marriage will take the form of a merger, with both parties benefiting from the contract."

Eden looked blankly at Neil for a moment before her long lashes swept downward to veil her eyes. She had barely heard Neil's discourse on marriage, intrigued as she was by other thoughts. Sexual attraction? Lust? The words and their meanings were foreign to her. Was that what she had felt when Neil had touched her? She had found it enjoyable, pleasurable. Was that lust?

"I still think you're too harsh," Eden said staunchly in spite of the bright, mocking laughter that leaped into Neil's eyes at her words.

"Do you indeed, my sweet innocent," Neil drawled as he pulled ashore.

Something in Neil's voice sent a shiver down Eden's spine and she brushed close to him as he helped her from the boat. "Have you ever been in love, Neil, even if just for a moment?"

Neil grinned wickedly. "There have been some moments . . . but I somehow doubt you would understand."

Neil purchased a bag of peanuts and they made their leisurely way across the park, pausing now and then to toss tidbits to the scampering squirrels.

"Tell me about your home, Neil. What's it like?"

"Our hacienda is on the coast. From the terrace you can watch the waves from the gulf break on the shore." They left the path, and Neil drew Eden down beside him on the grass beneath a tree. Sitting closely together, their shoulders touching, they were identical to the other young couples who had slipped away from vigilant chaperones for a few stolen minutes of privacy. "You can't imagine what it's like there, Eden. It's open, free; not like a city, with houses crowded on top of each other. There's a small mountain range on three sides of us—not that high, you understand, but tall enough to make each sunset a glorious sight. My brother and I used to camp and hunt and explore there when we were growing up. It served us well; during the Revolution we hid *Juáristas* in the caves we'd found. That was my brother's doing—he's the idealist in the family, not I.

"It's hot, believe me; if you ever came to Mexico your fair skin would burn in minutes. Maybe it's just my imagination—or my prejudice—but I don't think the sky is as clear and blue anywhere else in the world as it is in Mexico."

Neil stretched out on the ground and gazed up into the sky, his arms crossed beneath his head, with Eden sitting wide-eyed beside him. Neil seemed to have forgotten her presence as he described in detail his home. That he loved Mexico was clear from the way Neil brought each plant and animal to life with his words; he was fiercely loyal to the country that had nurtured him. Neil had been twenty-one when his younger brother had convinced him that Mexico's future lay in Juárez, that the time for legal appeals and inroads was long past and the only recourse lay in armed revolt. Two bloody years had followed, with Neil always in the thick of the fighting, fighting shoulder to shoulder with men for whom he once wouldn't have spared so much as a glance. Neil was one of the lucky ones; the wounds he received in the battles and skirmishes had healed quickly, leaving only a few scars in their wake. His brother had not been as fortunate; at the Battle of Querétaro a cannon ball had exploded directly in front of him, and a fragment had smashed its way through his thigh, leaving him with a less flamboyant memento of the Revolution, a limp that would remain for the rest of his life.

"My brother returned from Europe several months ago. He was studying medicine in Vienna. He plans to start a hospital of some sort on the estate. It's a good idea, I have to admit that. There's virtually no health care in the countryside—people sometimes develop blood poisoning from a cut simply because they don't know how to disinfect it properly." Neil's voice drifted off and he turned to look at Eden, a lean forefinger reaching up to tease the soft curls at her temple. "I've spent the entire afternoon talking about myself. Forgive me. I'm afraid I've bored you."

"Oh, no," Eden protested. "It's fascinating. The farthest I've ever been from New York is our country place, but someday I hope to see Europe. Maybe I'll even get to Mexico. Or China. Or Russia! Supposedly the Cossacks are the best horsemen in all Europe. Did you know that?"

"I know; I've seen them." Neil stopped Eden's exclamation by the simple method of placing a finger across her lips. "Enough about Cossacks and Russia and Mexico; I'm more interested in you, Eden, and you haven't told me anything about yourself."

"There really isn't much to tell," Eden hedged.

"I don't believe that for a minute. The heir to Thackery Ltd. must lead an interesting life."

Eden stiffened, instantly on guard. "How do you know about Thackery Ltd.?"

"I retained the firm to handle the legalities of an investment of mine." Neil smiled quizzically, wondering at Eden's sudden wariness. "I worked with Matthew Kelly—a good man, I think. He arranged my invitation to the garden party last Friday. Incidentally, he thinks quite highly of you."

"I should hope so—particularly since I have the power, indirectly, to replace him." In an effort to increase the physical distance between herself and Neil, Eden now sat so straight that her muscles cramped. Her voice was heavy with sarcasm when she added, "Did I meet your expectations, Neil? Or did Matthew lead you to expect more from me?"

Neil's expression darkened, anger rapidly pooling beneath his bewilderment. "I don't follow you."

"Oh, please," Eden said raggedly, her façade cracking. "No more games or lies; I've played out this scene more often than I care to remember! Whenever Matthew wants to impress a client he hauls out Locke Thackery's daughter for the client's inspection. The mere fact that I exist seems to serve as a reassurance that Thackery Ltd. is immortal." She gave Neil a brittle smile. "I must admit, though, your approach is ...innovative. Usually I'm presented somewhere between the dessert and the gentlemen's brandy and cigars. It never crossed my mind that a young, unmarried client would go through all these 'chance' meetings and feigned interest in the Thackery heir. You really needn't have gone to such elaborate lengths,

Neil. Matthew would have been only too happy to arrange one of his infamous dinner parties."

Neil turned so that his face was barely inches away from Eden's, and he recognized the pain she was gamely trying to conceal. "The firm has nothing to do with my interest in you." Eden turned away and Neil gently cupped her chin in his hand, forcing her to meet his gaze. "You're a beautiful, highly attractive woman, *querida,* but you jump to mistaken conclusions."

Somehow the words were not enough. Before he could stop himself, Neil leaned forward and pressed his lips against the softness of Eden's mouth. An explosion of desire surged through Neil with such intensity that he drew back, shaken. Eden's eyes fluttered open, their clarity replaced by a misty, languid gray.

"What does *querida* mean?" Eden whispered. Stunned by the overpowering pleasure she found in Neil's kiss, she sought sanity in conversation.

"It's a form of endearment," Neil answered in a roughened voice. He curved a hand behind Eden's head and drew her toward him. "You mimic the accent well—I'll teach you some Spanish if there's time. But for now, sweet Eden, you talk too much."

Their lips met again. All resistance and hurt drained from Eden at the gentle pressure of Neil's kiss, and this time Eden's arm stole around Neil's neck. Vaguely she was aware of a sudden warmth that seemed to encompass her entire body. It was a heady sensation, and when Neil's questing tongue darted against her mouth, Eden's lips parted of their own volition. An electric shock jolted along the length of Eden's spine and spread through her body, leaving her feeling strangely breathless and exhilarated—and disappointed when the kiss ended.

"I've been wanting to do that since the night we met." Neil's voice was husky. "Have you any idea how desirable you are— so coldly aloof one minute, all anger and fire the next? Someone like Jane I can understand, but you, Eden, you are a different matter entirely."

Eden's eyes widened in bewilderment.

"Do you know what I'm talking about?" Eden shook her head and Neil expelled his breath heavily. "It's probably just as well." He got to his feet and extended a hand. "I'd better take you home; it's getting late."

Eden rose, brushing the grass from her skirt. "I have my own carriage, but thank you." Neil was shrugging into his jacket, and Eden's heart twisted. The afternoon had fled; the present was rapidly slipping into the past, and she was powerless to stop it. Soon—in a matter of days, probably—Neil would leave New York, and the excitement he had brought into her life would be gone. Eden had never felt as alive as she had this afternoon, in Neil's presence. Sadly, she placed a slender hand on Neil's chest and smiled into the warm, golden eyes. "It was a lovely afternoon, Neil."

The glib response which sprang to his mind went unsaid. "Yes, it was," Neil replied sincerely, astonishing himself. "Will you believe me when I say I'm sorry it ended so soon?"

"Yes." Eden's smile wavered. "You aren't the cynic you claim to be, Neil."

Neil laughed but there was no amusement in his eyes. "There are those who would disagree with you—myself included."

"Perhaps," Eden conceded. A curtain had fallen across his eyes, a device Eden recognized because she had used it frequently herself, and instantly her heart went out to Neil. "But they don't know you as I do."

"You know me so well, do you?" Mockery danced in the golden depths.

Eden ignored the jibe. "Well enough, I think. I've thrown up enough barriers in my life to know when I encounter one." She smiled. "I like you best when you aren't playing the role of world-wise cynic."

The mocking gleam died, and Neil covered Eden's hand with his own. "And when the ice princess has melted, no woman I know has your gentleness and sincerity." He bent and kissed each of her fingers in turn. "I want to see you again, Eden."

"I'd like that very much," she conceded softly.

"Tonight?" When Eden shook her head, Neil chuckled and framed her face with his hands. "You always refuse my initial request. Why?"

"I'm seldom impulsive," Eden explained quietly. "I plan, I schedule, I make lists. My life runs very smoothly that way."

This time it was Neil who shook his head. "Schedules are for bankers, and lists are for spinsters. You, from what I see, are neither. We're going to have to change the way you live, Eden." He brushed his lips tantalizingly across hers.

From the concealing shade of a tree several yards away, Millicent nearly groaned aloud as the tall, dark man embraced Miss Eden once again. Millicent's eyes darted furtively, on the lookout for a familiar face along the paths—someone who could bring about her employer's downfall. A maid's unobtrusive presence, after all, had saved the reputation of countless young ladies. There was no one, the saints be thanked! The lovers were leaving now—the man's hand riding a bit too possessively at Miss Eden's waist—and Millicent jumped to her feet and followed at a discreet distance. Thankfully the afternoon was nearly at an end, but Millicent would not relax her vigil until she and Miss Eden were safely in the carriage. Something about this young man rubbed Millicent the wrong way—the predatory gleam in his eyes, perhaps; or the way he seemed to make Miss Eden forget about her surroundings. Kissing in public—imagine! A sigh of relief escaped Millicent as Eden was handed into the carriage and the gentleman departed. She would wait a few minutes before joining her employer. *Now* she could relax.

Millicent's security was false, although she did not realize it. In a vis-á-vis three vehicles behind Eden's *calèche,* Jane Gregory watched Neil Banning's retreating back. So Neil *was* interested in Eden Thackery. After this morning Jane had started to believe her instincts had been wrong. But now . . . a malicious smile curved Jane's lips. Perhaps she wouldn't be saddled with Eden Thackery for a sister-in-law after all.

The next two days swept Eden into an adventure which would have astounded her friend Meg, had she known, and which far exceeded Eden's own romantic fantasies. Mundane considerations such as Tim and the debut preparations fled before the whirlwind that was Neil Banning. True to his word, Neil casually appropriated nearly every waking hour of Eden's time and proceeded to throw her well-ordered life into chaos. Her plans and appointments meant nothing to Neil, and when he asked Eden to cancel or postpone her engagements she did so willingly. Neil's inevitable return to Mexico hung over both of them like the sword of Damocles, and Eden was determined to make the most of whatever time was left.

Eden was living in a dream world which neither Millicent's disapproving looks nor Hugh's uncharacteristic reserve could penetrate. She was in love—wonderfully, giddily, innocently in love with a man who made her feel vibrantly alive—and she planned to hoard that knowledge like a miser. Neil was her secret, a treasure Eden carefully guarded from prying eyes, even Millicent's. Despite her maid's objections, Eden adamantly refused to allow Millicent to chaperone any of her meetings with Neil. For Neil, Eden flouted all conventions, risking her position and reputation each time they met without giving the danger a second thought. Neil was a rebel and he brought out all of Eden's own rebelliousness. They were kindred spirits and Eden loved him more with each passing moment.

Their time together was marred only by the surreptitious nature of their meetings. Neil did not call upon Eden at her home, nor did Eden urge him to do so. She was content with the rapport which existed between them when they could be together. During their meetings—usually consisting of carriage rides and walks through Central Park—they talked constantly, freely, and Eden feared their cherished intimacy would evaporate should their names be linked together by society. If her fear was unreasonable, it was also quite real, and Neil seemed to understand. Apparently he valued their privacy as much as Eden did.

Only one thing disturbed their enchanted idyll: Eden's steadfast reluctance to tell Neil about herself. "Really, Neil," she would insist, "my past—my life—isn't all that interesting. Believe it or not, I've been very sheltered; I've led an extremely dull, proper life." Neil would sigh theatrically and their conversation would take a different direction. The patience Neil displayed at such times deepened Eden's affection toward him—aside from Hugh, Neil was the only man she knew who did not press for answers she was not ready to give.

Wednesday dawned, and not even the promise of a spring shower which hung in the air affected Eden's spirits. When Hugh informed Eden at breakfast that he would be gone all day and late into the evening, she felt a trifle guilty about her reaction. Today she wouldn't have to worry about returning home in time to have dinner with Hugh! The entire day and part of the evening would be hers to share with Neil. Eden was so excited at the prospect that she didn't even notice Hugh's expression when she kissed him good-bye at the door.

Eden dressed casually in a high-collared, yellow piqué walking dress and arrived in Central Park promptly at ten o'clock.

Neil was already there, leaning against a large tree just inside the park entrance. When he caught sight of her he smiled, and that was enough to double the already frantic tempo of Eden's heartbeat. She quickly dismissed her driver and hurried to Neil.

"I have the whole day, and the evening as well!" Eden said breathlessly before Neil could speak. "I hope you have something wonderful planned for today, because I intend to make the most of my freedom."

Neil grinned, affected by her excitement. "As a matter of fact, I do. How do you feel about a drive in the country and a leisurely picnic?"

Eden laughed. "I'd like that very much, but in case you haven't noticed, it looks like rain."

"I noticed—I hoped you wouldn't." Neil frowned and glanced at his surroundings. "We're doomed to the park again, I suppose."

His tone quelled Eden's laughter. "It's not so bad, Neil. I don't mind."

"But I do." Neil's frown disappeared as he caressed Eden's cheek with his left hand. "We're never alone, Eden, except when we take a cab from one place to another; and we're constantly looking over our shoulders to make sure one of your friends isn't around. Society and its codes are all well and good, but I'd like a little privacy. I had hoped the picnic would give us a little time alone."

Eden's mind raced. She shared Neil's frustration, but she was frightened as well. Victorian society simply did not allow the kind of privacy they both desired. Even their activities of the two days, innocent though they had been, could ruin them both.

"There is a place," Eden said slowly, "but we'll have to hire a cab."

"No, we won't. I rented a gig this morning." Neil's eyes glowed. "Tell me more."

Smiling, Eden took his hand. "Come along then. You're about to visit the Thackery mansion."

Both Neil and Eden were too intent upon each other to notice the closed carriage which followed them out of Central Park.

The rain had started by the time Neil drove up the wide, curving driveway and, leaning closer to him, Eden pointed to a partially concealed building behind the mansion. "That's the carriage house. We can leave the gig there."

Neil nodded, and when they reached the building he handed Eden the reins and jumped down to open the massive doors. Eden drove the vehicle inside and patiently waited during the few minutes it took Neil to unharness the team.

"This place doesn't see much use," Neil commented.

"No. When my father died, my guardian had the horses and most of the vehicles moved to his home. I wanted to sell them, but my guardian appreciates blooded stock."

Once the horses were secure in their stalls, Neil helped Eden alight. His hands lingered at her waist, sending a melting warmth up Eden's spine.

The gentle note which entered Eden's voice when she spoke about her guardian did not go unnoticed by Neil. "Your guardian is a good man, I take it."

"A fine man," Eden replied proudly. "His only fault is spoiling me outrageously."

Neil chuckled and released Eden. "I can't blame him for that." He reached into the boot of the carriage and withdrew a large, woven hamper. "Shall we dine here?"

Eden shook her head. "There is a parlor with a lovely fireplace on the second floor of the main house. It used to be my favorite place to spend a rainy day." Together they walked to the open doorway and paused. "The shortest way is across the back lawn to the French doors."

Eden's hand was engulfed by Neil's larger one, and the next moment they were running across the graveled drive and lush green grass. Eden lifted her skirt with her free hand in an effort to keep up with Neil's long, careless strides. She slipped once on the wet lawn, and gasped when Neil easily pulled her upright without breaking his stride. His iron strength surprised her— coming as it did from such a lean frame—but did not intimidate her. When they reached the French doors Neil freed her hand so they could walk single file beneath the shelter of the eaves. Eden mentally counted the doors they passed, then stopped.

"The lock on this one is loose," she explained. While Neil watched, she took a hairpin from her hair and inserted it into the lock. Moments later, after some careful manipulation, there was a soft click and Eden pulled the door open. "After you."

"What about the servants?" Neil asked as he stepped past Eden. "Won't they—" His voice died at the sight that greeted him. Slowly, cautiously, Neil walked to the center of the ballroom, the hair on the back of his neck prickling. There was a ghostly stillness about the house which grated on his nerves.

"The house has been closed for three years. There is no staff anymore, only Katrin." Eden closed the door as a bolt of lightning splintered through the sky. "And since she has Wednesdays off, we won't be disturbed."

She guided Neil through the mansion, up the staircase and into the small parlor which had been used by her mother. Two love seats flanked the marble fireplace and a half dozen chairs and tables were scattered around the room. A sudden chill shook Eden and she shivered. A long-forgotten memory had surfaced—a memory of a small girl snuggled close to her mother on one of the love seats, listening eagerly to a story told in a slow, gentle drawl.

"Cold?"

Neil's question startled her. For a moment Eden had forgotten his presence. She drew herself back to the present and smiled at him. "It's a bit chilly."

"That can be remedied." Neil gestured to the wood box beside the fireplace. "There's plenty of wood and I happen to be quite good at starting fires."

Eden's cheeks warmed, recalling the heat which had consumed her on those few occasions when they had kissed. "I'll bet you are," she said wryly.

Neil paused in the act of shrugging out of his suit coat. "You have an evil, wicked mind, my sweet," he teased, one eyebrow raised mockingly. "Why don't you unpack the hamper while I get the fire going."

"I'll open the window first; the room can use the fresh air." Eden walked to the parlor's only window at the opposite side of the room and pushed the drapes aside. She raised the frame a little and stood quietly by the glass panes, enjoying the downpour outside and looking across the mansion's front lawns to the rain-darkened street beyond. From behind her came the crackling of the fire and the sound of Neil adding more wood to the flames. A sense of peace crept through Eden.

"A penny for your thoughts."

Neil's voice—so close to her—was followed by a pair of strong arms encircling her waist, and Eden allowed herself to be drawn against his chest.

"I was just thinking how nice it is not to have to worry

about being seen." Eden felt, rather than heard, his low laugh. Sighing, she rested her head in the hollow of his shoulder. "We're breaking all the rules, you know."

"Yes." Neil's breath stirred the wisps of hair at her temples. "Does it bother you?"

Eden considered that. "A bit," she admitted. "I've heard terrible stories about young women whose reputations are blackened. Their families disown them and they're forced to . . . to find employment in exclusive houses. Some even kill themselves."

Neil studied her from his greater height, feeling a sudden protective urge. "We can leave if you like." The negative shake of her head surprised and pleased him.

"I thought you enjoyed flaunting convention," Eden teased.

"I do—or at least I've always done so without giving it too much thought." Neil turned her in the circle of his arms. "The consequences never bothered me until now."

The warmth in those golden eyes entranced Eden. "We're here," she said softly, "we have a fire and it's pouring rain outside. I don't see any reason to leave."

Neil smiled as he cupped a hand behind Eden's head. "I couldn't agree more." A gentle press of his hand lifted Eden on tiptoes against his chest and tilted her head back. Her lips parted slightly, invitingly, and Neil tenderly covered them with his own.

Eden's eyes fluttered shut and she brazenly curled an arm around Neil's neck and pulled him closer. She felt the change in Neil immediately—the arm at her waist tightened into a steel band, driving the air from her lungs. Neil's tongue sought her own, and a new kind of breathlessness seized her. Unconsciously Eden melted into his frame, enjoying the way their bodies fit together.

Breathing raggedly, Neil pulled his mouth away from Eden's and stared down at her. Did she have any idea of the extent of the passion she had aroused? God, how he wanted her!

"It's rude to stare." Eden's voice wavered and, unnerved by the hungry, amber gleam, she dropped her gaze to the open collar of Neil's shirt.

"I was admiring the way your cheeks turn a delicate shell pink. The color spreads from here," Neil touched a spot near

Eden's nose and lightly traced the curve of her cheekbone to the hairline, "over to here."

Eden swallowed hard as Neil's hand stroked her back, sending an involuntary shiver down her spine. "I think you're trying to seduce me," she whispered.

"Shh." One of Neil's hands threaded its way through the mass of Eden's hair at the back of her head. "Come here, sweetheart."

Eden gave in to the pressure, grudgingly at first, then willingly as Neil's lips moved gently upon her own and she allowed herself to succumb to the lover of her dreams. But Neil was no phantom lover; his embrace was strong and real and she felt achingly alive. Outside, the storm raged, but Eden no longer noticed.

"Enough," Neil muttered harshly, drawing away. Then, aware of the hurt in her eyes, he gentled. "Enough, *querida*, before I forget I'm a gentleman." He brought himself under control with an effort and managed a lopsided smile. "I promised you a picnic."

They left the window and retreated to the fire in their sanctuary without a backward glance.

Neil spread a tablecloth over the carpet and produced wine and an array of cold meats, cheese, bread and fruit from the hamper. "Come sit down." He patted the floor beside him and, while Eden carefully arranged her skirt, he uncorked the bottle and poured the wine. When Eden took her glass, he raised his own. "To us—and a pleasant afternoon."

The glass rims clinked together, filling the air with the sound of fine crystal. Eden felt as if she had just surfaced from a whirlpool and she went limp with relief. Nervously, hoping Neil wouldn't notice her shaking hands, Eden accepted the dishes he passed to her.

Knowing all the trouble Neil must have taken to arrange this lunch, Eden felt guilty when she could do no more than pick at her food. The afternoon was theirs but Eden knew, instinctively, that their time together was almost over.

"I suppose you're anxious to return home," Eden ventured as Neil refilled their glasses.

Anxious, Neil thought bitterly. Awaiting him in Mexico was marriage to Constanza. No, he was far from eager to return, but it was a fate he had already postponed as long as he dared. All that remained now was to tell Eden good-bye.

"I had a letter from Sebastian a few days ago. It seems my brother is managing quite nicely without me." Reaching out, he took one of Eden's hands and pressed a kiss into her palm. "But if I know Sebastian, the *hacienda* is probably falling down around his ears while he's off somewhere delivering babies and setting broken bones."

Eden smiled. "You're very adept at avoiding direct answers."

"I'm leaving New York the day after tomorrow."

Her heart twisted with pain and Eden felt the color drain from her face. "So soon!" She heard the dismay in her voice and immediately wished the words back.

"New York was my last stop—I've been gone for several months." Neil squeezed her hand. "I didn't mean to be so blunt."

"Don't be silly." Eden forced a stiff smile to her lips as she reclaimed her hand. "I knew you weren't staying forever. You made that quite clear when we met." *But I wasn't in love with you then.* The thought surfaced without warning and with such poignancy that tears started to her eyes.

Neil fell silent, giving serious consideration to an idea which had been in the back of his mind from the moment he had first laid eyes on Eden. They knew each other quite well by now, but most importantly Eden knew and understood the demands which were made upon a man of his position. While he hadn't mentioned his forthcoming marriage, he *had* pointed out during their boat ride that when he married it would be to someone of his own class in a merger of two aristocratic families. Eden must have gathered from that conversation that he would never even consider marrying her, Neil thought as he stared into the fire, but would she be willing to accept the position of his mistress?

"I'm ready to leave New York," Neil said at last, "but not you."

A choked sound came from Eden's throat; at the moment it was her version of a light laugh. "You can't leave one and not the other."

"I could," Neil replied slowly, his eyes locked with hers, "if you would come with me."

The proposal was made so calmly that it took a moment before Eden fully realized what he had said. When she did, an explosion of joy spread through her. Neil was asking her to

marry him! In spite of his embittered statements about love,
despite the fact that he spoke of marriage as if it were nothing
more than a business merger, somewhere, deep in his heart,
Neil believed in love as strongly as she did. She had known
all along that he wasn't the cold cynic he pretended to be—
and now he had actually proposed! Hard on the heels of her
pleasure came reality and all its complications, and worry
clouded her soft gray eyes. How would she explain Neil to
Hugh? Or to the rest of New York, for that matter? How . . . ?

Neil frowned at the abrupt changes in Eden's expression.
Setting his glass aside, he pried the wineglass from her fingers
and shifted his position so they faced each other. Neil took her
chin between the thumb and forefinger of his left hand and
stared into her eyes, seeking an answer to his question. Confusion marred the crystalline depths and Neil relaxed, sensing
the reason for her reluctance. She had been raised to think in
terms of marriage, not alliances; it was her Puritan conscience
Eden had to overcome. Neil had the solution. He slanted his
lips across Eden's, demanding nothing until her arms found
their way around his neck and he felt the stiffness ebb out of
her body. When Eden was totally pliant, Neil's lips explored
the slender white column of her throat. His leisurely kisses
tantalizingly traced along Eden's throat until their lips met
again.

Eden gave herself up to the sensations rippling through her
flesh. Her body seemed to thrill to each caress, like the strings
of a harp beneath the touch of a musician. Neil's fingers were
at the tiny buttons at the front of her gown; she felt them come
undone, but when she started to protest, Neil's mouth effectively stilled her voice. She was soaring! Their tongues met,
and Neil's hand slid inside her bodice. Eden sighed, then shivered as his fingers caressed her breast. She knew, in the recesses
of her mind, that Neil should stop—that she should make him
stop—but the thought quickly vanished, leaving Eden free to
concentrate on the shock waves which were making her head
spin.

Neil raised his head, viewing the woman in his arms through
eyes of molten gold. He hadn't meant to take them this far this
soon, but now . . . The dress slipped from her shoulders and
with a low groan Neil circled her waist and pulled Eden to her
feet. He brought his mouth to the valley which began just above
the top of her chemise and heard Eden's soft sigh. Stepping

back, he freed Eden's hands from the sleeves of her gown, kissing each palm in turn, and was rewarded by the dress sliding to the floor. The chemise quickly joined the gown and Eden gasped as warm hands grazed over her cool flesh.

"Neil—" She was shivering uncontrollably, torn between wanting to experience more and knowing she should stop before she lost her very soul to this man.

Neil forced himself into restraint, sensing her fear. "Do me, love," he urged in a thick voice. "Start with my shirt."

The buttons opened easily and, beneath Eden's now curious gaze, Neil shrugged out of the garment. Hesitantly, Eden reached out to touch the smooth, bronzed skin. Neil reached for his belt and was surprised to find his hand met by Eden's.

"It's only fair," Eden whispered, a hint of wickedness in her voice.

Neil tensed as her fingers worked at his waist, and in seconds he kicked free of his pants. He kissed away the fragile barrier of her undergarments and impatiently removed his own, anxious to discover how Eden's nude body would feel against the length of him. He drew Eden toward him with an intensity that surprised them both.

So this was how it felt, Eden thought disjointedly. A man and woman pressed so closely together that each could actually feel the texture of the other's skin. Neil's flesh was smooth and unmarred; his muscles rippled and corded beneath her touch. Only the rigid maleness prodding almost painfully into the sensitive skin of her abdomen caused her alarm. She knew, of course, from Meg's breathless explanations, the purpose of that particular appendage, but a hasty glance downward sent panic darting through her. Surely Meg had been mistaken! And if Meg hadn't . . . how would Eden ever be able to receive that tumescent part of Neil without being ripped apart?

Once again Neil seemed to read her thoughts. His mouth lifted from his exploration of the rosy peaks of her breasts and he took her hand. "Touch me, Eden," he breathed, but it was a command all the same. When she shook her head Neil guided her hand to the dark, crisp thatch of hair below his waist. "A man's body is very obvious, I'm afraid; so unlike a woman's, with all those hidden, secret places."

"It's so different from what I imagined," Eden whispered, thoroughly terrified now of the member standing so hotly erect in her grasp. "Neil, I can't possibly—"

"Gently, love." Neil's voice roared in her ear. He wrapped Eden in his arms and, over her fearful protests, sank with her to the floor. "You're ready. Just let yourself go and relax."

"But I can't, I—" How could she relax when . . . !

"Shhh, love. I'm sorry, *querida*, but it has to happen sometime." Neil positioned himself above her. For a moment, Eden was frightened by the intensity of Neil's need as, his eyes locked with hers, his trembling hands lifted her hips.

Pressure first, then a burning sensation deep inside made Eden cry out and, in a moment of madness, she sank her teeth into Neil's shoulder. Neil grunted softly at the pain, acknowledging her right to inflict it. Virgin's blood exchanged for his own.

Eden gasped as Neil moved inside her, creating a whirling vortex that coiled in her belly like a tightly wound spring. Breathing became difficult, the spring coiling tighter with each of Neil's thrusts. The pain was forgotten, forgiven. Neil found her lips, muting the cries that Eden vaguely realized she was making. She clung helplessly to Neil as the spring suddenly snapped within her, sending out fragments of pleasure so intense that Eden thought she would faint. She was barely conscious of the convulsive shudder tearing through Neil; only when he planted light kisses over her eyes and cheeks and brushed the damp hair away from her face did Eden open her eyes. Neil kissed her deeply and rolled onto his back, pulling Eden with him so that her head rested against his shoulder.

"My God, but you are beautiful, Eden." Neil's eyes raked over her slim body. "Just looking at you makes me want you all over again."

Eden surfaced slowly, struggling against the weight of her drugged senses. When she finally understood what Neil had said, Eden smiled and ran her hand across his bronze chest. "You are, too. Maybe 'beautiful' isn't the right word for a man, but that's how I feel right now. Do you understand what I mean?"

"I think so." Neil tightened his hold on Eden, finding himself unexpectedly touched by her words. "Thank you, love. No one has ever said that to me before."

"No one?" Eden's face was alight with impish curiosity. "Come now, Neil, admit it. With all the women you've undoubtedly had in the past, at least *one* must have—ouch!"

Neil had delivered a smart slap to her backside and now he

grinned at her pained expression. "That should teach you to doubt my word."

Eden laughed softly, but when Neil began removing what few pins remained in her hair, she sobered. "Is it always like this, Neil? I mean—" she blushed furiously beneath that amber gaze as she searched for the right words. "Is it always so perfect, so incredibly . . ." Her voice trailed off helplessly.

"Heartstopping?" Neil supplied the word while he thoughtfully drew his fingers through her thick curls. Strangely enough, the act of love never *had* been this explosively fulfilling with his other partners. "It should be."

"Even for the woman?" Eden blurted out.

Neil chuckled, the corners of his eyes crinkling in amusement. "Eden, love, you are priceless. Yes, it should be just as pleasurable for the woman as for the man, in spite of those old wives' tales I'm sure you've heard." He cocked an eyebrow at her. "You *have* heard those nasty lies, haven't you? About how a *lady* doesn't enjoy a man's bed, that a *lady* is all too happy to turn those duties over to a mistress as long as her husband is discreet?" Neil tangled his fingers in her hair, pulling Eden's head down until their lips brushed together. "I prefer a woman who is as natural in bed as out of it. And you, my sweet innocent, seem to have that rare combination."

His kiss seemed to last forever and when it ended Eden murmured, "Not so innocent, not anymore."

"Mmm." Neil buried his face in the fragrant, flaxen curls, one hand sliding down her side to rest possessively on her hip. "Still innocent," he contradicted, "in spite of what you may think. You have a lot left to learn." Neil rolled to his side, carrying Eden with him, and began reexploring her soft curves.

Gray eyes wide and searching, Eden followed suit. No longer afraid of his raw masculinity, she touched him freely, intent upon making some discoveries of her own. How wonderfully different men were from women, Eden thought as her palms slipped over the tanned skin. She felt so terribly insubstantial compared to the size of him, the breadth of his shoulders. His hands were large, with long, strong fingers, as capable of inflicting pain as they were of giving pleasure. Eden pushed the thought away and continued her study of the body which reclined so intimately against hers. At his waist the deep bronze faded to a lighter color which—though still much darker than her own flesh—looked almost white compared to the thick, black hair that coiled into tight curls and formed a trail downward across his flat belly. Eden's hand dropped lower, coming to a halt only when she heard Neil catch his breath.

Eden's hand jerked back and she looked up into Neil's half-closed eyes. "Did I hurt you?"

"No," Neil rasped as he returned her hand to him. "I just didn't expect you to learn so fast." He pulled Eden closer to rediscover the varied ways her body responded to his touch.

And respond she did. Eden's nerves leaped, her flesh tingled as Neil cast his sensual spell over her again. Eden would have been surprised had Neil told her that he was experiencing the same feelings. He could never have enough of her, Neil thought as Eden's delicate hands and body burned into his brain forever. Every instinct of his being cried out for release and it took a gigantic effort on his part not to give in at once. She's young, Neil constantly reminded himself while Eden unknowingly continued to raise merry hell with his self-control; she really has no idea what she's doing. But, God, if she's this way now, what will she be like when she knows exactly the effect she's having on me?

Eden moaned softly, her desire heightened by the leisurely way Neil was working his magic on her. She drew Neil down to meet her arching body. There was no pain at all this time, only wave upon wave of sensation that caught them both on the crests. Their pasts, their separate identities, their different worlds—these things no longer mattered as they clung tightly to each other. The waves peaked higher and higher until finally, shatteringly, an enormous breaker tossed them both breathless and sated onto a warm, golden beach.

"Eden, Eden," Neil whispered in a hoarse voice. He lay on his side, his long fingers smoothing her hair over the pillow of his arm. "To think I was certain you were made of ice."

She curled against him, sighing contentedly when Neil draped his arm around her waist. "For a very long time I was—or at least, that's what I wanted everyone to believe." Mist-gray eyes trapped the amber ones that watched her so avidly. "You make it very easy for me to be myself."

Neil's gaze was like molten fire. "You still haven't answered my question. Will you come with me to Mexico?"

"I . . ." Eden hesitated. "You don't believe in love, Neil."

"No, I don't," Neil agreed, thinking he understood the direction her mind had taken. Yet even now, knowing that a declaration of his love would make the idea of being his mistress more palatable to Eden, Neil refused to lie. "But I do know that I want you more than I've ever wanted any other woman. That's all I can offer, Eden. Is it enough for you?"

"I don't know," Eden answered truthfully, her eyes clouded. "Are you absolutely certain this is what you want?" There was no hesitation in Neil's affirmative nod, and Eden drew a shaky breath. "I love you, Neil. No, please don't laugh," she hastily added when his lips twitched. "It happens to be true, and it's not just because of today. I care for you, Neil; I love the man you are, not the man you pretend to be."

"I'm not laughing." Neil caressed her jawline with his thumb. "Will you come with me?"

Their marriage would be one-sided, Eden thought, at least at the beginning. But they could be happy—gloriously happy—she would see to that. In time Neil would come to love her. He would never regret marrying her. Eden smiled radiantly and ran her fingers through his black hair. "Oh, yes, Neil. Yes!"

Grinning, Neil cradled Eden against his chest and brushed a kiss across her forehead. "We have a lot to talk about, you and I. For instance, I hope you aren't prone to seasickness, because we'll be sailing to Mexico on one of my ships." His lips thinned briefly. "One thing you must understand, sweet. Your life in Mexico is going to be quite different from your life here. Rightly or wrongly, women in my country aren't allowed the kind of freedom you're accustomed to. You won't be permitted to leave the house unescorted, which means when I'm not with you you will have to be accompanied by a maid." Eden stirred, and glancing down, Neil saw that her lush sable lashes lay fanned across her cheeks.

Neil's expression softened as he watched the sleeping girl beside him. Girl? Woman, Neil told himself, a child-woman, not fully a woman because of her age, yet no longer a child in spite of it. The fire was dying down and Neil drew a dust cover over Eden. Rising, he added wood to the fire, found his shirt and selected a thin cigar from a gold case. His eyes caught sight of the red stain marring the white linen tablecloth on the floor and he winced with guilt. By God, he would not feel guilty! He had been honest with Eden and she had accepted his terms—it wasn't as if he had seduced Eden and *then* offered her the position as his *amante*.

Neil touched a match to the cigar and exhaled slowly, the smoke curling in the air. He seated himself in front of the fireplace and contemplated Eden's delicate profile. Outwardly relaxed, Neil's mind raced as he catalogued the preparations yet to be made. He already had a stateroom reserved aboard ship, so space was no problem. With little time to pack, Eden probably wouldn't be bringing along a great deal. Not that it mattered; Neil would attend to anything she wanted at the same time he found a house for her in Mexico City. Neil considered this briefly. It would be best if the house were furnished, to avoid wasting time buying furniture. He would have to find a tutor for Eden so she could learn the Mexican dialect immediately and she would need a small staff to maintain her residence. Neil studied the glowing cigar tip, frowning as he did so, adding to his mental list. A horse for himself, one for Eden. A matched team and a carriage for the times he wanted Eden with him but was unable to visit the city. She'd have to have a country place as well, someplace close to the *hacienda* yet far enough away so his visits could be carried on discreetly. It was a mixed blessing that Eden still slept, for had she awakened she would have questioned the ruthlessly arrogant light in Neil's golden eyes.

Neil shivered as a cold draft touched him. That damned open window! He flicked the cigar into the fireplace, padded to the window and closed it. The rain was still falling, in torrents now, with lightning arcing through the sky above the tree-lined avenue. Neil stretched, easing the muscles which had knotted uncomfortably between his shoulders. What had Eden said? That she had not only the afternoon but the evening as well? In which case, Neil thought wickedly, there was no hurry to get dressed. Smiling, he left the window to stretch out beside Eden. There was no reason to sleep away the hours that remained of their day.

# Chapter 5

Eden had just poured a second cup of coffee when Hugh entered the dining room, and she smiled brightly at him. "Good morning, Hugh. Coffee?"

"Please." Eden poured a cup while Hugh made a trip to the sideboard.

"Did you enjoy the play last night?" Eden asked when Hugh was seated. "Meg said her parents were looking forward to seeing it."

Hugh chuckled and shook his head. "I liked the play, but I wish Mrs. Lawson would stop playing matchmaker. You should have seen the one she fixed me up with last evening. Janet Lawson is a wonderful woman, but she has absolutely no idea what makes the world go round."

"She's only trying to be helpful," interjected Eden. "And honestly, Hugh, wouldn't you like to marry? I can think of a dozen women who would give their eyeteeth to become Mrs. Hugh Colter."

"Unfortunately the feeling isn't mutual. No, I'm afraid I'm too old, too set in my ways to let a woman come in and upset my life."

"You are not," Eden replied indignantly. "When you find the right woman she won't care two figs about your age. Just think, Hugh, I'll be gone soon and... well, wouldn't you like to have a family?"

"I already do." Hugh smiled and clasped Eden's hand. "I have you."

"I know," Eden's voice was gentle, "and I have you. I'll always be grateful for that. But don't you want children of your own? You'd be so good with them, and when I leave, my rooms would be perfect for a nursery. I can just picture you with a dozen children running around the house."

A sad smile curved Hugh's lips. "A dozen? Don't you think you're rushing things? I haven't even found a wife yet. Besides which, you're a long way from moving out."

Eden lowered her head, a guilty flush staining her cheeks.

How she wished she could tell Hugh about Neil and their plans. It seemed cruel to simply run off with Neil to Mexico tomorrow without letting Hugh know. "Think of it as an elopement," Neil had said on the drive home when she had wondered aloud what to tell her guardian. "Don't tell him anything. If he finds out about us, Eden, he'll try to stop us." The harsh note in Neil's voice had bewildered Eden but she had silently agreed. Hugh would probably insist they wait, to make sure that marriage was what they both wanted, and this was one time Eden didn't want to waste time thinking! Yet, Hugh was all she had in the world; she wanted him to be happy for her, to meet Neil and understand why she was so willing to leave her home and friends behind and follow Neil to a different country. If she didn't tell Hugh about her marriage and—as Neil had suggested—left only a note in explanation, Eden would never be able to forgive herself. She would feel as if she had betrayed the trust Hugh placed in her.

Eden stirred in her chair, distinctly aware of the soreness not even an hour's soaking in the tub had been able to alleviate. Had she and Neil really spent an entire afternoon and evening making love? And had she, Eden Thackery, actually been bold enough to reach for him when she wakened first? Eden sighed. They had and she had and until this moment she had been gloriously happy. Perhaps when she met Neil for lunch today she could convince him to speak to Hugh before they left for Mexico. Surely once Hugh saw how happy she was he would congratulate them and wish them well.

"I've got a surprise for you, dear heart." Hugh forced a cheerful tone to dispel his own dark thoughts. "I've commissioned a portrait of you for the study. It will look nice right above the mantel, don't you think?"

"A portrait?" Eden swallowed hard. "That's very nice, Hugh, but I really don't want a portrait of myself."

"It's not for you, Eden, it's for me; something I'll have long after you're married and gone."

"Hugh . . ." Her throat was tight and Eden had to work to clear it.

"Come, dear heart, you'll do this one thing for your old guardian, won't you?" Hugh teased lightly.

"Yes . . . of course." Eden felt like bursting into tears.

It was a somber, thoughtful Eden who met Neil for lunch

across from his hotel. "We have to talk, Neil," she said urgently as he helped her alight.

"After we've eaten." Neil paid off the cabdriver, and took her arm, steering Eden through the crowd on the sidewalk. "I've got a surprise for you back in my room."

Eden protested. "Neil, please, let's go someplace where we can talk privately. This really can't wait."

Frowning, Neil studied her pinched features. "What's the matter, Eden? There's something wrong, isn't there?" Eden nodded miserably, eyes misting with tears. Neil expelled his breath sharply. "All right, get hold of yourself; we'll go to my room. Come on."

Eden followed him wordlessly across the street and into the lobby of the hotel, too preoccupied to care if anyone saw them.

"Here, sit down," Neil said when they reached his room, guiding her to a chair. "I'd better get you a drink, sweetheart, you're pale as a ghost."

"I'll be fine." She took a swallow from the glass, choked, and gasped for air as the brandy burned its way down her throat. "What—?"

"Sorry, love, but I thought you were going to faint. Finish the brandy. You look like you need it."

Eden drained the glass, relieved that the last of the brandy produced only a cough instead of the initial choking sensation. "I've never fainted in my life and I have no intention of starting now," Eden said, some of her spirit returning.

"Good." Neil took the glass from her hand. "Now tell me what's the matter, love."

"It's my guardian." Eden rose and began to pace, unaware that Neil had stiffened. "Neil, I can't do it; I can't run off without telling him. It wouldn't be fair. Why, he told me today that he's commissioned a portrait of me. He expects me to be here to sit for it. Neil, I have to tell him!"

Neil shook his head and reached for a cigar. "Sweetheart, we agreed yesterday that your letter will do all that. He'll understand, believe me."

"He's my family, the only family I have, and I feel so *guilty* about sneaking off like this."

"My sweet, we've already been over this." In a few lithe steps Neil was behind Eden, his arms circling her waist. "He'd stop you if he knew. Do you want that?"

"No, of course not." Eden leaned back against Neil's chest. "I want to be with you forever. But I still feel guilty."

"Now listen to me." Neil turned her toward him. "There's nothing to feel guilty about. I'm sure your guardian is a nice man and I'm sure he's been good to you, but that doesn't mean you have to spend the rest of your life thanking him. We've got a chance for something good; I'd hate to lose that."

"So would I." Eden smiled slightly. "It's just that everything has happened so fast. I can't really believe it."

"Ah, but you must believe, darling Eden." Neil produced a jeweler's box from his coat pocket. "For you."

Trembling, her hands managed to open the box and Eden gasped. A choker of rubies and diamonds and matching earrings sparkled brilliantly against the velvet, beckoning for her touch. "Neil . . . I don't know what to say. They're beautiful."

"Just a token of my affection, as they say." Neil played with a curl that fell across Eden's cheek. "I thought they'd go well with your hair and coloring—something bold for contrast."

Setting the box aside, Eden opened her reticule and withdrew her own gift. Right up to the last minute she had meant to leave it for Hugh along with the letter but suddenly it seemed important that Neil have something from her. "I'm afraid it's terribly practical . . ." Eden blushed furiously, feeling desperately shy beneath Neil's unwavering gaze.

Neil took the case from the slender hand, part of him resenting the fact that her offering had the power to touch him. He almost regretted making Eden his mistress—she belonged in New York, with a husband and a couple of children. But hell, given time and more experience in the art of lovemaking, Eden would certainly make a captivating, seductive *amante*. Neil opened the lid and held the watch up for inspection.

"The . . . the back opens up as well." Neil opened the case, smiling at the inscription and miniature portrait. "If you don't like it—"

"But I do." Neil pulled Eden into his arms. "It's just that I happen to prefer the original." Neil kissed her deeply, thoroughly, letting Eden feel the desire that had been building since they had last seen each other. "You're not really hungry, are you?" he asked huskily. "Now that you're here it would be a shame to waste the opportunity."

"You mean I can't even try on my gift?" Eden teased.

"Later." Neil led her toward the bedroom. "I intend to hold you to that promise you made last night. The one about wearing your hair loose and flowing whenever I asked. I'm asking, my sweet."

"Umm." Eden's eyes lighted as she watched Neil unbutton his shirt. "If all your requests are this simple, I'm going to enjoy being married to you."

It was as if Eden had slapped him. *"What!"* The look on Neil's face rooted Eden to the floor. *"What did you say?"*

"Wh-when we're married," stammered Eden.

"What are you talking about? We're not going to be married; where did you get that idea?"

Neil's face was hard. He towered over Eden, his arms folded across his chest as she sank dazedly onto a chair. "You—you asked me to marry you, Neil, yesterday, at my father's house." Neil shook his head, and Eden hurried on. "You said we were eloping. Going to Mexico."

"I told you to *think* of it as an elopement. I sure as hell didn't ask you to marry me!" His voice had risen and Neil deliberately lowered it. "You wanted to tell your guardian about us, but I figured if you thought of it that way you'd keep your mouth shut. Christ, Eden, you acted like you knew what was going on."

"What about Mexico?" Eden asked stiffly. "Was that a lie too?"

"I never lied to you! I thought you understood that I wanted you as my mistress, nothing more. I still do."

"Your mistress," Eden echoed numbly, feeling as if the bottom had dropped out of her world.

"You'll have all the advantages of marriage without the drawbacks," Neil continued. "I'll give you anything you want—clothes, jewels, you'll have a house in Mexico City, servants..."

"What more could a woman ask for," Eden laughed bitterly, rising to her feet. "Tell me: Just how long do you think our little arrangement will last? A year, two? And your wife— what happens when she finds out?"

Neil shrugged and lit a cigar. "What can she do, divorce me? She's only my wife, not my keeper, and I'll do what I damn well please. After she gives me a son she can do the same, providing she's discreet about it. Besides, Constanza isn't even a problem yet—I won't be married for another

month. As for lasting, who knows? Until we get tired of each
other."

"Constanza! She's your sis—oh! Add up one more lie for
the *honest* Neil Banning!" Eden's eyes turned flinty. "What
did you do, Neil, come to New York to go mistress hunting?
Wouldn't any of the exalted ladies from Mexico accept your
offer? I guess they were all smart enough to see through you.
What a pity I wasn't that perceptive." Eden's eyes glistened
with tears, but her face was hard.

"I would never consider making such an offer to any of the
women of my position," Neil informed her haughtily. "A
woman of fine breeding would never accept such an arrangement."

"And you think I would!" Eden cried. "You had this all
planned, didn't you? Find a mistress before you get married;
you save a lot of time that way. Well, Mr. Banning, I may
have fallen into your lap like an overripe plum but I have no
intention of becoming your paramour."

"Take it easy, sweetheart, you're blowing this all out of
proportion," Neil said placatingly.

"Blowing—" Eden sputtered. "You bloody bastard! I *loved*
you! I loved you and you used me. I'm not going with you.
I refuse to be used and then thrown aside when you tire of me.
I made one mistake but I'm not stupid enough to make another
one."

Before Neil could move, Eden flung the jewel box at him
and ran from the bedroom. "Eden!" Neil ran after her, catching
her just before she reached the door to the hall. "Be reasonable,
Eden. You have to go with me."

"In a pig's eye!" Eden struggled to free her arm. "Not if
you were the last man on earth!"

"That's exactly what I am, for *you*," Neil ground out.
"Think about it, Eden. What man would marry you now?"

Eden stopped fighting, her gray eyes enormous. "What do
you mean?"

"You're ruined, Eden. You're not a virgin any longer. No
man wants secondhand goods."

"He wouldn't know—"

"The minute he made love to you he would know, the same
way I knew I was the first. You're no longer pure. He won't
like it."

"But that's not fair," Eden exclaimed. "My husband won't be a virgin either!"

Neil arched one eyebrow. "Fair or not, that's the way it is, love. You may trick a man into marrying you, my sweet, but once he finds out the truth your life will be hell. You'd be better off coming with me."

"No!" Eden snatched her arm from his grasp.

Neil's eyes flashed angrily. "Grow up, Eden, this is the real world you're living in. Face it; I'm the only choice you have."

"No!" Eden repeated vehemently. This time Neil didn't try to stop her as she seized the door.

"The ship leaves at ten," Neil called out mockingly. "Just tell the captain you're with me and he'll bring you directly to the cabin."

Fighting back tears, Eden faced Neil one last time. "I hope you fall overboard and drown."

"I'll see you tomorrow." Neil grinned infuriatingly. "Don't be late, sweetheart, I hate delays."

Eden slammed the door behind her.

By the time she got home Eden had worked herself into an explosive state. Even Simmons, who felt fully capable of dealing with anything, eyed her uncertainly as she stalked into the house.

"Is Mr. Colter home?" Eden snapped as she practically threw her reticule onto a table.

"No, Miss Thackery. He planned to go to the office and have dinner at his club. I don't expect him back until late this evening."

"Good! Inform everyone they have the rest of the day off. And tonight, too, for that matter." Eden all but tore her hat off. "What are you waiting for, Simmons?"

"But your dinner, miss," Simmons objected.

"I'll fix my own, Simmons. I'm not totally incapable!"

"Of course not, miss, but—"

"Simmons," Eden gnashed her teeth in frustration. "Do as I ask; I will not tell you again."

Simmons walked away stiffly and Eden fled to her room hoping to be alone. No sooner had Eden closed the door than Millicent appeared.

"Why, Miss Eden, I thought you were going to be out all

day." Millicent was obviously curious and Eden avoided her all-knowing gaze. "Are you all right, miss? You look so pale."

"I'm fine. My plans have changed, that's all!" Eden pressed a hand over her eyes. "Can't I change my plans without everyone in this house wondering why?"

"Of course you can, Miss Eden," Millicent began. "It's just that you said you were going to meet your young man—"

"I know what I said Millicent," Eden snapped.

"Then something has happened!" Millicent took a step forward. "I knew it; I knew that man was going to be trouble. He hurt you, didn't he, miss? He did something bad—"

"Millicent, *shut up!*" Eden began to shake and she hid her hands in the folds of her skirt before continuing in a quieter voice, "Take the rest of the day off and I'll see you tomorrow."

"But, Miss Eden, I've already had a day off this week and I think it would do you a world of good to talk about it."

"I don't want to talk, can't you understand that?" Eden shouted. "What I do want is to be left alone, *all alone*, Millicent! That means I don't want you or any of the other servants here. Will you please leave?"

"You're upset, Miss Eden, and angry. You're not acting like yourself and I think I'd best stay until—"

*"Get out!"* Eden threw open the door. "Get out of this house and don't come back until morning. Spare me your lectures and well-meaning advice and just get out of my sight!"

When Millicent had gone, Eden collapsed on the sofa and began to cry, the tears scalding down her face, the sobs wracking her whole body. She hadn't cried—truly cried—in years, not since she had first been sent away to school, and even that pain was nothing compared to this. She cried not only in pain but in anger as well, anger at Neil for having deceived her, and at herself for having allowed herself to be deceived.

Eden slammed her fist into a pillow. "Damn him," she sobbed brokenly. "Oh, damn him, damn him, *damn him!*" She rose and made her way unsteadily to the vanity, where she studied her reflection with blurred eyes. She looked the same—odd, somehow she had expected Neil's touch would show on her face. There was no change; no brand marked her as a loose woman. Hairpins gave way before her fingers as Eden undid the thick curls, remembering as she did that Neil had liked her hair best this way. Her heart shattered even further, the pieces finally settling into one huge, painful lump in her breast, and Eden swallowed back another sob.

"I'll kill him," Eden told her reflection, her knuckles whitening around the hairbrush. "He actually believed I'd be flattered to be his mistress, his whore! The bastard! I hope his wife castrates him, I hope he rots in hell. I hope . . . I hope . . . oh, damn!" Eden hurled the brush at the mirror, wincing as the smooth glass surface splintered into a bizarre cobweb. "Someday, Neil, I hope a woman does to you what you've done to me."

Blindly Eden turned from the shattered mirror and left her rooms. She was alone again, as she always had ended up when she had been foolish enough to place her trust in someone. But then, she had been alone all of her life and it had been ludicrous to think that would ever change. *Alone.* The word beat at her brain and Eden covered her face with her hands to hold back the scream that was forming deep inside her. Was it true what Neil had said? Would no man want to marry her now? That couldn't be right, Eden assured herself, not all men could be that unfair. But what kind of man would accept her now? And how could she face Hugh and tell him what had happened? She couldn't, that much was obvious. Hugh never would understand. Worse, he might even blame himself. No, this too had to be kept to herself. No one knew, and she would tell no one.

Eden blinked, brushed away the last tears and found herself in Hugh's study. The knot in her chest stubbornly refused to dissolve and Eden wished she just could forget the past few days and all that had happened. It would be so nice not to think about Neil, not to feel the pain just for a little while. . . .

Slowly Eden approached the cellarette and surveyed the selection of crystal decanters. One liquor was the same as another as far as she knew. Eden sorted through the decanters until she found the one Hugh always used for his Irish whiskey—she *knew* that was effective—then replaced the others in neat rows and closed the doors. The stopper came out with a soft chink of glass on glass, and Eden sniffed curiously at the contents, then shrugged. She poured a tumbler half full of the liquid and knocked back half of it as she had seen Hugh do. Instantly her chest exploded and her eyes watered so badly that the room blurred in front of her. Gasping, Eden grabbed the decanter and stumbled to one of the chairs. In a moment her hands no longer felt like blocks of ice, but her body still felt tight and rigid, like a mainspring that had been wound too hard. Eden swallowed the last of the tumbler's contents, nodding when a slight warmth crept into her veins. If her calculations were correct, two more glasses were all she needed to reach a state of oblivion. Resolutely Eden reached for the decanter.

Hugh returned well past midnight—much later than he had planned, but then that was one of the minor irritations of visiting one of the most respectable parlors in New York, despite the fact that the girls there were well worth it. His surprise at finding the house dark quickly gave way to annoyance when he had to fumble with the lock on the front door.

"Simmons! Where the hell—ouch! Damn," Hugh swore angrily as a table corner rammed into his thigh. "Simmons, if this hall isn't lit in one minute—"

"No use, Hugh."

Hugh peered into the blackness, his skin prickling at the caroling return. The voice was Eden's but . . . "Eden? Dear heart, is that you?"

"No one else." A giggle followed, which worried Hugh even further; he had never known Eden to giggle. "I'm in the study."

Cursing, Hugh groped his way through the hall and into the study. "Eden, for God's sake why haven't you lit a lamp? It's like a tomb in this place." A match flared and he lit the lamp on his desk.

"It was nicer in the dark," Eden grumbled.

Hugh turned around and nearly lost his grip on the lamp. Eden lay on the sofa, an empty glass balanced on her flat stomach, her hair falling into a cloud around her face and shoulders. A half-empty decanter sat on the floor beside her. Hugh walked over and picked it up, studying Eden as he did so. "As I remember, this was full this morning."

"You're absolutely right." Eden frowned, blinking at her odd speech, then shrugged. "I had Shimmons—Simmons fill all the decanters. Efficient little Eden. Eden the efficient." She giggled and held out the glass. "More, please."

Hugh fought back the smile that threatened to destroy the lecture he knew he should give his ward, and he put on his severest expression. "I think you've had your share for this evening, Eden. You're going to hate yourself in the morning—Irish whiskey has a way of doing that to a person."

"I don't care," Eden said mutinously. "When I wake up I'll take a headache powder and eat some toast and I'll be fine."

"Don't count on it," Hugh stated dryly.

Eden wrinkled her nose and held out her glass once more. With a sigh Hugh splashed in an inch of whiskey. If Eden was determined to find out what it was like to be drunk, she might as well do it under his care. Eden swallowed all the liquid and smiled fuzzily. "Thank you, Hugh. You're a grood grardian."

Hugh burst out laughing and dropped into a chair. "You won't say that tomorrow, darlin'; in fact, you will probably bite my head off, but I'll accept it for the present. Now, would you mind telling me where the servants are and why you are home alone drinking yourself blind?"

"One question at a time, please." Eden lurched to her feet and, while Hugh held his breath, weavingly began to light more lamps as she answered. "I gave the servants the night off. You don't mind, do you? After all, you were out and it seemed rather silly to have them stay when I wouldn't need them." The room began to spin and Eden leaned heavily on the desk until all the furniture fell back to its proper place.

"Are you all right, Eden?" Hugh's voice seemed to have to travel a long distance, and it occurred briefly to Eden that he sounded amused.

"Fine." The walls settled back on the foundation and Eden sighed gratefully.

"I'm glad. Now would you kindly answer my second question?"

Eden nodded, promptly deciding, when her head started buzzing, not to repeat such a drastic movement. "I wanted to be by myself, to think, to sort things out. . . ." Eden's eyes misted, her playful mood evaporating. "What's wrong with me, Hugh?"

"Aside from the fact that you're tipsy, not a thing."

"Yes, there is," Eden murmured. "Hugh, I'm not ugly, am I? I mean, wouldn't you say I'm fairly attractive?"

"Of course you are." Hugh studied her curiously. "Whatever brought this on?"

"I . . ." her voice cracked. "I've been seeing this man and I . . . I really liked him, Hugh. I fell in love with him and I thought . . . I thought . . ."

"Oh, Eden." The laughter left Hugh's eyes. "Darlin'—"

"I thought he felt the same way," Eden continued as if Hugh

hadn't spoken, her chin trembling. "I made a dreadful mistake; I never should have trusted him. I should have known better. With the shining example my father set for me, I should have remembered I can never trust anyone but myself."

Hugh gathered Eden to him, cushioning her head against his broad chest. Torn between his own selfish relief that Eden was still his own, yet angered that she had been hurt, Hugh could only pat her back consolingly. "Let it out, dear heart; I know it hurts, so go ahead and cry. I don't mind."

"No. I won't waste any more tears on the dirty bastard." Eden's voice was muffled against Hugh's jacket. "I hope he burns in hell."

"I'm sorry, Eden, I'm so sorry," Hugh commiserated. "You probably won't believe this, but in a little while you'll forget all about him. You'll find someone to love and he'll love you in return. Darlin', love doesn't have to be painful. It can be beautiful, sweet and warm."

"Not for me," Eden whispered. Her legs buckled and she felt herself lifted in Hugh's arms. "Not for me, never for me."

"For you too," Hugh said as he carried Eden to her bedroom. "Now, can you get ready for bed on your own?"

"If you do my buttons for me," Eden mumbled tiredly, all the liquor she had consumed catching up with her.

Hugh froze, his face reddening in the dark. "I think I'd better ring for Millicent."

"She's gone. Hugh, I don't feel very good."

Eden leaned weakly against him and Hugh sighed. "I was afraid of that. All right, turn around." Hugh fumbled with the buttons, his normally deft fingers turning clumsy when they accidentally brushed against a soft, exposed shoulder. The brief contact jarred along his spine and he was unnerved even further when Eden—now covered only by her chemise—fell back into his arms. "Oh, Lord—do you feel sick?"

Eden pressed a hand over her mouth and nodded.

"It's the best thing for you," Hugh told her. "Eden, I'm beginning to think you lost the sense God gave you. I thought you'd know better than to drink on an empty stomach." But he grabbed a pitcher and held her forehead while her stomach emptied itself and afterward he sponged her face and put her to bed.

"Don't go, Hugh." Eden's voice stopped Hugh at the door. "Please—stay with me."

Hugh retraced his steps and settled on the edge of the bed. "What is it, dear heart?"

"I'm afraid." Eden grasped his hand and brought it to her cheek. "You're all I have, Hugh, I don't want to lose you as well."

"That's the whiskey talking, so I'll pretend you didn't say that. Besides, there is nothing in the world that could ever come between you and me." Hugh squeezed her hand and smiled. "The man was an absolute fool not to snap you up and carry you off. But his bad judgment is my good fortune; I wasn't ready for you to leave just yet."

"You're shtuck—stuck with me now," Eden said sleepily. "I thought if I got drunk it wouldn't hurt so badly. I'm sorry, Hugh, I must be embarrassing you but I want you to understand why I did it."

"I understand, darlin', and I'm glad you trust me enough to tell me about it. Now close your eyes and get some sleep. I promise that tomorrow life won't look so dark and gloomy." Hugh looked down and saw that Eden was fast asleep, her breath falling gently on his hand. Carefully he brushed a strand of hair away from her face and lightly he pressed a kiss on her lips. "I'm sorry you were hurt, dear heart, but maybe once you've forgotten this lad you'll notice me." Hugh shook his head at his wishful thinking. He'd have to be content with a kiss stolen while Eden was asleep. Savoring the soft texture of her lips, Hugh kissed her again, storing the feeling in his memory to be recalled on some future, sleepless night. "Sleep well, my love."

Something penetrated the dense curtain surrounding her brain and Eden stirred reluctantly, wanting only to fall back into the blank, empty sleep from which she was being pulled. It penetrated again—the aroma of freshly brewed coffee. Eden rolled onto her back.

"Good morning, Miss Eden." Millicent primly set the bed tray across Eden's lap. "Shall I arrange your pillows, miss?"

"Yes, please." Eden sat up quickly and gasped as a bolt of pain sliced through her head. "Oh, Lord! Millicent, get one of those headache packets for me."

Millicent's lips pressed together in an I-told-you-so expression but she said nothing as she produced one of the packets from her apron pocket and added it to a cup of hot coffee. "Will there be anything else, miss?"

Despite the scalding temperature Eden drained the cup immediately and poured herself a second cup. "No, Millicent. When I'm finished you may help me dress—I'll ring when I need you."

"Very good, miss."

Eden sighed at Millicent's formal manner. "Is anything wrong, Millicent?"

"Not at all, miss." Millicent paused at the door and she looked pointedly at the chemise Eden was wearing. "Mr. Colter said you spent a bad night." Millicent's tone softened. "Is it anything I could help you with? You know I'll do anything for you."

"That's kind of you, Millicent," Eden smiled slightly. "But no, there is nothing you can do, except perhaps smile."

Millicent complied and moved back toward the bed. "It's that young man, isn't it? Oh, Miss Eden, I was afraid he was bad for you. Giving you the bum's rush, he was, and that kind always means trouble."

Eden sipped at her coffee, her eyes turning frosty gray as she studied her maid. "I don't care to discuss it, Millicent. The subject is closed."

"But, Miss Eden, if he did what I think he did, all you have to do is tell Mr. Colter and he'll put things right." Eden's look frightened Millicent but she doggedly continued. "It's only fair that he do right by you, and Mr. Colter will see that he does, you can be sure of that."

A look of understanding passed between the two women and Eden relaxed against the pillows. "I'm sure he would, Millicent, but I won't humiliate Mr. Colter that way. After all he's done for me it would be cruel of me to tell him what has happened. Mr. Colter would blame himself for my mistake, he would feel that he had failed in his duties. Would you have me subject him to that guilt, Millicent? How fair would that be?" Eventually Millicent shook her head and Eden breathed a sigh of relief. "You understand that our conversation must remain confidential. Not even your mother must know, as much as I trust her. You must tell no one."

"Of course not, miss," Millicent promised. But later, when she was helping Eden dress, a horrifying thought suddenly occurred to her. If Miss Eden turned up pregnant a month from now, there'd be no hiding her carelessness then!

Eden checked her appearance in the mirror and smiled grimly. Two dark smudges stood out beneath her eyes, and her face looked whiter than usual, due no doubt to the splitting headache, which was finally beginning to subside. Eden toyed with a small jar of rouge for several minutes before replacing it on the vanity. Hugh knew what to expect, and since she wouldn't be seeing anyone else today . . . Neil's smiling face materialized before Eden could stop her thoughts, hitting her almost like a physical blow. Trembling, Eden sank onto a chair and covered her face with her hands. This won't do, she told herself sternly. It's over. Forget Neil Banning but always remember the lesson he taught you. Don't allow him to ruin your life. Don't allow yourself to remember him at all—that is precisely what he would want you to do. Eden drew a shaky breath, collected her ledgers and started downstairs.

The door to Hugh's study was ajar, and Eden walked in without bothering to knock. "I have my books, Hugh. Are you ready—oh, excuse me." Hugh rose, as did the two men with him, Carl Gregory and his son, Tim. All three men wore grim expressions and Hugh looked as if he might explode at any moment. "I'm sorry, Hugh, I didn't realize you had company. Gentlemen . . ."

"Stay, Eden." Hugh gestured heavily to one of the chairs. "This concerns you, so you may as well hear what these two, ah, gentlemen have to say."

Eden went ice cold at the odd tone in Hugh's voice, and instead of sitting down she found herself standing rigidly beside Hugh. "I'll stand if you don't mind. But please, Hugh, Mr. Gregory, Tim, do be seated."

"I don't like this, Colter. Why does she have to be here? I say we come to a decision and then tell her what she has to do." Carl Gregory fixed Eden with a beady, self-satisfied stare. "Unless she can come up with a good explanation—such as a twin sister—" he laughed unpleasantly, "you may consider Tim's proposal withdrawn."

Confused, Eden looked first to Hugh, then to Tim for an explanation. "Would one of you please tell me what you are talking about?"

"Don't pull that innocent act, missy." Carl wagged a finger

in her direction. "We're onto you now. You're nothing more than a common streetwalker!"

"Wait just one minute, Gregory," Hugh snarled as he rose from his chair. "This is my home and as long as your presence here is tolerated you'll watch your mouth."

"Hugh, please," Eden placed a hand on his arm, her face deathly pale. "I don't understand, Mr. Gregory. If you will simply tell me—"

"You were seen, missy. The day before yesterday, you were seen by my son and Jane at your father's mansion with a man. Do you understand that?"

Hugh's arm circled her waist protectively but Eden barely felt it. She felt as if she had been turned to stone, unable to move or speak or breathe. They had seen her! But how . . . ? The window! She and Neil had stood at the window watching the rain and talking. And then Neil had kissed her. . . . Oh, my God, Eden thought wildly. Oh, my God, what am I going to do?

"You little slut," Tim's father sneered. "You thought you could slip between some man's sheets and then marry Tim. Well, I won't have it, do you hear? No whore is going to ruin our good name."

Hugh launched himself at Carl, tipping over his chair, and bringing both men to the floor in a jumble of arms and legs. Hugh sat on Carl's chest and delivered two punishing blows to the other man's face before the spell surrounding Eden and Tim was broken and they both sprang forward to separate the two men.

"Hugh, stop it, you'll kill him!" Eden pulled frantically at Hugh's arms. "You're only making things worse!"

"Let me go," Hugh panted as Eden and Tim finally succeeded in pulling him off Carl. "I'll fix it so he never says another word. Let me go, I say!"

"No!" Eden threw her arms around Hugh's neck. "Don't, Hugh, please. This won't do any good."

"It'll do me plenty of good!" Hugh said harshly, his hands clenched into fists.

"Come on, you Irish lout." Carl had regained his footing and he belligerently advanced toward Hugh. "I'm ready for you this time."

"Father, Mr. Colter," Tim pleaded. "You're both behaving like children."

"Stay out of this, boy." Carl Gregory drew a hand across his bleeding nose. "If you'd been man enough to hold onto your woman this wouldn't have been necessary."

"Hugh," Eden whispered, her eyes wide and terrified. "Don't fight him. It doesn't matter."

All the anger went out of him as Hugh stared down at Eden's drawn face. Slowly he pulled Eden's arms from his neck and pushed her aside. "I won't fight you again, Gregory, but I demand your apology to Eden." Hugh straightened his jacket.

"After what she's done," Carl sputtered, "I most certainly will not apologize."

"What she did was done out of love," Hugh replied. He felt Eden's eyes upon him and he spared her a brief, sad smile. "It was inevitable that we would be found out, darlin'."

"Hugh—"

Hugh silenced Eden quickly before her confusion could become apparent to Carl and Tim. "It's all right, Eden, we might as well tell them." He turned back to Carl. "The announcement will be in all the papers in a few days—Eden and I plan to be married in two months. I was the man in the mansion. I'm sure you can forget our little indiscretion." A sharp look at Tim effectively prevented any objection from him.

Carl smiled an oily smile that made Eden's stomach churn. "Well, well, congratulations. No wonder Tim here couldn't get a straight answer. We should have figured it out ourselves."

Eden didn't hear anything else that was said as Hugh ushered the two men to the front door. Completely numb, she sank into a chair and stared at the ledgers which still lay on Hugh's desk. What had happened in these few, short minutes?

"Tell me."

Eden jumped at the sound of Hugh's voice and found him staring down at her, his face set in a grim mask. "Wh-what?" She forced the word from between frozen lips.

"Did you go to the house with a man?" Hugh's blue eyes were unrelenting.

"Yes." She couldn't lie to Hugh; no matter what he would think of her, she couldn't lie to him.

"I see." Hugh turned away. "What they said is true, then."

"I thought—" Eden started to explain but Hugh savagely cut her off.

"No, Eden, you didn't think! That is the problem!" Hugh

rounded on her, a fierce gleam in his eyes. "Who is the man? Will he marry you?"

"I . . ." A clock chimed ten o'clock and she imagined she could hear a ship whistle its departure. Eden lowered her eyes. "No, he won't. He's engaged. He said he wanted to make me his mistress. I didn't know that when . . . when . . ."

"When you so willingly blessed him with your virginity," Hugh finished for her, his brogue thickening with each word. "Damn it, Eden, how could you do this? Didn't you have any idea that you would be ruining your life?"

"I thought he loved me," Eden whispered. "I thought he meant to marry me. Hugh, please try to understand—"

"Understand!" Hugh roared. "Understand what? That you climbed into bed with a man, that you dirtied your name and mine? And as for *love*, you can't begin to know what the word means! You don't think that Carl Gregory actually believed my story, do you?" Hugh poured himself a stiff drink and downed it in one swallow. "And if he does believe it, do you have any idea how it makes me look?"

"I'm sorry, Hugh."

"Sorry! That doesn't help a hell of a lot right now!"

"I know. But what do you want me to say? What would you have me do?" Tears streamed down Eden's cheeks, unnoticed by either of them.

"You've done quite enough, I think," Hugh told her unforgivingly. "Right now you better start thinking about your wedding gown and who is going to stand up for you."

"Hugh, you don't have to marry me."

"Oh, don't I," Hugh said cruelly. "If I don't, who will? You can be sure that if you stay single you'll have all kinds of offers from men, but not one of them will want to marry you! Or maybe you'd prefer to ply your trade in one of the expensive houses. God knows you'll bring a high price for your time!"

Hugh slammed out of the study, leaving Eden completely alone and utterly miserable. Neil had been right. Hugh's words kept repeating inside her head. I'm ruined, soiled; no man wants me now, not as a wife.

She wasn't certain how long she sat in Hugh's study. Eden remembered telling Simmons that she didn't want any lunch, and a long while later the butler came in to light the lamps and inform her that dinner would be ready in an hour. Eden heard the front door open and close and Hugh's voice in the hallway, but somehow she couldn't bring herself to go out to meet him.

"Miss Thackery." Simmons stood just inside the doorway. "Mr. Colter would like to see you in the parlor, miss."

"Thank you, Simmons." Eden rose and brushed the wrinkles out of her skirt. The parlor was the one room that Hugh rarely used, and she swallowed nervously. Whatever Hugh was going to say to her wasn't going to be pleasant.

Hugh was gazing out the window when Eden's knock sounded on the parlor doors. Mentally he braced himself. The blind rage of this morning had not subsided in the least, though he had been able to control it long enough to do what had to be done. But facing Eden again, knowing that she had betrayed him, had slept with another man . . . His control threatened to evaporate, and Hugh forced himself to concentrate only on what he had to tell Eden.

"You wanted to see me," Eden said unnecessarily, her heart pounding at the cold look on Hugh's face.

"Obviously." Hugh turned away from her, afraid that if he had to look at Eden for another minute he'd slap her. "Sit down if you like."

"No, thank you," Eden replied just as formally. The old Hugh was gone and this grim stranger who wanted to punish her had taken his place. He terrified her.

"I'm moving out tonight," Hugh said abruptly. "If for some reason you have to get in touch with me you can reach me at my club or my office."

"Do you have to?" Eden asked sadly, quietly. "I don't like being alone—"

"Be quiet!" Hugh bellowed. "Since we're going to be married I can hardly live in the same house with you, can I?"

"No, I suppose not." Eden bowed her head. "I hadn't thought of that."

"That figures!" snorted Hugh derisively. "I'll come around for you after lunch tomorrow and we'll pay a visit to that jeweler you're so fond of—what's his name?"

"Marcel."

"Right, Marcel. He does have wedding bands, doesn't he?" Eden nodded, choosing not to answer Hugh's sarcastic remark. "Good; we'll get that out of the way tomorrow then. I've already given the story of our engagement and forthcoming marriage to the papers. Since they all plan to run it within the next two days, if there's anyone you want to tell personally you'd better do it tomorrow morning. By the way, I told the papers we've been secretly engaged since you turned sixteen, so you should mention that."

"You've made it sound very...romantic," Eden commented, a hint of bitterness tingeing her voice.

"It does make our sudden marriage appear more plausible," Hugh returned sourly. "But people are still going to wonder why we're in such a hurry. Come in!" Hugh shouted when someone knocked at the door.

"Your bags are ready, sir." Simmons looked questioningly at Hugh.

"Put them in the carriage." The door closed and for the first time Hugh looked directly into Eden's eyes. "I assume you can run the household by yourself—or do you want me to bring Katrin here for the next few weeks?"

Stung deeply, Eden's cheeks colored. "That won't be necessary. I can manage quite well."

"I'm glad to hear it. At least there's one thing you're good at." Hugh brushed past her into the hallway and Eden followed.

"Will you at least stay for dinner?" Eden asked softly, hating the cowardly way her bottom lip trembled.

"No. The faster I get out of here the better I'll feel. Do you have any questions?"

"No." Hugh turned to leave and desperately Eden threw herself into his arms. "Oh, Hugh, I'm sorry. Please believe me, I never thought this would happen." She was crying openly now. "Hugh, I would do anything in the world to make it up to you."

Hugh's fingers closed painfully around Eden's jaw as he forced her face upward to meet his bruising, brutal kiss. There was no love in his kiss, no warmth; the kiss wasn't given or shared, it was inflicted by Hugh upon Eden, and when it ended she was sobbing brokenly. "I'm going to marry you, *dear heart*. I'll make you my wife; I'll give you my name to silence the scandal you've created." Hugh's eyes blazed like star sapphires. "Take my word for it, Eden, I'll make sure I'm paid back, with interest!"

When he was gone Eden fled to her room and locked the door. Not even Millicent was allowed into the room, although she knocked repeatedly and begged Eden to open the door. In her bedroom Eden cried until her eyes were red and swollen

and her head throbbed every time she breathed. It was over,
her life was finished, and all because she had been too willing
to give her heart and body to a man she thought she loved. But
the thought of Neil no longer had the power to hurt her; it was
Hugh—Hugh, the one person in the world in whom she had
had faith—it was his betrayal that caused the excruciating ache
which consumed her. Finally, a few short hours before dawn,
Eden cried herself into an exhausted sleep.

As fate would have it, Meg called early the next morning
and found Eden in her sitting room, a cold compress covering
her eyes.

"Eden, I have the juiciest bit of news that you'll just adore
hearing!" Meg's face was alight with excitement, her curls
bobbing madly as she settled onto the sofa.

Eden removed the compress and turned away to avoid Meg's
gaze. "I have some news of my own, Meg," she said in a thick
voice.

Meg's eyes widened. "Why, Eden, you've been crying!
What is it? What's wrong?"

"Nothing." Eden forced a smile as she began her charade.
"And I haven't been crying: I'm just coming down with a cold."

"Oh, dear, I hope not. Mama says a spring cold is worse
than any other. Have you tried tea and honey? Your throat
sounds awfully sore."

Eden's nerves frayed under the weight of Meg's chatter.
Today of all days Eden didn't need her friend's advice or inane
gossip. "Please, Meg. Do you want to hear my news or not?"

Meg stopped in midsentence. "Of course I do, but you must
hear mine first. It's so wonderfully awful that I just know you'll
forget all about your cold."

"Oh, go ahead then," Eden sighed and replaced the compress. "Out with it."

"Well," Meg leaned forward, "Jane Gregory has run away!"

"Who cares?" Eden said disinterestedly.

Meg looked nonplussed. "But, Eden, she's gone! Of course
her family isn't admitting anything, but Tim told Kevin that
she left a note behind saying she was going away with a man.
Anyway, she left yesterday morning and by the time her parents
found out, it was too late for them to do anything."

Something clicked in Eden's mind and she snatched the

compress from her eyes. "Did Tim say who the man is? I mean, it isn't Dan, is it?"

"Heavens no!" Meg exclaimed. "Jane's father is going to tell Dan today and Tim said that he's absolutely frantic. You can imagine why—the entire Gregory household was set on having Dan as a member of the family."

"I'm aware of that, Meg." Eden felt like screaming her frustration. "Will you please, please tell me who Jane ran off with?"

"I saved the best for last," Meg giggled. "It's that man we met the night of the ball. Remember him? Tall, dark, with those funny eyes...he was from Mexico, wasn't he? Neil something-or-other."

"Banning," Eden supplied the name dazedly but Meg was too excited to hear.

"Anyway, the whole thing is going to come out in a few days and the Gregorys are going to tell everyone that Jane is married to this Neil what's-his-name. She's completely ruined, naturally. I don't think she'll dare come back, even if everyone does believe that she really is married." Meg's expression altered. "You realize that you mustn't breathe a word of this to anyone. Kevin told me this in confidence but I know he won't mind that I told you—after all, the way Tim's been carrying on over you you'll probably be changing your name to Gregory before too long."

Eden pulled herself out of the trance into which she had fallen and fixed a falsely bright smile on her lips. "That's what I wanted to tell you myself." Eden drew a deep breath. "Meg, I'm going to be married."

"Married! Oh, Eden, how wonderful!" Meg impulsively hugged her friend. "I'm so happy for you—Tim didn't say a word when he talked to Kevin last night."

"That's because"— Eden swallowed, despising the fact that she had to lie to her only friend—"I'm not marrying Tim. I'm marrying Hugh."

The sentence fell into dead silence, and Eden forced herself to meet Meg's stare. "You might congratulate me, Meg. I'd like you to be my maid of honor."

Meg's mouth worked furiously, soundlessly, for at least a minute before she found her voice. "You can't be serious, Eden! You're teasing me, aren't you?"

"No, Meg, I'm not. Hugh and I will be married in two months."

"But, Eden, he's old enough to be your father! You've never even hinted that you felt something for Hugh, and now you're going to *marry* him? Your engagement hasn't been announced—"

"Neither Hugh nor I wanted a huge engagement party," Eden broke in quickly to forestall Meg's questions. "We knew what people would say if they found out about us and we wanted to avoid that kind of gossip. Actually Hugh . . . proposed the night of my sixteenth birthday party, so you see this isn't at all sudden."

"You do love him, then," Meg stated with relief. "And Hugh must love you."

"Yes, of course he does," Eden said quietly, although inwardly she shrank from the memory of Hugh's violent kiss.

"In that case, congratulations." Meg's eyes sparkled. "It sounds so romantic, Eden. You know, two lovers who have to hide their feelings from the rest of the world until the last minute. What was it like when Hugh proposed? Did he go down on one knee and pledge his undying passion?"

Eden felt the tears well in her eyes. That was how it should have been, a tender proposal of love and trust instead of recrimination and anger. She should be happy about marrying, not miserable and afraid of the man who would be her husband. But then, she should also be in love, and her life was devoid of that emotion.

". . . will happen to me one day," Meg said with a sigh. "As soon as Kevin gets his degree, but that's a whole year away. You must stand up for me then, since I'm going to be in your wedding. Oh, Eden, this is so exciting! You don't mind if I tell my parents, do you? And Kevin? And a few friends? I'm sorry, I know it's your news but if I have to keep it all to myself I'll positively burst!"

Eden laughed, although it came out sounding more like a sob. "I don't mind, Meg, and you may tell as many people as you like." Eden accompanied Meg downstairs to the front door. "Let's plan on picking out the material for our gowns in a few days, all right?"

"That will be fine. I'll ask Mama to come along, too; she always enjoys seeing you—if you don't mind, that is."

"You know I don't," Eden smiled but her face rapidly sobered when Hugh's carriage pulled up to the door and Hugh stepped out.

"Oh, Mr. Colter, Eden just told me about you two. Congratulations!" Meg's eyes widened and she giggled. "I can't very well call Eden 'Mrs. Colter' after you're married, so may I call you Hugh?"

"Thank you, Margaret." Hugh's easy manner was firmly in place and he gallantly kissed both her hands. "I would be honored. May I assist you into your carriage?"

They waved politely until Meg was out of sight, but once the door closed, isolating them from the rest of the world, Hugh dropped the facade.

"You look terrible," Hugh told her bitingly. "What did you do, my love, clean out my liquor cabinet again?"

"No." Eden flushed. "I didn't sleep very well last night, that's all."

"What a pity. Was your conscience bothering you?"

Eden flushed. "Not in the least," she replied hotly. "Was yours?"

"Why should it? I didn't do anything to you that hasn't been done God knows how many times before," Hugh jeered.

"That's not true!" Eden cried. "Hugh, you know it isn't true. I may not be a virgin any longer but I'm no whore either! You know that, Hugh, you know me."

"No, I don't!" Hugh shouted, his temper flaring. "I thought I knew you, but after yesterday I'm not sure of anything. For all I know you've been putting out to Tim and all his friends."

"So what if I had," Eden retorted angrily. "You can bet your bottom dollar Tim isn't exactly inexperienced, and neither are you, for that matter! Why is it that you can prowl from bed to bed and nobody condemns you for it?"

"That's different," Hugh said pointedly.

"Why? Because you're a man? Because with you there's no physical proof that you're not a virgin? Hugh, don't do this to me," Eden pleaded. "Don't crucify me because I made one mistake."

"I'm not crucifying you. I'm saving you." Hugh fought back the urge to shake Eden, and when she started to argue Hugh raised his hand to silence her. "That's enough, Eden. I don't want to talk about it any further."

"But we have to, Hugh. Don't you see? I understand why we have to get married and I know you're protecting me, but what kind of a marriage will we have if you can't stand to talk to me or look at me?" Eden caught Hugh's arm when he tried to walk away. "If you can't forgive me for what I've done, how will you ever be able to live with me?"

Hugh shook off Eden's hand. "I'll have what your lover had, and used or not, you're still a very attractive woman. You'll be here, wherever and however I want you. And I do want you, lovely Eden." Hugh's knuckles caressed her jaw. "Get your fill of sleeping alone because after we're married you won't have that chance again. You're mine, and when everything is nice and legal I'm going to remind you of that fact every night. Now get your things. We're going to the jeweler."

# Chapter 6

Neil Banning reined in his horse near the crest of the hill and relaxed in the saddle, a huge grin on his face as he studied the hacienda which loomed high above him. Home, Neil breathed deeply, savoring the clean, sweet scent that belonged only to this place. His bags had been sent ahead two weeks before when he had landed at Tampico, so Sebastian was probably expecting him at any time. For a moment the sun glinting off the red roof tiles reminded Neil of the ruby and diamond choker and earrings he had given Jane before leaving her at the hotel, and he passed a hand wearily across his eyes. What a scene that had been; the damages to the room alone had cost more than Jane had been worth for the weeks of the voyage and the few days beyond. Odd how Jane hadn't taken to the idea of being his mistress. She had certainly seemed eager enough when he'd found her in his cabin aboard ship. Neil shrugged and galloped the rest of the way to the hacienda. The courtyard was deserted when he arrived but as Neil dismounted the front door was thrown open and a slender, fine-featured young man hurried down the steps, a slight limp impairing his speed. Neil tossed the reins to a stablehand and, hands resting on his hips, waited for the younger man to reach him.

"It's about time, Neil, your room has been ready for a week!" At Neil's careless shrug Sebastian Saros laughed and hugged his brother affectionately. "It's good to see you. You've been gone a long time."

"Too long," Neil grinned as he met the golden gaze identical to his own. "I was afraid the place would be in ruins by the time I got back."

Sebastian looked affronted. "A Saros not take care of the family land? Neil, you know better than that. But enough— your note said you'd arrived with a guest. Where is he?"

"She," Neil corrected as they walked into the hacienda. "As far as I know she's still breaking all the furniture in Tampico. When she's finished with that, I guess she'll return home."

*"Dios mío!* Not another one!" Sebastian groaned. "You were
127

careful weren't you? No irate brothers or fathers are going to come knocking at our door in the middle of the night, are they?"

"Not unless they want to come all the way from New York. No, Sebastian, I'm sure dear little Jane will find some way to explain her disappearance. Here." They were in his bedroom now and Neil tossed Sebastian one of his bags. "Unpack this for me."

"Tell me, how was London?" Sebastian asked as he started putting clothes in a drawer. "Did you find him?"

"Finding him was no problem, but getting in to see him was another matter entirely." Neil's face turned grim. "I couldn't very well walk up to him on the street and say: 'Excuse me, but I'm the son you deserted almost thirty years ago.'"

Sebastian studied his hands intently, all too aware of the bitter resentment that constantly threatened to break through Neil's casual veneer. Finally Sebastian said, "We've argued that point so often that there's no sense in debating it all over again."

"You're right." Neil rubbed a hand across the back of his neck. "I managed an invitation to his home through a mutual friend shortly before I left England. I met him."

"And?"

Neil shrugged. "My father is older now, and somewhere along the line he gained a sense of responsibility. He asked me if I needed anything," Neil sneered. "I told him he was a couple of decades too late."

Sebastian shook his head. "Will you never change, Neil? You went over there to make peace with yourself and your father."

"It's no less than he deserved," Neil replied, a malicious glint in his eyes. "He owed me."

"So you alienated him? A brilliant strategy; I never would have thought of it." Sebastian slowly expelled his breath, abandoning the pointless argument. Instead he pulled a gold watch from Neil's bag and twirled it around his finger. "What's this?"

Neil's brows drew together as he studied the bright piece of jewelry. "A watch. What does it look like, Sebastian?"

A teasing grin played around Sebastian's mouth as he opened the watch. "Beautiful workmanship—and expensive, judging by these emeralds. Let's see if the back . . . ah, there it is." Sebastian gave a low whistle of appreciation. "This is what you left in a hotel room? You're out of your mind!"

"She's not the one," Neil snapped, grabbing for the watch, but Sebastian quickly pulled it out of his reach.

"No? My mistake." Sebastian ignored Neil's darkening features and assumed a grave, appraising expression. "Eden . . . a beautiful name for a beautiful woman. Blue eyes, I suppose."

"Gray," Neil corrected swiftly, a picture of Eden appearing in front of him. "Soft, like a mist that rolls in and traps you for hours."

"Oh?" Sebastian cocked an eyebrow at his brother but Neil didn't notice. "English or American?"

"American," Neil answered absently. "But she's not cold like the rest of them. She tries to be—she tries like the devil, but she's soft and warm."

"She sounds perfect. Why didn't you marry her?"

Neil angrily shook off his thoughts. "You're the one who's crazy. Marry an American!" Neil snatched the watch away from Sebastian and scowled at the miniature portrait. "She actually became angry when I offered to make her my mistress. Can you believe it?"

"No!" Sebastian feigned a horrified look. "Imagine that. I simply can't understand why she would turn you down. I assume you relieved her of her virginity and then handed her a nice little bauble before blithely proposing she come to Mexico as your mistress. What kind of a woman would turn her back on that kind of a life? All she'd have to worry about is keeping her self-respect. You must have lost your touch, Neil, if you couldn't convince her that sitting alone in the *casita* waiting for you to honor her with your presence would be infinitely preferable to living out a respectable life with a husband and family."

"Spare me the lecture, Sebastian, I know it by heart." Neil dropped the watch onto the bureau. "Besides, Eden got her revenge. I spent a lousy voyage with Jane as my cabin mate. God, but the woman is a bitch!"

Sebastian threw up his hands. "You're hopeless. Go ahead, have your Janes. But I'm through placating all the outraged male relatives and I refuse to sew you back together if you get shot or knifed."

"A small price to pay if I'm spared your sarcasm," Neil said, grinning. "Listen, I'm going to take a quick bath and then ride over to see Constanza. I brought her a few things that her avaricious side should appreciate."

Sebastian's expression changed rapidly. "I don't think that's such a good idea, Neil."

"Why not? Her family expects the eager bridegroom to rush into her waiting arms, and I'd hate to disappoint them." Neil glanced up. "I know you're not fond of Constanza—hell, neither am I—but it's all arranged and there's nothing I can do about it. Constanza and I will be married in a few weeks, so both you and I had better get used to the situation."

Sebastian looked at Neil calmly. "Constanza isn't there. She got married three months ago."

Neil was stunned. "She *what?*"

"I wanted you to get settled before I told you," Sebastian explained. "Señor Martinez came to me after it happened. You know that he breeds and sells cattle—don't interrupt," he ordered sternly when Neil started to speak. "Do me the courtesy of letting me tell this in my own way. Several months ago a man named Lathrop Williams showed up and said he was interested in buying some of Martinez's cattle. The old man was pleased, of course, and he invited this Williams to stay with them. After a week's stay Williams purchased half the herd and that night he told Constanza's father that he would let all of his friends know where he found such good stock. Martinez went to bed ecstatic—you know how desperate their finances were—and he thought this meant a change for the better. When he woke up the next morning Williams was gone and so was Constanza. A few days later they got a letter from her saying that she married Williams and that they're living in Texas. The contract's been broken, Neil. You're free to carry on as you always have."

"Damn it!" A porcelain vase smashed against the wall and Sebastian ducked to avoid the flying pieces. "That little bitch, I'll kill her! And that bastard Williams, too, when I find him. Who does he think he is?"

"Calm down, Neil," Sebastian said quietly. "You're not going to do anything because there is nothing to be done. I returned what passed as Constanza's dowry to Señor Martinez the day he told me what happened. I thought you would agree to forget the whole fiasco."

"Well, you thought wrong!" Neil stripped off his dusty

clothes, exchanging them for a pair of black pants and matching shirt and vest that he pulled from his closet.

"What do you think you're doing?" Sebastian asked in exasperation.

"What does it look like? I'm going to find my fiancée and bring her back." Neil absently attached Eden's watch to a fob and dropped it into his vest pocket.

Sebastian watched unbelievingly as Neil slapped a gun belt around his waist and yanked viciously at the tie-downs on the holster. "For God's sake, Neil, Constanza is married and there's nothing you can do about it."

"If Williams kidnaped her we'll find a way to annul the marriage."

"Kidnaped!" Sebastian struck his forehead with an open hand. "Neil, she went willingly."

"I don't believe that," Neil said stubbornly. "Constanza would never disgrace her heritage—our heritage—by marrying a *gringo*. She's too proud for that."

"Williams is rich," Sebastian pointed out. "You know Constanza well enough to realize that she is blind whenever a great deal of money is involved. You said it yourself, Neil: Constanza is greedy."

"But not so greedy that she would humiliate me this way," Neil countered angrily.

"That's really what rankles you, isn't it?" Sebastian said hotly. "Not the fact that Constanza married, but the fact that you feel humiliated by her choice. Your pride, not your heart, is hurt because she married an American. You wouldn't be reacting this way if Constanza had married a *criollo*. It's just fine for you to have affairs with any woman, anywhere, anytime—even to consider setting one up as your mistress—but when Constanza marries outside what you consider to be the upper crust of your society—" Sebastian stopped in frustration and raised his hands in a helpless gesture. "Your thinking is straight out of the Middle Ages! What do you think Juárez and the Revolution were all about? You—your way of thinking— are precisely what we fought to abolish!"

"It was your Revolution, not mine," Neil said. "I only went along to keep you from getting your head blown off. If you're finished, little brother, I'll be on my way. Trust me, Sebastian, I know what I'm doing."

"No, you don't," Sebastian told him as he followed Neil

out of the cool house into the blistering midday sun. "You and I both know Constanza. What Constanza wants, she gets, and she never has been forced to do anything in her entire life. The convent school was relieved to see her go. Damn it, Neil, listen to me! You're letting your temper control you again, and your thinking never is rational when that happens."

Neil threw a saddle on a fresh horse and tightened the girth. "My thinking is just fine, thank you, and I know exactly what I'm doing. I'm going to find Constanza and bring her back. And if I have to make her a widow in the process"—Neil shrugged and gave his brother a reckless grin—"so much the better. It'll save the time and expense of an annulment."

Neil swung into the saddle. "If I have to stay for any length of time I'll write and let you know where to send my things." He rested his hands on the saddle horn, the reins firmly wrapped in his fingers, and studied his brother. "In one of my suitcases there is a document that will tell you about the financial arrangements I made for you and your hospital while I was in New York—just in case." He leaned down and offered his hand to Sebastian. "Wish me luck."

"You know I do," Sebastian sighed and clasped Neil's hand. "It would be best to forget about Constanza; let her feed off this American." Neil was determined. Sebastian read it in his eyes and stepped away from the horse. *"Vaya con Dios,* Neil."

Neil rode west, crossing a low mountain range before turning again, this time to the north. The border wasn't far away—three days of riding at the most, two if he really pressed his horse and himself—but Neil wasn't in any hurry. He wouldn't have a hard time finding Lathrop Williams. Or Constanza. Neil fingered the watch in his pocket and frowned; between Eden and Constanza his homecoming had been anything but joyful. And somehow, in his mind, the two things were connected. If Eden had agreed to come back with him, Constanza would never have run off and right now he would be sitting on the terrace with a cold drink in his hand instead of riding his tail off across the wilds of Mexico. Hell, Neil told himself disgustedly, that wasn't exactly true. Even if Eden had returned with him he would still be following Williams and Constanza into Texas. Sebastian had been right about one thing: Neil's pride was involved.

Briefly Neil considered the validity of what Sebastian had said. Constanza *was* greedy, he couldn't deny that, but neither could he blame her. Señor Martinez had lost nearly everything during the Revolution—most of his land, his servants, his only son—and Constanza could not or would not accept the fact that her opulent, narcissistic world had vanished.

When a short time later—at his mother's insistence—Neil had offered his proposal to Señor Martinez, the old man had readily agreed. A great deal of Neil's fortune was to have been given to Constanza's father upon their marriage, enough money to enable her parents to live out their lives in comfort. The money didn't matter to Neil; most of it had been not earned but inherited from his mother, who had gotten it from that cold-blooded bastard sitting in his London town house who thought he could make up for his desertion with money. What had Eden said? That he was being too harsh?

Eden. His thoughts kept coming back to her. Neil grimaced and plunged his horse into the muddy water of the Rio Grande. Last night, alone beneath the stars, he had even taken out her picture and studied it, wondering what she was doing now, what had happened to her after he and Jane had left New York. That Eden hadn't shown up at the ship still angered him beyond reason—no woman refused him! The thought came perversely: Was Eden married to Tim by now? Tim wouldn't be man enough for Eden; she was too strong-willed, too independent to let a milksop like Tim ride roughshod over her. Eden Thackery needed a real man, someone who knew what he was doing and could keep her in line. Neil had to laugh—in his present situation he was hardly in a position to pass judgment on Tim Gregory.

Annoyed by the turn his thoughts had taken, Neil slapped his horse into a gallop. He was too experienced to be acting like a lovesick schoolboy. What he had to concentrate on now was finding Constanza and bringing her back to Mexico.

By midafternoon of the next day Neil was on the outskirts of town, looking with contempt at the name on the sign. "Welcome to Lathrop." Martinez had told him Williams was rich, but Neil hadn't believed the man would actually have the nerve to name a town after himself. Neil drew his revolver, automatically checking the cylinder to make sure it was loaded and assuring himself that the gun slid easily from the holster.

The saloon was deserted, except for a couple of drunks, the bartender and three or four working girls who were waiting for business to pick up. Neil sauntered carelessly to the bar.

"Whiskey." The bartender filled a glass and placed it in front of Neil. "Pretty slow today."

The bartender looked around and shrugged. "Roundup time. In a few weeks this place will be bustin' at the seams."

Neil sipped at his drink. "Interesting name for a town—Lathrop."

"Named for the man who founded it, Lathrop Williams." He carefully polished a glass and when he spoke it was a statement, not a question. "You're new here."

"For now." Neil pushed his glass forward and the man refilled it.

"You thinking of settling here?"

Neil shrugged. "Maybe. I heard there was a ranch for sale; thought I might take a look at it."

The bartender thought for a moment, frowning. "Oh, yeah, I know the place you're talking about. Borders on the Williams ranch and the old Mason place. Nice spread." He eyed Neil's dusty clothes. "You sure you can afford it?"

Neil laughed shortly. "If it's what I want. You know this Lathrop Williams?"

"Sure; ain't nobody in this town that doesn't. He came out here thirty years ago, fought the Apaches for the land and built this town." The bartender looked around and lowered his voice. "Take my advice, mister: If you're going to settle down beside Lathrop Williams, don't ever turn your back on him." Neil indicated his interest by casually dropping two coins onto the bar. The bartender quickly pocketed them and continued. "A friend of mine did—Art Mason, from the other ranch I mentioned—and his trusting nature got him killed. See, there's a nice, fat stream that runs through that property, and Art's father got to it before Williams. Water is precious around these parts and Williams wanted that stream. He offered Art money for his ranch, a lot of money, double what the place was worth, but the money didn't interest Art. It was his land and he wanted to keep it. He offered to share the water with Williams, but Williams ain't the sharing kind. It seemed for a while like Williams had forgotten about Mason and the ranch. A few months later they found Art with his head blown off."

Neil's eyes narrowed. "So Williams got what he wanted anyway."

"Nope. Art was the careful sort. After Williams' last offer Art did sell, to some fancy businessman back East. The new

...d to let Art ramrod the outfit for as long as he ...Course, when Art was killed the new owner just ...abled Mr. Randolph at the bank to hire a new foreman." The bartender paused, reflecting. "Art had a son; he must have been fifteen, sixteen, when Art died. The boy disappeared a few days later—never did hear what happened to him. Damned shame." The man shrugged. "Anyway, the Mason ranch is still going, and Williams still doesn't have the water rights."

"Interesting," Neil said consideringly. "What about Willams' family?"

"Ain't got none—not yet, anyhow. Went and got himself married a while back to some little Mex gal with a holier-than-thou attitude. Snooty little bitch; they say she married him for his money. 'Course, there could be another reason; Lathrop is quite a ladies' man, if you know what I mean."

"I know." Neil rose to leave. "Thanks for the information."

The bank was open. Neil strolled past the teller's cage and after a few pointed inquiries was standing before the president's desk.

"Yes, sir; may I help you?"

"If your bank holds the deed to a ranch that's for sale, then you can." Neil extended his hand. "I may be interested in the property. The name's Banning."

"A pleasure, Mr. Banning," the man said in a dry voice as he shook Neil's hand. "I am Lawrence Randolph. Won't you be seated?"

"Thank you, no. If you don't mind I'd like to take a look at the place right away. If it's what I want I'll return and you can draw up the papers."

The banker's voice was incredulous. "It's not quite that simple, Mr. Banning. First of all we must make certain that you can meet the mortgage payments as well as purchase the stock you'll need, the hired hands . . ."

"Allow me to simplify matters for you, Mr. Randolph. If I like the ranch I'll pay cash for it, in full." Lawrence Randolph's eyes widened behind his spectacles, and Neil smiled. "I'll give you the name of my bank in New York and you can telegraph them for confirmation while I'm gone. I will, of course, transfer a large share of my account to your bank *if* we do business. Now, may I have the directions to the ranch?"

Neil spent very little time inspecting the property before turning west. The ranch gave him the perfect reason for coming

to Lathrop. A feeling of recklessness welled up in
pinpoints of light dancing in his amber eyes. It felt
doing something. During the past three days he had felt so
damned helpless whenever he thought about Constanza and
Williams that he had ached to start a fight with someone,
anyone—exactly the kind of incident Sebastian deplored and
which Neil needed to work off his boiling temper.

But not this time, Neil resolved as he tied the reins to the
hitching post in front of the Williams house. This time he would
control his anger. In a few hours, once Constanza confirmed
that she had married Lathrop Williams against her will, he and
Constanza would be on their way back to Mexico. Her marriage
would be annulled and their lives would return to normal. While
the thought was not exactly a pleasant one, it did offer Neil
a kind of satisfaction.

Compared to the other homes Neil had seen on his way to
the ranch, Williams' house was palatial, its massive structure
comprised entirely of stone rather than the wood or adobe of
the other buildings in the area. Neil lifted the brass knocker
and let it fall heavily against the plate. He tried again, then
turned around to inspect the rest of the buildings.

"Yes? What do you want?" The female voice was low,
husky, with an unmistakable Spanish accent, and Neil smiled
at the trace of impatience in her tone.

"Just being neighborly, ma'am," Neil drawled as he pivoted
to face her. "And you must be the little lady of the house. How
are you, Mrs. Williams?"

"Neil!" Constanza Martinez Williams gasped and brought
a jeweled hand to her throat. "I . . . how . . . what are you doing
here?"

Neil's eyes were veiled by his long, dark lashes. "I might
ask you the same question. As I remember, you and I are
supposed to be married in a few weeks."

"It . . . it's not what it seems, Neil, I can explain—"

"I'm sure you can, my sweet Constanza, but does it have
to be on your doorstep?"

"No, no." Constanza stepped aside and hurriedly shut the
door when Neil was inside. "Lathrop . . . m-my husband is not
here; the roundup—"

"How convenient." Neil strolled through the house, casually
inspecting each room while Constanza nervously followed.
"You've done very well for yourself, Constanza, congratula-

tions. Dresden china, French crystal, and let's not forget those sparkling baubles you're wearing. A trifle overdone if you're only spending the day at home, isn't it?"

Constanza's hand flew to one of the oversized diamond teardrop earrings. "They are new; I was just trying them on."

Neil mocked her defensive tone. "I'm sure you earned them." When Constanza didn't answer, he shrugged. "You've forgotten your manners, Constanza; you haven't offered me a drink. I assume your husband does have a liquor cabinet."

"Let me explain, Neil—"

"In a moment. I want a drink first."

"In the library." Constanza led Neil to the room in a different wing of the house. Gesturing for him to be seated, she opened the ornately carved doors of a cabinet. "What would you like, Neil?"

"Brandy, if your husband has it. The whiskey I had in town left a bad taste in my mouth." Neil sipped at his drink and nodded approvingly. "Very good."

"Lathrop buys only the best." Neil's silence tore at Constanza's nerves and she sat stiffly in a chair, her hands clasped tightly in front of her. "Will you tell me why you have come here?"

"That should be obvious, Constanza. I returned home and found I was short a bride, so I decided to reclaim her."

"You cannot," Constanza gasped. "There is too much at stake, Neil. You do not know all the facts."

"No?" Neil smiled humorlessly and stretched his legs. "Why don't you explain it to me?"

Constanza wet her full, red lips. "I do not want you to hate me, Neil; please believe that I did not intend to dishonor you. You know that my family needs money, a great deal of money, and Lathrop has agreed to support my parents until they die. But that is not the reason I married Lathrop."

Her eyes filled with tears and Constanza dabbed at them with a lace handkerchief. "He is not an honorable man, Neil. When Lathrop came to my parents' house he was told I had a *novio*. He knew I was a virgin, and still he came to my room one night. . . . When he left me, I was no longer innocent of a man's touch. He ruined me, Neil."

Neil's eyes narrowed as he studied Constanza's pleading expression. "Why didn't you tell your father or Sebastian? They would have avenged your honor in my place."

"How could I do that?" Constanza's usually flashing eyes were subdued. "You were promised a virgin, Neil; I knew you would not want me after Lathrop." Constanza burst into tears and buried her face in her hands. "I could not bring such disgrace upon you."

"There is no disgrace," Neil said softly and, rising, went quickly to her side. "I thank you for your concern for my name. Despite what he did to you, I know it was done against your will. I would have married you regardless."

Constanza looked up, her smile bitter. "If I had known that I would never have married Lathrop. You are most generous."

Neil stroked her cheek gently. "It's over, Constanza. There is no need for tears. I've come to take you home."

"You cannot!" Constanza jumped from her chair and grasped his hand. "Oh, Neil, you cannot."

"Of course I can. We'll have your marriage to Williams annulled and then we can be married. Don't worry," Neil patted her hand. "I guarantee Lathrop won't come after you."

Constanza whirled and walked to the other side of the room. "Do you care so little for my reputation, my honor? Have I not had enough scandal attached to my name? We were married by a priest, Neil. The union is sacred to me. I did not take my vows lightly. No matter how I feel about Lathrop, in the eyes of the Church he is my husband. Would you disgrace me further? All our friends know about Lathrop—I do not think I could stand the gossip if I returned now. Please, Neil, is there not another way?"

Constanza warmed under his stare, her flesh tingling as she saw desire flare in the amber depths. She lowered her eyes and when she spoke her voice had a catch in it. "You do have certain rights, Neil. We could both take our revenge in the oldest way—and I do want to see Lathrop pay for what he has done."

Neil suppressed the urge to take Constanza's invitation at once. Time enough for that after Lathrop Williams was merely a vague memory.

"I am sorry," Constanza said quietly, humbly. "I should not have said that. I know that your feelings toward me have changed, but I have no other way to make things up to you. What Lathrop took from me by force I wanted to give to you willingly, even though in the eyes of the Church . . ." Constanza sighed and averted her face. "Perhaps I deserve what has happened to me; that I could suggest such a thing makes me no better than these American women."

"I understand," Neil replied at last. "You and I have always understood each other. I know how important your religion is to you and I admire you for that, Constanza. You were brought up properly. Neither of us had any illusions about our marriage but we would not have disgraced each other the way Lathrop has."

Constanza nodded and reached for his hand. "At least you know the truth now. That is all that is important. I knew what you would think when you learned of the letter Lathrop forced me to write." She rose and brushed her lips against Neil's cheek. "Thank you for coming here. The past few months have been a nightmare. To see someone from home—"

Her voice broke and Neil quickly put his arms around Constanza's trembling form. "It's all right, Constanza."

Constanza shook her head. "This is a savage place, populated by barbarians. They have not our heritage, our culture." She sighed wistfully and touched the handkerchief to her luminous eyes. "When you are safely home I hope you will spare me a few kind thoughts. God knows I have need of them."

"I shall think of you often, but not at home." At Constanza's obvious confusion Neil smiled and explained. "If you won't come back with me, I can't simply abandon you. You and I, Constanza, are about to become neighbors. I'm buying the adjoining ranch."

Constanza paled. "Neil, it is too dangerous!"

"Nonsense." Releasing her, Neil picked up his hat and grinned. "Lathrop won't suspect anything, even when he finds out that I'm from Mexico." Neil sobered. "I can't leave you here alone, Constanza. Honor demands I call Lathrop out, kill him and reclaim what is mine. But I realize that would only add to the scandal, so my only choice is to stay in Texas and offer you whatever protection I can."

Neil rode back into Lathrop and found that in his absence Lawrence Randolph had not only contacted his New York bank but had also drawn up the papers for the ranch. Neil's pretext for being in Lathrop had unexpectedly brought him full circle. He now owned land in the state where he had been born, and the irony of the events which had led him to this point was not lost on Neil. The realization that he was pursuing Constanza

just as his stepfather had pursued his mother grated on Neil
and he pushed it into the recesses of his mind.

The legalities concluded, Neil checked into the town's only
hotel and studied the map Randolph had given him. Ranch
boundaries, roads, a scattering of low hills, Neil absorbed the
locations of them all, storing the information in his mind until
he had the chance to see the environs for himself. He lit a cigar
and smiled; it wouldn't take long for Constanza to forget the
gossip she had caused—then she would be ready to dissolve
her marriage, Church or no Church. All he had to do was to
be patient and Constanza would come around.

From a window in Lathrop's office Constanza had watched
Neil ride away. Fool, she thought contemptuously. Did you
really believe I would settle for the crumbs you offered when
I could have someone like Lathrop? You would never have
given me what Lathrop will, and all I have to do for him is
give him an heir within five years. Then I will be free to do
as I please—and I will have the money with which to do it.

The curtain was pulled back farther from the window and
Constanza hastily withdrew her hand. "The abandoned groom,
I take it? You should have called me, Constanza. I would have
enjoyed meeting him."

Constanza shrugged. "You will meet him soon enough. I
believe he plans to destroy you, Lathrop."

Lathrop Williams laughed, but his pale blue eyes remained
cold. "Does he now? And did he ask you to help him?"

"Why would he do that?" Constanza snapped. "Neil does
not believe a woman capable of dealing with what he considers
men's affairs. ¡Idiota!"

"The man *is* an idiot," Lathrop agreed in his booming drawl.
"But then I don't suppose you told him about the bargain you
drove with me. If you had, his opinion of you would change
in a hurry."

"But I do not want his opinion to change." Constanza said
craftily. "He must always see me as pure, convent-raised and
helpless . . . and perhaps a bit spoiled. There may come a time
when I need Neil, and in order to use him for my ends I must
be able to appeal to his ridiculous standards. As you often say,
Lathrop, everyone has a price. All I have to do is find Neil's."

Lathrop snorted. "Just as I found yours. Now, Constanza,"
he warned at her affronted look, "we know each other too well

to pretend about our relationship. You flirted and teased your way into this little arrangement and you can't deny you've got a good deal. You'll recall that even if you don't produce a son for me in five years, you'll still receive a very handsome settlement; and in addition, as long as we're married you can have whatever you desire, provided you never lock your bedroom door to me. You and I both are opportunists; you should learn to appreciate that fact and enjoy your good fortune."

Constanza tossed her head. "You think too highly of yourself, Lathrop. And you are a very hateful man at times. In fact, you are much like Neil."

"With one exception: I don't have his blue blood. But that really doesn't bother you as much as you want Neil to think it does." Lathrop chuckled mirthlessly. "From what you've told me, Neil and your father are a lot alike—both of them refuse to believe that anyone outside their precious circle of friends is good enough to associate with. Take a look at your father. He's living in a house that's starting to crumble and he still can't see that his old way of life doesn't exist anymore. It seems Neil thinks he's just a little better than everyone else, too."

Lathrop fell silent and Constanza eyed him speculatively. "You are planning something, yes?" At Lathrop's nod, she settled herself suggestively on his lap. "Will you tell me, or is it going to be a surprise?"

"Of course I'm going to tell you. A husband and wife shouldn't have secrets from each other." Lathrop unfastened her dress and thrust his hands inside her bodice. "Seeing your old boy friend today excited you, didn't it?"

"You are crude—" Constanza moaned as Lathrop's fingers forced her nipples into hard, aching points.

"Which suits you just fine." Lathrop pushed her down onto the floor. "Since that first night you knocked on my bedroom door anything I've done has suited you."

# Chapter 7

"It's beautiful, Eden, just beautiful!" Meg exclaimed breathlessly. "Won't Eden be a lovely bride, Mama?"

Mrs. Lawson fluffed the veil around Eden's face and smiled. "Meg is right, Eden, you will be a lovely bride. Madame Du Prez must have worked day and night to finish your gown. Madame, you must agree to create my daughter's wedding gown."

Madame Du Prez finished pinning up the hem before rising from her knees. "I would be honored, Mrs. Lawson. Will the marriage take place soon?"

"Oh, my, no," Meg giggled. "Not for at least a year."

Eden stared at her reflection in the full-length mirror, the chatter going unheard as she tried to recognize the girl in the white wedding gown. I shouldn't be wearing white, she thought disjointedly. Red perhaps, or a nice rich burgundy.... Everyone suspects the worse, but they think that Hugh is responsible, and he's not. It's Neil's fault—and my own, because I was too eager to believe that I could be loved. But I'm paying for my mistake now. My God, how I'm paying!

Everyone had been shocked at their engagement, of course, but no one had dared suggest a scandal. How could they? Hugh was well liked, respectable, and he obviously was so adoring of Eden when they appeared in public that no one questioned their May-December romance. All Eden had to do was smile at the proper times and pretend that she was deliriously happy.

The formal engagement party had been the worst for Eden. All of Hugh's friends and their wives and Eden's former schoolmates—except Jane—had attended, and by the end of the evening Eden's face had ached from the hours of forced smiling. The Gregorys had come as well, even Tim, and Eden had worried all during the festivities that Tim would do or say something that would expose the charade she and Hugh were so carefully acting out. Thankfully Tim hadn't said a word except to offer his congratulations in a cold voice that the other guests had attributed to wounded pride. But then, after Jane's little fiasco, the Gregorys were keeping a very low profile.

143

Hugh had been right when he'd told her that their marriage would quiet any wagging tongues. Hugh! Eden shivered involuntarily as the seamstress helped her out of her gown. She feared Hugh more than anything else. He hated her passionately, vehemently, and he proved it every time he brought her home after an evening out. Hugh's brutal kisses left her weak and terrified of what would happen once they were married. Tears started in her eyes, and Eden fought them back. It seemed she was on the verge of tears all the time lately and Eden despised herself for being so weak. In three days she would be Mrs. Hugh Colter and she didn't want Hugh to know how much he upset her—it only would make matters worse. Hugh had to believe that while she might not be happy about their marriage she would at least accept it graciously. Lately, keeping up that gracious façade—despite all Eden's years of practice—seemed to require all her strength.

Mrs. Lawson volunteered to show Madame Du Prez to the door, and Meg handed Eden her dressing gown. "You've been awfully quiet, Eden. Aren't you feeling well?"

Eden sank wearily onto the bed. "I'm fine, Meg. I guess I'm just getting a case of prewedding jitters. I do get tired of all the fuss."

"Well, Eden, that's as it should be. After all, you only get married once. You should be floating on air."

"I know, and I am happy, but if I'm not having fittings on my trousseau then I'm working on the arrangements with the florist; if it's not that, then I'm seeing the priest for instruction; and if that's over, then someone is giving a tea. I tell you, Meg, my nerves can't take much more." Eden started to cry and Meg quickly put her arms around Eden's shoulders. "I'm sorry, Meg, I just don't know what's the matter with me lately."

"Oh, Eden, it's all right. It's just as you said: You're all nervous and jittery, that's all. I bet I'll feel the same way when I get married." Meg wiped Eden's face and smiled warmly. "You know, this is the first time you've ever cried in front of me and—I know this will sound silly—this is the first time I've ever felt that we're truly, truly friends." Meg started to cry as well and the two girls fell into each other's arms. "We've known each other for a long time but I never felt this close to you before and now you're going to be married and everything will change—"

"No, it won't," Eden managed to say. "We'll still be friends,

Meg; nothing will ever change that. You're the only friend I've ever had—in fact, you're more like a sister than a friend—oh, Meg, what I'm trying to say is that I love you. You are so dear to me."

Meg brushed at her eyes. "I love you, too, Eden, only I wasn't sure how you would react if I told you. I want you to be happy, Eden; after losing your parents the way you did, you certainly deserve to be happy. I just know Hugh will do his best to make your life together wonderful."

Eden tried to smile through her tears. "I'm sure he will. Don't worry about me, Meg, I'll be just fine. And when I get back from my honeymoon, let's spend an entire day together; we'll have lunch, do some shopping—"

"Yes, yes! And we'll go to the theater and perhaps the opera. Oh, Eden, promise we'll always be friends."

"Of course we will; I promise, Meg."

They both started to cry again until, gradually, their sobs turned to laughter, and by the time Mrs. Lawson returned to Eden's room they were laughing outrageously.

"What in the world!" Mrs. Lawson looked from one to the other. "What are you girls doing?"

"We were just talking, Mama," Meg finally gasped.

Eden struggled up from the bed. "Would you like to stay for tea, Mrs. Lawson?"

"Oh, no, dear. Thank you, anyway. Meg and I have several errands to run before dinner, and if we don't hurry, Father will be dining alone." Eden accompanied them downstairs and at the door Mrs. Lawson kissed her lightly on both cheeks. "We'll pick you up an hour before the wedding, all right? Now try to get some rest in the next few days, Eden. You look a trifle peaked."

When they were gone the silent, empty house took on sinister proportions for Eden as she started up the stairs to her bedroom. In the past two months the rooms had been empty except for the servants—no laughter or warmth welcomed Eden when she awoke in the morning, only stark terror as she realized all over again that the house which had once been her refuge soon would become her prison. How could everything have turned out so badly, Eden wondered for the hundredth time. She hadn't meant to hurt anyone, she had honestly believed that Neil would marry her. And yet now, incredibly, she was hurting the very person she had tried to spare. Hugh, oh, Hugh, why can't you forgive me? Why—

Eden gasped as a cramp doubled her over and she clung desperately to the banister, fighting off wave after wave of dizziness. She'd had the same pain off and on all week, but she'd ignored it until now. It always went away and it had never been this severe before. Maybe she should see the doctor just in case. Another cramp seized her, twisting through her abdomen, loosing a gush of warm, sticky liquid that soaked her dress. Eden lost her hold on the railing and suddenly she was falling...

Hugh burst into the house, Ian hard on his heels, before Simmons had a chance to open the door for him. "Where is she, Simmons? Has the doctor arrived yet?"

"Yes, sir," Simmons replied calmly. "The doctor arrived several hours ago, shortly after I sent a messenger for you. He's with Miss Thackery now, sir, in her room."

Hugh flushed dully at the implied criticism. "Ian, will you stay? You can wait in the study if you like, and Simmons will get you something to eat if you're hungry."

"Of course I'll stay, Hugh. I care for that girl almost as much as you do." The big man shook his head sadly. "You'd best get upstairs, man, I have the feeling she'll be needing you right about now."

Hugh took the stairs two at a time and found Millicent standing just inside the doorway of the sitting room, her eyes red from crying.

"Oh, Mr. Colter," Millicent wept. "I didn't know what to do, sir! I never thought anything like this would happen. I never... I never..."

"It's all right, Millicent." Hugh squeezed her shoulder reassuringly. "Tell me what happened. The note only said that Eden was taken ill."

Millicent struggled for her composure. "It was our day off, you know, sir, but I came back early to tell Miss Eden about the play I'd seen today. She'd found out that I'd never been to the theater and that I dreamed about going, so she bought me two tickets. I wanted to tell her..." Millicent swallowed a sob before continuing. "I got back around six and found her on the landing; all pale and still she was, so quiet I thought at first she was dead. But then she opened her eyes for a moment and said my name so I got her into bed and sent one of the stableboys for Dr. Sterling. She'll live, won't she, Mr. Colter?" Millicent asked fearfully.

"Millicent," Hugh said impatiently, "how badly was she hurt in the fall?"

Millicent blinked rapidly. "You don't know. I mean"—she searched frantically for the right words but she avoided Hugh's eyes—"it wasn't the fall, Mr. Colter, she doesn't have any broken bones or suchlike, it's just that she had already lost so much blood before we found her."

Before Hugh could ask Millicent what she meant, the bedroom door swung open and David Sterling stalked across the room. "Where the hell have you been?" he growled. "It's past midnight and I know damn well they sent someone for you at six!"

Millicent exited discreetly. "Get off your high horse, David," Hugh demanded, "and tell me what the devil is going on."

David glanced into the bedroom and lowered his voice. "This is going to be every bit as hard on you as it is on Eden. I'm terribly sorry, Hugh; Eden lost the baby."

"What!" The strength deserted Hugh's legs and he collapsed onto a chair.

"Look, Hugh, you don't have to be embarrassed about this." David clapped him on the shoulder. "A lot of people have 'premature' first babies; it's a story as old as time. I'm just sorry that this had to happen. I know it's a shock."

"A shock," Hugh repeated quietly. "That's an understatement, David." He ran a hand roughly through his hair. "What about Eden? Have you told her what happened?"

"I had to. She came to about three hours ago and wanted to know." David sat down on a chair next to Hugh. "I won't lie to you. Eden lost a lot of blood before she was found and she's terribly weak, but she will recover, given time and a great deal of understanding. That's the most important thing for you to remember right now. Be patient with her, Hugh, because she needs you now more than ever."

Hugh nodded. "Can I see her now?"

"Of course, but try not to stay too long."

Eden was awake, her eyes fixed blankly on the ceiling, and she appeared not to notice Hugh when he carefully lowered himself onto the edge of the bed. Gently, Hugh clasped one of her cold, lifeless hands between his own and pressed it comfortingly. Eden made no effort to return the pressure, but neither did she try to pull away. She simply lay there, unmoving, except for the slight rise and fall of her chest.

"How do you feel, Eden?" Hugh inquired softly. She didn't answer and after a long silence Hugh tried again. "I'm sorry I wasn't here before, dear heart, but they took quite a while finding me."

"It doesn't matter." Eden's voice was cold, unemotional. "There's nothing you could have done."

"I know, but at least you would have known that I was here."

Eden laughed feebly, a brittle sound that drew Hugh's attention from her hand to her face. "Thank God I was spared that! Your . . . concern these past months has been more than enough!"

"Oh, God, Eden," Hugh whispered, ashamed. "Don't do this."

She finally looked at him then, her eyes cold and unreadable. "I didn't know, Hugh. I didn't even know I was pregnant. Not that you asked. But then, whores never get pregnant, do they? And since that's what you think I am, I guess the possibility never crossed your mind." She turned away again.

"I don't think of you as a—"

"Of course you do," Eden interrupted bitterly. "And this act you're putting on now—you're not the least bit sorry about the baby, Hugh, you're just sorry I didn't die as well. I'm so sorry I disappointed you again, but with any luck you'll be left a widower shortly after the wedding."

"Stop it, Eden!" Hugh pulled her into his arms. "I don't want to hear you talk this way, do you understand? I'm not going to pretend that this miscarriage hasn't hurt me, because it has. You were hurt by it, and anything that hurts you hurts me as well."

"You seem to forget the baby wasn't yours," she whispered cruelly, "it was—" Eden stopped herself before she said Neil's name. "It was someone else's."

"It would have been ours," Hugh corrected her. "It was part of you, Eden, and I would have loved it as much as I love you. You're the most important thing in my life—I know I haven't acted like it lately," he admitted brokenly, "but I do love you, Eden, and I'll spend the rest of my life making up for what I've put you through."

"It doesn't matter," Eden repeated expressionlessly. "Nothing matters anymore. If you've come to me for absolution, Hugh, you needn't have bothered." Hugh lowered her back to the pillows and Eden closed her eyes wearily. "Whatever you've said or done to me makes no difference now. I don't feel anything anymore, not anger or hurt or pain. I just wish they'd found me a little later."

"You're tired, dear heart," Hugh said as he brushed the damp hair away from her face. "You need to rest, and in the morning we'll talk some more."

David entered the room in time to hear Hugh's comment and he smiled slightly. "A good night's sleep is exactly what I was about to prescribe for you, Eden. I'll leave a bottle of laudanum with you just in case you can't drift off, but I don't think you'll need it."

Hugh rose and shook the doctor's hand. "Thank you, David, I can't tell you how grateful I am."

"I'm just glad I got here when I did," David replied, then turned to Eden. "As for you, young lady, you're going to be fine, but I do want you to take it easy for a while, which means absolute bed rest for a week."

"I'll take care of it," Hugh assured him. "We'll postpone our wedding for a couple of weeks."

"No, we won't." Eden's voice was frail, but a thread of iron ran through her words. "Everything is set up for Saturday and I'm not about to undo all the arrangements."

"Now, see here, Eden. You've lost a lot of blood and until your body replaces it you're going to be weak as a kitten," David said crisply. "You won't have the strength to leave this room, let alone walk down the aisle. And if you try, I guarantee you'll pass out before you reach the altar."

"I appreciate your concern, Dr. Sterling, but the wedding will go on as planned." Eden turned her face away from the two men. "If you don't mind . . ."

"You'd better talk to her, Hugh," David advised before he left. "It's going to take longer than three days for Eden to get back on her feet, plus there's some danger of infection. I know it's a big day for her but—"

"I'll do what I can. Good night, David, and thanks again."

Ian sprang to his feet the moment Hugh walked through the study doorway. "How is she?"

"Asleep." Hugh went to the bar and poured a drink. "The

doctor says she'll be fine in a couple of weeks; all she needs is rest." His hand shook, spilling whiskey across the polished oak. "Lord, Ian, she was pregnant—Eden had a miscarriage tonight."

Ian expelled his breath sharply. "As if she hasn't been through enough. What a hell of a thing to have happen. I remember my mother losing a babe that way." Ian frowned, remembering, and fell silent for a moment. "How is Eden taking this?"

"I don't know," Hugh said bleakly. "She's closed herself off from me—from everyone, it seems. Eden isn't crying, she isn't sad or angry; I don't think she feels anything at all right now. God knows, these past two months I wanted to hurt her, to make her feel the pain I was feeling, but I never meant for something like this to happen!"

"Of course you didn't, Hugh. I understand and so will Eden when she's well. All you have to do is tell Eden exactly what you've told me."

"Sure! And then I'll explain that the reason it took me so long to get here was that you had to go to damn near every cathouse in New York before you could find me!"

"Take it easy, Hugh. Don't burden yourself with guilt when you don't deserve it."

"Don't I!" Hugh shouted. "Ian, I deserve everything Eden said to me tonight and more! You told me yourself I was acting like a damn fool, and you were right. The reason she's up there right now is because I put her through hell these last few weeks. I told her I loved her just now and she said it didn't matter." His voice caught and Hugh studied the whiskey in his glass. "I can't blame her for that; I haven't exactly been the loving bridegroom lately. Whatever affection Eden felt for me I've managed to destroy. Jesus Christ, Ian, what am I going to do?"

"Marry Eden," Ian said eventually. "You really don't have any other choice."

Eden woke up slowly, like swimming to the surface of a deep, dark pool which refused to release her even when she opened her eyes. Her eyes felt dry and gritty. She turned her head and saw the medicine bottle on the bedside table. It hadn't been a dream, then; what she had hoped was a nightmare had really happened. Oh, God, Eden cried silently. I didn't know, I didn't know! It never had even occurred to her. How could she have known? Such things simply weren't discussed. A tear trailed down her cheek and Eden wiped at it with the back of her hand. Neil's child. He had left his mark on her after all. How would Neil react if he knew? Would he be saddened? Probably not, she thought bitterly. No doubt Neil would shrug it off, as he did everything else that didn't matter to him.

"You're awake." Hugh's voice startled her, and Eden turned her head quickly. Hugh sat beside the bed, his eyes red-rimmed, the jacket he had been wearing the night before lying discarded on a chair. "How do you feel, dear heart? Would you like something to eat? Dr. Sterling said you should start off with broth or soup today, and if you tolerate those you can have solids tomorrow."

"No, thank you," Eden said quietly. "Perhaps later. What time is it?"

"Ten o'clock. You slept a long time." Hugh stirred uneasily beneath Eden's unwavering stare. "Would you like to sit up? I'm pretty good at fluffing pillows."

"I can manage," Eden told him coolly; but in the end she allowed Hugh to do it for her because she was too weak to sit up on her own. "I have several appointments for this afternoon that I'll have to cancel—"

"I'll take care of that for you," Hugh said quickly. "Do you want me to tell Margaret that you've been taken ill? I'm sure she would like to visit you."

"Good Lord, no!" Eden's voice was sharp. "I don't need Meg coming over here and asking a lot of questions."

"The questions will be asked eventually. When we postpone the wedding everyone will want to know what happened." He reached out to squeeze her hand. "I don't want you to worry about that, darlin'; I'll think of something to tell the people we invited, and then in a couple of weeks—when you're well— we'll be married."

"No! No postponement, no delays!" Eden's hands curled into tight fists on the satin coverlet. "I told you that last night. Why are you bringing it up again?"

"Why are you determined to kill yourself?" Hugh returned angrily. He jumped from the chair and began to pace. "You know you're not in any condition to go through a wedding and the reception we had planned. You heard what the doctor said: You need time to regain your strength. Two more weeks of waiting won't make any difference."

"It will to me," Eden said flatly. "You listen to me, Hugh Patrick Colter: I refuse to be humiliated by you or anyone else ever again. You and I are going to be married on Saturday if I have to crawl to the church. As long as we're going to do this, I want to do it right—and I won't have any more gossip spread around about our sudden marriage. Either we get married Saturday or we don't marry at all. This time it's my way, Hugh, and if you don't like it I'll be all too happy to leave."

Amazed by her vehemence, Hugh studied the pale, drawn features of the girl on the bed. "An ultimatum, Eden? You sound like your father."

Eden smiled coldly. "No, Hugh, if I were like my father I wouldn't be in this situation. To tell you the truth, I really don't care whether we get married or not, but for once in my life what happens to me is going to happen on my terms."

"I see." Hugh raked a hand through his hair, uncertain how to respond. "I do love you, Eden. That probably doesn't mean very much to you right now, but if we're going to spend the rest of our lives together it would be nice if we felt something for each other." He reached for one of her hands and held it gently. "You were right, you know; I was unreasonable and unfair when you told me about your . . ." Hugh stumbled over the words and he cleared his throat. "About the man. All the things I said to you—Eden, I was half out of my mind, jealous, angry, hurt, that's how I felt. I fell in love with you so long ago, yet for so many reasons I couldn't tell you about it. When this happened I couldn't control my feelings any longer. I don't hate you for what's happened, and I don't blame you, either.

"I think somewhere in the Bible it says, 'Let he who is without sin cast the first stone.' Well, God knows that's not me. I've done far worse things in my life than you have, for more self-serving reasons. I'm not lily-white, Eden, so who am I to tell you that what you did was wrong? If nothing else, at least we can start out our marriage being honest with each other, and maybe, in time, you'll at least grow fond of me."

Eden's face had remained expressionless while he spoke. She was too tired and too hurt to accept and believe all the things Hugh was telling her. And, predictably, Eden withdrew from anything and anyone that might cause her further pain. "Does this mean that you agree to my terms," she asked softly.

With a sigh, Hugh smiled sadly at Eden. "Yes, dear heart, that's what I mean. I don't have a choice, do I?"

# Chapter 8

Eden stretched luxuriously in the hot bath, the scented bubbles caressing her skin. She had been certain, after the drenching she and Meg had received this afternoon while riding, that she would never be warm again, but now, with a fire crackling in the fireplace and a half-empty pot of steaming tea beside the tub, the cold had ebbed from her body, leaving her cheeks delicately flushed and a few strands of hair curling damply around her face. It would be nice to stay home tonight—have a quiet dinner and curl up with a book, perhaps even play the piano Hugh had given her for her seventeenth birthday. Or simply have a pleasant evening of conversation with Hugh.

Frowning at her thoughts, Eden opened her eyes and reached for a towel. There were no pleasant evenings at home; such a thing didn't exist in their marriage—had, in fact, never existed, not even at first. Eden toweled herself dry by the fire and quickly slipped into fresh undergarments and belted a dressing gown around her waist. Not that their relationship was unpleasant. Whenever she and Hugh were together they were unfailingly polite; and when they were out in public or entertaining at home she and Hugh even managed to appear happily, lovingly married. But they weren't close, not in any sense of the word. They were remote, courteous strangers who occupied the same house and just happened to be married to each other.

Eden seated herself at the dressing table and began methodically opening the various jars that lined the mirror. She had rarely used cosmetics until nearly a year ago, on her wedding day—she had been so pale that day, so drained of all color except for the shadows under her eyes that Eden had given in to vanity and lightly rouged her cheeks and applied a hint of color to her mouth. Everyone had been fooled by her appearance except Hugh, and he made a point of being at her side throughout the entire grueling day. The next morning they had departed New York for a three-month honeymoon in the Orient. It was during that time that Eden recovered physically, despite Hugh's concern that a prolonged trip would do more harm than good.

From a business standpoint—Hugh had spent some time purchasing merchandise for his import business—as well as a sightseeing point of view, their honeymoon had been very successful. But for a man and woman who were supposed to spend this time adjusting to such simple things as sleeping together, the honeymoon had been a dismal failure. Hugh had reserved separate staterooms aboard the ship—because of her condition, Eden had assumed. All the time they were at sea Eden had worried about what would happen when they reached Hong Kong; by then she certainly would be well enough to consummate their marriage. She wasn't afraid Hugh would hurt her—he wouldn't be that cruel—but he would certainly demand his conjugal rights. How would she react when Hugh touched her? Would she, could she respond to him the way she had to Neil? Or would she merely endure Hugh's lovemaking? Eden had stewed and worried right up to the time they had been shown into adjoining but separate rooms in the Hong Kong hotel. Hugh hadn't said a word about the arrangements, merely smiled slightly and dropped the key into her palm before continuing down the corridor to his own room.

The huge, square-cut diamond on Eden's left hand flashed, drawing her attention. It was her engagement ring from Hugh, purchased during that terrible time when he had been determined to make sure that no one would mistake the fact that she was his. The jewelry box on the dressing table also was a gift from Hugh, as was the assortment of rings, bracelets, earrings and necklaces which filled it. If Hugh wasn't killing her with kindness, he was at least smothering her with it, Eden reflected. When they had returned from the Orient, Eden had been surprised to find that during their absence the master suite had been remodeled and, under Hugh's directions, enlarged to accommodate two bedrooms as well as a sitting room. Eden glanced at the door that connected her bedroom with Hugh's and sighed. That door had remained unused since their return, although Eden had carefully unbolted her side of it on the first night they were home.

Eden sighed again and began drawing a brush through her hair. How different her life would have been if . . . she shook her head. She tried not to think about Neil or the baby she had lost, but at times it was impossible for her to control the course her mind chose to take. Eden filled her days and nights with activities and people and it brought a certain amount of forgetfulness, but sometimes . . . Oh, God, sometimes . . .

As the weeks had passed, Eden had hoped to forget Neil and all that had happened, but she was slowly beginning to realize that it was impossible. Eden covered her eyes with her hand. The baby—that was the hardest part, the knowledge that she had carried a new life within her and hadn't known about it until it was too late.

She could have other children, Dr. Sterling had assured her, but what difference did it make, since Hugh wouldn't touch her? At least she no longer broke into a million pieces when she thought about Neil, Eden consoled herself, so she supposed she was getting over him. Besides, what else could she do? Spend the rest of her life wanting a man who was married to someone else by now and who, in any case, had never given a damn for her? Determinedly, Eden began pinning her hair into a simple chignon—she'd done more than enough thinking for one day and it served no purpose except to depress her.

Millicent paused in the doorway with Eden's freshly pressed gown over one arm, watching as Eden jabbed a final pin into her hair. So she was going out again tonight, Millicent thought disapprovingly. She cleared her throat. "Your gown, Mrs. Colter."

Eden caught the emphasis Millicent placed on her name and immediately bristled. Millicent made no attempt to hide the fact that she considered Eden's behavior scandalous. "Thank you, Millicent; stay and help me with the buttons, please."

Nothing was as it had been, thought Eden sadly as Millicent completed her duties and left the room. Once they would have chatted companionably, but now . . . Eden shrugged, picked up her cloak and went downstairs. She checked her appearance in the hall mirror, adjusted the diamond necklace that glittered at her throat and fidgeted nervously with the low, square-cut neckline of her lavender gown. Eden hated waiting for her escort like this; the tension shredded her nerves. Her foot tapped impatiently on the floor and Eden glanced at the clock. She'd done it again. These days she always was ready ahead of time. Twenty minutes to wait—she'd go crazy before Dan arrived.

She considered having something to drink and bit her lip. A small brandy, or perhaps a cognac, just to pass the time until Dan came for her. It might relax her as well.

Hugh and Ian stopped in midconversation when Eden burst

into the game room, and after a moment's startled hesitation they both rose to their feet. Eden's heart pounded and she felt the blood rush to her cheeks as she stammered an apology. "I-I'm sorry, Hugh; I didn't realize you were here." She started to back out of the room. "I'll just—"

"That's all right, dear heart. Stay." Hugh smiled and pulled out a chair for her. "You look beautiful this evening."

"I—thank you." Self-consciously, aware that both men were watching her, Eden poured herself a brandy from the bar before she sat down. "Ian, how are you? I haven't seen you lately."

"Aye—well, with your busy schedule and all, that's not surprising." Ian ignored Hugh's reproving frown and continued. "I was rather hoping you'd be here a week ago for our monthly poker game, but I guess something more important came up, eh?"

"No, not at all," Eden said quickly. "It's just that I had made plans for the evening and I really couldn't break them . . ." her voice trailed off and Eden studied the contents of her glass. Of all Hugh's friends, Ian was the hardest to face; just by looking at her he could make her feel guilty.

"Now, Ian," Hugh chided lightly, "how much fun do you think it is for Eden to sit around and watch five men play cards and drink? That's a bit like asking you to enjoy yourself at a sewing circle, isn't it? Tell me, Eden: Where are you off to tonight?"

"The theater." Eden looked up to meet Hugh's warm gaze, her own eyes wide with apology. "It's opening night and the house was sold out a month in advance. We were lucky to get these seats."

Ian's ears pricked up. "We? You're not going alone then?"

"No." Eden anticipated the explosion her next words would cause and said them as quickly as possible. "Dan Miller is taking me. He got the tickets from a business associate."

"Well, I—" Ian started angrily, but bit his tongue when Hugh warned him off with a shake of his head. "Ah . . . it's a good thing you won't be out alone, unprotected, I mean. You can't trust the streets late at night; all kinds of thieves prowling about."

"Yes, I suppose there are." Eden finished her brandy just as a knock sounded at the front door. "That must be Dan."

Hugh walked with her to the door of the game room. "Have

a good time, Eden. Give Dan my regards." He kissed her chastely on the forehead before opening the door for her.

"I will." Eden started through the doorway, then stopped, and turning back, said hesitantly, "Hugh, I . . ."

"What, Eden?" Hugh smiled gently at her.

Eden shook her head. "Nothing. I'll see you tomorrow morning."

"Only if you're up early. I have some things to take care of at the warehouse, and you," he laughed, "are becoming a late riser. Good night, Eden."

When she was gone, Ian stared curiously at Hugh. "I do not believe what my eyes have just seen. You *do* realize that your wife is spending the evening out, don't you? And that she is going to be spending it with another man while you sit at home with me and talk over old times and play cards? One of us has taken leave of his senses, man, and I'm sure it's not me."

"You heard Eden." Hugh shrugged, his gentle nature at odds with the jealousy he so diligently concealed. "It's opening night and I know she's been wanting to see this play. What's the harm?"

"The harm!" Ian bellowed. "The harm is that your wife is seeing another man, and people are beginning to wonder just how much of him she's really seeing. For God's sake, Hugh, put a stop to it."

"Why?" Hugh eyed him curiously. Ian began to splutter and at last Hugh spoke. "Ian . . . how can I explain this so you will understand? You're the only person outside of Eden and myself who knows the facts behind our marriage—"

"And I would think she'd be grateful to you after all you've done," Ian broke in.

"Will you shut up?" Hugh said in exasperation. "Think about it from Eden's point of view. She did what you and I have done hundreds of times ourselves except that she was in love. All right, she didn't stop to think, but Eden loved this man. She thought he loved her and that marriage would naturally follow. Now, can you honestly condemn her for her actions?"

"I guess not," Ian admitted slowly. "But that doesn't excuse her behavior now."

Hugh leaned back in his chair and stared at the ceiling. "It's taken me a long time to figure Eden out. It's damn hard to get through all those barriers she puts up, but I think I finally understand her. All her life Eden has had to please someone: her father, her teachers, her guardian, even society as a whole. Can you imagine the kind of pressure she's been under practically from the moment she was born? Locke beat it into her that she had to succeed, she had to be the best, she had to be perfect. I tell you, Ian, if that son-of-a-bitch were here right now, I'd kill him for what he put Eden through. I think what Eden needs—what she has always needed—is freedom. God knows she's had little enough of it.

"This social butterfly stage she's going through now doesn't bother me. Right now Eden needs to have a good time. Christ, she's been through more in one year than most people go through in five. And as far as what other people think"—Hugh pursed his lips, then smiled—"Let them think whatever they please about our marriage. I know the truth and that's what counts. Eden is finding out what is important to her and what isn't. All I have to do is wait."

Ian snorted. "I hate to put a damper on your happy little plan, Hugh, but what makes you so sure Eden is going to decide that you're what she wants?"

Hugh drew a hand wearily over his face. "I try not to let myself think about that."

"You look absolutely ravishing tonight, Mrs. Colter," Dan announced as he helped Eden remove her cloak and then steered her through the crowded restaurant to their table. "Everyone was watching you instead of the play, including me."

Eden smiled distractedly, "Thank you for the compliment, Dan."

Dan leaned back and studied Eden's profile in the soft light. "What's the matter, Eden? Did Hugh say something about our going out tonight?"

Eden twirled the stem of her wineglass between her fingers. "No. Hugh never objects, you know that. It's just that . . . I'm beginning to wish that he would! Have you seen the papers lately? Not the financial sections, Dan, but the society pages. 'What successful young banker has frequently been seen in the company of a recently married heiress?'" Eden quoted bitterly. "Do you realize that the gossip columnists are starting to link our names together? I detest having my life pawed over in public."

"You knew it would happen sooner or later; I'm just surprised that the press hounds held off this long. After all," Dan said half jokingly, half seriously, "we have been rather a twosome since your return. Even Tim has started asking me questions—I think he figures that when you and I are no more he can take my place. He's a little slow on the uptake, isn't he?"

"The nerve of him," Eden hissed. "How dare he assume that you and I are, ah . . ." Eden hesitated and glanced at Dan.

"Are lovers," Dan laughingly completed the sentence for her. "My dear Eden, half of New York thinks we are lovers—discreet lovers, but lovers nonetheless. Now, don't deny it, sweet, because I know that's precisely the impression you want to give everyone. The problem is, you wanted to get a little of your own back—which I don't hold against you—but you don't have the killer instinct when it comes to revenge."

"Is that what you think I wanted? Revenge?" Eden considered that for a moment before she asked, "Do you think I've been using you, Dan? If I have, I'm sorry."

"Lord, Eden, must you be so honest? I admire your candor but it doesn't do a thing for my ego." Dan picked up her left hand and studied her wedding rings carefully. "I haven't been used; I've enjoyed your company a great deal and I believe I even understand why Hugh hasn't tried to stop you from going out. I heard a rumor—from Jane, right before she disappeared—that you had done something outrageous. Then you suddenly married Hugh. I would guess that you were forced into the marriage, probably by Hugh, and this is your way of getting even. Am I right so far?"

Eden swallowed hard and looked away. "You know I can't answer you."

"*Won't* answer, you mean," Dan corrected. "Not that it makes any difference; I don't make a habit of prying into people's lives. What I'm trying to tell you, Eden, is that I've enjoyed our time together but I'll understand if you want to try to make something of your marriage."

"It's too late," Eden murmured helplessly. "Hugh and I only see each other in passing now. There are too many bad feelings on both sides."

"Then you'll make it up to each other," Dan said patiently. "You see, you really don't want to continue this way; you can't bear to inflict pain on anyone else. That's what I meant about your not having the killer instinct. Jane, for instance, never cared who she used or who she hurt as long as she got what she wanted. Would you like me to talk to Hugh to explain how things are between us—that we're just friends and nothing more?"

"No," Eden answered slowly. "If there's anything to salvage in my marriage it's up to me to find the way to do it. I truly don't want to spend the rest of my life the way I've spent the past year."

"Of course you don't and I don't blame you," Dan smiled. "For whatever it's worth, Eden, I think Hugh is just waiting for you to make the first move." He laughed suddenly. "Can you imagine what your reconciliation will do to the gossips in this town? That should put those old bats in their place."

They were still laughing when they left the restaurant, and when Dan went to hail a cab, Eden leaned weakly against the shadowed wall. People could say what they liked about Dan Miller—that he was cold, arrogant, had business before pleasure and occasionally instead of pleasure—but from the first time they had gone out together he had never pressured her for anything more than friendship. He seemed to understand how Eden felt without her having to explain it to him. *Revenge;* the word kept surfacing in her mind, and Eden closed her eyes. Perhaps she *had* meant to hurt Hugh, to pay him back for the way he had treated her before they were married.

"Did you see the way she carried on tonight?"

Eden started, looking around to see two women who were also waiting while their husbands went in search of transportation. The first woman spoke again and something in her voice caused Eden to retreat farther into the shadows. "I think it's disgraceful the way she flaunts her men right beneath our noses. Has she no shame?"

"Perhaps she has nothing to be ashamed of," the second woman said hesitantly. "Her husband apparently doesn't think—"

"Her husband is a fool! He should lock her up until she comes to her senses."

"Now don't be cruel, my dear. I'm sure Hugh Colter has his own reasons for wanting his wife out of the way." Eden pressed a hand over her mouth to hold back a cry of dismay. "Haven't you heard? Hugh hasn't been living the life of a monk these past months. Not only does he squire several women

around town but I understand—from a very reliable source—
that he visits that exclusive house on Trevor Street."

"No! I've heard things about that place and the woman who
runs it..." Eden stood rooted to the sidewalk as the women
disappeared into a carriage with their husbands and drove off.
Her head buzzed as she sought to regain her composure before
Dan returned.

Hugh was seeing other women. It shouldn't come as a surprise to her—she hadn't really thought that Hugh sat home
every evening, but still, she had felt better when she hadn't
known for certain that he was seeing other women. Fair was
fair, Eden realized, and yet...

"Eden? Come on, Eden, the cab is waiting. What are you
doing back here?"

"I—" Eden cleared her throat. "I'm sorry, Dan, I was thinking." She stared morosely out the window of the cab as it rolled
through the streets, unable to understand the different feelings
she was experiencing. Anger? Disappointment? Well, what did
I expect? she asked herself tartly. I haven't done anything to
make my husband want to stay home! Hugh had once said he
loved her, but Eden had allowed her bitterness over Neil's
betrayal to color her attitude toward love. She'd ventured nothing on her marriage. And now, almost a year later, what were
the chances that Hugh still cared for her? Had he found another
woman he could turn to, one who cared for him? "Dan," Eden
said quietly, "have you ever heard of Trevor Street?"

Dan's head shot up and he eyed her suspiciously. "Trevor
Street? Ah, yes, I think I've heard the name once or twice."

Eden's eyes narrowed at the evasive answer. "And?"

"And nothing. It's a street, that's all."

"Is it really," Eden retorted. "Tell me, Dan: How often does
a street come up in normal conversation? From the look on
your face, Trevor Street means something to you—just as it
did to the two women whose conversation I overheard while
I was waiting for you. They mentioned an 'exclusive house.'"

"Eden, I really wish you wouldn't ask any more questions,"
Dan protested.

"Why? What is it—some deep, dark secret place that only
a few people in New York are supposed to know about? I'll
tell you what," Eden suggested. "I'll guess what this mystery
place is, and if I'm right, just nod your head." Dan looked
unhappy but Eden ignored him. "A theater? No, of course not,

no owner in his right mind would want to keep a theater's location secret from the public. A restaurant? No, I suppose not. It can't be a tailor because I would have heard about it and besides, those women said that a woman owns the place. A gambling den? That would be kept quiet and it could be run by a woman." Eden chuckled as another thought crossed her mind. "It could be a den of iniquity, I guess; a place like that wouldn't want publicity, and a woman certainly would operate it." Dan suddenly went stiff and Eden's smile faded. "Oh, Dan, that can't be it."

"Sorry," Dan said candidly. "I told you not to ask questions, and now your delicate sensibilities have been offended. Oh, well, into the light of day, so to speak. So now you know where every man in New York likes to spend an entertaining evening once in a while. The, ah, house is run by a very personable woman named Libby, who is very, very discreet, and she wouldn't be happy if she knew that her place had lost its anonymity."

"I'm hardly in a position to go around giving this . . . this Libby person advertising," Eden snapped acidly. "You men and your damn prostitutes!" She drew a deep breath and carefully lowered her voice. "You needn't worry, Dan; believe me, I'm not going to mention this to a soul."

Dan politely declined Eden's invitation for a nightcap but Eden defiantly poured one for herself and carried it up to her bedroom. Now what? she wondered as she undressed and slipped a nightgown over her head. Eden pulled the pins from her hair and began brushing the pale strands distractedly. Looking in the mirror, she was suddenly reminded of her mother, sitting all alone in her bedroom while Locke made a night of it somewhere with his current mistress. Her knuckles whitened around the handle of the brush. I will not live like that, Eden told herself fiercely. I will not allow myself to be locked away and then taken out only when I'm needed. I want a marriage— a happy marriage—and I certainly don't want my husband frequenting a brothel!

Eden rose and began to pace the room, pausing occasionally to sip at her brandy. Now that she knew what she wanted, how was she going to get it? She could be a good wife to Hugh, she knew it! And it wasn't as if they were strangers; after all, they had lived together for several years, and Eden already knew most of his habits. They had enjoyed being together once;

they had the same interests, virtually the same likes and dis-
likes—surely it must be possible for them to try to make the
marriage work. Eden found herself standing in front of the door
to Hugh's bedroom, and she nervously bit her lip. He would
be shocked if she asked to come in, but then, maybe that was
part of the problem; maybe she was just too damn predictable.

With one hand around her glass, her other hand was almost
to the door before Eden snatched it back. Oh, Lord! What if
he had a woman in there? I'm being silly, she told herself.
Hugh would never do such a thing. But what if he weren't
there? Eden swallowed, and before she could lose her courage
again she quickly knocked twice on the wood.

"Come in." So he was there. Eden said a quick prayer and
opened the door. Hugh was in bed, reading, and he looked up
and smiled as if seeing his wife in his bedroom were the most
natural thing in the world. "Hello, dear heart, I thought I heard
you come in. How was the play?"

"The play," Eden repeated absently, unable to tear her eyes
away from the sight of Hugh's bare chest. She had never seen
him undressed before and somehow she had expected him to
look . . . different, less imposing. Neil had been the same height
as Hugh, possibly just as strong, but Hugh's build was massive,
imposing, and when he reached over to put the book on a table
Eden could see that the muscles of his arms and chest were
still firm and supple. But what fascinated her was the black,
curly hair that formed a triangle on the upper part of his chest
and slowly changed into a dark trail that abruptly disappeared
beneath the covers at Hugh's waist. Hugh was looking at her
questioningly and Eden forced herself to remember what he
had said. "Oh! the play. It was fine. Dan took me to dinner
afterward."

"Good; I'm glad you enjoyed yourself." Eden was still
standing uncertainly in the doorway with the light from her
bedroom turning the nightgown she wore into transparent noth-
ingness. Hugh shifted restively as his body responded to the
sight. "Would you like to come in and sit down? You can't be
very comfortable standing there."

"You're sure you don't mind? I mean, it is quite late and
you said you wanted to get to the office early."

"I don't mind," Hugh assured her, then caught sight of the
glass in her hand. "If you're having a nightcap, I believe I'll
join you. But first, would you mind turning around?"

"I beg your pardon?" Eden asked in confusion.

Hugh laughed softly as he sat up. "I may act like a refined gentleman, but there are a few things I refuse to give up for conventional society. One thing is the cigarettes that some of my friends find so distasteful, and another is the comfort and freedom of sleeping in the raw. So unless you want to see your husband naked as the day he was born, I suggest you turn around, my dear."

"Oh!" Eden turned bright red and whirled around to face the wall.

"There now," Hugh said a moment later as he took the glass from Eden's hand. "What are you drinking? Brandy?"

"Yes, please." Her eyes followed Hugh as he poured their drinks, admiring the way the quilted robe of royal blue satin clung to Hugh's broad shoulders and accented his silver hair. An odd warmth stole through her veins and before Hugh could catch her staring, Eden curled up in one of the huge armchairs that flanked the cold fireplace and tucked her feet beneath her. "Did Ian stay long?"

Hugh handed Eden her glass and took the chair opposite her. "He left about two hours ago, so I thought I'd try to catch up on some of my reading. What about Daniel? I expected you to invite him in for a nightcap."

The scent of Hugh's cologne teased her senses, making Eden acutely aware of how little physical distance actually separated them. "I really wasn't in the mood for his company." Eden swirled her brandy thoughtfully. "Dan and I aren't going to be seeing each other anymore."

"Why is that?" Hugh asked casually, although his eyes lit up at her words. "I thought you got along quite well."

"We do," Eden said hastily. "It's just that . . . well, it isn't quite right, is it?"

"I guess not. I suppose Daniel will start looking for a wife now." Hugh watched Eden closely for any sign of jealousy on her part. "Jane's running away must have hit him pretty hard."

Eden sighed. Neither she nor Hugh felt comfortable in this situation, that was obvious. "It was a shock at first but he's adjusted. Dan is a survivor; he doesn't let anything interfere too much in his life." Eden wet her lips. "Hugh, have you given any thought to . . ."

Her voice faded away and Hugh frowned at her troubled

expression. "To what, dear heart? Come on, now; something's bothering you, so you might as well tell me."

I can't, Eden thought desperately. I can't just walk in here and blurt out that I want to start living as husband and wife. "There are two things, actually. Meg's wedding is this weekend and I haven't found a gift for her yet. Would you mind coming with me tomorrow to help me pick out something? I have a few things in mind but I'd like your opinion. I could stop by your office and maybe we could have lunch together before we shop."

"That sounds fine," Hugh agreed. "What else?"

Eden's hands were shaking and she quickly set her glass down before Hugh could notice. "I know you were planning something for our anniversary, but I was wondering if you would mind terribly if we didn't have a formal celebration."

"Is there something else you'd rather do? I haven't made any definite arrangements, but I did assume we would be able to celebrate together."

"Of course we will," Eden exclaimed. "But I would prefer something private, something that just the two of us can share. You understand what I mean, don't you?"

"Eden," Hugh began, then shook his head. It was rapidly becoming impossible to concentrate on the conversation. The creamy skin exposed by the plunging V of her neckline fascinated Hugh, as did the way Eden's breasts jutted against the material of her nightgown. Hugh's fingers tightened around his glass as he struggled to ignore the desire which tripped his heart. She obviously had no idea how difficult it was for him to control himself when they were alone. If she had, Eden never would have come into his room clad only in a nightgown. "All right; if it will make you happy we'll plan on a nice, simple celebration." Hugh rose and pulled Eden to her feet. "And now it's time we both went to bed—if you're going to drag me around the city tomorrow afternoon we're both going to need our rest."

Eden tried to return his teasing smile but for some reason her lips refused to cooperate. Hugh walked with her to the door, kissed her lightly on the cheek, then gently but firmly closed the door behind her.

Confused, Eden stood in the middle of her room. Uncertain whether her visit had affected Hugh in any way, Eden swore she would never make such a blatant overture to him again.

If he loved her, Hugh wouldn't have pretended that he didn't know why she had come to his room. If he loved her . . . Tears pricked at her eyelids and she gave in to them. Let him have his women, she didn't care! She had survived all these months without a husband and she would manage quite nicely from now on as well. It wasn't as if she'd chosen Hugh, Eden thought petulantly, but he *was* her husband and they owed each other some sort of affection.

Eden threw herself onto the bed, refusing to listen to the tiny inner voices that were disagreeing violently with her definition of marriage . . . and love. She thought she had loved Neil—but wasn't it possible that she had only been infatuated with him and that his bringing her passionate nature to the surface had only magnified her feelings for him? Eden sat up and began drawing her fingers through her hair. She did miss that aspect in her marriage. At first it hadn't bothered her—it had been, in fact, almost a relief that a display of desire wasn't required of her—but recently she had become more aware of her body and her own desires. Any number of men had gallantly offered her their services, but she had turned them all down. She didn't feel comfortable with the idea of going from lover to lover in a series of mindless affairs without some kind of emotional commitment. But would she be able to make an emotional commitment to Hugh?

Questions and doubts nagged at Eden throughout the night, waking her whenever she fell asleep; and when she was too exhausted to awaken, the questions turned into frightening dreams in which the lonely years stretched endlessly ahead of her.

Eden woke with a smothered cry, relaxing only when she saw the sunlight flooding her room. It took her a few minutes to compose herself, only to find that last night's events were still weighing heavily upon her. She glanced down at her ring and frowned. There were answers to be found, she knew. If it was impossible to ask Hugh, then why not someone close to him? Not Ian, because Hugh would surely find out, but there had to be someone else. Eden's eyes lit up and she leaped from the bed and searched frantically through her wardrobe.

It took Eden just fifteen minutes to dress, during which time she also ordered Hugh's carriage and driver, and after thirty minutes and only some minor bullying on her part Eden found herself at the front door of a large house on Trevor Street.

Her knock was answered by a petite brunette—wearing a gaily colored day dress instead of the transparent nightdress Eden had expected—who smiled but eyed Eden suspiciously. Without inviting her in, she inquired, "Can I help you?"

The temptation to turn and run was overwhelming but Eden stood her ground. "I—I'd like to see Libby, please."

"So would a lot of people." The girl's eyes narrowed. "Is she expecting you?"

"No." Eden smiled self-consciously and held out a slip of paper. "But if you would give her my card I wouldn't mind waiting."

"Your card," the girl snickered. "Aren't you the one for putting on airs—oh, my!" The startled girl looked from the card to Eden. "You're Mrs. Colter! Lord, ma'am, we don't want any trouble here, so I think it would be best if you would leave."

"I don't want any trouble either," Eden said gravely. "All I want is to speak with Libby; I promise there won't be any kind of scene. Will you at least give her my card?"

The girl hesitated, then nodded and motioned Eden inside, where she was ushered into a drawing room. "I'm not saying Libby will see you, you understand, but I'll tell her you're here."

"Thank you." The girl left and Eden wandered about the room inspecting the furnishings. All the furniture was conservative, which was another surprise to Eden. She had expected something garish, tasteless, but this room could fit into any of the homes she had ever visited and no one would know the difference.

"I'm Libby." Eden spun back to the doorway and found a tall, red-haired woman about Hugh's age regarding her defensively. Libby tossed the calling card onto a table. "You don't have to introduce yourself; your card did that for you, Mrs. Colter."

Eden stared at the other woman in astonishment. Libby's red hair was a flaming crown above her fair complexion and, Eden noted with a pang of envy, Libby's figure possessed curves which made the word 'generous' seem an insult. The intelligent green eyes were snapping impatiently and Eden hurriedly found her voice. "I'm pleased to meet you, Libby—"

"I'll bet," Libby snorted and sat down on one of the chairs.

"I'd ask you to have a seat but I don't think you'll be staying that long. What do you want, Mrs. Colter?"

"I . . . " Eden hesitated. "I would like very much to speak with whichever of your women my husband . . . visits. Can that be arranged?"

Laughing, Libby took a cigarette from the silver case at her elbow and lit it. "Are you sure your busy schedule allows time for *all* those private interviews? And why, in any case, would you want to talk with a woman who commands your husband's attention?"

"It's personal," Eden said softly, "and I'd rather not discuss it with anyone else. Is what I ask possible?"

"Why should I do you any favors?" the older woman scoffed. "It's people like you who are all for running people like me out of town. Who sent you here? One of those groups of dried-up, sharp-tongued old cows?"

"No! No one sent me here!" Eden walked to the window and stared past the well-tended lawn while she struggled to bring herself under control. She never should have come here; it had been a terrible mistake to think any of these women would help her. But she'd be damned if she'd let Libby have the satisfaction of driving her out. "What I said is the truth; I simple want to talk to the lady . . . or ladies my husband has been seeing. Surely no harm can come of that."

"That depends. One of my girls was killed by one of you self-righteous wives, so if that's what you're planning, you can forget it."

Eden smiled in spite of herself and turned back to face Libby. "I assure you that's not the case. I can't even bring myself to kill a mouse and I loathe them. If you like, you can search me."

Libby appeared to relax a bit and she waved a hand to the chair across from her. "Why don't you sit down, Mrs. Colter. I'm having some coffee brought in in a few minutes."

"Thank you, that's very kind of you." Eden pulled off her gloves and laid them aside. "Your home isn't at all what I expected."

"Home? Hell, girl, this is a bordello and we both know it, so don't pussyfoot around the subject." The coffee arrived, brought by the same girl who had met Eden at the door, and Libby waited until the girl had left before resuming the conversation. She handed Eden a cup and then offered her the silver case. "A habit I picked up years ago. Care to try one?"

"I've never tried such a thing," Eden said in a shocked voice, eyeing the row of cigarettes suspiciously.

"I know." Libby smiled for the first time. "Hugh told me. Seems you don't have any bad habits, so maybe you should start one, just to keep up with the rest of us fallen angels." She watched as Eden copied her actions, then chuckled when Eden started to choke on the smoke. "Don't worry, it just takes some getting used to."

Eden's eyes watered horribly but she finally managed to gasp, "Why are you doing this?"

Libby sipped at her coffee before answering. "I'm not doing it to embarrass you, if that's what you mean. I guess I wanted to catch you off guard. Because, Mrs. Colter, I'm the one Hugh sees when he comes here, the only one, so whatever those questions were that you wanted to ask, I suggest you get to them."

Dumbfounded, Eden simply stared at Libby, unable to avoid her bright, all-knowing green eyes. She wasn't prepared for such directness and she floundered for the right words. "I don't know how to begin—it feels odd to be talking to a complete stranger about my husband, but I don't have any other choice. You see...I...Hugh and I, we're not exactly happy together. I mean, we are happy but not as happy as we could be, I think, and I'd like to try to change that....Oh, Lord, I'm not making any sense at all." Eden wet her lips and tried again. "I came here because I need to know if I can win Hugh back. I wondered if he had fallen in love with you." Eden dropped her eyes to her lap and braced herself for what must surely be Libby's reply.

"Hugh Colter in love with me?" Libby began laughing so hard that she had to set her cup down. "Mrs. Colter, it's very hard for a man to fall in love with someone else when he's constantly thinking about his wife. Lord, girl, is that what you thought? Who told you about this place? Not Hugh, surely."

Eden shook her head. "I overheard a conversation last night. At first I didn't believe it, but I can't very well blame him for it, not after the way I've carried on since we were married. But I haven't been unfaithful to Hugh, Libby, I hope you believe that."

"It doesn't matter whether I believe you or not," Libby

stated frankly. "It's what Hugh believes that's important. Let me explain something to you. Hugh and I go back a long way, almost as far back as he and Ian. Hugh brought me back here from the West. He bought my way out of a house where the girls only lasted six months, a year at the most. He bought me this house, even though he wanted me to try a 'respectable' trade, and gave me the deed without batting an eye. But, Mrs. Colter, romance is not part of *our* relationship. Why do you think Hugh lost his head when he found out about you and that fellow? Why did Hugh stand by you and marry you?"

"You don't understand," Eden murmured. "He wanted to hurt me, punish me."

"That's natural, isn't it? Hugh loved you for a long time, yet he couldn't do anything about it. What do you think it did to him to find out about you and your lover the way he did? He was hurt and he wanted to hurt someone back. I'm not saying what Hugh did was right, but I think you should at least try to understand how he felt. Hugh told me all about it the day he moved out of the house. Ian and I had our hands full that night; Hugh drank himself into a blind rage and was determined to track down the man and kill him. Well, we talked him out of that idea when he sobered up, but there wasn't a damn thing we could do about the way he treated you." Libby thoughtfully drummed her fingers on the arm of her chair. "Men are odd creatures; they can visit a place like this and expect their wives not to think anything of it, but let the woman they love stray from the straight and narrow and they're out for blood. I've often wondered what would happen if there was a place like this that was strictly for women—that would set the men on their ears!

"I'll tell you the truth, Mrs. Colter, I don't like you very much, not after the way you've treated Hugh. Are you so perfect that you don't have to forgive anyone else for their mistakes? From what I've heard you've been carrying on like a selfish, spoiled brat, and I happen to think Hugh deserves a lot better than you. You've treated him like a damned eunuch so he comes here to feel like a man, and now *you* come crying to *me* because your marriage isn't working the way you want it to. It's time you grew up, little girl, and stopped thinking that you're the only person in the world who's ever been hurt—or you're going to end up all alone." Libby stood up and walked to the door. "Hugh tells me you're a bright girl; myself, I can't see it, but if you're as smart as Hugh seems to think, you'll open your eyes and see just how much of a man you married. Personally, I don't think you're woman enough to handle him. Now if you'll excuse me, Mrs. Colter, I've had my say and I feel better for it so I'd like to finish the beauty sleep you interrupted. You'll have to show yourself out. Good day, Mrs. Colter."

The indignity of being dismissed as if she were nothing more than a maid—and by a common whore at that!—irked Eden all during the ride to Hugh's warehouse. Who is Libby to tell me that I don't understand Hugh? Eden thought indignantly. I know him! My God, I've lived with the man for years, I ought to know him well enough by now! Eden's eyes turned flintly with anger as she glared out the window. Spoiled brat indeed! Was it so selfish to want to be happy? That was what everyone wanted; no one wanted to be miserable. Was it so wrong for her to want what most people simply took for granted?

*But you're buying your happiness at Hugh's expense.* The thought hit Eden so suddenly that it made her gasp. A sick feeling washed over her and she pressed her fingers over her mouth. She had simply assumed that Hugh didn't mind the way they were living; he had his freedom and she had hers, with neither demanding too much of the other. Not once in the past year had she spared a thought for what her husband had been going through. All the publicity she had received when she had started appearing in public with other men, all the nights she had blithely sailed out of the house, leaving Hugh home alone . . . how had that made him feel? And she had been selfish enough to complain that her husband didn't care for *her!*

Hugh's office was deserted, so Eden wandered back outside and walked down to the wharf. Men were scurrying about unloading cargo from a ship and transferring it to the warehouse. From the size of the packing crates, Eden guessed that some of the teak furniture Hugh had ordered on their honeymoon had finally arrived. Eden smiled to herself; the pieces were lovely and should sell quickly. A shout went up from the men who were struggling to lift a particularly large crate onto one of the wagons, and Eden shielded her eyes from the glare of the sun. The crate was teetering perilously on the edge of the wagon bed, and several men dropped what they were doing to lend a hand. The crate slipped a bit more and Eden gasped when a voice she recognized as Hugh's called for another rope and more men. Eden saw Hugh then, his face set in grim, determined lines as he leaped into the wagon bed with an agility she had not known he possessed, wrapped the rope around the crate and wound the ends around his hands. The muscles across Hugh's back and arms knotted under his shirt as he strained against the rope, and slowly the crate started to right itself until it settled into place with a sudden lurch that nearly pinned Hugh against the wagon.

The men cheered and slapped each other on the shoulders as Hugh jumped back to the ground, and Eden slowly expelled her pent-up breath. Look at him, an inner voice prompted disquietingly. Look at him as if you were seeing him for the first time. See the man instead of the guardian. Stunned by this revelation, Eden found herself walking toward Hugh, uncertain what she would do or say once she reached him but unwilling to turn back for fear she might lose what she was only now discovering. Hugh's back was to her as he checked off more crates that were being unloaded and Eden touched him lightly on the arm to draw his attention.

"Are you all right?"

Hugh spun around so quickly that Eden was thrown off balance and he grabbed her around the waist to steady her. "Eden! Dear heart, what are you doing on the docks by yourself? I've told you before, it's not safe . . ."

Eden barely heard what he was saying; she was far too busy studying the face that was as familiar to her as her own and yet, because of Libby's accusations, now was strangely foreign. Odd how she hadn't noticed before that Hugh's eyebrows were black instead of silver like his hair; or that his eyes were a brilliant crystal blue that seemed to dance with a life of their own even when he was at peace with himself and the world. "Are you all right?" she repeated dazedly. "I saw what nearly happened with that crate."

"What?" Hugh asked impatiently. "Oh, that. Yes, I'm fine."

"I'm sure," Eden said dryly as she reached out and fingered one of the strips on his torn shirt. "Let me see your hands, please."

"They're dirty, too, if that's what you're looking for," Hugh growled, but he let Eden inspect them anyway, wincing slightly when she touched a raw patch of skin.

"Will you hush," she retorted. "You scared me out of ten years with your damned heroics, so the least you can do is let me see what kind of damage you've done to yourself."

Hugh's mouth snapped closed and he watched Eden curiously as she bent over his hands. What had gotten into her today? The way she had looked at him—as if she hadn't seen him before. Hugh watched her long, slender fingers turn back the cuffs of his sleeves and pause over the rope burns across his palms. Something was going on, he was certain of that; it wasn't like Eden to touch anyone so unself-consciously in public. How magnificent it would be if they were only someplace private and he could persuade her to try a less clinical examination—but unfortunately Hugh knew Eden well enough to be sure she would balk at that idea. "Well, doctor, will I live?"

"Never mind," Eden said in her sternest voice. "I thought owners didn't work on the docks."

"This one does," Hugh informed her. "Do you have any idea how useless I feel when I sit behind a desk shuffling papers?"

"Not really." Eden tilted her head back and smiled up at him, her gray eyes soft and warm. "But if you're not careful I'll come down and work on the docks beside you someday. I might even start a new trend—pants and open shirts for the hardworking woman."

Still confused by Eden's behavior, Hugh nonetheless grinned at her gentle teasing. "Minx! You were taught better manners than that."

"I was taught different manners," Eden corrected. "Not necessarily better ones. Would you be horribly disappointed to see me dressed that way?"

"I don't have to answer that." Hugh placed a hand under her elbow and steered her back to the office. "I keep a clean shirt here just in case. Give me ten minutes and I'll be ready for our lunch date."

Eden waited in the outer office while Hugh changed, taking advantage of the moment to check her appearance in the small hand mirror she carried in her reticule. It was up to her to make an effort, she thought once more as she carefully tucked a wisp of hair back into place. What had been between them as guardian and ward had been good—they had trusted each other, respected each other and Eden could see now that she had loved Hugh. Not in the same way she had loved Neil but . . . Eden sighed and put away the mirror. Emotions couldn't be forced, she knew that, but she *had* cared for Hugh once. Perhaps she could again.

"Eden?" She followed Hugh's voice through the door and found him looking at her sheepishly. "I can't seem to manage the collar button. Would you mind?" Laughing, Eden shook her head, and Hugh rested one hip on the corner of his desk to make it easier for her to reach. "And now, Eden, would you mind telling me what has happened?"

"Nothing." Eden glanced at him sharply before returning her attention to the stubborn button. "Why do you ask?"

Hugh covered both her hands with his left and cupped her chin with his right. "I may be approaching my dotage but I'm not there yet. Something is going on inside that pretty head of yours and I'd like to know what it is." Eden returned his stare silently for a full minute before the intensity of his gaze made her look away, suddenly disconcerted. "What is it, Eden? Have you overdrawn your account? Or is there a piece of jewelry that you'd like as a gift?" Hugh's voice lowered to a deep rumble. "If that's all it is, you know you don't have to play this sort of game with me. I'll be more than happy to buy you the trinket or cover the debt. All you have to do is ask, and I'll do whatever you want; but for God's sake, Eden, don't treat me as if I'm some damn gelding who doesn't notice the pretty filly prancing around him. It plays merry hell with my nerves."

"I'm sorry." Eden withdrew her hands and stood back. "I didn't realize. You never said anything, so I just assumed—"

"What was I supposed to say?" Hugh demanded, realizing there were many things he had been wanting to say to Eden for a long time. "You've made your feelings about our marriage quite clear from the start and it's obvious you haven't forgiven me for the things I said and did when the walls came down around our ears. Eden, dear heart, you wanted your freedom after we were married and I wanted you to have it. As a result we've lost everything there once was between us. There *was* something very good, even if you refuse to admit it—but now we are, at best, strangers. Do you realize that our way of life wouldn't be tolerated in any other marriage? We act like we approve of each other's affairs—even encourage them. I know twenty-four years is quite a gap between our ages, but I was hoping that, given time, you would stop noticing—"

"You're the one who can't let go of that bone," Eden cried. Hugh's apparent unwillingness to understand what she was trying to offer goaded her into anger. "Whenever we meet people, if they raise their eyebrows ever so slightly, *you're* the one who brings up that awful line about robbing the cradle. You seem to think that you're inferior to younger men, and I just don't understand why you feel that way."

"Oh, come on, Eden!" Hugh exploded. All the frustration of the past months boiled up inside him and he slammed his hand against the desk top. "Don't tell me you *enjoy* being seen with a man who is old enough to be your father! Aren't you just the least bit embarrassed that your friends aren't even sure what to say to me?"

"No more than you are when *your* friends look to you before they offer me so much as a glass of sherry," Eden shot back. "Can't you get it through your thick Irish head that I don't give a damn about your age?"

"Well, I do!" Hugh roared. "I can't compete with Dan or Tim, and you know it. I can't dance until two or three in the morning and be bright and chipper the next day. I can't—"

Eden stamped her foot impatiently. "To hell with what you can't do! How do you know I *want* to dance until four in the morning? You've never even asked me!"

"When have I had the chance?" Hugh lost the last shred of control over his temper and with one sweep of his arm sent the contents of the desk top flying across the room. "You've been gone so damn much I feel like I married a ghost! You've had more men courting you after your wedding than most girls do beforehand. My favorite pastime lately has been figuring out exactly how I'm going to kill your newest boyfriend. I swear to God, Eden, you're driving me crazy!"

"You . . . you . . ." Eden sputtered. Never in her life had she been so angry that words deserted her. In a blind rage she kicked out wildly at a chair and sent it crashing against the wall. "You want to trade lists of indiscretions? Let's try yours first—we'll start at the bottom and work up, which means we'll start with that red-haired *fille de joie* of yours. Don't you *dare* tell me what it's like to be married to a ghost. You haven't exactly been chained to the hearth. Just remember, you were the one who ordered separate bedrooms on our honeymoon; you're the one who never takes me anywhere! What do you expect me to do while you waltz off to Trevor Street? Sit by the fire and do needlepoint? From what I hear, you don't have to worry about growing old because you're going to wear yourself out long before then!" Unexpectedly Eden's chin began to tremble as she realized she sounded exactly like a jealous wife. "Hugh, you make me so mad I could . . . I could . . . oh, damn, I hate women who cry."

Before Hugh could stop her, Eden turned and ran from the warehouse, past the docks and the waiting carriage, out onto the busy street. Shouting her name, ignoring the stares he drew from passersby, Hugh raced after Eden for three blocks, but whenever he seemed to be closing in on her she either picked up her skirts and managed to put more distance between them, or she somehow disappeared briefly into the crowd. Just as Hugh rounded a corner he caught a glimpse of Eden entering a cab. Swearing—both at himself and Eden—he fumed his way back to his office, where he found Ian waiting for him.

"A grand show," Ian chuckled as Hugh stamped by him. "What the devil happened here? It looks like you two fought a war in this place. Don't tell me you finally came to your senses and told your wife where her place is?"

"Shut up," Hugh growled irritably. He threw himself into a chair and closed his eyes. "I have to see Libby. Do you want to come along?"

Ian shook his head. "Too early in the day for me but I hope you enjoy yourself." Hugh looked at him menacingly and Ian shrugged. "Sorry; I see you're in no mood for a joke."

"I'm in no mood for *anything*," Hugh emphasized. "Eden knows about Libby."

"What!" Ian's eyes bulged. "How could she?"

"I don't know how, but she does. I made a perfect jackass out of myself, telling Eden I didn't care for her going out with other men and all the while she knew about Libby. Lord, what a day."

"I take it Eden doesn't approve of your friendship with Libby." To Hugh's chagrin, Ian started to laugh. "I'd give a week's pay to find out who had the nerve to tell her—he's a braver man than I."

"What makes you so sure a man told her," Hugh said thoughtfully. "It could have been a woman, maybe even Libby herself. She's never been exactly fond of Eden."

"Either way, if this is Eden's reaction, then I'd say Eden

isn't as indifferent to you as she pretends to be." Ian's expression altered. "It could be she's jealous."

"Don't be absurd. Why would Eden be jealous?"

Ian grinned and helped himself to a cigar from the box on Hugh's desk. "Maybe she doesn't like her husband fooling around with another woman. Or maybe she's decided that marriage to a big, good-looking Irishman like yourself is just too good to pass up. How do I know what Eden is thinking? Why don't you ask her?"

When Hugh returned home early that evening he learned that Eden hadn't been back all day. To keep up a pretense of normalcy in front of Simmons, Hugh followed his usual routine, changing his clothes and then dining alone. Where was she? he wondered anxiously as he left the table and retired to the study. He should never have lost his temper; Eden always had hated arguments. She had told him once that even seeing two people fight made her feel sick inside. So why had she stood her ground when he started raising his voice, returning blow for blow? Hugh took Eden's card from his pocket and studied it. Of all the stupid things for her to do—leaving her calling card at a bordello! What if someone had seen it before he had? He'd asked Libby the same question, but she had been decidedly closemouthed about the whole affair and had told him bluntly to go home to his wife. Hugh picked up the book he had been reading and tried to concentrate on the words, but it was useless. The scene in the office kept flashing in front of him, jarring him away from Bryon's poetry.

Maybe he should try to find her—he didn't like the thought of Eden wandering around by herself at night. His hand was on the doorknob before he checked himself. She could have gone anywhere. He didn't have the faintest idea where to start his search. If she were just walking or riding around the city he would never be able to find her, and if she were visiting Meg, he certainly didn't want to barge in on her there. But at large in the city she could be in danger—the way she dressed, the way she carried herself, the way she spoke, everything she did made it clear that she was wealthy. Something could have happened to her already; she could be lying in a dark alley bleeding to death and no one would find her until morning.

"Ridiculous," Hugh growled at the silent room. "She's lived in New York all her life; she can take care of herself." But when eleven o'clock came and went, he rejected the idea of going to bed and poured himself another drink. If Eden wasn't home by midnight he'd go out and look for her, and when he found her . . .

His temper was starting to rise again and Hugh firmly tamped it down. The last thing he wanted was to have another fight with Eden when she finally showed up. Hugh folded himself back into his chair and, picking up his book, began to read aloud:

> "In secret we met—
> In silence I grieve,
> That thy heart could forget,
> Thy spirit deceive."

Hugh ran a hand angrily through his hair. Of all the poems in the book, he had to end up reading this one.

> "If—"

Hugh's voice caught and as he cleared his throat another voice took up the verse.

> "If I should meet thee
> After long years,
> How should I greet thee?
> With silence and tears."

Eden stood watching him from the doorway, her face half hidden by shadows.

Just looking at Eden made Hugh's heart lurch painfully and the anger that had been building ebbed away. "I was beginning to worry," he said softly. "May I ask where you've been?"

A flicker of a smile passed over Eden's face. "I had to buy Meg and Kevin a wedding gift, remember? After that . . . I don't know, I just hired a taxi and rode around the city. I wanted time to think about what happened this morning. It frightened me, Hugh."

"I'm sorry, Eden. I shouldn't have lost my temper."

"Oh, no." Eden moved quickly to the center of the room. "You don't understand—it wasn't you who frightened me, it was I. I've never been that angry before, or if I have I've always been able to control it. But today . . . it was like something snapped inside me. Hugh, I wanted to throw things!"

"As I recall you nearly did," Hugh chuckled. "I'm using what was once a chair as kindling for my stove." Eden's distress was so obvious that he stopped teasing her at once. "Dear heart, it's all right; we had a fight, that's all. Married people do fight, you know. It's the most natural thing in the world; two people can't live together day after day without getting on each others' nerves eventually."

"But to be so violent," Eden shuddered. "And what you said doesn't really apply to us, does it? I mean, you and I are in a unique situation."

"So we are." Hugh studied Eden as she moved restlessly about the room.

"I went to my parents' house today," she said finally. "I spent most of the evening there, staring at their portraits, wondering why they ever married in the first place. I ran across my mother's diary in her bedroom. I always knew my father was cold and ruthless, but until I read her diary I didn't know just how cruel he could be. Can you imagine how she must have felt when Grandfather Jessup told her that Locke Thackery would cancel his gambling debts if she agreed to marry him? Can you imagine marrying a man you don't even know and then moving away from everything familiar? But do you know what struck me as I read that diary? Not once did she blame anyone else for what happened to her—she didn't even accuse Grandfather Jessup of ruining her life. She was a remarkable lady trying to make the best of an intolerable situation, not allowing herself to become bitter over her life."

Eden looked at Hugh, her gray eyes large and sad. "I could never understand why you spent so much time at our house. I knew you and Father did business together, but even to a child it seemed odd that you would devote a great deal of your life to another man's wife and child. Mother loved you very much."

"No more than I loved her." Hugh's lips pressed together in a tight line. "Adria was an important part of my life. She taught me to appreciate art and literature—after she taught me to read, that is. I can't expect you to understand how it was between us, Eden; we loved each other but there was never anything . . . physical between us. We could enjoy being together without that side of it. Maybe that increased what we felt for each other, I don't know, but from the very first we both knew that an affair was out of the question."

"As it is with us?" Eden smiled faintly at his sharp look. "There's quite a resemblance between Mother and myself. Even physically—I never noticed it until today, when I compared her portrait to what I saw in the mirror. Is that why you wanted to marry me. Because I remind you of Mother? Please be honest," she said quickly before Hugh could answer. "I know that when you care deeply for someone those feelings don't simply disappear, and I think I'll be able to understand that you settled for me because you couldn't have Mother."

Hugh closed the book with a snap and began to fill his pipe. "You're asking a lot of me, Eden. You're prying into a part of my life—of me—that I've never discussed with anyone else, which is a liberty I've never taken with you. Whatever happened ten years ago has no bearing on you. However"— Hugh laid aside his pipe and fixed his sapphire gaze on Eden— "when you came to live with me you were a child, Adria's child, and that gave me two very good reasons to care about you. What I feel for you now has nothing to do with Adria. That, dear heart, for whatever it's worth, is the absolute truth."

Eden stared at the polished floor beneath her feet. "Thank you. I had to know."

"And you," Hugh asked carefully. "Now I have the right to ask. Do you still love that man? Honestly."

The question caught her unprepared and Eden went weak with shock. Hugh had never mentioned Neil, but how could she possibly refuse to answer him? "I don't know anymore," Eden said in a hushed voice. "A year ago I would have said yes without a qualm, but now . . . I really don't know."

"I see. Well, I can't say that comes as a surprise." Hugh massaged the tense muscles in the back of his neck. "What is it you want, Eden? A divorce? I'm sure you wouldn't have any difficulty in obtaining one—I won't contest it."

"You've missed my point." Eden spread her hands help-lessly. "I meant what I said this morning, Hugh; your age doesn't matter to me. What does matter to me is the fact that you and I made a commitment to each other. I know the cir-cumstances were unusual, even unpleasant, and I know that neither of us really meant our marriage vows, but that doesn't make our marriage less real.

"I've been doing a lot of thinking about us and about what

I've done to you." Eden took a deep breath before continuing. "I don't like the way we've been living, Hugh, and I hate what I've become over the past months. I realize now that I've been acting like a spiteful, spoiled child, refusing to acknowledge that I was creating problems, not solving them. If it's possible, if you would be willing, I'd like for us to try to work out our differences. Do you think we can?"

"Do you love me at all, Eden?" Hugh asked softly. "We're not discussing a business merger. If this doesn't work out we'll both lose a lot more than just money."

"I know that." Eden seated herself on the footstool in front of him. "Hugh, I respect you and I admire you and I like you, but I'm not in love with you. Oh, Hugh, don't look that way." Eden cried softly at his pained expression. "The last thing I want is to hurt you again; but I don't want to lie to you either; that would only make things worse. It doesn't mean I won't learn to love you. You're right—we would be taking a chance by trying to make our marriage work, but I think it's worth the gamble. We can't spend the rest of our lives bitter and angry and filled with regrets, wondering if we ever could have been happy."

"All I've ever wanted for you was happiness—preferably with me, but if that was impossible, then at the very least with a man you cared for." Hugh framed Eden's face between his hands. "If you want to take a chance on me, then there are some things you should know about me, about my past. You need to know how different we are. You have the right to know what kind of a man I am before you decide to spend your life as my wife."

"I know what kind of a man you are," Eden protested. "I know what you did, how you lived before you came to New York. You were a soldier—"

"I killed for a living, Eden, and I defiled the dead." Hugh held her face so she could not look away. "Did you know that?"

"You were a soldier," she repeated softly, afraid of what she saw in Hugh's eyes. "It was your duty to kill; the war forced you and thousands of others to kill. There's no shame in that."

"I'm not talking about the war. Before that, years before, when the Indians were still strong enough to fight against the white men invading their land." Hugh rose and walked to the window and stared into the darkness. "You can't imagine what it was like then. No place was safe, not even the army forts, although you stood a better chance of surviving an attack there than anywhere else. I can't blame the Indians for wanting the settlers to leave; I'd feel the same way if the land that had been mine for centuries was suddenly taken away by strangers who refused to let me live or hunt there any longer. But the fear, Eden, the fear was always there for us. A strange sound at night, a rifle shot—our first thought was an Indian attack, and we'd seen enough victims to forget that we were the invaders and that the Indians feared us as much as we feared them."

The demons that had first begun to haunt Hugh twenty years before returned with a sickening clarity and his mouth and throat went dry. "Everyone screamed for the army to exterminate the Indians or, if we couldn't do that, to drive them onto reservations where they could be watched. I was a good soldier, a good scout, too, with Ian's help. I followed orders, I . . ." His hands clenched into tight fists. "We set up an ambush for a band of Apaches who had massacred several farmers and their families. We waited all night for them high up in a ravine. I remember it rained that night and we didn't dare build a fire because the Apaches would spot it. A few hours after dawn they rode into the ravine. From my position they looked like toys, like dolls dressed up to look like the enemy." Behind him Eden closed her eyes, not wanting to hear what Hugh was telling her. "The captain waited until the entire band was in the ravine and then he gave the signal to fire. The Indians never had a chance. I think the entire action took less than ten minutes, but it felt like ten hours. Horses screamed and went down, thrashing their legs and pinning their riders. You couldn't help but hit something if you aimed in their general direction. When it was over, we were ordered down to make sure there were no survivors. 'Put the bastards out of their misery' was the way the officers put it.

"God help me, Eden, I'd thought they all were warriors, but there were women and children as well. I'd never killed before, and seeing what we'd done"—Hugh drew a hand across his eyes—"I found a woman still clutching her baby—"

"Don't," Eden said in a strained voice. "I don't want to hear this, Hugh."

"Ah, but you must, Eden love." Hugh turned and smiled grimly. Eden nodded her consent and Hugh turned back to the window. "Contrary to what you may have heard, no one ever

led him from the room and up the stairs. "I'll need help with my dress." She smiled gently. "You're not shy, are you?"

Hugh closed the door to his bedroom and watched nervously as Eden began to unpin her hair. "No, not shy." His hands were shaking and Hugh thrust them into his pockets. "Scared, I guess."

Eden's eyes widened in surprise. "Why?"

"Because I've wanted this for so long"—Hugh's voice faltered—"but now I can't help wondering if you're going to compare me to him."

"Oh!" Eden exclaimed quietly. "I see. Are you going to compare me to Libby?"

"Of course not! You and Libby are completely different—"

"Precisely." The pins fell onto the bureau with a metallic clatter and Eden walked toward Hugh, her arms outstretched. "I'm scared too, but I know that will pass if we help each other."

"I love you, Eden." Hugh slowly drew his fingers through the shining, flaxen curls and tugged gently on the ends that coiled around his hands, pulling Eden to him. "It's important to me you believe that. And trust me when I say I'll never hurt you again."

"I do," Eden assured him, her arms stealing upward to circle his neck. "If I didn't believe in you I wouldn't be here now."

Hugh stopped resisting then and lost himself in the experience of making love to his wife. Any awkwardness he felt at the sudden change in their relationship soon disappeared in the face of Eden's unspoken assurance that his actions pleased her. Between Hugh and Eden there was no uncontrollable need to hurry through this new facet of their marriage; instead both seemed to agree to linger over each movement, each discovery. Hugh's normally smooth voice assumed a gentle hesitancy as he lay beside Eden and stroked her alabaster skin beneath his hand with a tenderness she had never known he possessed. Simply lying together, their eyes locked in silent question and answer while they sought and gave responses with each delicate brush of their hands, brought a tingling awareness to each of them. Hugh fanned Eden's hair over the pillows, then buried his face in the soft, pale halo as she traced the rough edges of the scars that ridged his back and stroked the flesh beneath the mat of hair on his chest. Her slender body looked and felt so fragile that Hugh was certain it would snap under the weight of his own massive frame. To Hugh's surprise, he discovered that Eden refused to allow him to pull back. Her long, slender fingers learned the angles and contours of his face with the delicate touch of a butterfly's wings and then continued to caress the rest of him in unabashed fascination.

It felt good to be held in Hugh's arms, to watch the sparkling lights in his eyes turn into a smoldering blue glow when she quivered at his touch. Except for a few breathless phrases, they barely spoke, and yet Eden was certain they understood each other's feelings and desires. The shyness was dropping away now and she found that between kisses Hugh—in his odd, lilting brogue—was telling her all the things her heart had longed to hear. This first time he took her carefully, gently, as if he were afraid she might break if he allowed his passion free rein. With his own special, tender way of loving, Hugh carried her trembling to the brink of fulfillment and held her there for what seemed an eternity while Eden clung to him, softly crying his name. Coherent thought gave way to pure feeling when they both dropped over the edge and fell together through a starlit, velvet heaven.

There was no rude shock of return, only a sense of completion when Hugh cradled Eden in his arms and rested her head upon his chest. Her breath faintly stirred the short, crisp curls on his chest and Hugh opened his eyes to find Eden regarding him through half-closed, mist-gray eyes.

"I think I believe in miracles now," Hugh whispered.

The corners of Eden's mouth curved upward in an answering smile as she laid a hand on his shoulder. "I think I do, too."

Hugh drew the sheet over them and within a few minutes, nestled together, they both were asleep.

Meg's wedding day was overcast and rainy, but not even the weather could dampen Eden's spirits when she awoke in Hugh's bed. For the first time she truly felt married—the name felt married—the name Mrs. Hugh Colter really belonged to her now. Childishly delighted by the thought, Eden held her wedding rings up to the light and smiled happily.

"It's about time you woke up." Eden gave a tiny screech of alarm and flipped over onto her back to find Hugh grinning down at her. "Do you know, I've always wondered what you looked like when you first woke up in the morning. Now I know—you are incredibly beautiful, your eyes all soft and wide and your hair tousled." Hugh pulled her into his arms and kissed her deeply, thoroughly, using far less restraint that he had the night before.

"That was nice," Eden murmured when he released her. "Will you do that every morning?"

"I will," Hugh promised teasingly, "if you agree never to wear one of those cumbersome nightgowns to bed."

Eden slanted a wicked look at him. "I think that could be arranged, Mr. Colter, but is there a special reason for your request?"

"Sure and there is, Mrs. Colter," he rejoined with mock seriousness. "In the wee, small hours of the night I may get cold and need your body to warm me. This way I won't have to fight my way through layers of ribbons and lace and God knows what else in order to get a good hold on you." With a fierce roar that brought another shriek from Eden, Hugh pinned her against his chest and began tickling her until Eden cried out for mercy.

"Don't! Hugh, stop! Stop!" Eden giggled helplessly and struggled to break free. "Oh, Hugh, please! No more, no more!"

At last Hugh relented, but he did not release Eden until he claimed a kiss as his prize. "There now, you see? Until now I didn't even know you were ticklish."

"You could just have asked," Eden laughed as she brushed at her streaming eyes.

"Ah, but where's the fun in that?" Hugh reached out and toyed with a lock of blond hair. "Some things are better when they are experienced firsthand. Like last night, for instance. You are mine now—my wife, my love for all time. I never thought I'd be able to say that to you."

"Oh, Hugh," Eden exclaimed softly. "I've been away for such a very long time, but I'm home now. I've come home and there's no place I'd rather be than right here."

His eyes dancing, Hugh bent forward and kissed her lightly. "I'm glad—and I'll have you know I plan to keep you feeling this way. I plan to pamper you and indulge you in any way I can."

"That sounds wonderful," Eden purred as she curled against him. "Where will you begin?"

"I have a number of things in mind," Hugh said as he nibbled at the curve of her neck. "But right now all I can think of—"

"I know what you're thinking," Eden interrupted saucily. "It's becoming very apparent."

"That, too," Hugh chuckled; then he sighed and rose from the bed. "However, since I've already asked Simmons to serve my breakfast in bed, I suggest you at least put on a wrapper. Not that I don't enjoy the view, but . . ."

Eden hurled a pillow at his head and dashed into her bedroom. When she returned a few minutes later—demurely clad in a satin wrapper—Simmons had already arrived and was industriously arranging one tray beside the bed. Hugh exchanged an amused glance with Eden over the butler's head.

Straightening, Simmons asked, "Will there be anything else, sir?"

"Well, Simmons—" Hugh began.

"I'll just have coffee, Simmons," Eden spoke up brightly. "And you may tell Millicent to have my bath ready in half an hour."

Simmons' usual bland expression deserted him for a moment, and the cup and saucer he held rattled precariously. "Very good, Miss—Mrs. Colter." Eden hid a smile as Simmons backed uncertainly toward the door. "I'll see to it immediately."

"I never thought anything would shake him up," Hugh commented with a grin when they were alone. "I'll bet within ten minutes the entire staff is going to know."

Laughing, Eden walked into Hugh's waiting arms. "More like five. Even Simmons won't be able to resist this tidbit; and then our help will spread the news to other households and by nightfall *everyone* will know. Do you mind, Hugh?"

"Hell, no," he growled. "I'm going to be the envy of every man I see today. Why should I mind that? Do you?"

"Not a bit." Eden's eyes sparkled and she kissed him lightly. "After all, you're not the only one people are going to envy. I happen to be married to the most wonderful man in the world; I just didn't realize it before." Her wrapper fell away beneath Hugh's agile fingers and she laughed throatily as he lifted her against his chest. "What are you doing?"

"Having breakfast." Hugh nibbled at Eden's earlobe and sampled the tender flesh below. "You taste . . . delicious," he murmured against the fluttering pulse point in her throat.

The bed sank beneath their combined weight, and Eden's voice deserted her as Hugh's mouth closed warmly over one pink-tipped breast. The supporting arm beneath Eden's legs was withdrawn and she found herself sprawled across Hugh's lap with her head cushioned against his shoulder. Hugh's mouth sought her other breast, teasing the nipple into a hard point. Desire splintered through Eden, awakening a passion she had believed long buried. Her fingers tangled in Hugh's silver hair, pulling his head even closer. The stubble of his beard rasped across Eden's sensitive flesh and she moaned softly.

"All of you, Eden," Hugh demanded raggedly, his free hand gliding over her thighs. "I want all of you."

"Oh, Hugh . . . yes!" Eden's hands found their way inside Hugh's robe as his lips captured hers in a hungry kiss. She welcomed the invasion of Hugh's tongue with fierce delight, his display of raw need arousing an age-old response within Eden. Her fingers curled into the hard, masculine shoulders, driving Eden deeper into his embrace. Hugh's robe gaped open and Eden wantonly rubbed her breasts into the dark hair covering his chest.

"All of you," Hugh repeated when he finally released Eden's mouth.

Eden nodded, too giddy with desire to answer coherently. She struggled to her knees and stared into the glowing blue eyes, unaware that her own eyes were dark, heavy-lidded with passion. Her hands fell to Hugh's waist, untying the belt which held his robe together. A shrug of his shoulders sent the robe to the bed in a crumpled heap, and a moment later Eden was pinned between the mattress and Hugh's large form.

Naked flesh pressed against naked flesh, consuming Hugh's gentleness. There was no need to protect Eden—not now, when she arched upward to meet his every caress. Or now, when she caught at his mouth and her hand cradled that part of him which burned for release. Hugh trailed kisses along the mounds of her breasts, his fingers slipping into the triangle of blond curls above her thighs. Eden's nails bit into his shoulders, and Hugh uttered a low, savage growl as he reclaimed her lips.

Eden twisted wildly, seeking fulfillment. Her legs parted of their own volition, inviting, demanding. Hugh's hands raised her hips and when he thrust into her, Eden's cry was muffled against his lips. Eden found his rhythm, matched it. Hugh's tempo increased, carrying Eden into a dimension of pure sensation, and when the seemingly endless waves of pleasure welded her against Hugh, Eden gloried in the spasms which left Hugh vulnerable, buried deep within her.

Gradually their breathing returned to normal, their heart-beats steadied. Hugh kissed Eden's swollen mouth tenderly, cherishing the aftermath of spent passion. "Ah, darlin'," Hugh breathed at last, aware of the gentle flutter of Eden's hands across his back, "I must be crushing the life out of you."

"No." Eden splayed her fingers against Hugh's flesh, staying him when he made to withdraw. "Don't leave me yet."

Hugh quieted, his soul lost in the mist-gray gaze. "Did I hurt you?"

"No more than I hurt you." Eden traced a finger over the half-moons her nails had left in his skin.

"Marks of valor," Hugh teased. Eden smiled and he stroked the upward curve of her mouth with his thumb. "Darlin' Eden," he whispered, "I love you more than words can say."

Meg's wedding was little more than a blur to Eden since she had ended up rushing through her bath and toilette—as had Hugh—in order to make it to the church with a scant fifteen minutes to spare. Her heart was still pounding, her cheeks still flushed as she stood beside Meg and tried to concentrate on the ceremony. All Eden could think of was the miraculous transformation that had taken place between Hugh and herself. She had feared that Hugh would be offended by her obvious enjoyment of their lovemaking, had expected to feel ashamed when she had to face him afterward, but instead she had felt completely at ease lying nude in Hugh's bed and talking to him over lukewarm coffee and cold toast. They were comfortable with each other, and the discovery of such excitement with someone so familiar touched the depths of her heart.

The final prayer began, and when the congregation bowed their heads Eden stole a glance toward Hugh. He must have been reading her thoughts, because he was looking at her too. A knowing, devilish grin appeared on his face, reminding Eden of their wild joining, and he winked conspiratorially before lowering his head. Eden gripped the bouquet so tightly that it trembled in her grasp. He was wonderful—especially considering what she had put him through. I *will* be a good wife to Hugh, she swore vehemently as she stared at the gold cross, which reminded her too much of Neil Banning's eyes. Neil is the past and I have to forget him. I've given myself to Hugh every bit as freely as I did to Neil. Hugh is my life now, and my future as well. Neil Banning no longer exists for me, and I won't allow him to ruin my marriage!

Shivering in the thin, silk gown, Eden stood in the receiving line just outside the church, hoping fervently that the rain wouldn't start again until they were safe and warm in the Lawsons' ballroom. Why Meg insisted upon greeting everyone under such dismal conditions Eden failed to understand, and between smiling a welcome to the guests she tugged vainly at the wide, full-length sleeves to keep the cold breeze from blowing straight up her arms.

"Here, use this." Hugh's rich voice warmed her almost as much as the wool cape he draped around her shoulders. "Hold on, my love, only twenty people or so left."

"I love Meg dearly, but I could kill her right about now!" Eden's teeth were chattering and she burrowed into the warm folds. "'Apricot silk so everything looks sunny and bright,' that's what Meg said. Hugh, I'm so cold."

His eyes dancing, Hugh bent to give her a quick kiss. "You'll be warm enough soon. I keep a flask in the carriage just in case. And don't be angry with Meg—you are the loveliest woman in the wedding party, apricot silk and all." Regretfully, Hugh retrieved his cape. "I'll bring the carriage around."

Eden smiled ruefully at his departing back, then turned to greet the next guest . . . and the next . . . and the next, until her hand was grasped by a smiling Dan Miller.

"I ran into Hugh," Dan whispered as he brushed a kiss over her cheek. "He looks happy and you look radiant, so I assume Meg isn't the only one who should be congratulated. I wish you happiness, Eden; you deserve it more than anyone else I know."

"Thank you, Dan. I plan to be very happy with Hugh." Eden hesitated. "I enjoyed our time together. Thank you for taking me under your wing."

"My pleasure." Dan grinned broadly. "Just see that I don't have to do it again. The next time I might not let you go." His expression altered subtly. "I have some news of my own, but I don't know yet whether it's good or bad."

Eden tilted her head. "You look so serious, Dan. It can't be that bad."

"Jane came home yesterday. That's why the Gregorys didn't

make it to the ceremony. I thought I should at least warn you because the entire family is planning to attend the reception."

Every word hit Eden like a hammer blow, leaving her paralyzed. "I don't believe it," she said woodenly.

"I'm afraid it's true. I don't know the whole story yet, but Tim said she's a widow now. Apparently the man she ran off with died about three months ago and Jane has been trying to get back ever since. I'd better get going. I'm holding you up." Dan squeezed her hand reassuringly. "Don't worry; I'm sure she's changed a lot in the last year."

Hugh told her the same news as they drove to the Lawsons' home, but for a long time Eden was too stricken by the thought of Neil's death to think of anything but the fact that Neil lay dead in a grave in Mexico. At last Eden pulled herself together and replied in a bitter voice, "Why did she have to come back? And why now?"

"Her husband is dead, she's all alone; it's only natural she wants to be with her family at a time like this." Hugh wrapped Eden more securely in his cape and drew her against his side. "Don't let her reappearance upset you, darlin'; whatever happened a year ago, there's nothing Jane can do to hurt you now."

"She can drag up all the old rumors," Eden countered sadly. "They didn't get very far the first time because both Tim and his father held their tongues, but if Jane starts in . . . people may really talk this time." Eden kneaded her hands in her lap and fought against the sinking feeling in the pit of her stomach. Hadn't she just told herself in church that Neil would never disturb her again? Now he was dead; she could simply forget that Neil Banning had ever existed. Eden forced her thoughts away from Neil and concentrated on the man beside her. "I thought we stood a chance, Hugh. I really thought we could put the past behind us."

"And what makes you think we can't do that now?" Hugh admonished sternly. "Lord, Eden, I thought you had more courage than you're showing right now. Let Jane Gregory— or whatever her name is now—say what she damn well pleases. No one is going to believe her, not after that little disappearing act she pulled. I think she's smart enough to realize that if she starts throwing any mud around a lot of it is going to end up on her, and Jane isn't about to take that kind of risk." Hugh chucked Eden under the chin encouragingly. "Besides, I'll be with you, remember? I'm not going to let *anyone* jeopardize our marriage. So whatever happens, we'll meet it together."

Eden gratefully threw her arms around Hugh's neck. "Thank you, Hugh. I was so afraid—"

"Shh. You're my wife. Did you actually believe I would abandon you because of what Jane might say? She can't tell me anything I don't already know." Hugh tilted Eden's face upward. "You must learn to trust me, darlin'. We Colters don't turn tail and run when things get a little unpleasant. Come on, now; let me see you smile."

By the time they arrived at the Lawson mansion Hugh had teased and cajoled Eden out of most of her fears, so that when she glimpsed Jane and Tim standing just inside the ballroom Eden felt only a flicker of unease. Hugh must have seen them too, because he slipped a hand under her elbow and deftly steered her toward the buffet in the dining room.

"I never feel comfortable eating this way," Hugh confided as they made their way along the table. "The waiters always act as if they think I'm making a pig out of myself."

Eden compared his heavily laden plate to her own and grinned. "You should have eaten a larger breakfast."

"I know," Hugh said gravely. "Unfortunately, something came up which required my immediate attention, and by the time I got back to the meal I was too weak to lift the fork."

Eden's eyes widened and she retorted in a whisper, "You had enough strength left to throw me into the tub!"

"Delayed reaction." Hugh grinned. "I had to crawl back to my bedroom on my hands and knees."

In spite of herself Eden started to laugh. Then she added in an undertone, "You're terrible, Hugh. I suppose I'll either have to stay out of your bed in the mornings or make sure you're properly fed afterward."

"I'll take the latter," Hugh informed her as he brought his face level with hers. "Now that I have you where I want you, don't you dare try to escape."

The adoration reflected in Hugh's eyes brought a faint blush to Eden's cheeks. "I won't," she promised as their lips brushed together lightly.

"Look at her; just look at her!" Jane hissed to her brother as they witnessed the tender scene between Hugh and Eden. "Eden Thackery Colter certainly can act, I'll give her credit for that. If I didn't know better I would almost believe they were happy together. And will you look at how everyone practically kills themselves to get over there to say hello. The whole thing makes me sick!"

Tim shrugged. "Hugh has a lot of friends, and though you may not like it, so does Eden."

"Are you trying to tell me I don't?" Jane sniffed haughtily.

"I don't see anyone beating a path to your side. Do you?" Tim fixed her with a spiteful stare. "Eden at least had the good sense to keep her indiscretion private, but not you. Oh, no, you had to run off like a trollop and leave your family behind to face the scandal. Whatever Banning did to you served you right. Now that you're back, don't expect our friends to welcome you with open arms. In fact, I doubt any of them will even speak to you."

"Papa said he would take care of everything," Jane said sulkily. "He made up that story of my being married and then widowed. Dan believed it, didn't he? If we repeat it often enough, pretty soon everyone will believe it." Tim remained unmoved, so Jane forced tears into her eyes. "I don't understand why you insist on being so cruel to me. Mama and Papa forgave me last night. Why can't you? I told you that Neil Banning forced me to go with him."

"The same way he forced you to be outside the Thackery mansion that day?" Tim asked sarcastically. "Turn off the tears, Jane. Our parents may not see through your innocent act, but I did years ago. And you may as well know, the only reason I escorted you here today was because Father threatened to cut me out of his will if I didn't. Well, I'm here and you're here, but that doesn't mean I have to listen to you!"

Throughout the afternoon Eden stayed close to Hugh's side, enjoying the security she felt whenever he reached out and slid his arm around her waist. It was hard for Eden to adjust to such an open display of affection. The first few times Hugh pulled her to his side, Eden felt the blood rush to her cheeks. Surely everyone present must be staring at them and commenting on their behavior. Eden glanced around nervously and saw several raised eyebrows in the crowd, but when she looked up at Hugh and found the corners of his mouth trembling with suppressed laughter at the odd looks they were receiving, she relaxed and allowed him to lead her to yet another small group of his friends.

Finally, at eight o'clock that evening, the musicians arrived

and began setting up their stands and music in the ballroom.
Amid the general scurry of women disappearing to rearrange
their hair and check on their appearance Eden managed a few
minutes' conversation with Meg, then found a vacant chair and
collapsed gratefully onto the padded cushion. Her face hurt
from so much smiling and her feet ached miserably from standing all afternoon. Eden sighed wearily and closed her eyes for
a moment. So far she had managed to avoid coming face to
face with Señora Parral—as Jane now called herself—but
Eden was beginning to wish they had confronted each other
and gotten all the unpleasantness over with. Parral, Eden
thought contemptuously. Jane's fictitious name meant that her
widow's story was just another lie. Part of Eden had gone weak
with relief when she had heard Jane's "married" name. As
much as Eden hated Neil Banning, she certainly didn't want
to see him dead. Stop this, Eden told herself angrily. No more!
No more Neil. Concentrate only on Hugh and enjoying Meg's
wedding ball.

"Tired, dear heart?" Eden left her thoughts with a jerk,
relaxing when Hugh smiled down at her. "You look a bit pale."

"I'm fine, Hugh." Eden reached for his hand. "I was just
thinking about something Meg said a long time ago." Hugh
raised his eyebrows questioningly and Eden continued in a
hushed voice, recalling the day two girls had wondered about
becoming women, never dreaming of the transformation that
would take place in little more than a year. "Meg asked me
once if I ever dreamed of having an adventure. It sounds silly
now, I know, but she was in earnest. Meg has always felt I
was too contained, too much in control, to have any fun."

"What did you tell her?" Hugh asked curiously.

"I changed the subject. But I was just thinking how quickly
our lives have changed since then. The fantasies vanish to make
room for reality."

"Is that what it was like for you?" Hugh asked in a gentle
voice. "Did all your dreams turn into ashes when we were
married?"

"I . . . I suppose they did, but they had started burning long
before then," Eden admitted haltingly. As she fretfully twisted
the heavy diamond around her finger, Eden suddenly realized
that the loss of those girlish daydreams somehow had faded
into a bittersweet memory, and she amazed herself as well as
Hugh with her next words. "It doesn't matter to me now, not

really. You see, Hugh, I have other dreams, ones that don't disappear when I look at them too closely. I think of our life together now, of what will happen to us in the future. That's something we can share, and sharing makes a big difference. Don't you agree?"

Hugh nodded wordlessly and pulled Eden to her feet. "It's what I want for us, dear heart. Do you think we can manage it?"

"Of course we can," Eden responded adamantly. She stood on tiptoe and kissed his cheek. "What is there to stop us? And given enough time, who knows? Ours may be the greatest romance since Romeo and Juliet."

"I sincerely hope not," Hugh chuckled. "The idea of swallowing poison doesn't exactly intrigue me. And I'd hate to see you mar that lovely skin with a dagger. Would you settle for a long, happy marriage instead?"

"I think so," Eden teased in return, her eyes sparkling madly. "But right now I'd better freshen up. I must look like something the cat dragged in."

"Not to me." But Hugh didn't protest further when Eden slipped out of his grasp and up the stairs.

Three of the larger rooms on the second floor had been set aside for the ladies and, hoping to avoid the bulk of the guests, Eden made her way to the one farthest from the staircase. Only two other women had claimed this sanctuary, and Eden smiled politely at them before she sank onto a sofa and pulled off her shoes. Chatting quietly, the women departed at last, leaving Eden by herself, and with a groan of relief she swung her legs onto the sofa cushions. She'd rest for fifteen minutes or so, then check her face and hair before rejoining Hugh. Eden smiled, wondering if she would be able to persuade Hugh to leave early. . . .

"Well, well, so this is where you disappeared to. You're a difficult person to find. In fact, if I didn't know better, I'd swear you were avoiding me."

Jane's voice sent an unpleasant shock down Eden's spine, but she retained enough control to open her eyes slowly. "Why would I do that, Mrs. Parral?" she asked contemptuously.

Jane shrugged haughtily. "Maybe it's because you're jealous. Or maybe you're afraid."

"Of you?" Eden asked in a cold voice. "Not likely. Now, if you will excuse me, I have to fix my hair."

Undaunted, Jane followed Eden into the mirrored powder room and sat down on the chair next to her. "You can't get rid of me that easily, Eden. After all, we have a lot to talk about."

"I can't think of a single thing we have to discuss," Eden snapped.

"Oh, can't you," Jane sneered. "I want to know what you said to Dan that poisoned his mind against me."

For a full minute Eden stared at Jane in stunned disbelief before her composure cracked and she gave in to laughter. Hugh had been right after all—Jane was more concerned with salvaging her own reputation than in ruining anyone else's. Shaking with relief, Eden restrained the laughter that still bubbled in her throat, although a hint of a smile played at the corners of her mouth when she faced Jane. "Your nerve is unbelievable! I've scarcely spoken to Dan all day."

"I don't mean today. Tim told me that you and Dan saw quite a bit of each other while I was gone. How dare you do such a thing! You know Dan and I are engaged."

"Indeed," Eden interjected. "Well, as for the way Dan is acting, you have to admit your homecoming was quite a shock to everyone."

"I can't imagine why. My husband died, leaving me all alone, and I wanted to come home to be with my friends and family."

"My condolences," Eden mocked as her fingers drummed against the marble vanity top. "Tell me: What did the late Mr. Parral do for a living? Tim was convinced that Neil Banning was the culprit, and all along it was Parral. By the way, what was your husband's first name?"

Jane's mouth worked furiously and Eden smiled humorlessly. Apparently Jane hadn't expected such a direct approach, particularly from Eden. Good, Eden thought vengefully. Find out, Jane, what it's like to be faced by someone who would enjoy destroying you, because after what you and Neil did to me there's nothing I'd like better than to take my pound of flesh out of you.

"I . . . I don't care for the way you're acting," Jane blustered.

"No?" Eden gave a final pat to the wisps of curls that framed her face, then rose. "What a pity." Eden swept past Jane. "You won't mind if I congratulate Dan on your renewed engagement, will you?"

"No, Eden, wait." Jane grabbed Eden's arm just as she reached the door. "Please, Eden, I need your help."

Wary of the other woman's motives, Eden nevertheless let the door slam closed. "That's quite a switch. Of all the people in New York, I'm the last one you should come to for help. Besides, after what you did, give me one good reason why I should do anything for you."

"Because if you don't, I'll let all of New York in on your dirty little secret," Jane threatened wildly. "And now you have a husband to consider—you don't want Hugh's reputation ruined, even if you don't care about your own." Eden's temper flared and Jane paled as she realized she had said the wrong thing. For some reason, the threat of blackmail hadn't produced fear in Eden, only a cold rage that turned the gray eyes frosty with hatred. Belatedly Jane tried to correct her error. "I'm sorry, Eden, I didn't—"

"Keep your mouth shut," Eden commanded in a steely tone, "before I lose my temper and decide to ruin *you* permanently. I can do it, Jane. A few words to the right people and I'll drive you right back to Mexico. If you say one word about me I'll fix it so neither Dan nor any other man will look at you again."

"I won't!" Jane whined tearfully. "I won't say anything, I swear! Only promise you'll help me. I can't go back to Mexico—I won't go back! I was never married, not even to Neil. He abandoned me in a hotel when I told him I wanted to be his wife and not his mistress. Neil left me there, Eden. He just rode off and I never heard from him again. I waited for him for months, thinking he would come for me, and he never even bothered to write."

Eden gestured carelessly. "You're breaking my heart, Jane, but I can't understand why you're so surprised. You knew what Neil was like when you ran away with him."

"But I was certain he would change his mind when we got to Mexico; after all the time we spent together during the voyage I was sure Neil would realize that I would make an ideal wife. Then, when we arrived at Tampico, Neil finally told me he was already engaged. He even had the nerve to pay me off like a whore. Look!" Jane cried and pulled aside one of the ringlets at her cheek to expose a ruby and diamond earring. "He gave me these, along with a matching necklace. He said I could always sell them."

"I don't believe it," Eden murmured, the winking jewels

conjuring up a scene she had long tried to erase from her mind. Neil smiling, handing her a jeweler's box . . .

Not understanding the meaning of Eden's words, Jane nodded in agreement. "You see, Eden, neither of us knew how low that man would stoop. If we had, our lives would have been so different. We have to band together, Eden, so no one will ever have to know what fools we were."

"You mean what a fool *you* were," Eden said acidly. "You want my help? Fair enough. All you have to do is meet my price."

Jane's hopes plummeted in the face of the hard gaze. "I don't have much money, Eden, if that's what you want." When Eden remained silent Jane added desperately, "I could get more, though. I'm sure Father would give me some if I asked—"

"Fool," Eden spat derisively. "What do I need your money for? I know this may tax your limited brain, but do try to think, Jane. Think! What is it I could possibly want from you?"

"I don't . . ." Jane cast about frantically for an answer. "My jewels? Here, take them." With shaking hands Jane pulled the earrings from her lobes. Eden regarded the jeweled offering distastefully and Jane quickly withdrew her hand. "I don't know what you want."

"An apology," Eden said simply. "I'd rather you gave it publicly, but a private apology will do. After the bitchy little trick you set up with Neil, you owe me that much."

Jane gulped, quailing before the icy anger in Eden's gaze. She should have remembered Eden's cold, deliberate anger from their school days. Eden wasn't joking; Eden would destroy her unless she apologized. Jane's shoulders slumped in resignation. Hiding her irritation at being beaten, Jane mumbled, "I'm sorry."

"Louder," Eden snapped. "I can't hear you, Jane."

"I said I'm sorry!" Jane yelled back. Damn Eden for having gotten the upper hand and damn Neil for having gotten her into this in the first place! It was all his fault.

"Don't be uncivil or I may decide not to help you." Eden picked up her reticule and walked to the door.

"Wait, Eden, I haven't told you what I want you to do." Jane started forward, only to be stopped by the look on Eden's face.

"I think I can guess," Eden replied sarcastically. "Don't worry, as far as I'm concerned you're still the widow of the late, lamented Parral. That's what I'll tell anyone who asks. And as for Dan, if he's foolish enough to want to marry you . . ." Eden shrugged. "I pity the poor man."

Once outside the door Eden leaned weakly against the wall, listening as Jane stamped around the room indulging in a fit of temper. Her own behavior shamed Eden, and telling herself that Jane had long deserved to be taken down a peg or two did nothing to ease her guilt. Jane was one of Neil's victims, too—small wonder she wanted the security that marriage to Dan would provide. Her position was far more precarious than Eden's. By tomorrow morning the yellow tabloids would be having a field day with the story of Jane's return—unless Carl Gregory could buy them off as he had when his daughter had run off to Mexico.

Some of the strength began to flow back into Eden's limbs and she pushed away from the wall. Her gentle side urged her to go back into the room and try to make peace with Jane. Their bitter animosity had gone on long enough—she and Jane had left the schoolroom behind and it was time they learned to deal with each other. But not now, not yet, Eden's injured feelings cried out, and her hand dropped from the doorknob. If revenge were not completely sweet, at least it was better than letting Jane manipulate her life again. Before her resolve could weaken, Eden turned sharply on her heel and made her way back to the ballroom.

# Chapter 9

Neil Banning hunkered down in front of the early-morning campfire—the first in three days—and poured himself a cup of coffee. In spite of the heavy jacket he wore, the crisp mountain air made him shiver, and he gratefully sipped at the scalding liquid. A glance showed Neil that two of his three traveling companions still slept the same exhausted slumber which had overtaken all of them last night. If it weren't for the burning pain in his side, Neil would still be sleeping as well, but once he was awake it was easier to ignore the pain by concentrating on the problems facing the small band instead of coddling himself by staying in his bedroll.

"You are up early, *compadre*."

Before the quiet voice had finished speaking, Neil had pivoted on one knee and aimed his revolver at the man who had appeared behind him. "So are you." With a grim look, Neil holstered his gun. "You should know better than to sneak up on me like that, Julio. Next time you might not be so lucky."

"And you might not be so fast." Julio shrugged and helped himself to the coffee. "How is your side?"

"Better," Neil answered shortly, but he winced when Julio pulled aside his shirt and dressing to examine the wound.

"It's bleeding again," Julio stated matter-of-factly. "We'd better get you to Sebastian—I think we can make it by tonight if we push the horses."

"No! We've been tracking the rustlers too well. If the Rangers catch us now we'll be hanged as cattle thieves before we have a chance to explain that the real rustlers are half a day's ride to the south. Until I'm sure we've lost those damn Texas Rangers I will not take a chance on leading them to Sebastian; my side can wait another day."

Julio rose and motioned Neil to follow him to a heavily wooded ridge a few hundred feet from the camp. "They've been down there since sunrise sniffing around. We may have lost them in the shale, and with that stream they don't know which direction we took."

With his golden eyes narrowed against the glare of the sun,

Neil wriggled forward on his belly to get a better look at the men in the ravine below. The Rangers had been on their trail for over a week, but not until three days ago had they gotten close enough to fire at the small band. They hadn't even been close enough to be accurate, Neil thought ruefully; the bullet that had torn its way through his side had hit him only by the sheerest stroke of luck. When the four men stopped long enough for Neil to tear up a spare shirt to use as a bandage, he and Julio had decided to make a run for Mexico in the belief that the Rangers wouldn't follow them. Unfortunately, they had been mistaken.

"Damn," Neil cursed softly at the dozen men milling about below. "They should have given up days ago, Julio. Why the hell don't they go back home?"

"They must want the others badly, *compadre.* You said they would not follow us when we crossed the border."

"They shouldn't have. It doesn't make sense. Our government doesn't want them here, they don't have any jurisdiction in Mexico—damn it, Julio, if they're caught they may be executed. Don't they realize that?"

Julio glanced sharply at Neil, then turned back to study the men below. "You sound more concerned about these Texas Rangers than with the lives of your own men. Perhaps you have been living too long north of the border; four years is a long time."

"Not that long," Neil snapped defensively. "I don't like living in Texas now any more than I did four years ago. I just wish they'd leave so we can get out of these mountains." Wearily, Neil drew a hand over his week's accumulation of whiskers. "Keep an eye on them, Julio; I'll get back to camp and douse the fire. As soon as the horses are saddled we'll try to lose them. They'll probably think we'll try for the high country, so we'll go the other way—we should be able to double back and circle around before they figure out what we're doing."

Neil's plan worked, and by nightfall they had reached the plain and left the mountain range several miles behind them. The two other men separated from Julio and Neil and headed west to their homes and families. If the Rangers did manage to track the four men this far, they too would have to split up to continue their search, and Neil doubted the Ranger captain would take that large a risk.

"What about you, Julio?" Neil turned slightly to grin at his friend. "Shouldn't you be getting back to your wife?"

A rare smile flickered across Julio's normally somber features and he shook his head. "I'll go with you—like in the old days. Sebastian will be waiting for you—"

"Like in the old days," Neil finished for him. "All right, come along if you must. Far be it for me to deny you and Sebastian the satisfaction of gloating over this hole in my side."

Aside from stopping long enough to rest the horses or change the dressing on Neil's wound, the two men stayed in the saddle for nearly forty-eight hours. The strain did not show on Julio, but when the hacienda finally came into sight Neil was weaving in the saddle. Through a supreme effort of will he dismounted under his own power, but Julio had to help him up the seemingly endless steps to the front door.

"Sebastian must be off somewhere delivering a baby," Neil observed wryly as they stumbled through the darkened foyer.

"Once you're in bed I'll look for him," Julio said, then went suddenly motionless at a sound from the back of the house. "Sebastian?" he asked Neil.

"I don't think so, not at this hour," Neil said quietly, disengaging himself from Julio's supporting arm and drawing his gun, as did Julio. Icy fear gnawed at Neil's stomach as he tried to see into the dark hallway—not fear for himself but for Sebastian. Neil's finger tightened around the trigger; his mind raced as he tried to remember if he had said anything to anyone in Lathrop that could have led the Rangers to his brother and his home.

From somewhere nearby came the unmistakable sound of a gun hammer being pulled back. "¿Quién es?"

At the soft question, all Neil's tension evaporated and he sagged against the wall. "Sebastian . . . it's Neil and Julio. For God's sake, will you light a candle? I damn near blew your head off!"

Before Neil finished speaking, Sebastian had lit two candles and was walking toward them. "You should worry more about yourself," Sebastian grinned as he held up a shotgun for Neil's inspection. "I was asleep in my office when I heard your horses and seized the first gun I could find. I expected you days ago, Neil. What took you so long?"

"A small problem in the shape of a posse. Lucky for me they were lousy shots." Neil pulled his shirt aside and pressed his hand over the blood-stained bandage. "I need your help, little brother. I hope the time you spent in Vienna taught you something."

*"Dios mío,"* Sebastian breathed as he hurried forward. "Let's get you upstairs. Julio, give me a hand."

"Don't make such a fuss, Sebastian; it's just a little blood." Neil's reckless smile faded when the room abruptly tilted at an impossible angle and he groped blindly for the wall to steady himself.

"Grab him, Julio!" Sebastian sprang forward to catch his brother before Neil slumped to the floor.

Less than five minutes later Neil was lying upstairs in his bedroom with Sebastian carefully peeling away the sodden dressing. Frowning, Sebastian held a lamp closer to the wound and gently probed the bullet hole.

"How bad is it?"

Sebastian looked up to find Neil watching him and he smiled reassuringly. "It could be worse. You've lost some blood, I see, but the bullet passed right through. You're lucky—if you had ridden around with that bullet still in you, it probably would have killed you." Sebastian began unwinding the clean bandages Julio had brought from his office. "I'll clean up the wound, put in a few stitches, but from then on it's up to you."

"How long before I can travel? Damn!" Neil caught his breath as Sebastian applied antiseptic to his side.

"I don't know." Sebastian winced when Neil swore again, his yellow eyes narrowing in reflection of his brother's pain. "Give me a few days before asking for a prognosis. Besides, I'll enjoy having you here for a while. It's been a long time since you were home last. Roll over."

Neil obeyed, his long fingers twisting into the sheet as Sebastian repeated the cleansing procedure on his back. "Take it easy, will you?" he gasped. "I've seen horses shod with more care."

"Don't criticize," Sebastian shot back, "or I'll be a lot rougher. I hope this hole in your side clears up a few things in your muddled brain. Hell, Neil, Constanza isn't worth it. She never was."

Neil groaned as he turned onto his back so Sebastian could secure the bandage. "Spare me, little brother; a bullet I can survive, but I'm not so sure about one of your lectures." Neil

closed his eyes. "I'm tired, little brother, so tired. . . . I don't
want to argue."

With an effort, Sebastian held back his scathing comments
about Neil's behavior and contented himself with tucking the
sheet around Neil's waist. "No arguments, then, not even a
lecture—at least for tonight. We'll talk later—that is, I'll talk,
and this time you're going to listen."

"Sure. Whatever you say. My good-luck piece—" asked
Neil sleepily, "is it still in my vest?" Sebastian produced the
gold watch from Neil's vest and held it up for his brother's
inspection. "Good, good. I'd hate to lose that." Neil closed his
eyes, allowing the security of being home to dispel the turmoil
his nagging conscience had produced over the past months. As
long as he was here it was safe to forget about Constanza and
all the problems that accompanied their relationship. Here in
his own room, his own bed, Neil could relax and let himself
drift, just drift . . .

Sebastian watched the taut lines in Neil's face slowly relax
as he fell asleep, and Sebastian shook his head sadly. The past
four years had taken their toll on Neil. For reasons Sebastian
could not fathom, Neil viewed his role as Constanza's protector
with complete sincerity. As the years passed Neil's devotion
grew, and with it his blindness to Constanza's ways. Neil
defended her actions to everyone, denying her faults with a
vehemence which seemed to Sebastian to border on the insane.
The very fact that Constanza remained with Lathrop was proof
enough for Sebastian that she already had precisely what she
wanted, despite her laments to Neil. Sebastian had told Neil
exactly that four months ago, and for the first time in their
lives Neil had actually struck his brother. In a grim voice, Neil
had ordered Sebastian to stay the hell out of his life and without
so much as saying good-bye had saddled his horse and ridden
back to Texas.

Quietly, Sebastian placed a chair beside the bed and eased
himself into it. This time, by God, Neil wouldn't be able to
ride off; he would have to listen. There was a lot to be said
for a captive audience.

Sebastian's thoughts were diverted as he toyed with Neil's
watch. Odd how this one piece of jewelry had come to mean
so much to Neil. It wasn't like him to be sentimental or su-
perstitious. Had the picture and the words inside gotten under
Neil's skin? Sebastian pried open the back and studied the

timeless portrait. A lovely girl, to be sure, but Neil had always been involved with beautiful women and he'd never assigned any value to their various tokens of affection. This Eden must be someone special, someone that Neil couldn't get out of his mind. Sebastian flashed a grin at Neil's sleeping form and settled back to wait for morning.

The bullets whining through the air like vicious mosquitoes, the feeling of his own blood spreading warm and sticky down his side and chest—the whole damn thing was starting all over again, only this time Neil couldn't outrun the Rangers, and the terrifying knowledge that he was going to be brought to ground like a helpless rabbit tightened his throat until he could hardly breathe. A man should die in one of only two ways: in a fair fight, or in his own bed at a ripe old age. No man should be hunted down and torn to pieces like a buck caught by a pack of wild wolves.

Neil came awake with a jerk and found his throat so constricted it ached. Just a nightmare, he told himself. I haven't been frightened by a dream since I was eight years old. He forced himself to relax. The draperies were closed, allowing only a murky light to filter into the room. Neil passed a hand over his face and stretched, only to be brought up short by the outraged, protesting muscles in his side. Cursing, Neil pulled aside the sheet and gingerly explored his bandaged side with his fingertips. That much, at least, was real. To think he had made it through three years of fighting during the Revolution only to end up being shot by a *gringo*. Neil scowled menacingly at the bandage, then started at the soft chuckle that came from beside the bed.

"I'm afraid that won't help," Sebastian laughed as he leaned forward in his chair. "You can't intimidate a bullet hole, Neil. It has to heal in its own time."

Neil shrugged off the comment. "No thanks to you," he retorted as he pulled another pillow beneath his head. "I thought doctors were supposed to have a gentle touch."

"We do," Sebastian said in a wounded tone. "But when the patient rides around for five days before coming to us, he deserves everything he gets. Let's have a look." Sebastian cut away the dressing and examined the wound before he spoke again. "You might have died. You do realize that, don't you? Another day or two and Julio would have brought back a corpse."

"But he didn't, and I didn't," Neil countered. "I was only kidding, Sebastian, you're a fine doctor. I'm glad you're on my side."

"I'm not on anyone's side," Sebastian stated coldly. "Just remember: I can't breathe life into a dead man."

"I'll remember." Neil studied Sebastian's grim features. "You look tired, Sebastian. Don't tell me you sat up with me all night."

Sebastian glanced at Neil briefly before returning his attention to Neil's side. "Your calendar is off—you've been asleep for two days. Julio came by yesterday with a message for you. The men you were following sold the cattle at a very good price. Unfortunately the buyer doesn't know their names or where they went."

"As usual," Neil groaned. "Damn it, Sebastian, how do they do it? How is it possible for a band of rustlers to cross into Mexico and then just disappear?"

"They cannot; not if they are American," Sebastian replied absently.

"Which leads us back to the conclusion that they're Mexican." Neil winced as Sebastian tightened the bandage, then sighed. "I'm going in circles, little brother, and so are the Rangers. My neighbors and I are losing our stock and no matter how many precautions we take the rustlers seem to be one step ahead of us. We're no closer to stopping them now than we were when all this started nearly four years ago. There has to be a way!" Neil brought his temper under control with an effort. "When will I be able to travel?"

"Give it at least a week; two at the most." Sebastian crossed to the washstand to wash his hands. "Don't worry, I won't keep you here any longer than necessary. I certainly wouldn't want you to think I'm interfering in your life. Now, if you're hungry I'll send up a tray for you. I want you to stay in bed today and rest. Tomorrow, if you're well enough, you will be allowed to go downstairs." There was a certain malicious glint in Sebastian's expression, leaving no doubt that he was deriving a great deal of satisfaction from Neil's predicament. "And if you're a good *pequeño muchacho,* I'll even let you have dessert with your meal tonight." Sebastian made a hasty escape before Neil had a chance to reply.

"Like hell," Neil muttered aloud at the closed door. If Sebastian thought he'd stay in bed like some milksop invalid his little brother had better think again. Ignoring the leaping pain in his side, Neil swung out of bed, took a step forward and found the floor had rushed up to meet him. Panting, he rolled onto his back and stared at the ceiling. It crossed his mind to call for help—but that would bring Sebastian, who would undoubtedly find the situation hilarious. Groaning, Neil hooked an arm around the bedpost and dragged himself back onto the mattress. Conceding defeat, he wiped the beads of perspiration from his face and vowed not to ignore Sebastian's advice a second time.

Sebastian's attitude over the next ten days grated on Neil's nerves. Expecting an argument at any time, Neil mentally braced himself every morning before breakfast for Sebastian's attack, only to find his preparations unnecessary. Sebastian either skirted the issue of Neil's involvement with Constanza or avoided Neil altogether. More often than not Sebastian would be finishing his meal when Neil entered the dining room, and Sebastian would leave before Neil had a chance to say a word.

It had happened again at dinner tonight and now, several hours later, Neil lay propped up in bed trying to concentrate on the book he was reading while the sound of Sebastian's guitar drifted through the house. His patience at an end, Neil disgustedly tossed the book onto the bedspread and slammed out of the room.

Sebastian looked up in surprise when Neil burst into his office, then relaxed and resumed playing as Neil paced in front of the desk. "Is your side bothering you?" Sebastian asked sweetly, knowing full well what was on Neil's mind.

"Not exactly," Neil growled. "But you are, little brother. Are we going to have this out, or do you want to dance around awhile longer?"

Sebastian shrugged, his head tilted as if he were considering nothing more important than the melancholy strains produced by his guitar. "Can we talk calmly, rationally, without being treated to another display of your temper?"

Neil expelled his breath and folded himself into a chair. "However you want it. You're a very stubborn man, Sebastian."

Sebastian's eyes danced with laughter. "I come by it honestly, the same way you do. Don't look so sour, Neil. After all, this is the first time in my life that you have ever agreed with me."

Neil sobered as he studied his brother's face. "Sebastian, I'm sorry about what happened the last time I was home. No matter what you said, I shouldn't have hit you. You deserve better than that."

"So do you." Sebastian quit playing and propped his guitar against the wall. "At the risk of repeating myself, I don't like what you're doing, Neil. You covet your neighbor's wife, which breaks the tenth Commandment."

"You were in the Jesuit school too long, Sebastian; sometimes you sound like a priest." Neil rested his feet on top of the desk. "What comes next—the part about my being condemned to a fiery eternity in hell? Save your breath; I haven't believed in the concepts of heaven and hell since I was ten years old."

"How about the concept of dying at the end of a rope?" Sebastian inquired acidly. "It could happen to you very easily, you know. From what Julio told me, I gather the Rangers thought you were the rustlers. Had they caught you, you and Julio and the others would have been killed before you had a chance to explain that you've been following the rustlers as well. And the Rangers aren't the only danger you must face. Since Díaz took office his *rurales* have been patrolling the border with orders to kill any bandits who try to escape into Mexico."

"Then I'll just have to be more careful," Neil said casually. "Julio and I know this part of the country better than anyone, with the possible exception of yourself. Don't worry, Sebastian, no one will catch me."

"You were nearly caught this time. I am afraid for you, Neil, more so now than ever before. You have said yourself that the Ranger captain believes that you lead the rustlers and, quite frankly, his reasoning is understandable. The rustling started shortly after you moved to Lathrop; the rustlers disappear into Mexico, your homeland; and now, after the latest raid against the ranches, you've vanished. Constanza is not worth the risk you take by staying in Texas." Sebastian leaned back and stared at the ceiling. "Even when we were children you insisted upon having things your own way; that I could live with. At least then you had enough sense to know where pride ended and reality began. This . . . obsession you have with Constanza and Williams is destroying the man I knew as my brother."

"You don't understand," Neil argued. "Constanza is unhappy—desperately so. She is isolated in Texas, alone, trapped in a country whose ways are foreign to her. As for her husband . . . Lathrop abuses her, Sebastian; I've seen the bruises."

"Then she should leave him," Sebastian stated. "But you have noticed, have you not, that no matter how many tears Constanza sheds she remains with Lathrop?"

Neil's jaw tightened. "She was married by a priest, Sebastian; Constanza doesn't feel she can honorably have the marriage dissolved."

"Certainly not after four years," Sebastian commented sarcastically.

"She's doing what she feels she has to," Neil snapped. "Not even Lathrop can rob Constanza of her honor and pride."

"A truly exceptional woman!"

"I think so—considering the circumstances. Constanza depends upon me, needs me. She's been humiliated and degraded by Lathrop Williams and I'm the only one who understands that she didn't bring it upon herself."

Sebastian's disbelief showed clearly in his golden eyes. "Nevertheless, she is now her husband's responsibility. You have no part in her life."

Neil checked his steadily rising temper. That Sebastian failed to see his course as the only honorable one infuriated Neil. "I can't just abandon Constanza!"

"As you did the mysterious Eden?"

Neil went rigid with shock. "She was not *criollo*."

With an exasperated groan, Sebastian pressed the heels of his hands over his eyes. "You are impossible! You dare speak of honor, yet you act as if you have none." Sebastian slammed a fist on the desk. "I warn you, Neil, Constanza will be the death of you. Are you so blind that you cannot see that Constanza is using you? Surely in four years she has had an opportunity to escape her husband—or is it possible she is not as unhappy as she would have you believe? Must I repeat myself? Very well then: I think Constanza saw the opportunity of a lifetime in Lathrop Williams and she snapped him up before he could get away. And as far as Constanza needing your help . . . in my opinion she wants your body but nothing else. Williams can pamper and spoil her with all his money and you, my dear brother, can entertain her in that big, empty bed."

"That's enough!" Neil shouted. In one motion he was out of his chair, with one hand clenching Sebastian's shirtfront. "You don't know what you're talking about, Sebastian."

Sebastian returned Neil's menacing stare without flinching until, at last, Neil released him and subsided back into his chair. Slowly, deliberately, Sebastian readjusted the crumpled material of his shirt before he spoke. "Do you see now what I mean? Constanza is not only using your pride to gain what she wants, she is also slowly eroding your sense of humanity. Much as I hate watching you destroy yourself over a woman who couldn't care less about what happens to you, I'm through trying to reason with you. Go ahead and do whatever it is you feel you must do. If you succeed, and if you live through the experience, perhaps then you'll be rid of the demon that drives you to do such things." Sebastian rose and limped to the door.

"Sebastian, wait." Neil followed his brother to the door. "We've been through so much together—don't desert me now."

"Neil—" Sebastian sighed and shook his head. "I'm not deserting you. I simply can't watch you make a fool of yourself and perhaps die because of this coincidence with the rustlers."

Twin pairs of golden eyes locked together in understanding until, with a slight smile, Neil clapped a hand on Sebastian's shoulder. "I can't give this up, not yet."

"I know. And that saddens me." Sebastian squeezed Neil's arm. "Texas gave you life—I pray it does not bring you death as well. Be very careful, my brother."

When Neil finally returned to his ranch a week later, Sebastian's warning still was ringing in his ears. Sebastian was right about one thing: He should let the Rangers catch the rustlers and thereby prove his own innocence. Disregarding the Rangers' direct order that the ranchers let the law deal with the criminals, Neil had hired Julio and the others—old friends from the Revolution—to help him track the thieves. Had his plan succeeded the rustlers would have been in custody by now. Instead Neil's actions had probably served only to cast greater suspicion upon himself, and to confess now that he had formed a posse to track the rustlers would seem a lame alibi. But, damn it, a man could take only so much! Neil had worked hard to make his ranch a success, and to sit back and watch it being eaten away bit by bit was intolerable. But more important, Neil had to admit, he had been restless. Four years in Texas, forced into pretending a friendship with that snake Lathrop Williams, with only an occasional visit to Sebastian—at times Neil was more than willing to forget everything and return home. When he said as much to Constanza, however, her face registered such despair that he would take her in his arms and postpone the decision. To desert Constanza when she clearly needed him so much would be unspeakably cruel.

Neil turned off the main road and galloped the last few miles to his ranch. His ranch! In spite of himself Neil felt a quick burst of pride as he brought his horse to a halt and surveyed the buildings that made up the *Rancho de Paraíso*. When he had purchased this land, Neil had made a small wager with himself: to see if he could make the ranch a profitable enterprise without investing more money, other than what he needed to buy cattle and hire three men. The first year had been the worst. The house had burned to the ground one night, its dry lumber an apparent victim of the improperly cleaned chimney, so for the months remaining until the roundup Neil had moved into the bunkhouse. The loss of the house hadn't really mattered, since with a sizable herd the four men hadn't much time to spend away from the cattle. In retrospect, Neil's forced association with his men had been for the best. He had known how to handle the business end of raising and selling cattle, but he'd known almost nothing about what went on between calving and the marketplace. In Mexico the top *vaquero* had handled those details. So Neil had watched and listened, and by the time the herd had been sold—at a good price—and they were starting all over again, he felt that he finally knew what being a rancher entailed.

The second year Neil bought more cattle, hired another ten men and ordered the lumber for a new bunkhouse. They built it together, he and his men, working in shifts during the day and night, and when the structure was finished Neil threw a party for his men complete with whiskey and women from one of the better "houses." At the end of that year, the ranch was solidly in the black, despite the losses Neil had suffered from the evasive rustlers. Once again Neil increased the size of his herd and the number of ranch hands, and then he began work on a house.

Outwardly the house had the appearance of a Spanish mission with its whitewashed adobe walls and wrought-iron grilles covering the windows. Inside, the tiled floors and massive, dark furniture left no doubt that, aside from the housekeeper, this was a purely masculine household. Neil left his horse in the care of a stablehand and threw his saddlebags over his shoulder, a burst of pride swelling his chest again as he walked into the house. He and his men had built this structure as well. Neil could still recall how the bricks had torn the flesh on his hands, how he and his men had struggled to wrestle the heavy grillwork into place across the windows. Compared to the hacienda, this house was barely the size of a *casita*, but for some reason Neil couldn't fathom he felt more comfortable here than he did when he was home in Mexico.

Neil bathed, stretching out full-length in the Roman bath he had installed next to his bedroom. One of the hired hands had raised his eyebrows and asked blandly if Neil had stolen the bath from a bordello. The memory drew a chuckle from Neil as he stepped from the tub and toweled himself dry. He might have, after all, since the rooms above the city's one saloon—though hardly exclusive—had served his purpose over the past four years. The area around Lathrop wasn't exactly lacking in attractive women, but Neil had decided not to risk his standing in the area by seducing some virginal local miss who would run to her father. Far better to be seen discreetly courting several of the proper young women during the day, while the saloon girls vied for his attention in the evening.

Just as Neil settled behind the desk in one corner of the front room he heard several horses pull up in front of the house. He glanced out the window and cursed softly. Golden eyes narrowed angrily, Neil strode to the door and opened it before his visitor had a chance to knock. "Hello, Captain Gerald."

The lanky, sun-browned man lowered his hand and grinned. "Mr. Banning, this is a surprise. Your housekeeper wasn't sure when you'd be back, but I thought we'd take a chance and stop by. Your brother is well, I hope?"

"He's much better." Neil glanced at the three men still astride their horses by the hitching post. "Would your men like to step inside, Captain?"

Keith Gerald looked over his shoulder and nodded to the other Texas Rangers to dismount. "They won't come in, but I will—if you don't mind, I'd like to have a talk with you."

"Of course." Neil stepped aside so the other man could

enter, then escorted him to the front room. "How can I help you?"

"As you know, rustlers have been working this area, and several of the other ranchers have asked for our help. I realize you feel that you are capable of dealing with this problem, Mr. Banning; so if it's all right with you, I'd like to dispense with any protests you may feel obligated to make." Captain Gerald settled himself into a chair before continuing. "Shortly after you left for Mexico, five ranches were hit by the rustlers. My men and I trailed them for several days, even after they tried to throw us off by splitting up. The odd thing, Mr. Banning, is that after they split up, they all headed in the same direction. Mexico."

Neil stiffened imperceptibly, feeling Gerald's eyes bore into him, waiting for Neil to give some tremor of reaction that would betray him. Did Gerald know the Rangers had been following Neil's small band? Had he added Neil's so-called emergency at home to the timing of the raid and concluded—wrongly—that Neil was involved with the rustling?

Neil selected a thin cigar from a box on his desk. "I'm afraid I don't see what that had to do with me," Neil said through a cloud of smoke. "Unless, of course, you're suggesting that I have some connection with the rustlers."

"Not at all," Captain Gerald assured him quickly. "In fact, I was hoping you would be willing to help us catch these men. President Díaz is very touchy about any American lawmen violating Mexico's borders. He says the *rurales* can handle any bandits who escape into his country. Now, maybe they can and maybe they can't, but the point is, we never know for sure whether our criminals have been caught. Besides, the *rurales* are former criminals themselves and it's well known that those men aren't averse to accepting a bribe now and then."

"Excuse me," Neil broke in impatiently, "but I still fail to see what all this has to do with me."

Keith Gerald smiled faintly. "I'm going to get those rustlers, Mr. Banning. I take a great deal of pride in the fact that the area my company patrols has been relatively peaceful since I took over, and I intend to see that it stays that way. Branding time is coming up pretty soon, isn't it?"

"Six weeks or so. Why?" Neil's temper was rising.

"You usually hire a few extra men during branding?" At Neil's short nod, Keith Gerald replaced his hat and walked to the door. "I'm going to save you a little time and trouble by giving you three men. Don't worry about having to teach these men the ropes, Mr. Banning. They grew up on ranches."

"Now, wait a minute, Captain." Neil grabbed Keith Gerald's arm and swung him around. "I don't particularly care for the way you charge in here and start giving orders. This is my home, my ranch. What gives you the right to tell me what to do?"

"This." Captain Gerald tapped the badge on his chest, his blue eyes snapping in anger. Any pretense of civility between the two men was dropped, giving way to the instinctive dislike they had felt for each other upon their first meeting just over a month before. *"This* gives me the right, Banning. You and your neighbors are losing cattle to the outlaws. Over the past few years you've been incredibly lucky that no one has been killed or even wounded. One of these days that luck will run out, and suddenly the bodies will start to pile up. I want to put a stop to the rustling before anyone—including you—gets killed. Now, either you take my men or I'll haul you into headquarters right now and keep you there until we catch the thieves. This isn't Mexico, Banning; we have laws here that apply to everyone. You people may tolerate outlaws south of the border, but in Texas we see that justice is done."

Neil's lips thinned angrily. "I take it you're setting your men up at all the ranches."

"That is correct."

"Then you must suspect that someone who works on the ranches is passing information to the rustlers."

"I didn't say that," Captain Gerald countered. "But so far we've been in the wrong place at the wrong time whenever we've tried to catch them. This should at least give us some sort of jump on the rustlers, and if we don't get them this time we'll just keep after them until we do."

"As a matter of fact, Captain Gerald, I've tried following the rustlers, and they've always managed to elude me." Neil's tone grew skeptical. "Do you really believe that your Rangers will be able to accomplish what my own hunting parties could not?"

"Oh, we'll catch them, all right. Thanks to their last raid, we now know where they go. In fact, I even managed to fire a couple of shots. Don't worry, Mr. Banning, there isn't a Mexican alive who can outsmart a Ranger." Captain Gerald took one last look around the room before walking out the door. Seething with rage, Neil followed him outside and watched as he swung into the saddle. "See that my men are settled in with as little fuss as possible. And, Mr. Banning, needless to say you really should disband your, ah, hunting parties. I would hate to confuse you and your men with the rustlers."

Neil's ill-concealed displeasure over their encounter amused Keith Gerald as he rode back to Ranger headquarters in Laredo. If there was one person who rubbed Keith the wrong way on sight, it was Neil Banning, and his odd behavior aroused Keith's suspicions. In addition, Keith thought sourly, Banning was arrogant to the point of being rude whenever he was confronted with American authority; he seemed to think he was above the law, that the rules which had, for the most part, stopped Texas from being torn apart in bloody, private range wars did not apply to Neil Banning. Keith had felt the same way too, ten years ago, when he was a bitter, angry boy of sixteen crying over his father's body, the gentle face blown into bits of flesh and bone. He hadn't been known as Keith Gerald then—that name had been adopted years later when he had joined the Rangers—but as he knelt, pounding his fists into the newly turned earth covering his father, he had sworn to avenge his father's death. He knew who the murderer was, had given the man's name to the sheriff because that was what his father would have done. The sheriff had been sympathetic, had agreed that the man was probably guilty, but that was all. The law demanded proof, evidence that could be used in court before charging a man with murder, and the accusation of a grief-stricken boy was not evidence. No one had ever heard any threats being made against the boy's father, and worse, the killer had an alibi for the night of the murder. Nothing could be done—inside the law.

But if the legal recourses that Keith had been taught to believe in were closed to him, another way was not. In an act born of desperation, he had followed the murderer into town one day and shot him down in front of the sheriff's office. That is, he tried to. His father's gun misfired, and instead of cutting down the hated enemy, the gun barrel exploded and the fragmented steel had torn and gouged its way through his right arm. The shredded, bleeding wound nearly killed him. While Keith hovered between life and death, the murderer played the part of a shocked, concerned citizen, and in a magnanimous gesture had refused to press charges against the boy.

Despite his aching arm, when Keith regained consciousness his only thought was to get another gun and try again. He would have, too, had the sheriff not convinced one member of the Ranger squad patrolling the area to put the fear of God and the law into the young boy. Ted Gerald hadn't bothered to talk; instead he had dragged Keith out of his sickbed to the outskirts of town to witness a hanging.

"At least your father left something good and decent behind; and in the end he outsmarted the man who had him killed," Ted had stated calmly, ignoring the fact that the boy beside him was being disgustingly sick. "If you want to end up like this, tell me now so I won't waste my time on you. But if you're serious about seeing your father's murderer brought to justice, then I'll show you the right way to go about it."

With his good arm, Keith had brushed at his streaming eyes and stared at the man who was still watching the swaying body. "Why?" he choked.

For the first time, Ted Gerald had looked directly at the skinny boy. "I had a younger brother. He was hotheaded, like you are, and high-spirited. He found the life of a rancher a little too tame for his taste, but neither my parents nor myself could see just how desperately he wanted to get away from the cattle and the land. He ran away one night, along with some of his friends, and in order to get enough money to get them out of Texas they tried to rob a bank the next day. They were shot down when they ran out of the bank—only one of the boys survived, and he's been in prison for seven years. He's twenty-four now." Ted had turned away. "I couldn't stop my brother from making a mistake that cost him his life, but with any luck at all, I can stop you."

So it was that Keith had been introduced to the Gerald family. Ted had taken Keith to his parents' ranch, and there Keith had lived for four years. The Geralds were kind, gentle people who welcomed the orphan into their home and helped him recover from his physical and emotional wounds, but it was Ted who channeled Keith's anger into a deep, unwavering loyalty to the law and an unshakable belief that justice would eventually triumph—given time, patience and a great deal of help.

It was Ted who spent every spare minute he had teaching

Keith to shoot with the uncanny accuracy for which the Rangers were justly famous. In the evenings, while Keith cleaned and oiled the guns they had used, Ted would read aloud from the lawbooks he had somehow managed to buy with his meager salary. He wanted more for Keith than the brief career of a Ranger—at twenty-six, Ted knew that at best he had only another four years until his reactions began to slow down to the point where the men in his company wouldn't be able to depend upon him anymore. After twelve years of service, at the age of thirty, Ted would retire from the Rangers and find another career. Not ranching—Ted didn't care for the idea of punching cattle the rest of his life—but maybe he could start an agency like that man Pinkerton had done back East. Keith could go to college in the East to study law while Ted set up the business. But instead, Keith had chosen to follow in his friend's footsteps, his father's murder still not forgotten.

Keith finally rode into Laredo at midnight, and after stabling his horse he walked across the street to the building that served as the Rangers' headquarters and barracks. The man behind the desk didn't stir when Keith entered the office, but his easy manner didn't deceive Keith. Beneath the desk top a sawed-off shotgun was balanced across the man's lap. Keith had sat this duty often enough to know the procedure.

"Hello, Cal." Keith sank into a chair and propped his feet up on the desk. "Any business?"

"Nope. A couple of kids got hold of a whiskey bottle somewhere and stumbled in here about an hour ago, demanding a shoot-out with our best man." Cal had relaxed and now he grinned at Keith. "I told them to come back in the morning; that it's Ranger policy not to shoot anyone after sunset."

Keith chuckled and shook his head. "Don't I wish! How come you pulled the duty tonight?"

"We've only got six men available—three of them just got in a few minutes ago, and the other two were ready to drop when they rode in this afternoon. It was me or nobody."

"What's up? I thought Hastings was supposed to be here for another two weeks."

Cal grinned and got up to pour himself a cup of coffee. "Captain Hastings got all riled up because one of his men went off and got drunk a couple of days ago. Hell, Keith, you know Hastings, all spit-and-polish military discipline. Anyway, he

# Chapter 10

Hugh Colter shifted uncomfortably in his chair and for what seemed to be the hundredth time pulled out his pocket watch to check the time. Only fifteen minutes had elapsed since his arrival and yet Hugh felt as if he had been waiting for hours. He raked a hand through his hair, wanting to block out all the painful memories this meeting was going to tear open.

"Hugh?" David Sterling called gently. "Sorry I took so long. Come into my office."

"Thanks for seeing me, David," Hugh said when they were settled. "I know it's an inconvenience—"

Dr. Sterling waved Hugh's apology aside. "Think nothing of it, Hugh. I only wish this meeting were under happier circumstances. Tell me: How is Eden?"

"Better, I think, at least physically. She's going out tonight for the first time since . . ." Hugh bit his lip and brought his emotions under control before continuing. "In fact, I'm going to meet her when you and I are finished." Hugh's voice broke and it took a few moments before he felt strong enough to go on. "I don't know if Eden can survive another miscarriage, David, and to make matters worse, I'm not even sure I can."

"I understand," David said sympathetically. "The miscarriages have been rough on both of you. I wish to God I could do something about it, but medical science can only do so much."

Hugh nodded grimly. "That's what we learned after making two trips to Europe to consult with the specialists you recommended. All of them told us the same thing—that there is no reason Eden can't carry a child to term, that we should keep trying and eventually we'll succeed. Each time we came back with a different set of instructions. The first doctor told Eden to take long walks, ride for at least an hour a day and eat fish in place of red meat. Eden followed his advice to the letter and her next pregnancy lasted two months. Back we went to Vienna, this time to a different specialist. That one ranted and raved for an hour when we told him about his colleague's suggested regimen—he had Eden in tears. She still hasn't

221

recovered from the guilt he made her feel—as if it were her fault for losing the baby!" Hugh's voice had risen alarmingly, his lilting brogue echoing in the office. "What kind of a man would do that to her?" Hugh brought his voice and frustration under control with an effort. "At any rate, he told Eden to stay in bed from the moment she suspected she might be pregnant. So Eden tried it his way, but that didn't work either."

"Hugh, take it easy." David leaned forward and fixed Hugh with an unwavering stare. "You're tearing yourself apart with this, my friend."

"And what do you think it's doing to Eden? She can't sleep, can't eat—my God, David, I wake up in the middle of the night to find Eden gone and I don't have to wonder where she is. I know I'll find her in the nursery, holding some little thing she made for the baby and crying her heart out." Shaking, Hugh pulled his pipe from his pocket and began to fill the bowl. He was helpless in this situation, and that made matters worse. To have to stand by Eden without being able to do anything except hold her close when she cried—that was what made the situation doubly painful.

"There is another doctor," David suggested slowly. "In London this time, not Vienna. He may be able to help you."

"No," Hugh said quietly. "Eden's seen a battery of specialists already. I don't think she would agree to another trip abroad, not even for pleasure."

David Sterling rubbed his burning eyes, uncertain how Hugh would react to his next words. "The first time Eden miscarried I contributed it to her youth, but now . . ." David shook his head. "I don't know, Hugh. After this fourth miscarriage I checked her as thoroughly as possible. Quite frankly, I was certain I would find some kind of damage to her womb, but I didn't. Yet despite the evidence to the contrary, her medical problem is very real."

"I don't understand," Hugh frowned. "What are you trying to say?"

"I'm not certain." David fiddled distractedly with the pen and inkwell on his desk. "I've seen women who are childless for years suddenly become mothers and the unexpected pregnancy baffles everyone, including me. This could easily happen to Eden. You two might be trying too hard."

"But the miscarriages," Hugh interrupted impatiently. "David, I'd rather see Eden barren than watch her go through this kind of torment. Damn it, man, isn't there something you can do?"

"No, Hugh, I'm afraid there isn't. Aside from adding my prayers to yours." David sighed. "I'm sorry."

"Then tell me what *I* can do," Hugh begged. "Tell me to stop sharing Eden's bed or to destroy the nursery or to start breeding horses, but for God's sake tell me *something!* I can't stand by and watch Eden being ripped apart like this!"

David straightened. "All right. For what it's worth, this is all I have to offer: I think it would be best for Eden to leave New York—with you, of course. If the two of you could get away from here, away from the unpleasant memories, and make a new start somewhere, I think that given time Eden might be able to recover."

"How long do you think that will take? For myself, I don't care where we live. But Eden was born here; it's her home. I don't know if I can convince her to leave."

"We both know things cannot go on this way," David informed him sternly. "I nearly lost Eden this last time. She refused to believe it was happening again so she kept quiet about the miscarriage for at least eight hours. If she does the same thing next time—if there is a next time—she may very well die."

"I see." Hugh studied the embers in his pipe. "This move is that important then?"

David lifted his hands in a gesture of uncertainty. "I don't know, Hugh. I think so, though the specialists in Vienna probably wouldn't agree with me. I do know that staying here doesn't seem to be helping Eden, so what do you have to lose?"

Back in his carriage, Hugh carefully weighed what David had said. Aside from this one problem, the past three years of their marriage had been full and happy. No man had ever had a more loving, attentive wife than Hugh had found in Eden, nor was any woman more loved and cherished in return. Despite the difference in their ages—or perhaps because of it—they had become closer than most husbands and wives. Where their lives had previously revolved around the glittering diversions offered by New York society, Eden and Hugh soon discovered they preferred sharing their time with no one but each other. Most of their evenings were spent at home—they read, talked, played cards and occasionally Eden would play the piano while

Hugh sang, his rumbling bass filling the room with the haunting Gaelic melodies of his youth.

They had become companions, friends, lovers. The tenuous bond with which Eden and Hugh had begun their reconciled marriage had slowly strengthened until now their serenely content way of life was a source of astonishment and not a little envy. The cool, aloof Eden Hugh had married four years ago seldom surfaced these days, and in her place stood a vibrant young woman who often displayed a fine sense of humor. Somehow, in some way, Hugh had carried out his promise to Eden's mother—Eden could laugh at situations she would once have found intolerable, and better still, she could laugh at herself. The imprint Locke Thackery had left upon his daughter was slowly disappearing.

And now this, Hugh thought unhappily as the carriage rolled to a stop in front of the Miller mansion. Uproot Eden and move her...where? Someplace close enough so that they could return to the city whenever Eden wished? Or farther away? Europe? England? Hong Kong? Ireland? Darlin' Eden, Hugh sighed to himself. We've gotten through worse times. We'll get through this as well.

It took Hugh three days of virtually locking himself away in his study to come up with a solution to his problem, and then he stumbled across the answer by accident. "Eden!" Hugh roared as he separated a sheaf of papers from a file in his desk. "Dear heart, come in here."

A minute later the door to the study banged open and Eden flew into the room. "What is it, Hugh. What's wrong?" she asked breathlessly.

Startled, Hugh looked up to find that not only Eden but also Simmons and two of the maids had rushed into the study at his call. Hugh flushed as he rose and went to the door. "Simmons, you may go. I, ah, just wanted to speak with Mrs. Colter."

Simmon's mouth set in sour lines as he waved the maids out of the room. "Very good, sir."

"I hope you have a reason for all this commotion," Eden scolded when Simmons had withdrawn after an aggrieved look at Hugh.

"I'm sorry," Hugh apologized, chuckling.

"Well, you should be. I was on my way out to the rose garden when I heard you bellow—" Eden gave up trying to reprimand him and merely shook her head. "You are impossible. You do know that, don't you?"

Hugh nodded and reached out to grasp Eden's hand. "I know, but I love you."

"You always say that when you want to change the subject." Eden returned his light kiss and smiled up at Hugh. "So tell me: What is so important?"

Perched on one corner of the desk, blue eyes sparkling in anticipation, Hugh put his hands on Eden's shoulders and grinned down at her. "How would you feel about moving, dear heart?"

"Moving?" Eden's eyes widened in shock. "Why? You and I both like this house and we certainly don't need another place in the country."

Hugh paused and picked up the papers on his desk. "I was thinking of something farther away."

"Where?" Eden asked softly, completely taken aback by Hugh's idea.

"Texas."

Eden stared at her husband in stunned disbelief. "Texas?" she echoed weakly. "Oh, Hugh, you can't be serious! There's nothing in Texas but cactus and desert and"— Eden paled— "and Indians."

"It's not quite that bad, dear heart," Hugh assured her. "The climate is different from New York, but our ranch in Lathrop has a nice stream running through it so you can't really call it a desert."

"Ranch?" Eden sank onto a chair, her gray eyes enormous as she watched Hugh casually light a cigarette. "You bought a ranch? With cows and everything?"

Hugh restrained his urge to laugh at Eden's crestfallen expression and instead pulled another chair beside her. "First of all, darlin', they're cattle, not cows, and second, you don't have to worry about the Indians. The last warriors were put on the reservations two years ago." Hugh offered the papers in his hand to Eden and she took them reluctantly. "It's not as if we'd be starting from scratch, Eden, the place has been operating for years. All I have to do is write to the banker who has been handling the ranch's affairs and tell him to make sure the house is ready for us. No one has lived in the main house for a good ten years, but I'm certain Mr. Randolph is quite capable of making any necessary renovations."

"Wait, Hugh, please!" Eden jumped from her chair and began to pace around the room. "You're going too fast for me. This is all so sudden—one day we're making plans for the theater and the next you've got us moving halfway across the country. To a place named Lathrop, of all things! What kind of a name is that for a town?"

Hugh looked at her slender back. "I know this comes as a shock, but believe me, I have my reasons."

Eden turned around. "Can we at least discuss this, or is your decision final?"

"Of course we can." Hugh went to her and drew Eden into his arms. "You know me better than that. I'm not going to drag you away from New York if you don't want to go. Come on now, sit down and we'll start by looking over these papers."

Eden leafed through the papers, then, frowning, she studied the deed. "You've owned the ranch for nearly eleven years! I didn't know you had invested in anything like this."

"Investing in land was actually your father's idea." Hugh smiled, producing a map from among the papers. "Look at the size of the ranch, dear heart. You know, there is a part of me that still feels the measure of a man is in how he manages his land. Even during the bad times in Ireland there was a certain satisfaction in watching the fields you had sweated over and cursed at finally turn green with the crops. Texas isn't Ireland, of course, but still, it would be . . . well, it would be interesting to give ranching a try."

Eden watched the excitement in Hugh's face as he talked about the ranch. Texas! Her heart sank at the very thought of living there. If they moved to Texas Eden knew she would never again see this house or Meg and her brood of children. Tears stung Eden's eyes and she quickly lowered her head so Hugh wouldn't see them. She owed Hugh more than she would ever be able to repay. Hugh was more than just her husband; he was father, teacher, friend, lover and adviser all in one. Their marriage was a happy one, based on a solid foundation of honesty and genuine respect for one another—and yet, try as she might, Eden had not grown to love Hugh in the way she had loved a man with golden eyes. Not that she didn't care for Hugh. He was dear to her and in a very real way she loved him, but she also knew that her love didn't carry with it the fervent passion Hugh felt for her. This was the one truth Eden kept carefully hidden from him. She would die before she would hurt Hugh in that way. Anything she could do that would make Hugh happy she would do—even if it meant moving to Texas.

"Eden?" Hugh waved a hand in front of her face. "Darlin', you're not listening. What are you thinking?"

Eden smiled and leaned forward to kiss Hugh tenderly. "That I won't be here to see my roses bloom."

# BOOK II
## 1878

So we'll go no more a roving
   So late into the night,
Though the heart be still as loving,
   And the moon be still as bright,

For the sword outwears its sheath,
   And the soul wears out the breast,
And the heart must pause to breathe,
   And love itself have rest.

                —BYRON

# Chapter 11

Eden sat in front of the mirror and critically studied her reflection. After nearly a month on the ranch the sun had already left its mark on her. When they had first arrived, after a long, tiring train ride from New York, Eden had been pale and thinner than usual, but since then the days spent riding with Hugh had not only increased her appetite but had also brought a warm, golden glow to her face. Contrary to Hugh's fear—and her own—that she would find it difficult to adjust to such a different way of life, Eden was enthralled with the freedom and independence she now possessed. The vast scope of the land was indescribable, as was the tranquil silence which enveloped the ranch each evening.

At times it amazed Eden that her transition from New York socialite to Texas rancher's wife had been made so easily. Two months ago she had been living in a thirty-room mansion complete with butler and maids, and now—Eden glanced around the bedroom and smiled—now she lived in a two-story, four-bedroom house with only one servant, Millicent. She and Millicent shared the housekeeping duties, although Millicent put up a fuss whenever Eden ventured into the kitchen to help prepare a meal. Ian, too, had forsaken New York for Texas. Explaining that he was bored with the easy life of a gentleman, Ian had convinced Hugh that he would be useful on the ranch, and Hugh had sent him ahead with the furniture and orders to make any necessary repairs to the house. Eden suspected that Ian hadn't been all that bored, but he and Hugh had been friends for so long that a separation now would be intolerable.

Still smiling, Eden pulled the pins from her hair and brushed her flaxen curls until they shone. They had arrived just as the branding was about to begin, and during the hectic time that followed she and Hugh had met only one of their neighbors, Maude Barston. Maudie—as she insisted upon being called—was a widow of ten years who had taken over the ranch after her husband's death. Maudie was a strong-willed, fiercely independent woman who blithely disregarded

231

conventions and said and did precisely as she pleased. Eden and Maudie had hit it off immediately, like two kindred spirits who had known each other all their lives. As they had said their good-byes Maudie announced her decision to give a welcoming party for Hugh and Eden as soon as the branding was finished. If Maudie kept to her plan, it would be the first party Eden had ever looked forward to attending.

Eden slipped into a filmy wrapper and went downstairs. The lamps were burning in the combination library/study and Eden paused in the doorway to watch as Hugh, a frown knitting his brows, pored over the papers that had arrived in the day's mail.

"Problems, Hugh?" Eden asked softly.

Hugh looked up, his frown immediately vanishing at the sight of the beautiful creature gazing at him with such concern. "Eden love, I thought you went to bed an hour ago. Why are you still up?"

"You know I can't fall asleep when your side of the bed is empty." Eden went to Hugh and wrapped her arms around his neck from behind. "What are you doing?"

"The final papers for the sale of your father's house arrived." Hugh drew Eden to his side and handed her the papers he had been studying. "All these need is your signature and then we'll send them back to our lawyer. It's not too late to change your mind—you may want to go back to New York one day."

"If I do I'll stay in a hotel," Eden replied. With quick, decisive motions she dipped a pen into the inkwell and signed the paper. "Besides, I doubt we'll ever return to New York; we made up our minds about that when we sold our home."

"I was thinking more in terms of what you would do when I die," Hugh said slowly.

"Hugh!" Eden breathed, a horrified look on her face. "You're being morbid."

"I'm being practical, Eden love," Hugh corrected gently. "This is something we've never discussed and I think it's time we did. I'm more than twice your age, darlin', and it's a sure bet that I will die before you do. My will is already written and it's in the safe here—"

"Stop this!" Eden covered her ears and whirled away from him. "I won't listen to this, Hugh, I won't!"

"Eden, Eden," Hugh murmured and rose to gather her against his chest. "You must listen, just as I must talk, no matter how difficult it is. Everyone dies, Eden love, it's just a matter of time. If we face it now, it won't be so hard on either of us when the time comes to say good-bye. I don't fear death; I've seen it too often to be frightened by it anymore. It's you I worry about, darlin'. I worry about what will happen to you when I'm gone." Eden started to protest and Hugh silenced her by placing a finger across her lips. "My will is in the safe, and in the same folder you'll find burial instructions, what I want said and such. I'm leaving everything to you except for the import business—that goes to Ian. He helped run it from the start and after all these years he still hasn't put any money aside. I owe him something for saving my hide so often and this way I'll be sure he's taken care of for the rest of his life."

Eden was crying softly against Hugh's chest, soaking the fabric of his shirt with her tears. "No more," she sobbed. "Please, Hugh, don't say anything else."

"No more." Hugh raised her face to his and tenderly wiped away her tears. "I've had my say and I feel better for it. Now dry your eyes, Eden love, I'm planning to live for a very long time."

"I can't imagine life without you," Eden said in a choked voice. "I'd want to die, too."

"Hush," Hugh ordered. With an arm around her shoulders he drew Eden to the window. "Look at it, darlin', the infinite universe. A miraculous sight, isn't it? One that makes you believe in God's omnipotence and life everlasting. I want you to do something for me: Pick out one star that strikes your fancy."

"A star? Why?"

"Humor me." Hugh smiled down at her.

"Oh, all right." Eden brushed at her damp cheeks. "The little one off to the east. See it?" Eden pointed to a small star that seemed to burn with more intensity than the others. "He's off by himself, as if he's too proud to be lumped together with the rest."

"A good choice." Hugh nodded approvingly. "I want you to remember that star because when I'm gone and you feel you need me, all you have to do is go to your window and find our star. For as long as you need me, until you're ready to pick up your life again, I'll be watching over you and protecting you from that star."

"You can't believe that," Eden said incredulously.

"And why not?" Hugh asked with a smile. "When I was a small boy and my mother lay dying, she and I did the same thing. Do you know, her star stayed with me during my voyage to America and it followed me out West. Then suddenly, one night when I went to look for it, the star was gone. I guess she knew I didn't need her anymore, that I could stand on my own two feet. You must have faith, Eden love, and believe in the goodness of man. After everything I've seen and done in this life, I've learned that no matter how bloody awful things are, there always is one moment when the basic decency of man shines through. Can you understand what I'm saying?"

"I think so." Eden snuggled against Hugh and studied the heavens. "I'll remember your star, I promise. Although I'm not planning on using it for many, many years."

"That's my girl." Hugh took her hand and led her around the room as he blew out the lamps, then up the stairs to their bedroom. Eden was still upset by their conversation, her eyes clouded with bewilderment, and Hugh sighed inwardly. In New York he had given little thought to his own mortality, but the day they had arrived in Lathrop and he had strapped on a gun again after so many years, Hugh had become increasingly aware of the possibility of his own death. There were dangers in this land—he could be killed by a rattlesnake, trampled by cattle or, if he happened across the rustlers Ian had told him about, he might even be shot.

Hugh's own uneasiness notwithstanding, the change had done wonders for Eden. The depression that had plagued her since the loss of their last child appeared to have lifted, and the plethora of medicine David Sterling had insisted she take along had gone untouched for a month. Moreover, the enthusiasm Eden displayed for learning the business of ranching assured Hugh that he had made the right decision in bringing her to Texas. Eden was emerging from her chrysalis and becoming stronger every day. The strain that had been so apparent on her features when they had first arrived in Lathrop was gone, and the soft laughter which had been missing was now back, warming Hugh's heart as it floated through the house.

"What are you thinking about?" Eden asked when Hugh joined her in bed.

"What I always think about: you." Hugh smiled as Eden

rested her head on his shoulder. "You are happy, darlin', aren't you? You're not just putting on an act to please me?"

"Of course not. I think I am beginning to understand why you felt confined back East." Eden ran her fingers through the silver hair at Hugh's temple "It's so free here, so open. Sometimes I wake up in the middle of the night and just lie here and listen to the quiet. It's like being in my own private world where nothing bad can happen. I know I'm being silly, Hugh, but—"

"No, you're not. I like to think that here on the Emerald I all things are possible. Who knows? Your cooking may even improve." That brought an outraged shriek from Eden, and Hugh caught her hands as she playfully brandished a delicate fist beneath his nose. "Only kidding, Eden love. I wouldn't have passed up the meal tonight for anything. Forgiven?"

"Forgiven," Eden acceded good-naturedly. Then, with one hand toying with the dark hair covering his chest she asked softly, "Are you terribly tired?"

"No, not particularly." Hugh looked into the eyes that glowed silver in the moonlight. "Are you?" Eden shook her head, her soft hair falling across his chest. "Then let's listen to the quiet," Hugh said in a rough voice as he pulled Eden to him.

Eden and Hugh rode out early the next morning to check on the branding, and when they were finished there they inspected the corrals that were being erected for breaking the new horses. It was nearly time for lunch before they returned to the house, and when they did, they found a carriage tied up to the hitching rail.

"Maudie?" Hugh wondered aloud as they dismounted.

"Perhaps, but I doubt she'd use a carriage. Last time she just took her horse." Eden dusted off her shirt and riding skirt and made a vain attempt to brush her hair with her fingers.

Millicent met them at the door, her eyes shining with resentment. "It's guests you've got," she announced before either Hugh or Eden could speak. "And at this hour yet. Oh, they're a fine pair, Miss Eden, just wait until you meet them."

Eden suppressed a laugh. "Thank you, Millicent. Why don't you bring some coffee for us?"

"Very well." Millicent sniffed. "I put them in Mr. Colter's

study—I wouldn't give him the satisfaction of sitting in our parlor."

Hugh raised an eyebrow when Millicent turned and flounced off. "What's gotten into her? I can't remember Millicent ever being this put out."

"Not since she found out Dan and Jane Miller were buying my father's house." Eden chuckled softly. "I suppose we'd better see what's waiting for us in the study."

Two men rose from their chairs when Hugh and Eden entered, and the older of the two came forward, his hand outstretched. "The name's Williams, Lathrop Williams. And you, I assume, are Hugh Colter."

"That's right." Hugh took Lathrop's hand, then drew Eden to his side. "May I present my wife, gentlemen."

"Well, well." Lathrop's pale blue eyes traveled suggestively over Eden's face and figure. "I see I'm not the only man who likes his woman young. How are you, missy?"

Eden winced at Lathrop's unsavory comments and booming voice. She could see now why Millicent had taken an instant dislike to the man—Lathrop Williams was an overbearing, thoroughly repugnant creature, and Eden withdrew her hand from his grasp as quickly as possible. "How do you do, Mr. Williams," she said icily.

"Why, missy, you sound just as pretty as you look. Oh, and this is Vincent." Lathrop waved a hand at the grimly silent man behind him. "Vince kind of keeps an eye out for me; like a bodyguard, you might say." Vincent nodded slightly, his cold, flat eyes resting upon Eden until she shifted uncomfortably beneath his stare. Lathrop smiled humorlessly and added, "He doesn't say much, but Vince gets his point across. That's all, Vince; wait outside for me."

"Would you care for some coffee, Mr. Williams?" Eden asked when Vincent was gone.

"I'd rather have a glass of that fine Irish whiskey I see at your bar. The ride over here was mighty dry."

"In that case I'll leave you two alone," Eden said with a faint smile. "If you gentlemen will excuse me?" With a smile at Hugh, Eden closed the door to the study and strolled through the house to the kitchen. Millicent was just taking the coffee pot fom the stove, and Eden motioned to her to replace it. "Mr. Williams preferred something with a little more punch. Thank you anyway, Millicent. Just keep it warm and we'll have it with lunch."

"Will those two be staying for the meal?"

"I don't think so," Eden murmured absently a she rummaged through a drawer. "At least I hope not. Brr—that Vincent makes my skin crawl. Have you seen my gloves, Millicent? I want to work with the flowers before lunch."

"They're on the table outside, I think." Millicent turned as Eden started for the door. "You'd best wear a bonnet, Miss Eden, you're turning brown as an Indian."

"I know," Eden replied over her shoulder. "Isn't it wonderful?"

The one part of New York Eden had brought to Texas was flowers. A tall, three-sided enclosure with a burlap ceiling had been built against the house for the flower beds so that the plants could be protected from the scorching midday sun until they adjusted to their new climate, and Eden carefully drew the material across the supports before turning her attention to the flowers. Some of the plants were budding, and a few had already burst into bloom, Eden noticed as she retrieved her gloves from her work table and painstakingly began to ladle water around each of the stems. Water was precious here, the soil thirsty, and only the stream which ran through their land made Eden's colorful hobby possible. In a country where everything seemed to be some shade of brown, this one bright patch was a welcome change.

"That's mighty pretty, Mrs. Colter."

Eden gasped and whirled around to find Vincent leaning against one of the supports, watching her through hooded eyes. "You . . . surprised me, Mr., ah, Vincent," Eden stammered.

"Surprised? Don't you mean frightened, Mrs. Colter?"

His voice held no trace of emotion and Eden shivered, afraid of Vincent's watchful presence. "Very well then, Vincent, you frightened me. I assume that's one of the reasons Mr. Williams hired you." To hide the trembling of her hands, Eden knelt and continued working. "May I offer you something to drink, Vincent? There's coffee in the house or cold water from the well."

"No, ma'am, not just now." Vincent sauntered into the enclosure and seated himself on the table so that he could keep an eye on both Eden and the open side of the shelter. "You bring those flowers with you from New York?"

"Yes." Eden's head snapped up and she looked at him sharply. "News travels rather quickly around Lathrop."

For the first time a flicker of emotion passed across Vincent's features and he relaxed ever so slightly. "It's a small town; news doesn't have that far to travel."

"So I see," Eden commented drily.

"My wife used to grow flowers like these." Vincent shook his head. "They never did amount to much, though. The sun burned them into shriveled-up brown sticks."

"What a shame," Eden exclaimed quietly. "I'd be happy to give her some of these—they seem to be holding up quite well."

"That's nice of you, Mrs. Colter, but it wouldn't do any good. She's dead."

"Oh!" Eden looked away nervously and toyed with one of the blossoms. "I'm sorry."

Vincent shrugged. "It happens. Besides, that was a long time ago." He lapsed into a silence so forbidding that Eden was afraid to say another word. For what seemed like hours Vincent neither moved nor spoke and then, out of the blue, he asked, "Do you know how to shoot a pistol, Mrs. Colter?"

Eden was nonplussed. "No," she answered hesitantly. "Hugh—my husband—wants me to learn but I really don't think it's necessary. After all, what would I shoot?"

"Snakes, coyotes—men," Vincent told her impassively.

"Oh, I couldn't! How can you even say such a thing?" Eden admonished, her startled eyes wide. "Kill another human being? It's unthinkable!"

Vincent nodded, as if something Eden had said satisfied him, and without another word he rose and walked away.

"Well, what in the world..." Eden's voice trailed off and she stared after Vincent in disbelief.

A moment later Hugh ran into the enclosure. "Are you all right?" he demanded anxiously. "Millicent said she saw Vince out here. What did he want?"

"I haven't the vaguest idea." Eden pulled off her gloves with quick, jerky movements. "I think he just wanted company until his master was ready to leave. Why in the world does Mr. Williams need a bodyguard?"

"From what I've gathered, he's made a lot of enemies in his life." Hugh caught Eden's hand. "That Vince character didn't try anything, did he? He didn't hurt you?"

"Lord no, but he scared me half to death." Eden shuddered. "One minute I was alone out here and the next Vincent was standing there watching me. The way he looks at people is frightening. Did you notice, Hugh? It's like Vincent doesn't really see anyone."

Hugh grunted in agreement and they went inside for lunch. While Eden attacked her food ravenously, Hugh ate automatically, his mind still busy with their unexpected guests. Lathrop he could deal with—the man had an overblown image of himself that made Hugh wish he could wipe the ever-present smirk off Lathrop's face, but failing that, Hugh could ignore him. It was Vincent who really worried Hugh, particularly the interest he was displaying in Eden. Hugh had met Vince's type before and nothing good ever happened when a man like him was around.

Eden pushed her plate away with a sigh of satisfaction, then frowned at the way Hugh was absentmindedly spooning sugar into his coffee. "Sure and after all these years I thought you took your coffee black," Eden teased in the lilting Irish brogue she mimicked so well. "You may as well spit it out, me darlin', before you choke on what's bothering you."

Hugh chuckled and allowed the spoon to fall against the side of the cup. "You almost sound like you're from the old sod." The smile left Hugh's face and he gazed seriously into her soft, gray eyes. "I want you to stay away from Vince, Eden. He's a dangerous man."

"I'm hardly going to seek his company," Eden replied wryly. "But I think you worry too much. He's only a bodyguard."

"Vince is a killer," Hugh explained tersely. "A hired killer, a gunfighter. Did you see the way he wears his gun? Low on his hip, strapped down tight? The gun is the tool of his profession and I would guess he is very good at his work or Lathrop wouldn't have hired him. I don't care for Vince because of what he does, but more importantly, I don't like the interest he's shown in you."

"He just talked about his wife," Eden protested, but her throat tightened in alarm. "You don't think he means to harm us?"

"No, of course not," Hugh assured her. "But avoid him anyway."

"That shouldn't be hard." Eden relaxed in her chair and

grinned impudently at her husband's grim expression. "After all, how often will we see Lathrop Williams?"

"More often than you may think, I'm afraid. He and his wife are throwing a party for us on Saturday. It seems they want to make sure we're introduced to the citizens of Lathrop in style."

"But . . . Maudie wanted to do that!" Eden cried. "We promised her—"

"I know, and I am sorry about it," Hugh said quietly. "But Maudie wasn't definite about her plans and Lathrop was. I couldn't very well refuse him. Besides, Maudie will be at the party. I think Lathrop invited everyone in the county."

Eden threw her hands up in disgust. "All hail, King Lathrop. Honestly, the way he barged in here you'd think that's what he is."

"You're not too far off," Hugh agreed. "Lathrop owns 90 percent of the town, and his ranch is the largest one in these parts." At Eden's questioning look Hugh shrugged. "I asked around. Lathrop isn't modest about his holdings; he enjoys playing king of the hill."

"I thought we were finished with that kind of game when we left New York," Eden groaned. "Can't we just tell him— in a polite way, of course—that we aren't interested in joining his kingdom?"

Hugh's eyes darkened with concern at the strained note in Eden's voice. When it came to meeting new people and making friends Eden was still far too suspicious of people to let down her guard. Since they had arrived in Texas Eden had all but isolated herself on the ranch, not even caring to accompany Millicent when she went into town for supplies. It was a pattern of behavior Hugh didn't want to see continue. "I don't care for the man any more than you do, Eden, but I certainly don't want to offend him. We can't pretend the rest of the world doesn't exist."

"I realize that, Hugh. It's just that I've been so content these past few weeks." Eden sighed and began to clear away the dishes. "I've never had so much uninterrupted time to myself. That's one thing I don't miss about New York."

"Solitude is all well and good, but not in such a large dose. I'm rather looking forward to this party—I'd like to meet my other neighbors." Hugh curved an arm around Eden's waist when she walked past him and pulled her into his lap. "And you need to see other people besides Millicent and myself, dear heart."

Eden glanced away from the warmth of Hugh's gaze. "What if they don't like me, Hugh?" Eden's voice held a tremor of uncertainty. "I do so want to fit in here, to make you proud of me."

"I've always been proud of you, darlin'," Hugh stated quietly and dropped a kiss onto Eden's hand. "Nothing will ever change that."

For the better part of a week they had been trapped in the middle of a summer heat wave that had left Eden feeling limp and wilted. It was too hot to ride, eat or even move until the sun finally set each day. Never in her life had Eden experienced such heat—it sapped the strength out of animals and men alike. Even the cattle were content to stay by their water troughs rather than graze aimlessly over the range.

In a final attempt to be free of the heat, after a light evening meal Eden filled a tub with cool water and sank gratefully into it. She had exactly one hour before they had to leave for Lathrop Williams' party, and at this moment Eden didn't particularly care whether they went or not. Scowling, she fished the washcloth out of the water and laid it over her face. The door clicked open and Eden lifted a corner of the washcloth to peer up at Hugh.

"You shouldn't do that," Hugh admonished as he bent over the tub. "Jumping into cold water in this kind of heat can kill you."

"It's not cold, just cool," Eden replied petulantly. "I have to do something, Hugh. I feel like a steamed lobster."

"Luckily the party doesn't start until after sunset—it should be cooler by then." Hugh playfully splashed a handful of water at Eden's face. "What are you planning to wear tonight?"

"My chemise and nothing more if I can get away with it." Eden delicately wiped the water droplets from her lashes. "The party isn't formal, is it?"

"Formal enough." Hugh stripped off his shirt and tossed it onto the bed before crossing to the washstand to shave. "After issuing his invitation, Lathrop very politely implied that his wife is the only woman around here who knows how to dress fashionably. Lathrop seemed to think that your shirt and riding skirt were a bit unstylish."

Eden sat up so quickly that water splashed over the sides of the tub. "Oh, he did, did he?" she exclaimed, her gray eyes snapping.

"Un-huh." Hugh concealed a smile by vigorously applying the lather to his face. "I believe his exact words were, 'That little gal is cute as a mud hen.' Now, darlin'," Hugh cautioned as the sparks flew from Eden's eyes, "you have to admit you were not exactly a fashion plate at that moment."

"I had been riding for nearly five hours," Eden protested. "What did the man expect? Pearls and silk?" Eden snatched up a bar of soap and began to scrub herself furiously. "Mud hen indeed!"

Eden had never been particularly vain or self-conscious about her appearance, but the thought of Lathrop's condescending attitude was a spur set into her feminine ego. With a defiant toss of her head, Eden stepped from the tub and toweled herself off until her skin glowed, then pulled a clean chemise from the drawer. If Lathrop Williams or his wife expected to see a dowdy, windblown Eden Colter tonight they were in for a rude awakening. Eden threw open the doors to her closet and chewed thoughtfully on a fingernail while she mentally sifted through her wardrobe.

"Problems, dear heart?" Hugh chuckled as he climbed into the tub.

"You're really enjoying this, aren't you?" Eden shot over her shoulder.

"Ah, but you said you didn't miss all the primping you had to do in New York." Hugh's eyes danced with laughter as Eden inspected one dress after another. "Seems that most of the other women out here feel the same way—except for Mrs. Williams. Ian says she dresses fit to kill, especially when it comes to jewelry."

Eden ignored the remark about Mrs. Williams. "The women here don't have the time or energy to primp. What do you think of this one?" Eden held up a black satin trimmed with rows of white lace. "I wore it to the opening of the opera last season, remember? With the pearl necklace and earrings it's quite stunning."

Hugh shook his head. "I never have liked you in black, stunning or not. Try something else."

"What?" Eden asked in exasperation. "I left most of my formal gowns with Meg because I didn't think I'd need them."

"How about the silver silk you had made up for the reception Meg gave when her second baby was christened?" Hugh wrapped a towel around his waist and padded over to Eden. "You didn't give that one to Meg I hope."

"I don't think so—no, here it is." Eden took the silvery gown off the hanger and held it in front of her while she studied her reflection in the mirror. "Ah, yes, I remember this one," Eden said with a soft laugh. "I ended up repairing the sash because you were so impatient."

"And whose fault is that?" Hugh asked with a smug look. "After the way you teased and flirted with me all evening I had no other choice."

Eden recognized the gleam in Hugh's eyes and she warned him off with a wagging finger. "No, you don't, Hugh, we haven't the time."

"Damn party," Hugh grumbled, but after kissing Eden thoroughly he reluctantly let her go. "I hope this shindig is worth what I'm going to be missing—especially since we have to spend the night at the Williams'."

Laughing, Eden danced away from him and set about the business of doing her face and hair while Hugh dressed. Thanks to the sun she didn't need more color in her cheeks, but Eden critically applied a delicate shade of pink to her lips and then, with a narrow brush, she lightly dusted her eyelids with silver powder. The hairstyle proved more difficult and Eden tried a variety of swathes, coils, ringlets and combs before simply rolling her hair into a chignon. From the small lamp on the vanity Eden withdrew the curling iron that had been heating and in a few turns of her wrist the tendrils of hair at her temples became feathery ringlets that swayed whenever she moved.

The dress came next, and as she stepped into it Eden was grateful for the low neckline and for the cascading frills that served as sleeves. To be trapped in a long-sleeved, high-collared gown in this heat would be unbearable. Hugh came up behind Eden and buttoned the long row of tiny buttons running up the back of the dress—a habit he had acquired over the past years. When he was finished, Eden turned and knotted his tie. Smiling, Hugh dropped a kiss on Eden's forehead and took their bags down to the carriage. Seated once more at the vanity, Eden flipped open her jewelry box and surveyed its contents.

"And which of these trinkets will it be tonight, Eden lass?" she said aloud as she ran her fingers through the brilliant display. She would wear her engagement ring, of course, but what else? She didn't want to look as if she were competing with Mrs. Williams, especially since the woman must be twice her own age. Rubies? Eden discarded them with a shiver—rubies always reminded her of Neil, and she didn't need any unpleasant memories tonight. Diamonds then, Eden decided hurriedly when Hugh called upstairs to ask if she was ready. She quickly inserted the posts in her ears and clasped the close-fitting necklace around the base of her throat. Last, Eden touched her favorite perfume to her wrists and with a final glance at the mirror left the room.

"Finally," Hugh growled when he heard Eden coming down the stairs. "Why women take so long I will never—" The words died in his throat and he let out a low whistle of appreciation.

Eden snapped open a small fan with a careless flick of her wrist and struck a pose at the bottom of the stairs. Her eyes, reflecting the color of the dress, were a soft, fathomless gray that snared Hugh in their depths. The diamonds sparkled, but no more so than the cool, flaxen-haired beauty wearing them, and Hugh found himself momentarily speechless.

"Well?" Eden's lips curved into a seductive smile, her voice taking on a low, husky note. "Was it worth the wait?"

"Eden love, the things you can do to a man when you put your mind to it," Hugh rasped. "If you weren't already married to me, I would certainly find a way of seducing you tonight."

Eden laughed, deliberately breaking the spell she had woven. "Come along now. We mustn't make a bad impression by being late."

Had they been able to travel on horseback instead of by open carriage, the trip would have been considerably shorter, but as it was, they spent just over an hour on the rough road to the Williams ranch. But despite the bumps and jolts Eden enjoyed the ride, especially when the sun burned itself out in the sky in a final blaze of red, yellow and orange and was replaced by the far more companionable glow of the moon.

"That must be the place," Hugh said as he turned the team off the main road. Half a mile ahead light poured through the windows of what appeared to be a small fortress. Hugh nudged Eden and commented wryly, "I see King Lathrop has built himself a nice little palace."

"So it seems," Eden agreed. "The house looks so out of place compared to others I've seen, so"—Eden searched for the right word—"so incongruous. It's more like something you'd find back East."

They pulled up in front of the house and were instantly greeted by one of Lathrop's men, who took charge of their team and luggage; and before Hugh could use the heavy brass knocker, the door was opened by the butler who, to Eden's mind, bore a striking resemblance to Simmons.

"Ah, Mr. and Mrs. Colter," the butler deftly identified them as he took Eden's shawl as the sound of voices and music wafted into the entryway. "If you will wait here, I shall inform Mr. Williams of your arrival."

Eden exchanged an amused glance with Hugh before making a last-minute check of her appearance. "Why is it I expected him to sound British instead of Spanish?"

"Too many years with Simmons, I think." Hugh laughed. "And he's Mexican, dear heart, not Spanish."

Eden shrugged, then turned at the sound of footsteps. "Oh Lord," she whispered, "here comes Lathrop. I suppose it's too late to back out?"

"Definitely." Hugh smiled down at Eden as she tucked her hand in the crook of his arm. "Try to relax and enjoy yourself, dear heart; and just remember that I won't be far away."

"Hello, Hugh." Lathrop's roar drowned out the other voices and music. "Mrs. Colter, my, but you surely are a picture tonight."

"Thank you, Mr. Williams," Eden returned formally, coolly, even though the only thing she could think of was extricating herself from the sweaty hold Lathrop had on her hands. "But please, do call me Eden; Mrs. Colter is much too formal."

Her bright smile, concealing any other emotion Eden was feeling, disarmed Lathrop completely, and his eyes flared with undisguised admiration. "That suits me fine, Eden, as long as you call me Lathrop." Eden smiled again, and when she caught the laughter dancing in Hugh's eyes her smile broadened. Lathrop gestured toward an archway, and when Eden and Hugh fell into step on either side of him he continued, "My wife, Constanza, has been looking forward to meeting you, Eden. She's a very fashion-conscious woman, so be prepared. I'm sure Constanza will want to talk your ear off about bustles or something equally silly, but don't let her drag you into a corner for the whole evening."

"I won't," Eden assured him. They stepped into a ballroom that rivaled any Eden had seen in New York, and, pausing with Hugh and Lathrop just inside the door, for a split second she was afraid all conversation in the room would cease with Lathrop's rather dramatic entrance. When the conversation died down momentarily, then returned to its normal level, Eden slowly released her pent-up breath. Thank God for small favors, she thought gratefully. Already Eden realized that her gown and jewelry were horribly out of place here. Of the guests— which Eden estimated numbered seventy—nearly half were women and she could see no other woman wearing a dress of pure silk, although she glimpsed a few wearing satin and grenadine.

"Now, there's a man I want you to meet, Hugh," Lathrop said, oblivious to Eden's sudden silence. "If you haven't already had the pleasure. His name is Keith Gerald, and he's a captain in the Texas Rangers. But first"—Lathrop took Eden's arm and elbowed a path through the crowd—"I'd better introduce you to Constanza."

Constanza Williams was waiting—impatiently so, judging by the way one toe of her dancing slippers was beating a tattoo on the floor—but the surprise Eden felt when she was introduced to a woman only a few years older than herself was quickly replaced by irritation when she saw the haughty contempt flashing in the other woman's dark eyes.

"Eden," Constanza acknowledged in a lofty, heavily accented voice, offering a bejeweled hand. "I am glad we finally meet. I had hoped you would visit me before this."

Eden nearly choked on the cloying scent of Constanza's perfume. With an effort, Eden swallowed her anger and replied as cordially as possible. "I'm afraid I've been far too busy to visit anyone. You know what it's like to get settled in a new home—"

"No, I don't," Constanza said pointedly. "My servants have always attended to such trivial details. Do you not have servants, Eden?"

"Only a cook," Eden murmured, then after glancing over her shoulder to make certain that Lathrop was safely out of hearing she added, "I gave up the others for Lent."

"Pardon?" Constanza tilted her head and eyed Eden suspiciously. "I am not sure I understand."

"It doesn't matter, Constanza." Eden's lips twitched into

her first genuine smile of the evening, her eyes sparkling merrily. "Will you excuse me? I see Maude Barston waving to me."

Constanza raged for a good five minutes after Eden had left her standing all alone with her mouth half open. How *dare* that blond woman with the complexion of a dead fish treat Constanza Martinez Williams as if she were no more than a shopkeeper's wife! Lathrop had said that Hugh Colter had as much money, if not more, than he himself did. Impossible, Constanza consoled herself with a sneer. Eden Colter's dress might be in fashion and made of silk, but Constanza's gown was far more impressive with its rows of lace, pleats and gold-shot brocade. And Eden's jewels could not compare to the massive emeralds at Constanza's ears, throat and wrists. Constanza fingered her necklace possessively and sniffed at the sight of Eden Colter being warmly greeted by Maude's friends.

"Something wrong, Constanza?" The drawling voice so near her ear consoled Constanza's bruised pride, and smiling triumphantly she turned to face Neil Banning, who continued, "The last time I saw you looking like this you were fifteen and your horse had just had the audacity to throw you over a fence."

"And I sold him immediately," Constanza rejoined with a toss of her head.

"To me. He sired some of the best colts in my stable." Neil shrugged, his golden eyes narrowing when he saw Lathrop several feet away. The pretense of cordiality Neil had to maintain whenever he was with Lathrop left a bitter taste in his mouth. What kind of man, Neil wondered disgustedly, trusted a mere acquaintance to spend so much time alone with his wife. "So why the sour look, Constanza? Is Lathrop giving you problems?"

"No. I just met Hugh Colter and his bitch of a wife." Constanza's lower lip pushed forward in a pout. "I cannot see why Lathrop finds her so attractive. She is pale, drab, like a sparrow."

"While you are more like a peacock?" Neil smiled, taking the sting of sarcasm from his words. Getting into still another fight with Constanza was the last thing Neil wanted. In the past six months Constanza's temper had become unexpectedly shrewish, and whenever Neil tried to find out what the problem was, Constanza turned on him. Given her presently agitated state it would undoubtedly be wisest to compliment Constanza and take her mind off whatever was irritating her. "I don't think there's another woman here tonight who can hold a candle to you," Neil murmured. "I've never seen you looking lovelier, *querida*."

Constanza preened visibly and took Neil's arm. "I chose this gown particularly for you, Neil. Does it not remind you of home, of the way things used to be?"

"It does." Neil felt a stirring of impatience as Constanza wheedled more compliments out of him and soon he was replying automatically, though the attentive expression never left his face.

"But come," Constanza abruptly interrupted her own monologue. "I will introduce you first to Hugh Colter and then to his wife."

The gossip Neil had heard in town about Hugh Colter and his retiring wife did not prepare him for the easy good-naturedness displayed by the silver-haired Irishman. And when Constanza turned all of her sultry charms on Hugh, Neil's jealousy was laid to rest as Hugh politely and charmingly refused to be drawn into her game. Compared to Lathrop's swagger and bluster, Hugh's candid, open conversation was a welcome change and Neil found himself liking the older man.

"Be careful," Hugh warned jokingly when Constanza announced she was taking Neil to meet Mrs. Colter. "My wife is quite bewitching."

"I'll keep my guard up," Neil said with a laugh, amused by the idea of falling under a fortyish woman's spell. Still chuckling, Neil took Constanza's arm and started through the crush of people.

Hugh watched their progress, the laughter fading immediately from his eyes, until Neil and Constanza had reached the small knot of guests around Eden. With a sudden, barely controlled movement, Hugh spun back to meet another guest.

Constanza tapped Eden on the shoulder. "I have someone you must meet," she purred when Eden half turned to face her. "I hope we are not interrupting?"

"Not at all, Connie," Maudie piped up, deliberately using the nickname Constanza hated. "After all, you are the hostess." Maudie squeezed Eden's hand and whispered, "If you need help, Eden, just yell."

Eden laughed softly and nodded. "I will. I'll talk to you later, Maudie." A few minutes of Maudie's company had lifted

Eden's spirits considerably and she faced Constanza with a carefree toss of her head.

"Eden Colter, may I present—"

Eden didn't hear the rest of Constanza's introduction. Her heart gave one wild, sickening lurch and slammed into the pit of her stomach. *Neil!* His name beat deafeningly against her ears, drowning out all other sounds. Everything in the room seemed to spin crazily except Neil. This isn't happening, Eden told herself desperately while a pair of golden eyes locked with her own. Not here, not now. Let this be someone who only looks like Neil. Or better still, let her wake up and find that this was just a terrible nightmare; that the man who was so gallantly lifting her hand to his lips in an Old World, courtly gesture that sent a bolt of electricity jolting down her spine was a total stranger. He wasn't a stranger, though. Despite the fact that his face was leaner than it had been four years earlier and a thick, drooping moustache now curved down to the corners of his mouth, this man was undeniably Neil Banning. O God, Eden begged mutely as she tried to concentrate on what Neil was saying. Help me! Let him have forgotten about me. Help me get through this meeting without anyone seeing that I know him.

"A pleasure, Mrs. Colter," Neil drawled and bent over her hand to give himself time to mask the stunned recognition he knew was flaring in his eyes. The odds against Eden Thackery ever reappearing in his life were astronomical, and yet here she was, thousands of miles from New York, looking more beautiful than any memory Neil had of her and certainly more striking than the portrait in the watch he still carried. The girlish appeal Neil remembered had all but disappeared and in its place was the delicately refined, sophisticated patrician beauty into which Eden had matured. "Your husband said I might find you bewitching, Mrs. Colter, and may I say he wasn't exaggerating."

"Thank you, Mr. Banning." Ludicrously, Eden found herself noticing that Neil's crisp British accent had given way to a Texas drawl. "You're too kind."

"Neil is always gracious." Constanza hooked her arm through Neil's, disliking the attention Neil was paying to Eden. "His ranch lies just northeast of yours, Eden, which means Neil is your closest neighbor."

"How nice," Eden murmured weakly, her nerves fraying.

If only Constanza would stop talking and lead Neil somewhere else, she thought desperately. It was becoming impossible to think, let alone speak, with Neil staring at her as if he didn't quite recognize her. "I'm afraid I haven't had the chance to meet your wife, Mr. Banning."

"I'm not married, Eden. You don't mind if I call you Eden, I hope?" Eden shook her head and Neil smiled into the mist-gray eyes he remembered so well. "But I do have an excellent housekeeper, so you and your husband must do me the honor of having dinner with me one evening."

"I'm certain we would both enjoy that," Eden said as levelly as possible, choking back the irrational fear that was constricting her throat. "Will you excuse me, please? I . . . it's gotten terribly warm in here. I need to get some fresh air."

"There is a terrace just off the ballroom. I'll be happy to accompany you," Neil offered, ignoring the angry looks Constanza was giving him.

"No! Thank you," Eden said hastily. "I can find the way. Please, excuse me."

"Well," Constanza sniffed distastefully as they watched Eden hurry away, "I have never met anyone so rude, except Lathrop."

"She's not rude, Constanza, she's just not feeling well," Neil snapped. Frowning, Neil watched as Eden struggled with the door leading to the terrace.

"Why are you siding with that *gringa?*" Constanza demanded. "Her actions are unforgivable and I will not tolerate them."

"Sure you will," Neil said in a nasty voice. "Lathrops wants to deal with Colter about the water rights on his land, so you wouldn't dare alienate his wife." Neil sighed and brought his temper under control. "I'm sorry, Constanza. I know it isn't easy for you to act the part of a happy wife whenever Lathrop gives a party, but at times you play the role so convincingly—"

"Let's not talk about Lathrop now." Constanza tugged at Neil's arm. "Come dance with me, Neil. We will show these clumsy *gringos* how to move gracefully around a dance floor."

Hugh also had seen Eden struggling with the door and he excused himself and made his way toward her. "Eden?" Hugh placed a hand over hers and was shocked to find it was ice cold. "What is it, dear heart?"

Eden looked up and, when she saw Hugh, nearly sobbed out loud. "I . . . I don't feel very well," Eden said evasively. "The heat, I think. Constanza suggested I use the terrace to get away from the crowd."

"I'll come with you." Hugh frowned at the wild look in Eden's eyes.

"No!" Eden bit her lip at the sharpness of her voice. "No, Hugh, please don't fuss. All I need is a few minutes by myself in the night air. I'll be fine, Hugh, truly I will."

Eden's voice had a catch to it and Hugh looked at her sadly. "Something's upset you, dear heart. Why don't you tell me about it."

"It's nothing, Hugh." Eden looked into the gentle blue eyes so full of love and understanding and fought back the impulse to throw herself into Hugh's arms. No matter how much Hugh loved her, this was one thing Eden dared not share with him. "I just need a few minutes away from this crowd, that's all. Please don't worry, Hugh."

"All right." Hugh smiled down at her. "If you're sure nothing is wrong."

"I'm sure," Eden said gratefully. "I won't be long."

Eden stepped outside and quickly moved to the far end of the terrace. She was panicking, she knew, but her thoughts were such a jumble that she couldn't speak or act normally. This isn't fair! Eden all but screamed the words aloud. How could she possibly get through tonight without Hugh wondering what was wrong? And worse yet, how could she keep the truth from Hugh? She had never been able to lie to Hugh, and if she tried now . . . Eden leaned weakly against the rim of the fountain Constanza was so proud of and fought down the sob that was clogging her throat.

What am I going to do? Eden wondered desperately. I can't live here knowing that any time I go into town or to a party I'll run into Neil. She dipped her handkerchief into the fountain and pressed it against the ache that was forming in her temples. Eden drew a deep breath, tilted her head back to look at the heavens and immediately found Hugh's star shining bright and strong apart from the rest. No matter how she felt, no matter what her silence cost, Hugh had to be protected from finding out who Neil was. They were starting a new life here and if they were to succeed, Neil Banning had to be kept in the past, where he belonged.

"Hello, love."

The wickedly seductive voice jolted Eden out of her thoughts and, despite her efforts, sent her heart pounding wildly. With as much dignity as she could manage Eden slowly turned to face the golden eyes that fairly glowed in the dark, sardonic face.

"I still like you best in rubies," Neil commented softly as he came forward from the shadows. "Or perhaps emeralds. But not diamonds, love; they don't suit you. Neither does that old man you're married to." Neil came to a stop beside Eden and casually pulled a cigar from his jacket, lighting it while he studied her delicate profile. "You've changed, love. You're thinner than you were four years ago—but you're just as lovely."

Eden closed her eyes, fighting off the emotions Neil was evoking. "I'm surprised you remember," she said finally. "After all, ours was hardly an earth-shattering affair. What was it—a week? Not exactly a large portion of your life, or mine, for that matter."

Neil chuckled at the cool greeting. "You can drop the act, sweetheart; I know you too well to be put off by that look-but-don't-touch attitude of yours."

"Do you really?" Eden's voice dripped sarcasm. "Perhaps you'd better look again, Neil. This isn't a moonlit terrace in New York and I'm not sixteen anymore, so let's dispense with the charming banter at which you excel."

"You're still angry, aren't you, love?" Neil grinned audaciously at her. "I would have thought you'd have forgiven me long ago."

"Forgiven you?" Eden's eyes widened in affected bewilderment. "Whatever for, Neil? For seducing me? I can't blame you for that; after all, I wasn't exactly unwilling. For not marrying me? You never proposed, so I had no reason to believe you had honest intentions." Eden turned and walked around the fountain, her fingers trailing idly in the water. "No, Neil, I don't blame you or despise you for any of those things. But what I do hate you for—and what I will never forgive you for—is the way you and Jane set me up. I will *never* forgive you for that, even if I live to be a hundred."

The grin left Neil's face and in an angry motion he sent what was left of his cigar arcing through the night. "I had nothing to do with that, Eden. Jane had me followed. I didn't know she was spying on me until she told me everything during the voyage to Mexico."

"Spare me your explanation," Eden ground out. "I don't believe it."

"It's not an explanation, it's the truth," Neil snapped. "I don't practice seduction in front of an audience."

"No, you don't. Private, out-of-the-way places are definitely your style."

"And yours," Neil replied bitingly. "I seem to recall that you didn't want to cancel the picnic either."

Tears welled in Eden's eyes. "You haven't changed at all; you're every bit as cruel as you were four years ago."

"I don't mean to be." Neil reached out and touched Eden's cheek. "God, Eden, I can't believe you're really here."

Before Eden could react, Neil pulled her into his arms and brought his lips down upon hers. Holding Eden, kissing her, was something Neil had dreamed of continually. Neil's embrace tightened, crushing Eden against his chest, as his dream became reality. How Eden had come to be in Texas Neil didn't know, and at the moment he didn't care. The blood was hammering through his veins, his heart beating so rapidly that it caused an exquisite pain in his chest.

Gradually, through the mists that clouded his mind, Neil became aware that the pounding in his chest was only partially caused by his heart. Eden was pummeling at his shoulders, writhing in the steely prison of his arms.

Breathing harshly, Neil lifted his head and regretfully loosened his hold on Eden. "I suppose I should apologize," he began with a smile, "but sweetheart—"

Eden's hand flew outward and met Neil's cheek with a deafening crack. "I should have done that four years ago," she spat venomously.

Neil drew his hand back as if to strike Eden in return, then, slowly, lowered it to his side. "I suppose from your point of view I deserved that. But four years is a long time to hold a grudge, love."

"You arrogant, hateful..." Eden's voice choked on the words. "The slap wasn't for New York," she said in a strangled voice, "it was for what just happened. I'm married, Neil. *Married!* Doesn't that mean anything to you? Hugh and I have worked hard to make our marriage what it is and I'll be *damned* before I let a heartless bastard like you destroy it!"

"Are you finished?" Neil asked grimly when Eden paused to catch her breath.

"No!" Eden exploded. "By some trick of fate you and I have become neighbors, so I want to make a few things very clear right now. You may address me as 'Eden,' 'Mrs. Colter,' or 'ma'am,' but don't ever call me 'love' or 'sweetheart' again. Stay away from Hugh—my husband is a kind, trusting man and I don't want you contaminating him. And for God's sake, stay away from me. We may be neighbors but we are *not* going to be friends. Do you understand me?"

"Perfectly." Neil reached for another cigar. "And what do I say if your husband invites me over for dinner some night?"

"You accept," Eden snapped. "I'm certain that after spending one night putting up with your arrogant posturing Hugh will be more than willing to do without your company."

"Am I really such a monster?" Neil asked slowly when Eden turned and started toward the house.

"No." Eden stopped but didn't bother to face Neil. "You're no monster—just a person who doesn't know how to be human. You are selfish and self-centered; you care for nothing and no one but Neil Banning."

"What about you?" Neil sneered. "You married a man you didn't love, yet as I recall you were once very adamant about my views on marriage. Cold-blooded, I believe you called them. Just when did your happy union occur, Eden? I'll give you odds your guardian arranged for a husband who was leaving New York right after the wedding so your lack of virginity wouldn't be a source of embarrassment; and you agreed, to save your precious reputation."

Eden turned to him then, her eyes flinty with anger. "Since you seem so interested in my past, let me tell you what happened while you and Jane blithely sailed off to Mexico. Due to Jane's careful planning Tim decided not to keep our little affair a secret; he told his father, and then they both broke the news to my guardian. Oh, that was a scene you would have enjoyed. Hugh was in such a rage that he would have killed Tim's father if we hadn't managed to separate them.

"Do you know what Hugh did then? He lied. In order to protect me, Hugh lied and said that he was the man Tim had seen. Tim knew better, of course, but his father believed Hugh's story, and after Jane's little indiscretion they could hardly make a scene. Three months later, despite raised eyebrows and a few rumors, Hugh and I were married."

"Do you mean to tell me you not only married your guardian but you also told him that I was the man who—"

"Of course I didn't tell him," Eden hissed. "But I certainly didn't keep silent to protect you! Hugh and I had to make a life together and it was easiest to let you fade namelessly into oblivion." Eden's face suddenly crumpled and she caught her lower lip to still its trembling. "Please, Neil. What Hugh and I have is very special; I don't want my marriage destroyed because you or I might inadvertently let something slip."

"You're serious about this! Hugh Colter really is important to you, isn't he?" Eden nodded wordlessly, her eyes brimming with tears, and Neil cursed softly. "I don't remember your crying before—not even after that row we had in my hotel room—so for God's sake don't start now. Go back inside and find your husband. I'll follow in a few minutes and, if anyone asks, we spent a few minutes discussing the weather and this hideous fountain Constanza had imported from Italy." When Eden didn't move, Neil placed both hands on her shoulders, turned her around and none too gently pushed her toward the ballroom. "Damn it, Eden, will you do what I tell you!" As Eden paused in the doorway, Neil called after her, "Eden? I've done a lot of lousy things in my life, but I've never deliberately broken up a marriage. Our secret is just that—a secret."

Neil watched Eden disappear inside and then, frowning, he walked along the terrace to finish his cigar. Eden. He'd thought about her, dreamed about her for four long years, even though he had known there was no chance of ever seeing her again. He had even toyed with the idea of visiting New York once this business with Constanza was finished, just to find out what had happened to her. Damn, Neil swore silently as he ground his cigar beneath his heel. How *could* Eden have married Hugh Colter? Sure, he seemed nice enough, but he was also old enough to be her father. Hell, Neil hadn't even gotten back to Mexico before Eden had been planning her wedding and having fittings for her gown.

Neil took the watch from his pocket and opened the back of the case. The Eden staring up at Neil from the palm of his hand was far different from the Eden he had just confronted. Not that he had expected Eden to fall into his arms, but Neil certainly hadn't expected to see hate reflected in those mist-gray eyes. In the past women had either fallen for his careless charm or been intrigued by his devil-may-care attitude, but not one had ever hated him. Not until tonight.

She was doing it again, Neil thought ruefully as he absent-mindedly stroked his moustache. Eden was the only woman he had ever known who could worm her way into his mind and drive all other considerations straight out of his head. While Eden seemed to have been able to forget all about him, Neil hadn't been so fortunate. He had relived those three days in New York repeatedly during the long nights when sleep eluded him, and found himself wishing that Eden lay beside him, her pale hair fanned across his chest. And now she was here, looking more desirable than Neil remembered, married to someone else and seething with hatred for the man who had introduced her to the delights of passion. Scowling into the darkness, Neil admitted one final truth to himself: No matter how much time had passed since their last meeting, no matter how much Eden may have changed, he still wanted her, and having Eden this close would only serve to heighten his desire. So how, Neil wondered sullenly, would he be able to stay away from Eden now that the distance between them was only a few miles? With a disgusted snort Neil pivoted on his heel and followed Eden into the house.

"You know, of course, Texas wasn't always this civilized," Lathrop said exuberantly as he stepped on Eden's foot for the seventh time during the seemingly endless dance. "Not so long ago an affair like this would have been guarded by armed men whose only job was to be on the lookout for Indians."

"No!" Eden arranged her features into a feigned look of horror, then winced as Lathrop's foot crushed hers once again. "Everything seems so peaceful that it's hard to imagine that kind of danger ever existed here."

"It did," Lathrop assured her loudly. "Let me tell you, we had to kill a lot of those savages before the army finally drove them onto the reservations where they belong."

"Where they belong," Eden repeated in disbelief. "I was under the impression that the Indian was here long before the white man."

"What?" Lathrop dragged his gaze and thoughts away from the enticing display of Eden's neckline. "Sure, they were here, but they weren't using the land the way we are. They roamed from place to place, following the buffalo herds—hell, we couldn't have them living on our grazing land; they would have killed our cattle for food."

"So you tracked them down and put them in pens," Eden stated coldly. "The newspapers in New York carried horrible stories about the treatment the Indians received. I should think a more humane arrangement could have been made."

"You wouldn't say that if you'd ever seen what was left of a woman when the Apache finished with her," Lathrop said harshly. "If I'd had my way, we wouldn't even have bothered with reservations; it's a waste of land and money."

"That's awful!" Eden exclaimed. "You can't mean you would rather annihilate an entire race of people!"

Lathrop smiled patronizingly and shook his head. "I'd as soon kill an Indian as look at him, missy, and so would just about any man in this town. Only the strong survive out here, so don't shed any tears over those savages. We won, the Indians lost, and as they say, to the victors go the spoils."

"I see." Eden swallowed hard to rid herself of the bitter taste that was rising in her throat and glanced across the floor to where Hugh was dancing with Constanza. The dislike she felt toward Lathrop was shaping itself into a definite aversion for the man.

"You don't agree?" Lathrop questioned scornfully.

"Shouldn't there be a way we could live side by side with the Indians?" Eden returned thoughtfully. "After all, you seem to be able to exist alongside the Mexicans despite what happened forty-two years ago at the Alamo."

Lathrop chortled. "My neighbor Banning is only half Mexican, and he has spent more time in Europe and America than Mexico, so he really doesn't count; right now he's more Anglo than Spanish. As for my dear Constanza"—Lathrop shrugged and smiled knowingly —"she has a quality that defies all racial and national boundaries."

Eden caught the odd note in Lathrop's voice. While the words were what might be expected from a loving husband, there was something in his tone that made the compliment ring false. Be careful, a wary inner voice warned Eden abruptly. "I wasn't aware that Mr. Banning was from Mexico," Eden said evenly, although she could feel the blood rush to her cheeks at the lie.

"No?" Lathrop appeared surprised. "That's usually the first thing Constanza tells people when she introduces Neil. It was actually a blessing, his showing up like he did. As content as Constanza was living here, she still missed Mexico; having a fellow countryman to talk to made the adjustment easier for her. I'm sure you can appreciate how she felt; after all, you are in a similar situation. Texas is a far cry from New York. You must feel just as isolated and lonely as Constanza did."

"On the contrary," Eden corrected Lathrop softly, "I find ranching a welcome change from the city and besides, with Hugh I never have the time to be lonely."

"Spoken like a devoted wife."

Hugh and Constanza had made their way through the crowd as the dance ended and now Hugh curved an arm around Eden's waist. Grinning down at his wife Hugh said, "This dance is ours, I believe. Lathrop, Constanza, if you will excuse us."

Without waiting for a reply, Hugh swung Eden back onto the dance floor and she smiled gratefully into his blue eyes. "I was hoping you would come to my rescue—but what took you so long?" Eden chided.

"The enchanting Constanza couldn't bear to give up my company," Hugh teased, then winced when Eden playfully slapped his shoulder.

"You and your Irish charm," Eden retorted. "Leaving me to deal with that bore Lathrop while you have a good time with the ladies. You ought to be ashamed of yourself."

"But I'm not." Hugh laughed. "The night air did you some good, I see. Feeling better?"

Eden nodded and rested her head against his shoulder. "Have you met everyone yet?"

"I think so." Hugh idly scanned the other dancers. "Those Lathrop didn't drag over to me, Constanza did. Up to and including our resident Texas Ranger."

"Our what?" Eden looked up at Hugh in confusion.

"Texas Ranger," Hugh slowly repeated. "They're a cross between a sheriff and the army, and this one is on the trail of the rustlers who have been so active around here. You mean you've missed meeting Captain Gerald?"

"Apparently." Eden shrugged. "I don't think I care to meet him, either. I've heard quite enough about men hunting down other men from Lathrop. I don't want this evening ruined by any more talk of killing!"

"Ah, I see. Lathrop must have been expounding upon his belief that the only good Indian is a dead one," Hugh guessed.

"More than one person here feels that way, dear heart, and no matter how long you argue and reason with them, you will never change their minds. Let it go, darlin', you can't change what has already happened."

"Do you agree with Lathrop?" Eden asked, although she was half afraid of his answer.

"Dear heart, I've long since passed the age where I held a grudge or hated a man because of the color of his skin. That's one of the advantages of growing older—you grow more tolerant with each year." Hugh brushed a kiss across the top of Eden's hair. "You're trembling, Eden. Why?"

"Indians, rustlers, men carrying guns everywhere they go." Eden shuddered and gripped Hugh's hand tightly. "What kind of a place are we living in?"

"Shh," Hugh whispered soothingly. "I told you before, the guns are only precautions."

"I noticed you packed one of those 'precautions' in your valise," Eden whispered in return. "And I'll bet every man here tonight did the same thing. It frightens me, Hugh."

"I know." Hugh squeezed her hand reassuringly. "Give yourself time, darlin'—in a few months you won't think anything of watching men tramp into your house wearing their spurs and guns."

Eden smiled wanly and allowed Hugh to change the topic of conversation. How much simpler things would be if she could tell Hugh about Neil instead of deceiving him this way. Hugh's voice rumbled in her ear, its musical lilt wrapping Eden in a blanket of security even though she couldn't seem to concentrate on what he was saying. Suddenly bitter, Eden found herself wondering what Neil was doing here when he should be in Mexico. Why had he chosen this particular area? Neil's taste surely ran to more cosmopolitan diversions than the town of Lathrop had to offer, so why was he calmly living as a rancher in the middle of nowhere? Not that it mattered—whatever his reasons, Neil was here and Eden was going to have to deal with his presence. Even if Neil kept his promise about staying away—something Eden didn't believe he would do—in this small community an occasional meeting was inevitable. Eden could only hope that each time they met, the shock of seeing Neil would lessen until she would be able to treat him as she did everyone else.

Thankfully, Eden was spared the agony of a second con-

frontation with Neil for the remainder of the evening, but as
she was escorted into the late dinner by Lathrop it was clear
that she was also to be without Hugh's company. Constanza,
with Hugh seated on her right and Neil on her left, was in her
element, forcing both men to center their attention on her.
Constanza pouted, teased, flirted, and when Eden met Hugh's
eyes down the length of their table he gave her a despairing
look.

"Your husband seems to be enjoying himself," Lathrop
stated as Eden returned her attention to her own dinner companions. "Constanza appears to have made him feel right at
home."

"I'm certain she has." Before she could stop herself, Eden
laughed softly at the conceited note in Lathrop's voice. Surprisingly, her sarcasm went unnoticed by Lathrop, who nodded
in vigorous agreement, then applied himself to his food with
a relish that made Eden's stomach churn.

"We haven't met." Hearing a voice to her right, Eden turned
to the man at her other side and returned his smile. "I'm Keith
Gerald, Mrs. Colter, and may I be the last to welcome you to
Texas."

Eden's eyes widened in astonishment at the benign features
of the Texas Ranger. "You are Captain Gerald?"

"Yes, ma'am," Keith acknowledged with a grin. "I see my
reputation has preceded me. Except for the look on your face,
I'd be flattered that you know who I am."

"Oh, forgive me," Eden stammered. "It's just that I expected
someone much older with a fierce, deadly look in his eyes."

"Like our host's bodyguard?" Keith laughed and shook his
head. "I'm sorry to disappoint you, Mrs. Colter, but there aren't
many Rangers over the age of thirty, and as far as I know, very
few of us appear forbidding during our off-duty time."

"And the rest of the time?"

The corners of Keith's mouth twitched into a smile. "We
do look rather grim, I'm afraid. Tracking down other men, no
matter what they may have done, is rarely a pleasant job."

"Then why do you do it? Surely, Captain, you could find
another profession."

"Yes, ma'am." Keith nodded. "I intend to do just that as
soon as I tie up a few loose ends in this area."

"You mean the rustlers?" Eden smiled slightly. "From what
I've heard they hardly pose a serious threat. They steal a few

cattle, usually from the larger ranches, and then disappear without firing a shot. While the rustlers are an annoyance I can't see that they are much of a hazard."

"An outlaw, Mrs. Colter, is always a hazard, no matter how innocuous he may seem." The fire of controlled rage kindled in the Ranger's blue eyes. "And life, no matter how valued by some, is very cheap to others." Keith's gaze fell upon Lathrop Williams, and his expression hardened. "When the shooting starts, and it always does, it's the innocent who get hurt." Beside him the lovely Eden Colter had paled and Keith collected himself. "I've upset you, Mrs. Colter; please forgive me."

Eden waved aside his apology. "I appreciate your candor, Captain Gerald."

"Even if what I say frightens you?" Keith smiled gently. "I assure you, Mrs. Colter, that was not my intention."

"I'm sure it wasn't." Eden took a sip of wine before continuing. "What will happen to the rustlers—if they're caught?"

*"When* they're caught." The correction sounded so pedantic that Keith flushed.

Eden laughed, touched by the Ranger's unexpected vulnerability. Unaware that a pair of golden eyes had watched her every movement throughout dinner, Eden placed a reassuring hand on Keith's arm and leaned toward him. "Very well, *when* they're caught," she agreed, still laughing.

Keith studied the clear gray eyes, relaxing when he found no sign of malice in their depths. "If the law apprehends the rustlers, they'll be given a fair trial. However"—his gaze wandered back to their host as Keith spoke—"if Mr. Williams and the other ranchers catch them, I'm afraid the rustlers won't live to be arrested. I hope to prevent that kind of vigilante justice."

"I see." The Ranger seemed to tense whenever he looked at or spoke about Lathrop Williams, and his behavior puzzled Eden. "Of course," she observed, "either way you will be free of the rustlers."

"Perhaps," Keith replied enigmatically. Before Eden could pursue the subject any further, Keith graciously switched the topic of conversation to her trip from New York and her first impressions of Texas. Eden Colter's voice was soft, perfectly modulated, and no competition for Lathrop William's drawling intonations. In order to hear her every word, Keith bent toward Eden and soon found himself just as captivated by her beauty as by her speech. A pity the dancing was ended, Keith reflected as the candlelight played across Eden's bare shoulders. He would have given anything to know how it felt to hold Eden Colter in his arms.

Keith Gerald—his private thoughts well concealed—proved to be such an enjoyable dinner companion that for the most part Eden was able to ignore Lathrop's presence. Even the fact that Neil came into view whenever she exchanged a look or a smile with Hugh was beginning to have less impact upon Eden. The sheer, terrified panic had thankfully disappeared, and her heart no longer missed a beat at the sight of Neil's handsome face.

"Are you and your husband staying the night?" Keith asked as he held Eden's chair for her.

Eden nodded and walked with the lanky Ranger from the dining room. "And you, Captain Gerald?"

"I was asked, so I figured I might as well see how the rich and influential live," Keith grinned engagingly and shrugged. "So far it beats the barracks and the bedroll—at least where the food is concerned—and somehow I get the feeling that the pillows in this place are going to be a heck of a lot softer than the saddle I've been using."

"I'm sure," Eden agreed, then felt the smile freeze on her lips as Constanza, with both Neil and Hugh in tow, approached.

"You must not keep our delightful Captain Gerald all to yourself, Eden," Constanza reproved in a feline tone that made Eden's back stiffen. "Such a thing is too selfish."

"How thoughtless of me," Eden murmured mockingly. Ignoring the angry look that crossed Constanza's features, Eden's eyes slid past her hostess to sparkle up at Hugh. "But since you had the company of the most charming man here, I'm afraid I can't feel too guilty about monopolizing Captain Gerald. No offense intended, gentlemen."

"None taken, Mrs. Colter," Keith answered gallantly for both himself and Neil. Keith cleared his throat and turned to Constanza. "As enjoyable as this evening has been, Mrs. Williams, it's at an end for me."

"I'll have someone show you to your room, Captain," Constanza offered in her heavily accented voice.

"That won't be necessary, but thank you just the same. I found my way down here; I'm sure I can find my way back to my room." In a stiff, formal manner Keith said good night first to Constanza and then, in a voice that fairly bristled with hostility, to Neil.

"Good night, Captain Gerald," Eden said warmly when Keith took her hand. "I've enjoyed our conversation. If you ever grow tired of sleeping under the stars again, we have two guest rooms that have never been used. Please feel free to visit us."

"That's mighty kind of you, ma'am. I may take you up on that someday." Keith grinned and extended a hand to Hugh. "Nice meeting you, Mr. Colter. We'll be seeing each other soon. Good night."

Keith took the stairs in a leisurely fashion, ignoring the cold rage which clutched at his stomach when he viewed the luxurious surroundings. The first time he had seen the interior of this house Keith had been sickened by all it represented. He had, in fact, barely left the ranch site behind when he had to dismount and allow his stomach to disgorge its contents. Keith hadn't expected his reactions to be so strong, not after all the years that had passed, but each subsequent visit to the Williams ranch proved easier.

With a sigh of relief, Keith entered his room and divested himself of his suit coat and tie. The whiskey, thoughtfully provided by his host, washed the sour taste from his mouth, and Keith sipped a second glassful while he relaxed in a chair. It was revolting, he thought, what could be purchased with a stack of spent shotgun shells. Memories of his father surfaced, but the most vivid picture Keith had in his mind was the way he had stumbled upon his father's body. Keith grimaced, his hand tightening around the glass. The image of his father's lifeless body lying in the stream with his head half blown away was one Keith would carry with him for the rest of his life. Keith fought down his anger, his hatred, and with the sounds of the party floating into his room he prepared for bed.

Unhappily for Eden, another two hours elapsed before she and Hugh could retire, and throughout that time she was painfully aware of the piercing looks Neil sent in her direction. Even Hugh's presence offered no comfort—in fact, he only succeeded in making her feel terribly guilty about the way in which she was deceiving him. When they were finally alone in their bedroom, their bodies lightly touching as they lay side by side in bed, Eden's resolve to hide the truth about Neil weakened and she crept into the security of Hugh's arms. Help

me! she wanted to cry out to Hugh. I don't want to lie, not to
you. We've come too far together to let Neil Banning destroy
what we have. But how can I tell you? How can I jeopardize
our marriage with an awful truth we promised never to speak
of again? Hugh's breathing became deep and regular, and with
a shudder of relief Eden felt his arm relax its hold on her waist.
The need for a decision could be postponed for another few
hours, and perhaps by then some kind of solution to this dilemma would occur to her.

"Good morning."

Eden pried her eyes open, then winced at the sunlight flooding the room. Hugh chuckled, placed a hand on either side of
Eden's pillow and kissed her tenderly. "It can't be morning
already," Eden protested weakly when Hugh released her. "I
just fell asleep."

"Sorry, darlin', but one of the servants just knocked on the
door and announced breakfast." Hugh pulled Eden upright and
shook her gently. "Come on, Eden love, rise and shine—I've
been trying to wake you for fifteen minutes."

"Sleep," Eden murmured tiredly. With a sigh she snuggled
against Hugh's broad chest and closed her eyes. "Another half
hour."

"Not a chance. Breakfast won't be served until we arrive,
and you don't want the rest of the guests to go hungry, now
do you?" Hugh peered down into Eden's face, his lips curving
into a smile when a pair of gray eyes fluttered open.

"I hate it when you're so bloody noble," Eden groaned.
Yawning, she extended her arms and arched her back in a
feline stretch. "Have you been awake long?"

Hugh nodded and brushed back the pale wisps of hair from
Eden's face. "I watched the sun come up. Oddly enough, the
sight isn't any more spectacular from this fortress than it is
from our bedroom window."

"At least Lathrop and Constanza don't have a monopoly on
nature," Eden said acidly. "That's welcome news." Eden pulled
away from Hugh and slid from the bed.

Lips pursed, Hugh settled back on the bed to watch Eden
dress. "No need to bite my head off, dear heart."

Eden drew a hand across her forehead. Her head ached with
worry, her eyes were dry and sandy from lack of sleep and the

last thing she needed was to start a fight with her husband. "I'm sorry, Hugh, I didn't mean to snap."

"I know, darlin'." Hugh grinned at her reflection in the mirror. "You'll feel more yourself after you've had some coffee. Besides which, there are two young men downstairs who are expecting the same charming Mrs. Colter of last night."

"Only two? I must be losing my touch," Eden said with a wry smile.

"Not you, darlin'. You could charm the devil himself. I think Captain Gerald is hopelessly infatuated with you, and Neil Banning didn't take his eyes off you all during dinner last night." The hairbrush slipped from Eden's fingers and clattered to the floor. "Now, if I were the jealous type," Hugh continued teasingly, "there is a man I'd keep an eye on."

"Don't be silly." Eden bent to retrieve the brush as well as to hide the shock that drained the blood from her face. "Mr. Banning and I barely met. If he's intrigued by anyone, it's Constanza Williams."

Hugh raised his eyebrows at the strained note in Eden's voice. "So you noticed that, too? Apparently no one else has, or if they have, they're smart enough to keep what they see to themselves. Doesn't it surprise you that Lathrop hasn't caught on yet?"

Praying all the while that Hugh wouldn't notice the way her hands shook, Eden stood up and busied herself with adjusting the neckline of her dress. "Caught on to what?" She had to tell Hugh! The way she fell apart at the mention of Neil, Hugh was bound to see that something was wrong; and it would be best if he found out now, before she made the situation worse by lying further. Eden bit her lip and turned to face the man on the bed. "Hugh—"

"To the fact that his wife is having an affair with Neil Banning." Hugh's answer cut off Eden's confession. "I'm only guessing, mind you, but I've seen those kind of looks before, and if Constanza and Neil are only friends, then I'm the King of England. If Constanza were my wife I'd—"

"You'd what," Eden prompted breathlessly when Hugh fell silent.

Blue and gray eyes locked across the length of the room, and for the first time in years, Hugh's expression was cold as he gazed at his wife. "I'd kill Banning," Hugh said in a voice that would have seemed emotionless but for the thickened Irish brogue. "No matter what the law might do to me, I'd kill him."

Eden dropped her eyes to study the floor. "That's a bit harsh, isn't it?"

"Perhaps." Hugh rose and went to Eden, changing his tone. "It doesn't make any difference. Thankfully I'm not in Lathrop's position, nor is there any comparison between you and Constanza." Smiling now, Hugh gathered Eden into his arms and kissed her deeply.

Fighting back the sob that was threatening, Eden clung desperately to Hugh, her head buried against his shoulder. The decision had been taken out of her hands—no matter how badly she wished it otherwise, Eden had no choice now but to live with her secret. She swallowed hard and forced a smile to her lips as she raised her face to Hugh. "We'd better go downstairs."

Hugh nodded and cupped Eden's face in his hands. "I love you, Eden; always remember that."

The deadly expression on Hugh's face was gone so quickly that, as they left the bedroom and started down the stairs, Eden found herself wondering if she had imagined it. Their conversation had been real, though; the way her heart still hammered told Eden that. Get hold of yourself, Eden scolded herself silently. So Neil happens to be back in your life. That doesn't signal the end of the world! You've gotten through worse things than having a scoundrel for a neighbor.

A small knot of ranchers was clustered inside the front doorway and Hugh, frowning, drew Eden to a stop at the foot of the stairs. "Something's up," Hugh murmured, then swore softly as the crowd parted and Ian, obviously the source of the worried looks on the men's faces, came forward, accompanied by a grim and angry Keith Gerald.

"We've been hit," Ian announced as soon as he and Keith reached Hugh.

"Damn!" Hugh shook his head. "How many did we lose?"

"As near as we can figure, about twenty head. I've got some men tracking them right now, but I wanted to let you know what happened before I rode out."

"I'll be going with your foreman," Keith put in. "If Ian and his men catch these rustlers, I want to be there."

"To arrest them," Ian snorted derisively.

"I say hang 'em," demanded a voice from the crowd. The

ranchers had ranged themselves around the quartet, and Eden shrank from their violent expressions. Anger and frustration radiated from these men with such force that it was possible to feel the emotions crackling in the air.

"No!" Keith whirled around to face the men, his right hand brushing the handle of his pistol. "No vigilante justice. When we catch the rustlers, they'll be brought to trial in a proper court of law. You men know as well as I do that if and when they're found guilty, they'll be hanged. But if you don't leave the punishment up to the court, if you take the law into your own hands, then I swear I'll see that every last one of you is arrested for murder. Then you can experience justice firsthand. Now, does anyone still want to form a lynching party?"

Some of the ranchers muttered but not one of them dared to repeat the threat.

"My God," Eden murmured weakly when the crowd started to disperse. "I've never seen anything like this. Were they serious, Captain Gerald?"

Keith relaxed visibly, his gun hand falling back to his side as he turned to Hugh and Eden. He nodded grimly. "Yes, ma'am. If those rustlers aren't caught soon, this town is going to turn ugly, and then there won't be a prayer of stopping the ranchers from taking the law into their own hands."

"We'll just have to find them before they can steal more cattle," Hugh said easily when Eden's face paled. "That should be simple enough for Ian and me. Right?"

"Sure," Ian agreed wryly. "The Rangers can't find 'em; the ranchers can't find 'em; but two old ex-scouts like us will be able to track a band of rustlers in nothing flat." Ignoring Hugh's warning look, Ian jammed his hat onto his head and started for the door.

"Did you bring my horse?" Hugh called after him.

"Naturally." Ian paused at the door and gave Hugh a cha-grined look. "Have I ever left you behind? I'll wait for you outside."

"You're welcome to ride along, Captain," Hugh assured Keith. "Ian tends to overreact, but once he calms down he'll be glad to have you along. Stay out of his way for an hour or so and I guarantee you will meet a different man."

"Thanks for the advice—for a minute there I was sure your foreman was going to walk over anyone who got in his way."

Keith grinned at Eden and took her hand. "Good-bye, Mrs. Colter. It's been a pleasure meeting you."

Eden forced a smile which rapidly faded when Keith was out of sight. Some inner voice warned Eden that not even the Rangers could protect Hugh from the danger these rustlers presented, and her heart tightened painfully at the thought of Hugh being injured . . . or worse.

"I've got to change before I ride out." Hugh's voice jarred Eden away from her thoughts and she faced him bleakly.

"Do you have to go with them?" As soon as the words were out, Eden wished them back. She sounded like a whining, clinging woman, and although she hated herself for it, Eden couldn't help the way she felt.

"Yes." Hugh curled an arm around her waist. "I can't ask Ian to do something I won't."

"No, of course not," Eden said softly. "You'll wear that damn gun too, I suppose."

With a sharp intake of air, Hugh pulled Eden a short distance away from the others. His eyes sparkling angrily, Hugh told her, "I have to go and, yes, I have to wear a gun. Now, I don't expect you to be happy about the situation, but I do expect you to accept it gracefully. These thieves are parasites, Eden, and if they're not caught they will bleed this land dry. What do you want me to do, sit home safe and sound while other men do the dangerous work?" Tears welling in her eyes, Eden nodded miserably and the hard core of anger in Hugh dissolved. "Nothing will happen, darlin', believe me."

"I hope not," Eden replied in a choked voice, terror gathering like a flood inside her. "I'm sorry to be such a coward, but I can't help it."

Hugh shook his head and said gently, "You're no coward, Eden love, just easily frightened. Try not to make more out of this situation than there is."

"Take me with you," Eden begged. "I have a riding skirt packed."

"No." Hugh placed a finger across Eden's lips to still further protest. "A posse is no place for a woman—we'll be riding hard all day and probably most of the night as well."

"I can keep up, Hugh. I promise I won't complain or fall behind."

"No," Hugh repeated in the tone he used when a subject was closed. "You'll stay home and have a warm bath and a hot meal waiting for me. I'll find out if Lathrop can spare a man to see you home. I don't relish the idea of your riding around the countryside alone."

"If Mrs. Colter doesn't object, I'd be honored to see her back to your ranch."

Keeping Eden close by his side, Hugh pivoted to face the man who had appeared so quietly. "That's kind of you, Vincent," Hugh said hesitantly, "but I don't want to impose."

"No imposition." The bodyguard's voice was, as usual, expressionless, but for an instant Eden thought she glimpsed a flicker of understanding in Vincent's cold eyes. "Since Mr. Williams will be riding out with you, he won't be needing me."

Hugh shuffled uneasily at the thought of Eden being alone with the gunman. Vincent was dangerous and Hugh knew it. A gunman was the worst kind of predator, someone who killed not for survival or even revenge but for the pure enjoyment of killing. To put Eden into Vincent's hands would be like delivering the lamb to the lion.

From the look on Hugh's face, Eden judged that he was none too happy with Vincent's offer. Neither was she, but there seemed to be no gracious way to refuse Vincent and then turn around and ask Lathrop for an escort.

"Thank you, Vincent. I'll be ready to leave after I've seen my husband off." For a brief moment Eden's eyes locked with Vincent's and he nodded shortly at her polite acceptance before he sauntered away.

"I don't like this," Hugh growled when Vincent had disappeared. "I told you to keep away from that man."

"You also said he wouldn't harm us," Eden reminded him archly, "and I believe that. Oddly enough, I think Vincent, in his own way, would like to have us as friends."

Hugh snorted. "God help us both if that's what he wants. I'd sooner bed down with a rattler. I want you to take one of my guns for the ride back home."

This time it was Eden's turn to deliver an adamant refusal, and she did so with the accompaniment of flashing gray eyes. "Absolutely not! You can run off and play soldier with all the other men as often as you please, but I won't take one of those blasted things with me. And if you come home with a hole in your foot, don't say I didn't warn you."

They parted on that bitter note: Hugh tight-lipped because of Eden's lack of common sense, and Eden thoroughly fright-

ened and confused by Hugh's eagerness to help track down the
rustlers. I hate this country, Eden thought fiercely as she
watched the ranchers gallop off. Hugh, Lathrop, Captain Gerald, Ian, even Neil had been so anxious to be on the rustlers'
trail that they had scarcely taken the time to bolt down a quick
meal before swinging onto their horses. I hate this country, she
repeated silently, and I hate the people in it. She longed for
the familiar safety of New York, where Hugh had done nothing
more dangerous than visit his import warehouse and she had
spent her days tending her garden and listening to Meg's chatter.

Hastily brushing the tears from her lashes, Eden said her
good-byes and allowed Vincent to hand her into the waiting
carriage before climbing up himself. Early though it was, the
sun was already scorching, and the dust kicked up by the horses
and carriage hung in the air and left a film of grime on Eden's
skin and clothing. The heat made Eden increasingly irritable
and she shifted restively on the seat. Damn Hugh for being so
conscientious—that was one of his traits which Eden found
both endearing and annoying.

"He'll be all right, Mrs. Colter."

Startled, Eden turned toward the impassive Vincent and
found that a hint of a smile touched the corners of his mouth.
Can he read my mind? Eden wondered with a touch of fear.
"I—I'm really not worried about my husband."

"Sure you are," Vincent disagreed patiently. "Just like he's
worried about you being with me."

"Oh! Hugh's not—" The knowing look in Vincent's eyes
stopped Eden's explanation and she guiltily swallowed the lie
she had started to tell.

"No need to be embarrassed, Mrs. Colter. I'd feel the same
way if I were in his place." Vincent was staring straight ahead
while he spoke, and for a moment Eden wondered if he simply
were thinking out loud. "And you shouldn't be ashamed about
fretting over your husband. There ain't a man living who
doesn't feel flattered when his woman worries about him."

"But you don't have anyone," Eden felt compelled to say.

"In my line of work it's better that way. Attachments tend
to cloud a man's thinking, and that could get him killed."

"Oh." It was all Eden could think of to say. Her earlier
words to Hugh seemed more foolish than brave when she al-

lowed herself to remember that Vincent was Lathrop's hired
killer.

"You don't have to be afraid of me, Mrs. Colter." He had
read her mind once again and Eden gave a small gasp of alarm.
"But there are other things in this country that you should be
afraid of, and for good reason. These rustlers now, they haven't
hurt anyone yet, but with Captain Gerald after them there's no
telling what they might do if they're backed into a corner."

Vincent brought the carriage to a halt in front of the house
and sprang to the ground. He swung Eden down, unstrapped
the two valises from the back and dropped them onto the porch
beside Eden, before untying his own mount from the rear of
the carriage.

"Could I interest you in a cup of coffee?" Eden offered.
"And perhaps some breakfast as well? You didn't have much
time to eat this morning."

Vincent's mouth twitched into what, for him, evidently
passed for a smile. "I like eggs, bacon, a side of fried potatoes
and I take my coffee black. I'll just take care of the horses
first."

"Give your horse whatever he needs from the grain bins."
Eden whirled into the house and, after depositing the bags in
the hallway, hurried into the kitchen. "Millicent?"

Millicent looked up from her work and smiled at Eden.
"Welcome back, Miss Eden. Did you have a nice evening?"

"Lovely," Eden replied sarcastically as she set a frying pan
to heat on the stove. "I'll tell you all about it later. Right now
I've got to fix breakfast for Vincent, so will you cut some
bacon for me?"

"That gunfighter?" Millicent breathed, horrified. "What's
he doing here, and where's Mr. Colter?"

"Mr. Colter is out playing lawman," Eden said waspishly.
"Vincent drove me home."

"Mr. Colter won't like you entertaining that . . . that man,"
Millicent sputtered indignantly. "I say we feed him outside and
send him on his way."

"Absolutely not." Eden sliced potatoes into a second pan
with unnecessary vigor. "If Hugh doesn't care for what I'm
doing, then he can damn well stay home. Don't put on that
sour face, Millie," Eden rebuked when she caught Millicent's
expression. "Vincent was kind enough to take me home, and
the least we can do is give the man a decent meal."

"In the dining room, with the good china and silver?" Millicent's eyes were round as saucers.

Eden ground her teeth in frustration. "I don't intend to have him eat off the floor, for God's sake." With a withering look at Millicent, Eden finished her preparations and lifted the tray of food. "Bring in the coffee when it's ready, and do try to smile."

She managed to set the table moments before Vincent knocked at the front door, and with a hesitant smile, Eden led him through the house.

"You didn't have to go to all this trouble," Vincent said when Eden waved him into a chair.

"It's no trouble," Eden assured him.

He looked distinctly uncomfortable, she decided as she watched Vincent wolf down his food. The calculated certainty with which Vincent usually moved and spoke was gone, and he appeared almost intimidated by the imposing furnishings Eden had brought from New York. Eden glanced around the room—how hard it had been to choose which furniture to bring and which to leave. On Hugh's advice, only the most practical pieces had been packed and shipped and, except for the piano, the rest of the furniture and nonessentials had been given to friends or sold along with Hugh's mansion. Tears welled in Eden's eyes at the thought of Hugh now somewhere beneath the broiling sun, riding after a bunch of thieves with a gun in his hand. . . .

Eden wrenched her mind away from such unsettling thoughts and reached for the coffeepot. "More coffee, Vincent?"

"No, ma'am, this will do me fine." Gingerly, Vincent touched the linen napkin to the corners of his mouth. "There is something else you could do for me."

Curious, Eden tilted her head to one side and studied Vincent's implacable features. "And what is that?"

"Learn to protect yourself," Vincent said in a flat voice. "With your men gone—like today—you and your housekeeper are wide open for trouble."

"Your concern is flattering—"

"Don't be flattered," Vincent told her bluntly. "Just do it."

"No."

"Good for you," Millicent chimed in from the doorway.

"I've never heard such foolish talk. A fine lady like Mrs. Colter doesn't use firearms."

"Millicent, please," Eden murmured.

"A fine lady like Mrs. Colter could get herself killed because she can't use a gun," Vincent replied with more feeling than Eden was sure he had used in years. Answering the combative gleam in Millicent's eye with one of his own, Vincent scraped his chair back from the table and pushed himself to his feet. "It wouldn't hurt you to learn how to shoot either, Miss Millicent."

"Sure and I won't," Millicent answered tartly, drawing herself up to her full height. "We're safe here. If anyone threatens us, we can bolt the doors, close the shutters and wait it out until help comes."

"Hah!" Vincent gave a derisive snort. "You'd be burned out in half an hour."

"So you say. Your way—"

Eden's nerves gave under the strain of the rising battle and her concern for Hugh. "Stop it, both of you! Vincent, I appreciate your concern but I abhor guns and the violence which accompanies them."

"So did my wife," Vincent said woodenly. "I respected her wishes. She was murdered by renegades three days before her birthday. She would have been twenty-one."

Eden swallowed convulsively while Millicent's stare dropped to the floor. "I'm sorry," Eden whispered, feeling acutely the ache that Vincent must still be experiencing. "I'm so very sorry."

"Like I said, don't be flattered or sorry." Vincent's expression was blank once more. "Just let me teach you how to use a gun so the same thing won't happen to you."

His insistence sent a shudder of fear through Eden. It was as if Vincent were trying to warn her that she was in danger here—as if he knew, somehow, in some way, that her life was threatened. Eden jumped up and paced the room. It didn't make sense. Then again, after last night, nothing made sense in her world anymore.

"All right." Eden faced Vincent, a determined set to her jaw. "I will accept your advice. Since you think it necessary for us to defend ourselves, you may as well be the one to instruct us. I warn you, though, I won't be one of your better students. You will accomplish a great deal if I even learn to load a gun."

Vincent bowed his head stiffly. "We'll start right now. I'll meet you in back of the house in five minutes. Mrs. Colter, we'll start you out on a revolver and, Miss Millicent, you'll begin with a rifle. Bring a box of shells for each."

"Now?" Millicent objected. "The dishes—"

"They'll keep." Vincent's tone lashed both women into startled silence. "Five minutes, ladies." He left the room and moments later the front door opened and slammed shut.

With Millicent following her, Eden led the way to the study and unlocked the gun case with the key from her desk. She handed Millicent a rifle and then, shuddering, extended her hand toward one of the revolvers. It would have been easier to pick up a rattlesnake. Her courage fled and Eden's hand stopped a few inches above the handle.

"This is crazy," Millicent whispered when she saw Eden's hesitation. "If you ask me, the only thing we have to worry about is Vincent. He's just trying to scare us, Miss Eden; nothing bad will happen to us."

So Millicent, too, felt there was a definite purpose behind Vincent's warning. Eden's hand started to tremble and she hastily withdrew it from the case.

"You could always ask Mr. Colter to leave two or three men around the place," Millicent persisted.

And let Hugh know that she was afraid of being alone? Never, Eden decided finally. Such a thing was too childish to contemplate and Eden had indulged in enough childlike behavior for one day. She called herself a woman, but in many ways she hadn't ceased to be the sixteen-year-old girl Hugh had married.

"No." Eden reached into the case and extracted the revolver, though her skin crawled when her fingers closed around the cold metal. "Get the bullets, Millie."

"Which ones?" Frowning, Millicent pointed to the stack of shell cartons. "Which bullets for which gun?"

"I—I don't know." How could we be so stupid? Eden wondered as she opened several cartons. "I know these are for a shotgun but I don't know about the others. We'll just have to take the other three cartons and have Vincent show us which ones to use. Come on, Millie, we'd better not keep him waiting."

As Eden had privately predicted, Vincent didn't find their lack of knowledge amusing. He found it intolerable. Holding a sample of each bullet, he described in short, clipped tones the weight, muzzle velocity and force of impact each would have. Eden flinched as he graphically described the carnage the shiny pieces of lead could wreak upon the human body. Next, Vincent showed them how to oil and clean both weapons and then, when he was satisfied that they could perform that simple task, he taught them to hold and aim the empty guns.

Millicent turned bright red when Vincent, standing so close behind her that their bodies touched, guided her arms toward an imaginary target. Such intimacy was unnecessary with Eden's handgun. With his hand beneath her wrist, Vincent corrected Eden's aim by simply exerting a light pressure against her flesh. The gun drooped in Eden's grasp and, muttering something Eden didn't understand, Vincent took her left hand and curled those fingers around the gun handle as well. By the time Vincent allowed the women to load their weapons Eden's arms ached from the unaccustomed strain.

Aim, inhale, fire, exhale. Aim, inhale, fire, exhale. On and on went the drill, a relentless Vincent not allowing time for thought or a rest from the sun. The empty bottles Vincent had scavenged shattered, shards of glass littering the low garden wall and the ground below it. Runnels of sweat trailed uncomfortably down Eden's spine and between her breasts.

Aim, inhale, fire, exhale. With each shot, Eden's arms were jolted back by the pistol's recoil. What Millicent's shoulder must feel like Eden could only begin to imagine, but at least Millicent was hitting the targets.

"Don't close your eyes, Mrs. Colter," Vincent barked. "You won't hit a blasted thing that way."

Her face set, wincing at every round, Eden grimly forced her eyes to remain open as she squeezed the trigger. This time the bullet hit a bottle squarely in the middle, smashing the glass into a hundred pieces. Whatever pride Eden felt she could take in her newly found marksmanship was quickly dispelled when her next five shots slammed into the wall and the ground beneath it.

Finally, when Eden's ears were ringing so loudly that she could barely hear and her hands felt numb from the gun's recoil, Vincent called an end to the practice. It wasn't really the end, of course. She and Millicent still had to clean their weapons under Vincent's watchful eye, but at least they could perform that task in the shade of the flower shelter.

"You're learning," Vincent said at last. "What both of you need now is practice, and I'll see you get it. Neither of you is a crack shot by any means, but you'll sure worry the hell out of anybody who starts something. If you ever get to Dallas or Laredo, Mrs. Colter, find yourself a gunsmith and have him make you a revolver that's light enough for you to handle with one hand."

After Vincent left, Eden wandered aimlessly through the house, her thoughts constantly turning to Hugh and the danger he might be facing. Tears pricked at her eyelids and Eden fled to her bedroom, seeking reassurance where none could be found. Hugh's leather vest was flung carelessly on his side of the bed and Eden picked it up and held it tenderly against her breast. The scent of his tobacco still lingered in the material, causing a sob to choke Eden's throat. Although Hugh had never admitted it, Eden was fully aware that her health was the reason for their move to Texas. If anything happened to Hugh, the responsibility would be hers.

The sound of thunder dimly penetrated Eden's brain and she turned restlessly onto her side. The rumble persisted, an ominous sound that forced Eden to pry her eyes open and look toward the window. Sometime during the endless afternoon she had fallen asleep, and her dreams had taken her to their last night in New York, a night when she and Hugh had been caught in the garden by a spring shower. Like two children they had run laughing into the house and had warmed each other by making love in front of a roaring fire. Eden sat up, noting with drowsy surprise that moonlight was shining through the window, and listened more carefully to the rolling thunder. With a sudden exclamation she flew from the bed and down the stairs as she realized she was hearing the thunder of approaching horses.

"Hugh!"

Oblivious to the other men who had ridden in with her husband, Eden threw herself into Hugh's arms the minute he dismounted. Weak with relief, she clung to Hugh's neck while he kissed her deeply.

"Hello, darlin'," Hugh murmured against the soft, flaxen curls. "Lord, but you feel good."

Frowning in consternation, Eden pulled away. "Are you all right? You haven't been hurt?"

Hugh smiled and shook his head. "I'm fine—just bone tired and hungry, like everyone else. Think you and Millicent can whip up a midnight supper for the four of us while we take care of the horses?"

"Yes, of course." Reluctantly, Eden released Hugh and glanced through the darkness at the other men before running lightly up the steps to the house.

Half an hour later the men filed into the dining room, and Hugh waved them into their chairs as he sank into his own. Fifteen hours in the saddle was too much for a man his age, Hugh thought. He wasn't used to riding so hard and so long, in spite of the brave front he was showing the others. The table was already set with steaming coffee and Eden, bless her, had thoughtfully provided two decanters of whiskey.

"Drink up, gentlemen," Hugh instructed as he poured a glass of whiskey for himself and passed the decanter to Ian. "God knows you've earned it."

"Haven't we though," Keith Gerald commented wryly. "My apologies, Hugh, for dragging you on a wild-goose chase. I was sure we had a good chance of catching those rustlers today."

Hugh shrugged—more to ease the cramping muscles between his shoulder blades than to console Keith. "If not this time, then the next. Patience, youngster."

Keith chuckled and raised his glass in mock salute. "I bow to your wisdom, sir. Tell me: Where did you and Ian learn to track the way you do? Not in New York surely."

"The army," Ian growled. "In the old days Hugh could track a fish through water without getting off his horse."

Quiet laughter greeted Ian's loyal exaggeration but Keith sobered immediately. "I've been after these men for nearly a year and so far I haven't been able to catch even one member of the gang. Oh, we've gotten close enough to shoot at them— I even winged one of them a few months ago—but I'll be damned if we can bring one in."

Hugh scrubbed a hand over his face. "Seems like you've got yourself some cattle thieves who are either very smart or very cautious. You say they never returned your fire?"

Keith shook his head. "Not once. That's what really confuses me. If they're not above stealing a man's cattle, why are they above fighting to keep their loot?"

"Perhaps they simply don't want to hurt anyone." Eden stepped into the room and set the heavy tray on the table.

"My wife, gentlemen, has a very idealistic outlook on the rest of the world." Hugh rose and curled an arm around Eden's waist. "Eden love, I believe you know these two gentlemen. Captain Gerald, Neil Banning."

Eden's heart leaped in her throat as the two men stood politely until she was seated. "Do be seated, Captain, Mr. Banning," Eden said in a voice as calm as she could possibly manage.

"I offered our spare rooms to Keith and Neil," Hugh informed Eden as the dishes were passed. "It's late and Neil has as long a ride to his ranch as does Keith to the hotel in town." Eden quickly reached for a tumbler of cold water.

"I didn't think I'd be taking you up on your offer this soon, Mrs. Colter," Keith apologized. "I hope we haven't inconvenienced you."

"No—not at all." Eden swallowed hard, nearly choking from the lump in her throat. "You're welcome here anytime—both of you."

At her polite, albeit grudging inclusion of him in her welcome, Neil smiled and inclined his head mockingly to Eden. Blushing, Eden glanced away, and as the men resumed their conversation she had time to become painfully aware of her appearance. Her hair was loose, and the fine, softly curling locks cascaded down her shoulders and back to her waist. Her enormous eyes, still blurry from the long nap, appeared twice their size, and her dress had a distressingly slept-in look.

Hugh caught her eye while Keith was talking, and beneath the table he took her free hand in his and squeezed it warmly. Trembling, Eden returned the pressure, understanding the glow which darkened his eyes. I want you too, she answered silently as Hugh's fingers brushed her skin through the thin cotton of her skirt. At this moment she wanted nothing more than to have Hugh all to herself in the privacy of their bedroom. In four years of marriage Hugh had loved her to distraction, proudly declaring his love for her, never seeming to mind that Eden had never once said she loved him in return. It had taken the harsh realization that Hugh could be killed to make Eden realize how much she loved him. She had to tell him now, tonight, and she grew impatient with the way Keith and Hugh were compelled to discuss the day's events.

The affectionate byplay between Hugh and Eden was not missed by Neil. Content to let Hugh and Keith try to figure out where they had gone wrong today, Neil lit a cigar and settled back to enjoy what he guessed would be at least an hour of watching Eden at close range. Beautiful, Neil thought as Hugh's hand disappeared for a second time and the lights of passion danced again in the gray eyes. Simply beautiful. What a pity all that passion and beauty were wasted on a man old enough to be her father. Not that Neil didn't like Hugh Colter, but the fact remained that . . . that what? That it was sheer torture to sit idly by when his fingers ached to lock themselves in those silken, flaxen curls? That his sleep last night had been haunted by dreams of Eden? Dreams in which their roles were reversed—this time it was she who was the seductress while Neil gave his body up to the blood-pounding responses Eden was eliciting from him. Neil's groin tightened, hardening in exquisite pain, and he had his answer. He had tasted the girl years ago; he wanted to savor the woman now.

The reasons which prevented Neil from having an affair with Constanza—Constanza's honor, her faith in her marriage vows—did not apply when it came to Eden Thackery Colter, Neil reasoned arrogantly. She wasn't a *criollo;* she lacked the aristocratic blood which flowed through Constanza's veins and his own. Whatever guilt Eden had made him feel at Constanza's party had evaporated rapidly and Neil smiled to himself. He had been right four years ago—Eden would be the perfect mistress, but only a woman like Constanza was good enough to bear his name and his legitimate children.

Blessedly unaware of Neil's thoughts—although she could feel those golden eyes raking her from head to toe—Eden listened with growing concern to Keith and Hugh. They were planning to go after the rustlers again, as soon as the band struck and left a fresh trail.

"Why not let them keep those silly cows?" Eden demanded. With an exasperated sigh she rose and began pouring each of the men a fresh cup of coffee.

"Eden!" Hugh scowled at his wife. "You don't mean that."

Eden tossed her hair over her shoulder with a defiant shake of her head. "Yes, I do. Forgive me, Captain Gerald, I don't want you to think that I go through life disregarding the law, but you said yourself that the rustlers have only hit the larger ranches."

"Yes, ma'am." Keith regarded her steadily. "But I'm afraid I don't understand what that has to do with anything. It's still stealing."

"I know, I know. But it's not as if any of the ranchers have been deprived of their livelihood, and for all we know these men may have a perfectly good reason for taking the cattle."

"Such as?" Neil joined the conversation for the first time and Eden turned to him, her eyes wide and startled. "You are advancing a most interesting theory, Eden. Please continue."

"I—" Eden gestured helplessly. "They may need money for their families. If your family, your wife and children, needed food and clothing and you couldn't find an honest job, wouldn't you do anything you could to take care of them?"

She was serious, deadly serious, and recognizing this, none of the men laughed or even smiled at the naïve statement.

"In a situation like that, we probably would," Keith answered in an odd, quiet voice. "Unfortunately, I doubt these men are stealing for such a noble reason. Hugh, do you have a map of this area? I want to show you something."

Hugh nodded and led the way into the study. Behind his desk hung a map with the various ranches outlined and shaded in different colors. Keith took a pencil from Hugh's desk and began printing small x's across the map. When he had finished, Keith turned with a grim smile.

"If, as you suggest, Mrs. Colter, these men are desperate, they would have struck a few times and then disappeared. As you can see, that is not the case. These rustlers have been raiding this area for close to four years now. In other words, they found an easy prey and it's my guess they'll stay around until the carcass is picked clean."

"*If* that's their intention," Hugh commented softly as he stared at the map. "Look how often Lathrop has been struck compared to Neil and myself. Lathrop must have lost three times as many cattle as we have. It almost seems as if someone has it in for Lathrop and they're just stealing from Neil and me as an afterthought. Now, why would anyone be bent on destroying Lathrop?"

Keith's eyes sparkled in the light of the kerosene lamp, and his haggard features relaxed in a smile. "If I can discover that,

I should be able to capture them. Now, if you will excuse me, it's been a long day."

"Upstairs, first and second doors on the right," Hugh instructed. "Sleep well, Keith, and you, too, Neil."

"Captain Gerald must think I'm a foolish, empty-headed woman," Eden told Hugh unhappily when they were in their bedroom. Thoroughly humiliated by her behavior, Eden's cheeks still burned whenever she thought of the explanation she had given about the rustlers.

"I doubt that, dear heart." Hugh smiled indulgently and with a sigh of relief he settled into the tub of cool water. "I hope you provided Keith and Neil with this luxury."

"Naturally," Eden snapped, remembering the hurried trips up and down the stairs she and Millicent had made while the men had taken care of their horses. As far as she was concerned, Neil could bathe in the horse trough! Neil, Neil, Neil, Neil! Why did he have to plague her life, turning up like a bad penny when she least expected it?

"Darlin'?" Hugh studied the dark look that had settled over Eden's face. "Ah, darlin', I'm sorry to spring two guests on you like this but it couldn't be helped."

"I don't mind that," Eden said quickly. "Truly I don't. What I mind is that we can't share things the way we did in New York. You ride off with the other men and I'm left here to worry about you."

Hugh guessed what was coming and he held up a hand to ward off her next words. "Be that as it may, you still can't come with me."

"I know." Eden bit her lip nervously. Separations were something she would have to learn to live with. Eden knelt beside the tub and asked, half smiling, "Shall I do your back?"

"That, Eden love, would be pure heaven."

Hugh leaned forward and Eden applied the sponge and soap to his broad back. Sighing with pleasure, Hugh gave himself up to Eden's ministrations while her deft fingers drove the stiffness from his muscles.

"I love you," Eden said breathlessly, moving closer to the tub and sliding her hands through the dark hair on Hugh's chest.

Blue eyes snapped open and Hugh stared at Eden's flushed face. "What?"

"I love you," she repeated, her heart soaring. "Oh, my dear, darling Hugh, I love you so."

Hugh gripped her shoulders, his wet hands soaking her blouse while he rose, drawing Eden to him. "You're confusing love and sex," Hugh said quietly, afraid to believe what he was hearing. "What you feel now is—"

"—Is. love," Eden replied with a slow smile. "Forgive me for taking so long to recognize what I should have known years ago. And I do know the difference between loving you and wanting to make love to you."

Hugh stepped from the tub and, wet though he was, crushed Eden against his chest. "I always hoped, you know, always . . ."

"Dear, patient Hugh," Eden murmured, twining her arms around his neck. "Waiting for me to decide, never demanding, never pushing me. How painful it must have been for you."

"You never gave me a moment's pain, never."

"Pleasure then." Eden's lips fastened on Hugh's eagerly. She felt strange, not herself at all. Watching herself through Hugh's eyes as she drew out the motions of undressing, Eden felt something deep inside her heart break open and flow toward him. She was naked now, and with a deliberate sensuality she lifted the heavy mass of flaxen curls in her arms and let it fall in a shining veil around her body.

Hugh caught his breath when Eden reached for him, touching him boldly. Her mouth caught at his, then trailed down his chest and stomach, tracing delicate patterns upon the sensitive skin. Passion made her bold, drawing gasps of surprise and delight from Hugh, and her love made her lose any embarrassment she had felt. This was what love did, Eden thought dazedly as Hugh's fingers tangled in her hair. It transported them both beyond a world of conscious thought or action, giving them a freedom of expression previously forbidden by the small core of reserve in Eden's heart.

"Tell me again, darlin'," Hugh asked as he nibbled at the corners of her mouth.

"What?" Eden teased, running her hands lightly over his back.

"That you love me." Hugh caressed her cheek with the back of his hand. "That I wasn't imagining what you said."

The love shining in Hugh's eyes matched what was in her heart, and Eden replied softly, "You sweet, foolish Irishman—

I love you, I love you, I love you! I'll tell you every day, every night if you like."

"I like."

Their lips met and clung for a long moment before Hugh blew out the candle and, lifting Eden in his arms, carried her to the bed.

In the room across the hall Keith Gerald lay awake, listening for the faint murmur of voices which had ended so abruptly. A mattress squeaked—then silence fell once more. Jealousy swept through him, a raw, unsettling emotion which banished all hope of sleep. Keith pushed himself upright and stared blindly around the darkened bedroom. Hardly twenty-four hours had passed since he had met Eden Colter, yet Keith found her constantly in his thoughts. He knew virtually nothing about Eden, Keith reminded himself, except that she was married to a man he respected. Keith winced. Eden *was* married and, therefore, beyond his reach. Yet he couldn't help the way his blood heated whenever he saw her. Strange that Sandy, the young woman with whom he kept company back in Laredo, had never had that effect upon him. Keith's relationship with Sandy was . . . well, comfortable and undemanding, at any rate. At some point in time, Keith realized with a jolt, he should probably ask Sandy's father for her hand.

But not now. Keith swung his legs to the floor, lit the lamp on the bedside table and poured himself a drink from the bottle which had been placed there earlier. Until he understood the attraction he felt for Eden, Keith would back away from Sandy. It was, to Keith, the only fair thing to do.

Neil woke with a start, one fluid movement swinging him upright in the bed with his pistol leveled at the door. The sound of pots and pans being rattled in the kitchen came faintly upstairs and Neil leaned back against the headboard. Slowly expelling his breath, he holstered his gun and fumbled for his watch on the bedside table. Six o'clock. Time enough to shave, dress and get the hell out of here before the rest of the house awoke. There was too much to do today for Neil to be trapped into exchanging civilities with Gerald or the Colters.

Fifteen minutes later Neil strolled into the kitchen and casually dropped his hat onto the table. "If it's not too much trouble, miss, could I have a cup of coffee?"

Startled by the drawling voice, Millicent wheeled around

with a frightened gasp. "Lord, sir! You shouldn't do that to a body. You scared me near to death."

"My apologies." Neil grinned wolfishly, golden eyes narrowing as he assessed the generous curves beneath Millicent's dress. "I wouldn't frighten you for the world, miss . . . ah?"

"You!" Millicent's voice quivered with outrage as she recognized the tall, dark intruder and she hurled the plate she held at Neil's head.

Neil ducked, but not in time, and when the plate broke over his head one of the pieces gashed a trail down his cheek. "What's the matter with you?" Neil shouted as he touched the trail of blood with his fingertips. Then, remembering the people still sleeping upstairs, Neil lowered his voice to a menacing growl. "Are you trying to kill me, lady?"

"I wish I could," Millicent hissed, also mindful of the bedrooms within hearing distance. "Knowing what I do now I wish I'd killed you years ago!"

"What the hell are you talking about?" Neil pulled a kerchief from his pocket and pressed it to the cut. "I don't even know you!"

"Saints be thanked," Millicent spat. "You've got your nerve, coming into Mr. Colter's house and taking his hospitality after what you did."

"I haven't done anything . . . yet," Neil ground out. God, his face hurt! "But if you don't tell me what's going on I'm going to wring your neck!"

"Don't touch me, you . . . you heathen!" Millicent snatched up a butcher knife and waved it menacingly. "I'm not as innocent as Miss Eden was. Take one step toward me and I'll skewer you like a capon."

At Eden's name Neil went still as a rock. "You don't know what you're talking about," he said in a cold voice. "I just met Mrs. Colter two days ago."

"And you met her four years ago, only then she was Miss Eden Thackery," Millicent added relentlessly, relishing the opportunity to confront the man who had nearly destroyed Hugh and Eden. "I warned her not to keep company with you unless she had a chaperone, but she wouldn't listen to me." Millicent's eyes glowed spitefully. "Men like you—you all know how to make innocent young girls fall in love with you, and then you bed them and leave them without so much as a good-bye. It's just too bad you aren't more careful where you plant your seed.

You're worse than the bloody English lords who leave their bastards and used women all over Ireland."

Neil felt as if he had been shot. Involuntarily, he took a step toward the righteously indignant Millicent, stopping only when she brandished her blade. "Tell me what happened after I left New York," he ordered softly.

"No." Millicent's eyes were sparkling with victorious revenge. This man deserved every bit of pain she could inflict upon him. Mr. Colter didn't know him, and Miss Eden was too kindhearted to hurt *anyone* deliberately, so it was up to Millicent to see that this man didn't hurt the Colters again. "That's for Miss Eden to do."

"Since you seem to know so much, you should also know that Eden doesn't particularly care for my company," Neil said dryly. "Perhaps you are simply one of those servants who can't resist a tidbit of unfounded gossip."

Neil's quiet words were filled with menace and Millicent tightened her hold on the knife. "I'd rather cut off my hand than see Miss Eden hurt again, and I do not hold with backstairs gossip."

"But you won't tell me what I want to know."

Millicent shook her head and waved the knife toward the door. "You ask Miss Eden if you're so hot for an answer."

"Sure." Neil retrieved his hat and settled it on his head. "Tell Hugh I appreciate the loan of the bed for the night but I had some business to tend to this morning."

When he was well away from the Emerald I and heading south Neil finally let himself dwell upon the housekeeper's words, and not until then did their full impact hit him. A grim look froze Neil's features and a muscle worked in his jaw. Eden couldn't have been pregnant, Neil told himself over and over, not after only one afternoon! None of his lovers had ever had that happen—and until now it had been a blessing not to have to be responsible for an illegitimate family.

Neil turned off the road toward the Mexican border, cutting across land belonging to Lathrop. Children would come when he was married and had a wife to care for them. But suppose Eden had been pregnant. What would she have done? Given the child to an orphanage? Kept it herself? No, not that, because then Hugh would have had to accept it as his. Abortion? The thought settled like a dead weight in the pit of Neil's stomach. Not even Eden, for all her coldness, would do that. But Neil couldn't be certain. Millicent's vengeful seed had been planted, and she had no idea of the damage it would eventually wreak.

Neil crossed the border into Mexico and soon stopped at a small village. The streets were deserted but laughter echoed from the *cantina*, and Neil allowed himself a tight smile. At least some people were enjoying themselves. He sure as hell wasn't.

"Neil!" Julio's shout guided Neil through the smoky barroom to a table in the back. The *cantina* stank of stale smoke, cheap liquor and unwashed men, something that ordinarily would not bother Neil, but in his present mood it was just enough to set him off.

"Damn it, Julio," Neil snapped when he lowered himself onto one of the rickety chairs, "next time we'll meet in the stable. At least it will smell better."

Julio's eyebrows shot up. "The men were tired and this is the place you decided on, *amigo*."

"Sorry." Neil pulled a cigar from his vest and lit it, giving himself time to put a lid on his temper. "Did you find anything?"

"Nothing you will like." Out of politeness Julio poured a glass of tequila for Neil and watched in amazement as his friend downed the hated drink in one swallow.

Neil winced as the tequila burned its way down his throat and into his stomach. "And?" he questioned in a raw voice.

"And they crossed the border, divided the herd and scattered. The group we followed shot at us. With only three men . . ." Julio shrugged. "I thought it best not to take chances, so we came here." He lifted the bottle. "Another?"

"Are you crazy?" Neil growled. "You know I can't stand that stuff." He fell silent, smoking furiously.

Julio slowly expelled his breath. "So what do we do now, my friend? Give up?"

"And let that self-righteous Ranger hang me out to dry? You know he'd like nothing better than to pin the rustling on me. Not a chance." Neil rubbed a hand over his face, vividly recalling how Keith Gerald's gaze had strayed constantly to Eden during the previous evening. Unaccountably, Gerald's attentiveness toward Eden rankled Neil far more than the devotion Hugh Colter displayed. Hugh was, after all, Eden's husband. . . .

"Neil?" The sudden tightening of Neil's jaw worried Julio. "What is wrong? What has happened since we last met?"

"Nothing." Determinedly, Neil pushed all thoughts of Eden

to the back of his mind. "I want to catch those bastards, Julio. They've stolen from me long enough—I won't have them destroying what I've built."

Julio nodded. "What do you want me to do?"

"I don't know." Neil paused, frowning into his empty glass. "I thought having you at the ranch, ready to ride, would make tracking the rustlers easier. I was wrong. I think"—he raised his eyes to Julio—"I think I placed you in a dangerous position. You and the others deserve better. Go home, Julio, until I think of another way."

"But the Ranger captain," Julio protested. "We have to prove—"

Neil interrupted firmly, "Gerald has his suspicions but nothing more. He can't prove a damn thing." He shook his head. "When the rustlers are caught he will know the truth, but in the meantime I sure as hell don't intend to risk your life just to satisfy my ego."

Julio looked doubtful. "If I can help—"

"I'll let you know."

# Chapter 12

Indistinguishable from one another because of the heat, the days of that first summer in Texas all seemed to flow together for Eden. You'll get used to it, Maudie had assured her, but there were times when Eden felt like crying because there was no place she could go to escape the relentless heat. Some of her flowers burned to a crisp, in spite of the shelter, but miraculously the roses Hugh had had shipped from New York for her birthday had survived and were in full bloom.

Unfortunately, the Texas summer didn't affect the rustlers the same way it did Eden; if anything it made them greedy. The Emerald I was hit at least once a week, sometimes twice. It became a sort of ritual: Ian would bring the bad news, and a few minutes later Hugh and a dozen men would ride off. Eden would wave good-bye bravely, then worry herself sick until Hugh came home, dirty and tired but otherwise none the worse for wear. More often than not Keith Gerald was with Hugh—the man seemed to have an uncanny sense of where the rustlers would turn up!—and Eden routinely had a guest room prepared for the Ranger. Neil and Lathrop were victims too, but Lathrop was the only one who raged and bellowed when the men all met. Hugh sat quietly, making suggestions when Lathrop had to pause to take a breath, and Keith agreed with most of Hugh's ideas. Eden would listen to the discussions for hours, moving only to freshen their drinks, and gradually she began to understand the threat the rustlers represented to Hugh and the others.

Vincent, too, was a constant visitor, and though Hugh disapproved of the gunman's presence he could not fault Vincent's behavior or the fact that Eden had, under Vincent's tutelage, lost her fear of guns. Eden became a fair shot, and the knowledge comforted Hugh whenever he left the ranch site. Still, Hugh breathed easier when, after several weeks of gun practice, Vincent decided that Millicent and Eden could defend themselves and called a halt to the lessons. Much to Hugh's annoyance, the respite was short-lived. Vincent turned up the following evening—his hat in one hand and some wild flowers in the other—and haltingly asked Millicent's permission to 'come callin'.' Millicent blushingly agreed, Eden approved and Hugh ungraciously swallowed his objections. As for Eden . . . she kissed away Hugh's scowl and chuckled as Millicent led Vincent a merry chase.

If anything cast a shadow on Eden's contentment, it was Neil. He came and went with a casual air of possessiveness that set Eden's teeth on edge, and the fact that Neil had not tried to see her alone failed to allay the way her nerves jumped whenever he came to the door or stayed for dinner. Eden knew Neil was watching her, like a sleek panther waiting to pounce on his prey. Neil always managed to sit across from her at meals so that whenever she looked up Eden looked straight into those hard, golden eyes. When she was preparing drinks at the bar in the study for one of the men's late-night conversations, Neil always found some excuse to leave his chair and "help" her with the tray or make certain she poured him brandy and not whiskey. She had hoped that Neil would abide by his promise to avoid socializing with Hugh, but apparently he had chosen to forget. How foolish she had been to trust Neil, to believe for a minute any of the words which rolled so smoothly off his tongue! But chiding herself with that fact served no purpose, just as trying to deny that her heart raced whenever she saw Neil served no purpose. Hugh liked Neil, and Eden's only recourse was to treat Neil as coldly as possible without attracting Hugh's attention. Neil wanted something, Eden sensed whenever she caught him staring at her, but what?

Not surprisingly, Constanza was thinking the same thing, but she had no qualms about confronting Neil. Dressed in her newest riding habit, a striking affair of red velvet calculated to emphasize her dark, flashing eyes, Constanza appeared on Neil's doorstep one morning before he had finished breakfast.

Always quick-tempered, the past months had only shortened the fuse on Neil's anger. Plagued by the rustlers, Constanza's whining complaints and, most importantly, the knowledge that Eden and the secret she carried were still hauntingly beyond his reach, Neil had become disenchanted with his life and it showed in his greeting.

"What the hell are you doing here?" Neil growled when he answered the door.

"Do not be ill-mannered, Neil." Constanza swept by him and with an imperious wave of her hand sent the housekeeper back into the kitchen. "Since you have not visited recently I thought it best to come to you."

"You thought," Neil mimicked harshly. "As long as I have known you, Constanza, you have never thought. Now, at the risk of repeating myself: What are you doing here?"

"I came to see you. To find out why you have been spending so much time at the Emerald I when you should be with me." Constanza threw herself pettishly into a chair. "Four years ago you swore never to desert me, yet now you seem more interested in Eden Colter than in keeping your promise."

"Like hell! I've run my tail off for you in the past four years and been shot in the bargain, so don't tell me I haven't kept my word!" His face dark with anger, Neil hurled his napkin onto his plate. "Right now I'm ready to forget the whole thing and go back to Mexico."

"But you cannot! Not yet. You cannot abandon me so heartlessly." Tears glittered in Constanza's eyes. "You asked me to think about an annulment and I have, but I need more time."

Neil laughed harshly. "Time? How much of my life do you want, Constanza?"

"I should have known you would fail me," Constanza wept. "Why will you not help me, when it is your fault that I am married to Lathrop?"

"Would you mind explaining that?" Neil's eyes smoldered dangerously and he stalked across the room. "How in God's name am I responsible for Lathrop?"

Constanza ignored the anger in Neil's voice. She could deal with Neil's tantrums easily enough—like all men he was stupid and shallow, easily manipulated. "You fought for Juárez, you and Sebastian; and when the war was over you did not offer to help my family. While my father scratched out a living you and Sebastian went to Europe. Had you loved your mother more, and obeyed her, we would have been married long before Lathrop ever came to Mexico."

It was exactly the kind of twisted logic Neil had come to expect from Constanza, but even while his mind rejected her argument, part of him accepted the burden of guilt she placed on his shoulders. "All right," Neil sighed. "I'll saddle a horse, and by noon we can be across the border. Once we're back in Mexico I can pull a few strings and you'll have an annulment."

"No!" Constanza jumped to her feet and whirled away from Neil. "Not yet."

"Why not? Look—this game I've been playing with Lathrop on one side and you on the other was entertaining for a while, but enough is enough. Let's leave Texas and Lathrop behind."

"No!" Constanza repeated fiercely.

"How many ways do I have to explain it to you?" Neil shouted, all control deserting him. "I'm tired of living this way, Constanza! Either we get out now, together, or I leave without you!"

"I do not think so." A wild expression twisted Constanza's face. "If you disappear I will tell everyone what Captain Gerald suspects—that you lead the rustlers. He will believe me and hunt you down. Do not look so shocked, Neil, I will. If I have to endure Lathrop, I will make your life just as miserable as mine."

Icy fear trailed down Neil's spine, leaving him weak. "Do you know what you're saying? Constanza, men are killed for less than that. Is that what you want—me dancing at the end of a rope?"

"No, oh, no." With a small cry Constanza threw herself into his arms. "Forgive me, Neil. I would never do such a thing. But do you see what the thought of your leaving does to me? I would be all alone here, with no friends or family to rely upon." Constanza lifted tear-bright eyes to Neil. "Please, you must help me; I have no one else. Please, Neil, just a few more months."

Shaken by Constanza's threat, Neil automatically put his arms around her shoulders before he realized what he had done. She didn't mean it, of course; Constanza was frightened, afraid of what would happen to her if he went back to Mexico. Neil could feel the sobs wracking Constanza's body and in a comforting gesture he patted her hair. She was weak, Neil reminded himself, unable to defend herself against someone like Lathrop. It was at moments like this that Neil became the gallant gentleman he had been raised to be. "Don't cry, Constanza. I'll stay."

It was a smiling, confident Constanza who met Lathrop some time later at one of the branding sites. Wrinkling her nose in disgust, Constanza allowed Lathrop to help her from the saddle, but as soon as she was on the ground she brushed his hands away.

"You smell," Constanza stated disdainfully at his raised eyebrows. "The odor will cling to the velvet."

"Well now, since I paid for it, why don't you let me worry about ruining that fancy outfit?" Lathrop's eyes burned mockingly but he made no move to touch her again. "Did you talk to your boyfriend?"

"Yes."

"And?" Lathrop asked impatiently when Constanza showed a marked interest in adjusting her hat.

"And you were right. He wants to go back to Mexico." From the corner of her eye Constanza watched as Lathrop kicked the ground and swore softly. Constanza lifted her shoulders in an affected shrug. "He grows tired of the game."

"Damn half-breed Mex! You couldn't say or do anything to change his mind?"

"I did not say that," Constanza replied with a triumphant smile.

"Meaning what?" Lathrop looked at her sharply, his eyebrows knotted into a frown.

Constanza lowered her voice to a dramatic whisper. "Meaning I convinced him to say a few more months. Is that not what you wanted?"

Lathrop's face altered, his lips twisting into a faint smile at the victorious note in Constanza's voice. "And just what did you have to do to accomplish that little victory, my dear?"

"I cried," Constanza said simply. "I carried on about how I would be all alone if he left now. And oh, yes, I told him how awful it was being married to you. After that Neil could not help but take pity on me and agree to stay awhile longer. He wants to believe, you see, that he is a shining knight rescuing the fair damsel from a fate worse than death."

"Good, good," Lathrop murmured as he stroked his chin thoughtfully. "I must admit, Constanza, I didn't think you could handle him this easily. You have my congratulations."

"I would rather have the five thousand dollars you promised me. If you want my help again the price will be doubled."

"Judas only got thirty pieces of silver for his betrayal." Lathrop took Constanza's hand and squeezed it until she cried out softly. "Besides, you won't need the money, not if you're pregnant. Are you?"

Constanza stiffened. Every month Lathrop asked her the same question and every month she gave him the same answer in a sadistic ritual that Lathrop seemed to enjoy. "I—I do not know."

"You don't know," Lathrop echoed brutally. "You know, all right, and the answer is no, as always. You're running out of time, Constanza dear. Our agreement is for five years and you've already used up four. You and your boyfriend Neil deserve each other; you're both worthless." Lathrop dropped her hand as if it burned him, then smiled cruelly. "I'll give you the money tonight—after you've welcomed me home in an appropriate fashion. Take heart, my dear; with any luck at all you may be big as a house by the time our fifth anniversary rolls around."

"I shall do my best," Constanza replied stiffly. Lathrop started to turn away when Constanza caught at his arm. "You never did explain why it is so important that Neil stay."

"Because, Constanza, I think it's time our rustlers started stirring up a lot of trouble around here." With a not-so-gentle pat to Constanza's cheek Lathrop turned and walked off, leaving Constanza shaking with rage.

Someday, Constanza vowed silently, someday she would be free of Lathrop, free of his pawing, greedy hands and the malicious enjoyment he took in thinking he could manipulate her. What a pleasure it would be to see that leer, that condescending smirk wiped from his face once and for all.

"Your horse, Señora Williams."

*"Gracias."* Constanza accepted the reins casually, her eyes narrowing to conceal her recognition of the heavy-set man at her side.

"Can we meet tonight?" he asked softly.

"No. Lathrop will be home all evening."

"He is a pig." The man spat meaningfully into the dust.

"Shh," Constanza hissed. "Help me up, Manuel." The touch of his hard, calloused hands sent a shiver of pleasure through Constanza and she returned his broad smile. "Tomorrow night," she said impetuously. "He will be in town for at least two hours, playing cards. Come then."

Constanza spent the rest of the day preparing for Lathrop. She washed her hair, then relaxed in a tub laced with Lathrop's favorite scent. Dinner would be served in their sitting room, to serve her husband's purpose, so Constanza dressed in a transparent wrapper and brushed her hair until it lay like black silk down her back. Constanza smiled appreciatively at her reflection and applied a hint of red to her lips. Whatever else

she ventured quietly. "I mean, this won't exactly disappear overnight."

"I'm aware of that." Hugh exhaled slowly and stamped his cigarette underfoot. "I'll write to David tonight and ask him to be here for your confinement."

"I don't need David Sterling," Eden retorted with surprising vehemence.

"You cannot have a baby in the middle of nowhere without medical attention," Hugh insisted. "On second thought, maybe I should send you back to New York."

"Send me back!" Eden's eyes widened in dismay. "You will not—I won't go!"

"It's for your own good. You know what the doctors said, Eden."

"Oh, yes, I know what they said." Eden tossed her head angrily. "I was there, remember? Well, I did what all the doctors told me to and now I'm going to do things my way. I'm going to walk—even ride—instead of staying in bed like a frightened child. I'm going to eat what I want, when I want, and as much as I want. If I need a doctor, there's one in town who seems perfectly capable of dealing with a delivery, so you can just forget about packing me off to New York."

"Eden, I know how you feel," Hugh said slowly, his eyes dark and troubled. "But damn it, Eden, I'm scared."

Her anger dissolved and Eden laid a reassuring hand on his arm. "You don't need to be, not this time. Hugh, it's been four months already and I feel so wonderful. Look at me! Just last night you told me how healthy I look."

Hugh studied her for several minutes, his eyes taking in first Eden's glowing face, then traveling to her narrow waist which, Hugh noticed belatedly, had a new fullness to it. "Aren't you even the least bit frightened?" Hugh asked softly.

"At first I was terrified, but not now," Eden admitted. "David told me once that if I made it through the first three months I would practically be home free. Well, I held my breath every minute of every day for those three months and then I waited another month just to make certain. This time nothing will happen, Hugh, believe me."

Hugh smiled slightly. "What makes you so certain, dear heart?"

"Woman's intuition." Eden shrugged. "I just *know*, that's

all. Oh, Hugh, please don't look that way. Be happy for us. This is why we left New York, isn't it?"

"I thought that was my secret," said Hugh, amazed by Eden's power of deduction. "So tell me, Eden love, since you seem to have all the answers: How do I get rid of my fear?"

Eden opened her arms, and with an exclamation Hugh pulled Eden against him. "You see," Eden murmured against his shoulder, "when you hold me like this, nothing in the world can harm us. You taught me to believe in you. Now I want you to believe, as I do, that this child we created is going to come into this world whole and sound."

"I believe." Hugh said the words almost like a prayer. Then, suddenly, Eden found herself lifted into Hugh's arms and twirled around while she clung desperately to his neck. "A baby!" Hugh shouted, laughing, his face shining with excitement. "A girl—I want a girl, Eden."

"I'll see what I can do," Eden gasped. "But shouldn't we have a boy first? A son to carry on the family name and all that?"

"Definitely not." Hugh returned her gently to the ground and stroked the pale curls back from her face. "I want daughters, only daughters. Little girls I can pamper and spoil to my heart's content. Besides, boys are nothing but trouble—always getting into fights or wooing the girls to prove their manhood. No, dear heart, I much prefer a house full of girls."

"I should have known before now," Hugh commented hours later, when they were getting ready for bed.

Eden grinned, presenting her softly rounded profile to Hugh as he lay on the bed. "You've been so busy, love," she forgave him graciously. "You were just too tired to notice."

"Not a pleasant commentary on my performance as a husband," Hugh sighed ruefully. "I'll make it up to you, dear heart."

Eden blew out the candle, then stretched out beside Hugh and curled her arm across his chest. "You don't have to, you know, especially since I was trying so hard to keep it a secret from you."

Hugh's hand moved to her stomach and stopped, resting lightly against the slight mound. "You should eat more now; you're far too thin to be having a baby."

"Nonsense," Eden said defensively. "In a few months I'll

be so huge that you won't be able to stand the sight of me. We'll probably end up in separate bedrooms."

"Never." For added emphasis Hugh kissed her soundly and cupped her chin with his hand so he could gaze into her eyes. "I'm not exactly uninvolved in this little miracle, you know, and I'm claiming my right to see it through to the end."

Eden's heart swelled with happiness, bringing tears to her eyes. Giving Hugh a child had been her own very special, very private dream for so long that she hadn't truly allowed herself to believe that this time the seed within her was secure. Every night Eden, never a particularly religious person, had prayed for the tenuous life she carried. Her prayers, apparently, had been answered—unlike her previous pregnancies there had been no nausea to plague her mornings, and the cramps which she had come to recognize as the precursors of a miscarriage had not occurred. Not so much as a twinge, Eden thought with satisfaction as she snuggled against Hugh.

"I love you, Hugh."

Her voice was soft, fuzzy with sleep, but when Hugh's arms gently tightened in response Eden smiled into the darkness. How wonderful it would be when their child was born! Still smiling, Eden drifted off into a sweet land where dreams came true and men lived side by side in complete harmony.

The roundup began, bringing with it an end to the drowsy days and nights Eden spent with Hugh. He left early now, long before Eden was awake, returning dirty and exhausted when darkness fell. Scoldings, pleadings, all fell on deaf ears, so Eden had to be content with seeing that Hugh ate a hearty meal before he collapsed into bed. She worried about him and the way he threw himself so completely into making the ranch a success. It was for the child, he had said once when Eden chided him about working too hard; he wanted to leave a bit of himself behind in the form of the ranch so their child would always remember him. Eden had sighed and given up the argument. She knew Hugh well enough to realize that despite the physical demands of the ranch, he was happier working with his men than he would be relaxing around the house.

With Hugh's absences and with Millicent spending as much time as possible with Vincent, Eden found herself virtually isolated on the Emerald I. Not that she minded. The role of social butterfly had never appealed to her, and now Eden found other activities to occupy her days. The flower garden demanded attention, so she spent the mornings weeding, transplanting and generally coaxing the plants into riotous bloom. In the afternoons she retreated to the study and worked on the tiny shirts she was fashioning for the baby, a task which finally put to use the skills with a needle and thread she had dutifully learned so many years ago.

During the day, while her hands were busy with the mundane business of running the house, Eden's thoughts were full of the baby, who had started to move inside her. Neil, the rustlers—strange how she always thought of those two together—these concerns faded into the recesses of her mind, to be examined months afterward, when it was too late to rectify the events which had already been set in motion. But now there was no hint that the future would be anything less than perfect and joyous, and with a glad heart Eden allowed what remained of her protective shell to crumble away. She smiled through all her waking hours, at peace with herself and the surrounding world.

Hugh also—when he had time to dwell upon it—was content with the course their lives had taken. The roundup had gone smoothly, as he hoped the drive to Dallas would also. He felt vibrant, alive; the challenge of the land restored the zest for life he had lost in his comfortable mansion, and he found himself eagerly anticipating each day. This evening, finished with the paperwork from his business and investments in the East, Hugh unceremoniously shoved the folders into his desk and leaned back in his chair. Eden, her brow furrowed in concentration, was using the last rays of the sun to put the finishing touches on something for the baby, and Hugh silently marveled at the change this pregnancy had worked on her. No longer slender as a reed, Eden now moved with the slow, careful grace exclusive to women in her condition.

Glancing up from her work, Eden caught Hugh studying her and smiled. "It's quite miraculous, isn't it?" she asked with a soft laugh.

"It is," Hugh agreed, pushing out of his chair to join Eden and drop a kiss on her hair. "But then, we were due a miracle."

"True enough. Would you like a drink before you leave, or shall I make coffee instead?" Hugh would spend tonight camping with Ian and the others so they could leave before dawn the next day.

"A drink—but I'll get it," Hugh said firmly when Eden started to rise. "Do you want anything?"

Eden shook her head and folded away her sewing. "After you've gone I plan to eat my way through what's left of the pie we had for dinner." Gray eyes sparkled mischievously. "I'd hate to spoil my appetite."

"There's no danger of that, I'm thinking," Hugh grinned as he toyed with the decanters. His expression turned serious and he added, "I still don't like the idea of your being here alone while I'm gone. Eden love, why don't you take Maudie up on her offer and stay with her until I get back?"

"No," Eden replied lightly but firmly. "I'd rather stay right here. I won't be alone; Millicent will be here and a few of the men."

"A skeleton crew," Hugh snorted derisively. "I'd feel better if you were with friends who could keep an eye on you."

"And just who keeps an eye on me while you're out chasing rustlers?" Eden rejoined teasingly.

"No one," Hugh admitted, "but that's not the point, dear heart. Usually I'm only gone for a day, two at the most. This time I'll be gone for a month or more, and in your condition . . ."

"My condition, as you call it, does not make me a helpless invalid, Hugh. Neither do I need a nursemaid hovering about and getting in my way." Eden tossed her head in loving exasperation. "My darling, you cannot lock me away in some ivory tower to protect me from the world."

"I wish to God I could," Hugh said feelingly. "When I'm not around, you end up doing crazy things like having Vincent teach you to shoot. That's another thing—can't you do something about this little flirtation between Millicent and that gunslinger?"

"Not a thing," Eden said blithely. "Millicent is in love, and neither of us can fight that. Can we?"

Hugh groaned. "They're not planning on a permanent arrangement, I hope. Millicent's mother would never forgive me."

"Don't be silly. Beneath Vincent's grim exterior, I think there's a very kind, gentle man, despite the fact that he works for Lathrop Williams." Eden rose and walked across the room to Hugh. "Do you think that when Millicent and Vincent are married you could hire him away from that despicable man?"

"Eden!" Hugh's eyebrows shot up. "What would I do with

a bodyguard? No, absolutely not; having Vincent in this household is out of the question."

"Because he's made a few mistakes?" Eden persisted. "As you once told me, everyone makes mistakes. Please, Hugh, it would mean so much to me if we could offer him a job. I don't believe Vincent is all that happy working for Lathrop."

"All right," Hugh capitulated, "but I won't hire him as a bodyguard. I want that made clear right from the start."

Eden nodded and threw her arms around Hugh's neck. "Thank you, Hugh; I promise you won't regret it."

"I already do," Hugh sighed. "But if it makes you happy, darlin', that's what's important."

"One more thing," Eden said when Hugh had kissed her. "They'll need a place to live, and since Millicent's room is so tiny..."

"What do you want me to do? Build them a house?" Hugh's roar shook the glasses, and Eden winced. "Eden, you're trying my patience!"

"Please?" Eden's voice seemed tiny and weak in the wake of Hugh's explosion. "It wouldn't have to be a very big house, maybe four or five rooms. And if Vincent quits or decides not to work for you, we could always use it as a guest house."

"Saints preserve me from the plotting woman I married. Shall I provide a dowry for the blushing bride? Or, better yet, maybe I should buy the happy couple their own ranch!"

"Millicent has been with me for a long time. She's almost like a member of the family now." Eden smiled at Hugh's vexed look and ran her fingers through his silver hair. "Is it so much to ask, Hugh? Really? She's all alone out here, except for the two of us. Who else does Millicent have to give her a proper start in life?"

"That's enough," Hugh said sternly, but his expression softened. "If—and I mean *if*—Vincent asks for Millicent's hand, we'll discuss all this again; but until he asks, don't you go planning a wedding."

"I won't," Eden promised. Hugh's arms encircled her, and the minutes ticked by unnoticed while they held each other close, saying their good-byes.

"I'm going to miss you," Hugh murmured finally.

"Oh, I know, I know," Eden whispered. Until now she hadn't allowed herself to think about the impending separation, but suddenly the next few weeks loomed bleakly in front of her. "We've never been separated before, not for such a long time. Do be careful, Hugh."

"I will." Hugh peered down into her face. "That's why Neil, Lathrop and I decided to make this drive together—there's safety in numbers. Keith has promised to look in on you every few days, so if anything goes wrong be sure to tell him. Not that anything will," he said hurriedly when Eden's brows drew together. "But just in case."

"I understand." Eden kissed him gently.

Hugh returned the kiss and then slowly pulled her arms from his neck. "It's time, dear heart."

Eden nodded, her throat tightening as she watched him collect his hat and gun belt. Through a supreme effort she managed to hold back her tears when she walked outside with Hugh. Hugh kissed her once more, lightly, then swung into the saddle.

"I'll see you in a few weeks, Eden love." Hugh stared at Eden, burning her face into his memory.

Not trusting her voice, Eden nodded again and even managed a faint smile. Only when Hugh was out of sight did she allow the tears to fall.

Six long, miserable weeks—and one telegram—later, Hugh came home, looking fit despite the rigors of the drive. The worried frown he had worn throughout the trip, as well as the acerbic disposition he had sported, had eventually driven even the faithful Ian to avoid him as much as possible, but both dissolved the moment he saw Eden waving from the porch. With a wild shout Hugh spurred his horse into a gallop, leaving Ian and the others in a cloud of dust.

"Lord, but it's been a long time!" Hugh crushed Eden in his arms and kissed her thoroughly, desperately, as if he couldn't get enough of the taste and feel of her lips against his. "I was beginning to think we'd never get back, that I'd be stuck forever with those damn cattle."

Eden laughed and started to speak, only to have the word stopped by another kiss. Sighing, she gave herself up to Hugh's embrace, meeting his searching tongue with her own in a delightful flare of passion.

"That does it." Hugh was breathing heavily and in one easy motion he picked Eden up and carried her into the house.

"What about Ian?" Eden protested halfheartedly as Hugh climbed the stairs to their bedroom.

"Let him get his own girl," Hugh growled softly.

There was an urgency to their lovemaking this time, due, Eden supposed, to the long separation. Every nerve, every tactile facility was stretched to the limit until they could stand no more, and Eden's cry was drowned out by Hugh's harsh exclamation. They collapsed together, their legs and arms still intertwined, and Hugh shifted his weight from Eden.

"I missed you so," Eden murmured finally, her voice quite small in the silent room. "That's not a very brave thing to say, but it's the truth. Nights were the worst—the bed was so cold and lonely without you."

"I must have reached for you a dozen times every night," Hugh admitted, "and once we got to Dallas I went out of my mind."

"Poor Hugh," Eden teased, knowing full well his healthy appetite. "You should have sent for me. I was going a little crazy myself."

Hugh raised an eyebrow at her confession. "You've never said anything like that before, dear heart. I mean..." Hugh stammered, searching for the right words while his face reddened. "Well, I know you, ah, enjoy our...our..."

"You're embarrassed!" Eden cried, raising herself up on one elbow to look down at Hugh. "My goodness, Hugh, after all this time surely you must have known that our lovemaking is every bit as wonderful for me as it is for you. After all, I'm not exactly a nun."

"I know that, but..." Hugh swallowed. The only other woman Hugh knew who had ever admitted to wanting a man in her bed was Libby, and as far as he knew there were no similarities between a brothel madam and the sheltered, well-brought-up young woman beside him.

"But you're still shocked." Eden laughed, enjoying Hugh's discomfort. "Eden Thackery Colter, all icily proper on the outside"—her voice dropped to a husky note and she leaned over Hugh so that the tips of her breasts lightly brushed his chest—"all seething desire and fire on the inside."

Hugh's lips closed around a taut nipple, and the room fell silent again except for their murmured cries of love and need. Afterward, propped up against the headboard, Hugh placed a hand on Eden's gently ripening stomach, grinning foolishly when the child she carried moved and kicked against his touch.

"We won't be able to carry on like this much longer," Hugh commented thoughtfully when his hand jerked from a particularly violent kick. Then, frowning suddenly, he said, "I haven't even asked you how you're feeling, dear heart. I've been worried to death for weeks about you and the baby.... Have you seen the doctor since I left?"

"I did, and he says I'm the healthiest pregnant woman he's seen in years." Eden smiled affectionately at her burgeoning form and then slanted a look at Hugh from beneath her lashes. "Hugh, tell me about Dallas. What did you do there for three days?"

"Mostly I slept." Hugh chuckled. "One night the four of us—Neil, Lathrop, Ian and myself—treated ourselves to dinner at the best restaurant in town after we'd gone to the theater."

"Theater?" Eden's ears pricked up and she tried to ignore the sinking feeling in the pit of her stomach. "You went to a play?"

"Not a play, exactly—there was a singer from back East who's touring the country and she was performing in Dallas for a week."

"Did you have a nice time?" Eden asked stiffly.

"Oh, yes." Amused, Hugh watched her face tighten. "Neil was even considerate enough to supply Ian and me with feminine companionship for the evening."

Eden turned slowly toward Hugh, her gray eyes flashing. "Feminine companionship?" she inquired. "You took another woman to the theater and dinner while I sat home! Exactly what else did you do, Hugh Patrick Colter, when I was pacing the floor at night? Oh—I'll just bet you missed me. Now I know why you stayed in Dallas. You were probably having such a wonderful time you couldn't tear yourself away."

"My darling, you are a jealous woman." Hugh pulled her, resisting, into his arms and combed his fingers through the disarrayed flaxen curls. "Now, before you fly off the handle, let me explain something."

"Explain!" Eden shrieked. "Explain what? That four years of fidelity proved too much for you? Oh, Hugh, how could you?"

"How could I what? Eden, I was so miserable without you that I made the drive rough on everyone." Hugh looked at her patiently. "I made things especially hard on Neil, and I think a woman was his way of telling me there weren't any hard feelings. At any rate, a man as in love as I am doesn't have eyes for any woman except the one he loves. I sat through the concert and dinner out of politeness and escaped as soon as dessert was cleared away." Hugh peered into her face. "I wanted to tell you myself, before Lathrop made some crude remark in front of you. This way, if he does say something you'll know the truth."

Eden studied him and said softly, "I thought . . . well, with my being pregnant, I thought . . ."

"What? That I'd stopped loving you?"

Her lip was trembling and Eden fought to control it. "You didn't touch me for weeks after I told you about the baby," she protested. "What was I supposed to think?"

"My fault," Hugh sighed. "I was afraid it might hurt the baby."

"And just now?"

"Frankly, I wanted you so badly I never gave the baby a thought." Hugh pressed Eden against his chest. "If such a thing is possible, I love you even more now that you're carrying my baby."

"Truly?" Eden's voice was muffled.

"Truly," Hugh assured her with a light hug.

"Even when I'm so big that we can't be together like this?"

"Oh, I think I'll be able to manage." Above her head, Hugh smiled, blue eyes dancing with laughter. "Am I forgiven my indiscretion?"

"Oh, of course," Eden cried softly. She pulled away to gaze at Hugh, her eyes wide. "Have patience with me, Hugh; we pregnant women sometimes become fanciful creatures. Besides, if anyone is to blame it's Neil. Neil Banning and his way with women!"

Hugh laughed at her indignant tone, for which he received a withering glance from Eden as she climbed out of bed. "Careful, dear heart," he chortled, "you can't very well turn prudish after that little conversation we had earlier. You enjoy having a man, Neil enjoys his women. What's wrong with that?"

Eden tested the bath she had readied before Hugh's arrival and, finding it tepid but not cold, settled herself in the water before replying. "The difference is obvious. That man is positively immoral! If Neil had his way monogamy would have been dead and buried years ago."

"He's not the marrying kind; at least not yet." Hugh rubbed the stubble covering his face and decided a shave was in order.

He never will be, Eden thought sourly as she worked a generous lather from the bar of soap. It was all very well for Neil to play fast and loose with a woman, but unless her blood were as blue as his there was no way on earth Neil Banning would consider marriage.

"Now, Eden, there's no reason to look that way," Hugh chided when he caught her scowling. "I know you don't care for Neil very much, but I rather like him and I know the man thinks a lot of you."

"I'll bet he does." Eden's tone was colored by her bitter memories.

With careful precision Hugh began stropping his razor, a task which allowed him to avoid Eden's eyes. "Tell me why you don't like Neil, Eden. You two seem to strike sparks off each other whenever you're in the same room. I've never seen you react to anyone the way you do to Neil."

Hugh's voice was so quiet, so filled with love and concern that Eden was tempted to tell him everything. It would be best if she did—then their baby would be born without any lies between its parents. But she couldn't. Eden was too afraid of losing Hugh, of destroying her marriage over something that she knew still bothered Hugh.

"I wish you'd tell me, dear heart. Maybe I could smooth things out between you and Neil."

"There's nothing to smooth over." Eden was filled with self-loathing as the words came out. "You were right—I'm a prig and a prude and I don't care for Neil's cavalier attitude toward women."

Hugh fixed Eden with a cool stare. "Are you sure that's all there is to it?"

"Yes." Averting her face, Eden levered herself out of the tub and went about the business of dressing. "If we were in New York I'd cut Neil Banning dead and so would everyone else; his blatant carrying on with Constanza Williams simply wouldn't be tolerated the way it is here. If Lathrop wants to turn a blind eye to what's going on between those two that's fine, but I don't have to be charming and witty toward Neil Banning."

"They might be in love," Hugh suggested.

"For all I know they are," Eden replied. "But from what I've heard I think they're just playing a game and having a good time. Now, may we please drop the subject of Neil Banning?"

The subject of Neil Banning was happily dropped in the Colter household as Lathrop and Constanza Williams were just beginning to broach the same topic. They were seated on the terrace enjoying their after-dinner coffee when Lathrop, catching another of Constanza's contemptuous looks, decided it was time at last to end the charade between them. It was a pity, he reflected almost sadly. Constanza suited his jaded appetite admirably—she was delightful in bed. Submitting to his peculiarities without protest in the beginning of their marriage, Constanza was now as sadistically selfish as Lathrop himself. Not with Lathrop, of course—too much depended upon her ability and willingness to please him—but she demanded things of her lovers that made the blood pound in Lathrop's groin. Oh, yes, he knew all about her lovers, and in the past he had derived a great deal of pleasure from watching his wife and the other men with whom she entertained herself.

"Why are you laughing?" Constanza asked when Lathrop began to chuckle.

Lathrop shrugged and settled more comfortably in his chair. "I was just thinking what a deluded fool Neil Banning is when it comes to you. He really has no idea what a grasping little bitch you are."

"So?" Constanza faced him coolly. "That is to our advantage, yes? As long as I can manipulate him your plans for acquiring the Emerald I should be made that much simpler."

Lathrop puffed a fat cigar to life before replying. "You have been most, ah, helpful, shall we say? But unfortunately for you, my dear, I no longer require your assistance. You see, Constanza, I bought off all the men you supplied. They take their orders from me now."

"You cannot do that!" Constanza shrieked. Outraged, she jumped to her feet and began pacing the terrace.

"I've already done it," Lathrop pointed out. "They were mine anyway, right from the start. Don't look so surprised; the pittance you paid them wasn't enough to keep them in tequila."

"But they worked for my father," Constanza sputtered. "They are loyal to him, to me."

"Not anymore." Lathrop's mouth curled into a sneer and he rubbed his fingers against his thumb in an age-old gesture. "They are loyal to money and to the man who pays them. Your father treated them like animals and so did you. Now, why would they be loyal to either one of you? You can manipulate men like Neil because they still cling foolishly to ideals, but men such as our rustler friends have only one ideal—and that's to make as much money as possible. You can forget those tidy little sums you were collecting from our rustlers. I'm taking your cut and dividing it among the men—it makes for a smoother operation."

Constanza's lips pursed angrily, fine lines radiating in all directions from her mouth. Then, cursing loudly in Spanish, she brought her hand down hard against Lathrop's cheek.

Lathrop was on his feet before Constanza realized it. He trapped her wrists in one hand while his other hand cracked three times in rapid succession across her face. Crying, Constanza sank to her knees when Lathrop released her, her stinging cheeks buried in her hands.

"You stupid bitch," Lathrop snarled down at her. "I'm not like Banning. Did you honestly believe you could fool me the way you fool him? You, with your nose stuck up in the air and that blue blood you're so proud of—I've known better saloon girls!"

"I will tell Neil," Constanza threatened through her sobs. "When he hears what you have done he will kill you!"

"Not likely," Lathrop replied with a snicker. "Not when he hears about the kind of games you've been playing. How do you think he would like it if he found out that it is your rustlers who are stealing cattle around here and that you planned and arranged the whole thing not for revenge but for pocket money? Or I could arrange to have him meet your lovers. That should make a fine impression."

"You would not do that," Constanza cried, aware that once Neil heard the truth the control she had over him would vanish.

"Sure I would," Lathrop said cheerfully. "I don't give a damn what happens to you, Constanza. The past few years have been fun but I'm tired of you. I've decided to divorce you instead of waiting until next spring. Oh, don't worry. Since I'm the one breaking our agreement I'll give you an extra five thousand dollars above what I promised. That's fair enough, I think."

Constanza's weeping stopped abruptly at the mention of divorce. She got slowly to her feet, dark eyes flashing with resentment and contempt. How dare this swaggering _gringo_ think he could discard her so easily! She had invested time in this barbarian, too much time to be foisted off with a mere five thousand dollars. True, she would be able to take all her jewelry and clothing with her, but she knew that amounted to a drop in the bucket compared to what Lathrop had in the bank. "If I give you a child," Constanza proposed slyly, "will you abide by our original agreement?"

"No," Lathrop told her bluntly, a cruel gleam entering his eyes.

"But you said—"

"I know what I said." Lathrop started to laugh at his own private joke. "Can't you guess why I made that offer? If you'd produced a son in five years you'd have been set for life. You still don't get it, do you?" Lathrop chortled at Constanza's confused expression and brought his face within inches of hers. "I'm incapable of fathering a child. Now do you understand?"

Constanza stared at her husband for several minutes before she gasped, "You lied to me! For the past four years you've used me like a whore and all the time you were laughing at me!"

"That's right," Lathrop agreed maliciously. "You were so greedy, so eager to get your hands on my money that you didn't care what you had to do; and I enjoyed knocking you off your high horse every minute of every day."

"You _used_ me," Constanza repeated.

"Just like you wanted to use me—only you weren't smart enough to pull it off." Lathrop shrugged. "No need to look so miserable, Constanza. I've been buying and selling people like you for years."

Constanza's features sharpened with loathing. "Our agreement was for five years, Lathrop; I will not sign your divorce papers until then, not for five thousand dollars."

"You think you'll get more out of me by holding out?" Lathrop laughed unpleasantly. "You're a damn fool, Constanza. Come spring I'll have some heavy expenses—like paying off the rustlers for their last job, in addition to buying the Emerald I."

"*If* Hugh Colter changes his mind, you mean," Constanza said spitefully. "He has refused all your offers in the past and now with a child on the way, I am certain he is even more determined to stay on his ranch." At Lathrop's frown, Constanza smiled and pressed her point home. "Give me another forty thousand dollars and I will see to it that you have the Emerald I within one year."

"How?"

"What is it that Hugh Colter values above all else? Not money—he has all of that which he needs—but his wife. If he believes she's in danger, he'll be all too willing to sell." Constanza smiled mirthlessly. "It may be necessary to frighten Mr. Colter into selling his ranch, but in the end the Emerald I will be yours."

After a moment's contemplation, Lathrop nodded in a self-satisfied way. "Agreed, but I want it understood that you'll never come back here and never will ask for more money."

Constanza nodded, her eyes filled with a burning hatred which Lathrop, caught up in his own thoughts, failed to notice. "I will not be back, that I can promise you. Just have my money when I am ready to leave."

# Chapter 13

Rustlers, Lathrop's persistent offers to buy the Emerald I and all other worries dimmed in importance for the members of the Colter household when Eden went into early labor Christmas morning and delivered a delicate, squalling baby girl before a frantic Hugh could return with the doctor. By everyone's calculations the baby was premature, but from the moment she entered the world Shannon Patricia Colter clung tenaciously to life with a stubbornness Hugh claimed was purely Irish. When Shannon was a month old the doctor, admittedly surprised by the progress the infant had made, pronounced her healthy and sound, and both Eden and Hugh breathed easier.

"I knew Shannon would be all right," Eden murmured when the doctor had gone. Tenderly she lifted the crying baby in her arms and settled onto the rocking chair to nurse her.

"Of course you did," Hugh teased. "That's why she hasn't been out of your sight or hearing in the past month."

"Well, maybe I was a little worried," Eden confessed shyly. Hugh knelt beside her, one hand reaching out to stroke the fine down covering Shannon's head. The look on Hugh's face as he gazed at his daughter made Eden's heart swell with love for both of them. "She's beautiful, isn't she, Hugh?"

"Very." Dancing blue eyes locked with soft gray ones and Hugh leaned forward to kiss Eden. "Just like her mother."

"We have our miracle," Eden said, still half in awe of the tiny girl she had produced. "I've never seen a baby so perfect."

"Or so tiny. Shannon is going to take after you, thank goodness. Could you imagine how awful it would be if she grew up looking like me?" A small fist closed around his finger, and Hugh's expression sobered as he watched Shannon fall asleep. At Eden's nod, he carefully disengaged himself and waited while Eden laid Shannon in her cradle. As quietly as possible they left the nursery and went downstairs to the study.

Hugh poured each of them a drink and touched the rim of his glass to Eden's. "To Shannon Colter—may her life be long and happy."

"To Shannon," Eden agreed and sipped at her drink. As an

afterthought she added, "And to Millicent and Vincent, wherever they are. I hope their marriage is as happy as ours."

"Agreed." Hugh drained his glass and stared admiringly as Eden walked to the sofa. "I still wish they had postponed their wedding. You have your hands full taking care of Shannon without having to do the cooking and cleaning as well."

"I don't mind, and after all, it's only for three days." Beneath Hugh's stare, Eden arranged herself in a deliberately seductive pose, fully aware of the flame that kindled in his eyes. "Besides, don't you remember what it's like to be newly married and so in love? We spent so much time in our bedroom that Simmons was thoroughly scandalized and Lord knows how many visitors were told we weren't at home."

Hugh clamped a firm lid on the rising passion Eden was producing in him. To take his mind off the immediate problem Hugh said quickly, "Lathrop offered to buy the ranch again. He's increased his offer by half. Also, he pointed out that with the rustlers becoming more brazen, there is a certain risk for you and the baby."

"Oh?" The rustlers had become more daring since the cattle drive. Now they stole from herds grazing close to the building site and even took the risk of firing a few shots when they were followed. But none of that interested Eden at the moment.

"Maybe we should sell. Now that we have Shannon, it might be best to move back to New York so that she can have a proper upbringing."

"I don't think so." Lazily, Eden began unpinning her hair. "Shannon will be every bit as proper growing up here as she would be in New York. If you like, we can always send her back East to finishing school."

Hugh shot Eden a wry look. "Very funny—Shannon's only a few weeks old and you're planning her entire life."

"Mmm." Eden smiled invitingly. "Why don't we let Shannon decide when the time comes?"

"Fair enough." Hugh swallowed hard when Eden rose and glided to the door. "Where are you going?"

"To check on Shannon." Eden combed her fingers through the pale halo of curls while she boldly appraised her husband. "She'll be asleep for at least a couple of hours, so why don't your pour us both another drink. I won't be long."

After she had checked on the sleeping baby Eden hurried to the bedroom and changed into the new silk wrapper she had

ordered from New York. Carrying Shannon had changed her
figure, Eden saw as she surveyed her appearance. Her breasts
and hips were fuller now, even though her waist was rapidly
returning to its normal size. Eden quickly ran a brush through
her hair and touched Hugh's favorite perfume to her wrists and
throat. Hugh was so incredibly cautious these days, Eden
thought with a carefree chuckle, that he was afraid to touch
her. Well, it was high time they started living as husband and
wife again, instead of brother and sister, and if that meant
seducing Hugh, so be it.

The study door was ajar when Eden returned and, a smile
teasing her lips, she pushed it open a bit farther to see Hugh
standing in the middle of the room.

"I'm sorry I took so long, darling, but—"

The knob was torn from her grasp as the door was wrenched
all the way open. A startled cry escaped Eden as her wrist was
seized and she was thrown into a crumpled heap in the middle
of the room.

"What—" Eden started to say, only to be silenced by the
sight of a gun pointed squarely at her head.

"Don't try to scream, lady, or I'll blow your head off." Four
masked men had ranged themselves around the room and the
one who had just spoken—the leader, Eden guessed—now
waved his revolver toward Hugh. "Get over there with your
husband."

Hugh started for Eden only to find his way blocked by one
of the other men. "At least let me help my wife," Hugh pleaded.

"Not a chance," the leader snapped, and this time Eden
noticed the Mexican accent in his voice. "Stay where you are.
Come on, lady, hurry it up."

With as much dignity as she could muster Eden got to her
feet and made her way to Hugh, one hand clutching together
the low-cut neckline of her wrapper.

"She is beautiful," one man said in a loud, raspy voice.
"Let's take her with us. Make for a lot of fun during those long
nights."

"Why, you—" Hugh turned with a snarl and would have
gone for the man if Eden hadn't cried out and grabbed frantically at his arm. After a glance at Eden's frightened face, he
relented and curled his arms protectively around her. "Who are
you? What do you want?"

"Who we are is none of your business," the leader replied,

"What we want is your money. All of it. And your wife's jewelry, too. Hand it over and we'll go quietly on our way."

"I don't keep much cash here," Hugh said steadily. "And the more expensive pieces of jewelry are kept in town, in the bank."

"Now, that is strange. I heard just the opposite—and I can't hardly imagine that the *señora* would ride all the way into Lathrop just to get a few sparklers to wear to a party." The man leveled the gun at Hugh's chest and cocked it, leaving no doubt as to his intent. "Why don't you tell me the truth so we can be on our way?"

"Hugh," Eden begged softly, thoroughly terrified by the armed men, "let's give them what they want. Please." Hugh's arms tightened painfully around her shoulders, a mute warning for her to be silent.

"There's money in the desk, the lower left drawer," Hugh said finally.

The leader jerked his head and the man who had thrown Eden to the floor went to the desk and rummaged through it. With a shout he held the cashbox up for display before opening the metal container and rifling the contents.

"Well," the leader asked impatiently, "how much is there?"

The man's head came up, his eyes burning with anger and thwarted greed. In a tone that froze the blood in Eden's veins he answered his comrade in a heavily accented voice, "A hundred dollars."

"What?" The shout made Eden wince and she stifled a cry of alarm. "Are you sure?"

"'Course I'm sure. I can count. There's only a hundred lousy dollars here." He hurled the box through the window. "Where's the rest of it, old man?"

"There isn't any more," Hugh said evenly. "I told you I don't keep much cash here."

A hand grabbed her hair and Eden screamed as she was torn away from Hugh. Tears stung her eyes as her head was pulled backward until she was staring into the leader's face and she could smell the foulness of his breath.

"Leave her alone!" Hugh's enraged bellow was followed by the sound of wood hitting flesh and Eden heard something fall heavily to the floor.

"Hugh!" Eden—unable to see what was happening— twisted against the outlaw's grip but he was too strong for her, controlling her movements as easily as a puppeteer. "Hugh, what's happened?"

"Your husband just got a rifle stock in his gut," her captor sneered. "Hey, old man, get up. I want to ask you some more questions."

There was a scraping noise behind Eden as Hugh got to his feet and she fought back the hysteria that was rising in her throat. Please, God, Eden prayed desperately, don't let Shannon wake up until this is over.

"Let my wife go," Hugh ordered in a voice not quite his own.

"What's the matter, *señor?* Don't you like seeing me touch your woman?" The man's hand began caressing her breast, drawing a shudder of revulsion from Eden while the thieves laughed at her reaction. "Now unless you want me to do a whole lot more than just touch her, you better hand over the rest of your money."

"There isn't any more," Hugh ground out, a red haze floating in front of his eyes as he watched Eden writhe against the leader's humiliating embrace. "The jewelry is upstairs. For God's sake let her go and I'll show you!" Hugh lunged at the man, only to be kicked aside and he crashed painfully against the sofa.

"Keep ahold of him, damn you!" the leader shouted. Then, his grip tightening, he ordered Eden, "You show me where your jewelry is." Eden nodded. Her captor looked over her head to where Hugh was lying. "I'll only tell you once, old man, so listen good. If you try anything while we're upstairs I'll carve up your wife's pretty face so's you won't recognize her."

Eden was shoved through the doorway and up the stairs. On the top step her legs failed and Eden fell with a soft cry only to be brutally pulled upright a moment later by the man beside her. Shaking with fear, she stumbled into the bedroom.

"All right, lady," the man jeered as he shoved her onto the bed, "where's your jewelry?"

Eden's throat was so dry that she had to force the words out. "M-my dressing table. The teak box." As he began stuffing the jewelry into a sack, Eden ventured fearfully, "Hugh was telling you the truth. I don't have any of the expensive pieces here. Please—just take whatever you want and go away."

"Shut up." He grabbed Eden by the arm and half dragged

her back downstairs to the study. "Get over there with your husband."

Eden ran into Hugh's arms. "Are you all right? Oh, Hugh, your face!" Eden touched the bruise forming on his cheek.

"It's nothing." Hugh held Eden's hand, his eyes grave. "What about you? Did he——"

"No," Eden said hastily before Hugh could finish the thought. "Hugh, what's going to happen?"

"I don't know, but I won't let them touch you again." Hugh brought his lips to her ear, whispering so quietly that Eden had to strain to hear him. "If you get a chance, make a run for it. Get Ian."

Eden nodded imperceptibly, then stiffened when the outlaw demanded to know where the safe was. Hugh's eyes went flinty with anger and he pushed Eden behind him before he answered.

"There *is* no safe."

Her breath caught in her throat at the lie. There was a wall safe concealed by her portrait where they kept the bulk of their cash and Eden's most valuable jewelry. Tell them, Eden begged Hugh silently. I don't care about the money; I just want them to be satisfied so they'll leave us alone.

"Julio, I think you better teach Mr. Colter how we deal with liars."

The man called Julio took a menacing step toward Hugh, a knife gleaming wickedly in his hand, and the slim thread Eden held on her self-control snapped. "No! Don't hurt him!" She wrenched away from Hugh to face their leader. "I'll tell you what you want to know. The safe is——"

"Hallo." Ian's voice rumbled through the house, freezing the occupants of the study into a grim tableau. "Hugh? Eden?"

What happened next would, thankfully, always be a blur to Eden. As Hugh pushed Eden to the floor he yelled for Ian to get help and then a shot rang out. The thieves broke for the door and when Eden pushed herself upright she heard an exchange of gunfire coming from outside the house.

"Hugh, are you . . ." Her eyes widened in horror at the sight of Hugh lying flat on his back, a crimson stain spreading across his chest. Eden's scream echoed in the room, blotting out any other sound. "Hugh! Oh, my God, Hugh!"

Eden crawled to Hugh and with trembling fingers tore open his shirt. Blood swelled out of the gaping hole in his chest, covering her hands and soaking the sleeves of her wrapper.

Tears streaming down her face, Eden frantically tore strips from her wrapper and pressed the makeshift bandage over the wound.

"How bad?"

She glanced up and found Hugh watching her through half-closed eyes. "I don't know," Eden hedged. "You're bleeding and you need a doctor. Just be quiet, Hugh; save your strength."

Hugh nodded weakly and they listened to the gunfire slowly fading into the distance. "They must have escaped," Hugh whispered raggedly. "Damn! I was hoping Ian would catch at least one of them."

"It doesn't matter, Hugh. What's important is getting you to a doctor."

"I'd never survive the trip, darlin'." Hugh smiled sadly, trying to prepare Eden for what he knew was going to happen. "I don't feel anything, no pain, no burning. I'm going to die, Eden love."

"No!" Eden cried, feeling her heart being ripped into countless pieces. She took Hugh's hands and placed them over the bandage. "If you can't go to the doctor I'll have one of the men ride into town and bring him here."

"Darlin', it's no use. I'm asking you—please, Eden, let me die in my own way."

"Stop it!" Eden said sharply as she got to her feet. "Stop this foolish talk and let me do what has to be done!"

Ian, his left arm bloodied and hanging limply at his side, and several of the men were running toward the house when she stepped outside. Without wasting time she ordered four of the men inside to get Hugh into bed, sent one into town for the doctor and turned to Ian.

"Come inside and lie down, Ian. The doctor will be here soon." Eden draped his good arm around her shoulders.

"Send a man to the Banning ranch," Ian gasped as she settled him into a chair.

"What on earth for?" Eden demanded. "He's not a doctor."

"No, but his brother is. Banning's brother is paying a visit right now. For God's sake, lass, do it! They can be here in twenty minutes."

Eden obeyed him instantly, and then, leaving a man to watch over Ian, she raced up to the bedroom where Hugh was lying. He was unconscious, Eden saw as she bent over him, but whether that was good or bad she didn't know. The bandage was sodden and she folded a clean pillowcase and gingerly changed the dressing. Hugh didn't move or utter a sound as she worked over him. The sight of so much blood frightened her beyond words, but Eden forced herself to remain calm. The bleeding seemed to have eased somewhat, which brought her some hope.

Eden felt the first waves of helpless despair wash over her. This wasn't really happening, she told herself. In a few minutes she would wake up and find that she had been dreaming, that Hugh was safe and sleeping by her side. But this was no dream, she realized with revulsion as she caught sight of her stained hands and clothes. Hugh's blood was everywhere. What if he died . . .

No! Eden refused to complete the thought. She had to think of something else—Shannon! Her heart slammed painfully into her ribs and Eden ran to the nursery. She had totally forgotten about the sleeping baby. Eden bent over the cradle, sobbing with relief when she found her daughter still slumbering peacefully. Shannon would be awake soon, however, demanding to be fed, and Eden would have to change and wash before then. Glad to have something to occupy her thoughts, Eden hurried back to the bedroom. The water in the washstand turned red as Eden scrubbed her hands clean and took a washcloth to the blood which was spattered elsewhere on her body. Don't think about it, she ordered herself when her stomach lurched sickeningly. There's too much to be done right now. Eden discarded the ruined wrapper and dressed hurriedly, feeling herself begin to shiver despite the fact that the day was quite warm. She wanted to cry, scream, do anything that would relieve the excruciating pain twisting through her.

"Mrs. Colter."

Eden whirled, unable to control the frenzied jumping of her nerves.

"Forgive me, *señora*, I did not mean to startle you. I am Sebastian Saros, Neil's brother."

Sebastian's voice was so warm, so comforting that Eden's composure splintered. "M-my husband," she stammered, gesturing toward the bed. "He's been shot and there's so much b-blood and he said he couldn't feel anything . . ."

Without another word Sebastian limped to the bed and set about examining Hugh. Eden followed, stationing herself nearby. Sebastian worked rapidly, his slender hands moving with surprising gentleness as he cleaned and probed the wound. Hugh moaned softly and Eden made a whimpering sound far back in her throat, her hands clenched helplessly in the material of her skirt. Sebastian spared her a sympathetic look as he opened his bag and began arranging his instruments on the bed.

"I shall require two basins of water, one boiling, the other slightly cooler so I may use it for washing. Also alcohol if you have any, liquor will do if that's all you have, and clean towels and sheets." Sebastian took off his jacket and began rolling up his sleeves.

When Eden delivered everything Sebastian had requested, she found Neil and Keith helping Sebastian prepare Hugh for the surgery. The men looked up as she entered. Sebastian took the water and sheets from her arms while Neil stepped forward and led her back out to the hall. Neil returned to the bedroom and Eden leaned against the wall, the minutes ticking by with unbearable slowness while she stared at the bedroom door.

How could this have happened? Only a few hours ago she and Hugh had been laughing, delighting in Shannon and thinking about the shining future that lay before them. Sobbing quietly, Eden pressed her forehead against the wall, trying to pray for Hugh even though she couldn't find the words. Don't let him die, she begged despairingly. Please, God, he's all Shannon and I have. The door opened and Eden turned around, hastily wiping at her eyes.

Sebastian Saros approached her, his expression grim. "You may go in now, Mrs. Colter. Your husband is awake and asking for you."

"Then Hugh will be all right?" Eden asked urgently. "You removed the bullet?"

"Unfortunately, no." Sebastian's golden eyes widened in recognition as he got his first good look at Mrs. Hugh Colter. He forced his thoughts back to the reason for his presence. "I am afraid removing the bullet would do nothing to help your husband."

"But he *will* live," Eden insisted.

"No." Sebastian's voice was gentle but that single word hit Eden like a sledgehammer and she reeled visibly from the blow. "I am sorry, Mrs. Colter, but the damage is too extensive."

"Oh, my God," Eden murmured faintly.

"He is in no pain," Sebastian continued, trying to offer what comfort he could. "At the end he will simply fall asleep."

Eden didn't hear him. She brushed by the men and entered the room in which, only a few weeks before, a new life had been brought into the world. Shaking, Eden walked to the bed, trying to smile when Hugh's eyes fluttered open.

"Dear heart." Hugh took her hand. "He told you, did he?"

Eden nodded, her eyes brimming with tears at the sound of his familiar brogue. "Dr. Saros is mistaken," she said in a trembling voice. "When the doctor from Lathrop arrives—"

"It won't make any difference." Hugh brought Eden's hand to his mouth, placing a kiss in the palm before moving it to his cheek. "I've always loved the feel of your hands—they're so gentle, so comforting."

Eden combed her fingers through his hair, unable to speak because of the lump in her throat. Hugh smiled at her, his eyes already shadowed by death, and when Eden began to cry softly he brushed a hand across her damp cheek. Thank God he had been spared any physical pain, for the knowledge that he was leaving Eden alone was painful enough. His life shouldn't have ended like this, Hugh thought in a moment of self-pity. He should have died years later when Shannon was grown and Eden was better prepared to take care of herself.

"Oh, Hugh, forgive me. This is all my fault." Eden took his hand in both of hers. "If it hadn't been for me—"

"Shh. I won't have you blaming yourself, dear heart." His breathing was becoming labored and Hugh had to wait before he could continue. "I was lucky enough to be loved by the woman I loved. You made my life complete, Eden love; our marriage and Shannon are the two things I can look back on with pride and joy. I don't regret a single minute of the past few years."

"I love you," Eden whispered tearfully. "I love you so much."

"And I love you." Hugh's voice was strained. "I'm cold, dear heart. Hold me." Obediently Eden slipped an arm beneath Hugh's shoulders, cradling him against her breast. "Sweet Eden," Hugh murmured. "My sweet, sweet love."

Hugh fell asleep, resting quietly until he shivered once and then went limp in her arms. The rational part of Eden's mind told her Hugh was dead, that the essence of the man she had loved was gone, flown to a world far beyond her, yet she continued to hold him. Her heart would not accept what she knew to be true and she thought, desperately, that if she held him long enough Hugh's flesh would warm and his eyes would open and be bright again, sparkling with life. But Hugh didn't wake; instead he grew colder in her embrace. Eden cried silently, feeling herself break into pieces inside. Tenderly she brushed a lock of silver hair from the cool forehead and gently lowered Hugh onto the pillows. She kissed him lightly, the merest touch of her warm lips on his icy ones, and pulled the covers over his shoulders to conceal the hideous bandage marring his body.

Sebastian was waiting when Eden emerged from the room and after a quick glance at her ashen face he stepped forward to take her arm.

"Hugh is dead."

There was a scream behind the frozen words, but when Sebastian tried to put a comforting arm around her trembling shoulders Eden shied away.

"I . . . I don't want to be touched," she told him in a quivering voice.

Sebastian bowed his head and followed her downstairs to the study, where Ian and the others waited.

One look at Eden's tear-streaked face told the men what had happened and they fell silent as Eden stood stricken before them until Ian guided her to a chair.

"I'm sorry, lass," Ian said heavily. "I'm going to miss him too."

Eden looked up and nodded, her lips starting to tremble with renewed pain. "I don't know how to go about"—she gestured helplessly—"the arrangements, I've never . . ."

"I'll take care of it," Ian assured her.

"There are instructions somewhere," Eden remembered. "Hugh wrote everything out . . ." She stumbled to a halt, unable to continue. Ian patted her shoulder awkwardly and left to attend to the last service he would ever do for his old friend.

Keith knelt beside her and pressed a glass of brandy into her hands. Eden stared at it numbly until Keith brought it to her lips and she swallowed a bit of the liquid. Apologetically Keith said, "We have to ask you some questions, Eden. I'm sorry we can't wait until later, but if we're going to catch these men we have to start as soon as possible."

Eden stared at him stupidly, barely able to comprehend what he was saying. "Questions? About what?"

"About what happened." Keith's tone was patient. "Are you

up to it?" After a moment's hesitation Eden nodded and Keith drew a shaking breath, for the first time in his life hating the job he had to do. "How many men were there?"

Eden answered Keith's questions automatically, unaware that she was doing so. Hugh was dead—that was the only thing which registered in her mind. Nothing else held any significance for her; she didn't even realize that she was crying during Keith's interrogation until he placed a handkerchief in her hands. Hugh! Her heart screamed in agony and disbelief. Hugh! Never again would they laugh together or share the events of their day. She would never awake in the middle of the night to feel his arms around her, nor would his lilting brogue ever fill a room with its musical cadence. The world was splitting apart, leaving Eden suspended in a purgatory which took away her life while at the same time it withheld her death.

"Do you remember anything else?" Keith continued.

"No." Eden closed her eyes weakly. "They all looked alike with those kerchiefs over their faces. I didn't even hear them come into the house. Hugh must not have either, or he wouldn't have been caught the way he was. Will you catch them?"

"We'll try." Keith looked at the floor. "The money will probably be gone by the time we find them, but we may be able to return the jewels."

"I don't care about the jewels," Eden said with bitter hatred. "I want those men! I want to watch them die a slow death, and I want them to suffer."

Keith started to explain that a court would pass sentence on the men but thought better of the idea. Eden was in no frame of mind to have the judicial system detailed to her. Keith rose and started for the door only to be stopped by Eden's quiet voice.

"Julio. One of the men was called Julio."

Neil and Sebastian exchanged a stunned look which went unnoticed by Keith as he retraced his steps. "You're sure of that? You didn't misunderstand, or hear something that wasn't said?"

Eden shook her head. "Only two of the men said anything at all, and I distinctly remember the leader calling one of the other men Julio. And the two men who spoke had Mexican or Spanish accents." Her brow furrowed with a sudden thought and she looked up at Keith. "There is something else, but I don't know if it's important."

"Tell me," Keith prodded gently. "Anything you can remember may be of help."

"Well, it seemed like these men knew a great deal about us." Eden unconsciously wrung her hands as she relived the terrible event. "I mean, they *knew* that I didn't keep my jewelry in the bank, and when Hugh denied having a safe in the house they threatened—" Eden's voice broke and it was a moment before she could continue. "I had the feeling that they knew where everything was kept and that they were just playing with us. It was as if frightening us was more important than the money."

"I'll do what I can, Eden," Keith promised. "Some of your men took off at once after the thieves, and I'm going to catch up with them. At least this way the posse will be legal when we find those outlaws."

"I hope to God you find them," Eden said fervently. "And I hope you find it necessary to shoot each and every one of them."

Frowning disapprovingly at Eden's words, Keith left, closely followed by Neil and Sebastian.

Alone, Eden sat unmoving in the chair, staring blindly into space. Pure, white-hot agony coursed through her veins with each heartbeat until the pain made her gasp. She couldn't think, couldn't move—not until Shannon's cry penetrated the fog around her brain. Scalding tears poured down her cheeks as she ran to her daughter's room. Shannon began to mewl plaintively and Eden lifted the baby against her shoulder.

"Don't cry, little love," Eden murmured. "I'm here. I'm here."

An icy silence reigned between Neil and Sebastian as the brothers rode back to Neil's ranch, driving Neil into an ill-concealed, blistering rage. Sebastian's expression was one of open contempt, making it obvious that he blamed Neil for the events which had transpired. As they dismounted, two pairs of golden eyes locked in mute contention, which was relieved only when Sebastian turned on his heel and marched into the house. Neil followed, his lips compressed into a thin line.

"I'll order supper," Neil announced shortly as he strode past

Sebastian at the bar where the younger brother stood pouring a drink.

"Do not bother," Sebastian retorted. "Death does not make me hungry, only thirsty."

Neil spun around, his hands on his hips. "Spit it out, little brother. You've been aching to take me to task ever since we left the Emerald I, so let's get it off your chest."

"Why should I be upset?" The fury on Sebastian's face belied the silky tone of his voice. "I have just attended a man's death and been told by his widow that my old friend was partly responsible for that death. Add to that the fact that my brother is the one who persuaded him to come to Texas, and I see no reason at all why I should not ride back to the Colter ranch and tell that poor woman everything I know."

"What are you saying?" Neil demanded. "That I had something to do with Hugh Colter's death? Have you lost your mind, Sebastian?"

"I do not know. Perhaps." Sebastian thoughtfully swirled the contents of his glass. "Truthfully, I am no longer sure what I believe. Correct me if I am mistaken, but Mrs. Colter *is* the Eden whose picture you carry, is she not?"

"She is," Neil acknowledged tersely. "But I fail to see what that has to do with anything."

Sebastian shrugged. "Your women have always been a source of, how shall I say, pride, with you. You are, by nature, possessive, and I wonder if seeing her happily married did not cause some injured feelings on your part."

"So I went out and had her husband killed," Neil concluded with a tight smile. "Look, little brother, I may be guilty of coveting another man's wife, but I'm sure as hell not guilty of killing Hugh. I liked the man! No matter how I feel about Eden, I genuinely liked Hugh Colter."

"What about Julio? If those men weren't yours, as you say, why would Julio be riding with them?"

"Why ask me?" Neil threw himself into a chair and glared at Sebastian. "As far as I know Julio is in Mexico, waiting for his wife to have a baby. Maybe it's just a coincidence—there's more than one Julio in Texas, you know."

Sebastian shook his head wearily. He and Neil had argued constantly during this visit and he was tired of the bickering. Besides, in his heart Sebastian knew Neil would never have a man killed in cold blood. But the question of Julio remained, and Sebastian decided he would investigate it when he returned to Mexico. "This whole affair is becoming too complex for me, Neil, and I don't like it."

"Neither do I, especially now when the rustlers seem to be losing all fear of the ranchers and of the law." Neil sighed. "I'll be sorry to leave. Four years is a long time to invest in a place just to pick up and leave."

"Then perhaps you should stay," Sebastian suggested. "You never were content in Mexico—too many memories of my father, I think—and you would just be off again as soon as you began to feel trapped."

"And Eden," Neil said absently, his thoughts slipping unwillingly back to her. "Until today I never believed she really cared that much for Hugh." Sebastian eyed his brother curiously and Neil hurriedly went on, "I mean, the age difference between them was enormous, and then there was Hugh's lack of . . ." Neil's voice trailed off when he caught the recriminating look in Sebastian's eyes.

"Lack of what? Breeding?" Sebastian prompted acidly.

"I didn't mean it that way," Neil said. "It's just that I find it difficult to understand how she could fall in love with him."

"After you, you mean. It bruises your ego to know that she managed, somehow, to be happy without you." Sebastian's laugh held a trace of malice. "I applaud her. How refreshing it is to find a woman who refused to let her encounter with you stand in the way of the rest of her life. That is what really eats at you, the fact that she didn't lock herself up and pine away until you decided to find her again."

Neil's eyes burned like molten gold, and all signs of compassion vanished. "What bothers me, little brother, is the fact that Eden was pregnant when I left, although I didn't know it at the time. Since you understand people so well, why don't you tell me what she did with my child?" Neil brought his temper under control and unclenched his fists with an effort. "Until you have the answer, Sebastian, don't pry into things that don't concern you. Whatever I feel, or felt, for Eden Colter is no one's business. She loved her husband, so let's leave it at that."

"Can you?" Sebastian studied Neil carefully. "Can you simply write her off as an affair that went sour—forget her?"

A muscle worked in Neil's jaw. "Watch me."

* * *

Hugh's funeral service was held three days later, the length of time it took to find a priest from one of the border parishes. With Ian's help Eden had located Hugh's will as well as the instructions he had left for her. There were letters too, for Eden, Ian and, surprisingly, Neil. Eden had thought she had exhausted all her tears until she opened her envelope the night before the funeral. Her vision blurring, Eden had clutched the framed daguerreotype of Hugh she had had taken before they left New York and set about deciphering Hugh's scrawl. Now, standing beside Ian as the priest intoned words which were, to Eden, meaningless, she reread the letter in her mind, wondering at the man she had lived with for so many years.

*My darling,*

*Yours is the last letter I must write, and, I find, the most difficult. There are things I have tried to tell you only to find that when I look at you or hold you the words desert me. How do I tell you everything that is in my heart? How do I describe the wonder and love which fills me when I gaze at you and our darling, miraculous Shannon? Do you know, I wonder, that the past few years have been the best part of my life; that I clasp my memories of you to my heart and know that they will never fade from my soul even when I am dead?*

*Do not weep for me, my love, my life, although I know you shall. Start your life again, as soon as you can, disregarding those barbaric traditions which say that you must stop living for a full twelve months. You belong to the living, not the dead, and it is my most fervent hope that one day you will fall in love again. You must open your heart, my darling, because what a waste it would be—both of yourself and some young man who loves you—if you lived out the rest of your years in widow's weeds. And remember, Eden love, that I've always hated you in black!*

*And now, dear heart, I have worked up enough courage to make a confession. Since I am a blunt man, I shall say this bluntly and not hedge. Forgive me, but in those hellish months before our marriage I was driven to discover your lover's identity. Matthew Kelly happened to mention a client of his, a young man, who had shown a marked interest in you during his visit to New York, and I took the man's name to the Pinkerton Agency. Nearly a year later I received their report. I have known for several years who Neil Banning is and what he once was to you. In my safe there is a file on him which you may dispose of as you see fit. I would have told you this the night of Lathrop's party, but you were so obviously upset that I thought there would be a better time and a better place for the telling. I am glad you never felt compelled to bring up the subject of Banning. Once I was able to regard him without jealousy or anger, I found that I honestly liked the rogue, in spite of everything.*

*No more confessions, Eden, no more revelations. If I have one regret, it is that I protected you far too much, shielded you from whatever might have caused you worry or pain.*

*Remember the star, my darling, but remember also that there will come a time when you no longer need it. When that day arrives, say good-bye without regrets, without pain. Save only a few precious memories and walk whole into the sunlight.*

*Hugh*

If Hugh had thought to comfort her with the letter, to offer strength and hope when she was devoid of both, then Eden had failed him. There was no hope to be found, nor any comfort for the gaping hole in her chest where her heart once had been. The priest was staring at her, as were the others, Eden realized with a jolt. The black taffeta of her dress crackled as Eden knelt beside the grave to place a single rose near the wooden marker. In spite of her resolve to keep her grief private, Eden began to weep soundlessly when her fingers brushed the rough wood, and it wasn't until Ian pulled her to her feet that Eden discovered most of the strength had deserted her legs. Behind her Millicent was crying noisily, and though the sound increased the ache in Eden's chest and she felt a flicker of sympathy for Millicent, she couldn't bring herself to console her. Leaning heavily against Ian, Eden led the way back to the house where she checked on Shannon before joining the groups of mourners in the parlor.

They came to her one by one, expressing their sympathy in words that skimmed over her consciousness without leaving an impression. Eden sat stiffly erect, Ian at her side, receiving the condolences. Her face was pale, carefully expressionless except for the large, pain-filled gray eyes with the mauve circles beneath them. She neither saw nor heard anything or anyone until Sebastian took her hand in both of his.

"Please accept my deepest sympathy, Mrs. Colter."

The gentle, soothing tone penetrated through the grief, and with an effort Eden concentrated on the man in front of her. "Doctor..." Eden paused. "Forgive me, I seem to have forgotten your name."

Sebastian smiled kindly. "Sebastian Saros."

"Oh, yes, of course." Eden looked at him, her eyes brimming with unshed tears. "I want to thank you for everything you did for Hugh."

"You are most welcome. I only wish I had been able to do more."

Eden nodded, her lips trembling slightly. "Thank you for trying, for coming to the aid of a man you had never met. If there is anything I can do for you, Dr. Saros, besides your fee—"

Sebastian interrupted her offer with a shake of his head. "I am a doctor, Mrs. Colter; it is my duty to help anyone who needs me. I hope we shall meet again, under happier circumstances." He squeezed her hand and made his way to where Neil was standing.

"How is she?" Neil's tone was casual but Sebastian saw the quickly concealed flare of concern in his brother's eyes.

"Still in shock, I think." Frowning, Sebastian studied Eden from across the room. "And this ritual we practice when death strikes is making it more difficult for her."

"Look." Neil inclined his head toward Lathrop, who was now conversing earnestly with Eden. As they watched, Eden rose and accompanied Lathrop from the room. Neil thoughtfully stroked his moustache. "Now what do you suppose he wants?"

Eden was wondering the same thing as Lathrop closed the study door and unhurriedly walked around the room until he came to a stop in front of her portrait. "Well now, Eden, first off I'm mighty sorry about Hugh. A terrible thing, just terrible."

"Yes." A lump was forming in her throat and Eden swallowed several times before she could continue. "You said you had something important to discuss, Lathrop. I would appreciate it if you would be brief and to the point."

Lathrop shoved his hands into his pockets, his eyes glittering as he stared at Eden. "I know how you're feeling; I lost my first wife many years ago and I thought the world had come to an end. It's even worse for a woman, I guess, particularly someone like you who is used to living in a big city instead of being stuck on a ranch miles from the nearest town. Hell, Hugh would still be alive if you'd stayed in New York."

His words were like a knife twisting in her stomach. Eden closed her eyes and sagged weakly against the desk. "I realize that. If this is what you wanted to tell me, then I wish you would leave."

"Now, don't get uppity," Lathrop told her harshly. "I figure you aren't going to want to stay here, so I'm willing to take the ranch off your hands. For a reasonable price, of course."

Eden's eyes opened slowly and she stared at Lathrop, dumbfounded. "Mr. Williams," she said finally in a trembling voice, "my husband has only been dead for three days—"

"I know that," Lathrop broke in. "I figured you wouldn't be up to discussing this until today or I would have been here sooner. You don't have to give me an answer right now—take a couple of days to think it over."

"Leave me alone!" Eden cried. "How can you be so utterly heartless?"

"I'm being practical, girl. You can't run a spread this size and I want the land. You sell out to me and we both get what we want. I increase the size of my ranch and you can go back East."

"Why don't you give Mrs. Colter a chance to recover before you start pressuring her for a decision?" Unnoticed by either of them, Neil had entered the room, and he stood by the open door, one hand resting on the doorknob.

"Stay out of this, Banning; this is strictly between Eden and me."

"I don't think so." Neil sauntered closer, his golden eyes flicking contemptuously over Lathrop. "Although she probably doesn't realize it, whatever decision Eden makes will affect a few of the other ranchers around here. That's one of the reasons Hugh never sold out to you."

Confused, very much aware of the bitter undercurrent between Lathrop and Neil, Eden found herself saying, "I don't understand."

"It's quite simple," Neil explained while he kept an eye on Lathrop. "Our friend and neighbor here doesn't really want all of your land, just the stream. He and Hugh had quite a few good fights about that water because Hugh was letting the smaller ranchers like Maudie water their stock there when their own watering holes went dry."

Eden gestured helplessly. "What was wrong with that? If they needed the water, why shouldn't they share ours? They would have done the same for Hugh."

"Precisely. But Lathrop wants to add all those small ranches to the Lazy W." Neil smiled tightly. "Thanks to Hugh they were able to hang on this year, but I think Lathrop would like to make it their last."

"Is that true?" Eden faced Lathrop coldly. "Did you fight with Hugh over Maudie and the others?"

Lathrop shrugged. "I prefer to call it a difference of opinion."

"I'd hardly call trying to drive people out of their homes a difference of opinion," Eden snapped. "You can forget about owning the Emerald I, Lathrop; if Hugh wouldn't sell to you, neither will I. I'd give it to Maudie or one of the other ranchers before I'd sell out to you."

Lathrop's face hardened. "However you want it, missy, but you'll regret your decision. And as for you, Banning, you'll be dealt with in good time."

"Save your threats," Neil replied. "You're not dealing with a frightened, grieving woman now."

With an ugly smile for both of them Lathrop departed and, through the window a moment later, Eden saw him ride away.

"Thank you," Eden said as she turned from the window. "I didn't realize Lathrop had been doing such appalling things."

"Don't mention it." Neil stared at her through hooded eyes. "I'm sorry about Hugh, Eden. I liked him—he was one of the few people I've ever respected."

Memories stabbed at Eden and her hand flew to her mouth to hold back a cry of pain. When she was able to speak her voice was strained. "He left something for you. A letter." Stiffly erect, Eden went to the desk and produced an envelope from the drawer.

Neil took the envelope hesitantly, his brows knitting into a frown. "What does it say?"

"I have no idea," Eden said in a brittle tone. "The letter is addressed to you, not to me, and I am not in the habit of reading other people's mail." As Neil tore open the envelope she added, "Hugh knew about us, Neil; about New York."

Neil froze, eyeing the letter almost guiltily. "My God! How did he find out? When?"

Eden shook her head slowly, incapable of answering.

"I'm sorry," Neil murmured. "That was something I hoped he would never know."

"Yes." Tears began to fall from Eden's shimmering eyes. "I had hoped to spare him that as well."

"What will you do now?" Neil asked quietly after they had been silent for several minutes.

"I don't know. I'm not sure I can stay here after what's happened. I may turn the ranch over to Ian and take Shannon back to civilization. San Francisco, perhaps; we stopped there on our honeymoon—" Eden's voice cracked and she spun back to the window.

The sight of her vulnerability stirred something deep inside Neil and, despite the bitter feelings he harbored because of a child whose existence he could not confirm, he found himself wanting to take Eden in his arms and offer her some kind of comfort. He didn't, though—Eden's grief was a barrier which served only to intensify the mixed emotions Neil had toward her. "Eden . . . is there anything I can do?"

Eden bit down on her bottom lip until the salty taste of blood filled her mouth. "Thank you, no. I think that you and I, together, have done enough damage for this lifetime." She faced Neil slowly and his heart twisted at the sight of her agonized features. Eden answered his unspoken question in a soft, wrenching voice, although, Neil realized later, she was barely aware of what she said. "Millicent should never have found me when I miscarried your child five years ago. A few more hours and I would have bled to death and Hugh would be alive now. That's the hell I have to live with and there is nothing you or anyone else can do now. Good-bye, Neil."

# BOOK III
## 1879

What is love? 'tis not hereafter;
Present mirth hath present laughter;
What's to come is still unsure.

—SHAKESPEARE

# Chapter 14

Keith Gerald's efforts to find Hugh's killer proved as fruitless as Keith's search for the elusive rustlers, although he pursued the four masked men until his superiors ordered him to concentrate solely upon the rustlers. While outwardly obedient, Keith still managed to make a few discreet inquiries about the mysterious Julio when his duties took him close to the border.

"You're crazy, you know," Cal told him one night in late summer when Keith was resting for a week at the Ranger barracks in Laredo. "It's bad enough that you've been chasing all over Texas for over a year trying to catch a bunch of rustlers. Now you add these four to your problems. Hastings has been doing his best to convince the brass that you should be taken off the rustler assignment altogether."

"So he can take over, I suppose," Keith snorted. "I can see him now, riding in with his company and destroying everything I've set up."

Cal shrugged sympathetically. "Face it, Keith, you don't have any results to show for your work, not even a single arrest. Hastings is promising results within a week and you've had over a year."

"What Hastings promises and what he delivers are two different things." Keith swung off his bunk and drew a map from his footlocker. "Look at this, Cal. For four years only the three largest ranches have been hit with any regularity—the Lazy W, Emerald I and *Rancho de Paraíso*. Sure, there were occasional raids on the smaller, surrounding spreads but they seemed to be more of an afterthought than anything else, and a little more than a year ago, the smaller raids stopped completely while the big ranches were hit more often."

Cal stroked his lower lip thoughtfully. "So your rustlers got smart. They take less of a risk this way, unless the owners decide to hire their own private army."

"That's what I thought." Keith ran a hand through his tousled red-gold hair. "Then all of a sudden, a few months later, the number of raids doubled and the smaller ranchers were involved again."

"About the time your friend Colter was killed?" At Keith's nod, Cal studied the map attentively. "It's too much of a coincidence. Was he involved with the rustlers?"

"No," Keith said slowly. "Not the way you mean."

Cal moved his eyes away from the map and shook his head. "It's a regular battlefield down there, Keith; you'll never sort it all out."

"Yes, I will," Keith said grimly. "I think Hugh Colter knew who was behind the first group of rustlers—he may even have had proof."

"So they killed him," Cal concluded.

"I don't think so." Keith gnawed on a knuckle thoughtfully. "This is one time I think the original mastermind was set up, and set up good."

Cal expelled his breath noisily. "You just lost me."

Keith laughed. "It's confusing to me at times. I have a feeling this entire business is personal, probably done for revenge, but just when I think I have all the pieces figured out the puzzle changes."

"You'd better put your puzzle together, and fast; your men are going to be recalled in a month whether you like it or not." Cal raised an eyebrow. "What about Mrs. Colter? If her husband knew something he probably told her, right?"

Keith's expression sobered and he folded away the map. On his last visit to the Emerald I, Eden had been listless, unresponsive, and her despair and vulnerability had increased the affection Keith felt for her into love. Keith had thought himself in love with Sandy, but the raw passion that shot through him whenever he was with Eden had proved him wrong. Added to the force of his love was the burning knowledge that Eden was within Lathrop's ruthless grasp. Eden was alone and, to Keith's mind, completely defenseless against a man who got what he wanted at the end of a gun; and Keith knew, instinctively, that Lathrop Williams was every bit as responsible for Hugh Colter's death as he had been for the death of Art Mason ten years ago. And just as it had been ten years ago, Keith had no proof, only gut instinct. Cal was still watching him curiously and Keith sighed. "I considered that. Unfortunately, I doubt Mrs. Colter is of help to anyone right now, including herself."

Eden stared dully at the lunch Millicent had prepared and with a shudder of revulsion pushed the plate away. She couldn't eat; could, in fact, barely stand the sight of food. At first she had forced herself to eat because of Shannon, but in spite of her efforts her milk had dried up and she had been forced to hire a wet nurse. Though the nurse—a quiet, unassuming woman in her late twenties—had not disrupted the household, Eden was relieved that Shannon was nearly weaned. In another month the wet nurse could be dismissed and, with Millicent spending a great deal of time in the small house she now shared with Vincent, Eden would have the solitude she so desperately craved. Eden buried her head in her hands, the now-familiar depression settling over her like a shroud. Nearly nine months had passed since Hugh's death and still Eden found it impossible to put the pieces of her life back together. Decisions— any decisions—were postponed indefinitely or passed on to Ian. Simply getting dressed each morning was such an effort that Eden sometimes lay in bed for hours wondering whether she should get up. Visits from Maudie and her two sons and Kevin Gerald forced Eden to leave her shell temporarily, but when her visitors left, Eden retreated into her private despair. The only thing easy for her was taking care of Shannon. Holding her daughter, playing with her, all brought a spark of joy into Eden's life and except for the time it took for Shannon to be fed, Eden kept the baby constantly at her side.

Shannon gurgled happily in her basinette, briefly pulling Eden away from her dark thoughts. Smiling slightly, Eden picked the baby up and carried her into the study. The moment Eden set her on the floor Shannon made for the desk with its shiny, fascinating gold pulls. Oh, Hugh, I wish you could see her, Eden thought sadly.

There was a soft rap on the door and Eden turned to find Ian regarding her solemnly. "May I come in, Eden?"

"Of course, Ian. Come sit down." Eden waved him into a chair. "Have you eaten?"

"Yes, thanks." Ian picked Shannon up and tossed her shrieking into the air. He was one of Shannon's favorite playmates and it lightened Eden's heart to watch Ian playing the role of surrogate father.

At least Shannon would never lack love, Eden thought as she poured herself a drink. "Would you like something, Ian?"

With a final hug Ian returned Shannon to the floor and, straightening, walked to the bar where Eden was standing. "It's a little early in the day for me, Eden lass."

Eden flushed under his implied criticism, two bright spots of color appearing on her hollowed cheeks. "Well, you don't mind if I have one?"

"I do," Ian replied in his low rumble. "Seeing you stewed in brandy every day worries me."

"I don't drink that much," Eden said defensively.

"Yes, you do." Ian carefully removed his hat and placed it on the bar. "It's time we had a talk, Eden."

"There's nothing to talk about." Eden gasped as Ian suddenly tore the glass from her hand and slammed it down on the polished wood.

"Look at yourself!" Ian bellowed. "You don't eat, you don't sleep; in fact, you don't do much of anything except feel sorry for yourself. What the devil happened to the Eden I used to know, to the woman Hugh was so in love with?"

"She died," Eden cried out softly, the grief and pain twisting through her. "My God, Ian, you were Hugh's friend! If anyone could understand how I feel, you should. Hugh was everything to me; when he died I did, too."

"No, you didn't," Ian told her bluntly. "But you're doing your best to follow him to the grave. You're not grieving, lass, you're wallowing in self-pity and it's a sorry sight you are. Hugh would be ashamed of the way you've been carrying on."

Eden's face crumpled. "I killed him, Ian, don't you see that? He moved here because of me."

Ian swore, using a word that shocked Eden to the core. "Hugh did as he damn well pleased and you know it! He hated New York; he only stayed *there* because of you. Believe me, Hugh was delighted to have an excuse to leave."

"You're lying."

Ian shook his massive head. "You're a coward, Eden lass, though I can't blame you completely. You've had everything handed to you one way or another. You've never had to scrap or fight for what you really wanted; life always has been yours for the taking. You're weak, just like your father, only he hid his weakness behind the money and power he acquired. You hid behind Hugh for nearly five years and now that you have to stand on your own two feet and prove that you're all grown up you can't do it."

Tears splashed down Eden's cheeks. "You're not being fair, Ian. I'm a great, bleeding mess inside. I can't think, I can't function—there's an emptiness in me that never goes away.

There are days when I feel like an old woman and then suddenly I realize that I'm only twenty years old. In four years I've been a wife, mother and now a widow and I can't help but think that, except for Shannon, the rest of my life isn't worth living."

"Did you really love Hugh that much?" Ian asked quietly. "Or did you only make yourself love him because you knew it was safe?"

"I don't know what you mean," Eden said stiffly.

"I think you do. You never felt for Hugh what you felt for your first love. Now you're feeling guilty about that. There's no one else who blames you for not being able to force an emotion that simply never existed between you and Hugh—so you're punishing yourself."

"I did love him!" Eden cried. "I loved him as much as I could. It just wasn't enough!" Realizing what she had just said, Eden clamped a horrified hand over her mouth.

"We all have regrets, Eden, but we don't stop living because of them. Drowning yourself in liquor or dosing yourself with those powders isn't going to change the past. Whatever you gave Hugh made him the happiest man on God's earth. Don't you understand that? He never felt slighted or shortchanged." Ian drew a hand over his face. "If you cared for Hugh, Eden, you'll snap out of this and start taking care of yourself and everything Hugh left you. If you don't start showing some concern for the Emerald I, the ranch is going to come down around your ears and then Shannon won't have a damn thing to remember her father by. We have a drive coming up that's got the men so damned spooked quite a few of them will quit beforehand and the rest will quit once the herd is at market. They don't want to work for someone who doesn't care what happens to the ranch or to them, and once a reputation like that gets around you won't be able to hire good men for love or money.

"Another thing—Maudie and her friends want to combine with us for the drive, for safety's sake. You'd better make a decision about that. And you might think about asking Neil Banning if he wants to throw in with us like he did last year."

"I don't think I'm up to this," Eden said hesitantly, pathetically. "I don't know the first thing about running a ranch or hiring men."

"Then you damn well better learn, lass, and if you can't learn, then you might as well sell out to Lathrop now and save everyone the trouble of risking their necks for you." Ian picked up his hat and jammed it on his head. "When you decide to sell, let me know because I want to be a hundred miles away from here before that vulture takes over the land Hugh died for."

Afraid that he had been too harsh with Eden, Ian turned on his heel and left, his brow furrowed with the realization that his lecture might have just been enough to push Eden over the edge.

Bright and early the following morning Eden showed up in the stable, ready to ride out with a shocked Ian. Wordlessly he took her slowly around the herd—more, Eden thought later, to give the men a chance to see her than for her to learn the technicalities of a roundup. Still, meeting the men, talking with them took Eden's mind off her own problems; and if she wasn't exactly happy, neither was she adrift in a sea of self-pity. The men were understandably jumpy concerning the rustlers and when Eden broached the possibility of armed guards for the drive, most of the men heartily approved the idea.

Lunch was eaten with the men, with Eden using her saddle as a chair. The meal was plain but filling, and there was an inexhaustible supply of strong, hot coffee with which to wash down the food. Accustomed to dealing with men purely on a social level Eden found it odd and vaguely disturbing that these rough, work-hardened men looked to her for decisions. She was, Eden realized, responsible for their livelihood and safety as well as Shannon's. This was the legacy Hugh had bestowed upon her, and a determined core of steel began forming within her, drawing Eden back to the business of living.

"They seem like good men," Eden commented as Ian re-saddled her horse after the men had gone back to work.

"That they are. You won't find men more reliable or loyal than ours, except Neil Banning's." Ian gave the cinch a last pull, knotted the leather securely and handed the reins to Eden. "I'm glad you came today, lass. It may not show, but your being here is important to these fellows."

Eden nodded, fingering the reins. "They seem to like the idea of guards, Ian. Perhaps you should go into town and see if you can hire the additional men. No hired killers or drifters, though. But some of the men around town may be able to use the extra money."

"Whatever you say, lass. Do you want me to stop at Maudie's on my way in?"

"Yes. Tell her that she and the others are welcome to join us." Eden swung into the saddle with an easy grace, belying the fact that the muscles in her legs were already sore and beginning to stiffen.

"How about Neil Banning?" Ian asked before she could ride away. "Maudie will want to know, and we could sure use him and his men."

"Can't we manage without him?" Just the mention of Neil's name set Eden's nerves jangling and she knew it showed in her voice because Ian looked at her sharply.

"We could, but I'd feel a lot better if he threw in with us." Ian watched as a blush spread across Eden's cheeks and he frowned. "What do you have against Banning?"

"Nothing! I just think we can manage very well on our own, that's all." Eden fidgeted in the saddle under Ian's questioning gaze.

At last Ian shrugged. "If that's the way you want it, Eden. Sure and it's your ranch, not mine."

Eden glared at him. "You're not terribly helpful, Ian."

Ian shrugged and grinned up at her. "Like I said, it's not my ranch."

"Hugh trusted your judgment," Eden said slowly, weighing her own feelings against what was best for the ranch. "Until I know more about running this place I have to listen to someone's advice, and that someone might as well be you, I suppose." Eden sighed, brushing wisps of pale hair away from her face. "I'll talk to Neil Banning."

"If you'd rather I did it for you—"

"No! I said I'd talk to him and I will," Eden tartly interrupted Ian's offer. "Take yourself and your Irish blarney over to Maudie and tell her we'll be ready to leave in a week."

Seated across the table from Neil, the remnants of lunch littering the table between them, Constanza studied Neil through veiled eyes. He was changing, becoming more and more difficult to manipulate whenever she stalled for more time. If only Lathrop had bought the Emerald I when Hugh Colter had died. She could have been in Europe by now, far away from Lathrop's deliberate cruelty and Neil's demands for an explanation about why she wanted to stay in Texas.

Every month Constanza was tempted to take the money Lathrop gave her and catch the next train out of town, leaving Neil and Lathrop to play out the farce between them. She wouldn't do it, of course; Lathrop payed her too well for Constanza to leave simply because Neil was impatient, but still it was a tempting alternative.

"You owe me an explanation," Neil was saying when Constanza dragged her attention back to their conversation. "If you want out, now is the perfect time. Lathrop starts his cattle drive in two days—I can have you home in Mexico three days after that."

"I need more time," Constanza pleaded.

Neil's eyes smoldered angrily. "How much time? A week, a month, another year? Damn it, Constanza, you can't expect me to wait forever."

"Not forever," Constanza assured him. "Try to be patient, Neil."

"I've been more than patient," Neil ground out, "and I'm tired of waiting. Look, Constanza, if you've decided to stay here with Lathrop just tell me."

"How can you say such a thing?" Constanza gasped. "I hate the man and everything about him!"

"From where I stand it sure doesn't look that way." Neil paused to sip at his coffee and light a cigar. "I'm beginning to think I should have listened to Sebastian right from the start and left you to stew in your own juice. I'm sick and tired of dealing with Lathrop and Keith Gerald, of risking my neck over a woman who can't make up her mind."

Constanza shrugged helplessly. "Lathrop has me watched, Neil. If we did run away Lathrop would have his men after us before we reached the Rio Grande."

"For all his suddenly discovered jealousy Lathrop sure doesn't appear to mind your visits here," Neil said sharply. "How do you explain that?"

"Why must I explain anything?" Constanza asked pettishly. He didn't believe her protests, Constanza saw as Neil gave her a withering glance. She wouldn't be able to put him off any longer. Her days of playing Neil off against Lathrop were rapidly coming to a close. Nervously she wet her lips, deciding upon a different strategy.

"All right," Neil asserted in the face of Constanza's continued silence. "Just decide which one of us you want. Me or Lathrop."

"You, of course," Constanza breathed, her expression wistful. "I want nothing more than to return to the life I once had. I will make you a good wife, Neil, I promise. I will do all I can to repay your kindness of these past years."

"Fine." Neil nodded. "Now all you have to do is tell me when you'll be ready to leave."

"As soon as Eden Colter sells her ranch to Lathrop." Constanza widened her eyes appealingly.

The impact of Constanza's words left Neil speechless for nearly a full minute; then he swore violently. "Hasn't she had enough problems?" An awful thought struck him and he leaned forward to grab Constanza's wrist. "Did Lathrop have anything to do with Hugh's death?"

"I don't know." Constanza snatched her arm away. "All I know is that if I help Lathrop acquire the Emerald I, he will agree to an annulment instead of a divorce."

Neil stared at Constanza, his expression a mixture of disbelief and anger. "What are you saying? Lathrop knows about us?"

"No, of course not," Constanza replied placatingly. "I simply told him that I was unhappy here, that our marriage had been a mistake."

"And he immediately offered you a divorce?" Neil snorted. "Don't play games with me, Constanza."

"I am not playing games," Constanza exclaimed, her eyes filling with tears. "I know how long you have waited, how patient you have been with me, and I decided the least I could do was ask Lathrop for a divorce. He laughed; he said he was tired of me and would give me a divorce—but wouldn't I rather have an annulment so that I would be free to marry again."

"And?" Neil prompted when Constanza paused to wipe her eyes.

"I told him yes, of course." Constanza feigned a hurt look as she watched Neil's reaction. "That is what we both want, is it not? For me to be free so you and I can be married?"

Neil waved a hand impatiently. "Never mind that now. Tell me how you're supposed to help Lathrop get the Colter ranch."

"How doesn't matter. Lathrop is interested only in results." Constanza flashed him a sly smile. "I think I should be able to convince Eden Colter that she would be much happier somewhere else. Having lost her husband, she will undoubtedly want to protect her daughter. A few well-chosen words and I am certain she will go scampering back to New York. Then you and I can be together at last. In fact, since you were her friend, if you would talk to her—"

"No!" Neil slammed a fist against the table. "Count me out of this little scheme. Lathrop will have to get the Colter ranch without my help."

"But why?" Constanza protested. "Why should we worry about Eden Colter if we can have what we want in the end? Neil, Eden doesn't like me, and you could make things so much easier for us just by talking to her."

"No," Neil repeated coldly. "Lathrop will use the water on the Emerald I as leverage to drive out the smaller ranchers and I don't want any part of that business. My God, Constanza, these people are my neighbors; I've worked with them, eaten at their tables. I won't have any part in trying to destroy them. You got yourself into this mess, my dear, and you can damn well get yourself out of it."

Whatever scathing retort Constanza was about to make remained unsaid when a knock jolted both Neil and Constanza out of their argument. Angrily Neil hurled his napkin onto the table and strode to the door. Furious both with Constanza and the interruption, he jerked the door open only to find himself staring wordlessly at the delicate face before him.

"Hello, Neil." Eden's courage evaporated at the sight of his blazing eyes, but she managed to keep her voice level.

"Eden," Neil acknowledged finally, uncomfortably aware of Constanza standing a few feet behind him. "This is quite a surprise."

Eden swallowed. "I hope I'm not intruding, but I have some business to discuss with you—if you're not too busy, that is."

"No, of course not." Neil hesitated only a moment before opening the door to admit her, and he shot Constanza a warning look as Eden passed in front of them. "In fact, we were just finishing lunch. Will you join us for coffee?"

"Thank you, that would be nice." Eden worked to keep her expression bland when she caught the knowing, almost seductive look Constanza bestowed upon Neil. A flicker of anger stirred in Eden when Constanza, her lips curled in an arrogant smile, turned toward her. "How are you, Constanza?"

"Quite well, thank you." Contempt flashed in Constanza's eyes. "But you—why, you poor thing! I have not seen you since before your husband died, but surely you were not so thin and pale then. I am sorry I was not able to attend Hugh's funeral, but I was dreadfully indisposed that day."

Tears pricked at her eyelids at Constanza's cruelty and Eden fought them back.

"Constanza," Neil interrupted sharply, "didn't you say you had to get home right after lunch?"

"No, I did not," Constanza answered sweetly. "But if you two are going to talk about ranching and cattle, I believe I will leave. I find business so boring."

Neil escorted Constanza to the door—none too gently, Eden noticed, though she was trying to look at anything other than the two people speaking in hushed tones. A fragment of some distant memory tugged at her mind when she glanced at Constanza. She had heard that name or seen the woman before, years ago, but she couldn't quite remember when or where. The door closed behind Constanza, and Eden realized that Neil was staring at her.

"I'm sorry," Eden said hesitantly. "I didn't mean to intrude."

Neil shrugged. "It doesn't matter. Please, sit down. Do you take your coffee black?"

"Cream, please." Eden seated herself on one of the massive leather armchairs, nodding her thanks when Neil handed her the cup. "I've never seen your home before. It's very nice."

"Thank you." Neil stirred his coffee thoughtfully, trying not to stare at her slight figure. She looked so frail, so alarmingly vulnerable that Neil felt his heart thump painfully against his ribs. "In spite of what Constanza said, you look much better than the last time I saw you. How are you holding up?"

It was Eden's turn to shrug, and she did so with the barest lifting of her shoulders. "I never know how to answer that. I'm . . . coping. I think that word fits best."

"Have you decided what you're going to do?" Neil shifted his chair so that he faced Eden. "The last time we talked you were thinking about leaving Texas."

"The last time we talked," Eden repeated softly, "was the day of Hugh's funeral. I haven't seen or talked to anyone except Millicent, Vincent or Ian since then." She glanced up and smiled wanly at Neil. "So much for how well I'm coping."

"I'm sorry—"

Eden waved Neil's expression of sympathy aside and placed her cup on the low table in front of her. "I didn't come here for your pity or sympathy. I want to make a business proposition." Neil raised an eyebrow and Eden plunged ahead with determination. "We're going together with some of the smaller ranchers for the drive this year and Ian feels it would be best if you joined us as well. Truthfully I don't know why he expects trouble on the drive, but he does, and he thinks that if we join forces all of us will benefit."

Neil nodded. "I understand his reasoning—the rustlers have become more threatening lately. Three of my men have been shot since early summer and most of the others have been shot at."

"Good Lord!" Eden's eyes widened in horror. "I had no idea the situation had become so violent. Hasn't Captain Gerald been able to do anything?"

"He gets close enough to fire a couple of shots and then they disappear into Mexico." Neil shook his head. "Keith Gerald has been particularly ineffective, I'm afraid. Our only option now is to protect ourselves as best we can."

Eden frowned. "I thought the rustlers tried to avoid confrontations. I remember that was one thing that used to puzzle Hugh—the rustlers would turn and run rather than put up a fight for the cattle. Why would they suddenly change the way they operate?"

"There could be any number of reasons." Neil shrugged carelessly. "Maybe they got tired of losing what they had stolen. Whatever their reason is, right now we'll all be a lot safer if we stick together. I'll be glad to throw in with you for this drive."

"Oh, good," Eden breathed. "Ian will be so relieved."

"So will my men."

"Ian is hiring more men—guards for the trip."

"Good idea." Neil lit a cigar and smiled at Eden through the cloud of smoke. "Don't worry so much, Eden. At worst the rustlers will take a few of the stragglers, and once we're out of the area I'll bet money the rustlers fall back and don't bother us at all. Leave everything to Ian and myself and I promise you the herds will make it to Dallas in good shape."

Knowing that Neil and his men were going to be in the drive should have allayed Eden's fears, but it didn't. Riding home, Eden found herself glaring at the countryside, wondering why, exactly, Neil's last words had made her so angry. Everything was arranged the way Ian had suggested; she had carried out her obligation to the ranch. So why did she have the feeling that she was being patronized and humored every step of the way?

Maudie was waiting at the ranch house when Eden arrived, and with a slight smile Eden ushered the older woman into the house.

"Ian stopped by a little while ago," Maudie said without preamble. "I just wanted to thank you myself for what you're doing for me and the others."

"You're quite welcome, Maudie, but there's really no reason to thank me. Everyone involved will benefit from our arrangement."

"Ian said Neil Banning might be joining us. Is that true?" When Eden nodded stiffly Maudie gleefully clapped her hands together. "That only leaves a couple of other ranchers to join up with Lathrop. Damn, but I'd like to see his face when he finds out about this."

Eden's brows drew together and she passed a hand over her eyes. "I don't understand, Maudie. Why would Lathrop care about all of this?"

Maudie's jaw hung open in amazement. "My dear, where have you been all summer?" she asked when she found her voice. "Lathrop has long been offering people like me protection from those damn rustlers on the drive to Dallas. He's even hired an extra fifty men as guards for the cowboys and cattle. There's only one little catch. The fee he's asking—to help 'defray expenses,' as he puts it—is about half what most of us hope to earn."

"That's awful! How can he do such a thing to his neighbors?"

"Honey, Lathrop doesn't care two cents about us. Haven't you learned that by now? This is just another way to try to drive us off the land. Sure, I could pay him this time and hope next year would be different, but what if it isn't?" Maudie's eyes sparkled angrily. "My husband died making our ranch a profitable business and I'll be damned if I'll meekly turn belly up and let Lathrop take it away from us."

Eden sank onto the sofa and fixed cloudy eyes on the feisty widow. "May I ask you a question, Maudie?"

"Why, yes." Maudie sat directly opposite Eden and smiled encouragingly. "What is it?"

"Why did you stay after your husband's death?" Eden tilted her head thoughtfully to the side. "You must have had a family somewhere who would have wanted you back."

Maudie smiled wistfully and nodded. "I had two brothers back in Kansas. I don't know, Eden, I guess I didn't go home because I felt I owed it to my husband to see his dream through. That, plus the fact that my brothers would have tried to marry me off again and I just wasn't ready to share my life with another man."

"Didn't you ever feel like giving up? Didn't you ever wake up in the morning and think that the whole thing was"—Eden raised her hands helplessly—"pointless?"

"Never!" Maudie laughed. "You have to understand, Eden, I was all alone except for three hired hands. I had no foreman, like Ian, to help me out, tell me what had to be done. All I had in the world was that ranch. It was either sell it—to Lathrop, of course, twenty years ago he wanted it as bad as he does now—or make a go of it. I didn't have time to sit around feeling sorry for myself, not if I wanted to put food on the table and pay my men. My two boys helped as much as they could, but they were hardly more than babies then. Now, thank God, they're grown and healthy, but then they depended on me, too." She started laughing again and by the time she had controlled her mirth she had to press a handkerchief to her streaming eyes. "Why, do you know that for the first few years I actually went along on the drives? I had to, you see, because I couldn't afford to hire anyone. Lord, Eden, you should have seen me then, all dressed up like a man because it wasn't safe for a woman out there."

Eden was silent for a moment, fingering the material of her riding skirt. "You were very brave, Maudie; braver than I am."

Maudie made a rude noise and leaned forward. "I wasn't brave, I was desperate!"

"Are you going on this drive?"

"Heavens, no. I'm too old for that now, but believe me, if I were ten years younger I'd be right out there doing my share."

Maudie's words kept echoing in Eden's mind during the afternoon and evening. Maudie was living proof that being left a widow didn't mean that the rest of one's life was marred by tears and sadness. Perhaps if the circumstances had been dif-

ferent, if Eden had been left alone, without her father's or
Hugh's money to insure her future and Shannon's, she would
have thought about something besides her own grief. I'm weak,
Eden thought with bitter contempt as she stood at the window
of her darkened bedroom. For good or bad, all of my life people
have taken care of me. Decisions were made *for* me, not *by*
me—even Hugh, for all his love, took away a great deal of
my independence. Eden scanned the heavens, smiling when
she found Hugh's star. It's time to start picking up the pieces,
isn't it, Hugh? Time to see if some part of me can still exist
without you, without your love, your protection, your guidance.

Shivering, Eden crawled into bed and, in a soft brogue,
murmured to the empty pillow beside her, "Sure, and it's frightened I am."

# *Chapter 15*

Neil Banning rode out early to join the men for breakfast the day they were to start the drive. Cattle spread for miles in front of him, obscuring the sparse grass of the plain, and the sight caused his heart to expand painfully with a bittersweet pride. This would be his last drive—Constanza had agreed to come back to Mexico with him as soon as her annulment was granted. Even if she backed out again, Neil was still leaving. He felt a bit guilty about his decision, mainly because of Eden—once he was gone, Eden would have to stand alone against Lathrop. Sure, he would leave instructions for his foreman to offer Eden any assistance she might need, but he realized it wouldn't be the same as his being there if she needed him.

Hugh's letter nagged at his conscience as well, Neil admitted to himself as he found one of the cook wagons and dismounted. The burly Irishman had harbored no bad feelings toward Neil over what had happened in the past. Instead, he had asked Neil to look after Eden, to help her if necessary. Then he had hit Neil with a theory about the rustlers. Suppose one of the ranchers was behind the operation? Wouldn't it be natural for the rustlers to make their escape over his land, where they could be sure they wouldn't encounter any resistance because all the men would have been pulled out of their way? It has to be Lathrop, Hugh had written, but I can't prove it. Perhaps you can.

"Hey, Neil!" Ian's voice carried over the general noise of the camp, and Neil turned to find the foreman of the Emerald I waving to him. "Grab yourself a plate and come on over."

Grinning, Neil took a tin plate and cup from the cook and wound his way toward Ian. "How are you, Ian? Ready to spend four weeks whispering endearments to these bovine beauties?"

Ian's eyes danced merrily. "As ready as you are, I'll wager. Did you say good-bye to the girls above the saloon last night? Sure and we were missing your smiling face around the campfire."

"I made your farewells as well," Neil retorted, accepting the ribbing with good humor. "They all send their regards."

"Ah, well," Ian chortled. "At least this year we'll have a pretty girl to look at instead of our own ugly faces."

"What happened? Don't tell me you hired women cooks this time—although I have to admit that strikes me as a good idea."

"Not exactly." Ian scowled at the toe of his boot. "A week ago I had a talk with Eden—you know, to try to get her interested in the ranch? Well, I must have been more persuasive than I thought, because she showed up about ten minutes ago with a bedroll and a change of clothes."

Neil choked on a mouthful of coffee. "What the hell for?" he sputtered.

"She's going along," Ian explained, "and she's not about to change her mind."

"Then I'll change it for her," Neil growled. He spun on his heel and stalked off, leaving Ian shaking his head.

"What the hell do you think you're doing?"

Braced against her horse, one hoof resting against her thighs, Eden looked up to find Neil towering over her. "I'm trying to dig a stone out of this hoof," she said primly. "What are you doing?"

"Watching a fool," Neil snapped. From his boot Neil produced a knife and motioned her out of the way. "You won't get it out with your fingers. Let me do it."

They exchanged places and Eden watched intently as Neil flipped the stone out with a twist of the blade. Straightening, Neil met her calm gaze and they stared at each other for a long moment before Neil looked down and returned the knife to its sheath.

"Thank you." Eden reached up to stroke the soft nose of her horse. "I'll have to remember how you did that in case it happens again."

"You can't go along," Neil told her bluntly.

Eden's eyes widened. "Don't be silly. Of course I can. Half of these cattle are mine and I want to see them get to market."

"That's what you're paying Ian for." With his thumb, Neil pushed his hat back on his head, trapping her in his golden stare. "He'll look after your interests. He'll get a fair price for the herd and pay off the men. It's not necessary for you to come along."

"Yes, it is," Eden argued steadily. "It's necessary for me."

Neil's lips compressed into a thin line. "You just don't

understand, do you? This drive could be more dangerous than most and if the worst does happen we'll have our hands full controlling the herd and defending ourselves. We won't be able to play nursemaid to a woman."

"You won't have to; I can take care of myself," Eden retorted archly.

"Sure you can," Neil sneered, unwittingly taking exactly the wrong approach to talk Eden out of anything. He looked pointedly at the empty rifle holster on her saddle. "I see you're prepared to defend yourself to the end."

Eden flushed dully. "I don't like guns—"

"Then you better learn to like them, and fast," Neil interrupted. "Can you use that rope, or is it just decorating your saddle? When was the last time you spent twelve hours on a horse? Will you be able to ride down a stray and bring it back to the herd? In other words, Eden, will you be more of a hindrance than a help?"

Although her chin was trembling when Neil finished his relentless questioning, Eden defiantly met his hard gaze. "I shall do whatever I can. Now, I grant you, I may not be much help at first, but I plan to learn a few things along the way. And I promise you, I won't slow you down."

"You'll understand if I find that rather hard to believe," Neil said in a deliberate voice. "Besides, there's another reason why you can't come along. Some of the men we just hired may decide that you're fair game. Neither Ian nor I can be with you twenty-four hours a day. This isn't a holiday, Eden; it's tough, demanding work. Do you understand now why you have to stay at home?"

"You're trying to frighten me," Eden hissed, gray eyes flinty with anger. "You're being patronizing and overbearing and I will not stand for it! I don't have to explain myself to you and I certainly don't intend to argue with you. I have just as much right to be here as you do, and that's the end of it." She snatched up the reins and mounted her horse. "Just take care of yourself, Neil, and I'll do the same."

Years later she would look back upon her first cattle drive and laugh at the experience, but now, caught up as she was in a struggle to prove herself not only to the hundred-odd men but also to herself, everything that happened during the drive seemed to be part of an elaborate plan to show her how correct Neil had been. Herding the cattle was a hot, dirty job, the main challenge of which, Eden decided early on, was learning how to breathe without choking on the dust. Stubbornly she gasped and coughed her way through the first two hours until Neil—it would have to be him, of course—happened to ride by while she was having a coughing fit. Looking smug, even though most of his face was covered by a bandanna, he drew abreast of Eden and gallantly handed her an extra bandanna from his saddlebag. When she hesitated Neil shook his head in disbelief at her stupidity, wrapped the material around her saddlehorn and galloped off before Eden had a chance to thank him. Injured pride kept Eden from using Neil's kerchief for a while longer, but in the afternoon the dust was so thick that, pride or no pride, she gratefully tied the bandanna around her face.

Neil had been right about other things, too. Eden wasn't used to spending entire days in the saddle, and by the time the cattle were bedded down and the campsites set up on the second night Eden found that she was practically numb from the hips down. To save face she dismounted behind the cover of the cook wagon. Actually, she fell out of the saddle more than she dismounted, but at least no one witnessed the humiliating sight so she was spared that indignity. Or so she thought until, leading her horse, she limped around the wagon and found Ian and Neil blocking her way. They didn't say a word, just stepped apart so that she had to pass between them, and Eden swore she heard Neil chuckle before she was out of earshot.

As much as her outraged muscles hurt that night, Eden managed to feed and water her horse, unsaddle him and still have enough strength to eat her own supper, but the next morning when she woke Eden was so stiff and sore that she could hardly move. Huddled under her blankets on the cold, hard ground she was feeling very sorry for herself when Neil strolled by and raised an amused eyebrow at her.

"Better roll out of there if you want a hot meal," he advised mockingly. "We're breaking camp in fifteen minutes."

Cursing Neil, the blankets, which were tangling her legs, her sore muscles, the angry headache, which was already gripping her temples, and anything else that happened to come to mind, Eden struggled to her feet. She quickly forgot about her aches and pains, however, when she learned five head had been stolen by rustlers the night before.

"Why weren't they stopped?" Eden demanded. "With all the men we have, surely one could have gotten off a shot."

"Sure, and stampeded the entire herd," Neil replied sarcastically. "You'd better not carry a loaded gun, after all. We'd end up selling our horses to get back home."

Stung, Eden stalked off with as much dignity as she could muster. Later that day she tried to redeem herself by riding down a stray and discovered the task was more difficult than it looked. After several attempts, she managed to get the beast turned around and headed back to the herd, but on the way back the stupid animal kept veering off in every direction but the one Eden wanted it to take. She circled around the steer, gently waving the coiled rope as she had seen the cowboys do, but despite all her actions and cajoling the animal eventually came to a dead stop and stared balefully at her.

"You dumb cow," Eden cried in sheer frustration. "I hope the rustlers get you! It would serve you both right!"

Eden glanced away from the steer and to her horror saw Neil and another man bearing down on her. If she had ever before wished the earth would open up and swallow her, the fervency of that wish was now doubled as the cowboy easily maneuvered the steer back to the herd, leaving a thoroughly embarrassed Eden to face Neil.

"Damn it, Eden, are you crazy?" Neil exploded. "That steer was a perfect target for the rustlers."

"Precisely why I went after it," Eden retorted.

"I don't suppose it ever crossed your mind that they might take you as well as the steer, did it?" Eden's expression froze and Neil nodded in satisfaction. "I didn't think so. Until you know what you're doing, which I doubt will ever happen, don't wander off."

"I was only trying to help," Eden protested, tears sparkling in her eyes.

"Do me a favor," Neil said bitingly. "Don't help anymore. That way the men won't have to waste time getting you out of trouble."

With that Neil wheeled his horse and rode off, leaving Eden to fume silently.

True to Neil's prediction, they weren't bothered by the rustlers after their fourth day out. Grateful for any good news, Eden relaxed a bit and turned her attention to learning how to handle the cattle. One of the men—she was never sure who he worked for—took Eden under his wing and taught her the way to drive a stray back to the herd as well as the art of roping. True, her ability couldn't compare with that of the veterans, but Eden was justifiably proud when she neatly dropped a rope around the neck of a recalcitrant steer and returned it to the fold. For her efforts she received a slow wink from her mentor and a few calls of congratulations from some of the other men. Neil hadn't seen her accomplishment, of course, and Eden found herself wishing she had dragged the steer back right beneath his nose. Now let him say something, Eden thought smugly. I'll show him I can hold my own.

But Neil didn't speak to her for more than a week. If he and Ian were chatting after a meal or sitting around the campfire at night, as soon as Eden joined them Neil always made some excuse to leave. Not that she cared; but at the very least he could be civil.

The silence between Neil and Eden continued throughout the drive. If Neil wouldn't condescend to speak to her, Eden certainly wasn't going to make the first move. What she didn't realize was that Neil knew exactly where she was at any given moment during the day; and at night, from beneath the brim of the hat he tilted over his face, Neil watched her as she sat by the fire. Sometimes she talked quietly with Ian, raising an unexpected twinge of jealousy in Neil, but often she simply sat and gazed into the flames. Neil enjoyed watching Eden, studying her, memorizing the delicate lines and hollows of her face. After three weeks of watching her, Neil knew all of Eden's mannerisms: the faint knitting of her brows, the way she chewed on her lower lip, the gentle movement of her hand as she brushed strands of flaxen hair back into place. In spite of the fact that she was as weary and dirty as everyone else, Eden still took the time to pin up her hair every morning. The ritual fascinated Neil and, without appearing to, he watched in the mornings as the shining mass was pinned in place, and again in the evening when the pins were removed.

Eden was an amazing woman, Neil grudgingly admitted to himself. Where nearly a month ago she had been a pale, hesitant ghost, now she was very much like the self-assured Eden Neil remembered, but with one difference. There was a new confidence in the way she moved, even in the way she talked, and Neil savored the few remaining days of the cattle drive. Circumstances being what they were, Neil could hardly propose a relationship with Eden now. She had too many memories, both of himself and Hugh; and unfortunately, Neil was certain that all her memories of him were unpleasant ones. It was just as well he would be leaving soon, Neil reflected. Eden was a temptation he would find hard to resist for any length of time.

Just when Eden was sick to death of cattle, dust, Neil's arrogant snubbing and Ian's fatherly lectures, they reached Dallas. As much as she longed for a hot bath and the feel of clean sheets against her skin, Eden was also determined to see the drive to an end and waved aside Ian's suggestion that she go to the hotel while he sold the herd. If such a thing were possible, she was even more out of place at the stockyards than she had been on the drive. The men who were lounging around the pens until their employers paid them off stared at her so avidly that the blood rushed to her cheeks, and when one or two of the wranglers let out a low whistle of appreciation, Eden felt a prickle of fear creep up her spine. She was safe enough as long as Ian was within earshot, Eden knew, but she was still uneasy as the stares followed her into the manager's office.

The manager stared at Eden as well, but her initial embarrassment changed to annoyance when the man was so busy eyeing her that he fumbled around for several minutes before settling down to processing their herd. She finally understood why Maudie had disguised herself as a man all those years ago—men simply couldn't keep their minds on the business at hand when there was a woman around, even if the woman was as dirty and trailworn as they were. Finally the manager handed Eden the bill of sale for her signature and when she returned it, he gave her a bank draft for the cattle along with an invitation for dinner. Judging from the look in his eyes, dinner wasn't the only thing he had in mind, and Eden's refusal was prompt and curt.

"Hugh has an account with—"

"—With the Cattlemen's Banking Association," Eden finished the sentence for Ian as they stepped outside. "I do know a few things about the workings of my ranch, Ian."

"Sorry," Ian apologized, a wounded look on his face. "I was only trying to help."

Eden sighed, brushing at the stains on her riding skirt. "I know you were, Ian. I'm sorry. Friends?"

Ian looked down at the slender hand extended to him and, grinning, he took it in his own massive paw and shook it heartily. "You did all right, lass, for a greenhorn. I didn't think you'd make it through the first two days."

"Truthfully, neither did I," Eden admitted, remembering the beating her muscles had taken.

"You have every right to feel proud of yourself," Ian told her in an admiring voice. "And if you're not, your men are proud enough to make up for it. All but two of the men who said they were going to quit after the drive have changed their minds."

"That's good." The nervous energy was starting to ebb and for the first time since the drive began Eden felt herself relax.

"I'll pay off the men, if you like," Ian offered. "You must be dead tired."

Although an easy, genuine smile was still beyond her, Eden's gray eyes sparkled in knowing amusement. "Ah, and just where will you transact this business? In the local saloon, by any chance?"

Ian removed his hat and ran a hand through his hair. "Well, now, lass, it's been a long, dry ride. You wouldn't begrudge a man a drop or two of the brew to wash away the dust, would you?"

"Never. Come with me to the bank and then I'll leave you to celebrate."

Half an hour later Eden watched as Ian rode down the street in the direction of the saloon. It dawned on her, once Ian was out of sight, that she was completely on her own. She wouldn't see Ian or any of the others for at least three days—their kind of celebration hardly required her presence. Though she had looked forward to the stay in Dallas because it meant the end of the drive, Eden felt the familiar depression setting in. She sensed she was being stared at again, and turning slightly she caught sight of two men in business suits watching her from the doorway of the bank. To her horror, one of the men advanced toward her and before she could take a step toward her horse he had taken hold of her upper arm.

"Lonely, honey? Looking for a little companionship, maybe?" His leering expression sent the color rushing to Eden's cheeks and he grinned down at her. "You just might be passable once we scrape some of that dirt off."

Temper flaring, Eden dug her fingernails into the man's hand until he grunted in pain and released her. "And you, sir, might be passable once you've been civilized," she spat, eyes flinty. As his hand reached for her again Eden warned, "Don't lay a hand on me again or I'll bring this whole damned street down on your head!"

Her would-be accoster stood speechless with shock while Eden, using every shred of dignity she possessed, mounted her horse and rode away. Once she was safely out of sight, a hint of a smile tugged at the corners of her mouth despite the trembling that was the residue of her anger. Pride surged through Eden's blood at the small but important victory. How long it had been since she had relied on no one but herself! The independence which had defined her early years reasserted itself, nudging her away from self-pity.

A dress shop caught her eye and impulsively Eden drew her horse to a stop. After brushing off as much of the dust as possible she entered the building. The welcoming smile on the proprietress' face when the small bell above the door signaled another customer rapidly changed at the sight of the dusty woman who stood in the doorway.

"May I . . . ah, help you, miss?"

The look of disdain hadn't escaped Eden's notice and while at some other time it might have sent her temper soaring, she accepted the look with wry humor. Not five minutes ago two men had been eager for her company, dirty as she was, and now this woman was uncomfortable with Eden's presence in her shop.

"We don't sell riding apparel," the woman continued, eyeing Eden's serviceable but unstylish riding skirt and shirt. "At least not the kind you obviously are accustomed to wearing."

Eden's tolerant sense of humor disappeared at the rude statement, as did the faint sparkle in her now wintry gray eyes. "I'm not interested in a riding habit," Eden said caustically, the cultured tone of her voice bringing a shocked expression to the other woman's face. "I want three gowns, at least; possibly more. Yes, more, I think. Three for evening, three for day. Gloves, stockings, shoes to match, of course. Also a nightgown and wrapper." Eden's stare was frosty as she rattled off the list and when she was finished she almost felt sorry for the pale, shaken owner. "I'll need one of the evening gowns immediately, as well as the bedclothes. The rest must be delivered by eleven tomorrow morning."

"B-but that's impossible," the owner stuttered. "I can't possibly—"

"What a pity. But then I'm sure I can find a shop that is more cooperative."

"Wait!" Hand on the doorknob, Eden half turned, her expression impatient. "I can meet your order, miss. There is a blue silk I have been working on which, with minor alterations, would be very becoming on you."

Eden shook her head and returned to the middle of the shop. "All the dresses must be black."

"B-black?"

"I am in mourning," Eden said with a defiant lift of her head. "And the name is Mrs. Colter." Without waiting for a reply she walked around the shop picking out material and, last, patterns. Eden laid the sketch of the more elaborate gown in front of the owner. "This one for tonight; the others by eleven tomorrow. Can you still meet my schedule?"

The owner nodded slowly. "It will be more expensive, you understand, because of the time limit."

Eden fished into her pocket and slapped a stack of bills onto the counter. "My evening gown no later than six—and I'll take my wrapper now."

The poor woman went white, and after measurements had been recorded and the name of Eden's hotel noted, Eden walked out of the shop carrying a small box. By the time she arrived at her hotel, she was humming jauntily.

The desk clerk raised his eyebrows at the slender young woman who deposited a dusty saddlebag on the gleaming wood of the reception desk. "Good afternoon, madame. May we be of service to you?"

"You may indeed," Eden replied brightly. "You have a reservation for me—Mrs. Eden Colter."

The clerk flipped through a file and then turned the registration book toward Eden for her signature. "You're in room 306, Mrs. Colter. I'll have one of the boys carry your bag."

"That won't be necessary." Eden draped the saddlebag over her shoulder and held out her hand for the key. "I'm expecting a parcel around six this evening and another tomorrow morning."

"I'll see that they're brought up immediately, Mrs. Colter. Enjoy your stay with us."

Enjoy she did, beginning with a most luxurious bath and headwash, which made Eden feel like a new woman, and followed by a nap on a soft bed covered by clean sheets. Her gown was delivered promptly at six and Eden felt positively buoyant as she dressed and descended to the hotel's restaurant. Conscious of the curious, inquiring looks she was receiving, Eden held her head high as she was led to her table. Let them stare, Eden thought defiantly as one by one conversations were resumed and the curious eyes were lowered. Social conventions notwithstanding, Eden was discovering a certain enjoyment in her newly discovered independence. She recognized the man who had propositioned her that afternoon dining with a woman who, Eden guessed, was his wife. He didn't recognize Eden, however, and she toyed vindictively with the idea of going to his table and letting his wife know exactly the kind of man she had married. Sighing regretfully, Eden turned her attention to her meal.

The food was delicious, the atmosphere festive, and Eden lingered over her coffee. She had never been one for socializing, and since Hugh's death she had become a virtual recluse. That had to change, Eden decided abruptly. Self-pity was a very cold companion.

"Well, well, this is an unexpected pleasure."

Lathrop Williams' booming voice startled Eden and she looked up to find him looming over her, a leering smile curling his lips. The woman beside Lathrop clung to his arm, and Eden surveyed the pair coldly.

Lathrop disengaged himself and rested both hands on the table. "Where's your manners, girlie? Aren't you going to invite us to join you?"

"You won't be staying that long," Eden told him in a glacial tone. "What do you want, Lathrop?"

"Mr. Williams to you, girlie," Lathrop snarled menacingly. "You and me got a few things to talk about."

Eden returned the cup to its saucer and daintily touched the napkin to her lips. "I can't think of a thing we could possibly have to discuss, Lathrop," Eden responded pointedly.

"I want the Emerald I," Lathrop growled. "When are you going to sell?"

"To you? Never!"

Lathrop straightened and lowered his voice to a more acceptable level. "Be sensible, girlie, you can't run a spread like the Emerald I—men won't work for a woman who doesn't care if they get shot to pieces by rustlers, and you just don't have the guts to give orders and make decisions. Play it smart; sell to me before you drive that ranch into the ground."

That did it! Eden rose and hurled her napkin onto the table. "I'll sell to you when hell freezes over!" Fuming, she brushed past Lathrop and stormed up to her room. Of all the nerve, she raged silently as she undressed and slipped into her wrapper. How dare Lathrop accuse her of incompetence! Hugh's blood had paid for the Emerald I. The ranch was all she had left of Hugh; it was all Shannon would ever have of her father. What did you expect? a merciless voice inside her asked. You let the ranch fall apart for nine months while you walked around in a drugged daze, so why shouldn't Lathrop assume you'd be willing to sell?

Her wedding band drew her attention and Eden twisted the thick ring around her finger, remembering the day Hugh had placed it there. Abruptly Eden blew out the lamp and went to the window to study the night sky. After a few moments of searching she found Hugh's star, her eyes misting as she stared at the winking blue-white light.

"Oh, I miss you," Eden said softly. "I miss your strength, your courage, but most of all I miss your companionship. I'm so alone and there's so much I have to learn, so many decisions to be made. I'll never sell to Lathrop, but should I stay on the ranch? Help me, Hugh; tell me what to do." There was no answer, just the faint sound the breeze made as it played with the curtains of the open window.

Recapturing the past was impossible, Eden realized with a sudden pang. That part of her life which had centered around Hugh was over, but her life itself was still intact. She had fond memories, loving memories of Hugh which would stay with her always, and she had Shannon. Eden gazed fondly at Hugh's star but her thoughts were busily assessing her situation. Thanks to her father and Hugh she was financially independent, a blessing few other women in her position could claim. If she wished, Eden could live anywhere in the world. London, Paris, New York, Rome—no city or society would be closed to her or Shannon. In a matter of weeks they could be far away from Texas. She wouldn't be forced to deal with Lathrop and better still, Neil would be out of her life once and for all. Shannon would have the finest dresses and tutors; she would attend private schools and have every advantage Eden could give her.

But not in New York. That decision surfaced unbidden and

Eden blinked in surprise. Nor would Shannon be raised in a foreign country. She had been born on the Emerald I and that was where she would be raised. So it was to be Texas, then. For all its problems it was definitely preferable to returning to a life Eden had never regretted leaving.

The decision was made and a feeling of relief and contentment washed over Eden. It was time to put away the sorrow and bitterness—far past time, in fact. With a final, gentle smile for Hugh's comforting star, Eden sank into bed. Her sleep that night was natural and undisturbed for the first time since Hugh's death.

Eden slept late the next day and then spent the afternoon shopping for gifts for Millicent, Shannon and Maudie. Ian would grouse when he saw the extra packages but, as Eden knew full well, they had extra horses for the return trip, so her extravagances actually wouldn't pose any problems. Her last stop was a bookstore and when Eden left, her arms so filled with purchases that she could scarcely see over the boxes, Eden collided with a passerby. Boxes flew in every direction and she would have fallen into the street had not a pair of strong hands pulled her back from the edge of the sidewalk.

She turned, words of apology and thanks half formed on her lips and found herself staring straight into Neil's golden eyes.

"No serious damage, I hope," Neil said lightly, a mocking gleam entering his eyes when he recognized Eden. He released her so quickly that Edén stumbled backward, tripping over one of the parcels, and Neil quickly reached out to steady her again.

"Sorry," Eden muttered when she regained her balance. "I'm not usually this clumsy."

"Forget it." Neil bent and started retrieving the packages.

"I can do that," Eden protested, shamefully aware of the way her heart was pounding.

Neil shook his head, looking askance at her when their hands touched on the same package. "I'm partly responsible for this. The least I can do is try to set things right." Rising, Neil handed Eden a small box but kept the rest firmly in his grasp. "Where are you staying? I'll walk you back to make sure nothing else happens."

Swallowing another protest, Eden told him the name of the hotel and fell into step beside Neil. They were silent for the duration of the walk and from time to time Eden nervously glanced at Neil's stony expression from beneath the curtain of her lashes.

What the hell was he doing? Neil wondered irritably as they entered the hotel and Eden led the way to her room. He had sworn to stay away from Eden, to keep his distance from this woman who proved such a fascinating distraction.

When she had unlocked the door to her room Eden reclaimed the packages from Neil's arms. "Thank you," she murmured uncertainly. "I'm sorry to have caused you so much trouble."

Neil shrugged carelessly, unwillingly snared by the mist-gray eyes gazing up at him. "Watch where you're going after this," he said unkindly. "Next time you might end up under the wheels of a carriage."

Eden bristled immediately. "Which would please you to no end, I'm sure."

"Did I say that?" Neil retorted, a muscle working in his jaw. "Did I? All I did was give you some friendly advice."

"Keep your advice," Eden snapped. "I've managed quite well without it. Thank you again and good-bye!"

Before Neil could reply the door was slammed in his face. He stared at the wood for several seconds, cursing himself because the simple act of walking away was beyond his power.

Her eyes still spitting sparks, Eden answered the knock on her door to find Neil waiting in the hall. Eden surveyed him coldly, taking in the rakish tilt of his hat and the way his thumbs were negligently hooked through the belt loops of his trousers. Gold eyes locked with gray, neither gaze wavering as they stared angrily at each other.

"I have two tickets for the theater tonight," Neil announced in his soft drawl.

Eden glared at him mutinously. "Enjoy yourself."

"*Two* tickets," Neil repeated. "I thought you might enjoy seeing a play, and perhaps having a late dinner afterward."

Some of the anger faded from Eden's eyes and though her spirits lifted at the thought of going to the theater, she knew it was impossible. "It wouldn't be appropriate." She glanced away from those piercing eyes and studied the pattern her finger was tracing on the doorjamb. Grudgingly she added, "But thank you for asking me."

"I didn't ask you just to be turned down." Neil raised an

eyebrow as understanding dawned on him. "I'm not going to try anything, if that's what you're thinking."

"I never—" Eden swallowed, horrified to feel a blush steal across her cheeks. "I'm still in mourning, Neil; it just wouldn't be right."

"Would you go alone? Or with Maude Barston?" Neil queried mockingly. "Of course you would. I'll pick you up at seven."

"But I—" Eden began. It was too late; Neil was already striding down the hall.

She wouldn't go, Eden told herself throughout the afternoon. Even if she weren't in mourning she would refuse to go out with Neil Banning—once burned, twice shy as the saying went. Defiantly, Eden took a leisurely bath and then, clad only in her wrapper, she set about wrapping the gifts she had purchased. One item was not a gift, however, and Eden carefully lifted a gleaming revolver from its box. There were guns aplenty at the Emerald I, but this one was special: Its weight and balance suited Eden's strength and she would be able to handle it with a minimum amount of awkwardness or strain. With her bottom lip caught between her teeth, Eden studied the deadly weapon lying so innocently on the bedspread. As much as she loathed guns—a hatred which had been increased by Hugh's death—Eden feared another invasion of her home far more. She was now Shannon's only defense, as well as her own, and that knowledge overcame any reluctance she harbored.

There was an impatient knock on the door and without thinking Eden opened it, only to wish a moment later that she could melt into the floor. Neil's golden eyes raked her from head to toe.

"You're not ready," he stated unnecessarily, his gaze hopelessly riveted on the thin wrapper.

Eden swallowed and brought a hand up to close the neckline of the dressing gown at the base of her throat. "I told you I couldn't go."

Surprisingly Neil grinned and reached out to clear a strand of hair from her face. "It doesn't matter—I'm early, so you have ten minutes to get ready." Eden started to protest but Neil warned silkily, "I'm prepared to stand out here all night if I have to. Now, which is worse—going to a play and dinner with me, or having people wonder why I'm standing here?"

"You wouldn't!" Eden challenged bluntly.

"No?" Neil raised a dark eyebrow. "Mrs. Colter, ma'am, you have no idea of the lengths I'll go to for an enjoyable dinner companion."

Her mouth formed a soundless "oh" and Eden's eyes widened in exasperation. Neil grinned audaciously. "Ten minutes or I tell everyone who walks by that you trifled with my affections."

A bubble of laughter burst from Eden's throat and she shook her head helplessly. "I need at least half an hour."

Neil smoothed his moustache, considering her surrender with an affected air which drew another low laugh from Eden. "Fifteen minutes," he compromised at last. "And if you don't mind, I'll just wait right here until you're ready."

Exactly fifteen minutes later Eden emerged from the room looking as cool and unruffled as if she had spent the afternoon in preparation. Her composure fled momentarily, however, when Neil offered his arm, but after a brief hesitation Eden placed her hand in the crook of his elbow.

They created quite a stir in the theater lobby—the tall, dark man and the slender blond woman in black. Neil guided Eden through the crowd with an air of propriety, and when they were seated in their box several pairs of opera glasses were trained on them.

Eden toyed with her program, embarrassed by the attention she and Neil were receiving. "I shouldn't have come," she murmured weakly.

"Nonsense." Neil leaned toward her, protecting her from the greater share of prying eyes. "We're neighbors; we've just finished a cattle drive together. It's perfectly natural for us to celebrate."

"Is it?" Eden smiled ruefully. "If I were a man, perhaps, but I'm not. I'm a widow."

A genuine smile lifted the corners of Neil's mouth. "Take a chance, Eden; thumb your nose at convention."

"I did that once," Eden reminded him softly. "And as I remember, you were present then, too."

"And was the outcome so awful?"

Eden thought about that for a moment, expecting to feel the old rage and bitterness against Neil fill her heart. But the anger didn't appear. The pain and hurt of his betrayal had been lost somewhere, fading in the light of everything else that had transpired over five years. Eden raised her eyes to Neil, a tremulous smile on her lips. "Do you mean at the time, or now?"

Neil was spared from replying by the rising curtain. Starved for the excitement and drama of a stage production, Eden was immediately engrossed in the play to the exclusion of all else. She did not notice that Neil watched not the play but her reactions to it, committing to memory her varying expressions. It had always been like this for him when he was with Eden—surroundings and people faded until they were but dimly perceived, leaving only an image of the flaxen-haired beauty who had claimed some unnamed part of him so long ago.

The intermission was upon them before Eden realized how much time had passed and turning, she found that Neil had ordered champagne. Smiling, he handed her a long-stemmed glass and they sipped their drinks in companionable silence. Had Neil teased her or even tried to make light conversation the spell would have been broken, a fact he apparently understood. He, too, seemed content for the moment. Whether it was the champagne or his amiable disposition Eden wasn't sure, but her spirits were considerably higher during the second half of the play. When the final curtain call had been taken, Neil draped Eden's shawl around her shoulders and they joined the throng of people exiting the theater.

"Did you enjoy yourself?" Neil asked when they were out onto the street.

"Oh, yes." Eden's smile was bright and easy as she lifted her face to Neil and watched him light a cigar. "Thank you so much, Neil."

"You're most welcome." Neil grinned. "Now, if you'll come with me, I intend to buy you the best dinner Dallas has to offer."

They dined by flickering candlelight in a restaurant where Neil was obviously well known and liked, judging from the attentive service he received. Curious looks were directed toward them here as well, Neil pointed out wickedly, but oddly enough the raised eyebrows and whispered gossip failed to produce any reaction in Eden except for a slight shrug.

The food was excellent and the company undeniably charming. There was no hint of the strain which had existed between them during the cattle drive, and Eden found it hard to believe that the attentive Neil who sat across the table was the same man who had repeatedly lashed out at her during their weeks together. Eden realized with a jolt that there seemed to be a new tenderness about Neil, a gentleness Eden did not remember from their time together in New York. Had he changed, she wondered, or had this side of him existed all along, carefully concealed behind a façade like the one Eden herself had used for so many years?

"You're very quiet," Neil commented with a smile, leaning back in his chair so that his face was shadowed. "I offered you a penny for your thoughts once, as I recall. Shall I do so again?"

Eden shook her head, her slim hands playing with the stem of her wineglass.

Faced with her continued silence, Neil struck a match, touched the flame to his cigar and studied the glowing tip. After several minutes he leaned forward and said softly, "I want you to know I think you handled yourself quite well on the drive."

"Better than you expected, you mean," Eden teased, her expression lightening.

Neil bowed his head. "I stand corrected. You managed admirably, all things considered."

"All things considered?" Eden rested her chin on the heel of her hand, eyes alight as Neil became hopelessly entangled in his choice of words. "Exactly what 'things' are you referring to, Mr. Banning?"

"Your lack of experience, Mrs. Colter," Neil replied in a bantering tone. "Nothing else. To be perfectly honest, I was afraid we'd lose you the day you could barely stay on your horse." Gray eyes widened in astonishment, and Eden's delicate oval face registered such dismay that Neil laughed softly.

"You knew," Eden said accusingly.

Neil nodded, covering her clenched hand with one of his in a pacifying gesture. Laughter subsided as the contact sent a flood of warmth through him. Forcing his thoughts back to the conversation, Neil confessed, "Of course I knew. Why do you think Ian and I stayed so close to you? Both he and I have gone through what you did, although not to such a painful extent. No one would have blamed you for riding in one of the wagons for the next couple of days. Why didn't you tell me?"

"I couldn't do that, as you very well know."

"Why not?"

"Because Ian would have fussed," Eden explained, gently

reclaiming her hand from Neil's far too enjoyable hold. "And you were so perfectly hateful that I would rather have been trampled by the herd than admit you were right."

"I'm sorry. You had enough problems without my adding to them." The apology came readily, as if he had spent time rehearsing the words, and Neil retired to the shadows once again. "I'm sorry for what I did to you five years ago as well—believe me, Eden, I never meant to hurt you. Try not to hate me too much."

"Oh!" The soft exclamation barely carried over the hum of conversation as Eden dropped her gaze to the table. Her voice, when she found it, trembled faintly. "I don't hate you, Neil, for the drive or anything else. In a way I should be grateful. Because of you I married a man who taught me more about loving and living in four years than I had learned in the first sixteen years of my life."

"May I tell you something?" When Eden nodded, Neil said quietly, "Hugh may have taught you a lot, as you say, but he had a lot to work with. You're an amazing woman, Eden; I've never known anyone quite like you."

Eden canted her head to one side, trying to read Neil's expression through the obscuring smoke and deep shadows.

"You see," Neil's voice touched her as surely as if he held her in his arms, "I've learned quite a bit in five years as well. Tell me, Eden: Did you ever think of me?"

Uncertainty and apprehension clouded the mistlike depths as gray eyes met gold.

"I thought of you," Neil continued when it became obvious Eden either would not or could not answer. "I guess this is a strange time for me to tell you this, circumstances being what they are, but you and I never did straighten things out between us."

"There is nothing left to straighten out," Eden replied in a hushed voice, memories descending in a kaleidoscopic explosion.

"Perhaps not for you, but for myself..." Neil allowed his voice to trail off and he laughed softly. "In my mind there remains a picture of a young woman in gossamer, her hair silvered in the moonlight as we stood on a terrace in New York. I remember her watching me through the most beautiful eyes I'd ever seen, half of her frightened innocence and the other half righteous indignation."

The mesmerizing drawl continued, sending Eden's mind whirling. Somewhere during the course of the evening she had lost her defenses against Neil; he had managed to turn back time, making her every bit as vulnerable now as she had been when she was sixteen.

"Do you remember our picnic?" The corners of Neil's moustache lifted as he smiled. "You told me you wanted to see Europe, and Russian Cossacks, I believe. Did you ever go?"

He was drawing her into his game, wearing at her resistance until Eden gracefully capitulated when she realized her silence gained her nothing. Eden shook her head. "No, I never did go to Russia. And as for Europe . . . we went there on three separate occasions, but on two of them the circumstances were somewhat less than enjoyable."

Neil's expression was openly curious. "Would you like to tell me about it?"

Again Eden shook her head. "It was a terrible time, best forgotten now." She put away the bleak memories as a question of her own took shape. "I remember a few things, too; such as the fact that when we met you were engaged. Why didn't you marry?"

"Would you believe me if I said I remained single because of you?" Neil countered.

"Hardly," Eden said drily, but a flicker of laughter appeared in the unfathomable gray eyes.

Neil laughed. "You always did want the truth, no matter what the knowledge might cost you."

"And you always scrupulously avoided it," she reminded him tartly. "Or ignored the question, just as you're doing now."

Golden eyes gleamed from the shadows. "You remember more than I thought. Very well, since you will settle for nothing less than the truth: I returned to Mexico to find my bride-to-be had married someone else in my absence. Ironic, isn't it? While I was busily making plans to be unfaithful to my future wife, she was deciding on another husband."

Embarrassed, Eden lowered her head to study the weave of the linen tablecloth. Whatever had possessed her to ask such a question? She didn't care why Neil had remained a bachelor, she told herself fiercely. His affairs were none of her concern.

"Let's go." Neil rose abruptly and rounded the table to hold Eden's chair. Being alone with Eden like this was bringing too many long-forgotten emotions into play and it wouldn't do to become involved with her again, not if he planned to make a clean break when he left Texas.

They were outside now, and Neil watched as Eden tilted her head back to study the evening sky. A frown crossed her face, drawing a similar response from Neil. "Eden, is something wrong?"

With an effort Eden dragged her thoughts back to her companion but her gaze remained fixed on the empty space where Hugh's star had been only the night before. "It's gone," she murmured, more to herself than to Neil.

"What's gone? What are you talking about?"

"You wouldn't understand," Eden replied. "And I'm afraid I'm not in the mood for explanations right now. Will you please take me back to the hotel, Neil?"

"Certainly." Neil drew her arm through his; and although he never would have admitted it, the pensive look on Eden's face tugged at his heart. She was so incredibly complicated, Neil thought with a glance at the delicately molded profile. Worse than that, whenever they were together common sense and sanity deserted him. He wanted to see her laugh and smile; but even more, he wanted Eden to care for him the way she had in New York, in spite of the fact that he knew he could make no long-term commitment. The consequences could be devastating if he became involved with Eden Thackery Colter a second time. He knew the risks, the pitfalls, and yet there was a demon inside him that refused to be silenced.

Caught up in her own thoughts, Eden instinctively fell into step with Neil. Hugh's star was gone! That solitary thought kept running through her mind. She knew, logically, that some upheaval in the universe had caused the phenomenon, but at the same time Eden couldn't shake the feeling that in his own way Hugh was freeing her from the last remaining bonds of their marriage. There would be no star to talk to now, no crutch on which she could lean.

"Room 306."

Neil's voice jerked Eden out of her reverie and for a moment she stared blankly at the key Neil pressed into her hand. Neil studied her thoughtfully, one hand stroking his moustache as he racked his brain for a way to end their evening. At last he took her free hand in his and began in a gentle voice, "Eden, I—"

"Mrs. Colter!"

Eden jumped at the sound of her name and as she turned toward the voice Eden was certain she heard Neil swear softly in annoyance. Looking dusty and weary, Keith Gerald strode across the lobby and after an icy glance at Neil, the Ranger gave Eden a tight smile.

"Keith, what on earth are you doing here?" Eden took in his bedraggled appearance with wide, questioning eyes.

"Looking for you. Sorry I didn't have time to change into something more presentable, but I had to get to you in a hurry."

Eden's heart slammed into her stomach, fear spreading like liquid ice through her veins while the color drained from her face. "Shannon! It's Shannon, isn't it? Something's happened to my baby!"

Keith reached out to steady the white-faced Eden only to find Neil's arm already curled protectively around her shoulders. Through sheer force of will Keith stopped the bitter words that sprang to his tongue and concentrated instead on reassuring Eden. "Shannon is fine, Eden. I'm sorry; I didn't mean to frighten you."

Eden nodded jerkily, trying futilely to control the trembling which coursed through her.

"Now that you've scared the lady half to death," Neil growled menacingly, "suppose you explain this display of theatrics, Gerald."

"My business is with Mrs. Colter, Banning, not you." Keith fixed Neil with a blazing sapphire stare. "Suppose you leave us alone."

Sensing the hostility between the two men, Eden swiftly intervened. "Keith, please. Neil is a friend. Anything you have to say can be said in front of him."

Keith's glare didn't falter, but after a moment's consideration he nodded shortly. "A week ago I arrested four men. They're in jail now, in Laredo, charged with robbery and Hugh's murder."

The room and its occupants abruptly receded and Eden felt her legs start to give way. Neil must have felt her weakness, too, because his arm tightened, supporting her while Keith's voice continued to beat at her eardrums.

"They made the mistake of paying for a night in one of the brothels with your emerald brooch. When the, ah, madam tried to sell it the next day, the jeweler became suspicious and contacted the sheriff. The sheriff, in turn, contacted me. The brooch matched your description and I arrested them."

"I see," Eden said shakily. "Will the men be brought to trial?"

Keith nodded. "If you can identify the brooch and the other pieces, our case will be very strong."

"Strong enough to convict them?"

"They'll have to come up with a damn good explanation of how your jewelry came into their possession," Keith hedged. "I seriously doubt any jury will believe some story about finding the jewelry in a sack by the side of the road."

"Is that what the men claim?"

"Not exactly." Keith flicked a look of pure hatred at Neil. "It would be a big help if you could identify even one of the men, Eden."

Eden swallowed convulsively and passed a shaking hand across her eyes. "I didn't see their faces, Keith; I told you that."

"But you heard their voices," Keith persisted. "Surely you could recognize that much."

"I don't know," Eden cried softly.

"Come on, Gerald, leave her alone," Neil interrupted. "Can't you see this is enough of a shock for Eden without your badgering—"

"What I see is you're interfering, and if you shoot your mouth off just once more I'll throw *you* in jail with those other four Mexican bastards. You should feel right at home!"

"Stop this, both of you!" Eden wrenched herself away from Neil and faced both men, gray eyes flashing with anger and fear. "I refuse to listen to this petty bickering any longer. Neil, I appreciate your concern, but I'm perfectly capable of listening to what Keith has to say without your help." At Keith's smirk, Eden turned her flinty gaze on the unsuspecting Ranger. "And as for you, Keith, I told you before that Neil is a friend and I will thank you to treat him as such." Neil and Keith subsided into a glowering contest that at some other time Eden would have found amusing, but at the moment it served only to shred further her already lacerated nerves. "Now, if we can conduct this conversation in a civilized manner, perhaps you will tell me what you want me to do, Keith."

"I need you in Laredo, to identify the jewelry and the men, if you can." Keith dismissed Neil with a contemptuous look and turned his attention to Eden. "There's a train leaving in half an hour. Can you be packed and ready to leave?"

Eden nodded, desperately wishing she could avoid the up-coming confrontation.

Upset as she was, Eden managed to fall asleep during the train ride, and when Keith gently shook her awake the next morning as the train screeched to a stop she felt better able to handle what was to come. Resolutely squaring her shoulders, Eden followed Keith through the streets to the Ranger jail. Nothing about Laredo registered in her mind—the town was simply a collage of faceless people and faded, colorless storefronts until they entered the brick jail and Eden was given a seat behind a battered desk. Keith crouched in front of a safe and, after a few spins of the dial, the metal door opened and he produced a small sack from the interior. The door to the room opened and, straightening, Keith directed Eden's blank gaze to the stranger.

"Eden, this is Cal. He helped me bring in these four men. Cal, this is Mrs. Eden Colter."

Cal touched the brim of his hat, then awkwardly took the slender hand Eden offered. "Did you have a good trip, Mrs. Colter?"

"Nice enough, I imagine. I'm afraid I slept through most of it." Her tentative smile faded as Keith deposited the sack on the scarred desk top.

"Sorry, Eden, but this has to be done," Keith said when she made no move to open the sack.

"I know." Taking a deep breath, Eden carefully upended the sack and sorted through the sparkling display. Tears stung her eyes and she brushed furtively at her damp lashes. After a few minutes she said in a choked voice, "These are mine, Keith."

"You're sure?"

Eden nodded, selecting an amethyst necklace for Keith's study. "All my jewelry is from one shop in New York. You can see here on the clasp the initial M—that stands for Marcel. If you need further verification you can write to Marcel." She frowned suddenly and looked through the jewelry again. "Some pieces are missing, Keith."

Keith reached into a drawer and withdrew a sheet of paper.

"This is the list you made up for me, but I haven't had a chance to check it against what's in that sack."

"I don't need that." Eden waved aside the paper Keith offered her. "I can tell you right now what's missing. A square-cut emerald ring, teardrop diamond earrings, a diamond bracelet, and a matching set of choker, earrings and bracelet made of emeralds and diamonds."

Keith checked off the items on the list and then counted the pieces on the desk. "Looks like you're right, Eden. They must have sold or traded off those pieces before I caught up with them."

"They showed excellent taste," Eden commented bitterly. "All the most expensive pieces are gone."

"How much were they worth?"

Eden's shoulders lifted in a gesture of despair. "The money is secondary. The missing jewelry was from Hugh—how can I place a value on things which were a token of love?" Eden sighed. "Besides, I don't see what the price has to do with anything."

"These men probably never had more than fifty dollars in their pocket before they 'found' your jewelry," Keith explained patiently. "Doesn't it strike you as odd that they stayed in Texas instead of crossing the border into Mexico?"

Eden raised clouded eyes to Keith. "Keith, at this point nothing makes any sense to me. Could we please just get the rest of this over with?"

Keith led her from the office to a back room which housed half a dozen cells. Heart pounding, Eden watched as the four men in the last cell turned to follow her progress down the narrow aisle.

"All right, on your feet." Keith's voice held a grim, inflexible note Eden hadn't heard before and she shivered at the deadly gleam that appeared in his eyes. When the men were on their feet Keith stepped away from their cell to lean negligently against the bars of the cell behind Eden. "Take your time, Eden. There's no hurry."

Eden studied the four menacing faces as calmly as possible, desperately trying to match them with the blurred pictures in her mind. It wasn't possible. These might well be the men who had killed Hugh, but there was no way in the world that Eden could identify them as such.

"Step forward one by one and tell the lady your name."

Four intractable stares greeted Keith's order and when obedience was not forthcoming the unmistakable sound of a gun being cocked split the air. "One by one, and tell the lady your name," Keith ordered in a steely voice. "I'd hate to have to kill you for trying to escape."

This time his order was grudgingly obeyed and Eden closed her eyes as each man identified himself. Perhaps if she weren't confused by the faces the timbre of the voices would strike a chord of recognition. At the name Julio, Eden's eyes flew open and she pressed an icy hand to her lips. The man met her terrified gaze with a contemptuous, leering smile and she recoiled with a gasp.

"Sit down," Keith barked at the man. Placing himself between Eden and the cell he ushered her back to the office. "Cal, get Mrs. Colter some coffee."

Eden sank numbly onto the chair Keith held for her, nodding her thanks, unable to force a single word from her constricted throat. Cal handed her a steaming mug and Eden gratefully wrapped her icy fingers around it.

"Well?" Keith asked when some color had flowed back into Eden's cheeks.

"I'm sorry." Eden drew a shaky breath. "I didn't recognize any of them, Keith. I told you I never saw the robbers' faces."

"Not even the one named Julio?"

Eden shook her head. "I wish I could be of more help, but I honestly can't. Everything that happened is a blur, and after ten months even the voices don't sound familiar. Keith, believe me, if I truthfully thought I recognized them I wouldn't hesitate to say just that in a court of law."

Over the top of her head Keith exchanged a look of frustration with Cal. "You'll still have to testify, Eden. Will you be able to swear that the two men who spoke had Mexican or Spanish accents?"

Eden nodded. "My memory hasn't totally deserted me, Keith. It's just that I can't positively identify those men."

"I guess that's better than nothing," Keith stated bluntly, his ill humor showing.

Eden's temper snapped and she slammed the mug onto the desk with such force that coffee sloshed over the rim. "Damn it, Captain Gerald, what do you expect from me?" The men's eyebrows flew upward at her choice of words but Eden ignored their shocked expressions. "Have you any idea how often I've relived that day, how many times I've watched my husband die? For months that was all I saw when I walked into the study and all I dreamed of when I finally fell asleep. How dare you act as if I'm withholding evidence!"

"I don't want those four set free so they can make some other woman a widow!" Keith shouted.

"Neither do I," Eden replied sharply. "But neither do I want innocent men hanged for a crime they didn't commit."

"Keith, ease up," Cal's smooth drawl entered the conversation for the first time. "Mrs. Colter, ma'am, why don't you come with me and we'll get you a hotel room."

"What's the matter with him?" Eden blurted out when they were out of the jail. "Keith acts as if it's my fault I can't identify those men!"

"Don't take it personally, ma'am, he's been like this ever since we arrested them." Cal registered Eden at the desk and walked with her to her room. He paused outside her door. "Maybe I shouldn't tell you this, but you might understand Keith a little better if you know more about this case from his point of view. He got raked over the coals pretty good by our superiors when we rode into Laredo with our prisoners."

"Why?"

"Because he was ordered off your case months ago. When they found out Keith hadn't stopped his investigation, all hell broke loose. If those four men aren't convicted Keith will be asked to resign."

"Oh!" It was all Eden could think of to say.

"Keith usually is able to keep a professional detachment about his work, but your husband's death was a different matter. He's put everything on the line for you, ma'am, and it eats at him that he won't be going into court with something more solid than circumstantial evidence."

Eden wearily massaged the aching muscles at the back of her neck, managing a faint smile for Cal. "You must be good friends."

"We joined the Rangers at the same time," Cal explained. "Look, Mrs. Colter, I've never seen Keith this riled up before. Nothing has gone right for him lately. Aside from the problems with those four men, he's also been ordered to pull his command from the ranches in the Lathrop area and just trail the rustlers when they strike. Keith believes in the letter of the law down to crossing the final 't,' but with everything that has happened he's feeling frustrated and angry."

"It seems I'm not the only one affected by my husband's death," Eden said quietly. "Do you think Keith would be willing to drop by so I can apologize?"

Cal's eyes sparkled. "I'll mention it to him, ma'am."

The man called Manuel lounged negligently on his bunk, one foot braced against the cell bars, watching expectantly as Keith made his way toward the cell. "So, the lovely *señora* did not recognize us, eh, Captain?" Black eyes glittered insolently. "Why don't you let us go now, Captain, before you make a fool of yourself?"

Keith resisted the urge to pull Manuel out of the cell and beat him within an inch of his miserable life. A muscle ticked in Keith's cheek and his voice crackled with hatred when he spoke. "You're going to hang, Manuel; you and your friends. I'll see to it."

"How?" Manuel asked with a sneer. "You have no evidence, Captain, only a bag full of baubles which we found by the road."

"You didn't find those jewels," Keith growled, "you stole them and killed an unarmed man in the process. He left behind a widow and a baby."

Manuel directed a glob of spit at Keith's feet. "So a *gringo* died. We had nothing to do with it."

"That's not what you said a week ago," Keith countered. "If you tell a jury what you told me, things may go easier for you."

"Ah, I may go to a *gringo* prison for life instead of the gallows?" Manuel's lips curled. "I prefer the sweet scent of freedom to the stink of prison."

"You won't go free, that I promise you. Not unless you testify about Neil Banning's part in the Colter murder."

"Neil Banning?" Manuel echoed. "The name is not familiar."

"Like hell," Keith snarled. "You told me yourself Banning hired you to kill Hugh Colter."

"Did I?" With an affected air of confusion, Manuel tapped a finger against his temple. "Strange, I do not remember saying anything like that."

Keith nodded grimly and took a step toward the cell. "Have

it your way," he said in a menacing voice, "but remember, Neil Banning will be watching you swing from the end of a rope."

"You do not frighten me, Captain."

"No? I'll try harder." Keith held up a piece of paper, a menacing smile twisting his lips. "The prosecuting attorney requested, and obtained, a change of venue. You'll be standing trial in Lathrop, nor Laredo."

Manuel raised his hands in a gesture of indifference. "One *gringo* court is the same as another."

"Not quite. Hugh Colter was a popular man; his friends and neighbors will like nothing better than having his murderers stand trial in their town." Manuel paled visibly at the words and Keith allowed himself a wide grin. "If they don't lynch you before the trial I'll give you odds you'll be found guilty before the jury is out five minutes. I suggest you and your friends start making out your wills."

Keith departed, leaving a heavy silence in his wake. After several minutes Julio rolled from his bunk and made his way to Manuel's side, a worried frown knitting his brow. "What will happen now, Manuel?"

Manuel shrugged. "We will go back to Lathrop."

"But we will be recognized," Julio hissed. "The men we worked with on the Williams ranch—"

"Do not worry so," Manuel interrupted. "The boss will take care of everything."

"You place too much trust in another, Manuel; the time has come for us to save ourselves. If we tell Captain Gerald everything, if we give evidence in the *gringo* court—"

"Silence!" Manuel grabbed Julio's shirt and dragged the heavier man toward him. "Have you forgotten it was my bullet which killed the old man? Be patient, *amigo;* no harm will come to us. Remember, we have an important friend who will take care of us."

"Mrs. Colter wants to see you," Cal informed Keith on his return.

"What about?" Scowling, Keith poured himself a cup of steaming coffee.

Cal shrugged. "Our prisoners, maybe, or the rustlers. Maybe she just wants to know about the trial. How should I know?"

Keith barely heard Cal, his mind still on the man called

Manuel. "Damn," he muttered. "I was so sure I was right. One man behind the rustlers, another behind Hugh Colter's murder."

"What are you talking about?"

"The murder—and my brilliant deductions concerning it." Keith's voice trembled with self-mockery. "Hugh Colter wasn't accidentally killed in a robbery, Cal; his death was planned by Neil Banning, the same man who's backing the rustlers."

Cal had been lazily balancing his chair on two legs but at Keith's statement he returned to the floor with a crash. "Neil Banning? Jesus, Keith, have you lost your mind? Banning is a solid citizen."

"With ties to Mexico," Keith put in grimly. "Just like the rustlers and our friends back there in the cell. The one named Manuel even admitted that Banning hired them to stage a robbery and kill Hugh Colter. Unfortunately," he added when Cal started to speak, "Manuel has suffered a memory loss. He denies having said anything about Banning."

"I don't understand," Cal said slowly. "Why? Why would Banning involve himself in the rustling or a killing?"

Keith exhaled loudly. "I don't know. He's a blue blood, a member of the old aristrocracy. Maybe he was bored and wanted a little excitement, wanted to make fools of the Texas Rangers. He's like that; contemptuous of everything that doesn't meet his arrogant code."

"But why kill Colter?" Cal mused, accepting Keith's conclusions. "Was that part of his game? Or did Colter find out Banning was behind the rustlers?"

Keith shook his head. "I don't think so. My guess is that Banning is hot after Eden Colter, and Hugh was in his way."

The two Rangers sat silently for several minutes, sipping their coffee, until Cal spoke up. "Do you have any proof, Keith?" he asked in a hushed voice. "Anything solid?"

"Not a thing," Keith replied. "All the pieces fit but I can't arrest a man on conjecture. Banning's covered himself too well." He paused, thoughtfully swirling the remains of his coffee. "My only hope is that Manuel or one of his cronies will break down and confess."

"You think that's likely?"

Keith shrugged. "Men do strange things when they're faced with the gallows. Anything's possible."

Cal nodded in agreement. "What if they don't break? Will you go to the old man with your theory?"

"And be laughed out of his office? Hell, no!" Keith sneered. "I'll sit back and let Hastings ride his ass off between Texas and Mexico. By the time the rustlers are finished with him, Hastings won't know which way is up."

"You mean he does now?" Cal inquired, and both men laughed. The laughter eased the tension in the room, and Cal tipped his chair back against the wall once again. "Don't forget about Mrs. Colter."

"I haven't." Rising, Keith strode to the washbasin in the far corner of the room and rolled up his sleeves. "What do you think of her?"

"She seems like a fine woman," Cal answered, amused by the care Keith was taking with his appearance. "A little bewildered and frightened by everything that's happened to her, but it looks like she can hold her own. Any lady who survives a trail drive has my admiration." When Keith nodded, Cal added, "She's also the prettiest woman I've ever seen. I could spend a week just looking at her. I can see now why you broke it off with Sandy."

Keith half turned from the mirror. "I didn't—" His denial faded under Cal's knowing stare. "Is it that obvious?"

"To me, yes. But then, we've been friends for seven years. You in love with her?"

"Yes." Keith's voice was low, steady. "I plan to marry her."

Cal pursed his lips. "Go slow, Keith; the lady may be gunshy this soon after her husband's death."

"I know." Keith settled his hat on his head and started for the door.

"By the way," Cal said before Keith could leave, "you said something before about being wrong. If you didn't figure Banning for Colter's murder, who did you suspect?"

Lathrop Williams. The name sent a wave of nausea through Keith, but he couldn't say it aloud. To do so would require explanations and an unveiling of his own past. Keith wasn't ready to do that—not until he found an airtight way to reveal Lathrop Williams for the scum he really was. "It doesn't matter now. I'll see you later, Cal."

The sick feeling in Keith's stomach persisted until Eden opened the door to her hotel room and he lost himself in the mist-gray eyes that gazed up at him. Belatedly Keith removed his hat and smiled. "Cal said you wanted to see me."

"Yes." Eden returned his smile and stepped aside. "Come in, Keith."

Keith started forward, then hesitated. "I don't think that's such a good idea. Laredo's a small town, Eden; people might get the wrong impression."

"I don't particularly care. Come inside—unless you want me to apologize here in the hallway," Eden teased gently.

Keith shook his head and entered, surveying the room in a glance while Eden closed the door. "I'm sorry a better room wasn't available."

"It doesn't matter; I won't be here that long." Eden motioned to a chair. "Would you like to sit down?"

"No, thank you." Oh, God, but she's beautiful, Keith thought as he watched Eden take his hat and place it on the hat rack. Dressed in a divided riding skirt and a long-sleeved white shirt, Eden appeared almost frail, and it was all Keith could do not to gather her into his arms. Eden wasn't meant for this kind of life—she was too delicate to have to run a ranch or deal with rustlers. She deserved to wear silk, not cotton, and be pampered in every possible way. Eden needed a man to hold her, to relieve her of the burden of responsibilities she carried. In short, she needed Keith Gerald, only she didn't know it yet.

Blissfully unaware of Keith's thoughts, Eden turned to face him. "I'm sorry for the way I behaved this afternoon, Keith. I had no right to snap at you the way I did." She looked down at the worn carpet beneath her feet. "Seeing those men, the jewelry—I guess it was all too much for me."

"My badgering didn't help," Keith reminded her gently. "I'm the one who should apologize."

"No," Eden said quickly. "You were only doing your job, I know that, and I know how frustrating it must be for you. I want to help, Keith, honestly I do, but . . ." Tears welled in her eyes and she tried to swallow a sob. "I had stopped thinking about them, even stopped praying for their arrest, and now . . . now suddenly it's all happening and I can't do a damn thing to help."

"It doesn't matter." Keith took one of Eden's hands in his. "They're guilty and a jury is sure to convict them. Don't worry."

Eden nodded, grateful for his understanding, and slowly

withdrew her hand. "Cal tells me you've been ordered to leave the Lathrop area. I'm sorry."

Keith gestured impatiently. "I failed; it's as simple as that."

"Where will you go now?"

"Wherever I'm ordered, at least until my enlistment's up. Then . . . who knows?"

"I'll miss you," Eden said softly. "Your visits over these past months have meant a great deal to me."

"I was worried about you," Keith admitted. "Hugh's death was quite a blow." Eden paled and he hastened to make amends. "I'm sorry, Eden. I didn't mean to upset you."

"You haven't," Eden assured him. "I cherish Hugh's memory, but I'm finally getting on with the business of living."

Keith smiled, silently admiring the brave front Eden was putting up. "It's getting late, Eden, and you haven't had anything to eat all day. The hotel has a passable dining room. I'd be honored if you'll have dinner with me."

"I had planned to eat in my room." Eden glanced at her attire. "I'm afraid I don't have anything else to wear."

"You look just fine." Keith grinned boyishly. "And I could do with some pleasant company for a meal."

"In that case, I accept."

They chatted amiably during dinner, avoiding, by tacit agreement, any reference to the men in the jail just down the street. Instead they talked about New York, Keith's life as a Ranger and, finally, Eden's plans for the Emerald I.

"I plan to stay," Eden replied firmly to Keith's question about her future. "There's a lot I don't know, of course, but I can learn."

Keith leaned forward, fascinated by the way the light played through the pale curls framing her face. "Tell me: How did you end up on a cattle drive?"

Eden laughed quietly and Keith found his gaze riveted to the hollow at the base of her throat. Her explanations fell on deaf ears as Keith allowed his eyes to drop lower, to the open top two buttons of Eden's shirt. The flesh beneath the cotton fabric was gold-tinged, impossibly smooth, and Keith's eyes lingered over the tantalizing shadow which started just above the first closed button. Keith allowed his imagination to roam, to speculate on the gentle, full curves contained within the well-tailored fabric. Regretfully, and through a supreme effort of will, he dragged his attention back to Eden's face. Eden apparently hadn't noticed his wandering thoughts, and Keith forced himself to concentrate on what she was saying.

". . . Ian and Neil didn't think I could do it, of course, but I proved them wrong." Eden leaned forward, gray eyes sparkling with an excitement that had been missing since Hugh's death. "I even received a grudging apology from them both."

"Is that why you were with Banning last night?" Keith asked with affected nonchalance. "To accept his apology?"

Eden stiffened. "Not that it's any of your business, Captain, but I'll tell you anyway. We were celebrating the end of a successful trail drive." She drained the remainder of her coffee and returned the cup to the saucer with a loud chink. "It's late, and my train leaves early tomorrow morning."

Keith escorted Eden back to her room in silence, his thoughts roiling. He had to protect Eden from Neil Banning, but Keith was beginning to wonder if he wasn't already too late. Though he had no solid proof against Neil, he had to try to warn Eden before she found herself caught in Banning's snare.

When Eden had unlocked the door to her room, Keith gently took her arm. "I didn't mean to pry, Eden. I apologize."

Eden nodded, some of the coldness leaving her eyes. "You don't care for Neil, do you?"

Keith laughed harshly. "Not much."

"You two are very much alike, you know," Eden said thoughtfully. "You're both stubborn and very loyal to what you believe in. And if Neil were here, I think he'd be every bit as unhappy with the comparison as you obviously are."

"That's probably the only thing Banning and I would agree upon," Keith admitted.

"I won't argue the point." Eden chuckled. "Good night, Keith."

"One more thing: When you get back to Lathrop . . . be careful." At Eden's questioning gaze Keith explained, "Until the rustlers are caught, that area is a powder keg. Stay on the ranch as much as possible, and if you have to leave it, for God's sake take someone with you. I don't want anything to happen to you."

"You are so suspicious," Eden chided lightly. "Don't worry, Keith, I can take care of myself."

Not against Banning, Keith thought sourly. He could only hope that Eden would be safe until he himself returned to Lathrop for the trial.

\* \* \*

*All the world's a stage.* The Shakespearean quote echoed through Eden's mind as she drew her mount to a halt and shakily dismounted. Today four men would be executed, their lives snuffed out at the end of a rope. The men had been found guilty of the murder of Hugh Colter in court only two days before. A sudden wave of weakness washed through Eden and she leaned heavily against the hitching post. Events were moving too quickly for her. It had taken over ten months to find Hugh's killers, yet within a week of their arrest Eden had gone to Laredo, identified the jewelry, returned to Lathrop and testified at the trial. Now the men she had not been able to identify would hang. You are not responsible, Eden told herself. A jury convicted those men, not you. Lathrop Williams had testified that the men had worked for him, and Keith had given an emotionless recounting of his investigation and the subsequent arrest.

"Eden lass, are you sure you want to go through with this?" Ian's gentle query pulled Eden back to the present and she managed a wan smile for her foreman. "Yes, Ian, I'm sure."

"You don't have to go through this alone," Ian reminded her. "It would be better if we could stay with you, lass, all things considered."

"Because I might faint or become ill?" Eden asked in a vain attempt at humor, her soft words sounding more like an accusation than a light joke. "I saw Hugh die, Ian; I think I'm capable of watching this. Now why don't you and Vincent do whatever it is men do to pass the time and stop following me around. I'll meet you both after the"—the words stuck in her throat and she continued haltingly—"afterward. By the horses."

With a faint smile for her would-be guardians, Eden turned and made her way through the crowded streets. "Let her go," Ian advised when Vincent started after her. "Nothing is going to happen in a town full of people."

Vincent stared unhappily after the departing figure. "Mrs. Colter is in danger, Ian, whether you believe it or not. We have to guard her twenty-four hours a day."

"Aye, so you keep telling me." Ian sighed. "We're doing what we can, Vincent. One of us is with her whenever she rides out around the ranch, and we keep men around the house and stable during the day. Sooner or later Eden is going to become suspicious and then there'll be the devil to pay. Eden is bound and determined to have things done her way, and her way does not include having a bodyguard dog her every step." Ian regarded the gunfighter-turned-cowboy steadily. "Now if you would be after telling me exactly why you're so sure Eden's in danger, I might be able to convince her to stick close to home."

Vincent's expression did not alter. "No reasons, Ian, just a gut feeling."

"Uh-huh. That's what I figured you'd say." It was plain Vincent would not share whatever information he possessed, so Ian retreated gracefully. "Eden carries a gun with her all the time now, and seeing as how you taught her to shoot, I'll wager she's safe enough. Come on. I'll buy you a drink."

From a table by the window in the crowded saloon in Lathrop, Neil had seen Eden ride into town. Through narrowed eyes he watched as Eden made her way toward the gallows site. At least, he thought with some relief, his doubts about Julio's part in Hugh's death had been resolved. Neil remembered all too well the sickening knotting of his stomach at the trial when he had recognized the four defendants. The men had once worked for Constanza's father in Mexico, but until the trial Neil had known only their faces, not their names. Neil had felt Keith Gerald's eyes upon him when the defendants had entered. It dawned on Neil then that the Ranger suspected him of dealing with these men. But the blatant connection with Mexico bothered Neil even more than Gerald's unspoken accusations. Neil was being framed with extraordinary care and he could think of only one person who knew enough about him to accomplish the frame so neatly. One other person also had ties in Mexico. His eyes had settled on Constanza, and Neil was suddenly aware of a feeling of keen disappointment. There was a malicious enjoyment glittering in the depths of Constanza's eyes as she viewed the proceedings, and Neil had seen the truth there as well. For nearly five years Constanza had used him. He had stood motionless in the back of the courtroom, waiting for one of the defendants to implicate him in Hugh Colter's murder.

Neil had been dumbfounded, therefore, when the man called Manuel had met his eyes after the sentence was pronounced . . . and smiled. Why, Neil had asked himself repeatedly throughout the remainder of the day. Why? Why had

Lathrop been so eager to help Eden bring her husband's killers to justice? And what did Constanza stand to gain by participating in the rustling or by killing Hugh Colter? None of it had made sense at the time. Neil slowly expelled his breath, trying to control the violence sweeping through him as he recalled how his questions had been answered that same night.

A few voices were raised in greeting as the double doors of the saloon swung open to admit still another thirsty witness of the hanging. Neil glanced up at the disturbance and groaned inwardly. Keith Gerald, the pride of the Texas Rangers, stood at the bar. Their gazes met, and while Neil calmly sipped his whiskey he watched Keith elbow his way through the swarm of people to his table.

"We missed you at the trial, Banning." Keith hooked the toe of his boot around the leg of a chair and pulled it beneath him. "Or I should say the lady missed you—I found the atmosphere improved by your absence."

Neil raised his glass in a mocking salute. "I felt the same way about this place, until now. For a man who hates my company so much you've sure gone out of your way to find me." The two men eyed each other coldly. Their animosity had taken on a new dimension since Keith had returned the prisoners to Lathrop for trial, and Neil knew why. Eden. The way Keith hovered around Eden struck a chord of antagonism Neil hadn't known he possessed. "But just to set the record straight, Captain, I did attend the trial. I stood well back in the courtroom. I found your testimony absolutely riveting."

Jealousy played havoc with Keith's already foul humor and he leaned forward, an ugly glint in his eyes. "We have a few things to straighten out, you and I."

"Like what?"

"Like Eden Colter," Keith growled. "Stay away from her."

The Ranger's words dropped into a deadly silence which Neil prolonged by pouring himself another drink and lighting a cigar. "Go to hell," Neil said tersely, anger heating his blood. "And while you're at it, pick up your glass and find another table."

"I'd like nothing better," Keith replied, "but first I want your word that you'll stay away from Eden."

"Not a chance—not unless Eden tells me herself that she doesn't want to see me."

"I can arrange that," Keith snarled. "I'll tell her a few things about her 'friend' Neil Banning that will change her mind about you."

"What are you talking about, Gerald?"

"Get off it, Banning; your innocent act doesn't cut it with me anymore." Keith downed his drink in one gulp. "You're too smart for your own good, and one of these days I'm going to have enough evidence to take you into court and charge you with rustling. When Eden finds out exactly what kind of a bastard you are, every minute of my past year will be worthwhile."

"You're crazy." Neil studied the glowing tip of his cigar with detached interest. "The only connection I have with any rustlers is that I've spent a lot of hours chasing them, just like you."

Keith snorted. "When I finish with you, not even the town drunk will believe that story. Manuel told me everything—how you hired him and his friends to get rid of Hugh Colter, how you told them to take Eden's jewelry and then get out of Texas. I'm going to nail your stinking hide to the wall, Banning, for everyone—including Eden—to see."

"She won't believe you," Neil said in a low voice. "And neither will anyone else."

"Maybe, maybe not." Keith gave Neil a cold smile. "If I were you I wouldn't want to take that chance."

Any fear Neil had felt at the mention of rustlers now turned to icy rage. "You want Eden all for yourself, is that it?" Neil asked, golden eyes molten in his tanned face. "Sorry. No deal, Gerald. I don't like being told what to do, and I especially don't like being threatened. Of course, if you'd care to stop hiding behind that badge we can settle this right now."

"Our weapons are impounded," Keith reminded him.

"We still have these." Neil curled one hand into a fist on the table. "Or are you afraid that I'll mess up your pretty face?"

For an answer Keith scraped his chair back from the table and rose, Neil following suit. No one noticed as the two men weaved their way through the saloon and out the back door to the alley.

"This is going to be a pleasure," Keith jeered as he stripped off his jacket and faced Neil.

Keith had barely finished speaking when Neil swung, his fist connecting with painful accuracy against Keith's jaw. The Ranger staggered backward and before he could recover Neil delivered a blow to his stomach and another to his cheek. Sheer, blind rage overwhelmed Keith and in the blink of an eye his fists had landed a combination of blows on Neil's ribs and face, and the fight began in earnest. The men were equally matched in height and weight and it was only a few minutes before both Keith and Neil were bruised and bloody. They stood facing each other like two Titans, each refusing to give ground or admit that this fight could only end in a stalemate. Each believed he had right on his side, just as each saw before him a competitor who threatened his tenuous bond with a flaxen-haired woman named Eden. It was Eden for whom they fought, driven by an instinct as old as time though they deluded themselves into thinking the cause was a conflict between a man of the law and a man of ideals. They fought with mounting passion, exhilarated every time their fists drew a grunt of pain or left a crimson break on the skin of their opponent.

At last, gasping, Keith threw a final punch only to find his arm caught by Neil's hand. "What the hell—"

"Listen," Neil panted, making no move to strike.

Over the sound of their ragged breathing came pounding footsteps and someone yelling, "They're ready! Hanging's gonna start in five minutes!"

Neil laughed and shoved Keith backward. "Sorry, Gerald. I'm afraid we'll have to settle this at a later time." He drew a handkerchief from his pocket and dabbed at the blood seeping from a cut in his lower lip.

"I'm not finished with you—" Keith began.

"Stop by my ranch anytime," Neil invited. "I'll be happy to finish this—but right now I plan to see your justice carried out." With a contemptuous smile, Neil turned on his heel and left the alley.

"I'll get you, Banning," Keith swore vehemently. "No matter how long it takes, I'll get you!"

Eden found a place to stand far back from the gallows, safe from prying eyes and jostling elbows. Odd how something this macabre could become the town's source of entertainment, turning otherwise sane people into creatures eager for the sight of death. There were children present as well, their eyes wide with curiosity as they surveyed the rough planks and dangling ropes above their heads. Eden thought of Shannon, blissfully unaware, so far, of the darker side of human nature, and shivered. How sad that her trusting innocence would have to be lost.

The door of the jail opened and an expectant hush fell over the crowd as the condemned men stepped into the street. Closely flanked by the sheriff and his deputies, the men approached the gallows with seeming indifference. All but the man Julio, Eden noticed. He kept looking around, as if he expected rescue. The other three appeared to think their up-coming execution was nothing more than a joke. One—the leader—even paused beside the four ready caskets and spat contemptuously into the dirt beside them. Up the dozen steps of the gallows they went, footsteps echoing, and as the thick ropes were draped around their necks their confidence suddenly gave way to sheer horror. One of the men screamed something unintelligible and Eden's mouth went dry with fear. Suppose these were the wrong men? Suppose—?

The trap door swung open and the four men plummeted downward only to be brought up short with a sickening sound which reminded Eden of dry wood snapping. Now Eden understood what the phrase "dancing at the end of a rope" truly meant and with a choked cry she spun away from the scene.

"Come with me, Eden." The voice was familiar but Eden couldn't put a name to it, and her eyes were blinded by unshed tears.

"I . . . I have to stay," Eden stammered. "I h-have to see this through."

"You already have." A firm, gentle hand was placed beneath her elbow and she was led, unseeing, from the execution. "Is your stomach churning?" She nodded and the voice, softened with understanding, resumed. "Take deep, even breaths. Are you going to faint on me?"

"No! At least, I don't think so." Eden wiped the back of her free hand across her eyes and was appalled to discover that her cheeks were wet. More tears followed those she had just wiped away, and something soft was pressed into her hand.

"For the life of me, I cannot understand why women never have a handkerchief when they need one."

"Neil!" Eden worked furiously to clear her vision. All other concerns fled when she looked up to meet that mocking, golden gaze. "What do you think you're—oh! Neil, your face!"

"It's nothing." Neil grinned carelessly, then winced as Eden touched the bruised and swollen flesh.

"Nothing!" Eden exclaimed, her eyes widening as she took in the extent of his injuries. "It looks like someone used you for a punching bag!"

"Sweetheart, you should see the other guy." Neil's golden eyes danced with laughter and after a moment Eden's lips twitched into a tiny smile. "That's better. You've got some color back in your cheeks now."

Beneath his frank, admiring stare, Eden reddened but she refused to be sidetracked. "What happened, Neil?"

"Didn't anyone ever teach you it's rude to pry?" Neil countered evasively.

"Never," Eden blithely replied. "And don't use that one with me."

Neil grimaced in exasperation. "I had a fight. There—does that satisfy you?"

"I figured that much out on my own," Eden said drily. She returned his gaze openly, unafraid of the scowl settling over Neil's face. "You should learn to control your temper, I think. Next time you may not be so lucky."

"My temper didn't get me into this," Neil informed her stiffly.

"Of course not; you were just an innocent bystander." Disbelief stood out clearly in her wide eyes.

"I did not instigate the fight," Neil elaborated. "I took as much as any man would have before accepting the challenge."

"I'm sure you did," Eden said with mock commiseration. "Who did you fight with? I'd like to take a look at the loser—just to compare cuts and bruises."

"Stay the hell out of it!" Neil exploded, his vehemence destroying Eden's bantering mood. "I can handle Keith Gerald quite well without your help."

"Keith!" Eden's eyes widened even further. "Why in the world would Keith pick a fight with you?"

"We fought over a woman," Neil said brutally, wincing at the pained expression which came into Eden's eyes before she dropped her gaze. "Now are you satisfied?"

"Yes." Eden's voice was barely audible. "My mistake. You were right—I shouldn't have pried." She turned away.

Neil swore, placed both hands on her shoulders and spun her back to him. "I didn't come into Lathrop for the hanging, Eden; I came to find you."

Eden refused to look at him, silently cursing herself for caring. "Why?"

"To say good-bye." She looked at him then, confusion and pain marring the gentle gray depths, and Neil pulled her from the main thoroughfare to a side street where they had a relative amount of privacy.

"Good-bye?" Eden echoed numbly. "Where are you going?"

"Home—to Mexico." Neil released her, his self-control badly strained when he touched her.

"For how long?"

"A few months. Maybe longer." Neil shrugged, jamming his hands deep into his pockets to stop himself from reaching for Eden when she shook her head in bewilderment. "Not because of the fight, if that's what you're thinking. It was all decided before the drive."

"Why?" Eden took a step toward Neil, unaware of the effect she was having on him. "Because of the rustlers?"

"No." Neil paused, wondering how he could possibly explain everything that had happened. Neil sighed. An explanation would be futile. "I guess I'm just homesick. I want to spend some time with Sebastian."

"I see." Eden's gaze dropped to study the toes of her boots. "Are you selling the ranch?"

Neil shook his head. "I thought about selling it, but I found I couldn't part with it. Strange how a person gets attached to a piece of land . . . and his neighbors."

"Well." Eden forced herself to look at him, fighting back the absurd desire to cry. "We'll miss you, Neil. I . . . I'll miss you."

Ridiculous as it seemed, that pleased him, and Neil smiled tenderly. "Visit us if you like," he said, "and bring Shannon. Sebastian would like that." She nodded and Neil produced a slip of paper from his vest pocket and handed it to her. "If you should need me, if there's ever any trouble you can't handle, send a telegram to me at this town. I can be here in two days."

Shaking, Eden put the paper in her skirt pocket. "You're very kind. Thank you."

"I ran out on you once before—I figured you deserved better this time." Neil tore his gaze away from the drawn face in front of him.

"When—" Eden's voice cracked, forcing her to start over. "When are you leaving?"

"Today. As soon as I clean up some business."

"Will you say good-bye to Ian? He's grown rather fond of you."

"I'll write to him instead, once I'm back home. Say good-bye for me, will you? Tell Ian I was anxious to get started. He'll understand." A small sound like a sob came from Eden's throat and before he could stop himself, Neil cupped her face in his hands. "I'll write you, too, if you don't mind."

"You're not coming back, are you?" Eden asked tremulously.

"No," Neil answered finally.

Eden gave him a tearful smile, her thoughts spiraling back in time to another parting. Then she had been angry, hurt, consumed by hatred for this man and his betrayal. Now . . . now she felt only sorrow. "Good luck, Neil. I wish you only the best in life."

"Thank you, love. I want the same for you." The endearment slipped out, startling them both. Simultaneously Neil dropped his hands and Eden retreated in confusion. He ruthlessly ignored the torment in her eyes and said softly, "It's still there, love; five years may have gone by, but every time I look at you I remember how good it felt to hold you, how right it was. Do you remember?"

"No," Eden whispered. "No!"

"Don't lie, sweetheart, not to me or yourself." His face hardened and Neil cautiously stepped forward, his eyes snaring Eden in their tawny depths.

"I—I'm not lying," Eden stammered.

"Then prove it." Neil's face was suddenly within inches of hers. "Kiss me, Eden, and then tell me, if you can, that what was between us is gone."

"No!" Before he could touch her Eden turned and fled. A glance over her shoulder assured Eden Neil had not followed her, but she found no consolation in that. *I responded to him,* Eden thought as a mortified blush colored her cheeks. I wanted him to kiss me, make love to me! What kind of woman am I?

Too occupied with her own tumultuous thoughts to make even an attempt at conversation, Eden rode back to the Emerald I in silence while Ian and Vincent exchanged worried glances behind her back. Damn you, Neil, Eden thought angrily as she dismounted and entered the house. Why did you have to spoil everything at the last minute? We could have said good-bye in a civilized manner but no, you had to dredge up the past and all the feelings that went with it.

Lunch was a tedious affair which Eden barely noticed. Even Shannon, babbling merrily on Eden's lap, proved to be only a momentary distraction as Eden offered Shannon her locket for a toy and retreated again to her thoughts. Neil! Eden's cheeks flamed. Neil had the uncanny ability to tear away her safe and secure grip on reality and put in its place this mixture of volatile desire and keen longing that left her feeling breathless and rather intoxicated. Damn him, Eden moaned silently when her heart involuntarily contracted at the thought that she would never see Neil again. He had no right to make her feel this way.

Shannon's nodding head drew Eden's gaze. The baby was asleep, the thumb of her left hand firmly lodged in her mouth. A smile curved Eden's lips and, humming softly, she rose and carried Shannon to the nursery.

Millicent had gone to her own home by the time Eden descended the stairs, and for several minutes Eden wandered aimlessly around the study. The silence of the house bothered her today, the very absence of sound making her ears ring. It was too much like the day of Hugh's death, and that unexpected thought set Eden's nerves on edge. Suddenly uneasy, she walked through the house to close and lock the kitchen door, telling herself to remember to unlock it before Millicent returned to make supper. Back in the study she took her pistol from the desk drawer, checking the load before slipping it into the generous pocket of her riding habit. The clock suddenly struck the hour and Eden turned with a smothered gasp. I'm being silly, she chided herself when the wild jangling of her nerves lessened. With deliberate calm she forced herself to sit at the desk and work on the ledgers, a task which had been set aside until the trial was over, and when that was finished Eden answered Meg's last letter.

Paperwork from Thackery Ltd. and Colter Imports also demanded her attention, and as Eden signed the various contracts a phrase in one of Matthew Kelly's letters leaped off the page. Her face pale, Eden carefully reread his closing paragraph, which stated that a prospective client had been pronounced sound for further investments after a preliminary investigation by the Pinkerton Agency. With a gasp of horror Eden flew across the study and swung her portrait away from the wall, revealing the safe. The dial spun easily beneath her touch, the steel door opened and Eden rifled through the contents until she came across a long-forgotten file.

Emblazoned on the cover in bold, stark lettering was the name Neil Banning and, lightheaded, Eden sank to the floor in front of the fireplace and began reading the age-yellowed pages. Nearly every aspect of Neil's trip to New York was chronicled therein, from his arrival in New York aboard a ship from London to his departure ten days later. The hotel staff had been questioned, as had the other guests on Neil's floor, and Eden's heart pounded wildly as she read a description of herself given by a man who had seen her entering the hotel room with Neil. Some things the agent hadn't been able to ferret out, thank God, like the time they had passed in the Thackery mansion and the afternoon they had spent in the park, but even so, the report was damning. Small wonder Hugh had been in such a rage, Eden thought miserably. She had remained stubbornly silent, hoping to salvage some scrap of dignity, and Hugh had learned the story from a dispassionate piece of paper which made her sound like a loose woman.

But there was more, Eden realized, and with a sinking heart she found herself reading about Neil's trip to Mexico—Jane Gregory in tow—and finally Neil's purchase of a ranch in Texas. The agent must have worked for Neil in order to be so thorough, Eden thought, frowning, and when she stumbled across the name of Julio in the report she paled even further. A coincidence? Was this Julio the same man who had hanged today?

If this report should ever fall into Keith's hands . . . Eden's heart slammed frantically against her ribs. Whatever Neil might have done—and the report proved nothing—at this point Keith did not need to be involved. Eden meticulously crumpled a sheet of paper, placed it in the fireplace and touched a lighted match to its edges. The paper flared briefly, then withered as the flame greedily converted paper and ink to ashes. She added another piece of stationery, and then another, and another, stirring the charred remains with a poker occasionally to be sure nothing escaped the flames.

Assailed with doubts about Neil, Eden nonetheless kept at the task. Hugh had kept Neil's file a secret and so would she. Neil was gone—out of Texas and out of her life. For the second time in her life Eden resolved to bury the past and forget Neil completely. The feelings he had aroused in her this afternoon were merely memories of what they had once shared. If she was to put her life in order, she had to erase Neil from her thoughts.

A knock on the door sent Eden flying from the chair, but for a full minute she found she couldn't move. Unreasoning panic filled her, and when Eden finally walked from the study to the front door the sound of her own heartbeat thundered in her ears. Summoning her courage, Eden opened the door but when she didn't recognize the man in front of her, her right hand unconsciously slid into her pocket.

"Miz Colter?"

"Yes." Her fingers tightened around the pistol grip.

The man pulled off his hat. "I'm George, ma'am, George Hawkins. Mr. Garrison hired me a few weeks back."

The name rang a bell and Eden released her pent-up breath as well as her hold on the gun. "Yes, of course. What is it I can do for you, Mr. Hawkins?"

"Well, ma'am, we've got a problem with that new well you're trying to sink and Vincent wants you to come take a look."

"I see." Eden sighed. "Very well, you ride back and tell Vincent I'll be there as soon as I can."

"Beggin' your pardon, Miz Colter, but Vincent, he said I was to ride back with you. Said he don't want you riding no place without an escort."

"Oh, for heaven's sake," Eden burst out. "That's ridiculous!"

"Maybe so, but I sure don't want to tell him." George raised his shoulders in a gesture of helplessness.

"All right," Eden capitulated, her gray eyes stormy. "I'll tell Millicent to watch the baby while you saddle my horse."

"You can't ride out there alone," Millicent protested when Eden told her the latest turn of events.

"Alone?" Eden protested. "Who's alone? Vincent ordered George Hawkins to wet-nurse me all the way to the well! I told Vincent I didn't want a bodyguard."

"He's just concerned about you," Millicent started to explain. "He and Ian—"

"Concerned, are they? I'll show them concern. When Ian gets back you tell him to be in my study at six o'clock sharp.

The three of us are going to have a nice, friendly discussion about who runs the Emerald I, and when I'm finished with those two they'll be lucky if they can still stand!" Muttering furiously, Eden stomped off and all but tore the reins out of George's hands. "Let's go, Mr. Hawkins, we don't have all day."

Millicent watched the pair ride off. Eden Colter didn't lose her temper often, but when she did, the wisest course of action was to stay out of her way. Millicent pitied the two men who would be on the receiving end of that withering anger.

Neil Banning's golden eyes were incandescent with rage as he faced Constanza and Lathrop across the expanse of the drawing room. "Have you both lost your minds?" he shouted. "What in God's name were you thinking of when you decided on this scheme?"

"The Emerald I, what else?" Lathrop sounded amused. "If you don't have the stomach for the truth you shouldn't have asked the question."

Neil's foot sent a small footstool crashing against the wall as he advanced on the pair. "You killed a man, don't you realize that? You killed Hugh Colter!"

"An accident," Constanza said airily. "He was only supposed to be frightened into taking his family back to New York. Those were my orders."

*"Your orders?"* Neil thundered.

"That's right," Lathrop said coolly. "Let's give credit where credit is due." Lathrop waved a hand toward Constanza. "My lovely wife arranged that by herself, but as Constanza said, Colter was only supposed to be scared. And if you're wondering why sweet, innocent Constanza is involved in this, I'll tell you. There was money to be had, and wherever there's money you'll find Constanza."

Neil glared at Constanza. "I should have listened to Sebastian—he tried to warn me about you. My congratulations. You've been playing me for a fool all these years. I was blind not to see what was going on; the excuses, the delays, all strictly for your benefit. You've been playing me off against Lathrop from the very beginning."

Constanza raised her hands in a gesture of indifference. "You have always done as you pleased, Neil, without a thought for anyone else. I learned a great deal from you."

"I've never had an innocent man killed," Neil snarled.

"I keep telling you that was an accident," Constanza pouted.

"Nor have I held the life of four men in my hands and allowed them to think I would save them when I never had any intention of doing so."

Constanza jumped out of her chair and sashayed arrogantly around Neil. "Why should I have saved them? Manuel and his friends were nothing but peons, hired hands. They enjoyed themselves enough before Captain Gerald caught them."

Neil stopped Constanza's strutting by seizing her arm. "Is that what you told them that night outside the jail? That's right, Constanza, I was there," Neil told her when she looked at him in alarm. "I was in Lathrop—I saw you talking to Manuel. But that surprise was nothing compared to the one I got when those four men died instead of escaping, as you had so faithfully promised."

"Lathrop," Constanza called anxiously to her husband when Neil showed no sign of releasing her.

"Just relax, my dear, Neil isn't about to harm you." Lathrop raised an eyebrow at the younger man. "Are you, boy?" With a curse Neil thrust Constanza away from him, and Lathrop nodded approvingly. "Very wise. Now I think it would be best for everyone if you left. You heard Constanza: She wants to stay until the Emerald I is mine, at which time she collects a tidy sum for delivering the ranch into my hands."

"I don't believe this!" Neil grabbed Constanza by the shoulders and shook her angrily. "Five men are dead, Constanza, and you and your husband are responsible. How can you live with that?"

Lathrop's ugly laughter filled the room. "I'm not responsible for anything, boy, except initially hiring those four murderers. Their leader, by the way, was Constanza's lover for several months. No, if there is any guilt it belongs squarely upon Constanza's shoulders. I can produce witnesses to Constanza's meetings with Manuel both before and after the murder of Hugh Colter."

"Witnesses you bought and paid for, I suppose," Neil sneered.

Lathrop shrugged. "Does it matter? The point is that I have them, just as I have witnesses who will swear that you're the man backing the rustlers. The frame is perfect. Run back to Mexico, sonny, and mark the past five years up to experience.

You can take comfort from the fact that neither Constanza nor I can go to the law without implicating ourselves. Who knows? When all this is over I may just pay you a visit to let you know how things turned out."

"You'll never get the Emerald I," Neil said confidently. "That's my one consolation—Eden will never sell it to you."

Lathrop began laughing again and this time Constanza joined him. Shrugging out of his grasp, Constanza faced Neil contemptuously. "She will sell. I've already made the arrangements and you can do nothing to stop what is happening even while we speak."

A shaft of fear stabbed at Neil. "What are you talking about?"

Constanza glanced at her husband. "Shall I tell him?"

"Why not?" Lathrop's eyes danced with depraved amusement. "There's nothing he can do, and for all we know he might enjoy what is happening to the very desirable Eden Colter. She is lovely, isn't she, boy, with that exquisite hair and soft, satiny skin?"

The tone of Lathrop's voice sent a wave of apprehension through Neil, as did the satisfaction with which Constanza described her plan.

"Kidnaping!" he shouted when Constanza was finished. "It will never work. Keith Gerald will move heaven and earth to find her."

"Which is why we're taking her to Mexico," Constanza explained. "Captain Gerald has no authority there. A few days at the hands of our friends and Eden Colter will be only too happy to sign over the Emerald I to Lathrop."

"You can't do this," Neil protested ineffectually.

"Of course we can," Lathrop gloated. "Who's going to stop us?"

Neil picked up his hat and started for the door, only to be brought up short by Lathrop.

"Don't be a hero," Lathrop warned. "Gerald wants the leader of the rustlers so bad he can taste it, and believe me, I'll find a way to hand you over without a second thought if you get in my way."

"Who's going to get in your way?" Neil forced a twisted smile to his lips and faced Lathrop. "I just want to get back to Mexico and forget about Texas, Keith Gerald and both of

**you.** I don't care what you do with Eden Colter . . . or Constanza, for that matter."

"Do you believe him?" Constanza asked as they watched Neil ride away.

Lathrop nodded. "He's not about to get into trouble over an American—after all, we don't have the distinguished, honorable bloodlines you and he share. Eden Colter is nothing to him, just like you're nothing to me. No, Neil Banning won't cause us any trouble."

Shortly before sunset Vincent and Ian returned home, weary but exuberant that the first of several wells Eden planned to drill for watering the cattle was proving successful. The two men stabled their horses, and when the animals had been fed and curried, Vincent produced a bottle from his saddlebag and solemnly passed it to Ian.

"What's this for?" Ian turned the bottle over in his hand.

"For taking me on," Vincent replied. "For giving me a chance. Not many men would."

Ian shook his head. "Eden's the one who gave you a chance, not me. I just follow orders."

"You could have fought against me," Vincent countered. "You didn't, and I'm grateful."

Ian considered the mask that was Vincent's face. "You're a strange kind of gunslinger, Vince. In the nearly two years I've been here, I've never seen you draw on anything except empty bottles. Now, I think that's downright strange."

"I haven't had a reason lately," Vincent replied evasively.

That answer, apparently, was the only one Ian was going to hear, and with a wry smile he pulled the cork from the bottle and took a healthy swallow. Wordlessly he handed the bottle back to Vincent, who did the same.

"I'm not going to cause trouble," Vincent assured Ian as he passed the bottle back.

"I never thought you would." Ian smiled and led the way to the house.

Millicent met them at the kitchen door, concern turning to bewilderment as neither man appeared in the least upset. "You two certainly don't seem worried. Or has Miss Eden finished with you already?"

Ian exchanged a confused look with Vincent. "You have any idea what she's talking about?"

"None." Vincent turned his attention to his wife. "What's all this about, Millie?"

Millicent frowned, pulling an inquisitive Shannon away from the vegetable bins. "Didn't she tell you to be in the study at six?"

"It doesn't matter," Ian said and began inspecting the contents of the pans on the stove. "It's six now. We'll go talk to her and find out what this is all about and then sit down to supper."

Millicent's frown deepened. "Vincent, didn't George Hawkins tell you how upset Miss Eden was?"

"How could he?" Something flickered across Vincent's face, turning his eyes cold and flat. "Ian! You better get over here. Where's Mrs. Colter, Millie?"

"She's supposed to be out with you," Millicent whispered fearfully. "George Hawkins came for her after lunch. He said you were having a problem with the well."

"Did you see the man?" Vincent asked sharply.

"No, not really. I was too busy with Miss Eden. Even if I had, it wouldn't have made any difference. I don't know all the men who work for the ranch."

"Neither does Mrs. Colter." Vincent glanced at Ian. "One of us had better ride into town and get the sheriff—and Captain Gerald, if he's still around."

"What for? Eden's with George. She's all right," Ian ventured.

"No, she isn't." Vincent stated in a grim voice. "George Hawkins was my partner at the well today. We were working on the scaffold—we were twenty feet in the air together, when Mrs. Colter supposedly rode off with him."

"Oh, my God!" Millicent sank weakly onto a chair and pulled Shannon onto her lap. "Why would anyone use George's name?"

"Because Mrs. Colter would be familiar enough with it to believe whatever the man said." Vincent started for the door. "I'll get the sheriff. In the meantime, Ian, start questioning the men who were around the buildings this afternoon. Maybe one of them saw which direction they went in."

"Wait! Maybe Millicent got the name wrong. We can't assume something bad has happened just because a message wasn't delivered."

Both men turned to Millicent, who slowly shook her head,

her eyes filling with tears. "Miss Eden said George Hawkins—I remember because she was furious that George, or whoever he is, told her that Vincent wanted him to escort her out to the well." Millicent sobbed. "I didn't pay any attention, I thought—"

"It's all right, Millie," Vincent murmured soothingly. "You couldn't have known; no one could."

"I'll talk to the men." Ian jammed his hat on his head. "Looks like your instincts were right, Vincent."

Vincent jerked his head toward Shannon. "I just hope Mrs. Colter's been kidnaped for a good-size ransom—because if she hasn't, chances are that little tyke is an orphan."

Hands bound behind her back, Eden watched helplessly as the man she knew as George Hawkins secured a length of rope around her ankles, cutting off the circulation in her feet. She whimpered and the man looked at her angrily.

"Please, the rope is too tight," Eden implored him.

"Don't matter—you ain't gonna need your feet." Eden started to protest but George cut her short. "You open your yap or start screaming like you did a while back and I'll gag you again. Understand?"

Terrified, Eden subsided and waited until he returned to the campfire before she tried to find a comfortable position on the rocky ground. Anger and fear roiled inside her and she desperately fought against the rising panic. If she could just remain calm she might think of a way to escape, although her present state didn't lend itself to overpowering two armed men.

There had been no sign of danger, Eden recalled, not until the other man had appeared out of nowhere and George had grabbed for her reins. She had managed to evade him and had kicked her horse into a gallop, riding as fast as she could toward the site of the new well. But in less than a mile they had overtaken her, and George had dragged her twisting and screaming from her saddle onto his own. Frantically, Eden had raked her nails across his face, and George had slapped her so hard that she went limp in his arms. She had remained conscious, fully aware of what was taking place, but she was too weak to struggle. Later, when her ears had stopped ringing and some of her strength had returned, her hands had been tied and George had thrown her back on her own saddle to ride between the two men.

Eden had waited and watched, biding her time until George relaxed his hold on the reins of her horse, and then she screamed and sent her mount flying past the two startled men. She knew, logically, that no one could hear her, but she screamed all the same until her horse stumbled, throwing her to the ground with such force that she twisted her ankle and scraped her cheek. Moments later the men caught up with her and shoved a foul cloth into her mouth. Even then victory hadn't been completely theirs—when George was trying to gag her she had caught the fleshy part of his hand between her teeth and held on with every ounce of strength she possessed. George had screamed even louder than she had. They had forced her mouth open eventually, but she had bit through a fair amount of flesh by then, and George now sported a gun hand which was swathed in a makeshift bandage.

"You want some food?" Eden looked up to find George towering over her, a steaming plate in one hand. She shook her head. "You better eat. We got three more days' hard riding."

"How do you propose I eat?" Eden inquired sarcastically.

George's free hand came up and a knife blade glinted in the firelight. "I'm gonna cut you free, but you make one wrong move and I'll kill you."

The knife flashed once and Eden's hands were free. While she rubbed the feeling back into her wrists and hands George went to the fire and returned with a cup of coffee. Eden reached for the plate but hesitated when George crouched beside her.

"Go ahead." George waved his knife toward the food. "Eat up before it gets cold."

Eden returned her hand to her lap. "Must you watch me?"

"'Fraid so." George's gaze left her face and fastened on the material covering her bosom. "You're easy to look at, girl, real easy. Almost tempts a man into forgetting what he's paid to do. I'd bet that once you got to know me you wouldn't mind me watching you--you might even get to likin' it."

Fear tightened her chest and Eden nervously wiped her damp palms on her thighs, starting when she encountered something hard in the pocket of her skirt. Her gun! She wasn't helpless after all!

"What's the matter?"

George had seen her startled movement and as Eden floundered about for some plausible explanation he moved closer.

She had to come up with some excuse before George decided to tie her up again. "I thought I heard a rattlesnake," Eden whispered at last in a strained voice.

"I didn't hear nothin'." George eyed her suspiciously.

"Listen," Eden demanded. "I'm sure there's something out there."

George cocked his head, straining to hear the unmistakable rattle. "Like I said, nothin'."

Several hundred yards away, Neil lay full length against the ground, golden eyes alight with fury at the scene in front of him. Neil eased himself back down the slight incline and carefully removed the spurs from his boots. Off came his hat and jacket and finally his gun belt, leaving nothing on his person to reflect the moonlight or the flames of the campfire. The blood was singing in his veins, carrying a reckless excitement through him as he crawled back up the incline and began to inch his way toward the camp on his belly.

Only two men, Neil thought confidently, one of whom seemed more intent upon retiring to his bedroll than on guarding the prisoner. Neil's eyes flicked to where Eden sat, and what he saw started a muscle working in his cheek. Backed helplessly against her saddle, Eden was enduring the man's touch as he combed his fingers through her riotous mass of curls. Neil paused, his eyes narrowing as he drew the knife from his boot. He had planned to wait until at least one of the men was asleep—but if he waited too long, Eden would probably be raped right in front of him.

"Please, don't," Eden breathed, shrinking from the man's touch.

"Now, girl, I ain't gonna hurt you none, not unless you try and fight me." George's hand slid to the buttons of her shirt. "You and me's just gonna have a little fun, is all. It ain't like you never had a man before, so you just relax and let me do what I want and you'll live to see that baby of yours again."

"Don't," Eden warned hysterically, her right hand stealing into the pocket of her skirt. "I won't let you touch me."

The knife appeared in George's hand, cutting through the bonds at her ankles. "Just how you gonna stop me, girl? I sure would hate to slice up this pretty face of yours, but I will if you don't leave me no choice." He backed off and began unbuckling his belt with his free hand. "Stand up and take off your clothes; I want to see what you kept hidden under them widow's weeds."

Eden swallowed her panic and tightened her grip on the weapon in her pocket as her finger curled around the trigger. If she was lucky, very lucky, at this range she could kill George and still have time to turn the pistol on his friend before the other man could draw his gun.

"I said stand up!"

Impatient, half naked, George was reaching for her. "You want me to tear your clothes off, that suits me—"

The gun roared once, putting a hole in Eden's skirt and an even larger one in George's left shoulder. Time was frozen as Eden stared in horror at the blood dripping from the wound, and George looked stupidly from the hole in his shoulder to the wide-eyed woman on the ground. The man at the campfire rose, pivoting toward the explosion and drawing his gun in the same motion.

"Shoot, Eden!"

The cry broke her trance, and as George took a step forward Eden snatched the gun from her pocket, steadied it with both hands and squeezed the trigger. George's face dissolved into pulp and thankfully the force of the bullet threw him backward, away from Eden's sight.

"I'll kill the woman," the man at the fire threatened the shadows, his gun pointed at Eden. "Come on out or—"

His voice suddenly ended in a gurgle and he dropped the gun to claw at the knife hilt which protruded from his throat. Retching, he fell to his knees and slowly toppled to the ground, where he shuddered convulsively and finally went still.

"Oh, my God," Eden murmured over and over, sickened. "Oh, my God, what have I done?"

Neil was beside her, prying the gun from her stiff fingers. "What the hell's the matter with you?" he demanded angrily. "You could have gotten yourself killed pulling a stunt like that! Why didn't you wait for help?"

Eden stared at the two bodies, then at Neil. "He said he was one of my men so I rode out with him. I thought we were going to the new well, but then the other man appeared and I forgot about the gun. I almost got away but my horse stumbled and they had tied my hands so I couldn't fight them. But then I told them about the snake. . . . He was going to touch me. . . . I couldn't let him, I couldn't.... They took me by surprise, you see, and I forgot about the gun. I don't know why."

She was rambling, completely disoriented, and Neil watched her with growing concern. "We've got to get out of here. Can you walk? Are you going to faint?"

"I never faint." Eden laughed spasmodically. "Hugh always said I was amazingly strong that way. Of course, I'd never killed a man, either." She looked down at the grisly stains on her shirt and began to shiver uncontrollably. Her arms flew outward in terror. "There's blood all over me! Get it off! *Get it off!*"

"I will, love, I will," Neil promised. "I have an extra shirt in my saddlebag; just wait—"

"No!" Eden screamed. "I can't stand it! Help me, please— I can't stand it touching me!"

Neil brusquely pulled off her shirt and tossed it to the ground out of sight. He stripped off his own shirt and with surprising gentleness dressed Eden in it.

"Listen to me." When Eden didn't respond to his voice, Neil lifted her to her feet and shook her urgently. "Damn it, Eden, listen to me! I'm going to saddle you a horse and then we're going to get away from here, but I can't do that if you go wandering off. You've got to stay right here. Do you understand? Don't move."

Eden touched the sleeve of the shirt and then examined her fingers. Apparently reassured that there was no blood, she calmed a bit, although the gray eyes still were dazed. "I can't walk. I twisted my ankle when my horse fell." She sank to the ground. "I'll wait."

Neil started for the horses, pausing to retrieve his knife from its resting place and wipe it clean against the man's clothing. He worked quickly, first saddling Eden's horse and then running back for his own mount. He would have to lead Eden's horse, Neil realized when he returned a few minutes later and found her gazing numbly into the fire. In her present state she would have all she could do just to stay in the saddle. Neil pulled on a shirt and then gently draped his jacket around Eden, an action which drew her attention, and she watched as he put on his gun belt and secured the holster to his leg.

"I want my gun," Eden told him unexpectedly. "Where is it?"

"Let me keep it for a while," Neil advised soothingly. He

brushed the hair away from her face, alarmed by her pallor and the icy feel of her skin. She didn't press the issue but instead turned her attention back to the fire, which worried Neil even more. Eden needed to have her ankle attended to, as well as the scrape he had noticed on her cheek, and he didn't dare try to deal either with those injuries here or with the shock she was obviously slipping into. Knowing Lathrop, additional men were probably on their way, and Neil and Eden had best be long gone when they arrived. Neil helped Eden to her feet. "Come on, Eden, we have a long ride ahead of us."

Eden felt herself lifted into a saddle, and she looked down into a pair of glowing, amber eyes. Hesitantly she reached out and touched the lean, tanned face. "Neil? Are you in my nightmare, too?"

Neil grimaced, covering the frigid hand with his. "I'm afraid this is one nightmare I helped cause. Forgive me, love."

"Yellow eyes—cat's eyes." A hint of reason returned and Eden glanced at the two bodies. "They're dead, aren't they?"

"Yes." Neil mounted his own horse and tied the reins of Eden's horse around the saddle horn.

"Where are we going? Home?"

The question was asked with such childlike trust that Neil's heart twisted. "Not yet. First I'm going to take you someplace safe."

"Oh." Eden didn't protest, although somewhere in the back of her mind several questions about Neil and his arrival were forming. Right now it was enough that he was someone who spoke tenderly to her and occasionally reached out to draw the jacket back up around her shoulders whenever it slipped off. By first light they were across the border, several miles inside Mexico.

Eden and Neil weren't the only ones who had stayed in the saddle all night. After notifying Keith Gerald and the sheriff, Ian and a few of the men from the Emerald I had ridden to the neighboring ranches in the faint hope that Millicent had been mistaken and that Eden had simply gone visiting. They all knew the act was futile—all the signs pointed to a well-planned kidnaping—but the questions had to be asked just to be sure, as Keith said. The answer was the same from all the neighbors: They hadn't seen Eden Colter. A solicitous Lathrop Williams placed himself and his men at Keith's disposal, and Keith gratefully accepted. It was the news that Neil Banning had left for Mexico early in the day, however, that brought a vengeful light to Keith's eyes and he fingered his bruised jaw thoughtfully.

"We'll split up our men," Keith announced to Ian, Vincent and Lathrop in Eden's study. "Start a sweep to the border with parties of four. That way when we pick up the trail three men can ride ahead, and one can ride back for the rest. Tell them to be sure to mark a trail we can follow."

Ian frowned. "Shouldn't we try the other directions as well, Keith? They could be headed anywhere."

"Just south—they'll head for Mexico."

"Maybe not," Lathrop interjected. "If they want to ransom Mrs. Colter, they'll have to be close enough to communicate with her friends. I think Ian has a good idea."

"Mexico," Keith maintained stubbornly. "You offered to help, Mr. Williams, which means you do as I say. Is that clear?"

Lathrop's eyes narrowed. "Clear. But you're making a big mistake."

Keith turned on his heel and stalked from the room, closely followed by Ian. Vincent pushed away from the wall and started to do the same, but he halted abruptly in front of his former employer. "That Ranger does have the bit in his teeth, doesn't he?"

"He's wrong about the direction they took." Lathrop's expression twisted contemptuously. "By the time he does find Eden Colter she'll be dead."

"She better not be." Vincent's hand blurred and before he finished speaking his gun was pressed beneath Lathrop's chin. "If you've got a way to get word to your men you better use it, because if anything happens to that woman I'm going to separate your head from the rest of your body."

Lathrop's eyes bulged alarmingly. "What are you talking about? I don't know who—"

The pressure of the gun barrel increased and Vincent smiled coldly when Lathrop fell silent. "No? In that case you better pray we find her safe and sound." Vincent holstered his gun. "By the way, I'm not letting you out of my sight. You and I are going to ride with Ian and Captain Gerald."

They rode through the small hours of the morning, until they ran across an abandoned campsite with its still-glowing coals. Circling warily, guns drawn and pointed at the two prone figures, Lathrop, Vincent and Ian waited while Keith cautiously approached the camp. After a quick inspection of the two bodies Keith returned his gun to the holster and motioned to the others.

"They're dead," Keith proclaimed. He dropped to one knee and stoked the fire into life.

"What the hell happened here?" Ian muttered when the perimeter of the campsite was illuminated by the flames.

Vincent let the reins of his horse trail and sauntered forward to examine the bodies while the others opened the saddlebags of the dead men and sorted through the contents. Vincent noted with interest the position of each man's body and weapons. Frowning, he tore open the shirt of the man farthest from the fire, oblivious to the blood and splintered bone which covered the cloth. He sensed a presence behind him and turned to find Lathrop staring down at the body.

"Recognize this one?" Vincent inquired softly, lifting the bloody mass which had once been a man's face into the light for Lathrop's inspection.

"No," Lathrop lied, nudging the body with the toe of his boot. Fools! Lathrop thought viciously. Eden Colter was gone now, beyond his reach, and he had a nagging feeling that Neil Banning was responsible for this massacre. "I told you before, I don't know anything about this."

"Sure." Vincent rose and draped a blanket over the dead man before joining Keith and Ian. "Find anything?"

Keith shook his head. "No letters, no papers; nothing that could identify these men."

"We did find this," Ian put in quietly as he passed Vincent a blood-spattered white cloth.

Vincent turned the shirt over in his hands. "Mrs. Colter's?"

Ian nodded. "She was wearing it today."

"This fits in with what I found." Vincent jerked his head toward the blanket-covered body. "From what I can see, that one got a bullet in the shoulder first, took a few steps, and then took a round full in the face. That has to be Mrs. Colter's doing." When the three men looked at him questioningly, Vincent elaborated. "Mrs. Colter tends to shoot high and to the right. Judging from the trail of blood he left, her first shot didn't stop him, but she had enough presence of mind to correct her aim and try again."

"Then she's free," Ian said hopefully.

"We won't know that for some time." Vincent gazed

thoughtfully at the second body. "This one here was killed with a knife, which means someone else stumbled across them and gave Mrs. Colter a hand."

"Or someone was waiting here," Keith theorized. "Possibly the leader, who didn't need these two anymore. This way he can collect the ransom and not have to split the money."

Vincent shrugged. "No use wasting time with guessing games, Captain. If Mrs. Colter was rescued we'll know soon enough, and if she wasn't...well, we'll find that out, too. Right now I suggest we notify the others, get some rest and then see if there's a trail we can follow come morning."

"Do as you please." Keith checked the cinch on his horse and swung back into the saddle. "I'll leave a trail for you to follow."

"And if the trail leads into Mexico?" Ian folded his arms across his chest. "You don't have any authority there, Captain, and if we ride in there armed to the teeth we'll do Mrs. Colter more harm than good."

"Then don't come...any of you," Keith told them shortly. "In fact, I order you to stay out of it. Stay at the ranch and wait for a ransom demand. If I can't find Eden then we'll have no choice but to do as the kidnaper demands."

"Let him try it." Vincent placed a hand on Ian's arm when the Irishman started after Keith. "He's not going to find her, but trying will make him feel better."

Ian's eyes narrowed. "You know something I don't, I'm thinking. Eden's like a daughter to me, so if you know anything that can be of help..."

Vincent clapped Ian's shoulder reassuringly. "Trust me, my friend. She'll be returned safe and sound."

"Tell me," Ian demanded harshly.

"Not yet—you'll know everything in good time, which is when Mrs. Colter is at home with her daughter. Until then, let me handle things my own way." Vincent smiled coldly. "I have been known to get results. Come on. Let's get these men buried before we end up fighting off the coyotes."

They worked at the grisly task and when Ian stepped out of hearing, Vincent spoke to Lathrop in a quiet, lethal voice. "Find her. Don't argue and don't waste your breath on denials. Just find Mrs. Colter and make sure she gets back to the Emerald I without so much as a scratch, because if something happens to her you're a dead man. Understand?"

# Chapter 16

Eden's leg throbbed angrily with every step her horse took. Only pain seemed to penetrate the fog surrounding her brain, no matter how hard she tried to put her haphazard thoughts in order. She remembered putting Shannon in her cradle for a nap, but after that, events seemed disjointed, tinged with a nightmarish quality which made her shiver. How long had it been since she had slept? Eden wondered. She was so tired that every beat of her laboring heart sent shock waves through her body. Maybe she was asleep now, only she didn't realize it. That would certainly explain the presence of the grim-faced man who rode beside her.

"Please." Eden forced the words through frozen lips and discovered her throat was dry as sand. "Could we rest? Just for a few minutes? My ankle hurts terribly."

Neil looked at her swiftly, the tension in his face easing somewhat at the first words Eden had spoken during their ride. "Sure. I could use a rest myself, and so could the horses."

He dismounted and lifted Eden from the saddle, scowling as she cried out when she tried to put her weight on the damaged ankle. Eden felt giddy, lightheaded, and she did not protest when Neil lowered her to the ground.

"Just lie back and watch the sunrise," Neil ordered gruffly, "while I take a look at your leg."

"It feels funny," Eden murmured. "Do you suppose it's broken?"

"I can't tell through the boot," Neil replied wryly, wondering if Eden fully understood yet what was happening. He pulled out his knife and quickly sliced through the laces before attempting to remove the boot. "I don't know if it's broken, but it's swollen to twice the size it should be."

"Can we stay here for a while?" Eden asked pitifully. "I honestly don't think I can stay on my horse much longer."

Neil shook his head, casting a glance over his shoulder. "Sorry, love, but we don't dare." He rose, pulled a pair of binoculars from his saddlebag and studied the terrain they had just covered. "Take heart, though; a few more hours and you'll be safe and tucked into a nice, clean bed."

"Neil?"

He turned at the sound of his name, vastly relieved that a portion of Eden's sanity had returned, and found her propped up on one elbow watching him. "Yes, Eden?"

"Who's after us? Do you know?"

"By now, probably half the state of Texas, with Keith Gerald leading the parade." Neil put away the binoculars.

"Shouldn't we wait, then?" Eden struggled to sit up. "Keith will know what to do."

"Sure—hang me and marry you," Neil muttered under his breath.

"What?"

"Nothing." Neil handed his canteen to Eden, then took a long drink himself. "We can't wait because we can't be sure who's behind us."

"I don't understand," Eden said quietly. "Nothing seems to make any sense right now." She buried her face in her hands. "If I could only think straight I might be of some help to you."

"Listen to me." Neil knelt beside Eden and pulled her hands away. "The best thing for you right now is *not* to think. Let me take care of everything and when you're stronger I'll help you sort out all the pieces."

Eden stared at him through wide eyes and nodded. "I'm glad you're here, Neil."

"I aim to please," Neil teased in a faint attempt at levity. He lifted her onto his horse and then swung up behind her. "Lean against me and try to rest."

She did as he asked, finding the hardness of his chest oddly comforting. Neil's arm tightened around her waist, drawing a tiny sigh from Eden, and, glancing down, Neil watched her eyes flutter shut. Darling Eden, he thought unexpectedly. How did I ever leave you five years ago?

Sebastian was just sitting down to lunch when he heard the approaching hoofbeats. With a wistful glance at his plate he tossed the napkin aside. Fully expecting to find another patient waiting on the doorstep, Sebastian limped to the door, only to be brought up short by the sight of Neil carrying a woman up the steps. Her appearance—with a man's shirt and jacket, a dusty riding skirt and only one boot—was, to say the least, disheveled, and Sebastian blinked rapidly.

"Now what have you done?" Sebastian groaned when Neil crossed the threshold.

"I haven't *done* anything," Neil snapped, pivoting so that Sebastian could see Eden's face. "She's hurt and she needs a doctor."

Sebastian was already moving and he called over his shoulder, "Take her to Mother's room while I get my bag." By the time Sebastian entered the long-unused bedroom, Neil had removed Eden's travel-stained clothes and had replaced them with a clean nightgown from the bureau.

"Her ankle is twisted, but I don't think it's broken," Neil explained. "She took a bad fall when her horse threw her."

"Thank you, Dr. Banning," Sebastian replied, a cutting edge to his voice. "But if you don't mind, I prefer to make my own diagnosis." He fell silent for several minutes while he meticulously examined Eden's ankle and scraped jaw. Frowning, Sebastian reached for a roll of bandages, glancing at his brother for the first time. "I think it would be best if you explain what is going on, Neil."

Neil ignored the question. "How is Eden?"

"Aside from the sprained ankle and a few scrapes and bruises, she appears to be fine."

"That's a relief." Neil expelled his breath slowly and sank onto the edge of the bed. "She fell asleep a couple of hours ago, but when I tried to wake her she just wouldn't come around."

Sebastian drew the covers around Eden's shoulders and tucked the covers securely under the mattress. "Let her sleep. We'll try to wake her tonight and see if we can get some food into her." He studied Neil's battered face. "You look like you could use a doctor, too."

"Because of this?" Neil touched his swollen eye and shook his head.

"In that case, come downstairs with me and have some lunch."

"Shouldn't someone stay with Eden?" Neil brushed the tangled curls away from her pale face.

"The best thing for her right now is rest. She's not in any danger, Neil, not from a sprained ankle; and I would guess she's sleeping for the simple reason that she's exhausted."

When Neil made no move to leave, Sebastian added, "I'll have one of the maids stay with her. Will that make you feel better?"

"Yes," Neil admitted grudgingly. "But the minute she wakes up I want to be told."

"As you wish."

Satisfied, Neil accompanied Sebastian to the dining room. A second place had been set and Neil applied himself ravenously to the food, bracing himself for the barrage of questions Sebastian was obviously preparing. Neil felt like a fool. Five years wasted; five years! Neil thought of Eden lying upstairs and groaned inwardly as guilt washed over him. For the first time he acknowledged the castastrophic effect he had had on Eden's life. In a very real way he was responsible for Hugh's death as well as Eden's kidnaping.

"Care to discuss Mrs. Colter now?" Sebastian poured himself a brandy and offered the decanter to Neil.

Golden eyes locked over the crystal, and Neil nodded slowly. He filled a glass and leaned back in his chair. "She was kidnaped—no, not by me, so you can lower your eyebrows—by two men working for Lathrop and Constanza. Wonderful woman, Constanza. Quite willing to arrange anything up to and including murder if the price is right. But then, that shouldn't surprise you, little brother. After all, you warned me about her years ago." Neil's tone turned bitter, filled with loathing and self-contempt. "The little bitch! I risked everything for that woman—I gave up my home, my family, years of my life, because I believed Constanza would never lower herself to marry outside our class. Now I discover that not only was Constanza not forced to marry Lathrop, she engineered the entire thing!" Neil laughed shortly. "I made a perfect jackass out of myself, riding to her rescue like some damned knight in shining armor. And Constanza loved every minute of it— for five years she played me against Lathrop. She sold me out for a fat bank account and a ticket out of Mexico! And did you know she's had lovers all this time?" He snorted in disgust.

Sebastian rubbed a hand across his forehead. When Neil paused to catch his breath Sebastian said bluntly, "Tell me what, if anything, this has to do with Eden Colter."

Neil's eyes blazed angrily but he controlled his temper long enough to explain what he knew about Lathrop's plan for acquiring the Emerald I, and Constanza's part in the plan. "According to Constanza, her men were only supposed to scare

Hugh into taking Eden and the baby back to New York. The murder was not part of the plan. I guess they figured Hugh would sell the ranch to Lathrop just to be rid of it.

"Thanks to our brave Captain Gerald, the men were caught and brought to trial, which left Constanza and Lathrop with a rather large problem. Not only hadn't they acquired the Emerald I, but if their men were convicted they just might turn in their employers to lighten the sentence. Darling Constanza took care of that by telling the outlaws exactly whom to implicate—me, of course—and by promising a last-minute rescue which, not surprisingly, never came off. The death of four men took care of one problem, but—"

"—But Lathrop still didn't have the ranch," Sebastian finished, disgusted by the story Neil had related. "So he decided to kidnap Eden, with ownership of the Emerald I his ransom price. Tell me: Once Lathrop has what he wants and Constanza is free, will you marry her?"

"Of course not," Neil growled. "Do you think I'd lower myself to marry the likes of her?"

"Her blood is pure, no matter how black her soul. That's all you care about," Sebastian retorted brutally. At Neil's distraught look Sebastian relented. "What will you do now?"

"I don't know." Neil slowly refilled his glass. "I meant to stay in Mexico but now . . . I can't send Eden back to Texas to face Lathrop all alone. I'll have to go back."

Sebastian's lips compressed into a thin line. "I wonder if that might be rather difficult, under the circumstances."

"I don't follow you."

"The men who were hanged told Captain Gerald that you were responsible for Hugh Colter's death. Whom do you think he's going to blame for Eden's disappearance?"

"Me," Neil muttered. "Look, Sebastian, what Gerald suspects doesn't matter. Once Eden is well I'll take her back to Texas and she can explain everything to the proper authorities. That should satisfy even Captain Gerald."

"It should," Sebastian agreed. "But what will you do about Constanza and Lathrop?"

"Damn it, Sebastian, I don't know!" Neil replied harshly. "I haven't had time to sort it all out yet, so stop asking questions!"

"You used to have all the answers," Sebastian reminded him.

"All of them wrong—is that what you're going to say?"

"That isn't what I meant."

"It's exactly what you meant," Neil shot back. "Go ahead. Say, 'I told you so' and get it off your chest."

"I want to help you, Neil," Sebastian said quietly, "but I can't unless you tell me how. For once in your life forget your pride and admit that you need someone."

"I'll handle it—by myself. There's no reason for you to be involved."

Sebastian stared at Neil for several moments. "As you wish." He rose and limped to the door, where he paused. "You might remember, however, that Eden Colter also is involved, whether you like it or not. Don't do anything that will place her or her child in jeopardy."

"Sebastian!" Neil's voice was drowned out by the slamming of the dining-room doors.

Enraged, and chafing under his brother's rebuke, Neil tossed off his drink and stalked out of the house. From Eden's bedroom Sebastian heard Neil gallop away, and with a sigh he returned to the window and his gloomy contemplation of the sea below. Once, years ago when they were children, he had fallen into those turbulent waters when he and Neil had escaped the eagle eye of their tutor and climbed down the cliff, an adventure expressly forbidden by their parents. Sebastian could still recall the heart-stopping panic he had felt when the waves closed over his head and the way the undertow had threatened to drag him out into the bottomless sea. Neil had saved him that day, Sebastian learned later, diving into the swirling water when his brother failed to reappear. Not only had Neil saved his life, but later Neil had taken the full responsibility for the escapade and had borne silently the whipping that followed—when in fact the entire affair had been instigated by Sebastian.

Sighing heavily, Sebastian massaged his aching thigh, remembering another time when Neil had saved him from certain death by risking his own life. The Battle of Querétaro still haunted Sebastian's dreams at times like these, when his leg pained him. Wounded himself, Neil had crawled through the battlefield to find Sebastian and drag him back to what passed as a field hospital. Even in those days some demon had lurked inside Neil, driving him into defiance of all authority and luring him into situations that were at best volatile, at worst explosive. Neil had had some control over his demon then, but now . . . now the demon seemed to be in control and there was hell to pay for those who stood in the way.

But still they were brothers, and friends as well. Sebastian's jaw set in a determined line. Perhaps there was still time to save Neil from himself, still a chance that the brother he had known could be resurrected. It was a slender thread of hope indeed, but Sebastian clung to it throughout the afternoon as he waited at Eden's bedside for Neil's return.

While her mind fought against the shock of killing another human being and wrestled with the trauma of her own abduction, Eden lay enveloped in dreams. Events straightened themselves out, forming an orderly chain that left her terrified when George's face loomed above her. There was no choice but to use the gun clutched tightly in her hand, and after the deafening roar of the shot Neil was beside her calming her with the simple force of his presence. The nightmare receded at the soothing touch of his hands as they brushed back the hair from her face. His voice was gentle, tender, the way it had been after their first lovemaking, and Eden wanted so badly to see his face, to see if Neil were smiling. . . .

"Hello."

A pair of golden eyes floated in the mist in front of her, and Eden tried to clear her vision. "Neil," she said in a cracked voice.

"Sebastian," a warm voice corrected, and Eden relaxed at the familiar name. The twin gold objects moved away briefly and then reappeared. An arm curled beneath her shoulders, lifting her upright, and a glass pressed against her lips. "Drink this. Are you having much pain?"

"No." The words came easier now but her eyes refused to focus properly. "Where is Neil?"

"Asleep." Had there been hesitation in that reply? She heard Sebastian move away, and a moment later her left ankle was being deftly examined. "He will look in on you the moment he awakens. Tell me when this hurts." Eden gasped in pain despite Sebastian's gentle touch and he eased her leg back onto the bed. "Forgive me for the pain, but you will be glad to know your ankle is only sprained, not broken. Given a few days in bed, it will heal nicely."

"I seem to be having trouble with my eyes, Sebastian," Eden said quietly.

"Ah, my fault." Sebastian's voice held a trace of laughter and was followed by the sound of a match being struck. Seconds later the room was illuminated as different lamps flared into life. "Better now?"

"Yes, thank you." Eden struggled upright in the bed. The room and its furnishings, though unfamiliar, were a welcome sight and she gave a sigh of relief.

Sebastian smiled and limped to the chair beside the bed. The smile gave way to a thoughtful expression as he checked Eden's pulse, heart and finally the pupils of her eyes. "Very good. Aside from your ankle there seems to be no lingering effect of your ordeal."

A chill ran through Eden at the thought of the two men lying dead and she shivered.

"Are you cold?"

Eden shook her head, realizing she had a few questions of her own. "How long have I been here—wherever here is?"

"About eight hours, and 'here' is my home and Neil's in Mexico." Sebastian paused. "Neil told me you rode all night."

"I really don't remember," Eden admitted ruefully. "What concerns me is going home. I just want to forget that any of this happened."

"You won't be able to travel for a couple of days, not without a great deal of discomfort, at any rate." Sebastian raised his hands helplessly at Eden's cry of protest. "I know you are anxious to return home, but I think it best to wait to give your ankle time to heal before you spend any length of time on a horse."

"My friends must be frantic by now," Eden pointed out. "They have no way of knowing that I'm safe. Is there some way I can get word to them?"

Sebastian shifted uncomfortably beneath the crystal gray stare, and after a prolonged silence he informed her, "There is a telegraph office about fifteen miles from here. If the lines haven't been cut by bandits and if the operator isn't drunk, you may be able to send a message to your friends."

Eden frowned, confused by his less than optimistic tone. "Sebastian, what is it? What's wrong?" She paled at a sudden, dreadful thought. "Is it Neil? Has something happened to him?"

"No, no." Sebastian hastily assured her. "When I last saw him he was fine; a trifle angry, perhaps, but in good health just the same."

"I don't understand." Eden's frown deepened. "Only a moment ago you said Neil was asleep and now you sound as if you don't know where he is."

"I don't," Sebastian confessed. "Neil and I argued and he rode off. Don't worry, though; he'll be back sometime in the morning, if not before. He just needs time to cool down."

"This sort of thing has happened before, I take it."

A grin surprisingly similar to Neil's own appeared and Sebastian nodded. "All the time, especially when we were growing up. He's probably in some *cantina* right now getting drunk and picking a fight."

"Oh!" Eden swallowed her surprise, despising the way her heart sank because Sebastian was at her side instead of Neil.

"Don't be concerned, Eden. Even when he's drunk Neil can handle himself better than most men when they're sober."

"I'm not worried," Eden replied caustically. "Though I would have thought one fight this week would have been enough."

"Is *that* what happened to his face?" Sebastian chuckled. "I hope he enjoyed himself."

Eden's eyes threw sparks into the room. "I'm sure he did. He and Keith Gerald fought over a woman."

Her tone warned Sebastian to change the topic. "Would you like dinner?" He rose, disappeared into an enormous walk-in closet and reappeared with a silver brocade dressing gown draped over his arm.

"I'd rather discuss arrangements for returning home." Wincing, Eden pulled herself to the edge of the bed.

"As you wish," Sebastian graciously conceded. "There are several riding habits in the closet. You are welcome to choose whichever one you like."

Biting her lip from pain, Eden slowly eased her legs to the floor. "I'm not trying to be difficult, Sebastian, and please don't think I'm not grateful for what you've done, because I am. It's just that . . ." Her voice trailed off. How could she possibly explain to Sebastian the mixed feelings being in this house aroused? Worse yet, how could she explain that she and Neil had once been involved with each other? She could remember all too well Neil sitting on the grass in Central Park, his eyes glowing as he described his home to an attentive young girl. Buried deep in her heart—shrouded in time and by another, gentler love—was the knowledge that Neil was a fever in her blood, the one grand passion of her life. A passion which, if allowed to run unchecked, would consume her all over again.

"You were saying?" Sebastian prompted when Eden's silence stretched to a full minute.

"I can't stay," Eden said firmly. "My daughter will be one year old in a matter of weeks. I want to be with her."

"And away from Neil as well?"

Eden looked at him sharply. "Don't be ridiculous." She jumped to her feet, only to fall heavily into Sebastian's arms a moment later, when her leg refused to bear her weight.

"Dinner first, I think," was Sebastian's only comment as he generously offered the silver brocade to a blushing Eden.

Still defiant, Eden stared at the garment with loathing. "Whom did it belong to?" she asked with a sniff of hatred. "One of Neil's mistresses, I suppose."

The tinge of jealousy in her voice startled, then amused Sebastian as he helped her into the dressing gown. If the lady were jealous then she must feel something for his profligate brother, and from the way Neil behaved whenever Eden was around, the feeling was mutual. With any luck at all, she might be the one person to reach Neil. Smiling, Sebastian replied, "She was a very important part of his life. In fact, you might even go so far as to say she made him what he is today."

"I can well imagine!"

Sebastian lifted Eden in his arms, silencing her protest with a stern look. "Do you really feel like debating your ability to walk?" When she shook her head, Sebastian grinned and started downstairs. "As I was saying about the former owner of that garment—"

"I don't care to hear about her," Eden said coolly.

"She was a fascinating woman," Sebastian continued. He carried Eden down the wide, curved staircase, past the framed portraits of the Saros ancestors, and paused near the bottom of the steps. "Charming, intelligent, witty; she influenced Neil and myself more than I could possibly explain. When she died Neil felt as if she had deliberately deserted him." Sebastian nodded toward the painting of a beautiful woman with golden eyes. "Our mother, Alicia. In some ways you are very much like her."

"Alicia," Eden murmured, intrigued by the face which stared at her from the canvas.

"Neil loved her very much—although he would not admit that to anyone, including himself." Sebastian smiled when Eden turned her gaze back to him. "You see, you need have no reservations concerning the garments at your disposal—they were Mother's."

Eden smiled faintly, wondering if she had betrayed her feelings to Sebastian. Beneath his alert gaze she flushed brightly, well aware that he was waiting for some response. She was spared the effort of making an oblique reply because Neil chose that moment for his return. The front door slammed shut, the jingle of spurs echoed through the foyer and moments later Neil appeared. Grim-faced, he froze at the sight of Eden in his brother's arms.

"Well, well." Neil smiled unpleasantly, leaned an arm on the balustrade and fixed Sebastian with a cold stare. "You must be a better doctor than I thought. I see the patient is already up and around."

"Welcome back." Sebastian's tone was equally cool. "We were about to go in to dinner. Care to join us?"

"Might just as well." Neil's eyes flicked over Eden, golden depths murky with what Eden thought was anger, and when she involuntarily cringed against Sebastian, Neil's expression hardened. "Feeling better?"

Eden nodded jerkily. "And you?"

Neil raised an eyebrow. "Never better." He turned on his heel and stalked off.

Dinner—once Eden was comfortably seated with her injured leg elevated on a chair—was an awkward affair which tore at Eden's nerves. So thick was the tension between the two men that Eden, trapped between Neil at one end of the table and Sebastian on the other, could scarcely taste the few bites of food she managed to force down. Sebastian, to his credit, made several attempts at light conversation, but Eden's replies fell far short of being scintillating and the withering glares Neil divided between his brother and the pale woman on his right effectively destroyed any pretense of civility.

"Well, pleasant as this has been, I'm afraid I must leave you two alone." Sebastian touched a napkin to the corners of his mouth and rose. "There are two patients in my hospital and I must look in on them before it gets too late."

"Must you go?" Eden blurted out. The moody silence Neil had maintained during the meal, as well as the amount of whiskey he had consumed, frightened and confused her, and she had no intention of being alone with him if she could help it. At Sebastian's curious look Eden hastily explained. "I mean . . . of course you must go, but could you take me back to my room first?"

"Is your leg bothering you?" When she shook her head, Sebastian glanced at his brother and smiled slightly. "Finish your coffee," he suggested, "and then have Neil take you to the library. As long as you are going to be our guest for a few days you might find a book for an entertaining diversion. I'll look in on you when I return."

When he was gone Eden concentrated on stirring cream into her coffee, all too aware of Neil's intense observation. Her ankle twinged painfully and she winced.

"That position can't be too comfortable."

She had been forced to sit parallel to the table in order to keep her foot elevated, and at Neil's words she stared ruefully at her bandaged limb. "It's all right. Sebastian said the worst should be over by tomorrow."

Neil lifted his glass in a mocking salute. "To Sebastian— would that we were all as perfect as he." Neil drained the liquid in two swallows. "What else did my brother tell you?"

Eden frowned. "I don't understand?"

"What did Sebastian tell you about the kidnaping?"

"Nothing." Eden eyed him warily. "Why are you acting this way? You practically drove Sebastian out of the house!"

"He's a big boy now," Neil sneered. "Sebastian can take care of himself. The problem is: What are we going to do with you?"

*"Do* with me!" Eden shrieked indignantly.

"You present a problem," Neil went on in a calm voice. "I'm not sure it's safe for either one of us to go back to Texas, yet obviously you can't stay here. Without a proper chaperone your reputation would be in shreds by the time you went home."

Eden laughed, genuinely amused. "Do you think for one minute that after what I've been through I give a damn about my reputation? What concerns me most right now is getting back to Shannon and forgetting this ever happened. Sebastian says I'll be ready to travel in a day or two, so I fail to see what problem I present. The journey back has to be easier than was the one coming here."

"The men who kidnaped you may try again."

"They are dead," Eden reminded him, confused by Neil's attitude. "Honestly, Neil, I should think you would jump at the chance to wash your hands of this business."

"You have no idea," Neil told her savagely, "how glad I'll be to forget about you and Keith Gerald and all the rest! My life was relatively simple until you dropped back into it. Why the *hell* did you have to come to Texas, Eden?"

"What does that have to do with anything?" Eden yelled. "Neil, you're not making sense. All I want is to go home and I don't understand why that's so difficult." Eden struggled to her feet and, clutching the table and chairs for support, started for the door. "I don't understand you, I never have. You are the only man I have ever known who deliberately complicates my life."

In a few long strides Neil was in front of her, golden eyes blazing angrily as he blocked her path. "You can't go back to Texas, not until I've checked a few things out."

Shaking with anger and sudden weakness, Eden reached out a hand to push Neil out of her way. "I intend to go home, with or without your help. I'm certain Sebastian can help me hire an escort back to the Emerald I."

Ignoring her feeble attempt to brush him aside, Neil framed Eden's face with his hands, forcing her to meet his gaze. "The two men we killed were hired to do a job, that's all. Don't you understand? Someone else planned the kidnaping."

Dumbfounded, Eden stared at Neil for a full minute while she struggled to regain her voice. "Who? Who planned it?"

"That doesn't matter," Neil said wearily. "What does matter is putting a stop to the whole thing before someone gets hurt."

"Two men are dead," Eden pointed out. "Someone has already been hurt!"

"I was thinking of you."

Eden shook her head dazedly. "If you know who planned this, then let's go to Keith with the information. Surely that's the simplest, most intelligent thing to do."

"I can't." As he spoke, Neil reluctantly pulled his hands away from her face.

"Why not?"

"Because by now Keith is certain I'm the one who kidnaped you. And because he would never believe the correct name." Neil drew a deep breath and continued in an emotionless voice.

"Sell the ranch, Eden. Give it away if you have to. A piece of land isn't worth your life, too."

Stunned, Eden sank into a chair, unable to believe what she was hearing. "Are you telling me that everything that has happened was over the ranch?" When Neil nodded it was as if a stake had been driven through her heart. "And Hugh? Was Hugh killed for the same reason?"

Neil nodded again, hating himself more each minute as Eden's eyes filled with tears. "I know it doesn't help, but Hugh's death was an accident. He was only supposed to be frightened into taking you back to New York."

"How do you know all this?" Eden forced the words through stiff lips, more than a little afraid of hearing the answer.

"I was told."

"When?" Struggling for composure, Eden clenched her hands in the folds of the dressing gown.

"Sweetheart, don't do this—"

"Tell me," Eden demanded shrilly. "I have a right to know!"

Neil took the chair next to Eden and studied the pattern of the polished wood as he spoke. "I found out yesterday when I asked Constanza to return to Mexico with me."

"Constanza?" Eden fought to retain what self-control she still had. "What does she have to do with this?"

"She was my fiancée." Neil sighed and as briefly as possible described to Eden the bizarre events of the past five years. The arrogance and self-pity which had been present in his conversation with Sebastian disappeared as he explained everything to the woman at his side. The plan of which he had once been so proud sounded tawdry now, and any redeeming qualities it might once have possessed evaporated in the face of that steady, icy gray stare. Only when he told Eden the story about the men who had hanged for Hugh's murder did a flicker of emotion enter Eden's eyes. When Neil was finished, Eden remained stonily silent and he felt compelled to add, "Try not to judge Constanza too harshly, Eden. Her family nearly lost everything to the Revolution, a loss she simply couldn't accept."

The flintiness in Eden's eyes increased until they looked like chips of crystal. "Don't defend her actions to me, Neil; don't paint her as a blushing innocent. And you—all this time you knew what was happening. The rustling, my men being used for target practice, you *knew* all about those things! How could you live with yourself? And what about Julio? You claim that you didn't know him, yet his name is in a report on you that was filed with Hugh by the Pinkerton Agency five years ago! I don't believe anything you're saying!"

"Sweetheart—"

"Don't call me that!"

"All right," Neil conceded. "Eden, I didn't know until yesterday who was behind the rustlers. Maybe if I hadn't been so damn blind I would have figured it out a long time ago. But I didn't. As for Julio, the man who was hanged just happens to have the same name as a friend of mine. I can introduce my Julio to you tomorrow if you like."

"So my husband loses his life while Lathrop ends up with everything he wants. What a pity you had to discover your precious Constanza had feet of clay." Eden rose and hobbled to the door, unmindful of the shooting pain in her leg.

"Eden, wait! I didn't know about the circumstances of Hugh's death until yesterday, I swear."

"The same old Neil," Eden said dully. "Always proclaiming his innocence. Have you ever in your entire life spared a thought for the people who pay the price for your snobbery?" She sighed heavily, feeling the tears start to her eyes. "I hope Keith does arrest you—and Constanza and Lathrop, too. That's one trial I'd enjoy attending. In fact, I may just turn you in myself."

"Listen to me, Eden. Please."

"*I can't!*" Eden's voice was brittle. "I can't listen to this any longer!"

Neil had followed Eden and now stood behind her, resisting the impulse to take her into his arms. "You shouldn't be using that leg. Let me take you back to your room."

"Don't touch me!" Eden shrank from the outstretched hand. "Don't come near me—the very thought of you makes my stomach turn."

"I'm sorry," Neil said quietly.

"You always are," Eden returned bitterly. "Unfortunately, by the time you're sorry the damage has already been done."

She limped out of the room, the tears which streamed down her cheeks unseen by Neil. With one hand gripping the door he listened until the halting footsteps were out of hearing. Eden hated him now, that much was certain, and the knowledge left Neil with an overwhelming sense of loss.

"So you told her."

Neil looked up to find Sebastian studying him and nodded. "I told her. Isn't that what you wanted?"

"Not what I wanted, Neil, but what had to be. Judging from your expression I would guess Eden took it badly." Sebastian crossed the foyer to stand in front of his brother.

"What did you expect?" Neil ground out. *"Damn!* I never intended to hurt her again."

"I know. The situation is doubly painful because you love her."

Neil's eyes flashed. "You don't know what you're talking about."

"No?" Sebastian reached out and flicked the watch out of Neil's pocket. "Why do you carry this, then?"

"It's a good timepiece, that's all." Neil shrugged. "No sense in letting it sit in a drawer when I can use it."

"Sure, and I suppose this is your good-luck piece because it keeps such accurate time."

"Leave it alone, Sebastian." Neil snatched the watch back, but both men knew he wasn't talking about the piece of jewelry.

"Why don't you stop trying to prove what an unfeeling lout you are?" Sebastian asked with a touch of anger. "You're only fooling Eden and she is the last one you should lie to."

"Mind your own business," Neil growled. "Besides, it's too late."

"Then turn back time. Use that single-mindedness you possess to your own advantage for a change. For the first time you have something you should fight to keep and you are giving up before the first blow. If you let her slip through your fingers you are a fool."

When Sebastian knocked on the door, Eden hastily wiped at her damp cheeks and turned to the window before he entered. "Come in."

"You shouldn't be on your feet," Sebastian chided, frowning when the figure at the window didn't budge.

"How are your patients?" Eden asked, unwilling to be drawn into any conversation which might turn personal.

"Obedient, for the most part." Sebastian straightened the covers of the bed and fluffed the pillows. "Come lie down."

"I'd rather not." Eden pushed the mass of blond hair away from her face. "I detest lying in bed when I can't sleep."

"Insomnia?" Sebastian inquired solicitously. "I can give you something for that."

"No, thank you." Eden pressed a hand to her burning eyes. "I'd just like to be left alone right now."

"He's not all bad, you know." The soft words drew a harsh laugh from Eden, and Sebastian stared thoughtfully at the carpet. "Do you hate him so much?"

"Sebastian, *you* don't understand." Eden groaned, the sound a mixture of despair and anger. "How could I have been so blind? After all the discussions Hugh and Keith had about the rustlers, I should at least have been bright enough to connect what they said about an 'inside job' to Lathrop. Keith did, and I'll bet Hugh did, too."

"You could not have known. Constanza and Lathrop planned well; they made all the evidence point to Neil. Had you suspected anyone it would have been Neil; and you would have been wrong, just as Captain Gerald is wrong."

Eden shook her head. "This is all happening so fast—there's so much I don't understand. Why did Neil stay in Texas all this time?"

"He stayed out of pride and honor. He believed Constanza was desperately unhappy, that she needed him. Would you not want Neil to do the same for you?"

Eden whirled and faced Sebastian, eyes sparkling with fury. "In my case," she informed him with a grim smile, "Neil was less than heroic! When I needed him most he was sailing to Mexico with another woman. Even after he told me the truth about Constanza—something I would have done well to remember—I still loved him. On my wedding day it wasn't Hugh I thought of, it was Neil! Just when I thought I was over him, just when my life had regained a semblance of normalcy, he had to reappear and turn everything upside down again!"

"Neil is not responsible for Hugh's death," Sebastian said. "Nor was he responsible for your kidnaping." Eden gestured impatiently but Sebastian continued. "I know him. Neil will do everything in his power to stop what is happening."

"How noble!"

Sebastian smiled faintly. "He is not noble, Eden. Who knows that better than we? But at the same time we expect him to be better than anyone else. I expect more from him than I do from my friends, and you expect him to be perfect. Both of us know better, but still our folly continues. Why do you suppose that is?"

"Maybe because he has more room for improvement than anyone else," Eden responded acidly.

"I prefer to think it is because we care about him—love him, if you will."

Eden snorted. "Not a chance. For two cents I'd hand him over to Keith right now."

"Would you indeed?" At her gathering frown, Sebastian decided a strategic retreat was called for. "You are not Constanza. You would not cause an innocent man's death."

During a restless, sleepless night Eden tried to examine Neil's information with logic rather than emotion, but the dawn found a thoroughly confused Eden sitting in a chair by the window. The gulf waters sparkled far below, and Eden shifted uncomfortably. For all the questions she had asked herself during the night, she had found an answer to only one: There was a portion of her heart which still loved Neil.

She also knew Lathrop had to be stopped. Financially the Emerald I could stand the loss of some stolen cattle, but Lathrop presented a greater threat than that. Because of Neil, Eden could not go to Keith—yet neither could she think of a way to stop Lathrop without involving the law.

"Morning."

Eden jumped at the sound of Neil's voice and, twisting around in her chair, she found Neil standing just inside the open door. "Don't you ever knock?" she asked sharply, hoping her sudden breathlessness didn't show in her voice.

"I did." Neil sauntered across the room. "Three times. When you didn't answer I thought I'd better see if you were still here."

"Where else would I be?"

Neil shrugged. "You have a habit of doing the unexpected, Eden. You could have been halfway to Texas by now." He contemplated the mauve shadows under the clear, gray eyes. "How are you feeling?"

"Better." Eden toyed with the folds of the gown's skirt. "Where's Sebastian?"

"Attending a delivery. I'm afraid you're stuck with me." Neil extended his hand. "I'll take you down to breakfast if you're ready."

Eden pulled herself out of the chair, pointedly ignoring Neil's proffered hand. She didn't dare allow Neil to touch her, not if she wanted to keep a clear head. There was too much at stake to risk falling under Neil's spell again—too many questions had gone unresolved last night, and Eden needed answers before she could return home.

"Let me help." Before Eden could sense his intention, Neil had scooped her into his arms and was holding her against his chest.

"Put me down!" Eden ordered indignantly.

"Sorry, but I can't do that." Neil's expression softened, although his eyes remained hooded. "Sebastian wants you off your feet for another day and he'll have my hide if I don't follow his instructions."

"I'm not an invalid," Eden protested, "and I resent being treated like one."

"Resent it all you like," Neil returned, all too aware of the way Eden's body fitted against his own. The blood surged through his veins, carrying an immediate response to her closeness.

Eden averted her face as Neil carried her through the house, chastising her capricious, wanton body with every step. After all she had learned about Neil, how could he still wield such power over her? Why did the icy hatred she had willed herself to feel toward him evaporate the moment she set eyes upon him?

"I stayed up most of the night," Eden said unexpectedly, midway through the meal. Neil stopped chewing, golden eyes suddenly wary as he studied her, and Eden concentrated on circling the rim of her cup with a slender forefinger. "What I said to you last night about turning you in to Keith . . . I wasn't thinking clearly just then."

Neil's gaze suddenly pinned her to the chair. "What about Constanza and Lathrop?"

"I don't know." Forcing a look of composure, Eden returned Neil's gaze steadily, ignoring the erratic beating of her heart. "Obviously I can't go to Keith because of the way Lathrop has framed you, but neither can I allow Lathrop and Constanza to go scot-free. They deserve to be punished."

"Yes, they do," Neil agreed softly. "Look, Eden, the simplest way out of this is to go to Keith Gerald and tell him everything."

"That won't work," Eden argued, dreading the thought of Neil being tried and sentenced to prison—or death.

"Why not?"

Eden gulped, casting about for a reasonable answer. "Well . . . to begin with, Keith would need evidence or witnesses, something we can't provide. Even if you testified, it would be your word against Lathrop's, and a good attorney would cut your story to ribbons. Second, Lathrop owns most of the county and the people in it. Any trial would be a mockery of justice."

"Then try for a change of venue—hold the trial in Dallas or Laredo."

"I said no," Eden replied vehemently, her nerves stretched to the limit. "I won't have it! Keith holds a personal grudge against the rustlers, and he thinks you're behind them. Do you really think your story would change his mind?"

"Maybe, maybe not." Neil shrugged. "It's worth a chance. As long as Lathrop is free you'll be in danger, and that, sweet Eden, is a fact."

A challenging light flared in her eyes. "If Lathrop is brought to trial, Constanza will be implicated. Will you testify against her as well?" When Neil didn't answer after several minutes Eden sighed, wishing the unforeseen ache in her heart would disappear. "You see, the legal way won't work."

Neil must not have heard Eden's last statement because he finally answered, "Constanza will have to stand trial as well. She's as guilty as Lathrop." He pushed at the food on his plate, speaking more to himself than to Eden. "I've been wrong about Constanza and a lot of other things in the past. Oddly enough, I used to consider myself a very good judge of character, but where Constanza was concerned I had a blind spot a mile wide and just as deep. Do you suppose Keith and the other ranchers would understand if I told them I was insane for the past five years?"

Eden bowed her head. "People in love have been known to commit strange, inexplicable deeds. I doubt there is anyone alive who hasn't done something in the name of love." She drew a shaky breath. "We've strayed from the subject, I'm afraid."

"Have we?" Neil watched her intently. "I don't think so."

"About Lathrop and Constanza," Eden reminded him, anxious to turn his thoughts away from herself. "What can we do?"

Neil smiled indulgently, willing to abide by Eden's wishes,

at least for the moment. "Since you're against going to Keith Gerald, all we can do is play by Lathrop's rules, which means arming ourselves to the teeth."

"You make it sound like a war."

Neil looked thoughtful. "It will be, don't delude yourself. Lathrop has no qualms about killing to get what he wants, so we have to be willing to fight for what is ours."

Eden raised her eyes to Neil. "Ours? This isn't your fight, Neil. There's no need for you or your men to be involved. I can handle whatever Lathrop throws at me."

"Of that I have no doubt, love, but in any war it helps to have an ally. Maudie and her friends would be more than willing to help, but that would place them in danger, too. Besides they don't have the men or the money I do to back you up."

"Money isn't everything," Eden grumbled.

Neil laughed. "Maybe not, but it certainly helps. Suppose we have to hire a killer to deal with Lathrop?" At Eden's gasp he nodded sympathetically. "I don't like the idea any better than you do, but once we're into this thing we'll have to ignore the fact that we are supposedly civilized people."

"What about Keith?"

"What about him?" Neil demanded. "If he's very lucky he won't get killed in the crossfire."

Eden buried her face in her hands. "All this over a piece of land! I can't bear the thought of people being killed because of Lathrop's greed and my stubbornness."

Rising, Neil went to her side and gently pulled her hands away. "Then let me go to Keith and tell him everything—he may hate my guts but he'll listen to me. Even if Keith doesn't believe me, Lathrop will know Keith is suspicious of him, and that may be enough to make Lathrop pull back."

"Or it could make Lathrop completely ruthless." Her eyes dark with fear, Eden gazed at the tanned face.

"That is a possibility," Neil conceded, fascinated by the play of sunlight through the shimmering mass of golden curls. "But I don't think even Lathrop would be stupid enough to take such a risk."

"You could wind up in prison," Eden pointed out in a barely audible voice.

"In which case you can come on visiting days and tell me what a fool I was," Neil said in a lame attempt at humor. Eden didn't respond and Neil added, "I'm willing to take the chance, sweetheart."

"No," Eden whispered, shaking her head. "There has to be another way." Neil's hand slipped beneath her chin, lifting her face to meet his own, and Eden knew she was powerless to stop what would surely follow.

"It's the devil or the sea, love. We've run out of choices, but we'll stand together." He meant only to brush his lips over hers in a reassuring, comforting gesture, but when their lips met an explosion took place inside Neil's head. His free arm found its way around Eden's shoulders, and he pulled Eden upward to savor the wild delight of her body. Neil waited for her to pull away, to pummel his chest with her fists, and was shocked when instead Eden's arms circled his neck. Her lips parted softly beneath his own, and with a muffled exclamation of pleasure Neil found himself going back in time as his tongue plundered the recesses of her mouth.

For Eden, the kiss erased all other considerations from her mind. Her head fell back against Neil's arm as she passionately returned his caresses, unaware of time or place. There was no guilt, only a sense of peace and the exquisite knowledge that she was, at last, exactly where she belonged.

His senses reeling, Neil pulled back first, shaken by the force of Eden's response and his own alarming emotions. "It's been a long time," he managed to say.

Eden nodded in solemn agreement, wondering if Neil could hear the thunderous beating of her heart.

"You've changed," Neil added, trapped by a pair of mist-gray eyes which, somehow, demanded that there be no misunderstanding between them this time. "I guess I expected the Eden I knew five years ago."

"Disappointed?" Eden asked.

Neil smiled wickedly, his golden eyes cloudy with passion. "It's too soon to tell. Can I answer that later?"

"Of course." Eden's gaze shifted to his lean, brown hands. "You must understand one thing, Neil: This won't be New York all over again. This time we have to know each other first."

Neil's smile changed rapidly into a frown. "If you're talking about marriage—"

"Did I mention marriage?" Eden interrupted. "I'm sorry to disappoint you, but I have no intention of marrying again. Even if I did, I rather doubt I would want to marry you; you're very poor husband material. And aside from that, I have to think of Shannon—somehow I can't see you as a father."

Neil's frown deepened and Eden smiled, remembering very well Neil's view of marriage. The question was: How would he react when the tables were turned?

Neil eyed her curiously. "Then what do you mean by our knowing each other?"

"Simply that." Eden traced his throat with one finger. "Choosing a lover is something which requires a great deal of thought. Don't you agree?"

Neil stared at her in disbelief. "I suppose so, but—"

"Then you must also agree that we must first see if we are as compatible out of bed as we are in it."

Neil took a step back. "I'm afraid I don't follow you, sweetheart."

"Let me explain." Eden's voice held a note of exaggerated patience. "Some women are quite content to enter into casual love affairs. I am not. We could go upstairs right now and I'm certain we would both enjoy the lovemaking tremendously; but I'm not in the market for stud service."

"You want some sort of commitment, then."

Eden smiled. "Exactly."

"A marriage without the license." Neil snorted. "You'll still be putting a ring through my nose."

"Not at all. If you find a woman more to your taste, you will be free to terminate our relationship without any arguments or recriminations on my part."

"What's the catch?"

"No catch," Eden assured him. "As you once said, there is some sort of attraction between us from which we cannot escape. You wanted to explore it with me as your mistress; I am simply proposing a more balanced relationship."

"I see." Golden eyes narrowed, Neil thoughtfully stroked his moustache. "You make it sound like a business merger."

Laughing, Eden extended her hand and drew Neil back to her side. "That, lover, is because when you touch me all reason deserts me. I just want everything clear before I fall under your spell again."

This time it was Eden who initiated the kiss, and when she allowed her passion free rein it was not only Eden who lost all sense of time and place. Would he ever love her? Eden wondered desperately as Neil's kiss became more demanding. Given enough time, could there be more between them than just desire?

"This won't be like New York," Neil promised, his lips leaving a scorching trail down the slim column of Eden's throat. "This will be far better."

Eden's eyes closed, the back of her head coming to rest in the palm of Neil's left hand. This is madness, Eden thought dazedly as his moustache brushed sensuously across her flesh. There were so many reasons to keep Neil at arm's length, the most compelling of which was the love she bore him. She was no longer a naïve sixteen-year-old; she was a woman who understood the rules governing men and women. She was . . . Neil's mouth was on her own, seeking, probing, and desire shivered along Eden's spine. No, Eden told herself desperately as reason fled; I won't be taken this easily! She meant to push Neil away, to halt the responses weakening her limbs— but when her hands encountered Neil's chest she did no more than caress the muscles which rippled beneath his shirt.

"Oh, Neil . . . don't," Eden protested weakly when he lavished feathery kisses upon her upturned face. Words were her final weapon—surely they would penetrate Neil's ardor.

"How do I stop, love?" Neil murmured, his right hand sliding upward from her waist to cup her breast. He caught Eden's lower lip in his teeth and tugged gently. "All these months, watching you . . . not being able to touch . . ." He crushed Eden against him, inflamed by the press of their bodies. "God, Eden, it's so good to hold you again!"

Neil's mouth descended once more and Eden met it with undisguised hunger. He had deflected her weapon, turned it back upon her with devastating accuracy . . . and Eden found it didn't matter, not now. She grew pliant in his embrace, wanting to lose herself in the lean, hard frame. Eden stroked his shoulders, then tangled her fingers in the waves of his black hair as his tongue took urgent possession of her mouth.

Neil pulled away with a groan, then traced the inviting curve of Eden's ear with his lips. "Eden, *querida*—"

Eden melted in his embrace, the last of her stubborn resistance evaporating. My love, Eden answered silently as she was lifted high in Neil's arms and carried through the hacienda. My own, dearest love. Neil's heart was pounding against her breast, and Eden turned her face into the taut muscles of his neck. The

fragrance of his cologne bit into her nostrils—a clean, masculine aroma which imprinted itself upon her senses. A door
closed, a distraction that brought her eyes open. They were in
her bedroom, Eden noted, and then her breath caught sharply
when she encountered Neil's molten gaze. His eyes were a
golden snare, tempting Eden with the promise of passion, and
the embers of her own desire caught flame.

Their clothing fell away, no barrier to Neil's eager fingers,
and Eden sighed as the bed replaced the cushion of Neil's arms.
She ached for Neil's touch, and moaned softly when his caresses unleashed the full tide of her desire. Her hands skimmed
the length of him, enjoying the rippling muscles beneath the
bronze flesh. The hard proof of Neil's desire burned against
her hip and, purring, Eden stroked him with loving care.

Past all rational thought, Neil tightened a hand in Eden's
hair and rolled her onto her side. His mouth greedily claimed
her breasts, torturing the rosy peaks until her cry filled Neil
with the savage need to make Eden his. Eden's leg swept
upward over his own hard-muscled limb, inviting possession,
and with a harsh growl Neil buried himself in the soft, welcoming flesh. Eden gasped as Neil filled her, awed by the
pleasure which engulfed her senses. Passion rose in ever-increasing waves and Eden clung desperately to Neil, their
mouths muting each other's ecstatic cries when the fury of their
joining broke over them.

Trembling, Eden lay in Neil's arms, her leaping heart slowly
falling into a steady pattern. She was trapped against his hard
form, acutely aware of the way their bodies fit together, of the
way her leg hooked wantonly over Neil's lean hip. A slow
flush spread upward from the base of Eden's throat but when
she tried to pull away Neil pressed his hand into the small of
her back, stilling her movement.

"You, my love, are beautiful," Neil whispered against her
ear. Too embarrassed to answer, Eden buried her face in his
shoulder and was incensed at the laughter her action provoked.
"I was right, sweetheart, you have changed . . . and I'm anything but disappointed."

"Neil, don't," Eden whispered. Torn between basking in
the afterglow of their passion or crying over the destruction of
her good resolutions, Eden wanted only to be left alone.

"Shh." Neil stroked her hair comfortingly, mistaking the
emotion behind her broken whisper. "I've dreamed of this,

Eden, of having you respond the way you just did. Your pleasure increases mine, love." He raised Eden's face to his and
kissed her gently, thoroughly. "As I promised, my sweet, this
time will be far better."

Eden thought to explain but Neil's kiss left her confused,
lightheaded. His embrace was warm, comforting, and in spite
of her turmoil Eden quieted. Neil's breath stirred the hair at
her temples and with a sigh Eden rested a hand on his neck.
Her eyes slowly closed and she drifted into a dreamless sleep.


Sebastian returned that afternoon to find Neil lounging on
the terrace. Neil looked so damnably content that it irked Sebastian no end. Just like Neil, Sebastian thought with an annoyance born of a night without sleep. He comes home, throws
the entire household into disorder and then casually waits for
the dust to settle. Vexed, Sebastian dropped his medical bag
on a table with a clatter. Neil was out of his chair in the next
instant, his gun drawn and pointed toward the disturbance.

"How heartwarming to see your reactions have not deserted
you," Sebastian commented drily. "Must you wear that in this
house?"

"Sorry—force of habit, I guess." Neil holstered the gun
before he leisurely unbuckled the gun belt and laid it aside.
"What put you into such a foul humor?"

"Two hours' sleep and a difficult labor," Sebastian replied
bitingly. "Add to that the fact that I have to worry about you—
just what kind of a mood would you expect me to be in?"

Neil grinned infuriatingly and pushed a chair toward his
brother. "Sit down, little brother, and have a drink."

Sebastian grunted and sank wearily onto the chair. "Where
is Eden? I want to check her ankle while I can still see straight."

"Upstairs, asleep. She didn't get much rest last night." Neil
took the chair across from Sebastian. "We're going back to
Texas as soon as Eden can travel."

"We? You and Eden?" Sebastian raised an eyebrow.

Neil shrugged. "Once Eden sets foot on her ranch she'll be
in danger again. I can't just take her back and dump her into
Lathrop's lap."

"Of course not." Sebastian chuckled. "Have you discussed
your gallant plan with the lady in question, or are you planning
to bull your way into her life again? From what Eden said last

night, I think she would be quite happy if you dropped off the edge of the earth."

"Is that so?" Neil leaned forward and trapped Sebastian with a knowing look. "Women are such mercurial creatures, Sebastian. You mustn't believe everything they say, particularly when they're angry."

"A fascinating observation," Sebastian remarked. "But you still have not answered my question."

Neil grinned. "Let's just say . . . Eden and I have formed an alliance."

"Against Lathrop?"

"Partly." The grin abruptly left Neil's face and he scowled into his glass. "She's gotten some silly notions into her head, though."

"Are you going to tell me, or do you plan to stare at your drink until your eyes cross?" When Neil didn't answer, Sebastian prodded, "Don't tell me you are finally going to do the smart thing and marry her?"

"Don't be absurd," Neil snapped. Then after a long pause he added, "Besides, Eden said she's not ready to get married again. She told me straight out—before I even had a chance to tell her I wasn't interested in marriage."

Sebastian choked on his drink and the coughing fit which ensued thankfully covered his glee. So Eden was using Neil's own strategy against him! Shrewd woman, Sebastian applauded silently. In a matter of weeks Eden would drive Neil to distraction. Sebastian eyed his brother furtively, fully enjoying his confusion.

"Where are you going?" Neil inquired when Sebastian rose and started to go inside.

"To check on Eden," Sebastian called over his shoulder. "Then I am going to bed before I fall asleep on my feet."

"But I want to talk to you," Neil objected.

"About what? You are the ladies' man in this house, not I." Sebastian threw Neil a jaunty salute. "I wish you luck, big brother. God knows you are going to need it."

Eden was awake when Sebastian tapped on her door, and when he entered she greeted him with a smile.

"How are you feeling, Eden?"

"Much better, thank you." Eden watched as Sebastian, whistling merrily, unbandaged her ankle. "I must say, Sebastian, you don't sound as awful as you look."

Sebastian's eyes danced with laughter. "I received some interesting news upon my return that improved my outlook immensely. I understand you and Neil are joining forces against Lathrop." Eden nodded and Sebastian helped her to her feet. "Walk around the room, please." As she complied, Sebastian resumed nonchalantly, "I thought you were going to turn Neil over to Captain Gerald."

Eden shrugged. "I changed my mind."

"You can sit down now." Sebastian gently examined the puffy flesh and nodded approvingly. "If you are still anxious to return home, you can leave day after tomorrow. How does that sound?"

"Marvelous," Eden exclaimed. "I'm tired of being carted from one room to another like a invalid."

"From now on you are on your own." Sebastian smiled. "If you like I will order a bath for you, and you are free to wear any of the clothes in the closet."

"Thank you, Sebastian. You're very kind."

"It is the least I can do—after all, you have to put up with my brother as your dinner companion this evening." Under his frankly curious stare Eden reddened and Sebastian patted her hand encouragingly. "Don't let up on him, Eden. Between the two of us we may knock some sense into Neil yet."

Eden blushed even harder but she managed to keep her voice level when she spoke. "I don't hold out a lot of hope for that particular miracle, Sebastian."

"But you have accepted his offer of help all the same, yes?" After a moment's consideration, Sebastian counseled, "You need only have patience, Eden. Neil does not give his loyalty or affection lightly, but once he does, he is unwavering in his devotion."

"A fact to which Constanza can surely attest," Eden retorted acidly.

"If you cannot forgive him for that error in judgment, blatant though it was, then perhaps it would be kindest if you did not allow him to become involved with you again."

Eden sniffed. "Apparently you don't know the nature of our liaison a few years ago. It was terribly one-sided—all on my part. This time I intend to take a few precautions, Sebastian. I'm not going to run into the same brick wall twice."

"I see." Sebastian rose and limped to the door, where he turned and regarded her thoughtfully. "Believe it or not, the 'liaison,' as you call it, was not entirely one-sided. Neil is not the easiest person to fathom; at times he can be a mass of contradictions. Have you seen the watch Neil always carries, the one he calls his talisman? No? Then I suggest you ask him for the time when you are together tonight."

Eden frowned at the curious advice. "Why on earth should I do that?"

"Doctor's orders," Sebastian replied enigmatically. With a slight bow he was gone, the door closing softly behind him.

Sebastian was playing matchmaker, Eden thought as she bathed and hunted through the closet for a suitable gown. His good intentions notwithstanding, she fully intended to be on her guard with Neil. If Neil ever discovered how she truly felt she would be utterly defenseless and then, when he left her as he had before, there would be no way to deny the pain. She was not going to be used and tossed aside again.

Despite the exacting rules Eden laid out for herself, she dressed with special care for dinner. Much to her surprise, Eden found that the gowns and matching shoes all fit her perfectly and she tried on one after another before settling on a burgundy taffeta with a plunging décolletage. If the bold display of gleaming, alabaster skin caused Eden any discomfort after nearly a year of being swathed in widow's black, she rationalized that in two months—the end of January—her period of mourning officially ended. Still, as she walked along the veranda which adorned the second floor, Eden's conscience continued to nag at her. This was the wrong time to become involved with Neil; to even think of such a thing when Lathrop posed such a deadly threat seemed pure folly. And what of Shannon? The thought of her daughter brought a sharp pang to Eden's heart. In dismay she came to an abrupt halt. By confronting Lathrop would she be placing Shannon in danger? Was Lathrop so demented that he would imperil a child's life to gain a parcel of land?

Heartsick, Eden gazed at the crashing waves far below. Whatever she felt for Neil, no matter how badly she wanted things to work out between them, Shannon was her first consideration. At the first sign that Shannon was in peril because of her mother's defiance, Eden would capitulate to Lathrop's demands.

The pungent scent of a cheroot intruded upon her thoughts and Eden spun around to discover Neil standing in the shadows behind her. "Must you sneak up on me like that?" Eden questioned angrily in spite of the wild lurch her heart gave.

White teeth flashed in the twilight as Neil smiled and moved forward. "My apologies—but you brought this upon yourself, love."

"I did not!"

"Ah, but you did," Neil countered in a tone of mock reproof. He stepped to the railing and tossed the cheroot into the sea before facing Eden. "You ventured into my territory, sweet; these doors lead to my bedroom." At her apprehensive look, Neil's smile flashed again. "I have a very good sherry inside if you would care to partake before dinner."

"I think not," Eden retorted, taking a step backward. "Your bedroom is hardly conducive to rational conversation."

Neil laughed softly. "How do you know, my sweet? Have you been snooping about during my absence?"

"Of course not," Eden replied indignantly, the color rising in her cheeks.

"Then you can't possibly know whether this bedroom is a den of depravity or simply a room which contains a bed." Smiling, Neil playfully chucked Eden under the chin. "Wouldn't you like to find out?"

"Not on your life!" Eden batted his hand away. "In spite of what happened this afternoon, I meant what I said about this not being New York."

The golden eyes lost their teasing light. "You want to be wooed and courted like some simpering virgin, is that it?"

"Not at all," Eden shot back. "I just want us both to be sure this time around. Now that we know what we can ... be like together"—Eden had the good grace to blush—"we have to see if it will last."

"I see." Neil eyed her thoughtfully.

"No, you don't, or you wouldn't have made such a ridiculous suggestion! I'm not going to hop into bed with you just because you snap your fingers, Neil."

The fine state of outraged emotion Eden was embarking upon vanished when Neil muttered, "Oh, the hell with it," and pulled her lips to his own.

It was like being consumed by liquid fire and, helpless, Eden melted against Neil, all prudent thought receding beneath the onslaught of his kiss. Only when Neil drew back did Eden remember all her protests and by then it was too late—she was too weak to say what should have been said minutes before.

"You can slap me if it will make you feel any better," Neil said after a long pause.

She was, in fact, ready to do just that, but for some reason her arm refused to obey her command. At last Eden shook her head and asked dully, "What purpose would that serve?"

Eden drew a deep, deliberate breath to steady herself and discovered she was totally unprepared for what happened next.

"You, sweet Eden, are the only woman I have never been sure of," Neil informed her in a voice lower than his normal register. "Five years ago you hid behind so many reflections of yourself that I felt I was talking to a different girl every time we met. One day you would be so cold that I was frostbitten if I came within three feet of you, and the next . . . the next you were like flame, searing my brain with the memory of a single afternoon. No matter how hard I tried to forget you, no matter how many women I had, that one damned memory always burned in my mind." He stopped, angry that he had revealed more of himself than he had intended, and lit another cigar. For several minutes Neil smoked in silence before adding, "You're my one weakness, sweet; too bad I'm not yours."

"How do you know you aren't?" Eden asked in a trembling voice.

"Then why are you resisting what we both know is inevitable?" Neil ground out. "Damn it, Eden, I want you! I could make love to you right now, with or without your consent, and I *swear* I wouldn't have any regrets afterward."

"That's the problem," Eden pointed out in an icy tone. "I'd be just like all the others and nothing would have changed between us."

Neil groaned in sheer frustration. "I don't understand you! First you say you want the same thing I do and the next minute you say just the opposite. Woman, what the devil do you want?"

"Dinner," Eden replied with a lighthearted smile. Apparently unintimidated by the dangerous glint in Neil's eyes, she took his arm. "I'm absolutely famished. Aren't you?"

Thwarted by her rejection of intimacy as well as her tacit refusal to be drawn into an argument, Neil could only lead her down the steps from the veranda to the patio, where dinner had already been laid.

"How romantic," Eden said archly as Neil handed her into a chair. She lifted her wineglass and sipped at the contents while Neil took his seat across from her. "Excellent. Is it your intention, sir, to ply me with moonlight and wine?"

"If that were the case, madame, I would have selected a much stronger liquor, since moonlight plainly has no effect upon you," Neil returned in a low growl.

Eden chuckled and raised her glass, reminding him in a soft voice, "You once asked me if we could exchange more than two words without one of us becoming angry. Do you remember?"

Neil inclined his head. "I remember."

"I thought you might—we agreed upon a truce and we managed to spend a pleasant afternoon together. Do you suppose we might reach a similar understanding now?" Neil's glowering expression remained intact, despite the gentle, teasing smile which curved Eden's lips. Stubborn man, Eden thought as she leaned forward, purposefully placing herself in his line of vision. "We can make no progress, Neil dear, if you refuse to speak to me. Truce?"

The neckline of Eden's gown dipped lower as she moved, displaying the alabaster swell of her bosom. Adjusting his position to accommodate the suddenly restricting material of his trousers, Neil wondered if Eden had the slightest idea of the effect she was having on him. Neil's hand tightened around the stem of his glass and in a hushed voice he warned, "Don't push me too far, Eden dear."

Surprisingly, Eden laughed. "I have no intention of pushing you, lover. It's just that this time around you and I are going to understand each other." She moved her glass a fraction of an inch closer to his. "Agreed?"

The crystalline gaze refused to waver and Neil capitulated with a sigh, touching the rim of his glass to Eden's. "Agreed. You leave me no choice, Eden; either I abide by your rules or I lose you."

"Exactly." Eden sipped at the wine, then returned her attention to the meal. "I hope that situation sounds vaguely familiar, Neil. You offered me a similar one in New York."

"You rejected it, I seem to recall," Neil said pointedly. "Maybe I should do the same."

Eden's shoulders lifted slightly. "As you wish."

"Damn it, Eden!" Neil began, only to swallow the angry

words when a pair of gray eyes riveted him to the chair. "My apologies; I forgot we are under a truce."

"Forgiven." Eden accepted the apology with undisguised generosity. "I'm certain I'll have my lapses as well."

"Let's hope so," Neil muttered, decidedly uncomfortable with his new role of supplicant. It appeared that for the first time in his life he was not going to have everything his own way.

They succeeded in getting through the meal without further mishap, although Neil's replies to Eden's comments about the weather and the hacienda and surrounding land came with a great deal of effort.

"I noticed a path along the cliffs," Eden said as Neil politely held her chair when the meal was completed. "Could we go for a walk there?"

"It's not much of a path," Neil informed her gruffly, "and you're not exactly dressed for blazing a trail."

"Neither are you," Eden retorted, indicating his suit. "But I'm game if you are."

"Your ankle—"

"I'll let you know if it bothers me." Gray eyes flashed challengingly before Eden bent to remove her shoes and silk stockings.

A slender, infinitely tempting leg was bared to Neil's smoldering gaze and he fought to keep an iron hand on his passion. "Jesus, Eden," he murmured thickly. "What are you trying to do, drive me crazy?"

"A gentleman would turn his back," Eden bantered lightly, not ceasing her movement even when she felt Neil take a step toward her.

"I'm not a gentleman."

"I know—I was simply giving you the benefit of the doubt." Eden straightened and smoothed her skirt back into place. "Besides, since you've seen far more of me than just my leg, modesty at this point is rather superfluous."

"That all depends on how you feel about being ravished," Neil replied harshly. Shrugging out of his jacket and tie, Neil reached for her hand and started toward the cliff. "I feel like a damnfool kid."

"Why?" Eden panted, breathless from the pace he was setting.

"Hell if I know." Neil came to an abrupt halt and stared down at Eden. "I only feel this way when I'm around you."

Hesitantly, Eden brought a hand up to caress Neil's cheek. His strong, bronze hand covered her own, moving it from his cheek to his lips, where he pressed a warm, deliberate kiss into the palm. Eden sighed. "You don't give up easily."

"Never," he whispered against her flesh. Slowly Neil's free arm circled her waist, drawing her toward him.

"You promised," Eden protested weakly, the buttons of Neil's shirt pressing against her bare skin.

"So I did—but I didn't promise I wouldn't touch you, or hold you... or kiss you." Neil's lips grazed Eden's, leaving them both breathless despite the briefness of the contact. His golden eyes unreadable, Neil gently released her. "I keep my promises, my sweet; just tell me when you're ready to end this charade." When Eden simply stared at him, Neil took her hand again. "Come with me. There's a place farther down the path where we can rest and... talk."

She followed him mindlessly, fully aware that she was courting her own seduction yet unable to save herself. Amazingly, Neil was true to his word, for when they reached a spot where the ground leveled off, Neil sat down and indicated the spot beside him.

"I can't," Eden demurred. "I might ruin the gown."

Neil gave her an odd smile. "It's yours to ruin, love. Sit down." When she hesitated Neil gently but firmly pulled her down to his side.

"What do you mean?" Eden struggled against the force Neil was exerting. "I thought the gown was your mother's."

"Is that what Sebastian told you!" Neil stared at her, then threw back his head and laughed. "Remind me to speak to my brother about the sin of lying."

Frowning at this impudent display of hilarity, Eden demanded, "Will you please tell me what you find so amusing?"

"Certainly, my love." Before Eden could rise, Neil gave a hearty tug on her arm which sent her spilling onto the ground next to him.

"Let me up!" Eden clamored when Neil rolled to his side and pinned her between his arms.

"Don't you want to know the story behind your gown?" Neil teased.

"Yes, but—"

"Then listen," Neil commanded with a grin. "Five years ago I met a most enchanting woman in New York, and when it seemed that she was going to return to Mexico with me, I purchased an entire wardrobe for her. A surprise, you might say, for when we reached Mexico." With a lean forefinger Neil traced the neckline of the gown, chuckling when he felt Eden shiver. "All for you, sweet Eden. You left me with a closet full of clothes and no one to wear them. I think you owe me at least a kiss for that. Don't you?"

Eden's eyes widened in alarm as she stared at Neil. "I had no idea—"

"Of course you didn't. That was, I thought, the beauty of my plan." Neil touched his lips to the valley between her breasts. "Didn't you find it the least bit odd that all the clothes fit you so well?"

"How did you manage all that in such a short time?" Eden questioned, anxious to distract Neil. "How did you know everything would fit?"

Neil sighed in affected exasperation and propped his chin in one hand. "For the first, as you are undoubtedly aware, enough money makes anything possible."

"And for the second?" Eden prompted when he fell silent.

"Guesswork, for the most part." The offhand reply didn't quite ring true even to his own ears, and Neil smiled lamely. "Must I confess all to you?"

Eden swallowed nervously. "Not if you don't want to."

The golden eyes glowed, raking Eden from head to toe before returning to her face. "I remembered you," Neil said slowly. "Every curve, every hollow—I remembered them all. For the seamstress I simply had to convert my memories into inches. Five years is a long time to live on memories, Eden; at least it is for me."

It was an enormous confession for Neil to make, Eden realized, but there was a question in his words as well. She had no intention of giving him the answer that easily.

Her silence brought a scowl to Neil's face and he sat up, presenting his back to Eden as he gazed at the sea. "It wasn't the same for you, was it?"

Eden sat up, too, and shrugged, hugging her knees to her chest. "I had a husband, and a marriage I thought would last forever. When I lost your baby I came very close to hating you—and then, when one of the specialists in Europe told me that the reason I was losing Hugh's babies was due to that first miscarriage, I really did hate you. Eventually, after the last two miscarriages, I didn't even hate you anymore. I was simply numb."

Neil turned and found Eden with her head cradled in her arms, her eyes closed. "I'm sorry, Eden."

Eden nodded but kept her eyes tightly shut. "By the time we moved to Lathrop I was sure I didn't feel anything for you; but that night at Constanza's party, when I saw you again, the entire world turned upside down.

"Don't misunderstand me, Neil. I cared for Hugh very much; over the years I grew to love him. But I guess you were always there, hidden away in the back of my mind where I didn't have to examine how I felt about you." Eden's eyes flickered open and she thoughtfully studied the movements of the waves. "That's why I want to get to know you before . . . well, before. I have to find out if I like you as you really are, or if I'm still caught up in some adolescent fantasy. At sixteen you were my one adventure, but I'm twenty-one now. I have to know, Neil, or nothing will ever work between us."

They sat in silence for several minutes, each caught up in thought until Neil slowly nodded. "I think I understand. Hard as it is going to be, I won't push you for an answer."

Their eyes met and Eden smiled tremulously. "Thank you. Believe me, Neil, I'm not playing the tease."

"I know that, love; you're not the type." Neil rose and offered his hand. When Eden was on her feet he added, "I still want you, Eden. Remember that when you're sorting everything out."

Eden nodded and they walked back to the hacienda.

From his bedroom Sebastian watched as Neil bid Eden good night on the patio without so much as a chaste kiss. A complacent smile lifted the corners of Sebastian's mouth. It appeared to be a promising beginning.

# Chapter 17

Captain Keith Gerald, his bland expression betraying nothing of his inner rage, was seated in an armchair in Neil Banning's ranch house awaiting the owner's return. A murderous glint entered his blue eyes as Keith remembered riding onto the Emerald I and finding Eden standing at the well, deep in conversation with Vincent. Keith had been overjoyed when he'd learned from the sheriff that Eden was safe, but his initial reaction gradually had been replaced by anger as Eden had related how Neil Banning had miraculously come to her rescue. She so obviously believed Banning to be some kind of hero after this feat that Keith had wasted no time sharing his suspicions about Neil Banning with Eden, even including Manuel's confession that Neil had hired Hugh's killers. Eden's reaction had been to shake her head and tell Keith he was mistaken. As he waited, Keith clenched his fists, recalling the unshakable faith which had shone in Eden's eyes as she defended Neil.

At last, frustrated beyond belief, Keith had given up trying to prove to Eden what a bastard Neil Banning really was. Instead he had taken Eden's hand and, at long last, declared his love for her and asked her to be his wife. His proposal had rendered Eden speechless and Keith, thinking she might be unsure of his motives, had taken Eden into his arms and kissed her passionately. He told her of his love in a husky voice, asked for permission to court her properly.

"Oh, Keith, I'm sorry," Eden had replied, her eyes luminous. "You're a fine man. Any woman would be proud to be your wife but . . . I'm afraid I don't feel the way you obviously do. I'm honored and flattered that you asked me—"

He hadn't allowed her to finish, not when he knew why Eden had turned down his proposal. "You're in love with Banning, aren't you? I'll bet he 'rescued' you and then seduced you and you're so bewitched by the man that you can't see he planned the entire episode!" Keith had mounted his horse and stared bitterly at Eden. "We'll see how you feel when Banning is behind bars—when he's convicted of rustling, murder and

449

kidnaping. I'm going to put him away for a very long time—if he doesn't get a death sentence—and when that's done, you and I are going to have this discussion again!"

Keith came back to the present with a start. Drawing a deep, ragged breath, he brought his temper under control. There was no evidence on which to arrest Neil Banning, but until he managed to gather that evidence he could at least drive a wedge between Banning and Eden. Keith allowed himself a tight smile, relishing the upcoming confrontation.

The unfamiliar horse tied in front of the house put Neil on his guard and when, upon dismounting, he recognized the Ranger brand on the animal Neil swore to himself. Keith Gerald had come to pay his respects. No doubt the Ranger had returned from searching for Eden and had learned of her rescue. Neil thoughtfully stroked his moustache. He and Eden had told the sheriff the truth, although Neil had omitted the fact that he had actually been looking for Eden and had told the sheriff only that he had stumbled across Eden and her kidnapers while en route to Mexico. Everyone had believed the story. But would Keith Gerald?

Neil stared at the house for several minutes, considering the relative merits of making Keith Gerald wait. It wouldn't work, Neil admitted at last. There might come a time when he would need Gerald, so it would be best not to inflame their already antagonistic relationship. Steeling himself against what he knew would be at best an unpleasant conversation, Neil strode into the house.

"Good evening, Captain," Neil said coolly, the door closing softly behind him. "To what do I owe this pleasure?"

Not bothering to rise from the chair, Keith answered contemptuously, "This is no pleasure, Banning, believe me."

"My opinion exactly, but I didn't want to seem rude," Neil snarled in reply. "However, since you're here I assume you have some business with me." Neil unfastened his gun belt and tossed it carelessly onto the desk. "I would appreciate it if you would make it short, though. I have plans for tonight."

"With Eden?" Keith's mouth twisted into a smile. "Don't waste your time."

Neil shrugged, thinking he understood the venom in Keith's words. "It's my time; I guess I can spend it any way I please."

Keith's eyes filled with malice. "You were smart, Banning, telling Eden about my suspicions of you—you even managed to convince her of your innocence. Nothing I said or did shook her faith in you."

For a full minute Neil stared at the other man, his golden eyes growing as hard and flat as polished stones. "I take it you know that I'm the one who found her."

"I know."

"In that case I don't see that you and I have anything to discuss." Neil directed a pointed look at the door.

"I couldn't convince Eden that you were anything but a hero," Keith continued as if Neil hadn't spoken. "Even telling her about Manuel's confession had no effect. I did, however, manage to convince Eden that running a ranch was hardly a fitting occupation for a woman such as herself."

Neil's eyes narrowed. "I don't follow you."

"No?" Keith suddenly smiled. "Let me explain. I've asked Eden to marry me."

The casual words slammed into Neil like a bullet tearing through his vitals. The power of speech deserted Neil and he stared wordlessly at the Ranger.

"By the way," Keith added when it was obvious Neil intended to remain silent, "you'll find yourself short two hands. I ordered my men back to Laredo while you were in Mexico."

Neil ignored Keith's last statement. "What did Eden say?" he asked in something approaching his normal voice.

Keith's smile widened and, rising, he walked to the door. "She didn't say 'no,' Banning." It was the truth, in a way. Eden never had come right out and said "no," but Neil couldn't know that.

Every fiber of his being screamed out at Neil to wipe the smirk off Keith's face, and it took his last ounce of willpower not to strike him. This was one time he had to control his temper, because if he didn't Eden would be left to face Lathrop on her own when Neil was convicted and sentenced for killing a captain of the Texas Rangers.

For a long time after Keith's departure Neil stood unmoving in the center of the room, a muscle working furiously in his jaw. *She didn't say "no."* In a savage movement Neil lashed out at the closest object, a low table in front of the sofa. One kick of his foot sent ivory chess pieces skittering across the tile floor. Something withered inside him in the vicinity of his heart and Neil slumped into a chair. Part of him—a very large part—refused to believe what Keith had just said, but there was a nagging doubt in the back of his mind which threatened his confidence.

Eden was still shaken by her kidnaping; Neil knew that in spite of her brave front. And returning home to find that one of her branding crews had been shot up in her absence had done little for her state of mind. Groaning, Neil rubbed a hand over his face. Much as he wanted to, he couldn't burst into Eden's home and demand to know if she planned to marry Keith Gerald. He would wait for Eden, Neil decided; wait for her to come to him and tell him what had happened. They were still united against Lathrop, so she would have to talk to him eventually.

A full two weeks had passed since Eden's difficult encounter with Keith Gerald, and in that time she hadn't seen or heard from Neil. She heard *about* Neil, though, thanks to Ian and Vincent, and what they told Eden made her furious. It seemed Neil was dividing his time among drinking, carousing with the women above the saloon, taking pretty young girls for rides in the country. And, Ian had added with a slow wink when Eden had urged him to continue, rumor had it that Constanza Williams had paid Neil a visit and stayed longer than was quite appropriate.

Although her life resumed its normal pattern—playing with Shannon or chatting with Millicent when she wasn't overseeing the work on the ranch—Eden seethed inwardly. Only Vincent knew her true feelings, and he had learned them purely by accident. Vincent had, unbeknownst to Eden, gone to Lathrop Williams on the night Eden had returned home and had—by means Eden now wished she did not know—convinced Lathrop to disband his rustlers and give up any plans he had for obtaining the Emerald I. After due consideration, Vincent had come to Eden and told her of the bluff he had run with Lathrop—that if harm came either to Eden or Shannon, Vincent would see to it that Lathrop would not live to enjoy the Emerald I. And if not Vincent himself, then one of his friends from the old days.

"You did what?" Eden had exploded in so uncharacteristic a manner that Vincent's eyes had widened a fraction of an inch. "Damn it, Vincent, you had no right!"

"Yes, ma'am, I did," Vincent had argued. "You can't let a man like Lathrop Williams know you're scared. If he gets a whiff of your fear he'll be all over you like a coyote over a carcass."

Eden had gone suddenly still, her face ashen. "Vincent, how do you know Lathrop Williams had me kidnaped—or that he leads the rustlers?"

"I was Lathrop's bodyguard for seven years. After a while I was no more than a piece of furniture to him; he forgot I could still see and hear." Vincent shrugged. "He's a careful man, but in my case Lathrop Williams made a big mistake, a mistake he doesn't dare try to correct because he can't be certain how much I know or what I've told others."

"That's why you came to work here, isn't it?" Eden had inquired softly. "You were trying to protect me without letting me know."

Eden could have sworn Vincent reddened, but when he spoke there was no hint of embarrassment in his voice. "My first wife and I had a child—a little girl with pale curls and deep blue eyes. I like to think that if the renegades hadn't killed her she would have grown up to be something like you."

"Oh, Vincent." Tears shimmering in her eyes, Eden had placed a hand on his arm. "Thank you—for everything."

Vincent had smiled one of his rare smiles. "I'm glad you said that, Mrs. Colter, because when I was putting the fear of God into Lathrop Williams, I happened to mention that I was acting under your orders."

Eden had moaned. "You and Neil Banning are aging me rapidly! As if I don't have enough trouble with you making threats in my name, Neil—" She stopped abruptly, unwilling to admit to anyone how deeply Neil's absence hurt.

"Seems to me Mr. Banning's missing something in his life," Vincent had stated blandly. "Never did see a man as stubborn as that one, or so temperamental. Maybe you should ride over and see what's eating him."

"I don't think so," Eden retorted with a sniff. "I'm not the least bit interested in Neil Banning or his problems."

"That's a pity, considering how his ears perk up whenever Ian happens to mention you."

Again recalling Vincent's words, Eden rose from the chair behind Hugh's desk—her desk now—and blew out the lamps in the study. As she made her way to her bedroom Eden couldn't help wondering if Constanza had somehow managed to worm her way back into Neil's good graces. Surely not!

Eden sighed heavily as she undressed and slipped into her nightgown. She could speculate to her heart's content, even defend Neil to herself, but the fact remained that she had neither seen nor heard from him since he had delivered her safely back to the Emerald I. Well, she refused to go crawling to Neil and beg him to explain his absence. Neil could damn well come to her—as any *gentleman* would—and tell her that he had changed his mind since Mexico. Eden delivered a solid punch to her pillow and willed herself to fall asleep.

It was still dark when Eden awoke and she lay unmoving, heart pounding, listening to the sounds of the night as she tried to determine what had disturbed her rest. No cries or sounds of distress came from the nursery, so it could not have been Shannon. The night sounds were all familiar—nothing there that would awaken her. Then what? She forced her ears to hear every noise, suddenly wary of sitting up and looking around.

From behind her, Eden heard the faint click of the door, and her breath caught in her lungs. Someone was in her room! Frozen with terror, Eden now sensed rather than heard the intruder. He was standing at the foot of the bed, watching her, and Eden's mind raced frantically. She could scream, that would bring the guards who were supposedly patrolling the buildings, but if the intruder had made it this far the guards may have already been eliminated. Eden forced herself to lie still, trying to control the panic which flooded her as she resumed what she hoped was the normal breathing pattern of sleep. Her gun was her only hope of defense, but it lay on the nightstand at the other side of the bed. If she were careful she might be able to work her way across the mattress and reach the pistol before the intruder realized what she was doing.

Feigning sleep, Eden thrashed against the covers as if caught in the throes of a nightmare and turned onto her back. Her left arm was flung toward the edge of the bed now, and Eden flexed her hand, pretending to ward off some private horror. Just a bit farther, Eden told herself as she moaned softly, not daring to move any more just yet. She had to make the intruder believe her act, like setting the hook in a fish's mouth before landing it. A full minute passed before Eden turned again, this time onto her stomach, allowing her right arm to dangle limply over the edge of the mattress.

Although every nerve demanded action Eden bided her time, waiting for any opening the intruder might give. If his attention

wandered for even a second, her chances of reaching her
weapon would be greatly improved. Toward that end Eden
twisted slightly, allowing the shoulder of her nightgown to slip.
A good portion of her alabaster skin was exposed, and when
she felt the devouring gaze flicker over her partially revealed
breast Eden's hand flashed toward the gun.

With equal suddenness her arm was seized in an iron grip
and another hand was clamped firmly over her mouth. She had
misjudged! The intruder had not been at the foot of the bed at
all, but rather at its edge, and had caught her before she was
even halfway to her goal. Cringing, her right arm pinned behind
her back by an unyielding masculine hand, Eden was unceremoniously flipped onto her back, and in a last desperate attempt at freedom she sought to rake her captor's face with the
nails of her free hand. Again she misjudged, for where Eden
had thought to find vulnerable flesh she found only air as the
intruder jerked his head backward.

"Easy, sweetheart," came the harsh whisper. "I don't relish
having my face ripped apart."

Eden froze at the familiar voice and with a muffled cry she
stared unbelievingly into a pair of golden eyes.

Neil laughed softly, apparently amused by her reaction, and
easily lifted her stiff body upright. "If you promise not to
scream I'll take my hand away from your mouth. Promise?"

Silver-gray eyes narrowed defiantly and Eden raised her left
hand to strike again.

"I wouldn't, sweetheart." Neil increased the angle on her
imprisoned arm, drawing a whimper of pain from Eden. "I
don't want to hurt you, Eden, I only want to talk. There's a
hard way and an easy way to accomplish that, and right about
now I don't care which one you choose. Which will it be?"

After a moment's contemplation, Eden lowered her arm and
nodded slightly.

"Good." Neil cautiously removed his hand, smiling when
Eden sucked in a gasp of air. "Sorry, sweetheart; I didn't know
you were suffocating."

"A lot you care," Eden hissed, unable to steady her breathing.

"Oddly enough, I do."

"Sure," Eden replied acidly, her emotions in such a tumult
that she barely knew what she was saying. "That's why you
break into my house in the middle of the night and scare the

wits out of me. If this is the way you care for people, then thank God you don't love me—I don't think my heart could take the strain!"

"Don't be too sure," Neil said cryptically, pulling her upward until the tips of her breasts brushed his chest. "You may find my love easier to bear than my passion."

He freed Eden so abruptly that she fell back against the pillow. Her eyes wide in astonishment, she watched him move to the foot of the bed. A veil had fallen over those glowing eyes and Eden carefully eased herself into a sitting position.

"You're quite an actress, sweetheart," Neil congratulated her in a silken tone. "If I hadn't moved closer for a better look at what you were displaying you might have blown my head off. I guess there's something to be said for lust after all."

The moonlight, thankfully, concealed Eden's reddened cheeks, but just the same she hastily adjusted the revealing neckline of the nightgown. "Had I known it was you," she quipped in return, "I wouldn't have bothered with the dramatics, since you seem to be able to see right through a woman's apparel."

"Not all women," Neil corrected with a sardonic smile. "And where you are concerned I have an insatiable curiosity, despite what I already know."

Eden sniffed and pulled her knees up to her chin, arranging the folds of her garment so that when she looked at him again only her face and a modest portion of her neck were revealed by the long-sleeved nightgown. With deliberate impudence Eden allowed her eyes to wander over Neil in the same fashion he had just assessed her. Handsome is as handsome does, Eden thought flippantly, but just the same she couldn't deny the attraction she felt for the man in front of her.

"You look like you're going to a funeral," Eden commented saucily, noting Neil's unrelieved black garb. "No gun, no spurs, not even a hat—you must have had to dress in a hurry. What happened? Did the lady's husband come home unexpectedly?"

The odd note in her voice brought a scowl to Neil's face. "What the hell are you talking about?"

"Nothing," Eden muttered as she subsided back onto her pillow. Her position was far too vulnerable for the moment and it was making her defensive. The wisest thing to do was to let Neil say whatever was on his mind so that he could leave.

From his vantage point at the foot of the bed Neil watched

as Eden withdrew into herself. Like a flower drawing up all its petals against the night air, Neil thought irrelevantly. Neil couldn't fathom her injured dignity, and he propped a booted foot against the bottom of the bed. He had been stewing over Eden and Keith Gerald for a full two weeks until finally, in spite of his resolve that Eden would have to come to him, Neil could no longer stand the doubts which plagued him. It came to Neil, in an agonizing flash, that he cared for Eden. He didn't love her, of course, but he had a tenderness for her he had never felt for another woman, and the thought of losing her to Keith Gerald wounded him more deeply than had Constanza's betrayal. Might as well get it over with, he told himself now.

"Are you going to marry Keith Gerald?"

Eden's head snapped up and she stared unblinking into Neil's face. "Where did you hear that?"

"From Gerald, where else?" was Neil's cutting answer. "Is it true?"

Eden's jaw set defiantly. "You seem to have decided already, so why ask me?"

"Woman, I swear if you don't give me a straight answer in one minute you're going to be kidnaped again. This time by me," Neil warned.

"To what end?" Eden rejoined waspishly.

Neil's golden eyes narrowed wickedly, raking Eden from head to toe as he stripped her naked without even touching her. Eden shivered. "Now you know, sweetheart. This time my brother won't be around to play chaperone and your pleas and excuses won't mean a damned thing. I'll have you when and where I want, as often as I want."

"You're threatening me with rape," Eden cried softly.

"Take it any way you so desire." Neil shrugged. Their voices, out of consideration for the infant next door, had been kept low, but his next words flayed Eden's nerves in spite of their softness. *"Tell me, Eden, and tell me now before I lose my temper."*

Shaken, miserable, Eden shook her head. "Keith proposed, but I turned him down. If he told you anything else—"

"He told me you didn't say 'no'!"

Eden licked her dry lips. "Perhaps I didn't come right out and say 'no,' but Keith couldn't possibly have misunderstood. I refused."

Neil swore and Eden—wounded pride coming to the fore—

glared up at him. "Now that you have your answer you can get the hell out of my house," she hissed angrily. "Go back to Constanza or whoever your *entertainment* is for this evening."

Neil's face darkened. "What the hell are you talking about?"

"Oh, you miserable—" Modesty forgotten, Eden rose to her knees and shook her fist at Neil. "Don't you dare play innocent with me! You're the talk of Lathrop. Every woman—young or old, single or married—is fair game to you. I understand Constanza even paid you a visit."

"You're well informed, considering the fact that you haven't set foot off the ranch since we got back from Mexico."

"My spies are everywhere," Eden retorted. "Besides, you aren't exactly discreet! I find the situation appalling!"

"So do I," Neil answered quietly. "But not for the same reason you do. I've been waiting for you for two weeks, Eden; waiting for you to come and tell me that Keith Gerald proposed to you."

Eden gave a snort of disbelief and flung herself out of the bed. "You were well occupied during your vigil. How is Constanza, by the way? I hope she's not too disappointed that her plans for me didn't work out."

A muscle worked in Neil's cheek and he controlled his temper with an effort. "For your information, sweetheart, I've seen Constanza exactly once. She couldn't wait to tell me that Vincent broke into Lathrop's library, threatened him with a long, agonizing death at the hands of some of his old friends if Lathrop ever put you in danger again, then knocked him out and left him trussed up like a Thanksgiving turkey."

Eden paused in the act of shrugging into her robe. "Vincent did all that? My God, Lathrop must be mad as a hornet."

"Lathrop's more frightened than angry. It's Constanza who's fit to be tied." Neil watched as Eden firmly belted the robe around her waist. "Lathrop has called off his rustlers and he's keeping a low profile, but if I know Constanza she's doing her best to convince him that you and Vincent were bluffing."

"Vincent gets all the credit for Lathrop's change of heart—he decided to act in my name. At least he was kind enough to tell me about it. Although," Eden added thoughtfully, "he certainly omitted a few of the details."

"A sin we've all been guilty of," Neil said, taking a step away from the foot of the bed. "Between the things Constanza and Keith Gerald told me, I've been half out of my mind these past two weeks."

Wary of his movement and his words, Eden looked at Neil sharply. "You'll understand if I don't believe you."

"Is it so hard for you to understand that I was afraid Keith was telling the truth?" Neil countered. "Hell, Eden, what else could I think? It sure explained why I hadn't seen or heard from you."

She and Neil were, Eden realized with a pang, their own worst enemies. In a hushed, brooding voice she said, "We seem to be forever at odds, don't we? You distrust me, I distrust you, and that overshadows everything else."

Neil nodded, his thoughts running parallel to Eden's. "Any suggestions as to how we overcome this barrier?"

"Maybe we can't," Eden replied bluntly. "Learning to trust another person isn't easy under the best of circumstances, and we not only have to contend with Lathrop and Constanza and Keith but with our own past as well. I can't help remembering New York."

"Neither can I."

To Eden's surprise Neil took his watch from his vest and tossed it onto the bed between them. Curious, Eden picked up the watch, then gasped as the back fell open and she stared in shocked disbelief at the miniature portrait of herself. Sebastian's prescription flashed into her mind.

"I would have given it back," Neil said defensively, "but you ran out of my hotel room before I had the chance." Eden shook her head, transfixed by this moment from the past. Before she could marshal her chaotic thoughts, Neil rounded the bed and took her face in his hands. "We have an opportunity to be together again, yet we've already torn each other apart by holding back, by pretending that we don't care."

Eden, acutely aware of Neil's physical presence, sighed heavily and tried to look away, but Neil held her immobile. "I'm afraid of you, Neil; afraid of the power you have over me," she confessed at last. "And I'll never be sure of you. Your women—"

"Shut up," Neil ordered roughly.

In the next moment Eden was in his arms, her breasts flattened against his chest. Neil's lips ground angrily against hers for several seconds until, unexpectedly, the pressure lessened. He coaxed a response from Eden now, teasing her mouth lightly with his own until she strained upward to maintain the contact. It was exquisite torture, ending finally when Neil trailed kisses across her cheek and touched his lips to her eyelids.

Slowly, Eden opened her eyes and looked into the familiar golden gaze. "What happens next, Neil? A quick game of musical beds?"

Neil frowned, hating Eden's icy withdrawal. "I want you, Eden." His voice was ragged. "I won't deny that I've been seen with other women—but I haven't laid a hand on any of them, regardless of what you think. You're the one I want; not an endless parade of women." He gently stroked her cheek.

"You know how to find your way through all my defenses," Eden said in a trembling voice. "That's why I'm so afraid of you."

"Don't be," Neil whispered. "I've finally realized that when I hurt you I also hurt myself. Years ago Sebastian told me I was in love with you. Maybe I am—I don't know. I *do* know I can't stand the thought of losing you again."

Eden's anger melted away. "It's so very complicated, isn't it? Trying to deal with Keith and Lathrop while we learn about each other."

"No one said it would be easy, but I didn't risk my neck getting you away from Lathrop's hired thugs for Gerald's benefit." Neil smiled for the first time. "And since I can't send you someplace safe I guess I'll just have to stay with you as much as possible."

Still smiling, Neil lowered his head toward Eden. Sighing, Eden lightly rested her hands against his chest and gave herself up to Neil's kiss. How warm his lips were, how gentle as they pried her own apart. Like coming home, Eden thought as she twined her arms around Neil's neck. Some inner part of herself knew that she and Neil should be together like this. Their mutual desire allowed no other course. All her rationalizations and demands were unimportant. Neil had cared enough to come to her tonight, and at this moment nothing else mattered.

"Stay, then, for a few hours," Eden murmured when Neil's mouth left hers. She molded herself provocatively against him. "Protect me, keep me safe. Make love to me. I need you tonight."

Eden's lips fastened burningly on his and with a groan of despair Neil felt himself overcome by a sweet, aching passion. "Witch," he muttered thickly as Eden's hands slid beneath his shirt. He buried his face in the curve of her neck, senses reeling at the scent of her perfume, the pliancy of her body. Her touch seared Neil to the core of his being. He gasped with desire as his hands unerringly found the hollows and swells through the material of her robe. Neil endured the rapturous torment for as long as he dared and then gently, firmly captured Eden's hands in his and held them still.

"Come." Eden's voice was low as she drew Neil toward the bed.

It took every shred of self-control, as well as the unexpected appearance of a long-forgotten streak of decency, for Neil to deny his passion. With a desperate smile he backed away from Eden, longing to touch her again but not daring to do so.

"Neil?" Eden's eyes mirrored her confusion. "Don't you want me?"

"Oh, love," Neil replied in a strained voice. "You don't know how much I *do* want you. If I don't leave in the next few minutes I won't leave at all."

"It doesn't matter."

"Yes, it does, to me." Neil took a deep, steadying breath. "In Mexico you said we had to know each other first. Until a few minutes ago I didn't realize how right you were. I want you more than any other woman I've ever known—you're in my blood, Eden; but there's so much more I have to learn about you."

Incredulous, Eden watched as Neil retreated to the window. "You're not leaving that way!"

With one leg thrown out the window, Neil shrugged. "It's the way I came in. Unlike our days in New York, I had a care for your reputation tonight. I left my horse a good half mile from your house. I made it through your guards unseen and unheard, and I damned near broke my neck climbing up to your bedroom window. Now, after going to all that trouble, I'm sure not going to ruin everything by walking out your front door."

"You'll fall!"

"Not a chance." Neil balanced on the sill, golden eyes alight as they caressed Eden from a safe distance. "I'll see you tomorrow, love—or I should say, later this morning. Go back to bed now—dream of me."

A new door had opened on their relationship, and the thought brought a smile to Eden's lips as she returned to her bed. All she and Neil needed now was the patience to walk through that door together.

Somehow—through the arguments, recriminations and accusations of that night—Neil and Eden managed to achieve a lasting if tenuous peace. Their differing opinions often led to vociferous discussions, but if their disagreements were inconclusive they also unfailingly cleared the air between them. Neil curbed his impatience at such times, resisting the urge to take Eden and kiss her into submission; for he knew, instinctively, that resentment would follow any forced ardor.

He grew to know Eden, to learn the many facets of the woman who so intrigued him. He had already suspected that she possessed a strong business acumen, but the variety of her capabilities and the depth of her emotions were new to Neil. He watched as she signed the papers for the sale of Thackery Ltd. to Matthew Kelly without batting an eye, and then she was reduced to tears when she learned that one of the men seriously injured by the rustlers during the time of her abduction was facing the amputation of his arm because of infection. When her tears were dried she insisted on riding into town and talking with the injured man. She emerged from the interview with a grim set to her jaw and fired off a telegram first to David Sterling and later to Dallas, to a colleague Dr. Sterling had recommended. The doctor came and performed a second operation, and after several sleepless nights announced the ebbing of both fever and infection in his patient. Expecting Eden to be overjoyed by the news, Neil was astonished when Eden coolly thanked the physician and calmly escorted him to the door. Only when they were alone did Eden catch Neil's hands and dance with him merrily around the study until she collapsed in delighted laughter. So much for her imperturbable façade, Neil thought wryly.

There was, on the other hand, no facade between Eden and Shannon, Neil soon discovered. Shannon was obviously the joy of Eden's life, and Eden was fiercely devoted to her child. Such devotion did not, however, curtail sharp reprimands when they were warranted, and when Shannon's eyes welled with tears and her bottom lip quivered, Neil occasionally came to the rescue with some trinket magically produced from his pocket. At such times Eden felt duty-bound to make dire predictions about the effect such spoiling would have on her offspring, but Neil would simply grin and haul Shannon onto his lap while Eden shook her head in tolerant amusement. Had it not been for the fact that Eden paled whenever she encountered an unknown face among the hired men, Neil would have believed that she had put her kidnaping behind her. Instead, he watched as she subdued her fear and set about reestablishing a life for herself and Shannon.

Neil found himself spending more and more time at the Emerald I. He still was worried about Eden's safety—Lathrop had stopped his rustling, but he could be expected to make more trouble one way or another. More often than not Neil arrived at the Emerald I in midafternoon and stayed late into the evening. He enjoyed Eden's company—and Shannon's too—even though Neil and Eden sometimes did little more than discuss the day's events or read aloud from one of the books which lined the study. Shannon was usually patient with such foolish behavior, but at times she would loudly voice her desire for more rigorous entertainment, and Neil was only too happy to oblige. Shannon, to her delight, found a playmate whose stamina far outlasted her mother's, and after an hour or two of hard play she was more than willing to fall asleep in Neil's arms.

If—as Neil always had believed—familiarity bred contempt, he should have lost interest in Eden long before; but as Christmas approached and Eden gave no hint that he was to be invited to join the Colters' celebration, Neil's spirits plummeted. No matter how often he chastised himself for acting like a lovesick youth, Neil couldn't help feeling disappointed. Every time he looked at the cache of presents he had so carefully chosen and wrapped, the absence of Eden's invitation was rammed home with a vengeance. The tacit message was obvious: He was not welcome on this special occasion.

With Christmas only a few days away, Neil arrived at the Emerald I to find Eden with Millicent busily decorating the house, and Neil found it possible to hide his disappointment when Eden handed him a hammer and nail and asked him to hang the wreath on the front door.

"It won't last long, not in this climate," Eden said wistfully as she watched him work. "But just the same I'm glad Meg sent it. Right now I do miss the snow and the sound of sleigh bells—"

"Ouch! Damn," Neil swore as the hammer connected with his thumb instead of the nail.

"Neil! Oh, dear, let me see." Eden reached for his hand but was rudely brushed away.

"Leave it alone," Neil growled, holding the injured digit to his lips. "I've lived through worse."

"No doubt, but still it must hurt." Neil's affronted glare surprised her and Eden teased, "If you like, I'll bandage it and give you a piece of hard candy Meg sent." Neil's response was muttered but Eden was quite certain it was also incredibly vile. "What's the matter with you today?"

"Nothing." Neil retrieved the fallen hammer from the porch and sullenly completed the task. "Anything else you want me to do?"

"Millicent and I did some baking this morning." Eden took his arm and drew Neil into the house. "You can help Shannon sample the cookies and fruit bread."

Their entrance into the kitchen brought a quickly concealed flare of irritation to Millicent's eyes, and as Neil took his place in one of the chairs, she murmured a vague excuse and left the house. Shrugging, Neil took Shannon onto his lap and handed her a cookie from the plate Eden set in front of him. "Millicent really despises me, doesn't she?"

Eden grimaced. "She'll come around in time."

"I doubt it," Neil grumbled. "I half expect her to greet me at the door with a shotgun."

At his self-pitying tone, Eden eyed him curiously. "Millicent's attitude never bothered you before. Something else is wrong, isn't it?"

"No, everything's fine," Neil protested. "I got a letter from Sebastian today—he's going to come here for Christmas. Keep the family together for the holidays and all that."

"That's wonderful," Eden exclaimed. "I'd like to see Sebastian again. He and I keep meeting under circumstances which are less than ideal."

"Sure." Neil absently toyed with his coffee cup. "I'll bring him by before he goes home."

"I suppose that would be best," Eden said softly, drawing an odd look from Neil. "I mean . . . well, now that Sebastian will be here I don't suppose you'll want to spend Christmas Day with us."

Neil stared at her. "I didn't know I had been invited."

"Of course you are!"

"You never said one word," Neil told her in an accusing voice. "Not one."

Eden looked at him dumbfounded. "I guess I just took it for granted. You've been here so much that I just assumed..." Her voice trailed off and she brushed at the tears which stung her eyes. "I'm sorry! I should have known better. Of course you have plans of your own. After all, we agreed that there would be no strings attached to our relationship. I just thought..."

She was struggling gamely to conceal her disappointment and it dawned on Neil that once again they had presumed a great deal without bothering to gather all the facts. Neil shook his head. "Eden, my sweet, what am I going to do with you?"

"I don't know." A single tear trailed down her cheek. "We agreed that we were both free to do as we please—"

"To hell with the damned agreement," Neil interrupted. "Don't you understand that I've been waiting for you to tell me that I was welcome here?"

Eden's eyes widened in astonishment. "But what about Sebastian? You said—"

"I said he was coming to spend a few days, but Sebastian or no Sebastian, I've still been waiting for your invitation." Neil lowered his gaze to Shannon. "I thought you didn't want me here."

"How could you think that?" Eden demanded. "Have I ever once made you feel unwelcome? Have I ever objected to your visits? Good heavens, Neil, you're practially part of the family." She stopped abruptly, remembering all too well Neil's opinions about wives and families. Above all else, Eden didn't want him to feel trapped. "I—I didn't mean that the way it sounded, Neil. I only meant that you and Sebastian are more than welcome to join us on Christmas."

Slowly Neil shifted his gaze from Shannon to Eden, understanding that his arrogant proclamations of the past were stumbling blocks now and that only time and his own actions would remove them. "In that case, my sweet, you can plan on two extra guests."

Christmas Day—which was also Shannon's birthday—brought rain and an unexpected chill to the air, but inside, fires crackled gaily in the fireplaces, and laughter echoed through the rooms. Vincent and Ian amused Shannon in the parlor while

Eden and Millicent prepared the meal, and by the time the women had finished in the kitchen there was a loud banging on the front door.

"I'll get it, Millie. You go ahead and join the others." Drying her hands, Eden ran to the door and threw it open.

Two pairs of golden eyes—all that were visible above a giant tarpaulin-draped cargo—sparkled down at her and Eden hurriedly stepped aside so the men could enter. "What is all that?"

"Presents, of course," Neil's muffled voice informed her. He proceeded to pull off the tarps and the two men marched off to the parlor. When they returned a few moments later, both were grinning widely. "I hope you don't mind," said Neil, "but I gave Shannon one of her presents early. By the time we get back she may have gotten the bow off."

"You are impossible," Eden chided lightly before turning to take Sebastian's coat and hat. "Hello, Sebastian. Merry Christmas."

Sebastian bowed slightly. "Your invitation is a godsend, Eden. I had nightmares of being forced to spend the entire day with only Neil for company." He bent over her hand and kissed it gallantly. "Many thanks. And may I say that you are even more ravishing than I remember."

"Ah, at last: a true gentleman," Eden bantered in return. She dropped into an elaborate curtsy and batted her eyes coquettishly at Sebastian. "You are most kind, sir, so speak on."

"I fear, madame, your beauty leaves me quite speechless. To speak of your beauty would be a great injustice." Sebastian chuckled, joining Eden's laughter, but when he glanced at Neil he was surprised to see the warning flash in his brother's eyes. Cheerfully he added, "My brother, however, may be able to find the words."

"Not me," Neil replied grudgingly when Eden's gaze came to rest upon him. "Sebastian is the articulate one in the family."

"I find that difficult to believe," Eden teased, not noticing that Sebastian had tactfully withdrawn. "As I remember you can be most eloquent when the occasion warrants."

"You remember too much."

"Do I?" Eden smiled, her eyes dancing madly. "I think I remember just enough." Unexpectedly she stood on tiptoes and pressed her lips against Neil's, catching him off-guard. Before Neil had time to respond, Eden pulled away and started toward the parlor. "Come along—before Millicent decides to hunt us down."

The small group spent the rest of the morning and early afternoon in light conversation, punctuated by spurts of laughter. An easy camaraderie prevailed, and even Millicent unbent far enough to give Neil a brief smile when he told her how pretty she looked. It was Shannon, however, who delighted everyone by taking her first halting steps toward Neil as he dangled another brightly wrapped package in front of her. She covered the short distance in a pitching gait that made Eden's heart lurch, but when Shannon triumphantly snatched her gift from Neil's hand, Eden laughingly applauded with the rest.

While Eden helped Shannon unwrap her packages the rest of the presents were distributed and soon the parlor was littered with discarded bows and ribbons, which fascinated Shannon far more than the gifts themselves. At last Eden gave up trying to keep a firm rein on her daughter and allowed Shannon to roam while she herself worked her way through the stack of presents Neil had brought.

Sometime during the commotion Neil sauntered across the room and sat next to Eden on the sofa. "What do you think, sweet? Can Shannon use all these things?"

Eden shook her head in mild exasperation. "Neil, what in the world possessed you to buy all this? You are spoiling Shannon rotten."

Neil looked smug. "Children are supposed to be spoiled, especially girls. Besides, what harm will it do?"

"None, I suppose." Eden glanced at him from beneath the veil of her lashes. "By next year I'll have plenty of time to repair any damage you may have done."

"Not even a thank you?" Neil raised an eyebrow. "I think I deserve at least that much."

Eden sobered. "Thank you, Neil, from both of us."

"Don't look so grim, my sweet," Neil said with a smile. "I was only teasing."

"But I'm not," Eden told him quietly. "You've been very good for Shannon these past weeks... and me." She reached into a stack of unopened gifts and handed Neil the heaviest of the lot. "I—I hope you like it, Neil."

Neil carefully unwrapped the package and then grinned as he pulled two leather-bound volumes from the paper. "Homer. *The Iliad* and *The Odyssey*."

"They reminded me of you," Eden said hesitantly. "As long as I've known you, you've been wandering; searching for"— Eden paused, floundering for the right word—"for happiness, I guess. Odysseus wandered for ten years; I hope your journey is much shorter and far less trying."

Neil eyed her strangely before he answered. "Thank you, Eden. For the books and especially for that kind thought."

Entranced, they stared at each other for a long time until the clamor of the others brought them back to the present.

"You will play, won't you, Miss Eden?" Millicent was asking. She picked up a stack of papers from the piano and offered them to Eden. "These were in with the Christmas things. I know you haven't played since Mr. Colter"—Millicent paused, flustered, before continuing determinedly—"well, in a long time. But I thought, after all, it *is* Christmas."

"Yes." Eden's reply was barely audible. She drew a deep breath and took the music from Millicent. Glancing at the others, she smiled wanly. "I can't promise a virtuoso performance—it's been quite a while."

"We'll manage," Ian boomed out. "Once I get warmed up, nobody will notice whether you're playing or not."

After the first few carols Eden's trepidation vanished and, with Neil at her side turning the pages, she lightheartedly joined in the singing. Predictably, Ian's basso profundo threatened the plaster on the walls, but the duet performed by Sebastian and Neil left even Millicent wide-eyed. *A cappella,* the two baritone voices blended in perfect harmony, evoking an unexpected tranquillity in the listeners.

"The next time Shannon wants a lullaby, I'll send for you," Eden told Neil when the caroling was finished. "I had no idea you were so talented."

"And I had no idea you played so beautifully," Neil replied. "You constantly surprise me, love. I've never met anyone quite like you."

Was there a hidden meaning in his words? Eden hoped so. "You're very special to me, too, Neil."

"To Shannon as well, I suppose," Neil added teasingly, although his heart lurched at her words.

Eden rested a hand on his chest and smiled gently. "I can't speak for my daughter, only myself. You know, I never dreamed you would fit so easily into my life. It feels right, truly right, to be with you."

Neil's eyes glowed and he curled a hand around the one Eden had placed on his chest. "That, sweet Eden, means more to me than you can possibly know." Difficult as it was, Neil suppressed the urge to pull Eden into his arms and instead merely tightened his grip on her hand.

Across the room, Ian glanced toward Neil and Eden and discreetly nudged Vincent. "Took them long enough, wouldn't you say?"

Vincent nodded, a rare smile appearing on his face. "I was beginning to wonder if he was blind or just plain dumb. No offense intended, Sebastian."

Sebastian too had followed Ian's glance and now he turned to grin at Vincent. "None taken. I know better than anyone how dense my brother can be."

Ian chuckled softly. "Do you think we should leave now, or should we stay and watch them make calf eyes at each other?"

"Let's stay." Sebastian's grin widened. "I've been waiting years for this day and I think it only fair that my patience be rewarded."

Millicent arrived just in time to hear Sebastian's comment, and though she sniffed at the sight of her employer smiling up at Neil she kept her comments to herself. Instead Millicent loudly cleared her throat and announced, "Dinner is ready, Miss Eden."

Eden blushed, but Neil, on the other hand, didn't appear to be the least disconcerted by the attention they had obviously been receiving. Allowing the others to leave the room first, Sebastian caught his brother's arm when Neil started through the doorway. "I hope your intentions toward Eden are honorable."

Neil frowned and shook off Sebastian's hand. "Not now, little brother. Save the lecture until tonight."

"I mean it," Sebastian said sharply, refusing to let the matter fall by the wayside. "If you still think to make her your mistress, you had better think again."

"Look, Sebastian," Neil sighed, "that's between Eden and myself."

"Oh, I trust *her* judgment," Sebastian agreed lightly as he started for the door.

Conversation soon gave way to the ravenous appetites as the traditional goose was reduced to a skeletal memory. Eden helped Millicent clear away the dishes and serve the pie and coffee; but before Eden sat down to her own dessert she gently carried a nodding Shannon upstairs to bed. No sooner had Eden returned to the dining room than there was a knock at the front door.

Ian frowned and exchanged a quick, worried look with Vincent. "Are you expecting someone, lass?"

"No one who isn't here," Eden replied, rising. "It's probably Maudie, wondering where you are. After all, Ian, two people who are engaged to be married usually spend the holidays together."

"I'm not due there for another hour," Ian explained. "Or am I? What time is it?"

Laughter greeted Ian's consternation, and Eden smiled as the sound followed her to the door. It was still raining and Eden hurriedly stepped behind the open door for protection.

"Merry Christmas, Mrs. Colter!"

The slicker-draped figure pulled the hat away from his face and Eden gasped as she recognized the telegraph operator. "Ben! What in the world—come inside." Ben happily complied, grinning at Eden as the warmth of the house enfolded him. "Take off your things, Ben, and have some coffee and pie with us. Or some brandy, if you prefer."

"No, ma'am, but thank you, anyway. The wife's waiting our dinner on me." Ben rummaged beneath his rain gear and brought forth a package and a telegram. "The telegram said this was to be delivered today, or I wouldn't have bothered you."

Eden took the package. "It's no bother for me at all. I'm just sorry you have to be out in this weather."

"It ain't a part of the job I like," Ben concurred with a laugh, "but at least I got steady work."

"Here." Eden took her reticule from the hall table, fished out a coin and pressed it into Ben's hand.

"You don't need—"

"Yes, I do. Merry Christmas, Ben." When he was gone, Eden eagerly ripped open the package. The hinged lid on the little box responded obediently to her touch and, her eyes wide, Eden stared in disbelief at the aquamarine and diamond ring nestled in the jeweler's velvet. This wasn't, as Eden had thought, a gift from Meg! Shaken, Eden tore open the telegram and as she read the message the color drained from her face.

*My darling Eden*. Stop. *Accept this as a token of my love and devotion*. Stop. *Miss you terribly*. Stop. *Will return Lathrop as soon as possible*. Stop. *Merry Christmas*. Stop. *All my love*. Stop. *Keith*.

"My God," Eden breathed, aghast at both the message and the gift. "How could he? How could he!" With her bottom lip caught worriedly between her teeth Eden glared at the sparkling ring.

"Eden love, you're missing the fun. Ian's telling—" Neil's grin faded when he caught sight of Eden's pale features and he hurried forward. "What it is? What's wrong?"

"I received another gift," Eden said in an odd voice. Without further explanation she handed Neil the box, a cold smile flitting across her lips when he glanced between herself and the ring in obvious confusion.

"Beautiful," Neil observed finally, jealousy clouding his amber gaze. "Very nice. Who sent it?"

"Keith Gerald." At Neil's sharp look, Eden shrugged. "You asked."

A muscle worked in Neil's cheek. "I see. And where is our noble Ranger that he couldn't deliver this in person?"

Eden consulted the telegram. "This was sent from El Paso. Would you like to read it?"

Neil snorted and glared at Eden. "No, thank you; I can guess what it says."

"Don't look at me that way!" Eden cried. "It isn't my fault Keith didn't take 'no' for an answer."

"Maybe you should have tried being more persuasive," Neil exploded. "You manage everything else in your life so well that I find it hard to believe you can't manage one Texas Ranger."

"That isn't fair," Eden choked. "I have no control over what Keith thinks or does."

"Sure." Neil plucked the ring out of the box and held it up to the light. "Every rejected man sends his woman an engagement ring."

"Are you implying that I didn't turn Keith down?" Eden questioned angrily.

"I'm *saying* you must have left the door wide open in order for him to walk through it with something like this!"

"Of course I did," Eden jeered, truly angered now. In a

high-pitched voice she mimicked, "'Oh, Keith, I can't possibly answer you now. Ask again in a month or so.' Hah!"

"Oh, hell!" Disgusted, Neil pivoted on his heel and stalked into the study, Eden close behind. Scowling, he splashed brandy into a snifter and downed it in one swallow before turning to face Eden. "Well?"

"Well, what?" Eden retorted defiantly, returning the golden glare with one of her own.

"What are you going to do with this?" Neil slapped the ring onto the desk and poured himself another drink.

Eden picked up the ring, carefully placed it in the box and closed the lid. "I'm going to send it back to Keith, along with a note explaining that I haven't changed my mind."

"Eden, I..." Neil shook his head, suddenly feeling very foolish, and passed a hand over his face. "I lost my temper, love; I'm sorry."

"So did I," Eden acknowledged. She went to Neil and slid her arms around his waist. "I understand—I'd feel the same way if the situation were reversed." Neil's arms circled her back and, sighing, Eden rested her cheek against his chest.

"He shows exquisite taste, I'll give him that much," Neil murmured against her hair. "I can't say I blame him for refusing to be discouraged. You're worth fighting for."

"I don't want to be fought for or fought over," Eden protested softly. "All I want is to love and be loved in return. I want a peaceful life which will allow me to raise my child without fear of rustlers or kidnapers. Is that so much to ask?"

"No." Neil raised her face to his and smiled. "I'll help if I can. Just tell me what to do."

Eden lifted a hand and combed her fingers through Neil's hair. "What you're doing now is nice."

"Only nice?" Neil teased. "I hoped for something a bit more complimentary, but perhaps I can change your mind. Wait here—I'll be right back." He left the room briefly, reappearing with one hand hidden behind his back. "Close your eyes."

"No more surprises," Eden laughingly implored. "My nerves can't take the strain."

"Close your eyes," Neil ordered again, smiling in return. "And hold out your hand." Eden obeyed, frowning when something heavy and square was placed in her hand. "You can look now."

Gray eyes opened, then widened at the small gold box in

her hand. The metal was ornately filigreed and the key, pro-
truding from one side of the box, was set with a single ruby.
"A music box." Eden smiled radiantly. "It's beautiful, Neil;
thank you."

"Not just any music box, my sweet," Neil corrected. He
opened the lid, watching her expectantly as the bright notes
filled the room. "Do you recognize the tune?"

Eden's brows drew together and she thoughtfully tilted her
head to one side. "I'm not sure. I mean, it's a waltz and I've
heard it several times but—"

"That, my love, is what we danced to a very long time ago.
Do you remember?"

"Oh!" Eden's breath caught in her throat and for some reason
she felt like crying.

A tear rolled down Eden's cheek and Neil gently wiped it
away with his finger. "I wanted to please you, Eden, not make
you cry."

Eden shook her head. "I'm not crying, it's just that I never
expected—" She laughed breathlessly. "I thought men didn't
remember details like that."

Neil said in a low voice, "I can even describe the dress you
were wearing. Does that surprise you?" Eden nodded wordlessly and just as silently Neil took the music box from her and
drew her into his arms for a tender, lingering kiss. Eden's
response was immediate and passionate, and with an effort Neil
forced himself to be satisfied with only one kiss. "Lovely as
you were at sixteen, Eden, the girl was a pale reflection of the
woman you are now. I find that I've grown quite fond of you,
love." Eden stood quietly in the circle of Neil's arms, conscious
only of the strength in his embrace and her own contentment.

And, in his palatial home, Lathrop Williams watched . . . and
waited.

# BOOK IV
## 1880

Oh mistress mine! where are you roaming?
Oh! stay and hear; your true love's coming,
That can sing both high and low.
Trip no further, pretty sweeting;
Journeys end in lovers meeting,
Every wise man's son doth know.

—SHAKESPEARE

# Chapter 18

If tongues had wagged over Neil Banning's heroic rescue of Eden Colter, and the couple's subsequent appearances together, the gossip flew fast and furiously when Neil and Eden attended Ian Garrison's wedding to Maude Barston. Still in mourning, Eden sat quietly on the sidelines during the wedding dance, but what surprised the other guests was that Neil Banning—the heartthrob of the unmarried women of Lathrop—stayed by Eden's side during the entire evening, except for taking one turn around the dance floor with the bride. Not that this was significant, the unhappy ones consoled each other. Neil Banning was merely being kind to a poor widow who would otherwise feel excluded from the festivities. After all, the rakish Neil Banning was hardly the type to court a widow with a small child.

It might have been true even a few short weeks before, but now, without warning, Neil found his thoughts turning constantly to Eden until at times he had difficulty concentrating on what was being said. Enjoying a woman's company when they were together was understandable, but to be so totally obsessed by one woman even when they were apart came as a nasty shock to Neil. Thoughts of Eden filled his days and nights, and Neil treasured their time together even though the physical side of their relationship never progressed past the point of exchanging a few kisses. Neil ruled his impatience in that area with an iron hand for he realized they were not yet ready to unleash the passion which seethed between them whenever they touched. Day after day Neil would recall their insatiable lovemaking in Mexico and would force himself to remember Eden's terms.

Exactly one year after Hugh's death, Eden placed flowers on his grave and spent the better part of the afternoon in unspoken communication with the man she had held so dear, while their daughter played nearby. Millicent sadly watched her employer, fully expecting Eden to fall to pieces in renewed grief; but although Eden's tears splashed against the flower-covered mound, her eyes were amazingly calm and serene when she returned to the house. Her farewell to the past was complete, and though Eden knew she would often remember Hugh in the years ahead, she was resolved to carve a new life for herself and for Shannon. Accordingly, the black gowns were packed away and, though she felt as if she had been stripped of a suit of armor, Eden began her reentry into the world.

She felt whole again, deriving a great deal of pleasure from running the ranch and raising Shannon. And there was Neil. With every day that passed Eden found her love for him deepening. Did he feel the same way? Eden wasn't sure. Neil often said he was fond of her, and the intense physical attraction which arced between them had if anything increased. But Neil never spoke of love, and Eden, in turn, kept her feelings to herself. Hers was a passionate nature, however, and Eden frequently chided herself for forcing Neil into an agreement which placed restraints upon their lovemaking.

While Eden's mind battled with her longings, a new set of problems confronted her in the form of would-be suitors. Eligible bachelors from Lathrop and the surrounding area suddenly turned up in town on marketing days or stopped by the Emerald I to water their horses on their way to some vague destination, and they were obviously not discouraged by Eden's lack of enthusiasm. Millicent, somewhat thawed by Neil's good behavior, was nevertheless pleased to see the competition. Eden found the situation rather amusing until she noticed that Vincent began staying close to her whenever she went into town and whenever strangers appeared on the ranch. Vincent eyed the men suspiciously, and after several days urged Eden to hire a few of his old acquaintances as bodyguards for herself and Shannon. When Eden objected, Vincent lost no time in pointing out that while Lathrop Williams might have crawled back into his hole for the time being, the visitors to the Emerald I provided the perfect opportunity for another kidnaping—and this time it could easily be Shannon who became Lathrop's victim.

Eden added to her payroll six men whose chilling expressions made Vincent appear tame by comparison. The bluff Vincent had run on Lathrop Williams so long ago was suddenly a reality. At Eden's insistence the guards were discreet, unobtrusive, and Vincent took one further precaution to safeguard his employer. To Lathrop Williams, Vincent reiterated his solemn promise that if any harm befell her, retribution would be swift and sure. Despite Vincent's wary attitude the days passed peacefully enough until one afternoon a familiar figure unexpectedly appeared at the Emerald I.

Preparing to go riding with Neil—and thinking the hoofbeats she had heard signaled his arrival—a smiling Eden led her horse from the stable but stopped dead when she saw Lathrop Williams coming down the steps of her house. While Eden debated yelling for Vincent or one of the other guards, Lathrop caught sight of her and strolled across the yard. Eden's jaw set in a determined line as her fear gave way to indignation, and her eyes turned flinty as she watched Lathrop approach.

"Afternoon, Eden." Lathrop stopped a few feet in front of her and tilted his hat to the back of his head. "Can you spare me a few minutes?"

"The question is not can I, but will I," Eden replied shortly. "Truthfully, Lathrop, I can't think of a thing we have to say to each other."

Lathrop's face reddened but he managed an affable smile. "Look, Eden, I know we've had our differences—"

"Differences!" Eden hissed. "You kill my husband and kidnap me and you have the gall to say we've had our *differences?*"

"Take it easy, girl." Lathrop glanced nervously around the buildings. "Wouldn't want those men you hired to think I was doing something wrong. All I want to do is talk."

Eden flashed him a contemptuous look. "If you're thinking of trying to buy the Emerald I again, save your breath. I'm not interested."

"No, no." Lathrop uneasily surveyed the buildings once more and took a step toward Eden. "I was hoping we could talk about your new hired men—in private."

It struck Eden that while Lathrop could employ others to do his dirty work without a second thought, when his own hide might be in danger he seemed to have all the courage of a rabbit. "Whatever you have to say to me can be said right here, in plain sight of anyone who happens by." Eden's voice was clipped. "And furthermore, I fail to see why you should concern yourself with my employees."

"Because they're a threat to me, that's why," Lathrop growled. "You hired them to kill me!"

"Did I?" Eden looked at him innocently. "You put too much

faith in gossip, Lathrop. The men needed jobs and I had jobs that needed filling, that's all."

Lathrop snorted. "I'm not fool enough to believe that— especially after what Vincent said."

"Dear Vincent," Eden laughed. "He is protective, isn't he?"

"This isn't funny!" Lathrop roared. "I have to look over my shoulder every time I leave the house! I used to enjoy riding over my land but lately I've been followed wherever I go, and I want you to put a stop to it. I don't like being hunted like some kind of animal."

"Neither do I," Eden replied tartly, but she was puzzled by Lathrop's dilemma. None of her men were following Lathrop—in fact, Vincent had given them strict orders to stay on the Emerald I unless Eden rode off alone, and even then only two men were to go after her. But if her men weren't following Lathrop . . .

"Well?" Lathrop demanded, jerking Eden from her thoughts. "What are you going to do about this?"

Eden shrugged carelessly. "Not a thing. It's high time the hunter became the hunted."

"Damn it, girl, you've got no reason to treat me this way!" Lathrop's face contorted in a mixture of bitterness and impotent anger. "I got rid of the rustlers just like you said, didn't I? And you and your daughter haven't been threatened, have you? Hell, you've got no reason to treat me like a criminal."

"I have all the reason I need," Eden corrected defiantly, eyes snapping. "As long as you're alive, neither Shannon nor I are completely safe and I intend to take any measures I feel are necessary. I will not be driven off this land by you or anyone else, so you better accept that fact and act accordingly. As long as you behave yourself you won't be hurt, but if you become greedy again you'll be the sorriest man alive. And that's not a threat, Lathrop, that's a promise!"

Slow, mocking applause followed her tirade and she and Lathrop turned to find Neil watching them from his horse. "Well said, Eden," he drawled, then turned his attention to Lathrop. "You're a long way from home, Williams. If you're lost I'm sure Eden would be happy to have one of her men escort you back to the ranch."

"You're mighty brave as long as you've got a woman's skirt to hide behind," Lathrop sneered. "If you were a man I'd challenge you right now and settle this whole damned business."

Amused, Neil dismounted and took several steps away from his horse. With his right hand dangling menacingly near his pistol, Neil offered, "Go ahead, Lathrop, make your move. This is what I've always wanted but Eden had had her fill of bloodshed. Fortunately I'm not as squeamish as she is."

Terrified, Eden started to intervene but held her tongue when Neil sent a warning glance in her direction. Lathrop's hand hovered near his holster, and for several seconds the men eyed each other grimly, the ringing silence jarring across Eden's nerves until she felt like screaming. Finally, thankfully, Lathrop backed down with a great show of contempt for his opponent, and Eden pressed her trembling hands to her sides.

"Some other time, Banning," Lathrop taunted. "When the lady is absent."

Lathrop walked away and had just settled himself in the saddle when Neil's calm voice answered. "Name the time and place, Lathrop. I'm always happy to oblige a neighbor." When Lathrop was gone, Neil turned to Eden and smiled. "Good afternoon, ma'am. May I say you're looking downright lovely today."

"Oh, Neil!" Eden threw herself into Neil's arms, her calm façade shattered as she clung to his neck. "Have you lost your mind? Lathrop might have killed you just now!"

"Not a chance." Neil pried her arms away from his neck and turned Eden until she faced the barn entrance. "Come on out, Vincent."

Vincent materialized from the gloomy interior of the barn and, much to Eden's chagrin, saluted her with a shotgun he carried. "Howdy, Mrs. Colter."

It took Eden a moment to find her voice but when she did her words emerged in an indignant howl. "Vincent, why in the world didn't you come out before? Lathrop scared me half to death and all the time you were sitting there with a shotgun!"

Eden sputtered incoherently and Vincent exchanged a grin with Neil. "She does carry on, doesn't she?"

Nodding in agreement, Neil winced as Eden—still in his arms—stamped her foot and ground the heel of her boot into his toes. "Calm down, sweetheart; there's no reason to work yourself up this way."

"No reason!" Eden screeched. "Vincent, you could have gotten Neil killed!"

"No, ma'am," Vincent countered, chuckling at her ire. "I would have stopped it before there was any gunplay. I waited to find out what Lathrop wanted. I figured it had to be mighty important to make him pay you a visit, and I was right."

"You must have taught your horse to walk on tiptoes," Eden grumbled to Neil. "I didn't even hear you ride in."

Neil laughed. "The way you and Lathrop were going at it a cavalry troop could have ridden by and neither of you would have noticed. Now, why don't you tell me what Lathrop wanted."

Eden forced herself to answer in a steady voice. "Lathrop believes he's being followed, and he thinks I'm responsible."

"Are you?"

"No. At least not that I know of." Eden shot Vincent a questioning look and when he shook his head Eden gave a sigh of relief. "I thought Lathrop was jumping at shadows but I wasn't sure."

Neil frowned and shifted his gaze to Vincent. "Are you sure none of your friends are taking their jobs a little too seriously, Vincent?"

Vincent shook his head. "It could be like Mrs. Colter says. Lathrop may be imagining things."

"Or," Neil prompted, feeling that Vincent had more to say.

"Or maybe someone else has a grudge against Lathrop," Vincent speculated. He broke open the shotgun, removed the shells and rolled them thoughtfully in the palm of his hand. "He's made a lot of enemies." Before Eden had a chance to question him, Vincent mumbled a few words about having work to do and sauntered away.

"I'm glad you have Vincent," Neil said as they watched him leave. "When I'm not with you, I know he's taking care of you and Shannon."

"I'm waiting for the day when all these precautions won't be necessary," Eden said softly. "I detest having my home turned into an armed camp, I hate the fact that Shannon's playmates are bodyguards. But most of all I hate having everyone in Lathrop think that I'm crazy." Neil chuckled and Eden shot him a quelling glance. "They do, you know—even Ian thinks I'm a bit odd for hiring these guards, but I don't dare tell him the truth."

Neil hugged her reassuringly. "This can't go on forever, love. I think Lathrop already understands that he might as well give up any hopes he had for the Emerald I."

"I wonder," Eden said thoughtfully. "I wish I could trust Lathrop when he says he's given up, but I don't. I have the awful feeling that he's just biding his time and thinking of ways to destroy us." She sighed and rested her head against Neil's shoulder. "When I first came here I loved the freedom of this land, the peace it seemed to bring, but now—"

"—Now what you need is to forget about Lathrop for a while," Neil ordered with mock severity. "Concentrate on something pleasant."

"Such as?"

Neil stroked his moustache thoughtfully, golden eyes dancing. "Such as me. I have been known to make the ladies forget their troubles."

"I can imagine," Eden retorted. "Unfortunately for you, I would rather go riding."

"I'll wait my turn," Neil assured Eden with a grin. "Sooner or later you'll give in."

They rode for enjoyment, with no particular destination, and Neil's teasing soon put Eden in a good frame of mind. If she tried very hard, Eden could almost imagine that Lathrop Williams and the problems he had created didn't exist. Thank heaven for Neil, Eden thought gratefully as she stole a glance at his profile. Without Neil to confide in, the past weeks would have been unbearable. They shared so much of their lives now that it was difficult to remember there had been a time when mere civility seemed beyond their reach.

Their wandering had taken them to the bank of the much-disputed stream. Neil dismounted and helped Eden from the saddle.

"All this fuss over so little water," Eden sighed as they walked along. "I wonder if it's worth it. I have dreams about Lathrop, Neil, nightmares in which Lathrop has killed you and is coming for Shannon, and I can't stop him. When I wake up, the nightmare seems so real—"

Her voice broke and Neil gently took her into his arms. "Shh. Nothing like that is going to happen, I promise. I know it's like living with a gun at your back, but this will soon be over. You have to believe that, Eden."

"When you're with me I do," Eden murmured. "I need you so much, Neil. That's a cowardly thing to admit, isn't it?"

"No." Neil tenderly stroked her back. "I need you too, Eden, but that doesn't make me a coward; it makes me human." Eden raised her face to his and Neil stared, mesmerized, into those crystalline eyes. "Do you have any idea how empty I feel when we're apart? It's pure hell leaving you each night."

"I know—I feel the same way." Eden smiled tremulously and placed a dainty hand on Neil's shoulder. "You're very different from the man I knew back East. That Neil Banning was cold, arrogant—I never felt for him what I feel for you."

"Eden—"

"Don't interrupt. Please." Ignoring the cautious voice which warned her to remain silent, Eden continued recklessly, "I know you don't believe in love or marriage and I'm not asking you for either one. All I ask is that you not laugh when I tell you how important you are to me." Neil stared at her so oddly that Eden dropped her gaze to his shirt, suddenly afraid that she was making a fool of herself.

"Do you honestly believe I would hurt you like that?" Neil asked softly.

"Our agreement—" Eden began.

"That bloody agreement," Neil groaned. "How long am I going to be hit with it? Can't you forget what I said?"

"Can you?" Eden countered.

"Hell, yes!" Neil framed Eden's face in his hands. "I care for you, don't you understand? I thought I had proved that to you—I thought I had showed you that you could trust me and depend on me."

"You have," Eden protested. "I value our friendship, Neil; it's very important to me."

"If that's true then you'll forget about the agreement; stop throwing it in my face every time I start getting close to you."

"I never meant to do that." Eden looked at him helplessly. "I'm sorry, Neil, I didn't mean to hurt you."

The apology was like a knife in his heart, and Neil winced. Eden didn't understand what he was trying to say, and Neil cursed silently. How could he explain that the admiring glances other men sent her way drove him into a towering rage? How could he tell Eden that seeing all the hopeful bachelors in the area descend upon the Emerald I had made him realize that she was the most important thing in his life? Somehow Neil had to erase any bad memories Eden still carried. In a bleak voice Neil said, "I'm leaving for Dallas tomorrow."

Eden nodded, troubled by the desolate expression Neil wore. "You told me a few weeks ago. The cattlemen's meeting."

"That's right." Neil's hands fell to his sides and he turned to study the stream. "I don't want to leave you here."

"I'll be fine," Eden assured him, trying desperately to fathom what had brought on Neil's dark mood. "Don't worry. Shannon and I will have a special dinner for you the night you return."

"You don't understand, sweet." Neil swallowed his pride and turned his amber gaze fully on Eden. "I don't want to leave you, but I can't miss that meeting. I want you to come with me." In the face of Eden's shocked silence, Neil added, "Bring Shannon if you like, and Millicent. I've already reserved a suite for you three, and I'll take another room for myself."

Eden swallowed hard. "I . . . that is, Millicent won't be able to make the trip. She's pregnant."

"I see—remind me to offer my congratulations." Neil smiled faintly. "That leaves you and Shannon."

"Neil, I don't think so." Eden nervously wet her lips and glanced away from those knowing, golden eyes. "How would it look?"

"I thought gossip didn't bother you," he countered.

Eden scuffed the toe of her boot against the ground. So Neil didn't love her after all, she thought wretchedly. True, she had already admitted to herself that she was willing to become his lover, but at the very least she had expected the moment to be spontaneous. Had all Neil's promises, all his tenderness been carefully planned to overcome her resistance?

Since his offer had been strictly honorable, it never occurred to Neil that explaining his intentions to Eden would change her mind. "I'm staying at the Fordham, in case you change your mind. Come on. I'll take you home."

They rode in silence, reaching the Emerald I just as a thunderstorm broke overhead; and without a moment to spare they galloped into the barn as the first raindrops splattered against the ground. A gulf had opened between them and, upset and bewildered, Eden attempted to set things right.

"Why don't you stay for dinner?" Eden suggested, a poignant tremor in her voice.

"No. Thank you." Neil's eyes were hooded as he lifted Eden

from her horse and quickly stripped the beast of its bridle and saddle. "I'd better get going."

"At least wait until the rain ends," Eden pleaded. "You'll catch your death riding home in this."

Golden eyes flaming with bitterness, Neil rounded on Eden. In one long stride he covered the distance between them, his hands closing painfully around Eden's shoulders. "Christ, lady, what kind of game are you playing?"

"I—I'm not—" Eden stammered.

"You're as bad as Constanza," Neil sneered. "You flirt and you tease and drive a man half crazy. Neither one of you has an honest bone in your body!"

"That's not fair!" Eden cried. "I've never lied to you!"

"Everything has to be your way," Neil raged, so furious that he didn't hear Eden's words. "Give me time, you said. Wait. Be patient. Don't press. Well, I did, and the first time I ask you to meet me halfway you act like I'm a leper!" Neil released her so abruptly that Eden staggered back against the wall. "The hell with it—I don't need this kind of aggravation." Before Eden could recover, Neil had swung into his saddle and cantered out of the barn.

"Neil, wait!" Eden raced from the building into the pouring rain and watched him fade into the distance. "Come back, damn you!" She shook a fist at his dwindling figure. "If you don't come back here, I swear I'll never speak to you again! Do you hear me?"

He didn't, of course, and a moment later Eden burst into tears. Sobbing, not caring that she was soaked to the skin, Eden stood in the downpour until Neil disappeared, finally turning and trudging into the house. Millicent, busy with the dinner preparations, looked up and found Eden standing miserably in the kitchen doorway, an ever-increasing puddle of water forming at her feet.

"Miss Eden, what happened?"

"I hate him," Eden announced forlornly. "I really do hate him. He's a boorish, insensitive clod who cares only about himself. What I ever saw in him I can't imagine."

Millicent looked at her employer in puzzled concern. "Who, miss?"

"Why, Neil Banning, of course." Eden's tone made it clear that Millicent should have known his identity. "You were right, you know. We were better off without him."

"If you say so, Miss Eden," Millicent answered doubtfully. "Don't you think you should get out of those wet clothes?"

"I will, Millicent; there's no need to treat me like a child." Eden sighed heavily and glanced at Shannon, who was playing quietly in the corner. "He was a bad influence on Shannon, too, spoiling her the way he did. Don't you agree?" When Millicent didn't answer, Eden looked at her sharply. "Well, don't you?"

"I don't think it did her any harm," Millicent stated bluntly.

"You certainly picked a fine time to switch sides," Eden grumbled. Glaring, she set water to heat for a bath.

Half an hour later Eden was relaxing in a hot, scented bath, her freshly washed hair draped over the back of the tub to dry. Now she allowed the tears to flow—large, scalding tears which did nothing to alleviate the searing pain in her chest. Things had been going so well! Why had he spoiled everything by making such a blatant proposition? If only his offer hadn't sounded so callous, Eden thought miserably. Even the tenderness Neil had displayed earlier in the afternoon paled in the face of the cruel things he had said upon their return.

The evening passed gloomily, particularly during dinner, with Neil's chair standing pointedly vacant. Vincent's curious looks were deftly fielded by Millicent, and she cautioned him to remain silent by an inconspicuous shake of her head. Eden stared morosely at the food in front of her and contemplated her own bleak future.

"Would you like coffee, Miss Eden?"

Eden looked up into Millicent's concerned eyes and shook her head. "Why don't you take the rest of the evening off, Millicent. I'll clean up."

"And let you take out whatever is eating at you on the china and crystal?" Millicent sniffed. "I'd best keep an eye on you. I'll wash, you dry."

"How are you feeling?" Eden asked as the two women worked in the kitchen. "You looked rather green at lunch today."

Millicent's nose wrinkled in disgust. "If I could skip directly from evening to afternoon there would be no problem, but heavens! The morning is just awful."

"Try eating a biscuit before you get out of bed," Eden suggested. "Luckily this phase doesn't last too long—in a few weeks you'll be back to your old self."

"That will be a relief." From the corner of her eye Millicent glanced at Eden's set features and studiously returned her attention to the pan she was scouring. "What about you and Neil Banning?"

Eden's lips set in a thin line. "What about us?"

"Now, Miss Eden, it's plain you two had a fight."

"Very perceptive," Eden replied acidly.

"Was it bad?" Millicent inquired softly, unafraid of Eden's biting tongue.

"Not in the least." With unnecessary vigor, Eden began returning the clean dishes to the shelves. "Neil finally showed his true character, that's all, and not a moment too soon. It must please you immensely to know that you were right about him all along."

Millicent flushed uncomfortably. "No, Miss Eden, it doesn't. I admit that at first I wasn't happy about your keeping company with that man, but he seems to have changed since New York. He's obviously fond of Shannon . . . and he's head over heels about you."

"Is he really?" Eden queried drily. "Then suppose you explain why, if Neil is so fond of me, he is quite willing to compromise my reputation by asking me to accompany him to Dallas." Millicent looked at her in shock and Eden nodded grimly. "That's right, Millie. So much for our heroic Neil Banning."

"I can't believe it," Millicent murmured. "He actually asked you to go with him without any sort of chaperone?"

"Yes." Eden set a stack of dishes into the cupboard with a loud clatter. "Of course, he tried to hide his motives by asking you and Shannon along, but when I told him you weren't able to travel he still insisted. Now I ask you, what kind of a man would suggest such a thing?"

"A man who loves you," Millicent carefully speculated.

"Hah!"

"I hardly think he planned to compromise you by dragging Shannon and me along," Millicent reasoned. "Did you stop to think that he just might want the pleasure of your company?"

"No doubt," Eden jeered bitterly. "And I can just guess what would happen after a few days in Dallas. I know exactly where I would spend my nights, and I guarantee it wouldn't be in my own room."

"That's between you and Mr. Banning," Millicent said

bluntly. "Frankly, I can't blame him for wanting a little privacy. You two get little enough of that around here, what with Shannon or Vincent or myself constantly about. The change would do you good."

"In your opinion." Eden's eyes glinted angrily.

Shrugging, Millicent dried the last utensil and faced her employer squarely. "You love him, Miss Eden; you have ever since New York, but now that he feels the same way about you, you're shying away like a frightened colt."

"I won't be used," Eden argued vehemently. "I know how Neil's mind works. A week in Dallas, a little careless seduction, and then he rides off again and leaves me with nothing!"

"Maybe, but you won't know that unless you go, will you?" Millicent prompted. "I think you should leave Shannon with me; meet Mr. Banning as an equal, woman to man. From what I've noticed, he hasn't had much of a chance to be anything to you but a companion, and you both need something more."

"You're telling me to go!" Eden cried, incredulous.

"No, miss, I'd never dream of interfering in your life," Millicent replied innocently. "I'm saying that you and Shannon could use a vacation from each other."

Sleep eluded Eden that night as her pride did battle with that part of her which longed for the presence of the man who made her feel truly alive. If Millicent were right . . . But, even worse, what if she were wrong? Eden shuddered, remembering the ache Neil had left in her heart years ago.

Seemingly, the answer lay in whether Eden was willing to gamble on the tenuous relationship she and Neil had established since their return from Mexico. If Neil were fond of her, as he proclaimed, then Dallas would mean far more to him than the end of the chase and there would be a chance to build a life together. If not . . . if not, the end would be swift and sure, and she would be forced to put Neil Banning out of her life once and for all.

Dawn streaked the morning sky when Eden descended the stairs, Shannon in one hand and a valise in the other. Breakfast was on the table and she met both Vincent's and Millicent's stares unflinchingly.

"If you're quite certain you can manage Shannon on your own, I believe I'll spend some time away from the ranch," Eden told Millicent calmly.

"Oh, I'll manage," Millicent assured her. "Don't you worry about us. You just go and have a good time."

The couple apparently had discussed Eden's problem, and before Eden could change her mind Vincent had carried the rest of Eden's luggage from her room to the waiting buggy, and Millicent all but shoved her employer out the door. A grinning Vincent handed Eden into the seat and, in a sudden state of garrulousness, kept up a stream of conversation during the ride to the train depot in Lathrop. His loquacity proved a blessing, for it allowed Eden to compose herself for the coming meeting with Neil. She would have to remain calm, and hopefully Neil would do the same.

When they arrived at the depot Eden was cool and collected, and without any outward show of trepidation she walked directly to the teller's cage. "I'd like a ticket, please. To Dallas—best make it one-way, since I'm not certain how long I'll be staying."

"Yes, ma'am." The teller accepted Eden's money and returned her change along with the ticket. "You going to that cattlemen's meeting too, Mrs. Colter?"

"No. I'm just taking a little holiday." Eden glanced at the crowded platform, her heart sinking. "Are all these people going to Dallas?"

"Most of them. Mr. Williams had his private car brought around not ten minutes ago." He nodded to the shiny car waiting on a side track. "I'm sure he wouldn't mind sharing his accommodations with you for the trip. That way you won't have to hunt for a seat in the passenger cars. Shall I tell him you're here?"

The thought of Lathrop Williams being so near sent a prickle of fear down Eden's spine but she managed a brittle smile. "No, thank you. I prefer to travel alone. By the way," Eden continued nonchalantly, "has Neil Banning purchased a ticket yet? I imagine he's going to the meeting as well."

"Mr. Banning's come and gone," the teller informed her helpfully. "He sailed in here last night looking black as thunder and left on the six-thirty train. I don't mind telling you, ma'am, I was mighty glad to see him go. That man has a mean temper."

"So I've heard. Good day, sir." Eden scooped up the coins and her ticket and made her way across the platform to where Vincent was standing.

"Another few minutes and you would have missed the train,"

Vincent informed her as the sound of the train whistle reached their ears. "Good thing you're an early riser, ma'am."

"Isn't it though." Eden drew a shaky breath and smiled. "You know where I'm staying, Vincent. Get in touch with me if anything happens."

"Nothing will happen here. You just watch yourself, Mrs. Colter." Vincent nodded toward the private car. "You stay away from that varmint as much as you can."

"I will," Eden promised.

"I can put a couple of men on the next train," Vincent offered. "Wouldn't be any trouble."

Eden shook her head and touched the pocket of her traveling skirt. "I have a friend with me and I'll use it if I have to. No guards, Vincent, not this time."

"Whatever you say, ma'am," Vincent conceded unhappily. The train screeched to a halt in front of the platform, and Vincent handed the baggage to the conductor before turning to Eden. "You take care of yourself, Mrs. Colter, and take heart. Neil Banning can't be as ignorant as he acts."

Impulsively, Eden threw an arm around Vincent's shoulder and hugged him lightly before disappearing up the steps and into the railroad car.

"Damn fool thing for her to do," Vincent muttered, pleased.

The journey to Dallas took several hours but the time seemed to fly past for Eden. She tried to think of what she would say when she and Neil came face to face, but the tight knot in her stomach was interfering with her thought processes. If Neil rejected her first overture she would have to try again, Eden decided, and she mentally reviewed the items she had packed. Although her gowns were flattering, none was particularly outstanding, at least not if a woman were bent on turning a man's head. With luck she might be able to order two or three stunning creations from the woman she had dealt with after the cattle drive, but Dallas was going to be teeming for the next week or so and all the money in the world couldn't force a seamstress's fingers to sew more quickly.

Eden's hands were icy and her heart thumping as the train pulled into the station. Once out of the car, events moved swiftly: a porter collected her bags and tossed them up to the driver of a cab, Eden tipped him and then Eden heard her own voice, sounding quite high and unnatural, ordering the man to take her to the Fordham Hotel. By the time Eden entered the bustling hotel lobby her knees were shaking and she had to brace a hand against the desk to keep from falling.

"Yes, ma'am, may I—" The desk clerk's face broke into a smile and he seized the delicate hand resting on the wood in front of him. "Mrs. Colter! Welcome back. It's so nice to see you again."

The double shock of being recognized nearly sent Eden into a dead faint until she realized with a jolt that this was the same hotel she had stayed at after the cattle drive. Her mind working frantically, Eden smiled weakly. "Thank you, ah, Dennis, isn't it?"

"That's right." Dennis beamed. "I'm flattered you remembered."

"How could I forget?" Eden chided, an enchanting smile replacing her previously wan expression. "You were so helpful during my last visit. I do hope you can come to my rescue again. I need a room, Dennis."

Dennis's face fell. "I'm sorry, Mrs. Colter, but—"

"I know you're undoubtedly full," Eden interrupted, "but surely you have *one* room available."

"No, ma'am, I'm afraid we don't. It's the cattlemen's convention, you see. All the rooms have been booked in advance."

"Oh, dear." There was no need to affect the dismay which altered Eden's expression. "I just decided to get away for a few days—an impulsive holiday, you understand. I completely forgot about that silly meeting." Eden sighed. "There's nothing to do but go home, I suppose. Can you tell me when the next train departs for Lathrop?"

The dejected look in those soft gray eyes brought out the gallantry in Dennis. If ever a woman needed assistance and protection this one did, and Dennis was not about to turn her away. "Wait here, Mrs. Colter. I won't be but a minute." He hurried through a door marked 'office' and reappeared a few moments later waving a key triumphantly.

"Dennis, how did you manage that?" Eden asked breathlessly.

Dennis leaned across the counter, laid the key in her hand and explained quietly, "The owner, Mr. Fordham, has delusions of grandeur. He always has one suite set aside in case the governor or President unexpectedly stops here." Dennis winked slowly, but it was a gesture of amusement, not lechery.

"I convinced him that you needed the room more than the President."

Eden laughed and at Dennis's request signed the register. As her bags were picked up, she gave the clerk a heartfelt smile. "Thank you, Dennis. You are truly a gentleman." When he grinned in return, Eden ventured offhandedly, "Considering the meeting, I would imagine several of my friends are in town. Could you check your register and see if they're staying here by any chance?"

"Of course." Eager to be of service, Dennis checked through the book as Eden reeled off her list, but at only one name did he answer affirmatively. "Yes, Mr. Banning is staying with us. Suite 409."

"Thank you, Dennis." With a final smile, Eden followed the bellboy to her room.

Like a general planning his battle strategy, Eden embarked upon her own preparations. She ordered a bath, sent her gowns to be pressed, then applied a bar of scented soap to her hair until the pale curls pronounced their cleanliness with a satisfying squeak. When the last of the soap was rinsed from her hair Eden stepped into the tub and worked a generous lather over her entire body. A brisk toweling brought a pink hue to her skin and she slipped into fresh underthings, belted a robe around her waist and brushed her hair until it dried. Her gowns were returned and Eden inspected them critically, settling at last on a lavender evening gown whose décolletage was far more daring than those Eden normally wore.

A sense of determination filled her and Eden set out the rest of her arsenal. The barest hint of color on her eyelids brought the cool, gray eyes to vibrant life, and though Eden decided against rouging her cheeks, she did apply a suggestion of color to her mouth. Her hair took longer as she worked first brush, then comb through the golden halo. Which was better, she wondered—something basic and simple, or a more ornate coiffure? Simplicity, she decided, sweeping the shining mass atop her head, allowing a few curling tendrils to fall at her temples. Amethyst teardrops were inserted into her earlobes and at last she stepped into her gown. After a small struggle, the last hooks were fastened and she appraised herself in the suite's three-sided mirror. The color and cut of the gown were flattering but the creamy expanse of shoulder and bosom the neckline provided made Eden swallow nervously. Perfectly ac-

ceptable though the display of the tops of her rounded breasts
and the valley between might be, it had been a long time since
Eden had worn anything this bold, and the matching amethyst
pendant she hung around her neck only accentuated the problem
as it settled into the faint hollow between her breasts.

The chiming of the clock drew Eden's attention. It was
dinnertime, and if Neil had any plans for the evening—which
was quite probable—he would already have dined and left the
hotel. She would be forced to dine alone and then wait until
she guessed Neil had returned; or, if it grew too late, there was
always tomorrow.

Having reasoned out the details of the evening to her satisfaction, Eden threw a shawl around her shoulders and went
in search of nourishment. She had drawn appreciative stares
as a widow, but her appearance at the restaurant tonight caused
heads to swivel and there was a definite upsurge in conversation
as the maître d' sought to find a table for the enchanting creature
who stood so patiently, waiting for him to accomplish his task.

Far from patient, it was with a great deal of consternation
that Eden waited for the maître d' to lead her to a seat. The
protective shawl had slipped during her progress from her suite
to the restaurant, and as she stood now only the deepest part
of her plunging neckline was concealed. The shawl brought
Eden little relief since the masculine stares directed her way
proved other occupants of the restaurant were imagining what
lay below the remaining concealment.

"This way, please, Mrs. Colter."

Relieved, Eden followed the man to a secluded table, trying
to ignore the avid looks of some of the men she passed. Even
after she had slid into her chair and ordered her meal, Eden
still felt the burning looks and she steadfastly retained the hold
on her shawl. How she would manage when her food arrived
she had no idea, but she had no intention of exposing herself
to those furious stares for any longer than was necessary.

Across the room the source of one of the devouring stares
touched a match to his cheroot and allowed the smoke to curl
before his face as he watched Eden being seated. Eden! The
wild leaping of his pulse had settled to a dull thud now, but
the golden eyes refused to tear themselves away from the vision
across the room. Eden! Eden! *Eden!* Her name beat like a drum
in Neil Banning's temples and he swallowed the last of his
brandy without tasting it. A simple, unobtrusive flex of his

index finger brought him a refill and as he drank, his gaze devoured Eden's beauty. She had come. Despite the violent argument and his wild accusations, Eden had put aside her pride and followed him.

When had Eden arrived? And why had she not sought him out before venturing into the hotel's dining room unescorted? Was it possible that Eden failed to understand what a tempting sight she made? The admiring, hungry looks directed at her were not missed by Neil, and a muscle worked furiously in his cheek. She never should have come here alone. Any one of the men present might easily misconstrue her unguarded state as an invitation to approach her with any kind of proposition. Neil drained his glass, signaled for another and tried to control the possessive rage building in his heart. Eden was the one woman whose charms he wanted displayed only when she was on his arm.

"Beautiful, isn't she?"

The comment from one of the men at the next table drew Neil's attention and without taking his eyes from Eden, Neil strained to hear the rest of the conversation.

"God, yes," a second man responded. "You know her?"

"Never seen her before, but I'd sure like to get acquainted."

Neil's eyes narrowed and he turned slightly to observe the two men. Without a doubt they were talking about Eden, and the gleam in their eyes sent a searing flame of anger through Neil.

"You don't suppose she's one of the hotel women, do you?" the second man was inquiring.

"Her? No, she's got too much class to be one of those. More than likely she's here with her husband for the meeting."

"I don't see a ring. Seems to me her husband wouldn't let her out of his sight for this long."

Neil ground his teeth in silent fury, his fingers whitening as they tightened around his glass.

"Well, there's a surefire way to find out," the first speaker reasoned. "I'll just go over, introduce myself and find out why a pretty gal like that is all alone."

Don't, Neil silently warned the stranger.

"Why not send her a note or a bottle of wine?" his companion suggested. "Kind of break the ice beforehand."

Neil, simmering with rage, sat unmoving in his chair, his

eyes fixed on Eden while he listened to the hasty scratching of pencil against paper.

Eden looked up when the waiter stopped at her table and, frowning, accepted the note he offered. Afraid that something had happened at home, Eden forgot her precarious hold on the shawl and allowed it to slip completely away from her shoulders as she opened the note. A moment later the frown disappeared and a faint smile curved her lips.

"Shall I open the wine, madame?"

Amused, Eden carefully refolded the note and placed it on the salver the waiter held in one hand. "You may return both the note and the wine to the gentleman, with my refusal."

"As you wish, madame."

Eden's meal arrived and she applied herself ravenously to the food, pushing the incident from her mind. Neil, however, was not so forbearing, especially when he heard Eden's refusal couched in the waiter's own words.

"The lady sends her thanks and her apologies, sir, but she must refuse."

"Damn!" The would-be suitor cursed under his breath when the waiter had gone. "I knew I should have gone straight over there. I'll bet she wouldn't have turned me down once she saw I wasn't old and diseased. In fact, I may do just that. What could happen if I pay her a friendly little visit?"

"You could get killed," Neil answered silkily, his voice so even that it took the two men several moments to realize they had been threatened. The two turned to stare at Neil and he smiled coldly. "You'll both do well to back off. The lady isn't available."

"Yeah?" The admirer jeered. "And just who are you?"

"A friend of the lady's," Neil informed him stonily as he rose to his feet. "A very good friend."

The man glanced at Eden and then back to Neil. "It appears she doesn't know you're here. Now, that strikes me as being a bit peculiar, seeing as how you're such close friends."

"If it's proof you want, I'll be happy to oblige," Neil replied, a deadly gleam in his eye. "Outside."

The man laughed. "Mister, you're crazy. I don't believe you've even met that pretty little thing. No, I think you just want some of that for yourself, and that being the case, you can just stand in line like everybody else."

Neil's temper flared. "She's mine, do you understand? If

I catch you sniffing around her again, I'll beat you to a bloody pulp!" With a last menacing look, Neil pivoted on his heel and strode across the room to Eden's table.

From the corner of her eye Eden saw a masculine figure approaching and, thinking it to be the author of the rejected note, ignored him, but the scraping noise of a chair being drawn up to her table made further pretense impossible. "Sir, I must protest this intrusion—" Her voice died as gray eyes locked with gold and Eden, her heart hammering against her ribs, watched helplessly as Neil smoothly seated himself across from her.

"Do continue, my dear," Neil invited mockingly. "You were saying?"

Eden, unaware that Neil had been watching her for the past half hour, floundered about for an answer. "I . . . I thought you were someone else."

"Who?"

The last thing Eden wanted was another argument; but judging from Neil's expression his foul mood was going to allow little else. She decided silence was the wisest choice. With an outward show of equanimity, Eden picked up her fork and resumed eating.

"You needn't worry about any further missives from your admirer," Neil announced when it became obvious Eden would not answer. "I took care of him."

Eden nearly choked on her wine, eyes widening in astonishment. "You did what?"

"I took care of him," Neil repeated harshly. "He was ready to come over and introduce himself. I couldn't allow that."

"You couldn't allow . . ." Eden echoed incredulously. "What did you do, Neil?"

Neil shrugged and casually lit a cheroot. "What any man would do when his woman is in danger of being pawed over. I threatened him." Neil exhaled a cloud of smoke.

Pure steel replaced the soft gray in Eden's eyes and she stared coldly at Neil. "You presume a great deal, Mr. Banning. For your information, I rejected that man's overture only a few minutes ago—and without making a scene, I might add."

"I know; unfortunately your admirer is not easily discouraged."

Eden set her fork down with an alarming clatter. "How long have you been spying on me?"

"Spying?" Neil snorted. "That's rather a harsh word, isn't it, my love? I was only doing what every other man here was doing—enjoying the sight of a beautiful, unescorted woman." Amber eyes dropped from Eden's face to the amethyst pendant nestled in the valley between her breasts, and Neil's face hardened. "I suggest you use that shawl for its intended purpose, my sweet, and stop displaying your undeniable charms for the rest of the men here."

Eden blushed furiously, but the shawl remained untouched. "I thought you had learned not to give me orders."

"And I thought you had learned not to push me too far," Neil retorted silkenly. "In case you don't realize it, you've created quite a stir among the men. Put an end to it, Eden. Now."

"Rage away, Neil dear; give commands to your heart's delight." Eden smiled sweetly but her eyes sparkled defiantly, and she moved so that the candlelight glowed against her bare shoulders. "Short of dragging me kicking and screaming through all these people, there's not a thing you can do."

"Don't tempt me, darling Eden. We both know how few compunctions I have when it comes to you." Neil flashed her a lecherous smile, then examined the smoking tip of his cigar before ruthlessly continuing, "If I were to drag you out of here, as you suggest, I assure you that your embarrassment would be far greater than mine. In fact, I'm not above explaining that you are my runaway mistress."

"You wouldn't dare," Eden gasped, but the challenging eyebrow Neil raised made a far different statement.

"You're welcome to test your theory, of course, but just remember that I gave you fair warning." Neil rose, snubbed out his cigar and circled the table to stand behind Eden's chair.

"I haven't had my coffee yet," Eden softly objected. Neil's hands passed lightly over the soft flesh of her shoulders and she felt her resistance crumble. This was, after all, why she had come to Dallas.

"You can have it later—in my room," Neil said in a low voice. His change of position had granted him a far more tantalizing view of Eden, and he fought to keep his desire from becoming blatantly obvious. Desperately in need of something with which to occupy his hands, Neil seized the treacherous shawl and draped it around Eden's shoulders. "Coming, my dear?"

Thankfully the lobby was nearly deserted as Neil led Eden up the wide, curving staircase; but when they encountered a group of drunken men on Neil's floor, Eden's cheeks burned with embarrassment and she shrank against Neil's side. A few lewd comments were directed toward Eden, which Neil, his golden eyes blazing, effectively silenced by pulling Eden behind him and staring menacingly at each of the men in turn. The group apparently thought better of pushing the tall, dark man any further, and with a sigh of relief Eden watched them retreat down the hall. Neil wordlessly unlocked the door and quickly ushered Eden into the sitting room.

The door closed behind them, shutting out the rest of the world, and Neil turned his amber gaze fully upon Eden. "The question is, ma'am, do I strangle you for the show you gave every man in that dining room or . . ." His voice trailed off and he reached out to tease a curl at Eden's temple.

"Or?" Eden prompted breathlessly.

Neil's voice dropped to a lower register. "Or do I kiss you and tell you how glad I am that you're here?"

"Oh!" It was all Eden had time to say because a moment later she was in Neil's arms, returning his kiss with an intensity which left them both trembling when they finally parted.

"I missed you, I missed you," Neil murmured over and over against her hair. "I was sure that after yesterday I had ruined everything. Forgive me?"

"Always," Eden replied, her voice muffled by Neil's shoulder. "It wasn't just your fault. I'm to blame, too. All these months I've been so caught up in myself that I forgot about your needs and desires. Can *you* ever forgive *me* for being so selfish?"

"As you said—always." Sighing, Neil raised Eden's head from his shoulder and smiled tenderly into the mist-gray eyes. "How long can you stay in Dallas, love?"

"As long as you want me to," Eden said softly. "I've taken a room here at the Fordham through the end of the cattlemen's meeting."

Neil's lips twisted into a smile. "How did you manage that little feat? Or should I ask?"

Eden laughed. "The desk clerk remembered me from the cattle drive." She widened her eyes innocently and was immediately transformed from a sophisticated, confident woman into an uncertain, helpless female.

Neil grinned, unconsciously stroking the satiny flesh beneath his hands. "I pity any man who has to negotiate with you—especially when you pull that poor, helpless widow routine."

"The end justifies the means," Eden murmured, melting at Neil's touch. "All's fair in love."

"And war." Neil was drowning—drowning in two fathomless gray pools, in the feel of Eden in his arms—and he fought to keep himself under control.

"We're not at war anymore, remember," Eden teased. She touched his cheek lightly, then ran her fingers through his dark hair. "We're allies, friends. It's so much better this way."

"I couldn't agree more." Was that really his voice sounding so calm when Neil felt his sanity abandoning him? As long as he kept talking he couldn't give in to the desire howling through his blood. "I promised you coffee, I believe. We'll have it here and then I'll take you back to your room before Millicent has a chance to add another black mark beside my name."

"Millicent isn't here and neither is Shannon . . . or anyone else from the Emerald I."

Trembling, Eden pressed herself against Neil and drew his lips down to hers.

Groaning, Neil slid his hands down Eden's back, molding her softness against his own lean frame. Holding Eden in his arms, feeling torn between ravaging passion and the drive to protect her from ravishment even at his own hands, was like sinking and flying at the same time. Eden's lips parted and Neil thrust into the recesses of her mouth, reality spiraling away in the face of Eden's eager response. Go slowly, his mind warned. Despite her words it may be too soon, she may not be ready. If you rush her as you did once before, you may lose her forever.

Desperately, before all reason deserted him, Neil broke away and purposefully held Eden at arm's length. "Eden, love, I—"

"Hush." Eden reached out and began unbuttoning his shirt.

"You don't know what you're doing," Neil pleaded in a harsh voice. Helpless, he watched as his jacket, cravat and shirt surrendered to her skillful fingers. "There is a limit, my sweet, to what a man can endure."

"Tell me when I've reached it." Neil's shirt slid to the floor and Eden, gray eyes alight, ran her hands over the smooth, rippling skin of Neil's chest. Neil gasped, eliciting a soft laugh from Eden. "So you are not made of stone after all, my darling." She pressed her lips against the bare flesh of his chest, tracing a path upward until their eyes met.

The blood pounded through Neil's veins and he surrendered to Eden at last. Amber eyes molten in his angular face, he slipped his arms around her and murmured accusingly, "Temptress. Seductress."

"Lover," Eden amended, quivering at his touch. "For you, my love. Only for you. Always for you." Her gown fell away, then her chemise parted with a faint rending of silk and it was Eden's turn to gasp as her breasts were crushed against Neil's chest.

"My limit has been reached," Neil informed her in husky tones. In a single, fluid motion he bent, lifted Eden in his arms and carried her to the bedroom.

A kick of his heel sent the second set of doors flying shut and Neil carefully returned Eden to her feet. Their seeking hands stripped away their hesitancy as easily as they removed what clothing still remained, and with a sigh Eden gave in to the passion she had so long kept in check. Entwined in each other's arms they sank to the bed, eagerly recapturing the all-absorbing bond which had begun so long ago.

Eden felt again the strength of his arms as he easily rolled her atop his chest; Neil felt again the softness of Eden's lips as they parted for his questing tongue. Dazedly Eden recalled how amazingly gentle his hands could be as they brought her to the outermost limits of pleasure; and Neil savored the peace only this woman had ever brought to his bed. Briefly Neil recalled the uncertain, troubled girl teetering on the brink of womanhood—she was a woman now, strong and proud, who had been tempered by fire and offered herself to the man she loved beyond all reason. She offered him strength and softness, love and lust—she gave Neil the whole woman she had become, and received in turn the complete man instead of the bitter shell he once had been. This was no ending of a companionable, chaste friendship, but rather the fulfillment of what had been unknowingly promised that day in New York.

"I love you," Eden whispered as Neil rose above her. "I love you."

"Sweet Eden," Neil murmured, his hands sliding beneath her hips. "Sweet, sweet Eden."

His entrance was skillfully gentle, filling him with the same sense of wonder he saw reflected in the soft eyes which fluttered open to meet his gaze. He moved carefully, experimentally, wanting to prolong the moment until he could comprehend the blinding joy which swelled his heart. Did Eden feel it too, this triumph that sent the blood singing through his veins? Did she feel, as he did, that the end to some long, painful search had been reached at last? She must, because a smile lay in the depths of those crystalline eyes—a smile which lingered long after they gave themselves up to the pleasure flooding over them. Eden succumbed first, half-formed words of love and delight escaping from her lips, and she in turn held Neil tightly in her arms as the spasms shuddered through him.

They lay in silence for several minutes, listening as their harsh breathing gradually returned to normal, until with a sigh of regret Neil kissed Eden tenderly and freed her from the burden of his weight. Propping himself up on one elbow, Neil ran a hand over the curve of Eden's waist and smiled into the clear eyes. "You never fail to surprise me, love."

"Because of this?" Eden queried.

"No." Neil shook his head and captured her hand in his. "What surprises me is that you cared enough to follow me after the things I said yesterday."

"I nearly didn't," Eden confessed. "By dinnertime last night I had consigned you to the deepest part of a very hot place."

"But you obviously changed your mind." Neil pressed a kiss into the palm of her hand. "Why?"

"Oh, my darling Neil," Eden sighed, tears starting to her eyes. "Have I really played my part so well that you can't guess what I'm trying to say?" She struggled upright on the bed and faced him seriously. "I started to tell you yesterday, at the stream, but I was afraid you would laugh at me and tell me I was being foolish." Eden drew a shaky breath and smiled faintly. "I had to follow you, Neil, because I love you. I don't want to spend the rest of my days hiding that love from myself or from you." Neil started to speak but Eden placed her fingers across his lips and shook her head. "Don't say anything—there are no strings between us, remember? All that matters to me is that I love you; and I'm not afraid anymore to show my love."

"That's why you came? To show me?" At Eden's nod, Neil sat up and kissed her deeply, searchingly. When the tender exchange ended he framed Eden's face with his hands and stared at her, his golden eyes burning with some unnamed emotion. "Do you know what you've risked by coming here? No matter how discreet we are, how cautious, there may be gossip."

Eden ran a hand through his dark hair and smiled. "I considered that, and I decided if I had to choose between my so-called reputation and being with the man I love, there could be only one choice."

"You're very brave," Neil said in a low voice, unwillingly touched by her honesty.

"Not brave," Eden countered. "Just terribly selfish. I couldn't bear the thought of losing you so soon after having found you."

"I might have disappointed you," Neil teased gently. "Given the mood I've been in for the past twenty-four hours, this might have turned out quite differently."

Eden laughed, vanquishing such dark thoughts with a wave of her hand. "You asked me to trust you. I tried not to think of anything else on my way here. And as for you"—Eden twined her arms around his neck and gazed at him happily— "this should teach you not to run off when we're having a fight. I don't give up that easily."

"Yes, ma'am, I'll remember," Neil assured her, grinning. A sultry gleam came into Eden's eyes, and as her hands began exploring his responses to her touch Neil fell back against the pillows, surrendering to the heated sensations Eden was evoking.

"My darling, we've always had the desire," Eden murmured as she impatiently guided his entrance into her. "Whatever else may happen, neither one of us can ever deny the passion."

Eden woke late the following morning and found, much to her disappointment, that the pillow beside hers was empty. Disappointment fled rapidly, however, as memories of the night before sprang to mind, and with a purr she stretched beneath the sheet. A wistful smile curved her lips and she rolled to her side. Pulling Neil's pillow into her arms, Eden found that a trace of his cologne lingered there and she breathed deeply of the familiar scent. Will Neil ever love me? Eden wondered with a sudden pang. It was enough for now that Neil met her love with fondness, but her mind could not help straying to the future. She understood and accepted the fact that marriage had no place in Neil's life—and therefore in her own—but Eden still hoped that, given time, Neil would return her love.

And if he did not? some traitorous part of her mind whispered. Her smile faded at the thought, her gray eyes darkening with sadness. Well then, she would have to be content with today and whatever tomorrows she and Neil had to share. She dared not forget that someday Neil might be lost to her; and though she would always love him, she had to steel herself against the time when they would part.

"Eden?"

The sound of her name softly called from the doorway drew her upright with a muffled gasp. Instinctively she clutched the thin sheet to her breast, turning her startled gaze toward the source of the disturbance. "Neil!" The breath left her lungs in a whoosh and Eden sank weakly against the headboard.

"Who else?" Grinning and fully dressed, Neil sauntered into the room and settled himself on the edge of the bed. "You, my sweet, are white as a ghost. Don't tell me I frightened you."

"You most certainly did," Eden responded spiritedly. "I didn't even hear you come in."

"That is because I've been back for"—Neil consulted his watch—"nearly an hour."

"An hour!" Eden sat up and examined the timepiece. "It's after noon! Why didn't you wake me, Neil?"

Neil shrugged and combed his fingers through the mass of pale curls. "After last night I thought you could use the rest. Besides, I had meetings this morning and I didn't relish the idea of your spending all that time cooped up in a hotel room."

"I appreciate your concern," Eden teased, "but you needn't have worried. I have things to do which will occupy at least a full day. I could have been up and about!"

"Even worse," Neil muttered, a shadow entering his eyes, "I don't want some gallant trying to turn your head when I'm safely out of the way."

Eden laughed. "You make it sound as if every man in Dallas is just waiting for me to set foot outside this hotel. Honestly, Neil, don't you think you're exaggerating the masculine response to a woman's presence?"

"Not where you're concerned," Neil informed her in a steely voice. "Too many men around here are too damn eager for your company to suit me."

A hint of anger flared in the gray eyes and, concealing her

ire, Eden leaned forward and drew a slender forefinger down the bronze skin which showed through Neil's half-open shirt. "Am I to gather from that statement, sir, that you feel my head is easily turned?"

The odd note in her voice should have put Neil on his guard, but, after having overheard some speculation about Eden's identity after the meeting just this morning, Neil's jealousy reared its ugly head once again. Obsessed with the need to keep Eden to himself, Neil blundered straight into her anger. "I am saying, sweet, that all women like being charmed and adored. That is a fact of life."

"You should know, *darling*. After all, your string of conquests alone is living testimony. *Myself included.*"

Her sarcasm was not unnoticed and with a jolt Neil realized he had vented his frustration on the wrong person. "Eden, I didn't mean—"

"Oh, yes you did!" With a snort of contempt Eden placed both hands on his shoulders and shoved Neil backward onto the bed. As he fell Eden disentangled herself from the sheet, flew from the bed and hastily snatched up his discarded dressing gown as protection against the wicked, amber gaze Neil leveled upon her. "If I wanted to be charmed and complimented and adored by someone I didn't give a bloody damn about, I would have stayed home," Eden railed. "I didn't come all this way to be accused of being a trollop, Neil! I came to you because I love you, because our chaste friendship wasn't enough for me anymore. And I came because you asked me, because I honestly believed I meant more to you than a woman you could buy for the night! Is this what you think of me after all this— that I'll fall into bed with any man who asks me?" To her mortification Eden felt the tears streaming down her cheeks and she brushed at them despairingly. "Damn it, Neil, I thought you understood me better than that!"

Neil's eyes clouded and he gestured helplessly, thoroughly shamed by her accusations. "I'm sorry, Eden." It was all he could think of to say.

"Are you really," Eden jeered. "Well, since we're on the subject of promiscuity, let me ask you a question: Are you sorry about all the women you've taken over the past few months?"

"No," Neil replied, a muscle working in his jaw.

His answer was not what Eden had expected and instead of

turning the sharp edge of recrimination against Neil she discovered that knife's blade was only lodged more deeply in her own heart. In a cracked voice Eden said, "I see. Now I suppose you're going to tell me that you had to have those women because your needs are different from mine."

"No," repeated Neil quietly. A sob escaped Eden before she could control herself and in desperation she turned her back on Neil. The move lost most of its defiance, however, because her slender back was without the concealment of the dressing gown. Neil eyed her uncertainly, torn between amusement and the earnest desire to ease the hurt she was obviously enduring. He rose from the bed, crossed the room, and stopped only inches behind Eden, both hands coming to rest upon her shoulders. "On that point, love, I have nothing for which to apologize. As I told you once before, I've laid a hand on no woman since our...agreement in Mexico." He turned Eden in his arms and forced her to meet his gaze. "Do you believe me?"

Eden studied him intently, searching for the truth in the fathomless golden eyes. He met her scrutiny unwaveringly and at last Eden nodded. "I believe you."

"Good." Neil kissed her gently.

"Your implications were still cruel," Eden said, unwilling to be totally pacified. "If you can't believe that I love you with all my heart, if you don't understand that my love makes me impervious to other men's overtures, then any trust or affection we built between us since Mexico is going to sour."

"I'm beginning to see that." Neil sighed and pulled Eden against his chest. "Be patient with me, Eden. When I could view life through cynical eyes everything appeared so simple, but somehow when I'm with you I feel as if my every nerve is exposed." He chuckled and briefly tightened his embrace. "I'll tell you a secret, love: I'm so jealous over you that if I catch another man even looking at you I see red."

"There's no reason to be jealous," Eden assured him. "No one can take me away from you. But you can drive me away with thoughtless, unfounded accusations. Don't do that to me, Neil; don't do that to us."

"I won't," Neil promised. "I just need time, love; time to hold you and make love to you. Time to learn that you'll still be mine even if I'm not with you every moment of every day."

Eden's heart softened at the gentle plea and she melted against Neil, offering him the only solace she could be certain he would understand—herself. The dressing gown fell away beneath Neil's fingers, the argument faded into memory as the shadows lengthened across the floor and for a time the man and the woman existed solely for each other.

"I'd like to keep you here forever," Neil murmured when they awoke as twilight descended.

Eden laughed warmly and ran a hand over his chest. "A lovely sentiment, but rather impractical. First of all, I have a child waiting for me at home; and second, at the moment I am famished."

"How can you think of food when we have the entire evening ahead of us?" Neil chided. "I offer you ambrosia and you ask for beer."

"I'm asking for food," Eden rejoined, deftly escaping his hands when Neil reached for her again. She slipped from the bed and began sorting through the pile of clothes which Neil had carelessly tossed upon a chair. "You at least had breakfast," she reminded him over her shoulder, "whereas I haven't eaten since last night. Even women in love need nourishment, and since I am most definitely . . ."

Eden's voice trailed off and with a smug grin Neil folded his arms beneath his head and watched a frown knit her brows. "Something wrong, sweetheart?"

"My gown," Eden muttered. "Have you seen it?"

Neil assumed a thoughtful expression. "I may have. What did it look like?"

Eden stared at him in disbelief. "That is the silliest question I've ever heard! Unless you've taken to wearing women's clothing, I don't see how you could overlook my gown." She started toward the sitting room only to be brought up short by Neil's drawling voice.

"You won't find it out there, love; it's gone." Neil rose and, unconcerned with his state of undress, strode past a blushing, speechless Eden into the sitting room, reappearing a moment later carrying a valise Eden recognized as her own. "I took the liberty of removing a few things from your room this morning."

Wordlessly, Eden accepted the bag, rummaged through it, then turned perplexed eyes on Neil. "Unfortunately I can't set foot outside this room dressed only in my camisole."

Neil's eyes danced with amusement. "Did I forget to pack a dress? How careless of me." Grinning, he lifted a handful of pale curls from Eden's shoulder and thoughtfully rubbed them against his cheek. "I've never kept a woman prisoner in my room before—the idea presents endless possibilities."

Was Neil teasing, Eden wondered, or was he serious? Those golden eyes told her nothing... except that he wanted her again. The amber gaze locked with her own and the breath caught in Eden's throat as unspent passion rose between them. Liquid fire surged through her veins and Eden reached out to touch Neil, to further explore the body she was learning to know so well. Dimly, Eden became aware that something was intruding upon their isolation, but only when Neil unwillingly pulled away and hurriedly dressed did she realize there was a discreet tapping on the door.

Murmuring an apology, Neil stepped into the sitting room and pulled the bedroom door firmly shut before answering the persistent knock. Cursing the binding cut of his trousers, Neil nonetheless greeted his visitor with faultless aplomb. "Good evening, Mrs. Alderson."

"Mr. Banning." The woman returned his smile with a speculative one of her own and entered the sitting room. A paper-wrapped package nearly the size of Mrs. Alderson was held carefully in her arms and she offered it to Neil. "Would you care to examine your purchase?"

"I think not. For the price I'm paying you I expect the merchandise to be no less than perfect." The feminine gaze lowered, taking in the half-buttoned shirt and Neil's general state of dishabille, and a knowing look spread over the woman's face. In embarrassment, Neil said stiffly, "You did include the matching shoes, I assume."

"Of course, sir; and the stockings and underthings as well." Mrs. Alderson draped her burden over the back of a chair and smiled at Neil. She was accustomed to dealing with men who enjoyed showering their mistresses with expensive gifts, and this man appeared to be no different from the rest. Her shop thrived on business such as this, and for the profit she would make on this one gift Mrs. Alderson was quite willing to overlook any display of hauteur.

Neil extracted a roll of money from his pocket, peeled off several bills and handed them to the woman. "You are most efficient. Thank you."

"My *pleasure*, Mr. Banning." Mrs. Alderson accented the word ever so slightly and with a meaningful glance at the bedroom door she dropped the bills into her reticule. "I'm certain your, ahem, *friend* will be quite pleased with your selection. Unlike most men, your taste in this matter is most refined. I find it refreshing to do business with someone who believes in the graciousness of understatement."

For some strange reason, the woman's chatter was diminishing the pleasure Neil had taken in finding a gift for Eden. "My *friend,* as you put it, is a lady, Mrs. Alderson—a lady who deserves only the best."

"Undoubtedly." The seamstress's tone held a smirk. "There's no need to be defensive, Mr. Banning. I understand the situation quite well."

"I'm sure you do." Neil's face was an angry mask as he opened the door. "Good night, Mrs. Alderson."

Her proper upbringing made eavesdropping and peering through keyholes unacceptable to Eden, but the moment Neil opened the bedroom door she flew from the bed and bombarded him with questions.

"Gently, my sweet," Neil teased lightly, managing a twisted smile and cheerful tone for Eden's benefit. While he had been busy with Mrs. Alderson, Eden had taken the opportunity to slip into his dressing gown, and the sight of her buried under the voluminous folds did nothing to brighten Neil's spirits. "I see you took advantage of my absence."

Eden fingered the material of Neil's dressing gown and tightened the belt more securely around her waist. "I had to wear something, Neil, and heaven knows you left me little enough to choose from. Do you mind?"

"No, of course not, I . . . Eden, I have a gift for you." Neil blurted the words out so unexpectedly that even he was surprised to hear them. Quickly, before that annoying feeling of guilt destroyed all his good intentions, Neil led Eden into the sitting room and waved a hand toward the package on the chair. "I hope you like it, love, but if you don't—"

"Of course I'll like it. Why wouldn't I?" Delighted, Eden tore off the paper; then stood silently, examining the gift with wide eyes. "Oh, Neil," she murmured finally.

"You don't like it."

"No, I do," Eden protested. "I just didn't expect . . ." Her voice trailed off and with a soft laugh Eden disposed of the rest of the paper and lifted a silk evening gown the color of pewter from the debris. Smiling radiantly, Eden held the dress up to her shoulders and danced across the room to stand in front of Neil. "Neil, it's beautiful! Thank you."

"You're welcome, love." Neil smiled down at her, a strange tenderness washing through him. Suddenly it was vitally important to Neil that Eden not misconstrue his gift as the seamstress had. "I want you to know that I ordered this for you yesterday—before I knew you were coming to Dallas. But this morning I stopped by the shop and asked to have it finished by tonight. It was intended to be a peace offering, Eden, not payment for what happened last night."

"I know that," Eden said quietly. She placed a light kiss on his lips and gazed at Neil through shining eyes. "I've stopped believing the worst of you, you know."

"I only wanted to make you happy," Neil added, still driven to clarify his motives.

"And you have." Eden smiled. "It's lovely, Neil, and I'll treasure it always. Not only because of its beauty, but also because you cared enough about me to do something you thought would please me. That means a great deal to me."

Some of the original enjoyment Neil had taken in his surprise returned, but as they lingered over a late dinner Neil found his thoughts straying once again to the seamstress and her innuendoes. Damn the woman, Neil cursed silently. Why couldn't she simply have delivered the gown and kept her comments to herself, instead of making such an innocuous present appear shamefully wicked? Guilt returned with a heavy hand, causing Neil to stir uneasily in the face of Eden's light spirits. The color of the gown set off Eden's eyes to a decided advantage, making them seem twice their normal size in her glowing face, and her slender figure lent the most tantalizing curves to the pewter silk. Tonight Neil didn't have to overhear the masculine conversations he was certain were taking place—he caught the covetous glances and frankly lustful stares, returning each with a menacing glower of his own. That golden threat sank the hopes of many; and while Neil was proud to be able to claim Eden as his, it was with a sense of relief that he escorted her from the restaurant and back to the seclusion of his room.

The few days they had stolen from the normal pattern of their lives were precious to both Neil and Eden, and they made the most of them. The transition from friends to lovers was smoothly accomplished and both took an unabashed delight in their new roles. Nurtured by Neil's passionate ardor Eden blos-

somed, holding nothing in reserve. She refused to worry about
what the future might bring, but instead reveled in the pure joy
which shot through her whenever she glanced at Neil. He had
tapped a hitherto unknown reservoir of love within her and she
gave herself to him willingly, no longer questioning his intentions. Nothing mattered save the love she felt for this man; and
in their priceless span of time, Eden unwittingly showed Neil
the quintessential beauty love could bring.

It came as a jolt to Neil to realize that truly no other man
existed for Eden. She seemed impervious to the admiring looks
turned her way, but his own admiration was greeted by a faint
blush and a soft expression in the depths of those mist-gray
eyes that sent his senses reeling. Jealousy no longer gnawed
at him when Eden announced she was going shopping or returning to her own room (for appearances, as she laughingly
put it) during the times Neil was caught up in meetings. With
a newfound sense of fairness, Neil discovered that to keep Eden
from occupying those hours in whatever way she desired was
selfish. She was always waiting in his room when he returned,
ready to listen to the events of his day, ready to erase the minor
irritations with a teasing word or sound logic. Eden did not
indulge in empty-headed chatter, but she could cajole Neil out
of a black humor before he knew what was happening.

And yet... what they shared was not enough for Neil. All
too soon they would return to Lathrop, and the thought unsettled
him. Here in Dallas they could be seen together at any hour
and remain anonymous, but once they were home such appearances would unquestionably cause gossip. If they continued
there as they did here, it would be only a matter of time before
Eden's reputation was shredded beyond repair. What would
happen to her then? How would Eden deal with the public
humiliation of being labeled his mistress? How would he, for
that matter? Worse yet, how could Eden explain the snickers
and whispers to Shannon when the child was old enough to
realize her mother's life was somehow different from other
women's?

The questions roiled within Neil, creeping into his consciousness when he least expected them. They destroyed his
concentration during the conference, and at night, with Eden
slumbering peacefully at his side, they drove Neil from the
bed. Robbed of sleep, deprived of the contentment and the
afterglow of their lovemaking, he spent his restless hours in

a chair by the window. With his golden gaze dwelling on the sleeping woman, he would wrestle with the emotions she had brought to the fore—emotions he had thought were long buried. Eden is mine, Neil would chide himself. She came to me freely, knowing that we would become lovers. This is how it should be—no ties, no strings, just two people enjoying each other as God intended. Sighing, unconvinced, Neil eventually would return to bed and take Eden into his arms. If this was precisely what he wanted, then why did he feel something important was missing?

It was their last day in Dallas and Eden, in high spirits, stepped out of the bookshop she had just patronized. Consulting the slip of paper on which she had listed her last-minute errands, Eden nodded in satisfaction, returned the list to her handbag and gave a sigh of relief. Now she was free to devote the afternoon to a luxurious toilette in preparation for the dance tonight. Neil—the cad—hadn't mentioned the fact that the cattlemen's association was holding a dance until this morning, when he had casually dropped the invitation into Eden's lap. Grinning, Neil had asked if she wished to dance the night away and had been answered by a resounding "yes!" Determined to look her best for meeting Neil's associates, Eden condensed a day's worth of errands into a few hours so that she could bathe, shampoo her hair and dress without the pressure of time. Her appearance tonight would be as flawlessly perfect as she could make it, and hopefully the scowl which occasionally crossed Neil's face when she caught him watching her would be absent tonight.

"Eden! Eden Colter!"

Eden paused in midstep, turned at the sound of her name and felt the blood drain from her face as a tall man waved at her and strode across the street. There was no mistaking the red-gold hair visible beneath his hat, or the badge glinting on the left side of his vest, and Eden shuddered as the man bore down upon her.

"Hello, Eden." Keith Gerald swept the hat from his head and took one of her icy hands in his. "Of all the people I thought I might see in Dallas, I sure didn't expect to see you. How are you?"

Eden stared blankly at Keith, scarcely hearing what he said. All she could think of was that Neil and Keith were in the same town and sooner or later they would come face to face. Probably sooner, Eden thought with rising panic, because she was on her way to meet Neil for lunch and she wasn't at all certain she could be rid of Keith by the time she got to the restaurant. In a voice which sounded painfully high and brittle to her own ears, Eden forced herself to speak. "Keith . . . this is such a surprise."

"A pleasant one, I hope." Keith smiled and pulled her arm through his. "Where are you going?"

"I planned on having lunch—"

"Splendid! I haven't eaten all day and I'm half starved. Mind if I join you?" Without waiting for a reply, Keith guided Eden into the flow of pedestrian traffic. "Which restaurant?"

Eden supplied the name woodenly, desperately trying to think of a way out of her dilemma. "W-what are you doing here?"

"Delivering a prisoner," Keith answered, pleased that his unexpected appearance was having such an obvious effect upon Eden. "Cal—you remember Cal, don't you?—was supposed to do it, but he got himself shot the night before he was due to leave Laredo so I ended up with the job." Keith grinned and pulled Eden a bit closer, adding, "Now I'll have to thank him for stopping that bullet. One man's loss, as they say."

Eden colored. "I'm sorry—he's not seriously injured, is he?"

Keith shook his head. "He'll be fine in a few weeks, no need for concern. Now tell me: What are you doing in Dallas?"

Eden swallowed hard. "Holiday . . . I needed to get away from the ranch for a few days."

"How long are you staying?" Keith inquired. "I might be able to get some time off myself."

"No!" Alarmed, Eden blurted out the word without thinking. "I—I mean, I'm leaving tomorrow. It's time I got back to Shannon, before she starts thinking Millicent is her mother."

"I can escort you to Lathrop then," Keith offered, oblivious to Eden's agitation. "We have some things to discuss, you and I."

"That's where you're wrong," Eden informed him coldly, her self-control returning in the face of Keith's casual presumptuousness. "We said everything we had to say months ago. And as long as you brought it up, I trust your Christmas gift to me was returned intact?"

Keith's blue eyes frosted but he managed a gentle tone.
"It was, and your note as well. The ring is in Laredo, waiting
to be worn."

"Not by me," Eden countered bluntly.

"*Only* by you," Keith returned sharply, brushing Eden's
defiance aside. "I'll grant you my timing was bad and I should
have delivered the gift in person, but I was halfway across the
state of Texas and I didn't want to wait until my job took me
back to Lathrop. Is that so hard to understand?"

"The last time we saw each other I told you I wouldn't
marry you," Eden reminded him. "Did you honestly think I
would change my mind because of a ring?"

"It was the only way I could think of to apologize for the
things I said to you and to let you know that I was dead serious
about wanting to marry you." Keith stopped in front of the
restaurant and faced Eden squarely. "I still am. You're all I've
thought about these past months, Eden." He looked pointedly
at her dress. "Now that you're out of mourning, there's no
reason for me to wait any longer. I want to marry you, Eden,
just as soon as you say 'yes.'"

Eden dropped her gaze to the sidewalk. "No."

"I'll be a good husband, Eden, I swear it. And I'll do my
best to be a good father to Shannon." Keith cupped her chin
in one hand. "I love you, Eden. I want you."

"No!" Eden pushed his hand away. "I don't feel the same
way about you, and I never will. Even if I did, I would never
marry a man in your profession—I need a man who can be a
full-time husband, not someone who drops into my life every
few months, as you seem prone to do. I have the responsibility
of running a ranch and raising a child of my own—I don't
need the additional burden of an absentee husband." They were
attracting stares and Eden deliberately withdrew her arm from
Keith's.

"Would it make a difference if I told you I don't plan to
reenlist when my hitch ends this year?" Keith asked quietly.
"I own part of a business in San Francisco, Eden. I'm more
than willing to give up this badge and build a life for us in San
Francisco. I'll be the kind of husband you want, darling; you'll
see."

Angered by Keith's stubbornness, terrified that Neil would
arrive at any minute, Eden became unmercifully blunt. "Keith,
I'm sorry you are forcing me to say this, but you could never

be the kind of husband I want because, quite frankly, you're not the kind of man I want. I hope I have made myself quite clear. Good day, Captain Gerald." She turned and hurried into the restaurant before Keith could stop her.

To Eden's dismay Neil was already waiting for her, and as she was led to their table in a secluded corner of the restaurant Eden fought to control the trembling which had seized her hands.

"Hello, love." Neil rose to hand Eden into her chair and he squeezed her shoulder affectionately before returning to his own seat. "Finish your shopping?"

"Y-yes." To her horror Eden's voice cracked and she avoided Neil's sharp look. "How about you? Did you finish your errands?"

Neil nodded. "It didn't take as long as I expected, so I went back to the hotel and returned your things to your room." He grinned and leaned forward to whisper, "I still think you'd enjoy sharing a tub with me far more than you'll like bathing by yourself. Are you sure you won't change your mind about this afternoon?"

"If I do, I can guarantee we'll be late for the dance." The bantering note in her voice sounded forced and, hoping Neil hadn't noticed, Eden reached for her water to give herself time to master her inner turmoil.

Her action backfired, however, because the delicate hand she extended trembled worse than her voice. Frowning, Neil caught her hand before it reached its destination. "Eden—good God, love, you're shaking like a leaf!" His golden eyes surveyed her attentively, the teasing light vanishing as he took in Eden's pallor and the tension in her face. In a low voice Neil questioned, "What happened to you?"

"Nothing."

"Forgive me, sweetheart, but I don't believe you." When Eden didn't meet his gaze, Neil's frown deepened. "I'll find out eventually, so why not save me the time and trouble of badgering you and tell me why you're so upset."

"It's nothing," Eden insisted, troubled gray eyes at last meeting his. Neil raised a skeptical eyebrow and Eden nervously wet her lips. "I just overdid it this morning, rushing around from store to store. That's all."

"That's an unlikely story coming from a woman who survived a cattle drive." Neil's face hardened. "You're lying to me, Eden."

"No, I'm—" Eden's voice died abruptly as she glanced over Neil's shoulder and she closed her eyes despairingly.

"What the devil is wrong with you?" Neil demanded, now more shaken than angered by Eden's evasiveness.

"Maybe it's me," said a deep voice behind Neil.

Neil swung around to find Keith Gerald standing behind him, and as he watched through narrowed eyes the Ranger folded himself into a chair at the table.

"I don't remember asking you to join us, Captain," Neil said coldly.

Ignoring him, Keith fixed his stare on an ashen-faced Eden. "You didn't tell me you were meeting someone for lunch. I'm terribly disappointed in you, my dear."

"Keith, please," Eden murmured weakly. "Don't cause any trouble."

"Trouble? My darling Eden, that is the farthest thing from my mind." Keith directed a stare at her hand, tightly clasped in Neil's. "Let go of him, Eden. It makes my skin crawl to see you touching an animal like Banning."

His demand unnerved Eden and, fearing a scene, she started to obey, only to have Neil's fingers tighten reassuringly.

"You're upsetting Eden," Neil said in a hushed voice. "I'd appreciate it if you would leave us, Captain."

"I'm sure you would," Keith sneered. "Unfortunately I don't plan to leave unless Eden comes with me." Eden shook her head and he cursed softly. "Damn! I knew I shouldn't have left you where Banning could get at you! What kind of lies has he told you, Eden? What sort of stories did he make up to get you to believe in him?"

"None," Eden replied faintly. "The only lie I heard was yours—the one about my agreeing to marry you."

Keith's lethal glare turned on Neil. "You bastard!"

A muscle worked in Neil's jaw, the only indication of the rage boiling inside him. "I'll meet you wherever and whenever you like, Gerald, if that's what you want. Just give me a chance to take Eden back to the hotel."

"I'm not about to let you get within three feet of Eden's hotel room," Keith ground out. "God knows what you might do to her!"

"You're digging your own grave, Gerald," Neil warned.

"What's going on between you and me has nothing to do with Eden, so why don't you have the decency to keep remarks like that to yourself."

"Why didn't you have the decency to leave her alone," Keith parried bitterly. "And you, Eden, how could you even consider being seen in public with this lowlife? He's a rustler, a killer. When you found out he followed you to Dallas why the hell didn't you go back home?"

"Gerald," Neil cut in, "if you say one more word, so help me I'll—"

"You'll what?" Keith taunted. "Call me out? You don't have the guts. Now you just sit here and enjoy your meal. I'm going to take Eden back to Lathrop before you trick her into thinking she means something to you." Keith's words brought a strange look to Eden's face, and his grim smile slowly turned ugly. "Or am I too late to save you from the disgrace of being Banning's whore?"

Neil started to rise and Eden desperately held him back, although her face burned with humiliation. Bravely she countered, "You don't know what you're talking about, Keith."

"Don't I?" Keith studied the couple intently, his blue eyes turning dark with contempt. "You should have told me you were Banning's mistress, Eden. I wouldn't have bothered to propose again." Keith rose. "When Banning gets tired of you let me know—I'll double whatever he's paid you."

The insult brought scalding tears to Eden's eyes and seeing them, Neil controlled the urge to put his fist through the Ranger's face. Eden was humiliated enough without adding a brawl to the confrontation. Seething inwardly, Neil had no choice but to hold Eden's hand and watch Keith thread his way through the restaurant. Damn him, Neil thought viciously. Damn him for showing up at this moment, for hurting Eden, for destroying the pleasure of the past few days.

"I'll kill him," Neil muttered, drawing Eden's misty stare. "I swear to you, Eden, I'll kill him for what he said."

"No," Eden replied softly, but vehemently. Her lower lip quivering, Eden reclaimed her hand and placed it in her lap. "It doesn't matter."

"It matters to me," Neil said harshly. "Gerald had no right to say what he did."

"Keith only said to my face what someone else might say behind my back. At least he was honest." The smile Eden attempted failed miserably and she looked away from those all-knowing golden eyes. "I'm sorry, Neil, but I seem to have lost my appetite. Would you mind terribly if I went back to the hotel?"

Neil's face contorted briefly but he managed to keep his voice level. "No, of course not. Just let me pay the check and we'll leave."

"No, you stay and finish your meal. I can find my own way." Rising, Eden gave Neil a wistful look. "I love you, Neil; always remember that."

She was gone before Neil could stop her, before he could tell her what he had discovered in his heart. I love you, Eden, he wanted to shout at her retreating back. I love you! But the words seemed unnatural, and because they distressed him, Neil's tongue remained chained. His meal arrived and he ate automatically, not realizing what he was doing. *I love you.* Neil had spent his life avoiding those words, avoiding the commitment which accompanied them. Love had destroyed his mother, and her tragedy haunted his own life as well.

*I love you.* Was it love to wake up in the morning and know pure joy because a woman with golden hair lay curled against his side? Was it love which lent an extraordinary splendor to their physical unions? No matter how often he took Eden, no matter how often the passion rose up between them, he was always astounded by the thunderous force of his own emotions. *I love you.* Imagine a life without Eden—imagine the lonely days stretching into bleak, empty years. Imagine never seeing her again, never holding her, never hearing the gentle cadence of her voice.

"I love you." Neil tried the words on himself in a barely audible whisper. His tongue didn't stumble over the words, nor did he feel less of a man. He felt, instead, an inner peace so deep and abiding that he found the strength to call himself a fool. He knew now, with unshakable certainty, that he had loved Eden from the first time they met—and that it had been his cowardice, not his wisdom, which had driven them apart. He had made a hideous mistake.

I cannot stay, Eden told herself, I cannot. The thought shattered her heart and her hard-won composure, and she surrendered to the tears she had managed to keep at bay before reaching her room. Sobbing, Eden desperately clutched the shawl she held—another of Neil's surprises—and stumbled to a chair. Through tear-blurred eyes she watched as her hands carefully folded the shawl and smoothed the material. It's been a lie, she thought wretchedly; a beautiful, magical lie, but a lie nonetheless. She had been wrong to believe that she could be happy as Neil's mistress. Oh, God, she had been so wrong!

Even if Neil came to love her, his love would not change the fact that she needed to be more than his mistress. How she wished it could be otherwise! How she wished she could be strong enough to believe that her love for Neil was all that mattered. For herself or her own reputation Eden cared not at all, but she did care about Shannon. It was Shannon who would be subjected to the gossip, the biting slander, and Eden found she could not bring herself to put her child through that ordeal. There would always be a Jane Gregory, Eden reflected dully, someone who took malicious delight in ravaging the guiltless. Perhaps, years from now, this choice would seem less bitter— perhaps the torment of choosing between her child and the man she loved so completely would ease.

But never to see Neil again! A sharp pain jarred through Eden at that thought and she cried out softly. To have to live on memories of what they had shared and dreams of what might have been . . .

But there could be no further delays. She had to escape now, while there was time. The break with Neil had to be quick and clean—later she could agonize over her decision.

Think of Shannon, Eden commanded her wayward heart. Think only of Shannon. She wildly packed her belongings, wrote a cold, heartless note and addressed it to Neil. It's better this way, Eden told herself as she sealed the envelope. After reading this Neil would damn her forever—his arrogant pride would never permit him to come after her. She would be spared the agony of explaining the truth behind this final separation.

A knock sounded at the door and Eden hastily brushed a hand over her damp cheeks before opening the portal. "That was quick, Dennis, I . . ." Her words died as Neil, his face grim, stared down at her.

"Dennis couldn't make it, sweetheart, so I volunteered to deliver this." Neil withdrew an envelope from his inside coat pocket and dangled it negligently between his fingers. "Will you tell me what's in here, or shall I look for myself?"

"It's a train ticket," Eden answered hollowly.

"I beg your pardon?" Neil tilted his head as if he hadn't heard her.

"A train ticket," Eden repeated with more force. Steeling herself against the weakness flooding through her at the mere sight of Neil, Eden arranged her features into an expressionless mask and held out her hand. "It was kind of you to assume Dennis's responsibility. May I have the ticket, please?"

"Ah, the ticket." Neil's mocking gaze contemplated her pinched face for a long moment before swinging back to the envelope. "Where are you off to, I wonder? Back to Lathrop? To Laredo, perhaps, to persuade the gallant Captain Gerald that he was mistaken about us and to accept his proposal of marriage?"

Eden's nerves frayed under Neil's cynicism and in sheer desperation she snatched for the envelope—a move she instantly regretted because Neil's free arm circled her waist and without so much as a by-your-leave he swept them both back into the room. Alarmed by his touch, Eden wrenched herself free and regarded Neil warily as he closed and locked the door. "You have no right—" she began.

A savage look from Neil quelled her protest. Satisfied, Neil prowled the sitting room, his long strides taking him to the bedroom doorway, where he paused to raise an eyebrow at the luggage on the bed. In a deceptively soft voice he remarked, "My, my. You don't waste any time, do you? You must be in one hell of a hurry, sweetheart."

"Neil, I..." Eden's voice faltered as twin flames of gold raked over her. She swallowed convulsively and tried again. "I—I'd like my ticket, Neil. Please."

A sardonic smile twisted Neil's lips. "Are you running to Keith Gerald?"

"That's none of your damn business," Eden snapped.

"Like hell it isn't," Neil ground out. He began to pace the room again, the suppressed violence of his movement reminding Eden of a caged panther. "You leave me sitting in a restaurant and when I get back here I find you planning to sneak off without so much as a damned note!" He paused in front of the desk and, snarling, seized the envelope Eden had so recently sealed. "What the hell is this?"

"The note you wanted," Eden informed him icily. "Must you swear so much?"

"Either I swear or break the furniture," Neil shot back.

"Which do you prefer?" Not bothering to wait for her reply, Neil slipped her ticket back into his pocket and tore open the envelope containing Eden's note. He read in silence for several minutes, his face going rigid with shock and disbelief.

Eden watched him cautiously, nervously edging her way toward the door while Neil's thoughts and eyes were occupied. If necessary she would flee without her luggage! She had enough money in the pocket of her dress, and the clothes she would be leaving behind were the least of her worries. Eden could deal with any advances Neil might make, but the loathing, the contempt Neil would feel for her once he finished reading the note—that Eden could not face. Eden reached the door and, keeping an eye on Neil, fumbled behind her back for the lock. She found the bolt first and fairly shook with relief when it slid noiselessly out of the slot. Now only the key was left and as her fingers searched for the suddenly elusive object, she turned her head slightly to aid her trembling fingers in their quest.

"I took the key."

With a gasp Eden spun around to find Neil watching her. "You can't keep me here!" she protested indignantly.

"Can't I?" Golden eyes hooded, Neil calmly lit a cigar and studied Eden thoughtfully. "If you can run off and leave me this"—Neil contemptuously crumpled her note in a ball, placed it in the ashtray and touched the glowing tip of his cigar to the paper—"then rest assured, my sweet, I can and I will keep you here as long as is necessary."

"I have neither the time nor the inclination for this silly game," Eden said waspishly. "I have a train to catch."

"So I gathered." Neil leaned negligently against the windowsill, indolently holding the thin cigar, and fixed Eden with a frigid stare. "Are you running to Keith Gerald?"

"What if I am," Eden challenged. "Keith has his faults but he loves me and he's willing to marry me."

"But do you love him?"

Eden shrugged carelessly. "As you once told me, love has nothing to do with marriage. I could make Keith happy, given the chance, and Keith would make a good husband."

"I don't believe you," Neil said flatly. "You're not the type of woman who can spend a week in one man's bed and then turn around and marry another man she doesn't even like." Neil stubbed out his cigar and regarded Eden skeptically. "In other words, my sweet, you are lying. You're not running to Keith, you're running away from me."

"Don't flatter yourself," Eden retorted. "And don't misjudge me. I meant what I said in the note—now that my curiosity about you has been satisfied I find the role of your mistress quite boring." Neil's face twisted with pain, and Eden forced herself to meet his gaze. "Enjoyable as your lovemaking during these past few days has been, the attraction is beginning to pall. In short, I find that you are the wrong man for me."

"And Keith is the right man for you?" Neil snorted. "The idea is absurd!"

"It is not," Eden stormed, her desperation to be rid of Neil changing to anger in the face of his calm rejection of her story. "Despite what happened today, I'll wager that in less than a week I could be Mrs. Keith Gerald."

"I don't doubt it," Neil conceded. "A man would have to be a fool to pass up the opportunity to marry you. The question is: How long would your marriage to Keith last? He's away twenty-five days out of thirty."

"Are you suggesting I wouldn't be able to hold onto my own husband?" Eden demanded.

Neil slowly shook his head, a hypnotic glow entering the amber eyes as he took first one step and then another toward Eden. "Keith would be your slave to the day he died. I wonder, though, if he could hold onto you."

"Of course he could," Eden replied, gray eyes blazing indignantly. Absorbed by her own anger and transfixed by the golden eyes which trapped her gaze, Eden failed to consciously realize that Neil had moved within arm's reach of her.

"Even with me as your neighbor?"

"You wouldn't be my neighbor," Eden loftily informed him. "In fact, none of your arguments are relevant! Keith offered to quit the Rangers and take me to San Francisco."

Neil appeared unperturbed. "Then I'll have to follow you, won't I?"

"In God's name, why?" Eden flared. "We both knew this couldn't last, so why are you so determined to hold onto what is already gone?"

"It's not gone," Neil said quietly. "Gerald's abuse proved that, at least to me. I don't believe you're running to Gerald, but if you are, you may as well know right now that I have no intention of losing you again."

"You're being cruel," Eden cried.

"Cruel, Eden? Shall we discuss cruelty?" Neil's hand closed painfully around Eden's chin, forcing her to meet his gaze. "Cruelty is telling a man you love him; making love with him; driving out the demons which have tormented him all his life until he finally, *finally* believes that this one woman can be counted on when all others fail him." Golden eyes molten, Neil roughly pulled Eden against him. "He believes, he trusts. He thanks some faceless deity for your existence. And then he discovers that you're leaving, that you're taking away the only thing in the entire world that he treasures." Neil paused. "To open my heart only to tear it into raw, bloody pieces—*that*, sweet Eden, is cruelty."

Tears shimmered in Eden's eyes and she quickly averted her face to hide the tears from Neil's gaze. She hadn't thought Neil would be hurt by her desertion—angered perhaps, but not hurt. Doubts began to assail Eden and she trembled in Neil's embrace, yet in her heart she knew that her decision to leave was the only possible solution. In time they would forget, the pain would ease—

"Eden."

Neil's gentle voice drew Eden back to the present and in a muffled voice she responded, "What?"

"Stay with me, Eden. Marry me."

Stunned, Eden raised her head and stared into Neil's eyes. "If this is some new game you've devised . . ."

"No game, Eden." Neil withdrew something from his pocket . . . and offered Eden a slender gold band.

Her heart gave one joyous leap before she brought herself under control. "You're only doing this because of Keith and because I'm leaving."

"Those conditions only forced me to propose sooner than I had planned—they didn't make up my mind for me." Eden looked unconvinced and Neil shook his head in exasperation. "Even I can't produce a wedding ring out of thin air, love. Is it so hard for you to understand that I love you?"

"But you've always said—"

"I know what I've said," Neil interrupted impatiently. "I was wrong. I'm not satisfied to have you just as my lover— I want to be proud of what we share and I want you to be proud of it as well. I don't want snickers and gossip to destroy what we have; I love you too much to let that happen." Neil smiled tenderly and brushed his lips across Eden's. "I want us to build a new life together, Eden. I'm not promising you a bed of roses, but I am promising that I'll try. I'll do my best to make you happy and to be a good father to Shannon."

"Are you sure?" Eden asked breathlessly, as she had years before. "Neil, are you really sure?"

"I'm sure." Neil's voice was soft but firm. "For the first time in my life I know exactly what I want, and that's you and Shannon. Marry me, Eden. Please."

Without a second thought Eden threw her arms around Neil's neck and in the fleeting seconds before Neil's lips slanted across her own Eden murmured, "Yes, Neil. Oh, yes!"

Half an hour later—kneeling beside Neil in a small, nearly deserted church—Eden heard her voice repeating the vows which joined her to Neil. His voice was hushed, too, yet also incredibly strong. Eden glanced at Neil's profile from beneath her lashes and, as if he felt her look, he turned and gazed down at her. His lips moved in recitation but Eden didn't hear the words—there was no need. Everything Neil was saying was reflected in his eyes, his face. In the flickering candlelight Neil's golden eyes glowed, overpowering all else. *I love you as I have never loved before and never will again. My love is real—reach out, touch it. It surrounds us, shields us. Nothing can ever change what we have found.*

The slender gold band was slipped onto her finger, and under the old priest's watchful eyes, Eden shyly offered her lips for Neil's kiss. Smiling, Neil bent his head toward Eden and tenderly, briefly claimed her mouth. The priest nodded, watching as the tall, dark groom rose and helped his new bride to her feet. The priest had wondered at the impetuousness of this wedding but now, feeling the emotion which charged the air around the couple, his doubts retreated.

"Come," he instructed Neil and Eden. "You must sign the certificate. And you as well," he added to the two old women who had witnessed the ceremony.

When the necessary papers were signed, Neil led Eden outside. There, in full view of anyone who happened by, he took Eden's face in his hands and kissed her thoroughly. "Hello, Mrs. Banning." Neil grinned at the color which rose in Eden's cheeks.

Eden laughed, the shawl which had covered her head during

the ceremony falling away to reveal the unbound mass of pale hair rippling over her shoulders. "You'll scandalize the priest."

"I think we already have, my love." Neil indicated the pewter silk evening gown Eden was wearing. "That is a most unorthodox wedding gown."

Eden's eyes sparkled. "Ours was a most unorthodox courtship. And do you know of any other bride who, at the groom's insistence, wore her hair down?" Neil shook his head and Eden teased, "And who ever heard of a groom forgetting his tie?"

Neil chuckled, fingering the open collar of his shirt. "I took it off when you insisted on changing and forgot to put it back on."

"So I'm to blame?"

Neil nodded, his eyes caressing Eden. "But I'm glad you chose this dress; and I'm glad you agreed to wear your hair down."

"Once, a long time ago, a man told me that he liked my hair best this way." Eden lifted their clasped hands so that Neil's flesh touched her cheek. "It seemed appropriate."

"Yes, it did." Neil lovingly adjusted the shawl around Eden's shoulders. "If Dennis is as efficient as you claim, there should be a bottle of champagne chilling in my—our room. Shall we go, Mrs. Banning?"

With Neil's arm curved about her waist, Eden walked contentedly at his side back to the hotel. "You realize we did this completely backward," Eden said gaily, tipping her head back to look at Neil.

"What do you mean?"

Eden smiled, eyes alight with mischief. "We had the honeymoon before the wedding. How do you plan to explain that to your son?"

Neil stopped dead, his eyes wide. "My son! Eden—"

"I don't know," Eden replied softly, forestalling his question. "Would it upset you?"

"No." Neil shook his head, suddenly aware of a new facet of their marriage. "What about you, Eden?"

"I think it would make me very happy," Eden said slowly. "In fact, I *know* it would make me happy."

"Then it's settled," Neil told Eden after a moment's silence. Grinning roguishly, he toyed with a lock of pale hair. "Our ranches can spare us for a few more days. No son—or daughter—of mine is going to say that I denied his mother a proper honeymoon." He raised a questioning eyebrow. "Do you agree, love?"

Eden squeezed his hand. "Completely."

# Chapter 19

Constanza Martinez Williams awkwardly dislodged a shovelful
of earth from the hole in front of her and, gasping, emptied
it onto the pile of dirt at her side. *You're digging your own
grave.* Lathrop's words of this morning echoed through her
mind. He had said that when he had discovered a substantial
amount of money was missing from his office safe. Constanza
grimaced. Lathrop was a fool, and she had told him so. Lathrop
had started divorce proceedings, but he was also trying to cheat
Constanza out of the payment he had promised. Suddenly the
money in Constanza's bank account had been transferred to
Lathrop's name. Lathrop had laughed at her outrage and told
Constanza she should have stuffed the money into her mattress.

Even now, remembering the conversation, Constanza's eyes
flashed indignantly. Lathrop had tried to cheat her, but he had
lived to regret his actions. After several midnight forays into
Lathop's office Constanza had discovered the combination to
the safe. That same night she removed not only all the cash
but also the jewels. Fool! Constanza thought once more as she
levered the final bit of dirt onto the pile. She had labored too
long and too hard as Lathrop's wife to meekly accept the scraps
he was now offering.

Smiling to herself, Constanza removed the carpetbag full
of riches from her saddle and placed it into the shallow hole.
This bag was the key to her new life; although Constanza
loathed having it out of her sight she dared not run the risk of
keeping it hidden in her bedroom. In two days she would sign
the divorce papers and would finally be free—free to put an
entire ocean between herself and the past and to live out the
rest of her days in luxury.

Gloating, Constanza imagined Lathrop's rage when he discovered, as he probably already had, that she hadn't been idiot
enough to hide her small fortune on his property. Lathrop could
tear her trunks apart, turn her bedroom into a shambles and rip
up the formal garden, but his efforts would be fruitless. Just
as she had done six years ago, Constanza now placed her future
in the hands of Neil Banning—or, more accurately, in his land.

Constanza pushed the dirt back over the carpetbag, placed several stones over the small mound and stood up. The shade cast by the nearby tree concealed the irregularity in the ground. Satisfied, Constanza brushed off her riding skirt, hid the shovel in the brush and mounted her horse. It had been a risk burying her fortune so close to Neil's house; but now that she had accomplished the task without being seen, Constanza's confidence soared. With a throaty chuckle she wheeled her horse and set off toward the Lazy W.

Lathrop was waiting in Constanza's bedroom when she arrived—waiting amid the clutter of packing crates, steamer trunks and baggage, all of which had obviously been searched. "Where the hell have you been?"

Constanza favored Lathrop with a contemptuous stare while she slowly pulled off her riding gloves. "It has been a long time since you concerned yourself with my activities. I am flattered, Lathrop."

"Don't be." Lathrop kicked one of the hat boxes across the room. "I want it back, Constanza—the money, the jewels, all of it."

Constanza laughed. "I haven't the vaguest idea what you are talking about."

"Tell me!" Lathrop roared. "Tell me or by God I'll—"

"You will what?" Constanza jeered. "Beat me? Kill me? No, you are too much of a coward to do your own dirty work, Lathrop. I think that is what I hate most about you: your cowardice."

"I'm not all that fond of you, either," Lathrop sneered in return.

"Then it is a good thing we will not be together much longer, isn't it?"

The inflexible note in Constanza's voice warned Lathrop that this strategy was useless and with an effort he held his anger in check. "Will you agree to a compromise?"

Constanza watched him suspiciously. "What kind of compromise?"

"If you return what you stole from my safe, I'll restore your bank account." When Constanza shook her head Lathrop added, "and I'll give you, in cash, 10 percent of the value of the jewels."

"Never." Constanza frowned. "Why are you so anxious to have the jewels back?"

Lathrop's face suddenly went blank. "Since you aren't about to turn them over, it doesn't matter."

"Yes it does." Constanza studied him intently. "You look frightened, Lathrop. Why?"

"Because those jewels can destroy us both." Lathrop's eyes narrowed. "You've forgotten, my dear, that our neighbor's emeralds and diamonds are mixed in with your treasures. I hope you hid them well, Constanza, because if they somehow come to light a lot of very unpleasant questions are going to arise." Lathrop walked to the door, then paused. "On second thought, you may have done me a favor. If the jewels aren't discovered, the evidence will disappear in a few days. Of course, if they are found, *you* will have to explain how Eden Banning's emeralds made their way into your collection." He turned and smiled coldly at Constanza. "And no one would ever believe that you stole them from my safe."

As the door closed behind Lathrop, a worried frown replaced the contemptuous expression on Constanza's face. She had forgotten about the damning emerald and diamond necklace and earrings. Even Manuel, before he had been arrested, had urged her to get rid of those jewels; but Constanza hadn't been able to bring herself to part with them. She still couldn't; the stones were too obviously expensive, the setting too exquisite. Constanza would simply have to make certain that her cache was adequately protected—and that meant a second trip to Neil's ranch. She smiled. Neil and his new bride were giving a party tonight, a celebration of their marriage three months ago. With all the excitement no one would notice any activity on the knoll behind the stable.

The *Rancho de Paraíso* was alive with the sounds of music and laughter. Lanterns illuminated both the house and the mock courtyard to the rear, where the celebration was taking place. Sebastian, his limp barely noticeable, twirled Eden through the final steps of a dance and then escorted her back to Neil's side.

Neil, looking handsome in a black suit, black vest and snowy white linen shirt, curled an arm around his wife's waist and smiled down at her. "As usual, you are the loveliest woman present, Mrs. Banning."

"Thank you, Mr. Banning." Her gray eyes sparkling, Eden kissed him lightly.

Sebastian sighed affectedly and shook his head. "Just when

I had given up on you both you surprise me by doing what you should have done six years ago. I shall never understand either of you."

"Ignore him," Neil ordered Eden with a grin. "He's still sore because he wasn't able to be the best man." Neil clapped a hand on Sebastian's shoulder and laughed. "You must strike when the iron is hot, little brother. Besides, I didn't want to give Eden time to change her mind."

"As if I would," Eden put in merrily.

Sebastian turned to Eden and took her hand. "Welcome to the family, Eden. You and Shannon are most delightful additions."

"Thank you, Sebastian."

"And now, if you two will excuse me, I believe I promised this dance to a very attractive young lady."

Sebastian departed and with a sigh of contentment Eden rested her head against Neil's shoulder. "I'm glad he was able to come."

"So am I," Neil agreed, shifting his gaze to Eden's face. "Happy, love?"

Eden nodded, smiling. "I think this is the first time in my life that I've ever been so content."

"I feel the same way." Neil's arms tightened briefly, possessively, around Eden. "I'm through running away from my past. Everything I want is here with you and Shannon—all I need is time to prove to you that I intend to fulfill all those promises I made in Dallas."

A soft glow entered her eyes and Eden placed a reassuring hand on Neil's chest. "You don't have to prove anything to me, Neil. I love you for what you are, not for any of those wonderful, silly, romantic promises you made."

Neil grinned. Sighing, he glanced at the guests and then lifted a questioning eyebrow at Eden. "I don't suppose we can send them home early, can we?"

"I'm afraid not." In spite of herself, Eden blushed at the hungry gleam in Neil's eyes.

"You're incredibly tempting, my love, particularly now. If we weren't a respectable married couple..." Neil's voice trailed off and, shaking his head regretfully, he loosened his hold on Eden. "I think we should dance, love, before my baser instincts take over. Will you do me the honor, Mrs. Banning?"

"Most certainly, Mr. Banning."

Neil swept Eden into the crush of dancers. It seemed impossible now, Neil thought as he gazed at Eden, that three months ago they nearly had lost one another. What a tragic mistake that would have been! Their marriage had brought Neil a happiness and serenity he had never known existed. They had buried the past; the painful memories which had threatened to keep them apart were forgiven. They had each other now, and Shannon, and a future that promised only happiness.

As if reading his thoughts, Eden whispered, "I love you, Neil."

"And I love you." Neil squeezed her hand. "I always will."

The evening was a whirlwind of gaiety, a time to put serious thoughts and troubles aside. Eden floated through the celebration with a radiant smile, exchanging light conversation with their guests. She had never been so happy. As she put Shannon to bed Eden thought of the years which lay ahead and smiled.

Eden carefully closed the door to Shannon's bedroom and walked through the house, her mind perversely dwelling upon Lathrop and Constanza. For well over six months there had been no rustlers in this area, nor had Lathrop made any further offers for the Emerald I. Even Vincent, with his suspicious mind, had finally agreed with Neil that Lathrop must have given up. A frown crossed Eden's face. She had been so wrapped up in starting a life with Neil that she hadn't bothered to examine Lathrop's motives in accepting defeat. What if he were still scheming? A chill ran up Eden's spine and she shivered. She still had nightmares about her abduction, nightmares which brought her jarringly awake to find Neil cradling her in his arms, driving away her demons with his soothing touch and deep, comforting voice. But those were only *dreams*, Eden chided herself; then she started as a knock sounded at the front door. Shaking her head at her own foolishness, Eden retraced her steps to welcome the late arrival. Eden's words went unspoken, however, as she opened the door and discovered Keith Gerald glaring down at her.

"Good evening, Mrs. Banning." Without waiting for a reply, Keith pushed the door out of Eden's grasp and strode into the house. "I hope I'm not intruding."

Eden gasped, "I . . . we're having a party—"

"So I heard." Keith stared down at Eden, fascinated by the daring neckline of her bright yellow satin gown. Black velvet bows and black lace accented the tiers of the skirt, and Keith watched as Eden nervously toyed with her cuffs. Suddenly the anger was gone from Keith's eyes and he smiled slightly. "Don't worry, Eden, I'm not here to cause trouble."

Eden watched him uneasily. "Why *are* you here?"

"To offer my congratulations—and to apologize for the things I said in Dallas."

"I don't believe you," Eden said flatly. "You didn't come all the way from Laredo to apologize."

Keith's face hardened. "I'm on leave for a week, then I go back to train a new man. After that I leave for San Francisco." He paused. "I came to say good-bye, Eden." The overwhelming relief flooding through Eden must have been obvious because Keith laughed shortly. "I can see I won't be missed."

Eden colored. "You're wrong. The ranchers here appreciate everything you did for them. Heaven knows the sheriff wasn't much help."

Keith snorted. "I didn't do a damn thing except run around in circles, and we both know it; just like we both know who was behind the rustling and Hugh's death."

"Don't start!" Eden stared at Keith defiantly. "How dare you come into our home and repeat those vile accusations!"

"I'm sorry," Keith said quickly—too quickly, in fact, but Eden was too upset to notice. "I shouldn't have said anything."

Eden bit back a sharp retort. "I know you dislike Neil, but you have no right to say such things, Keith. He's a good man—"

"You don't have to defend him to me." Keith shrugged. "It's quite possible I've been wrong about Neil, but at any rate, I'll be out of it soon. I'd like for us to part as friends."

Keith's overture didn't quite ring true but Eden pushed her doubts aside and accepted the hand he offered. What did it matter after all? As Keith said, he would soon be gone. Still, she would have to keep Neil and Keith apart.

Keith grimaced when Eden ushered him into the courtyard and then all but ran from his side. Before the night was over, she would believe all the things he had tried to tell her about Neil. Eden would be heartbroken, of course, but Keith would be there to lend her a supporting arm. He scanned the crowd, his eyes narrowing when he found Eden deep in conversation with Neil. She deserved better than Banning, much better, and once she was free he would take her and her daughter away from Texas. Turning away from the crowd, Keith withdrew the slip of paper which had been pushed under his hotel door. Until he received this note, Keith had had every intention of finding a way to say good-bye to Eden in private, for in spite of the things he had said in Dallas, Keith was still in love with Eden. But this, he thought triumphantly, this note had eliminated the need for farewells. Allowing himself a brief smile, Keith reread the hastily scribbled lines. *If you want Neil Banning be at Rancho de Paraíso tonight.* Nodding thoughtfully, Keith took a glass of chilled wine from a tray and settled back to wait for Neil Banning to be delivered into his hands.

Across the courtyard, Neil was speaking to Eden in a barely controlled shout. "I thought we were rid of that damn Ranger!"

"We will be," Eden said quietly, "as soon as the party is over. He only came to say good-bye, Neil; and when he leaves tonight it will be for good. Surely we can tolerate Keith for a few hours."

Neil swore softly, glanced in Keith's direction and then studied Eden's anxious face. "Is he bothering you?"

Eden shook her head. "I won't deny that I'd feel better if Keith hadn't come, but no, he isn't bothering me. Please, Neil, let's not ruin the party by having a scene."

Neil slowly expelled his breath. "I can't forget the names he called you, love. For two cents I'd throw him out, and to hell with his suspicions about me and the rustlers. I want him out of our lives—permanently."

"He will be, in a matter of hours. What can Keith prove in a few hours that he hasn't been able to prove in the past two years?"

"All right. For appearances' sake I'll put up with him. But," Neil warned, golden eyes sparkling wrathfully, "if Keith Gerald lays a hand on you, they'll ship him back to Laredo in pieces."

Eden sighed. "I don't want Keith here any more than you do. Perhaps if I steer some of the young ladies in his direction we can get through tonight without an incident."

With Keith's presence, Eden's enjoyment of the party waned. Eden avoided Keith but it seemed he was content simply to stand in the shadows and watch the festivities. He watched Eden as well—she felt his eyes on her as she moved through the guests or danced with Neil. Why had he come? Eden wondered, her nerves fraying under Keith's scrutiny as she looked up from her conversation with Millie and found him staring at her.

"You don't have to keep me company, Miss Eden," Millie said. "Captain Gerald's been watching you since he arrived. You should spend time with him as well."

Eden smiled weakly, knowing how rude her actions must seem to everyone. "Captain Gerald can manage quite well on his own."

Millicent shrugged, unable to fathom the strained note in Eden's voice. "Well, at least we don't have to put up with Mr. and Mrs. Williams," she said thoughtfully, trying to lighten Eden's mood. "Between his strutting and her prancing no one else would be able to dance. A hateful pair, the two of them."

Eden nodded distractedly, suddenly apprehensive. Millicent had meant to cheer Eden, but in fact her words had the opposite effect. Distressed, wishing she could recapture her earlier mood, Eden searched the crowd and discovered Neil talking with Ian and Vincent. Neil must have sensed her anxiety, because at the same moment he turned slightly and smiled, his gaze meeting Eden's. Her heart leaped. As long as we're together nothing can hurt us, Eden thought, returning Neil's smile with what she hoped was a convincing one of her own.

Eden had not meant to let her feelings show, but she must have done precisely that, for Neil abandoned his conversation and came to her side. With a word of apology to Millicent, Neil took Eden's arm and led her onto the dance floor.

"You haven't changed a bit," Eden admonished him in a bright, forced tone. "You still take it for granted that you can dance with a woman without asking her permission."

"You haven't changed either—but if you purposely step on my foot this time, I'll deal with you far more harshly here than I did in New York."

"And how do you propose to do that?" Eden bantered lightly.

"By making you explain what's troubling you." Neil frowned, but his eyes were gentle, questioning. "I don't like to see you worried, sweet. What's wrong?"

"Nothing," Eden protested, averting her gaze to study the cloth of Neil's shirt.

"The day we were married, you and I made a deal. Remember? We promised to share every part of our lives, good or bad." Neil peered into her face. "I have a right to know what's troubling you."

"I don't know. It's just a feeling that . . ." At a loss for words to describe what she felt, Eden shook her head and met his concerned gaze. "I think I just needed to be in your arms."

Neil smiled and pulled Eden closer. "Anytime, love. Anytime."

By the time the music ended, Eden's high spirits had returned. In a moment of devilishness Eden placed a teasing kiss on Neil's mouth when he deposited her on the sidelines, then laughed at her husband's shocked expression when she released him. "That, my darling husband, is to remind you just how married you really are."

"On the contrary," Neil drawled, golden eyes languorously caressing Eden's tempting curves. "That, my sweet, was an invitation."

Neil took a step forward and Eden placed a restraining hand on his chest. He covered Eden's hand with his, then brought it to his lips. "If you need to be held again, you know where to find me."

With a last smile, Neil returned to the guests while Eden went into the house to check on Shannon. The child was asleep and, glad of the respite from the throng of guests, Eden tiptoed to the window in Shannon's bedroom and stared at the heavens. A gentle breeze touched her face, and Eden turned her attention to the solitary tree on the knoll. Growing where it had, with only a slim chance of survival, the tree fascinated Eden. Now, in the broiling heat of summer, Eden watered it daily, in spite of Neil's repeated assurances that the tree's roots had long ago found their own supply of water. Eden had plans for that tree: In the years to come it would provide ample shade for a family picnic or for watching the men as they broke untrained horses to the saddle and bridle.

As Eden watched, the tree trunk moved, appearing to split in two. Eden blinked, then gasped as a figure of a man detached itself from the shadows and disappeared on the opposite side of the knoll. Who in the world . . . ? Eden started to wonder, only to realize with a jolt that the mysterious watcher was undoubtedly one of Keith's spies. Her eyes flashing indignantly, Eden tiptoed from the bedroom and left the house through the side door. If Keith planned to make trouble—to air his suspicions about Neil in front of their friends and neighbors—he was mistaken. Cursing herself for having allowed Keith to set foot inside their home, Eden lifted the trailing hem of her skirt and marched past the stable. The incline of the knoll seemed steeper in the dark than during the daylight, hampering her progress. She stumbled more than once, adding to her frustration and anger, and by the time she reached the crest Eden was furious enough to throw caution to the wind and stride boldly around the tree. The man, his back to Eden, was bending over, and Eden came to a stop just inches behind him. "I don't know who you are, but you have no right—" The words died in Eden's throat as the man spun around, a knife glinting wickedly in his hand. "Lathrop!" Eden's voice was a hoarse whisper. Rooted to the ground, she stared at Lathrop for several seconds before her eyes slid to a shape half hidden on the ground. A bare feminine leg was visible in the moonlight and Eden suppressed a shudder of fear. Terrified yet unable to stop herself, Eden moved closer until she was presented with an unobstructed view of the woman.

A scream rose from somewhere deep inside Eden, a scream that she fought to control by pressing a hand to her mouth as she stared in horror. Constanza Martinez Williams lay in the dust, her throat cut, her eyes staring sightlessly at the sky while a pool of blood gathered on the ground beneath her neck. A valise, half open, lay beside the body, its contents of gems entwined in the strands of Constanza's dark hair. Horrified, Eden returned her gaze to Lathrop and found him smiling, enjoying her revulsion.

The scream flooded Eden's lungs, rising in her throat, and as her lips parted she caught the flash of silver as Lathrop's hand came toward her. The next moment Eden's head exploded in blinding pain as the butt of Lathrop's pistol smashed against her skull.

It was some time before Neil realized that Eden was missing from the festivities. Concerned that Shannon might be ill, Neil went to the nursery and found his stepdaughter peacefully asleep. Curious now, Neil made his way to the master suite only to discover the room empty, and then quickly searched the rest of the house with the same result. Thinking he had missed Eden in the crowd, he wandered among the guests, golden eyes searching the sea of faces for Eden. Fighting back the unreasoning panic which closed around his heart, Neil made a second tour of the house and then, his face set, returned to the party.

Sebastian came to his brother's side and handed him a glass

of wine. "You look like you have just lost your best friend, Neil," Sebastian chided laughingly. "Perhaps you should get together with Captain Gerald—he's standing in the shadows looking nasty enough to start a fight."

Neil's fingers tightened around the glass, barely aware of Sebastian's last words. Forcing a light note into his voice, Neil replied, "I seem to have lost my wife somewhere along the way. Have you seen Eden lately?"

Sebastian thought for a moment and shook his head, not realizing that Neil was not indulging in idle conversation. "Perhaps she has decided to accept my offer to take her away from all this."

Neil didn't smile. "I'm serious, Sebastian. I can't find Eden."

Sobering, Sebastian scanned the guests. "I don't see her, but that is no reason for alarm. She's probably in the house with Shannon."

"I checked. She isn't there." Neil set his glass aside and distractedly lit a cigar. "Do me a favor, Sebastian?"

"Of course."

"Go to the stable and see if Eden's there. We have a mare that's about to foal—Eden may have gone to see if she was all right." At Sebastian's frown, Neil explained, "With Keith Gerald here, I want everything to appear as normal as possible—and that won't be the case if both Eden and I disappear. Get going, Sebastian."

It took less than five minutes for Sebastian to return from the stable and he gave Neil his answer with a shake of his head. "She may have gone for a walk, Neil, or perhaps—"

Neil silenced his brother with a grim look. "You don't believe that any more than I do. Something's happened to her, Sebastian."

Sebastian paled. "You can't be sure of that."

"Can't I?" A muscle worked in Neil's jaw as he surveyed the party. "The last time I saw Eden was over an hour ago and now she's nowhere to be found." He continued in a cold voice, "This has to be Lathrop's doing, or Constanza's. If they've taken Eden, I swear to God I'll kill them both."

Sebastian said quietly, "If you are right—and I hope you are not—our first concern must be Eden's safety as well as your own. If you charge out of here like a mad bull, Keith

Gerald will wonder where you're going and why, and so will the rest of your guests."

"I don't give a damn about Gerald or anyone else," Neil growled, fear lending a razor edge to his voice. "Eden is gone; she's in danger. I can't wait for Gerald or the guests to leave before I go after her!" Neil fought back the panic clawing at his heart. Suddenly the war was on again and Neil instinctively knew that Lathrop was a desperate man. Constanza may have threatened to expose him, or perhaps Lathrop had simply grown tired of waiting, but whatever the reason, Lathrop had felt cornered enough to kidnap Eden in the midst of a party in her own home. "I have to go, Sebastian. Cover for me as long as you can."

"And after that?" Sebastian inquired, his eyes bleak as he stared at his brother.

"After that you can start praying," Neil said grimly. "Give me fifteen minutes and then post guards around the house. I don't want to take any chances with Shannon."

Sebastian nodded. "I understand. This is the end, is it not?"

"Yes. One way or another, the charade is over. I only hope Eden hasn't been killed in the process." Neil's voice was tinged with despair and he quickly brought himself under control. "You know the truth and so does Vincent. If I don't come back, I want you both to tell Gerald what you know. This is one time Lathrop and Constanza won't walk away unscathed."

Sebastian nodded again, a lump rising in his throat. "You'll be back."

"Sure." Twin pairs of golden eyes met and Neil stared at his younger brother for several seconds. "Take care of yourself and Shannon, little brother." With that, Neil pivoted on his heel and disappeared.

The next fifteen minutes dragged by for Sebastian with agonizing slowness. Was it purely his imagination, or was Keith Gerald eyeing him suspiciously? The music and laughter wore on Sebastian's nerves and he found it next to impossible to engage in polite conversation. At one point he thought he heard the sound of departing hoofbeats and Sebastian pictured Neil riding toward Lathrop's ranch. A sinking feeling gripped the pit of Sebastian's stomach. The arrogant game Neil had started so long ago had turned into a tragic drama, with Eden's life hanging in the balance—as well as Neil's.

His thoughts weaving dark conclusions, Sebastian did as

Neil had asked and circumspectly ordered ᵃ
tioned around the buildings. The minutes tiᵉ
bastian found himself praying silently for Neil ᵃ
made excuses for their absence to a few of thᵉ
absorbed was he in keeping up the pretext of norᵐ
Sebastian failed to see one of the guards enter the ᶜ
and, after a moment of searching, head directly for Kerᵉ
ald. Thus it came as a nasty shock when, in response to a
tap on his shoulder, Sebastian turned away from a conversatᵗ
and came face to face with the lanky Ranger.

In clipped tones Keith asked, "Where's your brother?"

"Neil?" Sebastian glanced around the courtyard and shrugged
carelessly. "In the house, perhaps, with Eden and the baby.
Why?"

"We'll check, shall we?"

"By all means, go right ahead," Sebastian offered generously, his heart hammering painfully against his ribs. "I'm sure
Neil won't mind."

"I'm sure." Keith smiled coldly. "But just to be on the safe
side I'd like you to accompany me, Mr. Saros."

Sebastian had no choice. With a word of apology to his
companion Sebastian turned and walked with Keith into the
house. Away from the others Sebastian was less inclined
toward politeness and in a scathing tone he told Keith, "I
hope you have a good reason for dragging me in here, Captain
Gerald."

"A very good reason, I assure you." Keith looked around
the hallway. "Where's Neil?"

"I am not psychic, Captain. May I suggest you try the quaint
custom of knocking on doors if you must see my brother?"
Sebastian gestured to his right. "The library and parlor are this
way, the bedrooms to your left. Enjoy yourself, Captain
Gerald."

Keith's face hardened angrily. "He's not here, is he?"

"I have no idea."

"No? I think you're lying." Without warning, Keith twisted
Sebastian's arm behind his back, propelled him to the library
and shoved him into a chair. "I can arrange to have you named
as an accessory to rustling, kidnaping and two counts of murder.
Does that sharpen your memory?"

"I don't know what you are talking about." Sebastian rubbed
his injured shoulder. "Neil told me you have some insane idea

ie for the trouble in this area. Is your present
your delusion?"

elusions when it comes to Neil Banning," Keith
blue eyes flashing. "Now, where is he?" Sebastian
a sullen silence and Keith nodded bitterly. "I un-
you're a doctor. Tell me: Have you ever seen a person
naving her throat cut?"

ebastian's head snapped up. "What are you talking about?"
ore Keith could answer, a woman's scream carried through
he house, sending Sebastian straight out of his chair. "*¡Dios
mío!*"

Keith appeared unshaken. "I've taken the liberty of calling
a halt to the celebration. Apparently one of the guests caught
a glimpse of the body."

Sebastian blanched. "What body?"

"You'll find out soon enough." Keith sauntered to the door
of the library and paused. "Come along, Doctor. I think you'll
be interested in what Neil's men are doing out back."

Sebastian rose wordlessly and followed Keith to the quickly
emptying courtyard. It has to be Eden, Sebastian thought, feeling the gorge rise in his throat. This time Lathrop and Constanza
hadn't bothered with threats—they simply had destroyed one
of the people who stood in their way. The blanket-draped body
on the ground loomed into view and Sebastian clasped his
hands together in an effort to control their trembling.

Keith crouched beside the body and casually flipped back
a portion of the blanket. "Take a look, Doctor."

Sebastian drew a steadying breath and lowered his gaze,
expecting to see a tumbled mass of blond curls. He saw the
raven hair first, and then, as the sickening fear drained away,
Sebastian found the strength to study the face which was every
bit as haughty in death as it had been in life. "Constanza!"
Stunned, Sebastian noted the ugly wound in Constanza's throat
before looking up at Keith. "Where did you find her?"

"I didn't—one of the men did. Behind that tree on the hill."
Keith draped the blanket over Constanza's face and got to his
feet. Picking up the valise beside the body, Keith cleared a
space on one of the tables, emptied the bag and began sorting
through the contents. "Now will you tell me where your brother
is? And Eden, too; I want her to see a sample of her husband's
work."

"Neil did not kill Constanza," Sebastian protested.

"No?" Keith looked up from the evide[...] Sneering, he selected an emerald and diamon[...] held it up for Sebastian's inspection. "This is [...] stolen by the same men who killed Hugh Colter.[...]

"A necklace is a necklace."

"Not this time. Eden described the necklace in det[...] with the other jewels that were taken. When I arreste[...] men for Hugh's murder this was one of the pieces that wa[...] missing." Keith laughed triumphantly. "Now I've really [...] him! After all these years I've finally got the evidence I nee[...] to convict that bastard! The men he hired to kill Hugh told me Neil was responsible, but they wouldn't talk in court and I couldn't produce a shred of evidence. But now—now I can charge him with two murders. Even if the state won't prosecute for rustling or kidnaping I'll see him hang for the murders of Hugh Colter and Constanza Williams." Keith controlled his jubilation with an effort. "Where's Eden? It's time she faced the truth about that bastard she married."

Momentarily forgetting the circumstances, Sebastian lashed out, "You are the bastard, Captain, to deliberately want to expose Eden to this gruesome sight. Neil was right—you *are* insane."

Keith glared. "The way I see it Neil killed Mrs. Williams for one of two reasons. She may have accidentally stumbled over this cache, but I rather doubt it. A more reasonable conclusion is that they have been working together ever since Neil showed up here. In fact, they probably manipulated Lathrop into marrying Constanza, hoping or planning that he would die and leave the ranch to his poor widow. That's where the rustlers came in—if Lathrop was killed chasing a band of rustlers, no one would connect his death with Neil or Constanza."

Sebastian shook his head. "You are wrong, Captain. Horribly wrong."

"I don't think so." Keith thoughtfully stroked his chin, his mind racing. "Why did they wait so long? Why didn't they accomplish in six years what they could have done in a matter of months? Did one of them have a change of heart?" He poked absently at the jewels and money on the table in front of him. "They must have had Hugh Colter murdered because he somehow learned the truth and that opened up a whole new horizon for them—owning the Emerald I in addition to the Lazy W. Eden, widowed, was an easy target. Arrange her kidnaping

ride in and save her. Give Neil a few months
indispensable to Eden, and the next thing you
s Mrs. Neil Banning." Keith nodded, satisfied
clusions. "They must have planned to get rid of
d Eden—together they would have inherited a nice
pire—but I'll bet Constanza got greedy, or impatient,
. She decided to hightail it back to Mexico, and when
found out, he killed her. I'll bring Neil to justice one way
the other, Doctor, but your help can save us both a lot of
rouble."

Beneath Keith's stare Sebastian remained silent, wrestling
with the desire to correct Keith's mistaken conclusions and the
need to give Neil the time he required to find Eden. A decision
was forced on Sebastian, however, when Keith shot him a look
of disgust and started back to the house.

"Since you're determined to protect Neil, I'll do this my
way. First I'm going to get Eden and her child away from this
house and then I'm going to tell Lathrop about his wife's
death."

"Wait!" Keith paused in midstep and Sebastian gestured
nervously. "To do what you are planning will place Eden's life
in danger."

"Explain yourself," Keith demanded.

"I shall." Sebastian limped forward, golden eyes dull with
worry. "Come inside, Captain. There is a great deal you do
not know."

They spoke for over an hour and when Keith left the house
the victorious light had gone out of his eyes. Once on his horse
he rode not to the Lazy W but to the Emerald I, for confirmation
of a story which had shaken him out of his smug complacency.

Consciousness returned by degrees to Eden and she turned
painfully from her side to her back, trying to ignore the burning
ache slicing through her head and the deafening ringing in her
ears. Eden forced her eyes open and with a sinking heart surveyed the shabby room which was, she was certain, her prison.
She struggled upright on the cot, gasping when a fresh pain
lanced through her temple. Weak and dizzy, Eden sank back
and tried to order her jumbled thoughts. She remembered coming to at some point and finding herself slung across the front
of Lathrop's saddle like a sack of flour. She had struggled,

briefly, until Lathrop had reined in, fastened a hand in her hair and slammed his fist into her jaw.

Questions chased one another through Eden's mind. Why, after all this time, had Lathrop disposed of his wife? And why had he gone to all the trouble of taking Constanza's body to Neil's ranch? Surely no one would suspect Lathrop of killing his wife, even if she were found on the Lazy W's land. Eden shook her head wearily. How foolish she had been to investigate that shadowy figure on the hill! Had they missed her at the party yet? Oh, God, Eden thought with a pang, Neil would be frantic when he discovered she was gone. Would Neil ever find her here—wherever here was? Eden glanced around the room and shivered when the moon passed behind a cloud. One final question troubled her: Was this the place where she would die?

Fear returned with a heavy hand and Eden fought back tears. She was alone, and neither her hands nor her feet had been tied. There was no reason she could not try to escape. Better to run than to sit and wait for the inevitable.

Goaded by that thought, Eden ignored the pain of her protesting muscles and swung her legs over the edge of the cot.

"About time you woke up." Eden gasped, then quieted as a match was scraped into life and touched to a lamp. A moment later the room and its sparse furnishings were illuminated and Lathrop met Eden's startled gaze with a chilling smile. "You look surprised, girlie."

"I shouldn't be, but I am." Eden eyed him steadily despite the erratic pounding of her heart. "Where am I?"

"A branding shack just a few miles north of your home— but on my property." When Eden's eyes slid toward the door, Lathrop chuckled. "Don't try it, girlie. Vincent isn't here to back you up and I'd hate to have to knock you out again."

Eden clenched her hands helplessly in the skirt of her dress. "You killed Constanza, didn't you?"

Lathrop nodded. "I guess it doesn't matter if you know the truth. Constanza was a greedy little bitch—she thought she could rob me blind and get away with it. She even went so far as to bury her fortune on Neil's land so that I wouldn't find it."

"I remember seeing jewelry," Eden said quietly.

"Part of Constanza's hoard." Lathrop laughed, a brutal sound that made Eden tremble. "I followed her this morning.

I was planning to wait until Constanza left and then dig everything up; but then I realized that Constanza was solving all the problems you and Banning had created."

"I don't understand."

"Surely you don't think Keith Gerald showed up at your party by accident?" Lathrop got to his feet. Still talking, he carried the lamp to the cot and seated himself directly in front of Eden. "By now our good captain has arrested your husband for Constanza's murder."

"What!" Eden started to her feet only to have her wrists firmly and painfully grasped in Lathrop's hand. "What did you tell Keith?"

"Nothing—Captain Gerald will draw his own conclusions when he finds your emeralds among the other jewels. I think he will assume that Neil killed Constanza because she was going to run off with their fortune."

Eden shook her head wildly. "He won't believe anything of the sort. Your frame is too neat."

"Gerald will believe anything that gives him Neil Banning," Lathrop replied shrewdly. "I took Constanza to your ranch on my horse, dumped the jewels out of the bag to make it look like there was a struggle and then I killed Constanza. She came around just as I pulled my knife out of the sheath. You should have seen her, flopping around on the ground with her hands and feet tied and a gag in her mouth. She knew what was coming, all right, and I enjoyed every minute of it."

Horrified, Eden tried to jerk away from Lathrop's hold. "You're an animal!"

"I'm glad you think so. Maybe remembering what I did to Constanza will make it easier for you to do what I tell you." Gloating, Lathrop pulled Eden against him and ran a hand over her bare shoulder. Revolted by his touch, Eden shuddered, which only served to increase Lathrop's pleasure. "If you do as I ask, I'll see to it that Neil goes free. Would you like that, girlie?"

"Let me go!" Eden writhed in his embrace, sickened by Lathrop's closeness. Desperate to be free of him she kicked at his ankle, deriving a great deal of satisfaction from Lathrop's grunt of pain.

"You just don't learn, do you, girlie?" With his free hand Lathrop ripped apart the bodice of her gown and stared hungrily at the satiny flesh he had exposed. "So this is what that Mexican bastard fondles every night."

"I'll kill you," Eden spat. Then, realizing that her struggles were heightening Lathrop's perverted pleasure, she forced herself to stand motionless, to ignore the fact that only a thin chemise covered part of her breasts. "I swear, Lathrop, if you touch me, I'll kill you. Or Neil will."

Lathrop chortled. "I'm touching you now and I'm still alive. The game is over, girlie, except for a few last moves. Come morning I'm going to take you home and you're going to tell everyone how I saved you from being kidnaped by Constanza's accomplice. You're going to tell Captain Gerald how this outlaw bragged to you about the rustling and Hugh's murder. You're going to explain how you found him bending over Constanza's body, a bloody knife still in his hand. And then you're going to explain how I rescued you when we accidentally stumbled across each other on the range; and how, unfortunately, your kidnaper managed to escape."

Eden weakly shook her head. "I can't . . . I won't."

"You will!" Lathrop twisted a hand in Eden's hair and forced her to meet his gaze. "That little story will get your husband out of jail and leave me in the clear. After this neither one of you will ever be able to tell the truth about Constanza and me because no one will believe you."

"Neil will know the truth," Eden whispered. "When I tell him what you've done—" Lathrop's fingers tightened unbearably and Eden fell silent.

"You go ahead and tell him, girlie; but you tell him *after* you've both signed over your ranches to me and you're on your way out of Texas."

Eden paled. "Neil will never give up his ranch!"

"Sure he will," Lathrop assured her smoothly. "You see, if he doesn't I'll happen to find Constanza's diary, which implicates Neil in this whole mess. Now do you think you can get Neil to agree?"

All the defiance went out of Eden and she gave in to the tears which had threatened for the past several minutes. The land wasn't important, not when Neil's life hung in the balance. Perhaps it was better this way. She and Neil would be able to live out their lives without having to contend with threats and counterthreats. "I'll sign, and so will Neil, but I want the diary—which I'm certain you fabricated."

"You'll have it when you turn over the deeds to your ranches," Lathrop agreed. "I'm glad you decided to be reasonable about this."

"What other choice do I have?" Eden said dully. "Now let go of me."

"That brings us to the last part of our agreement." Lathrop's voice was harsh as he released Eden and shoved her back onto the cot. "No one makes a fool out of me and gets away with it. You made a fool out of me that night in the study when Vincent left me tied up—Constanza laughed herself sick when she found me the next morning."

Confused, Eden struggled to regain some semblance of modesty by holding the remnants of her gown across her breasts. "What more do you want, Lathrop? A pound of flesh?"

"That will do for a start."

Eden slowly raised her head and stared at him, her gray eyes wide with disbelief. "You can't mean..." Her voice trailed off and Eden bit down hard on her bottom lip to keep from screaming.

"This will give me a little extra edge, just in case you try to change your mind, or Neil's, about signing over your land," Lathrop explained brutally, leering into Eden's upturned face. "What do you think your husband would do if he found out I'd sampled his wife's charms? I have the feeling he'd come gunning for me, and then I'd have to have him killed." Slowly, deliberately, Lathrop began unbuckling his belt. "Or at the very least he'd always wonder if you sold your body in order to buy his way out of jail. I don't think you want to spend the rest of your life living with a man who doesn't trust you."

Sheer desperation jolted Eden out of her trance and with a strangled cry she kicked out at Lathrop, throwing him off balance. As he stumbled backward Eden sprang from the cot and bolted for the door. Eden's fingers had barely closed around the latch when Lathrop seized her by the shoulders and threw her to the floor. Her head cracked against the rough wooden planking and for a moment she lay stunned with Lathrop towering over her, his face contorted with rage and lust.

Lathrop took a step toward Eden, his menacing bulk looming over her. Unable to control her terror any longer, Eden screamed, a dark, primitive scream which echoed the helpless desperation of generations of women who had confronted the same brutality Eden now faced.

Lathrop chuckled mirthlessly. "Scream away, girlie. There's no one but the coyotes to hear you."

He might have said more and would certainly have found a way to increase Eden's pain and humiliation, but hard on the heels of Lathrop's words came the sound of splintering wood as the door flew open beneath the force of Neil's booted foot. Lathrop froze, a look of incredulity spreading across his face as he stared at the gun Neil had leveled at him.

"Stay right where you are, Lathrop. If you move I'll kill you." Neil edged into the room and dropped to one knee beside Eden. Not taking his eyes or gun from Lathrop, Neil extended his free hand to his wife. "Can you stand?"

"Y-yes." Eden slipped her hand into Neil's and with his assistance rose shakily to her feet.

With Eden safely at his side Neil motioned toward the door. "Let's go, Lathrop."

A confident smirk twisted Lathrop's lips. "Planning to turn me in and make yourself out to be a hero?"

Neil slowly shook his head, his golden eyes dark with a promise of death. "We're past that stage. I have something different in mind for you."

The lethal tone of Neil's voice warned her, and Eden clutched despairingly at Neil's free arm. "Neil, don't! I know what you're thinking and—"

"This is one thing we're not debating, Eden," Neil interrupted.

"But we have to," Eden countered. "There's so much you don't know—"

"I know enough." A savage light entered Neil's eyes and he spared Eden a quick glance. "My God, Eden, look at you!"

"Neil, I—" Belatedly Eden remembered her torn gown and bruised jaw. "Things aren't as they appear. Lathrop didn't . . . I mean, he . . . " Her voice broke and Eden pressed a trembling hand to her mouth.

"He would have, given time," Neil guessed rightly. Without waiting for a reply Neil gently pushed Eden toward the door. "Go outside and get on my horse."

"No, Neil, don't—"

"Move!" Neil's voice cracked like a whip. Choking back a hysterical sob Eden whirled and fled, and Neil smiled grimly at Lathrop. "You too. Outside."

Lathrop's face drained of color. "You're putting a rope

around your neck, Banning. You want to make your wife a widow?"

"She'll be free of you," Neil ground out, cold anger building into white-hot rage. "We both caused her pain, Lathrop; maybe this is the way it was meant to end all along."

"You don't know what you're doing—"

"Shut up or I'll kill you right now." Neil stepped backward and jerked his head toward the door. "Let's go."

Momentarily at a disadvantage, Lathrop obeyed, halting when he had progressed several yards. "What now?" Both men were standing in the pool of light which poured from the door of the shack.

"Now we find out how brave you are. Throw me your gun."

From the sidelines Eden watched in horror as Neil holstered his gun and picked up Lathrop's pistol. In a few swift movements Neil emptied all the bullets from Lathrop's gun, replaced one shell in the cylinder and then repeated the same procedure with his own weapon. Stop him, commanded a small voice inside Eden's head as she watched Neil return Lathrop's gun. But she realized it was too late even as she took a tentative step toward the two men.

"A duel?" Lathrop looked from the pistol to Neil. "You can't be serious!"

"We'll forgo the customary pacing off," Neil said evenly. Slowly, deliberately, Neil lowered his arm to his side, the gun dangling negligently from his fingers. "The distance between us is just about right, so whenever you feel lucky."

An eerie silence fell as the two men faced each other. Paralyzed, Eden offered up a prayer for Neil's safety. Not again, Eden implored, a sudden vision of Hugh floating in front of her eyes. Please, God, not again. For what seemed an eternity the three stood unmoving, frozen in time. Their concentration was so intense that all three failed to hear or see Keith and Vincent when they galloped up to the branding shack.

Keith started to dismount, only to be brought up short by Vincent's hand on his arm.

"Don't," Vincent warned. "You've seen enough gunplay to know what will happen if you barge in."

"I also know what will happen if I don't. Personally, I don't care if Williams and Banning kill each other, but I'm not going to take a chance on Eden's being hurt." Ignoring Vincent, Keith moved his horse closer.

Eden saw Keith first as he halted in back and to the side of Lathrop. For a moment a wave of relief washed through Eden until she realized, with shattering clarity, that an interruption now could cost Neil his life.

Keith pulled his gun from the holster and aimed it at Neil. "Banning! Williams! Throw your guns down!"

Startled, Neil made the error of letting his concentration slip for a fraction of a second, and in that time Lathrop brought his gun up and pulled the trigger. The bullet slammed into Neil's chest, lifting him off the ground before he fell backward and lay motionless in the dust. Eden screamed and rushed toward her fallen husband, blind to what happened next. Simultaneously Lathrop pivoted toward Keith—whether to surrender or run a bluff no one ever would know—but his gun was aimed directly at the Ranger. Suddenly Keith was sixteen again, confronting his father's killer; only this time there could be no doubt as to Lathrop's guilt. The proof was a man's body lying in the dirt; the evidence the weapon that Lathrop still held. Keith's gun roared, his years of practice sending the bullet directly into Lathrop's heart. Disbelief registered in Lathrop's eyes just before death left its glaze on them, and he pitched forward into the dirt.

Keith and Vincent dismounted but it was Vincent, his expression bland, who knelt beside Lathrop and rolled him onto his back. "He's dead." Vincent rose and handed Keith Lathrop's gun. "I hope Neil fared better."

They found Eden cradling Neil's head in her lap, trying to stanch the flow of blood from his chest with material she had torn from her petticoat. Wordlessly Vincent took Eden's hand away from the wound and examined what lay beneath the makeshift bandage.

Eden wrenched her gaze away from Neil's face and looked helplessly at Vincent. "Is it very bad?"

Vincent started to lie but the words stuck in his throat. "It's bad enough, ma'am." At the stricken expression in Eden's eyes he quickly added, "But then, I've seen men live through a lot worse. We're going to have to tie this bandage in place and get him to a doctor without jarring him around too much."

Restraining the blind panic sweeping through her, Eden forced herself to gather her scattered thoughts. "Home . . . we'll take Neil home," she decided in a hushed voice. "Sebastian will know what to do." Reluctantly she eased Neil's head to the ground and began tearing long strips from her gown. "We can use these to hold the bandage."

"I've got a couple of clean shirts in my saddlebag," Keith offered.

Eden's hands paused in midair, the bleak, wintry gaze she turned on Keith making him shift uncomfortably. "I don't need any more of your *help,* Captain. The best thing you can do right now is to stay away from my husband!"

"Mrs. Banning," Vincent interrupted gently, "I can't manage Neil alone. What's important is getting Neil to Sebastian as fast as we can."

"I . . . I know." Eden's chin trembled and she hastily resumed her work, heedless of the tears streaming down her cheeks. "We can use the shirts, Captain."

It took ten minutes for Eden and Vincent to bandage the wound, and then, with Keith's help, they settled the still unconscious Neil on Vincent's horse, and Vincent mounted behind him. Eden paused beside Vincent's horse, her heart constricting at the sight of Neil's ashen face.

"You'd best take Neil's horse and ride on ahead of us," Vincent quietly ordered her. "Tell Sebastian what to expect."

"I don't want to leave Neil." Eden reached up and took one of Neil's hands. His flesh was cold and Eden realized with a pang that Vincent was right. "Bring him home as quickly as you can, Vincent."

"Yes, ma'am." A brief, reassuring smile flitted across Vincent's lips. "Try not to worry—we'll have him home before you know it."

"I hope so," Eden whispered fervently. "Oh, Lord, I hope so." She pressed Neil's hand to her cheek, then turned and ran to her horse.

Eden drove Neil's horse unmercifully as she raced across the rangeland toward *Rancho de Paraíso.* Bending low over the stallion's neck, Eden prayed for Neil . . . and found herself remembering how a reckless, arrogant man with golden eyes had stolen her heart and become the love she never thought would be hers. Let him live, Eden begged silently, a cold weight settling in her chest. Please, God, let him live.

Eden slid from the saddle and raced into Sebastian's waiting arms. Sebastian swept Eden into the house and deposited her trembling form onto a chair.

"Thank God you are safe," Sebastian exclaimed. "Neil went

after you several hours ago, certain that Lathrop had kidnaped you a second time. And Captain Gerald—" he paused, suddenly aware of the frantic expression in Eden's eyes.

"Sebastian." Her eyes brilliant with unshed tears, Eden gripped his arm.

Mistaking the quiver in her voice for shock, Sebastian gently patted her hand. "You are safe now, Eden; there is nothing for you to worry..." His voice trailed off as Eden vehemently shook her head. A feeling of dread settled over Sebastian and in a cracked voice he requested, "Tell me."

"Neil's been shot." There, she'd said it—and hearing her own voice speak those terrible words shattered what remained of her composure. "Neil found us and—oh, God!—I've never seen him so furious. He challenged Lathrop to a... a duel and then Keith appeared and Lathrop fired and Neil fell—"

Alarmed, Sebastian took Eden by the shoulders and shook her. "Where is he? How badly is Neil hurt?"

"I—I don't know. Vincent said it was bad and Neil is bleeding so much..." Eden's voice caught and she shuddered. "Vincent is bringing Neil home. He sent me ahead to warn you."

His face drawn, Sebastian nodded and pulled Eden to her feet. "Come. You can change while I prepare the things I need, and then I shall see to your face."

"But Neil—"

"I can do nothing for my brother until he arrives," Sebastian reminded her. "And neither can you. Go, do as I say. It will make the waiting bearable."

Eden obeyed, grateful for anything which would keep her mind from the slow crawl of time. She exchanged her torn gown for a clean one, checked on Shannon and then made her way to the kitchen, where she found Sebastian sterilizing the instruments from his bag.

The smell of disinfectant was overpowering and Eden paused in the doorway. "Can I help, Sebastian?"

Sebastian looked up from a kettle of boiling water and shook his head. "Not just now. Come sit down and let me have a look at you."

"I'm only bruised," Eden protested weakly as Sebastian carefully washed her face and examined the ever-widening contusion on her jaw.

"Lathrop did this?" Sebastian asked grimly. When Eden

nodded, Sebastian cursed softly in Spanish. "He will not get away with this, I promise you. Lathrop will pay."

"He already has." A feeling of numb disbelief gripped Eden as she explained more fully what had happened at the branding shack. "I was so foolish, Sebastian. It never occurred to me that it might be Lathrop on the hill—" Eden's eyes widened in sudden remembrance. "Constanza! Sebastian, Constanza is—"

"Dead. She was found shortly after Neil went to find you." Sebastian's eyes turned bleak. "I was so concerned that Captain Gerald would kill Neil before he had a chance to defend himself that I sat the captain down and told him the entire story. I also told him that Vincent would confirm everything—that's where Captain Gerald headed after he left here. I forgot that Lathrop was a danger as well. It's my fault Neil was shot."

"Oh, Sebastian." Eden reached out to comfort him and they held each other tightly. "It's not your fault."

"Nor is it yours," Sebastian replied in a constricted voice. At last he pulled away from Eden and busied himself once again with his instruments. He dared not give in to his fear, not now; not while he could help his older brother.

"What can I do?"

Sebastian turned and studied Eden's anxious face. She, too, needed to feel useful. "I'll need clean linens for bandages— and a great deal of light next to the bed."

"I'll see to it."

Eden had hardly completed her tasks before she heard Vincent's shout and, her heart pounding, she ran through the house to the front door. Sebastian was already outside and Eden stifled a sob as he and Vincent carried Neil through the door. The makeshift bandage had done little good during the journey— the cloth was saturated with Neil's blood, and that same precious fluid now dripped to the floor.

Seeing where Eden's gaze had traveled, Sebastian ordered curtly, "The instruments are in the kitchen, Eden. Get them!"

All activity—her own as well as Sebastian's—blurred for Eden after that. She remembered bringing the instruments to Sebastian and watching as Neil's clothes were removed, and then she found herself standing outside the bedroom door. Isolated, Eden leaned against the panel and strained to decipher the occasional murmur of voices which reached her ears. How long she stood there Eden didn't know. One hour? Two? She found prayer impossible, and when the housekeeper came to offer her solace and support, Eden discovered she was too numb to speak. All the hands were awake, the housekeeper informed Eden, and they wanted Mrs. Banning to know that they were ready to track down the sidewinder who had put a bullet in Neil.

Eden wordlessly shook her head and eventually the woman left her alone with her thoughts. Why is Sebastian taking so long? Eden wondered impatiently. Angered by the lack of information about Neil's condition, Eden's fingers had closed around the doorknob before she checked her actions. No matter how she longed to be at Neil's side, Eden had to allow Sebastian the time he needed to repair the damage done to her husband. Reluctantly, Eden withdrew her hand and with a muffled sob sank to the floor. She would wait—there was nothing else she could do.

"Eden?" A light touch on her shoulder jerked Eden away from the dark thoughts which had filled her mind during the past hours and she looked up to find Sebastian bending over her. Sebastian's lips curved into a slight smile as he helped Eden to her feet.

"How is he?"

The smile faded but a hopeful light remained in Sebastian's eyes. "Weak but alive. He's lost a great deal of blood, but the bullet is out and I think I repaired all the damage. All we can do now is wait."

It was by no means a guarantee, but Eden breathed easier nonetheless. "May I see him?"

"Of course. I think seeing you will do more for Neil than anything I can do." Sebastian frowned as he studied Eden's pinched features. "You should try to get some rest, Eden."

"Later," Eden promised. Over Sebastian's shoulder she caught sight of Vincent waiting in the shadows and she extended her hand to him. "Thank you, Vincent. Thank you so very much."

Vincent took her hand and smiled, his eyes soft and gentle. "I should thank you, Eden. When we first met I was dead inside, a shell of a man waiting for a bullet to kill me. You and Millicent changed all that. I owed you a life, Eden."

Impulsively, Eden threw her arms around Vincent's neck and hugged him. Stepping back, she managed a wan smile. "It's been a long night, Vincent. Go home—Millie must be worried sick about you." With a grateful look at Sebastian, Eden disappeared into the bedroom.

The room was in semidarkness. The smell of disinfectant lingered in the air, and Eden moved quietly to the window, opening the glass panes to admit the soft breeze. Turning, she went to the bed, a sigh of relief escaping her lips as she saw Neil's bandaged chest moving slowly, rhythmically.

"My poor darling," Eden murmured. She perched on the edge of the mattress and took one of Neil's hands in both of her own. As if sensing her presence, Neil's face turned toward her and she smiled tremulously. Brushing back the dark hair that had fallen across Neil's forehead Eden whispered, "I love you, Neil; I always have. And I need you more than you can possibly know. If anything should happen to you . . ." Her voice broke and, unable to continue, Eden gently touched her lips to Neil's.

A feeling of staggering weariness stole over Eden and with a heavy sigh she rose and pulled a chair to the bed. Blowing out the remaining lamp, Eden collapsed onto the chair and laced her fingers through Neil's. I'm so tired, Eden thought dimly. If she could rest her eyes for a moment, just a few minutes . . . Carefully, so as not to disturb Neil, Eden lowered her head until it rested beside their joined hands. Within moments Eden was asleep.

That was the way Sebastian found them the following morning. Stopping just inside the door, Sebastian examined the scene in front of him with a slight pang. Eden was half sitting in a chair, half reclining on the bed, her hair fanned across the mattress. Her hands were locked around Neil's, a gesture of both hope and despair. Neil, Sebastian noted, had not stirred during the night, but his breathing appeared deep and even, and his color had improved. Thank God they have each other, Sebastian thought. Sebastian sighed wearily and limped to the bed, unable to delay his mission any longer. Unwillingly he gently shook Eden awake.

"Sebastian, what—" Eden's glance flew immediately to the man on the bed. "Oh, my God!"

"Hush," Sebastian ordered, taking one of Eden's hands. "He's only sleeping, Eden, nothing else." A single tear rolled down Eden's cheek and Sebastian handed her his handkerchief.

"I must have dozed off," Eden confessed guiltily. "How could I do such a thing!"

"The past few hours have been an ordeal for everyone," Sebastian said soothingly. "Particularly for you. It's not surprising that your mind and body demanded a release from the situation."

Eden nodded halfheartedly, her eyes riveted to Neil. "How is he?"

"He looks better, but I will know more once I have examined him."

"I'll help," Eden volunteered.

"You, unfortunately, must attend to your visitor." As Eden's gaze fell on him, Sebastian shifted uncomfortably. "Captain Gerald arrived over an hour ago and asked to speak with you. I am sorry, Eden, but I've stalled him as long as I can. He's waiting in the study."

"I see." A cold mask settled over Eden's face. "You can tell Captain Gerald for me that he can go straight to hell!" Sebastian's frame drooped, as if he carried a burden which had suddenly become too heavy for him to bear, and Eden frowned. "What is it, Sebastian?"

"I am afraid this is a bit more complicated than asking the captain to leave. Eden . . . Captain Gerald is here to arrest Neil."

"Arrest—" Eden paled so rapidly that Sebastian feared she would faint. "He can't mean it!"

"But he does," Sebastian dissented. "I think it would be best if you speak with him. I will stay here." Too dazed to reply, Eden nodded.

Numb with shock, she left the bedroom and walked slowly toward the study. Despite what Keith had been told by Sebastian and Vincent, he still meant to arrest Neil and charge him with rustling. How could he do such a thing? Was he so jealous that he would do anything to hurt Neil, to . . . a feeling of horror spread through Eden as she remembered Lathrop bragging about the diary he had forged. Of course Keith no longer believed Sebastian and Vincent: Keith had, at long last, evidence, written evidence, which condemned Neil as a rustler. And as Hugh Colter's murderer.

At the study door Eden paused to straighten her shoulders and comb her fingers through her hair. She would not allow Keith to take Neil. She would find a way, somehow, to prove Neil's innocence to Keith, and if that failed . . . well, she would convince Keith; she had to. Eden placed her hand on the doorknob and opened the door.

Keith was sitting in one of the armchairs, whiling away the time by leafing through a book, but when Eden entered he jumped to his feet. "I was beginning to think you wouldn't see me."

"You left me little choice," Eden replied. Her heart was beating like a sledgehammer and she fought to keep her voice steady. "I am surprised, however, that you can even look me in the eye after what you did last night."

Keith had the good grace to color. "I have a job to do, and part of that job is to stop the kind of wholesale murder that was about to take place. Lathrop had only one bullet in his gun. Did you know that?"

"So did Neil. Did *you* know that?" Eden retorted bitingly. From the deepening of Keith's flush it was clear he did not. "You must learn to check your facts, Captain. No matter how much you dislike Neil, my husband is a fair man. Neil would never face Lathrop, or anyone else, without giving him an equal chance."

"It was still my job," Keith maintained stubbornly.

Eden passed a trembling hand over her eyes. "In the course of carrying out your duty Lathrop was killed and Neil was gravely injured. You'll forgive me if I fail to see precisely what good came out of your interference."

"Perhaps none." Keith met the pain-filled gray eyes without flinching. "But at least my way it was legal."

"Legal." Eden repeated the word slowly, witheringly. "In the past year I've heard that word so often that I'm going to scream if you say it again! You are so damned concerned with legalities, with carrying out the *letter* of the law that you have forgotten about the *spirit* of the law. Where is your sense of justice, Captain?"

Eden's question rang through the house, reaching even the master bedroom with amazing clarity. Startled, Sebastian paused in the task of rebandaging Neil's chest and met the pair of golden eyes which had opened moments before. Astonished by the voice, Sebastian asked of his brother, "Eden?"

Pale but awake and amazingly clearheaded, Neil nodded. "Eden." Sebastian finished the rebandaging and Neil gave a sigh of relief as he was lowered onto the pillows Sebastian had fluffed behind his back. "Open the door, little brother; I want to hear the rest of that conversation."

"What you need to do is go back to sleep. Here, drink this:

You also need to start replacing the blood you lost." Sebastian handed Neil a glass of water but made no move to the door.

Neil drank half the glassful before replying. "You've already told me why Gerald is here, Sebastian; it's a little late to start protecting me." At Sebastian's gloomy look Neil managed a weak smile. "Since I'm in no shape to run from the law I might as well be prepared for whatever happens. Besides, I want to hear how Eden deals with our noble captain."

Sebastian capitulated, inwardly every bit as curious as Neil about the conversation.

Unaware of the eavesdroppers, Eden defiantly faced Keith across the length of the study. "You haven't answered my question, Captain."

"Because it doesn't deserve an answer and you know it."

"Yes, it does," Eden insisted. "You—"

"Eden, I didn't come here to arrest Neil," Keith interrupted. "I just told Sebastian that because I was afraid you wouldn't see me otherwise."

Now completely unsure of Keith's motives, Eden asked stiffly, "Then why *are* you here, Keith?"

"To give you these." Keith walked to the desk, picked up the two slim volumes he had deposited there earlier and crossed over to the window where Eden stood. "This morning I had the unpleasant task of going through Lathrop's personal effects and I found these in his desk drawer. Do you know what they are?"

Fear constricted Eden's throat and she had to swallow several times before she could speak. "N-no."

Keith propped the books on the windowsill. "They're diaries, written by Constanza Williams. Or rather, one was written by her." He opened the covers so that the first page of each book was exposed. "One of these is legitimate and the other a forgery—a very poor forgery at that. The one which I believe to be a phony is written in English and implicates Neil in nearly every crime committed in this area during the past six years."

Eden wet her lips. "And the other?"

Keith smiled slightly. "Written in Spanish, as you can see. It places the blame for the rustling, Hugh's death and your kidnaping directly on Lathrop and Constanza." He picked up the diary and fingered it thoughtfully. "They counted on my following the rustlers into Mexico and connecting the thieves with Neil, which I did. And then there was Manuel's confession, guaranteed to convince me but not give me any proof. It never occurred to me to suspect a woman. Lathrop yes, but not Constanza." Keith shrugged. "They threw me off by framing Neil, and of course, the way I feel about you . . . let's just say I found it very easy to believe Neil was guilty."

"I don't understand. You suspected Lathrop?" Eden stared at him in confusion. "Why? Lathrop had everything! He owned the largest ranch in this area; he owned a town and most of the county. I would think Lathrop would be far down on your list."

For what seemed an eternity Keith gazed silently out the window. "How much do you know about the Emerald I? About its history?"

"Aside from the fact that Hugh bought it about a dozen years ago, not a thing. Honestly, Keith, I don't see—"

"I was born on the Emerald I," Keith broke in, "only then it wasn't called the Emerald I. I grew up watching my father run this ranch, seeing the pride he took in making it a success." He drew a deep breath. "One day, when I was sixteen, Pa didn't come home for supper, so I rode out to the northern part of the stream where he was supposed to be working. I found him face down in the stream. He'd been killed by a shotgun blast to the head. Lathrop had had him killed because he wouldn't sell the ranch."

"Just like Hugh," Eden murmured.

"Yes," Keith agreed. "Lathrop wanted the water and killed two men to get it. The irony is that I couldn't prove Lathrop guilty of either murder. If he hadn't turned that empty gun on me last night he'd still be alive." Keith's smile was twisted. "You see, Eden, I waited eleven years for justice."

"Keith, I'm sorry," Eden exclaimed. "I didn't know."

"You weren't supposed to know, no one was. Not even Lathrop knew that I'm Art Mason's son. I dropped out of sight after Pa's death and took the name of the Texas Ranger who befriended me."

"I see." And she did. Eden began to understand what drove Keith Gerald to uphold the law. "It's appropriate that Lathrop met his fate at your hands."

"Yes, I suppose it is." Keith shifted beneath her gaze. "In any event, Neil has been officially cleared. I telegraphed Laredo before I came out here and told them about Constanza's diary. I'll be taking it back to Laredo as evidence."

Eden gingerly touched the forgery. "And this one?"

"It's yours, to do with as you see fit. I suggest you burn it." Keith turned, picked up his hat from the corner of the desk and walked to the door. There he paused and when he spoke his back was to Eden. "Sebastian told me that he thinks Neil will recover."

"Yes."

A shadow drifted across Keith's handsome features. "You love him very much."

"Very much," Eden repeated softly. She took a hesitant step toward Keith. "Thank you, Keith, for the diary and for clearing Neil. I think I know what it took for you to do this."

"Justice, remember? I'm sworn to enforce the law." Keith's voice roughened. "I'll always love you, Eden, that will never change. Keep that in mind and perhaps, in time, you'll find it in your heart to forgive the painful things I've said and done."

"Keith—"

"San Francisco will be a lonely place without you. Goodbye, Mrs. Banning."

He was gone. Stunned, Eden could only stare at the space Keith had so recently occupied while she listened to the sounds of the front door closing and the diminishing hoofbeats of his horse. Neil is free! That thought kept resounding inside Eden's head until she was able to believe that she had not dreamed the past few minutes. Neil is free! Eden smiled radiantly and, picking up the second diary, she walked out of the study. She would tell Sebastian the good news.

The door to the bedroom was open and Eden came to an abrupt halt just inside. She blinked twice, as if to clear her vision, and the two men in front of her grinned in delight. Neil's eyes danced with suppressed laughter as Eden stared at him speechlessly.

"In all the time I've known Eden," Neil mockingly confided to Sebastian, "she has never been at a loss for words. I would think that having her husband back from death's door would be worth an exclamation or two, or at least a smile. Wouldn't you agree?"

Neil was teasing, acting as if the previous night had been little more than an amusing diversion. After the strain of the past hours, it was too much for Eden—she burst into tears.

Sebastian rose and took the diary from Eden's hands. "I'll leave you two alone." He laid a reassuring hand on Eden's shoulder. "He is going to be fine, Eden, do not worry." The door closed discreetly behind Sebastian.

Neil stared at his sobbing wife, noting the dark circles beneath her eyes. Further teasing words went unsaid as he realized what a shock it must have been to find him not only conscious but also recovered enough to be eavesdropping. In a conciliatory gesture Neil stretched out his hand to Eden. "There's no need to cry, love, you heard Sebastian." When she shook her head miserably he added, "Ah, Eden, don't. Come here. Let me hold you."

Eden flew to the bed and took his outstretched hand in both of her own.

"Shh." Neil combed his fingers through the silken curls of Eden's hair. "It's over, my darling. We're safe now; and I promise I'll never let anything like this happen to you again."

Eden brushed at her tears and, sighing, gave in to the gentle pressure Neil was exerting. She sank to the edge of the bed and smiled tremulously. "I have so much to tell you, Neil. There's so much you don't know."

"And I want to hear it all, but not now." Neil brought Eden's mouth down to his and kissed her with exquisite tenderness, allowing their lips to cling longingly before releasing her. "I love you, Eden, and at this moment that love is all that matters. Just stay here with me, let me hold you. I need to feel you beside me."

"You're hurt," Eden protested weakly, but she permitted herself to be drawn down beside Neil.

Neil smiled roguishly, enjoying the way Eden's hair curled softly over his shoulder. "You're the best medicine for me, my sweet. None of Sebastian's remedies could do for my wound what the sight of you does for my heart."

"I do love you, Neil," Eden murmured, feeling herself relax for the first time in hours.

Nodding, Neil enfolded Eden's hand in his. There would be time later for explanations and to revel in the pure joy of being together. Neil smiled, recalling his first meeting with the woman who now lay beside him. How much pain they had both gone through to reach this point. Now they were as intricately joined to one another as the stars were to the sky. Their love had gone through fire and, instead of dying, had emerged stronger and brighter than Neil had believed possible.

He was a lucky man, Neil acknowledged silently. To love and be loved in return was the greatest gift any man could receive. Like Odysseus, Neil's journey had ended in the arms of his love.

# EPILOGUE

The night was cool, due to a late-afternoon shower, and a slight breeze billowed the curtains at the window. Eden stepped through the double doors of her bedroom and onto the veranda, where Neil sat smoking a cigar. She smiled, admiring the fine play of muscles across Neil's chest as he reached for his brandy. The red scar on his chest was gradually fading, and at times like this, with only the moon for light, Eden often found it hard to believe that a few short months before Neil had been in grave danger.

Sensing her scrutiny, Neil looked up and smiled. "I didn't mean to wake you."

"You didn't. I can't sleep either." Eden moved to the railing. "It is beautiful here, isn't it? And so peaceful."

"Yes." Neil stubbed out his cigar and, rising, went to stand behind Eden. His arms curled around her waist and Neil kissed the top of her head as she leaned against him. "Enjoyable as this sight is, sweet, it's not half as beautiful as you."

Eden laughed throatily and spun about to face Neil, her arms twining about his neck. "You're only saying that because I was such a mess after the roundup today."

"Not true. I found you quite attractive with that smudge of dirt across your nose," Neil teased. "But I must admit you're far more captivating right now." Neil's eyes raked Eden from head to toe, an admiring glow entering the golden depths as the filmy material of her nightgown—with the aid of the breeze—molded itself to her curves. He tangled his hands in Eden's waist-length hair. "I hope this is the way you plan to meet me in Dallas when the drive is over. Or are you still harboring the silly idea of going on the drive again this year?"

"It's not a silly idea," Eden countered with a sniff. "Besides, I have everything planned. Shannon and her nurse will meet us in Dallas and we'll all have a splendid time."

"As independent as the day I met you and twice as stubborn," Neil said, a hint of laughter in his voice despite the ferocity of his tone. "I suppose when Shannon is old enough you'll insist she go along on the drives?"

"I may." Eden raised her chin defiantly. "The Emerald I is Shannon's—she may as well know right from the beginning what it means to run a ranch."

Neil grinned and pulled Eden firmly against him. "All right, woman, have it your own way. No more arguing. I might as well get used to the fact that—"

"—That I'm independent and stubborn," Eden repeated mockingly. "Is that so terrible?"

"No." Neil sobered and gazed lovingly into the gray eyes so near his own. "Even if I could, I wouldn't change a single thing about you."

"Not a thing?" Eden inquired, running a hand over Neil's chest. "Surely I must have *one* fault you'd like to erase."

"Just one." Without warning Neil scooped Eden into his arms and strode into the bedroom. He gently deposited her on the bed and divested himself of his clothing. Golden eyes molten, Neil sank onto the mattress beside Eden and took her into his arms. "There are times, my darling, spirited wife, when you talk too much."